LONE STAR
BRIDES

LONE STAR BRIDES

TRACIE PETERSON

Three Novels in One Volume
A Sensible Arrangement
A Moment in Time
A Matter of Heart

BETHANYHOUSE
a division of Baker Publishing Group
Minneapolis, Minnesota

Previously published in three separate volumes:
   A Sensible Arrangement
   A Moment in Time
   A Matter of Heart

Published by Bethany House Publishers
11400 Hampshire Avenue South
Bloomington, Minnesota 55438
www.bethanyhouse.com

Bethany House Publishers is a division of
Baker Publishing Group, Grand Rapids, Michigan

Printed in the United States of America

Library of Congress Control Number: 2015938811

Scripture quotations are from the King James Version of the Bible.

This is a work of fiction. Names, characters, incidents, and dialogues are products of the author's imagination and are not to be construed as real. Any resemblance to actual events or persons, living or dead, is entirely coincidental.

3-in-1 edition cover design by Eric Walljasper
Original cover designs by Gearbox
Cover photography for *A Sensible Arrangement* and *A Moment in Time* by Steve Gardner, PixelWorks Studios
Cover photography for *A Matter of Heart* by Brandon Hills Photos

15   16   17   18   19   20   21   7   6   5   4   3   2   1

A SENSIBLE
ARRANGEMENT

Chapter 1

Marty Dandridge Olson looked over the letters once again. There were three, and each contained a variety of information meant to assist her in making a decision. A life-changing decision.

"Hannah would call me mad," Marty mused aloud. She picked up one of the letters—the latest—and noted the first line: *I have enclosed funds enough to cover your travels to Denver.*

Marty shook her head. *Am I mad? Crazy to seriously consider this matter?*

Putting the letter down, Marty got to her feet and paced the small kitchen. She put a few pieces of wood into the cookstove and stoked the fire. The chill of the day wasn't that great, but she was restless and it gave her something to do—something other than contemplate those letters . . . and what had happened four years earlier.

Now nearly thirty-five, Marty was a childless widow who was known for her spunk and ingenuity. She was the kind of woman who seemed destined to a life in Texas. Surrounded by family and friends, Marty had known a life of love and relatively little want. Why, then, was she so desperate to leave it all behind?

She had lived her entire life in Texas, or very nearly. Her birth in

Mississippi had taken the life of her mother, leaving her to be raised by a deeply saddened father and loving older sister. Hannah had been more mother than sister to Marty, and at nearly twenty years Marty's senior, Hannah's guidance and wisdom had seen Marty through many difficulties.

If only her wisdom could have saved the life of Marty's husband.

"Thomas." She whispered the name and smiled. "You were always so very stubborn. I doubt anything could have saved your life once you determined to die."

Her beloved husband had died four years ago to the day. Gored by a longhorn bull, Thomas had suffered massive internal injuries but had remained conscious until the very end. Even now, Marty could recall his final words to her.

"I reckon I've made a mess of Christmas, Marty, but never you mind. It ain't worth troublin' yourself over, so don't you go mournin' me for long." The pain had been clearly written on his face, but he'd held fast to her hand, although his voice had grown weaker. *"I've loved you . . . a long time . . . Martha Dandridge . . . Olson. Don't reckon . . . there's a . . . better wife to any man."*

"So don't leave me," she had begged, kissing his fingers.

He had given her a weak smile and then closed his eyes one last time. *"I gotta go, gal."* And with that, his hand went limp in hers and he exhaled his last breath.

Marty remembered it as if it had been yesterday. How she had mourned him—the loss unlike anything she'd ever known. Folks told her time would ease the pain, and in truth it had . . . a little. But time had done nothing to fill the emptiness. There were days when she feared the loneliness would swallow her whole.

She looked back to the table where the letters lay. Could this be the answer she sought? Could her decision fill the emptiness once and for all? The clock chimed the hour, and Marty knew it wouldn't be long before the Barnett carriage showed up to take her to her sister's for the Christmas celebration.

Marty took up the letters and tucked them in the pocket of her apron. There had been a time when she might have prayed about her decision, but not now. After God had refused her prayers to save Thomas's life,

Marty had hardened her heart. God was now only a bitter reminder of a trust that had been broken.

"I'm going to do it," Marty announced to the empty room. "I'm going to marry a man I've never met and do not love. I'm going to marry him and leave this place forever."

★

That evening as she settled in to exchange gifts with her sister's family, Marty looked for the right moment to break the news. She had already determined she wouldn't tell them about the classified advertisement that had started her plans. The Dallas *Daily Times-Herald* had run the request for a full week.

> Texas-born man now living in Colorado, working as a banker, wishes to correspond with a Lone Star lady. Seeking potential wife who would display the virtues, sensibilities, and wisdom of a strong Texas woman. Must be willing to leave Texas for Colorado.

Marty was more than willing. She didn't desire to remarry and still wasn't sure why she'd responded to that ad, but after the man's first reply, she had known it was fate that had brought them together. Jacob Wythe wasn't looking for romance or love—just a woman who would bear his name and act as his companion.

"You aren't payin' attention, Aunt Marty."

She looked up to find the entire family staring at her, her nephew Robert standing to her left with a gift extended. Marty flushed. "I am sorry. I was just thinking on . . . well . . ." She smiled and let the words trail off. "Let's see what we have here." She took the gift box.

Hannah seated herself beside her husband, William. "I hope you like it."

Marty pulled a bright red ribbon from the box. "I'm sure I will. You always have a way of figuring out just what I need most."

She opened the box to reveal a set of four small leather-bound books. Lifting one, she spied the author. "Jane Austen. Thank you."

"We knew you'd taken to reading more," William Barnett offered. "Hannah said these were some of your favorites years ago."

Marty nodded as she perused the titles. "Hannah used to read them to me. Andy thought himself above it all, but he always managed to sit close enough to listen in."

Hannah laughed. "Our brother was not half so sly as he thought himself."

"Speaking of Andy," Marty said, looking up from the box, "have you had word?"

William nodded. Marty had to admit she held her brother-in-law in great affection; his marriage to Hannah had been the best thing that had ever happened to the Dandridge family. After the death of their father, William had stepped in as protector and provider.

"We had a letter just a day ago. Hannah wanted me to save it for tonight—kind of like havin' Andy and his bunch with us."

"Now's just as good a time as any," Hannah declared. She pushed back a graying blond curl. At fifty-three and despite years of hard work, she was still a beautiful woman.

I envy her. I envy her peace of mind and happiness. Marty shook her head and looked away. Envy was a sin . . . but so too was lying.

William pulled the letter from his pocket and opened it while Robert took a seat. "Andy and the family send Christmas greetings from snowy Wyoming."

Marty shook her head. "I think he was ten kinds of fool to move his family up there. He never liked the colder weather."

"Yes, but since Ellen's family is from that part of the country, it seems only right," Hannah reminded. "And they did live here for the first five years of their marriage. Long enough that we got to know little John. I'd love to visit them and get to know Benny, as well. He must be six years old by now."

"Do you want me to read the letter, or would you rather talk about the family?" William asked with a grin.

Hannah elbowed him. "Read the letter."

William nodded.

"We are doing well. The longhorn seem to take the weather in stride. The herd increased again this year, and Ellen's pa is pleased

with the way things are going. John and Benjamin send their love. They both ride like they were born to a saddle. John can rope and help with branding as well as any of the hands. Benjamin isn't far behind in abilities, as he is in constant competition with John."

Marty chuckled. "Imagine that."

Hannah laughed, as well. "Given the way you two always tried to outdo the other, it's no surprise."

"Yes, but I was a girl, and it shamed him if I could do something better than he could," Marty said. "I wonder if he'll teach them steer-sliding."

"I still remember when they taught me," Robert said, joining in. "Seems like a mighty dirty trick to play on a fella."

Marty smiled fondly at the memory of her brother teaching his nephew to steer-slide. It was a joke they played on all the new greenhorns, telling them that they had to learn to slide under a steer just in case they found themselves in a perilous situation. To everyone's amazement, it had actually saved the life of one young fellow long ago, but Marty couldn't remember his name.

"It was just a matter of initiating you to ranch work," Hannah said, excusing the matter. "I've noticed it's not a prank you've given up. Weren't you showing young Micky how to slide under the fence just the other day?"

"I didn't attempt it myself," Robert replied. "I just told him it was something he needed to learn if he was gonna be one of our ranch hands." He gave them a mischievous grin. "I figure if it was good enough for me . . ."

"Do you want me to continue reading?" William asked.

"Sure, Pa. Go ahead." Robert settled back in his chair and folded his arms with a sly smile. "Didn't mean to stop you."

William looked down to the letter.

"Ellen sends her love, as well as good news. You'll remember our sadness three years ago when we lost our little girl just after birth. Then last year Ellen miscarried, and we feared we might not have another child. Well, the doctor just confirmed that she's expecting and due to deliver sometime in the spring. We are of course quite hopeful that all will go well."

11

"That is good news," Hannah said. "I know Andy wanted a big family, and Ellen was so sick after that miscarriage. It's an answer to prayer."

Marty bristled at the mention of prayer, but said nothing. William finished the letter with Andy sharing plans they had for celebrating Christmas, as well as his intentions for the ranch. Marty tried to appear interested.

"I'd say Uncle Andy has a good life in Wyoming," Robert declared. "He sounds happy with his little family."

"You should be thinking of getting a wife and family of your own," Hannah told him. "You are twenty-six after all, and you have proven able to take on a great deal of responsibility. Your father and I are quite pleased with your work here." She paused and gave him a knowing smile. "I believe Jessica Atherton would be even more pleased if you gave her a formal proposal."

"Jessica's still a child. Although I will say folks have been trying to pair us off since we were young'uns."

"That's hardly true, Robert. I have never wanted any of my children to feel that we were choosing their spouses. I never did abide arranged, loveless marriages. And I know Carrisa and Tyler don't feel that way."

"Then why are you trying to marry me off?" Robert asked with a smile. "I figured with my sisters gone from home, you would want to keep me around."

Hannah shrugged and scooted in closer to William. "It's not your company I mind, but I would like to see you happily settled."

"She wants more grandbabies," William declared.

"Well, we do only have the one. Of course, I was like a grandmother to Andy's boys, but now they're in Wyoming and so far away. Not to mention they have her parents there to spoil them."

Marty felt an aching in her heart at the banter between them. The thought of having children always made her sad. She and Thomas had been married for ten years but she had been unable to carry a child to delivery. Marty blamed herself, even though Thomas never did. The sorrow was one she had hoped to bury with her husband, but that hadn't been the case. Her niece Sarah, Hannah and Will's oldest girl, had just given birth in September to her first son. Hannah and Will had returned from Sarah's home in Georgia some three weeks earlier, and the baby was all that Hannah could talk about.

I would have made a good mother, but God apparently thought otherwise. I was a good wife, too. Thomas always said I was the best woman he'd ever known. I never gave him cause to doubt my love or my faithfulness.

"You seem so distant this evening." Hannah's comment brought Marty back to the present.

"I'm just tired." Marty motioned to the gifts she'd brought. "Why don't you open my presents now?"

Hannah nodded, and Robert jumped up to hand out the gifts. Marty had spent a fair amount of time on each of them. For William and Robert she had crafted warm robes, which quickly met with their approval.

"I've needed a new one for ages," William admitted.

"I know. I asked Hannah what I could make for you." Marty smiled.

Robert leaned down to kiss her on the cheek. "Thanks, Aunt Marty."

William nodded. "Yes, thank you very much."

Hannah opened Marty's gift and gasped. The bundle revealed a lacy cream-colored shirtwaist. "Oh, it's beautiful. Oh, Marty, your work is so delicate." She ran her hands over the intricately embroidered neckline. "This must have taken hours."

"I remembered you admiring something similar when we were shopping in Dallas last summer. I've been working on it, as time permitted, ever since."

"Well, this is by far and away grander. I shall cherish it always. Thank you."

The room grew silent, and Marty figured it was as good a time as any to share her news. She'd mulled it over at length and had concluded that the best thing she could do for herself, as well as her sister . . . was lie. Something she had always been quite good at.

"I have a bit of my own news to share," Marty began. All gazes were fixed upon her. "I'm going to be traveling soon."

"Truly?" Hannah looked stunned. "Where are you going?"

Marty drew a deep breath. "Colorado. Perhaps Wyoming to see Andy after that."

"Why Colorado?" William asked.

"I have friends there," Marty said. She had already planned for this part of the lie. "Remember the Stellington sisters? We were in finishing school together, and they were my best friends."

"I remember," Hannah said.

"Well, they've invited me to stay with them for a time in Colorado Springs. I thought it would be nice to get away from the ranch and . . . all the memories." She added the latter to appeal to Hannah's sensitive nature.

For several minutes no one said anything. Marty hoped it might remain that way. Though she didn't want to lie to Hannah, she knew her sister would never approve of Marty running off and marrying a man she hardly knew. In time, Marty would have to let her know the truth, but for now, this was much easier.

"I must say," Hannah finally said, "this is something of a surprise."

"Well, I'd been considering it while you were away, but I didn't want to leave before you'd returned. Now you're back, so it seems a good time."

"But winter will be a difficult time to travel," William said thoughtfully.

"I'll take the train, so it shouldn't be a problem."

Hannah frowned. "How long do you plan to be away?"

"Well, that depends." Marty shrugged. "I hoped that maybe you could run my few head with yours and keep an eye on the place." She didn't want to tell Hannah that she had every intention of selling the ranch. Hannah would know something was up if she made that kind of announcement.

"What's Bert got to say about it?" William asked.

"Well, he's all for returning to work for you." Bert Harris had come to help Marty with the ranch after Thomas's death. He'd worked a great many years prior to that on the Barnett Ranch, and Hannah had insisted Marty allow him to assist. "Bert said with expenses on the increase, it's probably for the best."

William nodded and rubbed his chin. "He's been worried about the low water levels. It isn't near as bad as the drought was in the '80s, but we're still suffering for water. I don't have a problem with this plan, Marty. You tell Bert he's welcome to bunk here again."

"And you'll put him on your payroll?" Marty dared to ask. She hoped the question wouldn't arouse suspicions. "I mean, since I won't be around to oversee him and you can use him to work for you, I just wondered . . ."

"Of course we'll pay his wages," William replied. "He'll do far more for me than he will for you anyhow. You haven't but about fifty head. We'll just run them with ours, and if you aren't back by spring, we'll separate them out and brand the new calves with your mark."

"Or you could just take them in pay," Marty said. "I don't mean for you to be out money on account of my . . . desire to travel."

"Surely you aren't planning to be gone so long as that," Hannah said, leaning forward. She gave Marty an intense look. "Are you?"

Marty shrugged and tried to appear unconcerned. "I might. Especially if I travel to see Andy, as well. I want to make provisions for every possibility. I figure I can close up the house and send the livestock to you. You can keep the animals as pay for checking in on the place from time to time."

"Nonsense. That's what family's for, Aunt Marty." Robert set aside the robe he'd been admiring. "I don't mind going over there to check things out. I'll see to it."

"Thank you, Robert. Thanks to all of you. I know it might seem sudden, but as I said, I've been considering this for some time now."

"I suppose if your mind is made up . . ." Hannah didn't finish her thought, and again the room fell silent.

Finally, William reached out and took up the Bible. "Why don't I read the Christmas story?"

"I'd like that very much," Hannah said.

Marty thought she looked worried. *I hope she won't try to change my mind on this. She always thinks she knows best, and this time . . . well . . . this time she doesn't.* Marty bit her lip and lowered her gaze to avoid giving Hannah any opportunity to question her further. She gave a silent sigh.

Just don't challenge me on this, Hannah. Just let me go without a fuss, and we'll all be a whole lot happier.

Chapter 2

Jacob Wythe couldn't help but pull out the last letter from Martha Olson. "Marty," he reminded himself with a smile. Rereading the beautifully penned script, Jake leaned back in his leather chair and breathed a sigh of relief. She had agreed to marry him, even knowing he wanted a marriage in name only.

"Mr. Wythe, I've brought the ledgers you requested."

Jake looked up to find Arnold Meyers, his secretary, standing in the open doorway. In the younger man's arms were several large record books. "Bring them in and put them on the table over there." Jake stuffed the letter into his pocket. He'd only been made bank manager in September, after the previous manager had died. Having worked for one of the other Morgan Bank branches, Jake was singled out to take the position due to the owner's high regard for his proven abilities. Given Mr. Morgan's faith in him, Jake had taken it upon himself to carefully study the bank's records. The more he familiarized himself with the details, the better he felt about his duties.

The younger man deposited the ledgers, then turned back to face Jake. "Mr. Wythe, I understand congratulations are in order. Mr. Morgan said that you are to be married."

Had anyone other than the bank's owner spread this information around, Jake would have reprimanded the man. Now, however, he supposed Morgan had made it public knowledge. "I am. My bride-to-be will arrive soon after the New Year, and we will marry immediately."

"Will there be a large wedding?"

Jake shook his head and got to his feet. "No. We've both been married before and are fine to wed without any fuss. Now, if you'll excuse me, I need to get back to work." He crossed to the table.

Arnold took the statement as his dismissal and left the office without offering further comment. Jake was grateful, as he had no desire to explain anything of his past to the young man. His past was, in fact, filled with more sorrow and poor choices than Jake cared to reminisce upon.

Picking up one of the ledgers, Jake returned to his desk and tried to focus on the task at hand. Instead, the past came unbidden and flooded his thoughts. Josephine was the first image that came to mind. She was his last attempt at falling in love. The lovely young woman had been the daughter of his father's good friend in California. She was flirtatious and flighty, but Jake had fallen hard for her. They'd married three years earlier, and Jake had never known greater happiness. At least for the first few weeks. After that Josephine grew bored and began to nag him about travel and finding a bigger and better house. Her expensive tastes were more than he could keep up with; however, it was her constant and loudly voiced disappointment in him that caused Jake to grow bitter.

At one time Jake had thought her very much like another young woman he'd fancied himself in love with years before. Deborah Vandermark lived with her family in eastern Texas. When ongoing drought caused Jake's father to sell their Dallas ranch and move to California, Jake hadn't wanted to leave Texas. So rather than join his father, Jake had gone looking for work elsewhere. Unfortunately, the ranching life he loved was not afforded him, and he took a job working for the Vandermark Logging Company.

He couldn't help but smile at the memory of Deborah and her family. The Vandermarks were good people—people he would have very much enjoyed remaining near.

"I would have loved to have married Deborah and called them my own family," he mused. But Deborah had married another, leaving Jake feeling more displaced than ever before. It was then that he had decided to join his family in California and return to college to complete his studies. At least that had been a wise choice. Perhaps his only one.

Opening the ledger and turning one dusty page after another, Jake noted the figures for the first quarter of the year. As they headed into 1893, he wanted to assure himself that the bank was completely solid. There had already been rumors of instability to come, and Jake wasn't about to wait until trouble was upon them to learn whether or not his bank could survive. But try as he might, Jake couldn't help but return his thoughts to Deborah and Josephine.

The two women he'd loved were both dark-eyed and dark-haired. Both were beautiful and intelligent, but where Deborah was kind and godly, Josephine had a wild streak that often made her seem cruel. Cruel and unfeeling. Barely six months after they'd married, while Jake struggled to establish himself in his new career, Josephine established herself with another man. Leaving nothing more than a hastily written note, Josephine deserted him for an adventure with this stranger. Less than six months after that, word came that she had died from some disease in a South American hospital. Jake hated himself for feeling more relief than sorrow.

But now I'm slated to wed again. And for what purpose?

As if on cue, Paul Morgan, the bank's owner and a distant relative of the well-known financier J. Pierpont Morgan, bound into the office without Arnold even having a chance to announce him. Josiah Keystone, branch bank president and board member, followed in the owner's footsteps.

"Mr. Morgan. Mr. Keystone," Jake said, getting to his feet. "I've just been going over this year's books."

"You're a good man, Wythe," the owner declared. "I was skeptical at first about promoting a junior officer to head manager, and had it been anyone but you, I would never have considered it. However, seeing your work and believing you capable of more, I'm glad to have taken the chance."

Keystone nodded. "Yes, in just this short time you have done a great deal to reorganize this establishment. It's to your credit that things are running so smoothly."

Jake was relieved to hear their praise. "I'm glad to know that, sirs."

"If I had ten more just like you, my other branches might run in an equally efficient manner," Morgan said. "But that's not why I've come today. With New Year's just two days away, I wanted to invite you to join us Sunday afternoon for tea. Mrs. Morgan hoped you might otherwise be uninvolved, as she wanted to know more about this new bride of yours."

Breathing a sigh of relief that there was nothing more pressing than an invitation on the old man's mind, Jake smiled. "I would love to join you on New Year's Day, but you will have to remind Mrs. Morgan that I haven't yet acquired my new bride. She is slated to arrive in the middle of January."

"Well, you know how anxious women can be."

"Bank boards, too," Jake murmured under his breath. He'd been badgered to marry since accepting the branch management position. An unmarried man in a position of such responsibility had worried the board members.

Apparently neither Morgan nor Keystone understood his muttering. At least neither acknowledged it, and for that Jake was relieved. He hadn't meant to be so flippant.

Morgan smiled and took a seat opposite Jake. The man's dark hair was graying at the temples, giving him a most distinguished appearance. This, coupled with the expensive cut of his suit and top coat, left little doubt that this was a man of means.

"Have you set the date for your wedding? You know the board is most anxious to see you settled."

Jake nodded. He was already settled, as far as he was concerned. He'd taken up residence in the house allotted him in a rather imposed manner. The board had presented him with loan papers and the keys on the day they'd promoted him to bank manager. He'd had little choice but to accept the offering. Even so, the house was quite lovely and positioned in the best neighborhood in Denver. It wasn't exactly what Jake would have chosen for himself, however. He was far more inclined to live modestly and save his extra money. He'd mentioned this to Morgan, only to receive a strict dressing-down on how a bank manager had a certain reputation to uphold.

"The wedding will take place when my fiancée arrives in Denver. As you know, I am a widower and my bride-to-be is a widow. We don't see any sense in making a fuss. We plan to be very quietly married in the rectory rather than the church as soon as Mrs. Olson arrives."

Morgan nodded. "I'm glad to hear it. It will put everyone's mind at ease once you are settled in as a family man. Married men are much better risks than bachelors." He smiled and cast a quick glance at Keystone. "I think we can all remember our wilder days without good women in our lives to keep us on the straight and narrow." Keystone laughed, but Jake only nodded. He couldn't agree with the men.

Josephine caused me more trouble than good. The straight and narrow wasn't a path she was at all familiar with, nor did she want it for me.

"So I will tell the board that you have arranged to marry by the middle of the month. Sunday you may tell Mrs. Morgan the same. I know she'll want to throw you a party."

"That isn't necessary," Jake protested. "I would never expect someone of your social standing to even give us a second thought."

"Nonsense. I believe you will make something of yourself in no time at all," Morgan stated, getting to his feet. "I have confidence in you, and I'm not one to be ashamed of small beginnings . . . just small endings." He gave Jake a nod. "I believe there are great things ahead for you, my boy. If I thought otherwise, you wouldn't be in my hire."

"Thank you for your confidence in me."

Morgan nodded. "We will see you Sunday, then. Good day." The men exited the room as quickly as they'd entered.

Jake sat back down and considered the bank owner's words. Great things for this man would no doubt be associated with banking, and that wasn't what Jake wanted for his future. Ranching was in his blood, and it was the same that called out to him on a daily basis. He longed to return to the land—to the hard work. He enjoyed fending for himself, sleeping out under the starry skies. He didn't even mind long hours in the saddle. It was office chairs that made his back ache. He'd only taken on this career in order to set aside enough money to purchase his own ranch. Unfortunately, it was taking a lot longer than he'd planned on.

"Sir?" Arnold peeked in through the open office door. "It's closing time. Will you be staying on this evening?"

Jake glanced at the ledgers and shook his head. "Lock these records up for the holidays. I'll get back to them when we return on the second of January."

"Very good, sir."

Jake paid little attention as Arnold scurried around to do his bidding. The younger man was small and pale and didn't appear to resent the business attire that threatened to strangle the life out of Jake. Neckties and stiff collars were akin to torture devices, as far as Jake was concerned.

How he longed for the days of a well-worn shirt, riveted pants, and a sturdy pair of boots. Jake gazed out the window for a moment and sighed. Would he ever see Texas again?

★

Sunday afternoon, Jake found himself seated in the grand salon of the Morgans' palatial home. Located near Sixteenth Avenue and Grant Street, the large Queen Anne was only one of many gems set in Denver's Capitol Hill crown. Most of Denver's high society held court on "The Hill." The opulent homes were graced by equally fashionable people who seldom left the confines of their wealthy estates except to visit other people of equal means. Jake thought it all rather nonsensical. In Texas, his father had been one of the wealthier ranchers before the drought. That didn't mean isolation, however. If anything, it sent people his way on a daily basis. He had good breeder cows and strong bulls. He grazed some of the finest beeves in the South and had made a small fortune during the postwar years.

"Mr. Wythe, I was just telling Mr. Morgan how happy I was to hear about your upcoming nuptials," Mrs. Morgan said, interjecting herself into Jake's memories.

An immaculately dressed servant offered Jake a cup and saucer. "Would you care for cream or sugar?" the woman asked.

Jake shook his head. He was no great lover of tea to begin with, but adding cream and sugar only seemed to make it worse. "No, thank you."

Mrs. Morgan frowned and cast a sharp glance at the servant. Jake had no idea what the woman had done wrong, but she quickly scurried back to the tea cart looking most dejected.

"As I was saying before my girl interrupted, I was glad to hear that you have the wedding date planned. Mr. Morgan tells me that your fiancée is to arrive around the middle of the month. Is that still correct?"

"That's correct, ma'am." Jake drank from the teacup and forced a smile.

"Why such a delay? Could she not leave her people in Texas?" Mrs. Morgan asked in a demanding tone.

Jake put the cup down. "She is visiting friends in Colorado Springs." He smiled and tried to change the conversation. "I must say, this is a beautiful drawing room. Is that Italian marble?" He nodded toward the fireplace.

"Oh goodness, yes," Mrs. Morgan said, looking down her nose at him. "We had an entire shipload delivered to America when the house was being built."

Just then Paul Morgan and several other men entered the room. Jake had no idea where they had been. Since his arrival, he'd only been in Mrs. Morgan's company and was beginning to feel uneasy.

"Mrs. Morgan, please forgive our delay." Mr. Morgan gave his wife a nod, then turned to Jake. "Mr. Wythe, may I introduce some of my associates. Just so happens they are my friends, as well." Jake got to his feet. "This is Mr. Charles Kountze, a man well known in our banking industry."

"It's nice to make your acquaintance, sir."

"Pleasure is mine. I've heard some great things about you from Paul."

Morgan ignored the reference and continued to make the introductions. "This is John Brown; he's the owner of that monstrous structure at Ninth and Grant. I've heard it said that folks call it 'the schoolhouse,' but I cannot say *I've* heard it said."

Brown laughed and extended his hand to Jake. "It's because I have so many children—nearly a dozen. It's good to meet you, Mr. Wythe."

"Likewise, sir."

"And this is Mr. Moffat." Morgan stepped aside so the two men could exchange pleasantries.

"A name I know well," Jake admitted. Fact was, he knew each of these men by name and reputation, although this was his first encounter with them face-to-face. The two men shook hands.

I'm standing in the presence of royalty.

At least Denver's royalty. Jake retook his seat as the men settled into chairs. He marveled at the collective worth of the gentlemen gathered there. Their fortunes came from banking, mining, railroads, and a vast number of other investments. Each was a savvy businessman whose actions had done much to develop Denver into a thriving metropolis.

"Again, I apologize for the delay in joining you here today," Morgan said, refusing a cup of tea from the servant. He motioned her instead to the liquor cabinet. "I had hoped to conclude our business prior to your arrival. After all, this is a holiday."

"A new year, 1893," Moffat said, shaking his head. "Hard to believe this century is nearly gone from us. This year stands on sandy foundations, but if wiser minds prevail, we will see it soon reinforced."

Jake had heard all manner of rumors concerning the state of finances in America. The government about to take office blamed the Sherman Silver Purchase Act, which had required the government to purchase silver using bank notes based on silver or gold holdings. People had been arguing for and against bimetallism as a major issue of politics since the act had gone into effect two and a half years earlier.

The servant returned with a bottle of amber-colored liquor and five glasses on a silver tray. She started to pour Morgan a glass, but he took the bottle from her and held it up. "Gentlemen, may I interest you in a drink?"

"Oh, Mr. Morgan, must you?" his wife questioned.

"My dear, it is a holiday, and we are celebrating. I promise we will only imbibe in one small sampling." He winked at the men and smiled, adding, "For now." The woman rolled her eyes but said nothing more.

Jake shook his head when Morgan looked his way. He held up his teacup. "I'm perfectly fine." There was no need to explain that hard drink had once been his downfall. He had sworn off the stuff ever since making a fool of himself in front of Deborah Vandermark. Even Josephine's nonsense had not caused him to forgo his promise to leave off all alcohol.

"I had forgotten you were a teetotaler, Wythe," Morgan said, as if

23

he disapproved. The man seemed to just as easily put it aside, however, as he moved on to the next man.

"We have a responsibility to our country," Brown declared, taking a glass from Morgan, "but more so to our own community and state. Silver is king in Colorado. We will see to it that Colorado stands strong. We have the resources here to back our financial institutions and must prevail in keeping order."

"What say you, Mr. Wythe?" Kountze asked. All gazes turned to Jake.

For a moment Jake wasn't sure what to say. He had no idea of his opinion mattering in the least. "I believe," he said in slow, measured thought, "that taking preventive measures is always preferable to reflecting on hindsight and regrets of what should have been done."

"Well said, young man. Well said," Moffat agreed. "I've been laying foundations for success since before I was your age. I went to work as a child in a nearby bank, and by the age of sixteen I was promoted to assistant teller. I have owned properties, created businesses, and now labor to see a railroad completed that will connect Denver to Salt Lake. This can only serve to benefit our fine city."

"Gentlemen, I have no desire to sit and listen to a business discussion," Mrs. Morgan interjected. "Today is a day of rest and a celebration of the New Year. I would ask you to postpone your choice of topics to another day."

Mr. Morgan smiled and nodded, while the other men offered their apologies. Jake felt a sense of relief as the conversation turned first to the weather and then to some of the artistic touches that could be seen in the architecture of the house. Even the liquor seemed to be forgotten.

"Yes, yes, the windows were something I had to have," Mrs. Morgan admitted. "After seeing your beautiful stained glass, Mr. Kountze, I could hardly do without."

Kountze chuckled. "I suppose it wouldn't be fitting to let our ladies' desires go unmet. I have learned in my lifetime that keeping the women of the house happy is almost certainly a guarantee of one's personal contentment."

"And shortly Mr. Wythe is to learn that lesson for himself," Mrs. Morgan said with a knowing smile. "He is to wed soon."

24

"Congratulations, Wythe," Morgan's associates offered nearly in unison.

Kountze nodded in approval. "This is indeed a day of celebration. And might I inquire after your young lady? Tell us about her."

"She's a widow from Texas . . . my home state," Jake added the latter as if it would matter to these men. "Her name is Mrs. Martha Olson."

"Is she of means?" Mr. Brown asked.

Jake didn't quite know what to say. He'd never really inquired as to Marty's financial circumstances. At first he'd figured if she was answering an ad for a mail-order bride, she couldn't be much to look at. Then she had sent her picture, and Jake knew that wasn't a problem. He figured she wasn't financially secure and needed to find a husband who could take care of her needs.

"Let us refrain from such vulgar talk," Mrs. Morgan said before Jake could reply. "I'm sure we shall enjoy getting to know Mrs. Olson—Mrs. Wythe—for ourselves."

"I hope so," Jake replied. "I believe Marty, uh, Mrs. Olson, will be a pleasant and genteel addition to my home. I've been too long without a wife, as your good husband pointed out."

Chapter 3

Marty shifted uncomfortably as the stage hit yet another rough spot in the road. Why she had ever allowed the Stellington sisters to talk her into taking the stage from Colorado Springs to Denver was beyond her. After several train delays, her friends had assured her that this service, for women only, was one their father had made available for ladies of means traveling unaccompanied from Colorado Springs to Denver and back. The journey, although not as fast as by train, would afford her comfort and amiable companions.

Looking across the enclosure at the three dozing old ladies positioned in the seat opposite, Marty couldn't help but smile. They had been all talk the first twenty or so miles of the trip. But now even the younger matron and daughter who sat beside Marty had stopped their incessant arguing and fallen silent. The only men were the stage driver and his shotgun rider. No doubt they were glad to be riding topside. Marty envied them.

Cradling her carpetbag, Marty considered what was to come. They had changed horses at the Seventeen Mile House; their next goal would be the Four Mile House, but Marty knew that was still more than an hour away. She was thankful that the weather had been so nice—though far colder than what she'd known in Texas, she knew the temperatures had been mild for the area. And though there was no stove on the stage as there had been on the train, Marty was used to taking such matters in stride. Much of her life had consisted of desperately hard work, along with occasional periods of ease and pleasure.

And now I'm to marry a stranger.

The thought left her feeling both nervous and excited. Jacob Wythe had promised her a life of ease in his last letter, a life filled with pleasantries and beauty. Marty wasn't sure what all that might involve, but it had to be better than life in Texas, where death stalked her at every turn.

She rubbed her gloved fingers along the ivory handle of the carpetbag and tried to imagine what her new life would bring. Mr. Wythe had told her of his lovely house and the servants who would see to their needs. She considered pulling out the letter again to read Jacob's descriptions of Denver, then thought better of it. To open her bag would cause her to jostle the matronly woman beside her, and Marty had no desire to stir up a conversation. Besides, she had nearly memorized the lines of each letter.

This decision had not come easily; neither had it come without a price. She could still hear Hannah's insistence that Robert accompany Marty at least as far as Colorado Springs. Marty knew her older sister was concerned for her safety, but Marty also knew it was important to make a stand. She had done her best to assure Hannah that she would be perfectly fine—that traveling by train in the 1890s no longer necessitated a chaperone for a woman in her position.

Hannah had been less than convinced, and Marty thought this almost comical for a woman who, during the War Between the States, had ridden off alone to help nurse a small band of hostile Comanche who were suffering from smallpox. Throwing out that memory in the face of Hannah's protests quickly quieted her sister, but still didn't win her approval. Nevertheless, Marty had her way.

I'll miss them.

There was no doubt about that, and Marty didn't pretend otherwise. She loved her family. It was Texas she hated. Texas and ranch life. She thought of Thomas again and gazed out across the landscape at the horizon. He would have liked Colorado—especially the snow-covered mountains. He might have even wanted to move there, Marty mused.

One of the old ladies began to snore, causing the matron's daughter to giggle. Marty had thought the silent young woman asleep, but even if she had been, her mother's sharp elbowing now put an end to that. The daughter straightened and gave a howl of protest, which only served to awaken the sleeping old women.

"Oh, do be quiet, Amanda," the matronly woman demanded. "You've disturbed the entire coach."

"It's not my fault! You hurt me. I am most likely bruised the full length of my side." The girl clutched her right side for emphasis. "I don't know why we have to go visit your aunt anyway. She's old and she smells funny."

One of the older women let out a *tsk*ing sound and turned to her traveling companions with a shake of her head.

"Oh, stuff and nonsense. You do go on." Her mother was clearly in no mood for her daughter's whining, and neither was Marty. She was prepared to say as much when the unmistakable sound of a shot rang out.

Before they could say another word, the shotgun sounded from overhead and the stage picked up speed. Marty leaned out the window and hollered up to the driver. "What's happened?"

"Bandits!" the man yelled. "Get down in there!"

Marty pulled back inside and turned to the other women in the coach. They were now all wide awake. "Do any of you have a weapon?"

The women collectively shook their heads. Marty opened her carpetbag and pulled out a Smith and Wesson revolver. "Well, I do." The matron gasped and her daughter pretended to swoon. Marty knew it was pretense, because the girl had given this performance multiple times on their journey.

With precise action, Marty loaded the .32 caliber top break without even doffing her gloves. Thomas had gifted her the gun the summer before his death. It was mostly for warding off rattlers and copperheads, but Marty had no difficulty protecting her welfare from snakes of the two-legged variety.

"You don't really mean to fire that thing, do you?" the matron asked.

Marty aimed the gun out the window as the first glimpse of a rider came into view. "I most certainly do." A bullet ricocheted off one of the hubs of the stagecoach. "You ladies would do well to keep your heads down." The shotgun boomed again, and this time Marty added her own precisely aimed shot.

Her traveling companions offered no further protest. Ducking low in their seats, they murmured prayers aloud instead. Marty could now see there were at least two riders. She hoped there weren't more. Surely between the shotgun rider and her own efforts, they would be able to hold the bandits at bay.

The bandits fired a flurry of shots in rapid order. Marty felt the horses pick up an even faster pace and fought hard to keep her aim straight. The shotgun echoed a reply, as did the little .32 revolver. Marty quickly ejected the spent cartridges and reloaded the gun. One of the riders had gained on them considerably and was nearly to the rear of the stage. Leaning as far out the window as she could manage, Marty aimed and fired again just as the shotgun blasted. The rider fell back, wounded. She had no idea if her bullet had helped to cause the damage, but she felt a sense of satisfaction as the shotgun was fired again and the rider dropped from the saddle.

"We got at least one of them," she declared to the women. Not even one of the formerly talkative old women responded. They were all terror-stricken and looking at Marty with new respect.

Marty smiled to herself and turned her attention back to the task at hand. There was no sign of the other rider. She wondered if he'd crossed to the opposite side of the stage. Unconcerned with the matron's protest, Marty threw herself across the older woman and her daughter to look out the opposite window. The stage was slowing now.

Straightening, Marty called up to the driver, "Are they gone?"

She heard the man calling out to the horses and the stage rolled to a stop. Without thought to her safety, Marty opened the door and jumped out. She wasn't used to the extra forty pounds of heavy traveling clothes and nearly went to her knees. Righting herself, however, she looked up to where the driver and his shotgun messenger sat. Only now the driver was slumped in the seat, clinging to the reins as the other man did his best to keep him upright.

"How can I help?" Marty called up.

"Mac's shot up bad," the man said. "I can't say I'm much better off. My arm's no good. We barely got the team stopped." His voice sounded strained.

Marty lifted her heavy wool skirt and tore a huge strip of petticoat. Casting a quick glance down the road, she felt relieved that no riders were in sight.

The matron and one of the old women had poked their heads out the windows. "What's going on? What is happening?" the matron demanded to know.

"Our driver and the shotgun are badly wounded," Marty replied.

"What are we to do?" the old lady asked fearfully. "Those men will soon return, and we will be . . . oh my . . . we might be . . . ravaged."

Marty would have laughed out loud had it not been for the precariousness of the situation. "I think they meant to rob us. Now, stay put while I help the men with their injuries."

She hiked her skirt again and put her booted foot on the hub of the stagecoach wheel. The wheel was nearly as tall as she was, and with the extra weight of her clothes it wasn't an easy feat. Not only that, but she was still trying to adjust to the higher altitude. She panted a bit as she struggled to place her right foot on top of the wheel rim itself. The nervous team refused to stand still and began to back up. Marty barely managed to grab hold of the rail at the front of the driver's box before she lost her footing. With strength she didn't know she possessed, Marty managed to swing her foot up to catch the edge of the front boot. All the while she vowed to herself that she would never again wear this many layers of clothing.

It seemed to take forever, but in fact only a few seconds passed as she hoisted herself awkwardly into the boot. Straightening, she secured the brake and took the bloodied reins from the wounded man and wrapped them around the rail. The shotgun rider cast her an apologetic glance as he slumped back. The driver was now unconscious.

"Sorry, ma'am. I couldn't hold 'em." Both sleeves were blood-soaked, and the man's face was nearly as white as her shirtwaist.

"It's not a problem. We have them now." Marty handed him the torn material. "Use this to stop the bleeding as best you can. How's the driver?"

"He took a bullet to the back and one grazed his head. I think he's still alive."

Even with the brake set, Marty knew it was dangerous to ignore the team of six, but she had to see to the driver. Doing her best to keep sight of the reins, she leaned across the slumped man and felt his chest. He was still breathing. Her gloved hand came away even wetter with blood, however.

"How far to the next stagehouse?"

"A good six miles," the messenger replied. "But I can't drive—not this way."

"I understand. I didn't mean for you to. I'll drive the team."

"You, ma'am? But you're just a little bitty thing." The man struggled to tie off the material around his wounded arm. "I can't let you do that."

"Nobody else is able to do it," she told him. "I've driven wagon teams before. I can handle this, as well. You just settle in and direct me."

Marty managed to straighten the unconscious driver enough that she could take a seat. Calling down to the passengers, she released the brake. "We're heading out, ladies." It was the only warning Marty gave before she snapped the reins. "Yah!" she bellowed and the team stepped into action.

By the time they reached Four Mile House, Marty's forearms burned and her hands cramped. She had pushed aside her discomfort, knowing that the lives of the driver and shotgun were reliant upon her getting them medical attention. She had pressed the team to their limit and couldn't help but sigh with relief at the sight of the station.

The stagehouse operators appeared for the relay change. They stared up in stunned surprise at the small woman. "We were attacked," Marty called down. "These men need a doctor fast!"

The two men who'd come to change out the team quickly went into action to retrieve the wounded men from atop the stage. Meanwhile, the women passengers spilled out from the coach. The matron and her daughter were sobbing in each other's arms, while the old women were chattering on and on about their brush with molestation and certain death. Marty waited patiently while the injured men were taken inside the house. She was relieved, however, when a young man bounded up the side of the stage and took the reins from her hands.

"I'll see to this now, ma'am." He gave her a grin as big as Texas. "You sure are somethin'. Ain't many women—especially one so purty—that could handle a team like this."

Marty looked at her bloodied clothes and thought of how disarrayed her hair and hat must be. She smiled and shook her head. "Perhaps you can tell me where I might clean up."

"I'll help you, ma'am," an older man called. "Let me get you down from there first."

Marty stepped to the side of the boot and allowed the man to help her from the stage. She felt her knees very nearly buckle as her feet hit the ground again.

"Easy there, ma'am." The man held fast to her arm as Marty drew in a deep breath and steadied herself.

"Thank you. I'm fine now." She allowed him to escort her into the house, where the other women had gathered. Everyone paused and turned their gaze to Marty. One of the older women came forward and took Marty's arm.

"Come with me, deary. I'll help you get cleaned up. You saved our lives, you know. You're a heroine!"

Marty shook her head. "No, I only helped our men. They are the real heroes."

The old woman kept moving Marty toward a stand with water and fresh towels. A woman Marty didn't know appeared and began to help.

"I'm Sallie," the woman explained. "I'm wife to the station manager here. What's your name?"

"Mrs. Marty Olson." She glanced around the room. "Was there someone nearby to help our driver and his man?"

Sallie smiled and stripped the bloodied gloves from Marty's hands. "Dr. Bryant is just a mile away. I already sent my boy to get him and the sheriff. You did real good in bringing them on in, Mrs. Olson. Probably saved their lives. I'll get these bloody gloves soaking in salt water. Since the blood is still fresh, I'm thinking we can get it out."

Marty's mind flew in a thousand directions. She worried that the men had no one to tend them while these women were fussing over her. She wondered if the boy would get the doctor in time and whether

32

the sheriff would be able to find the culprits who had attacked them. But most of all, Marty worried about what her betrothed might think once he heard about the commotion and how Marty threw propriety aside to shoot at the bandits and then drive the stage. He had wanted a proper lady for his bride—a Lone Star bride, to be exact.

Goodness, what will he think of me now?

★

"That's really all I can tell you," Marty told the sheriff the next morning. "I saw two riders. They were masked, and one had a sorrel mount, but I don't recall the color of the other horse." Marty continued to hold the mug of hot coffee she'd been given. From time to time she sipped the strong concoction and hoped it would give her the strength to complete this ordeal.

"That's quite all right, ma'am. You've done more than enough." The sheriff gave her a broad smile. "There aren't many women who could have done what you did. Thanks to you, both Mac and JR are gonna make it. Doc says they might have bled to death out there on the road if you hadn't gotten them in here. Oh, and JR says your shooting was probably what drove those men off. They most likely knew it was a stage full of women and figured to rob them of their jewelry and doodads. They sure weren't expecting there to be another armed protector inside."

"New driver's ready and the stage is set to head on to Denver," a man called from the door. Marty's traveling companions bustled off toward the stage, their babbling conversations creating quite a cacophony.

"They'll be talking about this all the way to Denver," the sheriff said, grinning Marty's way.

"No doubt." She put down her mug and got to her feet. The bloodstains on her traveling jacket and gloves had been scrubbed out the night before, and for the most part, Marty had been restored to proper order.

"Do you have friends in Denver, Mrs. Olson?" the sheriff asked, escorting her to the stage.

Without thinking she answered, "I'm to meet my fiancé. We were to have married yesterday, but with the train delay and then the attack on the stage . . . well, I suppose we will marry today. If he'll still have me." She had her doubts that a banker would appreciate her antics, even if they were heroic. But it was too late to worry about that now.

"Well, he'd be a fool if he didn't. In fact, I tell you what," the sheriff said, pausing at the stage with Marty. "If he doesn't want to marry you, you just make your way on back here. I know a dozen or more boys who'd snatch you up in a minute."

Marty couldn't help but smile at the man's expression of admiration. "Thank you, Sheriff. I'll keep that in mind."

Chapter 4

"Oh my, such excitement," one of Marty's gray-haired traveling companions declared.

"Why, we might all have been killed but for you," another said as the others agreed.

"I think it's scandalous," the woman who introduced herself as Mrs. Merriweather Stouffer announced. No one was sure if Merriweather was the name of her husband or the woman herself, and sadly no one really cared.

"Our father said that a woman ought to be able to handle a firearm," one of the old women commented, nodding to her companion. "Isn't that so, Ophelia? You remember, don't you? Papa always said that a woman with a keen eye and steady hand could take care of herself."

"Oh yes, sister. I do remember. Papa was always so very wise." The woman nodded with a look of absolute certainty.

Marty fought back a smile. The old women who had babbled most of the way from Colorado Springs were now even more infused with stories and tall tales. Not only that, but they'd made their admiration and gratitude toward Marty abundantly clear. The matron and her daughter still held her in contempt, and with exception to the occasional comment, they said little. Perhaps they feared Marty might turn her gun on them if they were to become too annoying.

The stage came to a stop, and in the time it took the shotgun messenger to climb down and open the door, a crowd swooped in and surrounded the stage. Questions were called out to the driver and his man. Marty could see there were several reporters, and two photographers were already setting up their cameras.

Good grief. That's all I need.

"Folks, if you'll calm down, I'm sure the ladies inside will be happy to speak to you," the driver announced. "Be polite, or otherwise you'll be escorted off the premises."

Marty clutched her carpetbag closer and leaned back further in her seat. The older women hurried from the stage as if all the world were waiting for them. They immediately launched into exaggerated accounts of the peril they had faced to anyone who would listen. The matron and her daughter disembarked and immediately began to wail in loud sobs that drew the attention of the reporters away from the babbling women. The older trio looked quite annoyed at this development.

The entire fuss, however, allowed Marty to slip from the coach and blend into the crowd of people. She searched each face, hoping to find Jacob Wythe and escape before the reporters learned her identity.

"Mrs. Olson?"

She startled and hesitated to answer.

The man smiled. "Mrs. Olson?"

"Yes?" She found herself gazing into the face of one of the handsomest men she'd ever met. His photograph did him no justice. She couldn't help but return the smile.

"Mr. Wythe?"

"The same." He let out a long breath. "We heard about the attack on your stage only this morning." He tugged at his starched collar, looking most uncomfortable.

"But you received my telegram? The sheriff assured me he would send one."

The blond-haired man nodded. "He did, ma'am. But it only said that you'd been delayed overnight. I assure you, Mrs. Olson, had I known what had taken place, I would have driven down to pick you up at Four Mile House."

"Marty," she corrected. "Please don't call me Mrs. Olson."

He grinned. "Marty. I don't think I mentioned in my letters how much I like that name. It suits you, too. Of course, you should call me Jake."

"I'd like that very much. I wasn't at all certain if you were that casual in your daily living."

"Ma'am . . . Marty, I would be nothing but casual if I could get away with it."

She relaxed a bit. "Well, I reckon I would, too."

"'Reckon,'" he repeated. "You speak like a true Texan."

"That's good, because I am," she replied, a bit curious at his comment. "Was I not supposed to?"

A chuckle escaped him, and his own drawl seemed a little more pronounced. "Well, you see, up here . . . in my new position as bank manager, 'reckoning' is reserved for bank ledgers and seldom mentioned in common speech. I've had to work hard to sound . . . well . . . less Texas cowboy and more Colorado banker."

"But I thought Denver to be a very western town. You mentioned mining and cattle as two of the larger industries." Marty glanced around her, noticing the buildings and well-orchestrated streets. "I suppose it is a bit more dressed up than I figured to find. Having grown up on a ranch, I didn't get into town all that often. Certainly not all the way into cities like Dallas."

"Oh, it does me good, ma'am—Marty—to hear you talk about Dallas. I have to say I miss Texas more than my own parents." He paused and gazed behind her. "Oh, it would seem you've caught the attention of the press. No doubt they want to hear from you. They're coming this way now."

"Oh bother." Marty cast a frantic glance in the direction of the reporters and then back to Jake. "I really don't want to talk to them. My family will worry. They . . . well . . . I didn't tell them I'd come to get married. I'm really sorry, but perhaps you could get me out of here without having to speak to them?"

"I can't see that happenin' now." He frowned. "Why don't you just tell them you came to Colorado to visit friends? Don't say anything about marryin' me."

She threw him a grateful smile. "Thank you, Jake. If it got back to my sister before I could write to tell her, she'd be hurt."

"Mrs. Olson! Mrs. Olson!" the men called to her.

The crowd parted, and all faces turned to Marty. She swallowed hard and waited as the gathering closed in on her.

"We understand you fought off the attackers with your own gun," one man said, giving a quick doff of his hat.

By now Jake had moved away from Marty and she stood alone. She glanced around for some sight of him and found him sandwiched between several curious onlookers. Marty looked back to the man who'd just spoken.

"I did."

"Tell us what happened," another reporter urged.

"We were attacked, and I helped to defend the stage," she said as though it were something she did every day.

"How many were there?"

She shrugged. "I only saw two."

"One of your traveling companions mentioned there being at least a dozen," the man said. The crowd seemed to hang on to his words.

Marty smiled and repeated, "I only saw two."

"And did you kill those two?" the reporter asked.

"Who can say? I fired my gun. Like my brother-in-law taught me, any time you draw a weapon, you have to be ready to use it, and you have to be ready to accept the consequences. I may have killed a man."

"May I quote you on that?" the man asked, writing furiously on a pad of paper.

"Of course," Marty said with a shrug.

"And then you nursed the unconscious driver and staunched the flow of blood from his associate's wounds—no doubt saving their lives—before risking your life to handle the fear-struck team and bring the coach and passengers to safety?" the first reporter questioned in rapid fire.

They made it all sound so dramatic, and while it had been a most anxious moment in Marty's life, she hardly saw the need to write it up in such a way. She had no chance to reply, however.

"Mrs. Olson, where are you from and what brought you to Denver?"

This question came from a new man, who looked to be acting in some sort of official capacity. He eyed her with marked intent.

"I beg your pardon?" Marty asked in return.

The man touched the brim of his hat. "The name is Haggarty. I'm one of the owners of this stage line."

"I see. To answer your question, I hail from Texas and am here in Colorado visiting friends."

"Will you be staying with your friends here in Denver?" the man asked. "I may have need to speak with you regarding this matter."

Panic struck Marty. What should she say? She didn't want to explain that she planned to be married as soon as she could get away from this interrogation. Realizing that everyone was watching and awaiting her answer, Marty shook her head.

"I . . . my plans are uncertain. Now, if you'll excuse me, I must arrange for my things. Once I'm settled with my . . . friends here, I can send word so that you can get in touch, should you have further questions."

"Mrs. Olson, we'd like a picture." The first and most annoying of the reporters took hold of her arm and moved her through the crowd back to the stage. "I wonder if you would climb back into the driver's seat—and hold your gun like you're firing it?" He looked at her with great anticipation. "Maybe over your shoulder like this." He acted out the pose he wanted.

"I should say not," Marty replied, rather appalled at the thought. "I only wish to get my things. No picture." She pulled away from the man and hurried toward the stage office. Several questions were hurled after her, but Marty kept moving forward, ignoring the clamor.

Mr. Haggarty appeared at her side and ushered her into the office. "You don't seem too excited to play the heroine."

She met the man's questioning expression. "Two men nearly lost their lives—they may still die. I hardly see this as an occasion for celebration and playing the heroine. We could have all been killed. My hope is that you would better spend your time seeing to the safety of your travelers."

"Pardon the interruption . . . Mrs. Olson?"

A large man with skin as black as coal called from the door. "Mrs. Olson, I's your driver. I has your trunks already loaded."

39

Marty breathed a sigh of relief. "Thank you." She gave Haggarty a nod. "Good day, sir. I'll be in touch."

She hurried from the office and allowed the stranger to lead her toward an enclosed carriage. The tall man slowed his step. "Mr. Wythe sent me. He be already inside."

A sigh escaped her lips. "Thank you. I think I would have risked traveling with the devil himself to get away from that ordeal."

The man laughed. "My mama done whooped the devil right outta me years ago. Name's Samson, ma'am."

Marty threw him a smile. "Glad to meet you, Samson."

Jake watched with pride as Marty Olson settled herself across from him in the carriage. Samson closed the door and had the carriage on its way before anything else could delay them.

"You handled yourself well, Marty."

She leaned back against the leather upholstery, looking exhausted. "I never anticipated such a grand welcome to Denver."

"I hope it won't put you off on our plans."

"If you mean do I figure to back out of the wedding, then the answer is no. I'm a woman of my word. I hope you are a man of yours."

Jake chuckled. "I most assuredly am. I wasn't raised to go back on my word."

Marty fidgeted with her carpetbag. "I'm glad to hear it, but I wouldn't blame you if you had changed your mind, given the situation."

"Marty, I think you figure me to be ashamed of what you did, but I'm not. You're exactly what I advertised for. A woman of character and ability. You evaluated the situation that life gave you, and you fought back. You probably saved lives in your actions. I can't be faultin' you for that."

"But a man in your position," she began, "a position that demands respect and . . . well . . . dignity . . ." She fell silent and looked toward the window.

"My dignity isn't hurt by your saving the lives of those people. Society will think what it will, but the way I figure it, we will just work it to our advantage."

Marty looked up, and her expression was one of confusion. Jake smiled. "The people of Denver are adventurers. This isn't that old of a state—nothing like our beloved Texas. Folks out here might put on the pretenses of being high society, but a good many of them started in places rougher than ours. They might make like they're shocked, but I'm bettin' most will hold you in esteem for what you did. I know the men will—if not the women."

"I hope you're right. I came to be a help to you in your social standing. You said you needed a wife to please the bank board. I hope they don't mind a woman who can shoot."

Jake couldn't hold back his laughter. "Marty, once they meet you they'll probably offer you a job at the bank. The first lady guard."

Marty giggled, and he could see that she was relaxing a bit. She was more beautiful than he'd anticipated. Her blond hair and blue eyes were a sharp contrast from the looks of Josephine and Deborah.

"So, are you . . . uh . . . ready to tie the knot?"

She nodded. "I suppose I am."

"We might as well get to it, then," Jake said. "We can marry on the way to . . . our house."

With those words, the atmosphere changed and the tension increased again. Jake realized that despite the easygoing conversation, they were strangers. Strangers who were to marry and share a home together.

Marty obviously sensed it, too. He saw her look away again, and this time she bit her lower lip. He wanted nothing more than to ease her mind.

"I meant what I said."

She threw him a cautious glance. "I don't understand."

"In the letters. I meant what I said. I intend for this to be a marriage of convenience—a union in name only. I don't want you thinkin' otherwise. I didn't get you out here on false pretenses. I don't intend for you to be a real wife to me."

Marty nodded. "I appreciate that you appear to understand my unease. I'm not generally a woman who does things in such a rash manner. Even so, answering your advertisement and coming here seemed . . . well . . . almost predetermined."

He wasn't at all sure he understood her meaning, but nodded just the same. "I want to reassure you that you'll have full access to a beautiful home, a bank account of your own, and the freedom to do pretty much as you please. There will, of course, be obligations—parties and other gatherings. I do have certain demands placed on my shoulders—demands that I'd just as soon forgo but find impossible to escape. You'll have demands, too."

"I understand. But I can't say that my wardrobe is exactly worthy of grand social events. I am a modest woman, and while I lived better than many in Texas, I was never one for fancy garb."

"That won't be a problem. I'll see to anything you need. My housekeeper already mentioned it, in fact, and I asked her to arrange for a dressmaker and so forth." The carriage slowed, and they heard Samson halt the team.

Jake looked out the window. "But besides that, Marty, I'd like it if we could be friends. My family's all back in California, and even though I've lived here a bit, I don't make friends easily."

Her sweet expression reassured him of his choice. "Of course we will be friends, Jake. I very much look forward to it, in fact."

The carriage halted, and Samson opened the door. "We be at the church."

Marty gazed at the large stone church in surprise. The huge steeple seemed to reach forever into the gray-blue skies. "A church wedding?"

"Actually, a rectory wedding, if you don't mind." Jake sounded hesitant—almost as if he feared her response.

Marty actually breathed a sigh of relief. "I don't mind at all. I was hoping we weren't going to make a circus of this."

He shook his head and offered Marty his arm. "No sense in it. We both have been married before, and we aren't children to be impressed by a lot of tomfoolery. You told me you liked to keep things simple, and I took you at your word."

For reasons she couldn't explain, his statement made her almost sad. They weren't that old and even if they had been married before, Jake made it sound as if they were past their prime. Were they really putting aside all the pleasures of youth?

42

"Frankly," Jake continued, "I find it kind of refreshing."

"What?" Marty asked as they moved toward the sandstone structure.

"That we don't have any pretenses between us. We both know why we're here. I like that."

For a moment, guilt washed over Marty. She managed to sidestep most of the reprehensive feelings, but one lingered. She had lied a good deal through the course of her life. Well, perhaps *lie* was too harsh a term; she often did nothing more serious than leave out important details—especially if they might get her into trouble. Marty had also been given to making mountains out of molehills, despite Hannah's attempts to wrest it out of her. But now . . . now she felt herself falling right back into her old ways. A lie had brought her here. Her life with this stranger would be a lie. The world would believe one thing, while in truth they would be another. It would be her greatest exaggeration.

"You don't think this is wrong, do you?" she asked without thinking.

Jake stopped. "You havin' second thoughts?"

Marty pushed down her concerns and smiled. "No," she lied, afraid it would be the first of many. "You?"

Jake laughed. "Hardly. I just wanna get this over with and get on with my life."

The door to the rectory opened just then, and a smiling dark-suited man welcomed them. "Ah, the happy couple. Come, come. I have the witnesses ready and the arrangements have all been made. Soon you will be joined in wedded bliss."

Marty looked away lest he see her roll her eyes. Wedded bliss indeed.

Chapter 5

Marty settled once more into the carriage seat. She was married. She stared down at the ring on her finger. It was a lovely piece of jewelry, a large emerald surrounded by smaller diamonds.

"I hope you aren't disappointed in the ring," Jake said.

She studied him for a moment. There was such a look of hopefulness in his expression that she couldn't have admitted to such an emotion even if she had felt it. Which she didn't. "Not in the least. I'm stunned. I've never had anything so grand. My other wedding ring was a simple gold band."

"I was going to buy you just that, but Mr. Morgan, the owner of the bank, insisted that I purchase something bigger and better," he explained. "He gave me a bonus, in fact, for just such a purpose."

"It's lovely and fits nicely." She pulled her gloves back on and smiled. "Almost as if it were meant for me. I will cherish it—thank you." Discomfort edged her emotions, and Marty quickly changed the subject. "So tell me about the place we are to live."

Jake shrugged. "There again, it wasn't what I would have picked out, but Mr. Morgan insisted. Fact is, it came with the job."

Apparently this Mr. Morgan had a way of bullying people into doing things they ordinarily wouldn't do. Marty made a mental note to remember that name.

"So is it all that bad?"

"No." He eased back against the seat, causing his hat to slide forward. He straightened again and adjusted the brim. "It's beautiful. It's grand and glorious, and in the words of Mrs. Morgan, 'It maintains the essence of elegance.'" His poor attempt to mimic the woman made Marty smile. Jake shook his head. "Much more so than I would have ever wanted. Mr. Morgan says that a man in my position has to live the part. For myself, I would just as soon live in a less pretentious neighborhood and save the money. That way, one day, I could buy my own idea of the perfect place."

She nodded. "So we're to live in a grand house. Is it very large?"

"I recall the paper work saying something about eight thousand square feet," he replied. "Seems like you could fit five or six families in there."

Marty's eyes widened. Her home in Texas had more than enough room and wasn't anywhere near that size. "Oh my. I suppose it will be a lot of work to keep up."

"That's why we have people to work for us."

"People?" She frowned. "Oh yes, I remember you said you had a staff to keep the house."

"You'll get to meet them soon enough. The house came with servants—again, something Mr. Morgan insisted on and not at all my idea. Look, we're just now arriving."

Marty glanced out the window at the three-story redbrick and stone house. There was a large porch on the front, some six steps up from the ground. An impressive turret stood to the right of the porch and a roofed balcony was atop the porch itself.

"The house is made of Colorado red sandstone," Jake announced. "The rest is local brick."

"It's quite lovely . . . and big." Marty quickly took in the dry brown grass contrasting with several large green pines. "I had thought there would be snow," she said.

"There was. We had a white Christmas, but a warm southwesterly wind melted it. Don't worry, we'll no doubt see some more."

She smiled. "I've never seen very deep snow. We only had small amounts in Texas. Well, there was one snow that proved worse than most, but even so, it melted quickly."

He nodded. "I think I know the one you mean. Well, around here you can never tell what to expect. The mountains make for interesting weather."

"They are beautiful . . . the mountains," Marty remarked. "I've never seen anything like them. My friends in Colorado Springs hoped I would return and go with them to the top of Pikes Peak. A local carriage company treats sight-seekers to the adventure. It takes all day, and at the top, they say you can hardly breathe. I can hardly breathe at this level."

"Altitude can be kind of hard on a body. We're not that high here, so it should be less troublesome. Even so, after a time you'll adjust." The carriage stopped, and Jake reached for the door before Samson could open it for them. "Come along, Mrs. Wythe. I'm anxious to show you your new home."

Marty allowed Jake to help her from the carriage. His hands held her waist for only as much time as was needed to plant her feet firmly on the ground. His familiarity surprised her, but Marty said nothing as he guided her to the front door.

A distinguished-looking gentleman, probably fifty or more years of age, opened the door and stood waiting. "Welcome home, sir. Madam."

"Marty, this is Brighton, my butler and valet. He sees to most of my needs."

"How do you do, Mr. Brighton."

The man's expression remained sober. "Madam, it is my pleasure to meet you."

"And this is Mrs. Landry," Jake continued.

Marty hadn't even noticed the three women who'd positioned themselves just in front of a grand oak staircase. The oldest of the three stepped forward. "I'm Mrs. Landry." She was an unassuming woman with a neatly coiffed head of gray hair. She wore a dark blue gown with a high collar. "I oversee the staff here, including Mr. Brighton, although he doesn't believe that to be the case." The older man gave a harrumph but said nothing.

"Mrs. Landry," Marty said, nodding. "I'm Martha Ols . . . Wythe, but everyone calls me Marty."

"I shall call you Mrs. Wythe," the woman said, giving the slightest smile. "We all shall call you Mrs. Wythe." She turned to the other two women. "This is Kate." The short redheaded maid bobbed a curtsy while Mrs. Landry continued the introduction. "Kate works with me to keep the house in order. She's fairly new but learning quickly."

"Very nice to meet you, Kate."

"Ma'am." The girl looked to Mrs. Landry as if further explanation were needed.

Mrs. Landry cleared her throat. "Yes, well, Kate will assist you as lady's maid until you can secure your own hire. Mr. Wythe let us know that you would not be bringing a woman with you."

Marty laughed without meaning to. "No, I don't have a maid of my own." Mrs. Landry frowned, as if this announcement lessened her opinion of Marty. "I'm really quite capable," Marty continued.

Jake interrupted. "You'll need a maid. The parties, teas, and other social functions will require you to dress for the occasion. I'm told women often change clothes as many as six times a day. You'll need a woman who can dress your hair and help you with your clothes and bath."

She tried her best not to look surprised by this news. Changing clothes more than twice in one day required a special event back in Texas! Marty supposed she should have figured on such a thing, but since she'd been old enough to dress herself, she'd been doing pretty much just that. The only time she'd had help was when she was first learning to wear a corset, and even then Hannah had taught her how to lace herself in after a time.

"I'll have the employment service send over some women for you to interview," Mrs. Landry continued. "Kate will need to return to her household duties as soon as possible, as I cannot manage this house on my own and Brighton believes a manservant should not have to attend to dusting the high chandeliers and washing the windows, although he is the best candidate for the tasks."

This time Brighton refused to remain silent. "I explained to Mrs. Landry that it is not expected of a proper butler. I trained with the best of instructors as a young man in England. I will not have this hoyden of a housekeeper poison your mind against me."

"Hoyden? You dare call me a *hoyden*, you English-trained ninny?

You pride yourself on going all the way to London to learn how to help a gentleman into a jacket or to open a door."

"Yes, and in England it is the butler who runs the household, madam. Not the housekeeper."

"Well, in case you didn't know it, Mr. Brighton, this isn't England. I can fetch a map if you doubt me."

Jake snorted and Marty turned to find him completely amused by the tirade. He shrugged at her questioning gaze. "I don't even bother to go to plays or operas. I can get all the entertainment I need here at home just watching these two."

"Such codswallop," Brighton declared. "Sir, if you need me, I shall be polishing the silver."

"At least he stoops to help me with that," Mrs. Landry spouted at Brighton's back. "I guess the English deem that an acceptable job for men."

Jake didn't bother to hide his grin. "See what I mean?"

Marty could only nod in agreement. In Brighton's absence, Mrs. Landry moved to the other woman. "This is our cook, Mrs. Standish. Up until now she worked alone, but Mr. Wythe has arranged for an assistant. She will arrive in three days—on the twenty-third."

"I would imagine Mrs. Wythe is quite exhausted," Jake declared, helping Marty from her coat. "Why don't we show her to her room."

Mrs. Landry nodded. Jake placed Marty's coat and his own on a nearby chair. He took off his hat and put that atop the coats before offering Marty his arm once again. "I hope you will enjoy living here." Mrs. Landry motioned Kate to see to the discarded wraps.

Marty looked around at the cream and blue colors of the entryway. "If this is an example of things to come, I'm sure I will." Although she was still rather stupefied by the jousting with words between the housekeeper and butler.

They began climbing the grand staircase, with Mrs. Landry leading the way. "As I mentioned in the carriage," Jake stated when they were nearly to the top of the stairs, "I have set up a bank account for you. Mrs. Landry has one as well for the running of the household, so you needn't share your funds."

"That really wasn't necessary," Marty replied. "Thomas and I always shared everything. I'm sure I could just come to you if I need something."

Jake nodded. "I understand, however, you will see the advantage of this soon enough. There's no need for you to check in with me and account for every penny you spend. First you will need an entirely new wardrobe. As I mentioned earlier, I had Mrs. Landry arrange for the dressmaker to arrive next week. Mrs. Landry tells me the woman knows exactly what you will need for your debut into Denver society, since she supplies clothing to many of the wealthiest matrons." Marty noted that his Texas drawl was once again carefully controlled. "Some gowns will have to be ordered from abroad, I'm told, but the dressmaker will see to all of that."

"Am I to have enough gowns to change six times a day?" Marty couldn't keep the teasing from her tone.

Jake grinned. "That and more. Mr. Morgan insisted I could not let you appear less than what your station demands."

"Sounds like Mr. Morgan insists on an awful lot," she muttered.

Jake didn't bother to respond but simply said, "I have also given you enough to do whatever you'd like with the house. If you prefer different rugs or draperies—even furniture—you should feel free to arrange for it. I have no preference. All that you see was in place when I arrived."

"I suppose Mr. Morgan was responsible for that, as well?" She met his amused expression.

"No, actually, Mrs. Morgan sent some of her people here to oversee the decorating. They did a nice job—don't you think?"

Marty glanced around as they made their way down the hall. There were beautiful carpets atop highly polished hardwood floors. Paintings graced the walls, and at the end of the hall a huge window was trimmed in billowing multicolored damask drapes. Why would she even consider changing it? It was all so very beautiful.

"They did, indeed."

"This will be your room," Mrs. Landry announced when they reached a door on the right. She led the way into the massive bedroom and stepped aside for Marty to inspect it.

A large canopied bed graced the space to Marty's left. On either side were beautifully carved side tables with fresh flowers. Marty had to smile. Jake had arranged for fresh flowers in the dead of winter. That was most considerate.

Opposite the bed, a beautifully tiled fireplace offered a welcoming fire to warm the room. The mahogany mantel held several knickknacks, including the statuette of a woman in Grecian fashion, a collection of cherubs surrounded by gold framing, and several other pieces that would require closer inspection.

"As you can see for yourself, you have a comfortable sitting area." Mrs. Landry moved to the side of the hearth. "If you need the fire built up, simply use this and someone will come to tend it." She showed Marty the servant pull.

Noise arose just beyond Mrs. Landry, and she turned to open a door not far from the fireplace. "This is your bathing and dressing room. Samson has just now deposited your trunks, and I have a warm bath waiting for you."

Marty looked at Jake and shook her head. "I had no idea."

He laughed. "I said it was a big house."

She explored the bathing and dressing area, an incredible room of marble and brass. There were large armoires, a chest of drawers, brass rails for hanging clothes, as well as a large tub for bathing and a sink and vanity where Marty could sit and fuss with her appearance for as long as she liked.

"Indoor plumbing, I see."

"Yes, we're thoroughly modern, although I didn't arrange for a telephone to be put in. I wasn't all that keen on people calling me at all hours," Jake admitted.

"I can understand. This is far more than I need," she said, shaking her head again. "I never expected anything so wonderful. We were still using a pump and outhouse in Texas." She smiled at Jake, who gave her a wink.

Mrs. Landry ignored the comment. "I'm afraid the fainting couch did not arrive in time, but is expected next week."

"I shall endeavor not to faint until then," Marty said most seriously before breaking into a giggle. She worried only a moment that Jake would be offended, but when she heard him chuckle, she relaxed.

Mrs. Landry ignored their merriment. "I will have Kate unpack your things and press them. Meanwhile, I will assist you into your bath." She went to the far wall, where another servant pull awaited. She signaled for Kate, then turned to face Marty and Jake. "Mr. Wythe, would you like me to show Mrs. Wythe your quarters, as well?"

Marty flushed and looked away. Perhaps the servants hadn't been informed of the arrangements. Jake seemed unconcerned, however. He moved to where Mrs. Landry stood by yet another door and motioned Marty to join them.

"This small passage adjoins your rooms to mine. There is a lock, as you can see, so that no one can disturb you." He opened the door and moved quickly to the end of the short corridor. Opening the far end exposed light from yet another large room. Marty walked into the expanse and marveled at the space.

It was a decidedly male room, done up in dark greens and heavy wood furniture. A desk stood against the wall at the far end of the room, and Marty could see from the look of it that Jake used it regularly for business. On the wall were oil paintings of Texas-styled cattle scenes as well as a stiff, but obviously much used, coiled rope. How strange to find it nailed to the wall of a bedroom.

For a moment Marty imagined herself back in Texas. She had nearly forgotten that Jake was a Texan. Spying a few books with ranch-related topics, a rather large yellowed map of Texas spread atop a nearby table, and an impressive bronze statue of a horse and rider, Marty knew she wasn't likely to erase Texas from this man's mind anytime soon.

"It seems very nice. Is it my imagination or is it smaller than my room?"

"A little bit," Jake admitted. "But it was the room I wanted when I moved in. The larger room seemed to be much more suited for . . . a . . . couple. I believe this was the nursery before I arranged for it to be redone."

Marty looked away in discomfort and pretended to study the bronze statue. "Very nice."

Kate appeared just then, and Mrs. Landry instructed her regarding Marty's trunks, while Marty could only look on. The two disappeared into the dressing room, leaving Marty and Jake alone. She saw the amusement in Jake's expression and couldn't help but question him.

"You look rather pleased with yourself."

"I'm just enjoying your surprise at everything." A clock chimed and he checked his pocket watch. "But now I will have to leave you in Mrs. Landry's capable hands. I have a meeting to attend. I will return to join you for supper. Enjoy the house, Mrs. Wythe."

Marty watched him leave out another door that she could see led back to the hallway. Mrs. Landry returned just then and directed her back to the bathing room. "I would imagine you are exhausted from your travels. Once you've bathed, I will pack you into bed and you can sleep until supper. Kate will come and help you dress for dinner and arrange your hair. It will be only you and Mr. Wythe dining, and Cook is preparing lamb. I hope that meets with your approval." All the while Mrs. Landry helped Marty from her clothes.

"Lamb is fine."

"In the future you and I will meet to discuss the menus for each meal. You must let me know if there are any particular foods that you abhor, or ones that you love, for that matter." She had stripped Marty down to her shift and corset.

"Now just sit here and rest while I see that the bath is still warm enough, and then we can finish with your clothes."

Marty did as she was told, knowing that the wheels of this massive machine could not be stopped even if she wanted them to be. No doubt Mrs. Landry was used to running this house as an army commander ran a fort. It wouldn't make sense to try and disturb the flow of things. At least not today.

After the bath, which Marty very much enjoyed, Mrs. Landry helped her into bed, then quietly exited the room. Marty marveled at the luxurious softness of the bed and the silky feel of the fine linens that graced it. She had never known such comfort, nor such exhaustion. She closed her eyes and tried to imagine how she would ever explain all of this to Hannah. Whispering aloud, she composed her letter.

"I'm to have my own maid, and a dressmaker will arrive to create a wardrobe fit for a queen. There are servants and eight thousand square feet of opulence to be explored." She yawned and tried not to fight the sleep that was gradually overtaking her.

"And Mrs. Standish will have a new assistant in the kitchen in three days' time," she murmured, smiling to herself. "On the twenty-third."

Speaking the date aloud caused Marty to reopen her eyes for just a moment. That meant today was the twentieth. The twentieth of January—her thirty-fifth birthday.

"Well, happy birthday to me," she murmured and closed her eyes again. "Happy birthday to me, indeed."

Chapter 6

Jake sat at work feeling rather pleased with the way things were progressing. The weekend had gone well, and he and Marty seemed able to share the house quite amicably. Because she had just arrived on Friday, Jake hadn't even approached the idea of them attending church services their first weekend together. He knew from things she'd said that while raised in a Christian home, Marty had very little interest in such matters for herself. There would be time enough to explain to her that proper society would expect them to be seen in services every Sunday.

He refused to worry about it, however. Reviewing the columns of numbers on the ledger, Jake instead thought of how surprised he'd been by Marty's quick wit and good nature. She even managed to take Brighton and Mrs. Landry in stride. No doubt in time she would come to find their mock arguments amusing. Truth be told, Jake suspected that the two held more than a passing fancy for each other.

A knock sounded on his outer door, and Jake looked up to find Arnold entering the room. "Mr. Morgan and several board members are here to see you."

Jake frowned and looked at the clock. They had no agreed-upon meeting today. He stood to receive the men as they filed into the room.

"Wythe," Mr. Morgan said with a nod.

"Mr. Morgan, gentlemen," Jake said, nodding to each man. He looked to Arnold. "Please bring in more chairs, Mr. Meyers."

Arnold hurried to do Jake's bidding and had everyone seated comfortably within a matter of minutes. Jake remained standing, wondering what this gathering was all about.

"So . . . what can I do for you today, Mr. Morgan?"

"Well, we have come, in fact, with congratulations." The older man smiled. "We understand you were married last Friday."

"Yes," Jake said, still guarded. "Mrs. Olson arrived by stage, and we were married immediately."

"We read all about a certain Mrs. Olson driving the stage," board member Mr. Palmer said with a sly grin. "Would that have been *your* Mrs. Olson?"

Jake swallowed hard. "Yes, sir. I must admit it was. Although I will add that the circumstances necessitated it."

"No doubt. We heard that she saved the entire stagecoach from a dozen armed marauders," Josiah Keystone added.

"I heard she single-handedly killed half of them by herself," the remaining man and former governor of Colorado, Mr. Cooper, declared.

"I assure you, gentlemen, it wasn't quite that dramatic. The stage was attacked, that much is true, but Marty . . . Mrs. Wythe tells me that she only saw two men approach. She fired at them, along with the men responsible for the stage. She has no way of knowing that anyone was wounded by her efforts, however. I also assure you that while she did find it necessary to take charge of the stage, she in no way sought publicity for her actions."

"Relax, Mr. Wythe. No one here is taking umbrage with you or Mrs. Wythe," Morgan interjected. "In fact, I find it all rather amusing. I can hardly imagine Imogene being as capable in her velvets and silks."

"You've got yourself a regular Annie Oakley," Keystone added. "Sounds like she's a woman who can hold her own. Did you see the picture they drew of her? I don't know if it's a good likeness or not, but she looked like she could have taken on an entire army."

Jake had indeed seen the drawing. He had purposefully hid the newspaper from Marty, however. He knew she had no desire for public attention, and this might only make her worry that her sister would learn the truth of what had happened before she had a chance to write and explain.

"I did see it. It looks nothing like her," he answered honestly. "And she only had one pistol, not two. I'm afraid the artist took great license with his rendition."

"Well, I enjoyed the article all the same," Mr. Palmer threw in. "I enjoyed it immensely."

Jake wasn't at all sure how to respond. Despite having told Marty otherwise, he had figured once word got out about her unseemly arrival, any desire to see him or his wife in public social settings would be discarded. But now it seemed as if these men were actually admiring Marty's performance. He sat down rather hard and awaited further comment.

"She's a real novelty," Morgan continued. "I can hardly wait to meet her. Imogene said that she must be a woman of divine courage."

That comment caused Jake to let out his breath in relief. If Mrs. Morgan hailed Marty as a conquering heroine, then all would be well. The community would no doubt take a cue from her.

"I believe she is," Jake replied. He rubbed his sweaty palms against his trouser legs. "Thank you."

"Well, that brings us to our other reason for coming by," Morgan continued. "Imogene is planning a party for Valentine's Day, as she does each year. Only this year, she wants to incorporate a celebration to honor you and Mrs. Wythe. There will be a supper and dance, although we will end the festivities by ten since the fourteenth does fall on a Tuesday."

Jake nodded and wrote a note to himself regarding the party. "That is very kind."

"We will expect you by six so that you and Mrs. Wythe might stand in the receiving line and greet our guests. It will be the perfect way to introduce you. It will be a formal affair, so you will be expected to attire yourself accordingly. Do you have white tie and tails?"

"I do. If you'll recall, you helped me arrange a very fine suit of clothing for the Christmas season," Jake replied.

"Of course." Morgan nodded and looked to his friends. "My tailor is the best in town." He looked back to Jake. "That will be exactly right for the Valentine's party. I'm sure that Mrs. Wythe will have something lovely to wear."

"But tell her to leave her six-shooter at home," Cooper teased. "We wouldn't want her rewarding us with a repeat of her arrival into our great city."

The other men laughed, but Jake could only muster a smile. He still felt uneasy with these men and their place in society. He was a fish out of water, and they knew it as well as he did. Truth be told, Jake was almost certain they preferred it that way. It gave them a sort of edge—a pretense of control.

But that was all it was, Jake assured himself. A pretense. Nothing more. These men did not own him, even though he was greatly indebted to them. There wasn't a single thing they had offered him that he couldn't walk away from. And while they didn't know his real purpose in accepting the high-paying job, Jake felt no remorse.

I'm only here as long as it takes to put aside enough money for a ranch. No longer. Texas is my home, and that is where I'm bound to return.

★

Marty smiled at the sour-faced woman. "Well, Mrs. Sales, it would seem your references are in order. I appreciate your taking the time to speak with me today."

"Yes, madam."

Uncertain what else to do, Marty looked to Mrs. Landry for help. "If you'll come this way, Mrs. Sales, I will see you to the door. Mrs. Wythe will notify the agency if she wishes to retain your services." Mrs. Landry led the way and the seemingly unhappy woman followed. She was the fifth woman sent over by the agency, and Marty liked her no better than the first four. Most were quite dour and rigid. All had worked for numerous years as ladies' maids and were well versed in their duties, even if Marty wasn't. They impressed Marty as women who would impose their will upon her rather than take instruction.

Mrs. Landry returned. "There's one final applicant."

Marty sighed and looked beyond the housekeeper to where a young woman stood with her face turned slightly to the right. She was staring at the floor, as if too shy to meet anyone.

"Miss Alice Chesterfield," Mrs. Landry announced. She turned to the girl. "Give Mrs. Wythe your references."

Alice stepped forward, but her gloved hands were empty. Marty could see that the small woman couldn't be very old.

"I'm pleased to meet you. May I call you Alice?"

The girl nodded, but still refused to lift her head. "I wanted to apply for the job, but . . . well . . . I have no references."

"Why would the agency send her to interview for this position?" Mrs. Landry interjected. "I'll turn her away and send a letter of reprimand to the employment official."

"No," Marty declared, seeing something in the girl that touched her heart. "That won't be necessary. Alice, have a seat."

The girl looked up in surprise. It was then that Marty caught sight of the scar that ran down the right side of her face. The nasty pink scar was evidence that the wound had not healed that long ago.

"Please sit, Alice. I'd very much like to talk to you."

Mrs. Landry was less than pleased, but instead of saying anything, she positioned herself in a chair by the archway and waited for Marty to continue. Alice took the offered chair and licked her lips in a nervous fashion. Her dress was too short for her and rose to reveal tattered boots, but Marty pretended not to notice.

"So tell me about yourself, Alice." Marty smiled, hoping it would relieve the girl's fear.

"I want to say that I know it was wrong of me to come here. The agency . . . they didn't send me. I was there and heard some of the other women getting their instructions to come. I . . . well . . . I need to work, and I thought I would . . . apply, as well." She straightened her shoulders and fixed Marty with her gaze. "I know that wasn't right, but I need this job."

"Well, Alice, why don't you tell me about yourself." Marty noted her clothes were frayed and far from the latest fashion. They were, in fact, too immature for the young woman, but Marty supposed they were all she had. "I'd like to know about you and why you want to work as a lady's maid."

"I . . . well . . ." She cleared her throat and seemed to carefully consider her words. "I'm seventeen. I know how to work hard, although I don't have experience as a lady's maid. I'm a good learner, and I have an eighth-grade education." The latter she said with some pride, and Marty couldn't help but smile.

"That's wonderful. So you can read and write should I need you to handle correspondence for me."

"Yes, ma'am. My penmanship is quite good."

Marty nodded. "That's definitely a benefit to us both." She could see this bolstered the girl a bit and hoped to encourage her further. "I've always appreciated those who understood the value of education."

"My father saw schooling as very important."

"And who is your father?"

The girl frowned. "Mr. George Chesterfield, deceased."

"I am sorry." Marty could see the pain in Alice's expression. "Has it been long?"

"No. Just about five months ago. He was . . . murdered."

Mrs. Landry let out a gasp that echoed in the room. Marty tried to handle the news in a less stunned fashion, although she was rather shocked to hear the declaration. "Can you speak about what happened?"

Alice nodded. "We were walking home in the evening. My father was carrying some papers for a banker named Mr. Morgan."

Marty immediately recognized the name. Apparently Mr. Morgan was a very busy man. Alice continued to speak.

"Father often carried papers and money for Mr. Morgan—it was his job as a bank manager. I suppose the men who attacked us knew that. The men stopped us and demanded that my father turn over the satchel he was carrying. Father refused and they took hold of me and . . ." Her voice faltered.

Marty thought to stop her, but for reasons she didn't entirely understand, she remained silent and let the girl struggle through her explanation.

"I . . . tried to fight them off." She paused and bit her lower lip. The pink scar seemed to pale a bit as Alice clenched her jaw. "I wasn't strong enough," she finally said. "One of the men held me while another put his knife to my face." She touched her hand to the scar. "He . . . he . . . cut me before I even realized what was happening."

"I'm so sorry, Alice. What a terrible thing to endure."

Alice looked Marty in the eye. "My father screamed at the men to take the satchel and let me go. He rushed them, and the men forgot about me and pushed my father away. He fell to the ground and hit his head. I don't remember anything after that because I fainted. When I woke up again, I was in the hospital. They told me Father had died from striking his head. They weren't even sure I would make it. Honestly, at that point I didn't care if I did."

"I can well imagine," Marty replied. She looked across the room to where Mrs. Landry was dabbing tears from her eyes. "Mrs. Landry, would you arrange some refreshments for us?"

"Of course. Poor wee girl," the housekeeper said, heading from the room.

Marty turned back to the blond-haired girl. "Do you have no other family?"

"No. No one. I'm alone and I need to work in order to support myself. Up until now, some friends from church have helped me get by, but they're moving away and I have no one else. I'm sorry if I've wasted your time." She looked up with an expression that seemed to plead for Marty to assure her that she hadn't done wrong.

"Nonsense. You haven't wasted my time. In fact, I'm very honored that you would share your story with me, Alice. I know it couldn't have been easy for you."

"I'm a quick learner, Mrs. Wythe. Truly I am. I know how to sew and clean. I can fix your hair and maybe even learn some of the new styles. I'm pretty good at figuring things out. If I can see some of the new magazines, I'm sure to be able to copy the fashions."

Marty smiled. "I bet you could. You strike me as a remarkable young woman, and I think you're exactly the kind of employee I could use."

Alice's expression cheered. "I promise. I would do my best. I would give my all."

"You need not convince me," Marty assured her. "I can see that you are very determined."

Alice leaned forward. "I wasn't sure if the job included room and board, but I need a place to live. After the first, my friends will be leaving Denver and I'll be . . . alone."

"We have quarters for you here. A salary, too. Mrs. Landry will see you settled in."

"Of course I will," Mrs. Landry said, bringing a silver tray with refreshments. She placed the tray atop a small table and immediately set to work pouring tea. She handed a cup to the young woman, but Alice shook her head.

"No, if I'm to start right away, I should go get my things." Alice hesitated a moment. "I can start right away, can't I?"

Marty chuckled. "Of course you can. I'll have my driver assist you, but wouldn't you rather have some refreshments first?"

"No, ma'am. I want to get back here as quickly as possible and start learning my job." She stood and touched her hand to her face. "Thank you. Thank you for giving me a chance . . . even though . . . ."

"Even though nothing, Alice. You have presented yourself as the better candidate for my needs," Marty said, standing. "I am certain that we will get along famously. Mrs. Landry, would you see that Samson drives—"

"No, that's all right." Alice was already halfway to the door. "I'll walk. It's not all that far." She very nearly flew out the front door, not at all the shy, reserved young woman who'd entered.

Marty exchanged a look with Mrs. Landry. "I know you must think me a fool, but I couldn't stop myself. That poor girl needed our help."

"I don't think you a fool at all, Mrs. Wythe. You have a tender heart, as do I. It will no doubt be the death of us both, but we could hardly send that girl out into the cold with no hope." The housekeeper handed Marty a cup of tea. "We'll need to get her some uniforms. She's smaller than Kate, but perhaps she can borrow one of hers temporarily."

Marty nodded. "And some new shoes. Hers looked rather . . . worn."

"I can take her shopping tomorrow, if that's what you'd like."

Marty thought about it for a moment. "We can both take her."

Mrs. Landry shook her head. "Mrs. Wythe, that wouldn't be acceptable. Mr. Wythe needs you to be . . . well . . . respectable . . . to your position. There are certain rules to your station in life, and I won't have Mr. Wythe shamed because I was remiss in explaining them."

The housekeeper shifted uncomfortably, and Marty couldn't help but feel sorry for her. She barely knew the woman but already liked her no-nonsense style. "Very well, Mrs. Landry. I shall keep to my place. I cannot say I approve of this world of rules, but since I agreed to take it on when I married Mr. Wythe, I suppose I should keep my word." Marty sipped the tea and gave a sigh. "I don't know that I'll ever get used to having servants or rules."

Chapter 7

"I didn't know Mr. Chesterfield," Jake said at breakfast the next morning.

Marty found this surprising. "Apparently you were the replacement for his job after he was murdered."

"I do recall someone saying the former bank manager had died, but little else." He took a drink of his coffee before continuing. "And your maid is his daughter?"

"Yes, and I like her very much. She was injured in the robbery that claimed her father's life. She has a scar that runs the length of her face. When you meet her, try not to be . . . surprised."

Jake smiled. "No worries. I've probably seen worse. And by the way, Mr. and Mrs. Morgan have invited us to their Valentine's ball next month and would like us to arrive by six in order to receive the guests with them."

Marty looked at her husband for a moment. "Is this to be a regular occurrence?"

He seemed confused. "Valentine's parties?"

"No, being summoned by the Morgans," she replied and took a bite of her toast.

Jake shrugged but gave her a grin. "It does seem to be the pattern. You'll get used to it. Mr. Morgan has a way of seeing to it that folks do what he wants. I'm really not sure why he's taken such a likin' to me, but I have to say he's generous to a fault where it's concerned us. Just look at all he's done on our account, and always with the requirement that I not give him credit for his generosity. He's a humble man."

"I can see that you're right about that," Marty said. "I suppose I'm still stunned by my new life here." With Mrs. Landry, Kate, and Alice busy transforming the front sitting room into a fitting area for the expected dressmaker, Marty leaned forward in hopes of not being overheard.

"I know that he believes us to be a love match, but . . . well . . . do the servants know about our . . . situation?"

"You mean do they know our sensible arrangement? This marriage of convenience?"

"Yes."

He shook his head. "No. I think Mrs. Landry might suspect, but I haven't told her outright." He put down his fork. "See, when they promoted me to bank manager and started in on my need for a wife, I lied and told them I had a fiancée in Texas."

"And that's why you placed the advertisement."

"Exactly." This time he leaned in to speak in a hushed tone. "You have no idea what Morgan and his cronies had planned for me. There were entire parties full of eligible young ladies for me to court."

"Sounds like torture," Marty said, smiling.

Jake grinned and relaxed in his chair. "I thought so. Anyhow, I made this big fuss about how I was promised and I couldn't be unfaithful. I told them we planned to marry in another year, but that didn't sit well with them. They started in on insisting I move the wedding date up. They said it worried the board to have a single man in a position of such great responsibility—even a widowed man."

"I suppose there is some merit to that. Married men do present themselves as more stable and respectable in their activities."

"Some married men do," Jake countered. "But certainly not all. There's scandal aplenty in this town, and marriage doesn't seem a sturdy boundary marker for many."

"I'm sure you're right. Just the same, I wanted to know what you'd told folks. I don't want to cause problems by not getting the story straight."

"I appreciate that. I don't want to outright lie if I don't have to—I've already done that in telling them we were engaged. But if you can abide it, I'd appreciate it if we'd say as little as possible."

"It's been my experience, however," Marty said, pushing her eggs around on the plate, "that sometimes details help to keep stories from unraveling. I suggest we agree to certain things, such as when we first met and how. Women are always asking after that kind of thing."

Jake nodded. "Well, we both lived in Texas . . . Dallas area, to be exact. That helps a great deal. We needn't lie about our youth."

Marty considered the story for a moment. "We could say that we grew up not far from each other, implying but not outright stating that we knew each other. I am a bit older than you, but we needn't make too much of that."

"True." He seemed to like her thoughts on the matter. "And we could say that time separated us and we married other people, but we always held fond thoughts of each other." He grinned. "There wasn't a pretty gal in Texas I didn't hold fond thoughts of."

"Exactly." Marty was confident it could work. "We'll say that we corresponded, mentioning we had both lost our mates and after that we got in touch with each other. That's all quite true."

"Seems simple enough."

"Simple details are the best," she assured him. Just then Marty heard a knock at the front door. "I suppose that's for me." She dabbed the napkin to her lips. "I want to thank you for your generosity, Jake. I had no idea I'd be treated to so many fine things. It really isn't necessary."

"Unfortunately, it is," Jake declared. "Mr. Morgan has plans for me—at least that's what he's always telling me. I just go along with things for now."

"What do you mean?" she asked.

"Well, my plans and his don't exactly line up. What I want in the long run—"

"I am sorry to interrupt," Mrs. Landry declared, entering the room, "but Mrs. Davies has arrived, and she is anxious that we should begin your appointment, Mrs. Wythe."

Marty looked to Jake. What did he mean his plans didn't line up with Mr. Morgan's? "I suppose we can resume this conversation tonight at supper."

Jake smiled and got to his feet. He came around the table to help Marty up. "I shouldn't be too late." He surprised her by giving her cheek a light peck.

Her face grew hot at the kiss, and Marty ducked her head like a shy bride. Mrs. Landry only chuckled. "Come along now."

Marty followed the housekeeper through the house and into a sitting room that now looked nothing like it had on Marty's first inspection. Most of the furniture had been moved aside, and several tables were positioned in their place. The women who'd accompanied Mrs. Davies were busy spreading out fabrics, trims, and a large portfolio of dress designs.

"Mrs. Wythe, this is Mrs. Davies," Mrs. Landry introduced. "Mrs. Davies, this is the lady of the house, Mrs. Wythe. She will require a complete social wardrobe, as well as personal items. Mr. Wythe has instructed that one gown in particular is needed for the Morgans' annual Valentine's ball. The gown should be appropriate to the event, of course, and the cost should reveal quality, as this will be Mrs. Wythe's first formal appearance."

The dark-eyed woman nodded and clapped her hands. "Girls, come quickly and meet our client, Mrs. Wythe."

Marty scarcely had time to acknowledge the bevy of women before they were undressing her down to her shift and corset. Mrs. Davies herself took the measurements. She chattered on with her team, making suggestions as she completed her tasks.

"You are so lovely and have a most enviable figure, Mrs. Wythe. Your petite frame will be a delight to clothe."

"Thank you," Marty said, uncertain what else she could say. She'd never thought of her figure being anything special. She was petite, just as her sister, Hannah, but she never considered herself anywhere near as pretty. Where Hannah's features were delicate—like a fine china doll, Marty thought of herself as more earthy and plain.

"Now that we have your measurements," Mrs. Davies continued, "I will show you my book of designs. I have created a great many gowns in my day, so you will be pleased to note that these sketches are quite up-to-date and will reveal the latest in fashion."

She didn't give Marty a chance to reply before pulling her toward the table. "Lynette, bring Mrs. Wythe her dressing gown lest she catch her death of cold."

Marty slipped into the robe, grateful for the extra warmth. The fire had been lit to warm the room, but the temperature outside had dropped considerably since Marty's arrival. She hugged the robe to her neck and took a seat as she waited for Mrs. Davies to lay out her drawings.

"This gown in a silk taffeta would be quite appropriate for the Valentine ball." She placed the drawing on the table in front of Marty. "Note the fur trimming the hem and the sleeves. Ermine will give added warmth, as well as a look of opulence. Accompany it with a velvet cloak, and you'll put all the other women to shame."

Marty studied the gown for a moment. She'd never known anything so elegant. Life in Texas had never been this grand—at least not for her and Thomas. She'd generally avoided events that required formal garments.

"It's beautiful," she finally said, seeing that Mrs. Davies was anticipating a comment.

"The low neckline is perfect for showing off your lovely shoulders."

"I wouldn't want the neckline to be too low," Marty replied. "I'm not comfortable with that."

Mrs. Davies nodded. "But of course. We can trim the bodice with ermine, as well. I believe the gown is well suited for a dusty rose color. It will work perfectly with your complexion and hair." Only then did Marty notice that a young woman stood directly to Mrs. Davies's left, writing down most every word the woman said. "We will set out to create this gown immediately. I will return for a preliminary fitting this time next week.

"Now, here is another gown that I think will be perfect for you," Mrs. Davies said, turning several pages. "Note the full sleeves and high neckline. The bodice is sewn with permanent pleating."

Marty nodded and Mrs. Davies hurried to turn the page. "And here is a gown very similar to one created by the designer Charles Worth. Of course you have heard of him." Marty had no time to reply as the woman continued. "You will note the cascading bustle. This gown is done in two pieces, and I believe it would show off your tiny waist to perfection."

"All right." Marty then found herself studying numerous other sketches and designs. Mrs. Davies kept her so busy and focused on the order of the new wardrobe that Marty lost track of time.

"I believe a dozen shirtwaists in varying styles will suffice for now," Mrs. Davies stated to her assistant. "And a half dozen woolen skirts. Three heavy and three of lighter weight. We can arrange for other skirts in the months to come." She touched her finger to the table. "Oh, we will also need to create undergarments. Please note that," she told her assistant.

Marty tried to protest the number of pieces, but Mrs. Davies waved her off.

"I believe you'll find these color swatches to your liking, Mrs. Wythe." She picked up a board that revealed a vast number of colors. "These will be serviceable skirts that should work well for your informal times. Might I suggest the burgundy, brown, gray, black, and of course the dark navy. I would have two in the black and brown, as they will go well with many of the jackets we will make for you and would be appropriate for walking out."

"All right," Marty simply replied, not feeling capable of demanding her own way. It was a strange position for her to be in, for she'd often stood up to Hannah and Will, and even Thomas to a certain degree. Folks around the ranch knew she wasn't one to argue with, so they generally gave in to her desires—but here, that wasn't even a consideration.

The appointment continued with orders for nightgowns, robes, cloaks, and coats. By the time the clock chimed noon, Mrs. Davies and her merry employees were once again packing their wares and hurrying to return to their sewing house.

"I will see you in one week for the first fitting," Mrs. Davies declared at the threshold, and Mrs. Landry closed the door behind her while Marty sank into the nearest chair.

"Goodness, but that was an ordeal. I can't imagine going through that again."

"It won't be quite as bad next time." Mrs. Landry offered Marty a gentle smile. "Come now. Luncheon is ready, and you must eat before the milliner and cobbler arrive."

Marty had hoped that the departure of Mrs. Davies would signal her freedom for the rest of the day, but it wasn't to be. "I suppose I must choose hats and shoes next?"

"And gloves, stockings, and any other needed accessories. Mr. Wythe said we were to spare no expense."

"Yes, but I'm sure he didn't mean for me to have so much. A dozen shirtwaists! Who needs a dozen? Goodness, but where will I even put a dozen?"

Mrs. Landry gave a tolerant nod. "That is our duty, Mrs. Wythe, and we will arrange for everything to have a proper place. Now come along. Cook has your meal prepared. We mustn't let it grow cold."

The rest of the day passed much as the first part. People were in and out of the house, measuring, marking, fussing over Marty until she wanted to scream. Finally by four in the afternoon, she was allowed to retire to her room for a rest. She fell into the bed without even caring that she was fully clothed.

"What have I gotten myself into?"

"Ma'am?" It was Alice. She stood by the door to the dressing room and bath. "Did you call for me?"

Marty sat up. "No, I didn't call. I suppose, however, if I'm to have a proper rest, I should undress."

Alice smiled and came to help Marty with her buttons. "You will have such a lovely wardrobe when Mrs. Davies finishes. I doubt any other woman in Denver will look half so fine."

"I can't understand all the fuss. I'm not a grand lady, and while I've lived in a house with help, I certainly never needed servants to take charge of everything."

"So you are unhappy?" Alice asked and immediately apologized. "Sorry, ma'am. Mrs. Landry said a lady's maid was not to ask personal questions."

Marty laughed. "Please, you needn't worry about my taking offense. Frankly, I'd like very much for us to be friends."

"But that isn't proper. Mrs. Landry made it very clear that while I am to assist you and be a companion to you if needed, I'm supposed to mostly stay in the shadows and anticipate your needs."

"I'm sure Mrs. Landry did state that. I'm sure it's written up in the rules somewhere, but that isn't how I prefer it. Frankly, trying to keep up with all the rules is giving me a headache." Marty allowed Alice to help her from the modest gown she'd worn that day. Thinking about this dress compared to the other things that had been ordered, Marty felt rather shoddy.

Slipping beneath the covers to ward off the chill of the room, Marty gave a sigh. "I've never been one for napping, but it seems this life is quite tiring."

"It's the mountains, too, ma'am. If you don't mind my saying so."

Marty closed her eyes. "Yes, Jake mentioned that. I should think now that I've been in Colorado for a few days, I should be adjusting. However, I'm beginning to wonder if I'll ever adjust."

★

Jake sat across the beautifully set dining table in moody silence. Marty hadn't yet seen this side of him. He was obviously troubled about something, and she didn't know if it would be deemed appropriate to ask or whether she should remain silent. It seemed only natural that she would question him about his day. . . . Didn't all wives do that? She and Thomas always had.

After being served the soup, Marty picked up her spoon and dared a question. "You seem tired. Did you have a difficult day?"

"It's not important." Jake attacked a piece of bread. "There are problems that I have to resolve, and you don't need to worry about it."

"I wasn't worried," she countered. "I simply noticed that you looked tired. I presumed the day had given you some problems. I'm happy to listen if you'd like to talk."

He looked at her for a moment, his brow knit together as his frown deepened. "No. There's no reason to involve you."

"But I want to be involved."

Jake slammed his hand down, causing all of the dishes to rattle. "I said no!"

Marty straightened in defense. She wasn't used to being treated in a harsh manner. Up until now, this man she'd so quickly married had seemed quite lighthearted and easygoing.

With a sigh, Jake put down the bread and shook his head. "I'm sorry, Marty. I had no right to act that way. You're just showing concern for me and I shouldn't have snapped at you. Sometimes I open my mouth just wide enough to stick my boot in."

She could see he was truly sorry. The expression on his face and his tone of voice made it clear that his reaction had been a surprise even to Jake. "I shouldn't have pried. My Thomas and I used to talk out our problems over supper. I learned that from my sister and her husband. I suppose it's an old habit."

"My folks did much the same," Jake admitted. "Supper was about the only time they saw each other for any length of time. Breakfast always seemed rushed so that we could get to work, and lunch was often elsewhere on the range."

Marty nodded. "And while everyone was tired from a day of arduous tasks and difficult trials, supper gave us a time to sit back and review the good and bad of the choices we'd made."

Jake smiled for the first time that evening. "Supper was always my favorite time." He picked up his soup spoon. "I can remember my mother having the table set in beautiful china with a fine tablecloth. Father would admonish her, saying that such things should be used for special occasions. But Mother said every time we came together as a family was a special occasion."

"I never knew my mother and barely remember my father," Marty told him. "However, my sister always tried to make us a comfortable home. She was more mother to me than sister. . . . Hannah gave up a great deal to care for my brother and me."

"That's what family should do."

"Do you have any brothers or sisters?" Marty asked.

"No, it was just me."

Marty hoped that might be the start of a new conversation, but it wasn't. Before long, Jake was lost in his thoughts again, and Marty had no luck in drawing him back into a conversation.

"The dressmaker said she would come next week for my first fitting." She waited until the new kitchen assistant, Willa, served the main course of roasted game hen before continuing. "The gown she suggested for the Valentine's ball is quite lovely. I'm sure I've never had anything so grand."

"Hmm," Jake murmured without even looking up. He cut into the meat and continued to eat in silence.

"It's going to be a lovely color—a sort of rose. A dark, pinkish rose. There will be white fur trimming the gown." She knew he wasn't listening, so she reverted to a childhood habit that she'd used on Hannah when she wouldn't give Marty her full attention.

"Then Mrs. Davies suggested we turn snakes loose in the music room."

"Whatever you decide is fine," Jake said.

"I suppose they are smaller than bears and won't make as much mess."

Jake looked at her for a moment, and Marty was certain he would call her comment into question. But instead he gave a sigh and got to his feet. "I'm sorry to be such poor company. I think I'll make an early night of it."

Marty watched him leave the room. His meal was barely touched. Whatever troubled him had robbed him of his appetite as well as his personable mood. Perhaps he'd be more willing to explain in the morning.

"But what if he isn't?" She frowned. She really knew nothing about this man. Anyone could put up a pretense for a few days—but what if this was the way Jacob Wythe generally acted? What if she'd married a man of unpredictable moods?

It was only then that the full impact of her decision to leave Texas and marry a stranger hit her. He had seemed nice enough in his letters and even the time they'd shared here thus far had been pleasant. Still, what if he were unstable? That kind of thought had never come to mind until now.

"Perhaps I've been most foolish."

Chapter 8

As the days slipped into February, Marty saw less and less of Jake. When she did see him, he was quite resigned but not harsh. His duties at the bank often kept him there late into the evening, and Marty found it necessary to find ways to busy herself. She read through the Jane Austen volumes her sister had given her at Christmas, then ventured into the library to see what other tomes might hold her attention. If this was to be her life, at least it was peaceful.

Mrs. Davies had come and gone many times since her first appointment. She had arrived for fittings and to get Marty's approval on materials, but otherwise had not delivered a single item. She promised, however, that the rose and ermine gown would be ready in time for the Morgans' party, and that was truly all Marty cared about. But not as most women might. Marty wasn't concerned with looking beautiful or being held in high regard for her taste in fashion. She just wanted to please Jake and not cause him any problems with this elite circle of friends. Thankfully, Alice had been true to her word and had learned her duties quickly.

Marty patted her artfully styled hair and smiled. Hiring Alice had proven to be one of the wisest choices Marty had ever made. It made Marty happy, too, just knowing that they could somehow extend assistance to the daughter of George Chesterfield. Although neither she nor Jake had ever known the man, they were in a way benefiting from his demise. It seemed appropriate that they should help Alice in return.

Truly, Marty's only complaint was the boredom. The days here in Denver seemed longer than any Marty had ever known in Texas. At the ranch there had always been something to work at—cooking, cleaning, caring for the animals, gardening. Here, there was always someone else to do the work.

Mrs. Landry suggested she get started in remaking the house into her own style, but Marty thought it suited her well enough. For reasons she couldn't explain, there was a feeling of the temporary in this place. Perhaps it was Jake's admission that he didn't care for the place and that he would prefer to live a simpler life. Perhaps now that they were married, Mr. Morgan would understand if they decided to sell this house in lieu of another.

Mrs. Landry suggested various outings, but Marty found the cold difficult to get used to. There'd been no more snow, so the town looked all gray and brown—with little to entice her outdoors. There was also no occasion to entertain or receive guests—she didn't know anyone. The fact that no one had come to present themselves made her feel like an outcast. Mrs. Landry, however, was quick to explain that most people were waiting to be introduced to her at the party or in church. She'd managed to avoid the latter for a second time the previous Sunday, but that would unfortunately not be a luxury she could oft repeat.

"You're expected to show yourself as a respectful, godly woman," Mrs. Landry had told her. "Whether you agree with the sentiments of the pastor or not, you need to be present in the pew."

"I have no interest in church," she'd replied. "God and I have an agreement. I stay out of His way, and He stays out of mine."

She could still see the look of surprise on Mrs. Landry's face. She hadn't argued with Marty, but her disapproval had been evident.

Since it was Saturday, Marty presumed that Jake would be free of bank business, but she hadn't seen or heard from him so far. Not that she really expected to, given his recent moodiness. She hadn't bothered to go down for breakfast, telling Alice that she wanted to just linger in bed for a time. Much to her chagrin, Alice took this to mean she wanted breakfast in bed. The young girl showed up with a tray shortly thereafter, and Marty didn't have the heart to refuse her efforts.

"If you're finished with breakfast, I will take your tray," Alice said, entering the room.

Marty smiled at the young woman. "Thank you. I truly hadn't meant for you to do this, but it proved to be rather enjoyable."

"Mrs. Landry said it's quite routine for a married woman to take her breakfast in bed. I'm happy to bring it up for you every day."

"Goodness, no," Marty declared, pushing back her covers after Alice took the tray. "Eating in bed is for invalids and the sick, neither of which applies to me. I was just being a bit lazy today. It seemed colder and since I had no plans, I thought this to be as good a place as any to remain."

Alice headed for the door. "I'll be right back to help you dress and arrange your hair."

She was gone before Marty could say another word. Walking to the window, Marty could see that it was snowing. In fact, it had apparently been snowing for some time because the grounds were covered in a blanket of white. The snow cheered her, somehow, and she couldn't help but touch her hand to the frosty glass and smile. What a difference from her home in Texas.

Alice returned in short order and went into the dressing room. Marty followed after a moment and found the seventeen-year-old busy arranging hairpins on the vanity. She looked up and pointed to the brass rail, where Marty noted her dark blue gown was ready to be donned.

"I'll be glad when Mrs. Davies gets me some additional petticoats. I have a feeling I won't be very warm in this today."

"I'll keep the fire built up in your room, if you'd like," Alice said, helping Marty to disrobe.

"That's probably a good idea. I have no plans to leave the house. It doesn't even look safe to do so."

"The roads do get very slick at times. Sometimes there are accidents with the carriages."

Marty slipped into a shift and allowed Alice to help her with the corset. "I'm sure people take a great many falls, as well. I remember once in Texas when I lost my footing on an icy path."

"I've never been to Texas," Alice commented. "Is it pretty there?"

"Not to my way of thinking. I was glad to leave it. It's mostly range and farmland, with some of the hottest temperatures you could ever want. The summer days feel damp, even when a drought has split the dusty earth."

"How can that be?"

"The air blows in from the Gulf. It combines with the heat, making you feel as though you're being steamed alive."

Alice continued to dress Marty. "Denver can get very hot in the summer, but it doesn't feel like that. It's hot and dry here. Sometimes the sun just feels like it's sitting right over your shoulder. My skin burns if I'm not careful."

She did up the back of the gown and moved to the vanity. "Shall I do your hair now, or would you rather attend to your stockings and shoes?"

"Let's do the hair," Marty said, pulling the ribbon from her long blond braid.

Alice picked up the brush as Marty took a seat at the vanity. Once settled, Marty gave herself over to Alice's gentle care. For someone who'd never trained as a lady's maid, she certainly managed Marty's needs well.

"Alice, when I interviewed you for this position, you said you were alone in the world. Might I ask about your mother?"

"She died a few years ago—my younger brother, too."

"How did it happen?"

"My father said they died in an epidemic."

"Your father said?" Marty questioned. "Were they not with you when they passed?"

"No."

Marty saw Alice's reflection in the vanity mirror. She looked sad, and yet there was something else. For a moment neither woman said a word.

I've overstepped my bounds. I should never have brought up the subject. Marty immediately tried to think of a way to change the topic of conversation.

"My mother died when I was born," Marty offered, not really knowing why. "My sister, Hannah, helped my father raise me and my brother, Andy. He's a little older than me. Hannah's the only mother I ever knew. Then our father died when I was just five. I never mentioned this before, but like your father—mine was murdered."

Alice stopped in her preparations and met Marty's eyes in the mirror's reflection. "Truly?"

Marty nodded. "Yes, he had a business partner who was a very bad man. That man arranged to have my father killed. Though I was young, I keenly felt his loss."

"My father was my whole world." Alice began arranging Marty's hair once again. "I didn't really have any other people in my life. Your sister must be so special."

"She is, but why do you say that?"

Alice shrugged. "She could have abandoned you and your brother—put you in an orphanage or given you over to strangers."

The thought of Hannah's sacrifice caused Marty a moment of shame. She had lied to the only person in the world who had gone beyond duty to see Marty cared for and safe. Hannah probably wondered even now how Marty was doing, and Marty had been remiss in her communications.

"That reminds me that I need to write to her. I'm going to need some paper and ink. I can go out and purchase some in the future, but would you mind seeing if Mrs. Landry has some she can spare? After we finish here, of course."

"Certainly." Alice twisted Marty's thick hair atop her head and began pinning it in place. Once she'd finished, she stepped back to assess her work. "It's very simple. Would you prefer I do something more?"

"It's fine. As I said, I don't intend to go out today. Besides, I seldom wore it much different in Texas. I often just braided it down the back and pinned it on my head. That usually kept all the wild strands in place."

"You won't be allowed to be so simple once Mrs. Morgan gets ahold of you. At least that's what Mrs. Landry says." Alice put her hand to her mouth. It was clear she hadn't meant to speak that information aloud.

"It's all right, Alice. As I've said before, I want you to feel free to say what you think needs saying. I want us to be friends."

Alice relaxed. "I know, but I need this job. Mrs. Landry says that familiarity breeds contempt."

"Well, she's not the first one to say that, nor will she be the last. Familiarity can also encourage love and trust. So I am going to keep my sights on those types of things."

Alice smiled, and Marty glanced again at the scar on her face. The poor girl had suffered so much. The loss of her mother, her father's murder, her own injury . . . they were terrible burdens to carry. Still, the young woman maintained a sweet and gentle spirit.

"Thank you for being honest with me, Alice. Honesty doesn't come easy—I know."

★

By late afternoon Marty had still seen nothing of Jake. Brighton had told her that Jake had gone out early that morning and hadn't left word as to when he'd return. Mrs. Landry berated the man for not having more information to give and the two launched into one of their debates on Brighton's responsibilities as he knew them versus what Mrs. Landry presumed them to be. Marty took that moment to escape and explore the house a bit more.

Finding herself at the kitchen, Marty looked around for some sign of Mrs. Standish or Willa. Neither seemed in residence, but then Marty caught the sound of voices coming from just off the far right of the room. Investigation proved that this was the pantry, and Mrs. Standish and Willa were busily taking inventory.

"Oh, Mrs. Wythe, ma'am. Did you need something?" Mrs. Standish questioned.

"No, I'm sorry for the interruption. I was just doing a bit of looking around. I hope you don't mind."

"Not at all, ma'am." Mrs. Standish looked most uncomfortable.

Marty gave her a smile. "I know sometimes women tend to be very possessive of their kitchens."

This caused the older woman to smile in return. "I am at that, but I don't imagine you'll take up a skillet and start in."

"You might be surprised. I did all my own cooking in Texas."

"Well, you aren't in Texas anymore," Mrs. Standish replied. "We'll have none of that here. You're a fine lady with an important husband. Folks will be looking to you for an example."

Marty frowned and nodded. Why was it that this luxury and opulence was starting to feel more like a ball and chain? She'd never wanted to be seen as a standard for others, and the thought made her feel most uncomfortable.

She made her way to the back door, and only then did she notice how deep the snow had gotten. She'd had no idea it could accumulate so fast. They certainly had never seen snow like this in Texas—at least not in her part of Texas.

Fascination drew Marty from the safety and warmth of the house into the outdoor celebration of winter. Without proper boots on her feet or a coat to ward off the cold, Marty immediately felt the chilled dampness. Even so, this didn't stop her moving out into the yard. She marveled like a child at the snow coming down around her. Never in her life had she seen such a wondrous thing. Reaching up, Marty caught multiple flakes. She laughed and kicked one foot at the white blanket. The snow felt wet and heavy.

Whirling around and around, Marty couldn't help but cast her worries to the wind and enjoy the simplicity of the moment. For the first time since coming to Colorado, she felt carefree and happy—truly happy. She closed her eyes and lifted her face to the sky. The wet snowflakes fell against her skin. Without warning, a large amount of snow hit her arm.

Marty's eyes snapped open, and she found a grinning Jake reaching down to scoop up a handful of snow. Without taking much time at all, he formed it in a ball and lightly tossed it at her shoulder. She ducked and by the time she rose up, he was already forming another.

"I don't imagine you've ever had a snowball fight, have you?" he said in a teasing tone.

"I haven't. But I must say it does get one's blood up." She reached down and pulled a handful of snow into her fist. She flung it at Jake as his third snowball met the target of her hip.

He easily sidestepped her attempt and laughed. "You need practice, Mrs. Wythe, and a lot of it if you're going to hit your mark."

"If you'll recall," Marty said, hurrying to form another snowball, "I'm a pretty fair shot. At least enough of one to scare off bandits."

He laughed again. "But you weren't throwing snowballs at them."

"I'm sure to get the hang of this, as well." She tossed the missile and this time hit his leg. "See, what did I tell you?"

Jake reached down with both hands and formed a massive ball. Then to Marty's surprise, he lifted it and came running in her direction. Uncertain what to do, she froze in place until he was nearly upon her. Only then did her senses return and she began to run, slipping and sliding on the snow-covered ground.

Jake's chuckles filled the air. It was a magical moment, and Marty found herself laughing with delight. This was the Jake she enjoyed, the man she was glad to have married.

"You can't outrun me," he called, gaining on her.

"Oh, you think not? I have an older brother, and you should probably compare notes with him. Dress or no dress, I can move pretty fast when I need to." Just then, however, the wet snow seemed to take hold of her and Marty lost her footing. She fell face-first into the cold white depths.

"Marty!"

Jake sounded terrified, while Marty laughed so hard it must have sounded for all the world as if she were sobbing. He came to her and lifted her in his arms. "I'm so sorry. Are you hurt?"

She tried to sober and answer his question, but the moment got the best of her and laughter spilled from her like water over a falls. Seeing that she was all right, Jake joined in her delight and carried her back to the house.

"You're soaked to the skin and will be half dead by night if you don't get into a hot bath." Jake hurried up the back stairs and into the house, much to Mrs. Standish and Willa's surprise.

"Mr. Wythe! Mrs. Wythe! Whatever happened?"

This only caused Marty to laugh all the harder. Jake carefully lowered her feet to the floor, but the water-soaked skirt acted against her and, combined with her shaky legs, Marty's knees buckled. Jake caught hold of her and hoisted her into his arms again.

"Willa, have Mrs. Landry see to it that Alice gets a hot bath arranged for Mrs. Wythe. Mrs. Standish, we'll need something warm to drink. I believe Mrs. Wythe is quite overcome by her introduction to Colorado winter weather." He gave Marty a wink. "I shall play the hero and carry her to safety."

Marty felt her heart skip a beat at the gleam in Jake's eyes. She was beginning to wonder if safety around this handsome man would continue to be possible. Apparently bandits robbing stagecoaches weren't the only perils of which she should be aware.

Chapter 9

Jake's mood lightened considerably after their snowy encounter, and Marty stopped worrying about whether she'd made a mistake in coming to Denver. What was done, after all, was done.

There remained a great deal they didn't know about each other, a lot that they would need to learn, but she hoped in time they could at least be good friends. She liked to imagine them growing old together in an amicable friendship. Perhaps they would travel, as Jake had mentioned in one of his letters. Marty found the idea intriguing.

Jake proved an honorable man. He never suggested their marriage be anything more than they had agreed to, his character proven daily in his kindness and generosity to her—and without expecting anything in return. Well, anything other than keeping up appearances. With this in mind, Marty agreed to attend church at Trinity Methodist Church when Jake asked her to do so the Sunday before Valentine's Day.

Truth be told, Marty had no desire to pretend her heart was in it. She had told Jake very frankly that she remained at odds with a God who listened to one person's prayers and seemingly ignored another's, answering in whimsical fashion at His leisure. Jake listened and nodded, not disagreeing. When Marty had concluded her comments, he simply told her to do what she felt best. She was touched that he wouldn't impose church services on his wife—the wife demanded by the bank board, the wife required to meet society's expectations.

It was with this latter thought in mind that Marty finally acquiesced. Part of their marriage agreement was for Marty to fill exactly this role. She had given her word, and if that meant she had to sit through stuffy, meaningless church services to prove to society that she was a proper and fitting wife to Jacob Wythe, then that was what she would do.

Attired in one of her new gowns, a powder-blue worsted-wool suit, and white velvet cloak, Marty felt rather like a princess. The enclosed carriage had been readied with blankets and warming pans so they could ride to the church in complete comfort despite the rather blustery day.

"They certainly do not have weather like this in Texas," Marty marveled. "I've known some cold days, but nothing like this."

"Mr. Morgan tells me it can get much worse," Jake replied. "Last winter was my first here, and it wasn't all that bad. Sure wasn't as cold as this."

"You came here from California, didn't you say?"

He raised his eyes to meet hers. "I did. That's where my folks moved after they sold off our ranch. But my heart's in Texas and always will be—much as I appreciate the beauty of Colorado."

Marty frowned. "What do you mean?"

He seemed to lose himself in thought for a moment. "Well, it's like I've said before—ranching is in my blood. I grew up on a ranch my grandfather started, and I plan to one day return and buy it back or at least buy something nearby. I have my heart set on it. Ya'll can take the boy outta Texas, but ya can't take Texas outta the boy."

His drawl reminded her of his origin. She bristled and tried to stay calm. "You've never mentioned that before."

"I haven't? I thought I wrote to you about that first thing. That was one of the reasons I wanted a Texas bride. I knew she would understand my love for Texas and want to return there one day. It was a particular bonus to me that you'd been a rancher's wife. You already know how to do the job." He grinned.

"But not all women love Texas," Marty dared to say. Jake didn't seem to notice, however.

"It's like I told you a while back, my plans and Mr. Morgan's take two different directions. Mr. Morgan would see me continue to seek social status and civic popularity. At least that's what he says. I'm not sure why he's taken such an interest in me, but I suppose it had something to do with my father's influence and that of his California business cronies. Anyway, he sees me continuing in the business of banking."

"There's nothing wrong with becoming successful in the banking industry."

"No, of course not. Not if that's your calling."

"I see. But it's not your calling?" She got a sickening feeling in the pit of her stomach.

"No. My calling is to return to Texas. I've always known I would. I'm a cattleman. As soon as I have enough money to buy a ranch, that's what I plan to do. I figured I'd made that clear—and I apologize if I didn't." He smiled. "But you're a Texan, very nearly born and bred. You've known ranching all of your life. You know how it gets in your blood."

"I do, and that's just the problem."

The carriage stopped and Jake appeared completely oblivious to her comment. "Ah, we're here. Now you can see the inside of the church. It's quite amazing."

Marty wanted to stop him—to demand he listen to her and understand that she had no desire to return to Texas. If this was his plan, then they would need to revisit his dream and their marriage of convenience. But instead, she allowed him to help her from the carriage.

Stepping onto the cleared sidewalk, Marty noted what seemed like a hundred carriages lining the street around the church. Gazing upward, she was again taken in by the tall steeple.

"They say it's nearly two hundred feet in height," Jake whispered, as if reading her thoughts. "Can't really see why it needs to be that high. I suppose it's their little tower of Babel," he mused aloud.

"It's beautiful. I've always liked church steeples," Marty said, remembering her childhood. "It always made me think of us somehow reaching up to God."

Other well-dressed people made their way into the church, barely pausing to offer nods. The wind was growing stronger, and no one desired to endure its chill for long. Inside, Marty allowed Jake to lead her into the massive sanctuary. He stopped at a pew about halfway up on the right-hand side and stepped back to allow her admission. The other occupants nodded in greeting and scooted down to make room.

Marty had barely had time to take her place when music started booming out from the organ. Glorious music filled the air, unlike anything she'd ever known. The entire congregation rose to its feet for song.

Without any prompting, the people began to sing the doxology in perfect pace with the music. Marty knew the words, but had no desire to partake.

"'Praise God from whom all blessings flow.'"

She didn't feel much like offering praise. For all the blessings that God gave, He also took away. Didn't Job even speak to that? She recalled the verse. *The Lord gave, and the Lord hath taken away; blessed be the name of the Lord.*

"'Praise Him all creatures here below.'"

Discomfort crept up her spine. Marty would have exited the row had Jake not blocked her. Coming here was a mistake. She'd not been in a formal service since Thomas died. That was when her anger at God had reached the boiling point. Until now, she'd been fairly good at keeping that rage under control.

"'Praise Him above ye heavenly host.'"

She tried to calm her breathing and silently wished she'd thought to include a fan in her new white velvet purse. *I can do this. I can do this.* She focused on breathing in and out. *Just a little longer.*

"'Praise Father, Son, and Holy Ghost. Amen.'"

The music and singing ended, and from the front of the cathedral a prayer began. Marty bowed her head, not to pray or even out of respect, but mostly because it helped to calm her nerves. Why was this happening? Why had Jake talked about moving back to Texas—to own a ranch, no less?

I own a ranch—a Texas ranch.

It was one of the little facts she'd not shared with her husband. No doubt if he knew, Jake would insist on throwing off his banking duties to move her back to Texas that very day.

I won't go back.

Jake tugged on her arm, and Marty could see that everyone was now taking their seat. The pastor welcomed the congregants and spoke of how the blessings of God were upon them that day. She ignored his words and tried instead to figure out what she might do to persuade Jake that remaining in Colorado was the better part of wisdom.

Hadn't he mentioned something about the country struggling with certain financial problems? She tried to recall the conversation they'd shared a few nights back. Jake had spoken of several concerns the bank had regarding railroads that were facing receivership. It was the main reason he'd been under so much pressure. She hadn't completely understood the implications of such actions, but it was obviously not good. If the entire country was having trouble related to money, then Texas would be suffering right along with the rest of the states. Not only that, but there were still problems with the lack of predictable water. Her brother-in-law had been concerned about that even when discussing running her cattle with his.

The congregation rose to listen to the Word being read and then the organ boomed out again with a rousing arrangement of "Onward, Christian Soldiers." Everything seemed to vibrate, as if a part of the music itself. Marty glanced around at the vast sanctuary. Jake had told her the church held over a thousand people. The beautiful and intricate woodwork of the interior was unmatched by anything Marty had ever seen. Someone had taken great pains to make this an incredibly beautiful place of worship.

Seated once again, Marty's mind remained on what she should do regarding Jake's desire to own a ranch. She didn't hear anything of the sermon, and when the service was over, Marty was no closer to figuring out what actions she should take.

When at last they were dismissed, several of societies' finer attendees commented in passing that they would be eager to spend time with Marty at the Valentine's ball, but they didn't linger to talk. With the weather colder than ever, most folks were happy to move on. For this, Marty was truly thankful.

Jake helped her into the carriage, then settled down beside her. "We might as well try to stay warm together," he said, throwing a blanket over their legs. "Sure don't get this cold in Texas."

"I heard talk that the water shortages in Texas are worsening," she blurted without thinking.

"It'll never be as bad as when my father up and sold our ranch. It took me a long while before I could forgive him for that."

"I suppose it would be hard to lose your home."

Jake shifted his weight. "It wasn't just my home. That ranch had been owned by my grandfather and father. It was my birthright—and my father sold it. If he'd just held on a little longer, we . . . Well . . . he didn't hold on, and now I'm here."

"But you seem well suited to banking."

"The ranch was always what I loved most. It was the reason I went off to college in the first place. I wanted to learn more about the business side of things and about any new methods to make the ranch more profitable. Banking was never in my plans." He sounded almost disgusted. "I just happen to be really good with numbers."

"That's a very valuable skill," Marty pressed. She hadn't meant to get him dwelling on the past and all that he'd lost—she'd only wanted to remind him of how difficult things were in that ghastly place.

"Might be, but it doesn't hold my interest like ranching does."

"My brother-in-law owns a ranch, and they aren't doing all that well," she lied. "The drought ruined a lot of water sources, and they are still struggling to get enough water for the cattle. And I don't need to tell you that the price for cattle has gone down considerably. It's a hard time for everyone, but especially folks in ranching. That's one of the reasons I was anxious to answer your advertisement for a wife."

"Agriculture is suffering, too," Jake agreed. "I was just reading that the price is bottoming out for cotton. But these things do tend to cycle around."

"I know you've voiced concerns for the economy and the railroads folding. I think you should count yourself fortunate to have a solid position at the bank." *Please let him see the truth in what I'm saying.* Marty wasn't at all sure to whom she was speaking, but she wished with all her heart it might be so.

Jake looked away and nodded. "I suppose I am. What was it that the pastor said this morning in his sermon . . . about wisdom?" He shook his head. "Something about God giving it if you ask."

Marty hadn't heard the sermon, but she had been well schooled in the Scriptures. "It's from James. It tells us that if we lack wisdom, we should ask for it from God because He gives it liberally."

Jake smiled. "Yes. Yes, that was it. I suppose I should just ask for wisdom about my situation and seek God's direction. I haven't done a whole lot of that, though I know it's what's right."

Marty couldn't hide her frown fast enough, and Jake's brow rose in question. "You seem to be angry at God. Why? I know you said you weren't much for church or religion, yet you know the Scriptures."

"I suppose I'm angry at God because I believe Him unjust and unfair. The Word talks about how He sends the rain where He will. He loves whom He will. He saves one life and lets another die—and very often the innocent suffer."

"But that's not all there is to God. Why would you focus only on that? I mean, I'm not a deeply spiritual man, but I do revere the Lord."

Marty didn't wish to get into a discussion of religion. "My first husband was a God-fearing man. He read the Bible and worshiped God in his heart and in the church. But God didn't save him from being gored to death by a riled-up longhorn. I'm sure you could offer something similar about your first wife. Do you not ever wonder why such a loss was visited upon you at such a young age? The Bible says that God is love, but I see nothing loving in allowing such sorrow and pain."

Jake frowned, and Marty feared that she'd touched a nerve. She'd never discussed his first wife with him prior to this. He'd shared very little regarding the first Mrs. Wythe in his letters. And, because he was new to Denver, she couldn't even question the household staff about the woman. None of them had ever met her.

After several minutes of silence, Marty apologized. "I'm sorry. I often speak my mind without thinking of where it will take me. I shouldn't have expressed my feelings in such a bold way."

"Of course you should have," Jake replied. "I want there to be honesty between us. I've been deceived in the past, and I don't like it. I'd prefer we always be truthful with each other. Don't you think that's best?"

Marty swallowed her guilt. "I do," she lied again. "I think honesty is always best."

"Well then, let me just say that my marriage was not a happy one. Not like yours. My wife was only interested in the next sparkly thing. I guess that's why I'm pleased with your reserve. That's why I wanted a Lone Star bride," he said, seeming to forget she was even there. "Josephine didn't love me. She loved what she thought I could give her. I was ten kinds of fool. Even her folks were embarrassed by her attitude . . . and actions."

"I'm sorry." Marty looked at him, but he continued staring at the carriage top.

"She found someone else and ran off not long after we married. I didn't know where she'd gone, but a part of me was glad to have her gone. She made me so miserable with her nagging about wanting a bigger house in a better neighborhood." He gave a harsh laugh. "She would have given her buttons and bows to be in your place."

Jake finally seemed to realize he was rambling. "I didn't mean to go on like that."

"It's all right. I want to know about you," Marty admitted.

"Well, now you do."

"Where did she go? Did she come back?"

He shook his head. "She ran off with another fella, and then got herself sick in South America. South America of all places! Who even wants to go there?" He shrugged. "She caught some disease, and it killed her. A priest sent us a letter and her things. Her mother cried for weeks on end and very nearly ended up dead herself. Me, I was . . ." He let the words fade. "Never mind. We're home, I see, and Mrs. Standish promised us a wonderful Sunday dinner."

Marty said nothing, but nodded. She couldn't help but wonder what Jake might have said. Perhaps one day he would tell her.

★

Later that evening as Alice helped her ready for bed, Marty remembered her words to Jake and stuffed down an overwhelming urge to seek him out and confess.

It won't do any good to tell him that I own a ranch. I'm not willing to move back to it, and it would only be a source of argument between us.

"Better to leave it be," she murmured.

"What did you say, ma'am?" Alice asked.

Marty suppressed a yawn. "Oh, nothing of importance." Alice finished braiding Marty's hair and secured it with a ribbon. Rising, Marty gave the girl a smile. "Thank you. You've proven yourself quite capable these last few days, and I couldn't be more pleased."

"Thank you," Alice replied. "I know you took a big chance in hiring me."

"We all need a big chance now and then. I don't understand why the bank didn't compensate you somehow for your loss—especially since your father was in their employ and it was their goods that attracted the attention of thieves. But in a way, they are providing now, since Mr. Wythe also works for Mr. Morgan doing your father's old job. It's Morgan money that pays your salary."

Alice nodded. "I thought of that after I learned about Mr. Wythe's position. God knew exactly where to bring me."

Marty found the girl's comment strange. "Why do you say that?"

"I was in need, and the future looked grim. I didn't see a way out or a hope for making things work. I was broken in spirit, and I wasn't in very good shape—even physically—for several months. Though friends were helping, I knew that soon I'd have to take care of myself. And frankly, as I told God one morning, I wasn't at all prepared to do the job." She smiled. "God knew I was speaking the truth, so He put you in my life. Now you and Mrs. Landry take care of me, and so I am safe once again."

Marty didn't want to discredit the girl's faith, so she only nodded and started for her bed. Alice's next words, however, caused her a great deal of discomfort. "God always knows best. He knows just what we need—even before we know it. He's always making provision for us."

Like He did when Thomas got killed? Like He did when your father and mine were attacked and murdered?

"And don't forget to write to your sister, ma'am. Mrs. Landry put some fine stationery on your desk, and there are several choices of pens and ink. She wasn't sure what you preferred."

Marty glanced across the room to her sitting area. "Thank you. I suppose I should write that letter first thing tomorrow."

Alice nodded and made her way from the room. Marty settled into bed, wondering if she'd be able to find any peace for her soul. The lies she had told and the truth she had concealed rose up to accuse her. Jake wanted honesty between them, but Marty couldn't give that.

She glanced in the darkness toward the connecting door to her dressing room. She could easily cross through to knock on Jake's door. The thought of trying to explain left her without courage, however.

"I can't tell him the truth," she whispered in the dark. "I can never tell him the truth."

Chapter 10

The Valentine's party at the Morgans' residence was unlike anything Marty had ever attended. Even during her time in Georgia while attending finishing school, she had never seen such evidence of wealth. There were at least twenty servants moving in a carefully choreographed dance as they went about their duties. Most were men dressed in smart black suits and white gloves, while a few were women in fashionable black dresses and white aprons. It seemed that the women, however, disappeared with the announcement of the first guests, while the men remained to take outer garments, direct guests to the receiving line, and offer any other needed assistance.

Overhead, massive crystal chandeliers spilled light upon the visitors. Marty thought the crystals sparkled like diamonds and even wondered if, given the Morgan wealth, they weren't exactly that.

Mrs. Morgan greeted Marty with practiced charm, expressing her utter delight to introduce Martha Wythe to society. "I seldom invest my time in these matters," Mrs. Morgan told her in confidence, "but my husband expressed his desire for young Wythe to be well received." She smiled in a knowing manner. "And that, of course, demands that his wife be." She assessed Marty from head to toe. "I can tell we shall be good company for each other."

Uncertain how to respond, Marty simply offered her thanks. Mrs.

Morgan didn't seem at all concerned with her silence. Perhaps this was expected. Marty allowed the older woman to position her in the receiving line and make suggestions for how to greet the arriving public.

"What . . . what should I do?" Marty asked in a hushed whisper.

"It's best to keep your comments to a minimum," Mrs. Morgan advised. "I shall conduct the introductions, and you follow my lead."

Marty wanted to laugh. No doubt she feared that Marty and Jake would make unforgivable social mistakes. However, Marty was happy to limit her replies. Most of the people, particularly the women, seemed far more interested in Mrs. Morgan and what she thought of their expensive new gowns.

"Mrs. Keystone, this is Mrs. Jacob Wythe. She and Mr. Wythe were recently married, as I'm sure you will remember."

The pinch-faced woman eyed Marty carefully. "Mrs. Wythe, I've heard . . . about you."

Marty wasn't at all sure if that was a good or a bad thing. "Mrs. Keystone, I've looked forward to meeting you."

The woman nodded and turned her attention back to Imogene Morgan. "Mr. Keystone is unforgivably late, but plans to join us for dinner. He was delayed with some sort of business matter."

"Our men must attend to duty," Mrs. Morgan replied. She dismissed Mrs. Keystone by looking to the next couple in line. "Governor and Mrs. Cooper, this is Mrs. Jacob Wythe."

"Oh, Mrs. Morgan, you should remember I'm no longer the governor," Mr. Cooper responded, giving Marty a half bow. Mrs. Cooper smiled rather uncomfortably and bobbed her head in acknowledgment. Marty did likewise and remained silent, since no one had really spoken to her.

"I want to thank you for joining us tonight." Mrs. Morgan reached out to touch Mrs. Cooper's arm. "I know that you've had a very busy schedule."

"Oh, but I wouldn't miss your Valentine's ball for all of the world. I simply couldn't. I so look forward to this event, and just look at your beautiful gown."

Mrs. Morgan touched the edge of the flowing gold-toned fabric that fell from either shoulder to the ground. "Isn't it marvelous? Mr. Worth's creation."

"But of course," Mrs. Cooper replied, touching the bodice of her own lavender gown.

Mrs. Morgan smiled knowingly. "I recognized his work immediately. I must say that color goes well with your complexion."

Marty tried not to appear bored at the banter. She thought back to times when Hannah and Will had entertained some of the area's wealthier ranchers and their wives. There had been social circles in Texas, but life had a way of being less pretentious. Maybe it was because folks there knew they often depended on one another for their very lives.

The receiving line went on and on until Marty thought she might very well scream in exasperation of the façade of pleasantries. When dinner was finally served, Marty found herself sandwiched between Mr. Cooper and a Mr. Sheedy. And while both were amicable enough, she longed for Jake's company. The men offered pleasantries, asking how she liked Denver and her new home. Sheedy spoke about some of the houses being built nearby, and Cooper added his thoughts on the growing city. It wasn't until Mr. Cooper leaned close to comment on her unusual arrival to the city, however, that Marty grew uncomfortable.

"I must say, I thought you would be a much fiercer-looking woman." He smiled. "When I read of your heroics in the paper, they made you sound larger than life."

Marty paled. "They wrote about me in the paper?"

"Oh, surely Mr. Wythe showed you the article. He said, of course, that the drawing looked nothing like you. I can see that for myself now. You are a delicate and beautiful woman, and I don't say that lightly. Sweet talk has never been my style."

She glanced around the table to where Mr. Cooper's wife sat laughing at something the man to her left had said. Marty swallowed hard and met Mr. Cooper's gaze. "Thank you, I think."

He chuckled. "I merely stated the obvious. You hardly seem capable of handling a two-team carriage, much less six large stage horses."

Marty smiled finally. "I grew up on a ranch in Texas. I know very well how to handle horses—cattle too. Does that also shock you?"

Cooper shook his head. "No, Mrs. Wythe, I'm beginning to think you could say most anything, and it wouldn't surprise me in the least. You are quite a woman."

"What was that, Cooper?" This came from a man opposite the table. Marty struggled to remember who the man was, but she couldn't place a name with the face.

"I was merely commenting on our heroine, Mrs. Wythe. Many of you may not realize it, but this elegant young woman is the one and same Mrs. Olson who saved the stagecoach a few weeks ago."

There were several gasps from the women; obviously they found Marty's exploits to be unacceptable table conversation. Some women looked away, as if Marty's actions were vile and unmentionable, while others merely frowned. It was apparent that everyone knew only too well about the incident. Most of the men seemed quite supportive, however—most were nodding their heads and offering her a smile.

"Is it true that you singlehandedly foiled the stagecoach robbery?" a man at the far end of the table asked.

"Did you really handle two pistols at once?" someone else asked. It was as if a dam had burst. Questions came at her from every direction.

Marty looked to Jake, who appeared as uncomfortable as she felt. He pulled on his collar and stared at his plate. Marty didn't know what to think or say, but the entire party awaited her response.

"I . . . I should say . . . no. I was only one passenger among many, and I had only one revolver. The driver and his associate were the heroes of the day." She fell silent, hoping she hadn't caused problems for Jake. Goodness, why hadn't he shown her the article in the paper? At least then she could have been ready for this.

"Well, I heard that the driver and his man were shot nearly to death," Mr. Morgan threw out.

Mrs. Morgan and her friends seemed appalled at the reference. She hushed her husband with a look. He shrugged. "I beg your forgiveness, ladies. I did not mean to be crude."

Marty would have laughed had the situation not been so important to her husband. So instead, she bolstered her courage. Amidst the fine china, silver, and crystal, she was the odd wooden bowl accidentally left in plain sight.

"I'm afraid it all happened quite fast. The men were wounded and because of that, someone had to get them to safety," Marty finally replied. "I did what anyone would have done."

"Few women would have known how to drive a team of stage horses," one of the men commented.

"Perhaps that's true, but I grew up on a ranch in Texas. We often found it necessary to learn . . . irregular duties."

"However could you manage climbing up that monstrous contraption?" Mrs. Cooper questioned. "I haven't ridden a stage in years, but I know them to be quite large."

Marty nodded. "It wasn't easy. It took all the strength I could muster. Even so, I'm just happy to know that my efforts helped those men."

"I should say so. The paper," Mr. Morgan said in a voice that suggested his approval, "said that if it were not for Mrs. Olson . . . pardon me, ma'am, *Mrs. Wythe's* actions, those men would have died and the stage occupants would have been left to the mercy of the bandits, who might have returned to the scene. Mrs. Wythe deserves our congratulations and admiration."

Mrs. Morgan agreed. "She does, indeed. She's a heroine, and we are glad to have her among us."

There was a great deal of murmuring and nodding. Marty offered them a smile. If the Morgans said she was a heroine, then these people were happy to conclude nothing less. The opinion of the Morgans mattered more than the shocking actions Marty had given the city to talk about.

After that, no one seemed inclined to comment, and the guests returned to more private discussions. Marty found herself engaged in conversation again with Mr. Sheedy and Mr. Cooper. Sheedy, it seemed, had once been a rancher himself. Now, however, he was vice-president of the Colorado National Bank.

"Of course, I made my fortune in cattle and mining. Good money in ranching if you have the right people involved."

Marty nodded but said nothing. She was relieved when someone else spoke to Sheedy and drew his attention from her. Focusing on her plate—a beautiful gold-edged bone china—Marty toyed with her food.

"Do you not care for the fish?" Mr. Cooper asked.

Marty shook her head. "It's not that. With the excitement and all, I find that I'm not very hungry."

"These parties can be quite exhausting, so it's best to keep up one's strength—especially since there is to be dancing."

Course after course was served, and Marty did her best to nibble a little of each offering. She was momentarily relieved when the women were excused to ready themselves for the ball while the men smoked cigars and enjoyed a good brandy.

Finding herself in a room of strangers, Marty readied herself for the onslaught of questions she feared would come. Mrs. Morgan, however, was good to engage her first. She complimented Marty's gown, which prompted the other women to do so, as well.

"I find Mrs. Davies to be the most capable of seamstresses and designers. She is quick to understand exactly what I'm seeking," the woman introduced as Mrs. Katherine Sheedy commented.

"Personally, I'm spoiled," Mrs. Cooper started. "For formal occasions, I must have Worth, or I'm completely out of sorts. The man is a positive genius of design. I believe his creations only get better each year."

"Oh, I agree wholeheartedly," Mrs. Morgan answered. "I daresay there will never be another designer quite so talented. It will be a sad day indeed when we lose Mr. Worth."

A rather mousy but opulently jeweled woman interjected, "He surely must have a great many students learning from his creative talents. It wouldn't be right to lose such insight—such vision."

"They can learn to emulate the man's designs," Mrs. Morgan replied, "but when Charles Worth dies, he will no doubt take his biggest secrets with him to the grave."

"Such a disparaging conversation," Mrs. Cooper said, *tsk*ing her disapproval. "We are here to welcome Mrs. Wythe."

"Indeed we are." Mrs. Morgan stepped closer to Marty. "I believe we will all enjoy getting to know you better in the months to come."

Marty wasn't entirely sure that she could offer the same comment and so merely gave her thanks.

The women contented themselves with allowing maids to retouch their hair and help them into ornate gloves for the ball. Marty was assisted by a very plain young woman who knew her duty well. She had Marty fitted and buttoned in no time at all.

The beautiful gloves now gracing her hands were quite foreign to Marty. She had owned riding gloves most of her life, and in finishing school she had learned the requirements of wearing gloves for various occasions. Back on her ranch, though, gloves were used for work, and there were very few times she donned them for special occasions. Especially after she stopped going to church. However, her trip to Colorado had changed all of that. Now gloves were almost her constant companions—so much so, in fact, that she gave serious thought to giving them names. She looked around the room at all of the elegant pairs and couldn't help but smile at the thought of them each having names. What would the social etiquette be for introducing one's gloves?

She suppressed a girlish giggle at the thought and tried instead to focus on the conversation directed at her.

"I visited Texas once," Mrs. Keystone said. "I didn't appreciate the climate."

Marty nodded. "Many people don't."

"I also didn't appreciate the insects. You would think they could do something about that."

She wasn't entirely sure what the woman expected, but not wanting to make trouble, Marty only nodded again.

"I saw Texas as a dry and desolate place." Mrs. Cooper shook her head. "Mr. Cooper found it necessary to journey there several years ago, and I accompanied him. I was most miserable. The people were some of the strangest I've ever met." She looked at Marty. "At least your accent is tolerable."

Marty started to take offense at the remark. It was one thing that

Marty found Texas an abominable place, but that this woman should insult the people was another matter. Mrs. Morgan spoke up just then, however, and Marty had no chance to interject her thoughts.

"It is time. Let us meet our men for the ball."

★

Jake smiled at Marty from across the room. The evening was nearly over, and soon they would return to their home and the imposed pretense of the evening would be behind them. So far, no one seemed the wiser about their arrangement.

Retrieving a glass of punch for his wife, Jake was joined by Mr. Sheedy.

"Wythe, I was delighted to converse with your missus over supper. She's a smart one."

"She is indeed, and beautiful," Jake said without the slightest hesitation.

"You did well for yourself. I understand she hails from a ranching background. I was heavily involved in cattle at one time. Hard work, but it can pay off."

"Marty grew up ranching—it's in her blood. Her sister and brother-in-law still have the spread where she spent most of her life. I look forward to seeing it one day."

Sheedy took a glass of punch offered by the servant and nodded. "I don't imagine that will be very soon, however. Times are difficult, to say the least."

"Yes, sir, they are. However, I believe we can weather this storm, just like the others that came before. Folks say that things haven't been the same since the war, but our great nation is exploding with growth and development. Those are the very things that will see us through."

"I hope you're right, Mr. Wythe."

Marty joined them at that moment, smiling warmly at Jake. "I hope you don't mind the interruption."

"Not at all, Mrs. Wythe," Sheedy answered before Jake could. "Your husband and I were just discussing your upbringing on the ranch and how he looks forward to one day visiting that very place."

Marty threw Jake a quick glance, looking hesitant to speak. He

99

handed her a glass of punch, and she took a sip before addressing Sheedy. "I only hope there will be a ranch for him to visit. With recent hardships, I think my sister and brother-in-law are considering the possibility that they will need to sell."

This took Jake by surprise. She'd said nothing of the matter up until this time. "I had no idea things were so bad for them. Perhaps I should write to your brother-in-law and offer consultation. I know a great deal about ranching, and perhaps I could offer financial advice."

Marty shook her head rather vehemently. "It would shame him. Please don't mention it."

Sheedy nodded in agreement. "A man has his pride. Better not to step on it and cause more bruising than necessary."

Chapter 11

Fulfilling her social duties proved to be more and more exhausting to Marty. The endless visitations, gatherings, and changing of clothes left her feeling that her days were an utter waste of time, filled with pretentious people.

However, remembering Jake speak of Texas and his desire to one day return there made Marty more determined than ever to establish herself in Denver society. She always tried to receive her guests with the warmest of welcomes and even worked to tame her drawl and emulate the speech of her social peers.

Jake warned her there would be a great many responsibilities on her part, maintaining a presence at the social functions of the Denver elite. Marty would be expected to be seen at the proper events and reveal a knowledge of and interest in such functions in order to better fit into the social circles required for a woman of her position. Marty wanted to limit her participation, but she reconsidered every time she remembered how much Jake wanted to return to Texas. She vowed to herself that society and its façades would become as well known to her as ranching had once been. She would do her best to ingratiate herself with Denver's finest and prove to Jake that they belonged right where they were.

A little over a week after the Valentine's ball, Marty had attended yet another party celebrating George Washington's birthday. This one was hosted by the Sheedys and allowed Marty to see the interior of their elegant home. The house was palatial in size and was said to be a blend of Queen Anne and Richardsonian Romanesque architecture—although Marty wasn't entirely sure what that actually meant. The home had been completed just the year before, however, and was rumored to be one of the grandest in America.

As she had other events, Marty had endured that party rather than enjoyed it. Marty had found the house and its décor far more interesting than the people visiting it. The food, rich and overly abundant, had been delicious, but not to Marty's liking. It was only then that she realized just how much she preferred common things.

She awoke the next morning remembering the party and the unusual offering of multiple desserts. The dishes were lavish and presented in such a manner that they looked far more like pieces of art than dishes to eat. She sighed.

"I'd much rather have one of Hannah's good pies than whatever those concoctions were supposed to be."

Allowing Alice to guide her through the morning routine, Marty suppressed a yawn and wondered what was on her day's agenda. Alice was talking about something, but Marty didn't have any idea what the girl was saying. Already tired, Marty wished she could simply crawl back into bed.

She felt the same way much later in the day, when Alice helped her change clothes for the fourth time. Marty slipped into a stunning bodice that matched the skirt of green and blue tartan flannel. The simple cut of the skirt allowed her to wear a collapsible bustle, which would make it easy for Marty to spend time at her desk writing letters.

"I like the way the bodice lays," she commented as Alice did up the back buttons. The pleating was stitched into place with a rounded yoke trimmed in dark blue braid and a high lace neck.

"You look very pretty in it, ma'am," Alice replied. She secured a dark blue sash around Marty's small waist. "But you look lovely in most everything."

Marty could hear the longing in the girl's voice. "Alice, you are a very attractive woman yourself. That scar on your face does not take away from your sweet nature and spirit. The right man will come along one day and the scar will mean nothing to him."

"I pray that might be so," Alice admitted. She began to rearrange Marty's hair in a more intricate design. Taking up a curling iron, she carefully arranged some of the blond tresses around the rod. "As the pastor said at church just a few Sundays back, God isn't in the business of doing things without them having a purpose that will lead to His glory."

"Well, I don't know about that." Marty generally kept her religious thoughts to herself, but with Alice she felt she could be honest. "I've seen plenty of bad that has happened without any glory to God. There's a lot of suffering in this world. I find God cruel for not stopping it . . . or at best, insensitive to our pain."

"I beg to differ," Alice said, surprising Marty with her bold stand. "There will always be cruel and insensitive people, but those are not qualities that can be assigned to God. The Bible says that God is love. Love is never insensitive or cruel, so therefore I cannot believe God capable of such . . . human attributes."

Marty considered the younger woman's words. There was a time when she had accepted such thoughts herself. "So you believe God had you attacked and injured for His glory, and it wasn't an act of cruelty?"

Alice arranged a curl and pinned it in place before responding. "I don't think God had me attacked at all. I think the men who attacked me didn't much care what God wanted."

"But God could have prevented the entire situation."

"He could have," Alice agreed. "He could have done any number of things. And while I believe God did allow this to happen to me, I don't think it was His desire. I don't think He took any delight in the occurrence."

"Then why didn't He intervene to stop it? The Bible talks about how Jesus and the Spirit both intercede for us. Why not intercede to prevent an evil man from harming an innocent one?"

"Shall we receive good at the hand of God, and not receive evil?" Alice countered.

Marty studied Alice in the mirror. The younger woman seemed quite content in her beliefs and not at all shaken by Marty's questioning. "Isn't that Job?"

Alice nodded and continued to pin another curl. "It is Job. Second chapter, tenth verse. Job is suffering, and his wife wants him to curse God and die. That's how he answers her. To my way of thinking, evil will always be with us because of the sin of Adam. The world is not a perfect place."

"So your injury was just one of those things that happened because the world isn't perfect? Doesn't that alleviate God's responsibility in the matter?"

"And what would God's responsibility have been?" she asked.

"To keep you from harm. To save you."

"But He did save me, Mrs. Wythe. I very nearly died from loss of blood and then an infection."

Marty shook her head, causing Alice to jab a hairpin against her head. "Oh my. I apologize, ma'am."

"No, it was my own fault. I moved."

Alice gave a brief nod before her face lit up in a smile. "I suppose you could say that it was my fault or my father's for putting me in a position of danger. God didn't force us to go out that dark night. In fact, my father had commented that it wasn't a wise idea. However, he wanted to take care of business that evening. I decided to accompany him, even though he had suggested it would be better for me to remain home. So who is at fault?"

Marty was glad that the girl had gotten comfortable enough to debate such matters. "But my point is that if God truly is love, He would intervene and keep such bad things from happening to the innocent."

"Why?"

Marty turned and looked up at Alice. "Why? You ask why God should keep the innocent from harm?"

"Yes. He didn't keep Jesus from harm, and Jesus was completely innocent. He was beaten and spat upon and crucified. Does that mean God didn't love Him? Jesus is a part of God—how could He not love himself?"

Marty frowned as she considered the young woman's words. "You don't think that God . . . well . . . that He should keep the innocent from harm?"

Alice shrugged and moved toward the dressing room window. "If you are suggesting that God somehow owes it to us, then no. I think God has given us a great many blessings beyond what we deserve and yet has withheld a great deal of the punishment we *do* deserve." Her words resonated with conviction, something Marty had not yet witnessed in Alice.

The young woman tied back the drapes one at a time. Marty thought her quite delicate in appearance, yet there was a fierceness in the younger woman that she couldn't help but admire—even if Marty couldn't agree with her spiritual reasoning.

"And what about your mother and brother?"

Alice said nothing, simply stared out the window as if contemplating the question. Marty continued. "Do you believe it fair for a child to lose her mother and brother, as you did?"

"There's someone out there." Alice jumped back from the window. "A man. He's sneaking around. I saw him cross from the stable to the yard."

Marty got up and walked to the window. "Where?"

"I'm not sure where he's gone, but he was there just a little bit ago."

It was clear Alice was upset, but Marty couldn't help but wonder if it was just her way of changing the subject so she wouldn't have to answer the question. "I don't see anything."

"I'm certain he was there."

"Did you recognize him? Perhaps it was just Brighton or Samson."

"No." Then Alice's demeanor seemed to change abruptly. She shrugged and went back to the dressing table to straighten up. "Oh, you're probably right. Maybe it was just Mr. Brighton. He probably took something out to Samson."

Just then Mrs. Landry appeared. "Mrs. Wythe, I have the menus for the rest of this week for you to go over if you have the time."

Marty gave a quick glance toward Alice, who was now humming to herself and setting the vanity to rights. "I suppose it's as good a time as any," Marty said, turning to the housekeeper. "Shall we go to my sitting room?"

Mrs. Landry nodded and held out a large piece of paper. "Feel free to make any changes you wish. You asked me to prepare a menu much like those we'd had in the past, prior to your arrival. This is a typical arrangement."

Marty made her way back to the bedroom sitting area, studying the menu as she went. A wide variety of foods were listed, and while it was nowhere near the opulent affair of which she'd partaken at luncheons and suppers offered by society's finest, she found it appealing.

"I see my husband enjoys steak and ham."

"He does. He's not much for fish recipes."

Marty smiled. "Neither am I. My brother and brother-in-law were both quite fond of fishing and eating their catches, but I can't say I agreed. I'm glad Jake feels the same way."

"You will also note that he isn't much for desserts. However, I'm certain that if you wish to indulge in one each evening, Mr. Wythe would be amenable. He told me that he intended for you to adjust the menu in whatever manner would please you most."

Marty shook her head, amazed to have yet another thing in common with her husband. "I've not been one for them, either. Not that I don't enjoy a sweet now and then, but I hardly find it necessary at each meal." She continued to read the menu. "You haven't listed anything for Friday's supper." She looked to Mrs. Landry for explanation.

"That is the night Mr. Wythe plans to entertain Mr. Morgan and Mr. Keystone. I thought perhaps you would like to plan something special."

"He said nothing to me about this." Marty tried not to feel offended by her husband's omission. "Perhaps we should seek his advice."

"Oh, that wouldn't be proper. I can help you with some choices based on previous occasions, however. Mr. Morgan is fond of pork roast with a heavy sweet sauce. He also enjoys small roasted potatoes in dill, as well as asparagus in hollandaise sauce."

"I see. And will he desire a dessert?" Marty's tone was rather sarcastic. She wasn't sure why the subject matter put her at odds with her housekeeper, but it did.

"He does enjoy chocolate torte. Mrs. Standish has a delicious recipe, and I'm sure she will be happy to create it for the occasion. Other than that, I would suggest a cream of spinach soup and perhaps some fruit and cheese for those who would rather not partake of the torte."

"Whatever you think is best," Marty said, handing the paper back to Mrs. Landry.

The woman nodded and took her leave. Marty cast her gaze toward the writing desk. She still hadn't written to Hannah since arriving in Denver. She knew her sister would be most frantic for news, but she wasn't yet ready to tell her about the marriage. With a sigh, Marty made her way to the desk and took a seat.

"I'll simply tell her about the wonderful time I'm having in Colorado," she decided. Taking pen in hand, Marty consoled herself with the assurance that she needn't tell the entire truth. It seemed a reasonable compromise.

★

Alice Chesterfield pushed aside her fears and tried her best to focus on preparing for bed. The day had been long, and she had spent a good deal of time that evening reading a book given her by Mrs. Landry on how to be a proper lady's maid. Mrs. Landry told her that because Mrs. Wythe so desired Alice in the position, Mrs. Landry felt it important to educate her in her duties.

Gratitude didn't begin to explain Alice's feelings toward the older housekeeper. Mrs. Landry didn't hold it against Alice that she lacked training. Instead, she worked to teach the girl what was needed. Alice appreciated her kindness more than she could say. The employment company had been cruel in their assessment of her, chiding her for coming to them without any experience or references. Alice had tried to explain that up until a few months ago, she and her father had lived quite comfortably on their own. They'd even had a cook. The agency didn't believe her or else didn't care. Instead they had turned her away, suggesting that she get some type of experience working before returning.

If I'd had proper employment in which to gain experience, I wouldn't have needed to seek an agency's help in securing a position.

She carefully hung up the black dress that was her regular uniform.

She had a variety of white aprons to protect the body of the dress, and that way she didn't need to wash the garment more than once a week. The Wythes had very generously provided two uniforms for her use, as well as three other dresses. One was a beautiful striped yellow gown for Sundays and the other two were for her time off from work. But Alice doubted she would be using them anytime soon. She had no desire to leave the house. Especially now.

She cast a furtive glance at the window and shivered in the flannel nightgown she'd just put on. She'd seen a man out there earlier in the day. She knew he'd been there, and she knew that it wasn't Brighton or Samson.

Worried that her past was once again catching up with her, Alice dropped to her knees beside the bed and began to pray.

"Father in heaven, please deliver me from wicked men who seek to harm me. Deliver me from sin and from the temptation to do wrong. Please bolster my heart that I might not fear." She paused and gazed heavenward. "And please let my father know how much I miss him." She started to end her prayer and sighed. "My mother and brother, too. Amen."

She slid beneath the covers, grateful for the warming pan Mrs. Landry had suggested she use. The added warmth helped ease her weary body, and in doing so, Alice was able to put aside her fears and worries.

Sleep overcame her, but Alice's dreams soon turned to nightmares, as they often did. She remembered in detail the events of the night that took her father's life. . . .

She could feel the dampness around her. It had been rainy that night, and cold. Father had been so determined to make his delivery.

"It's critical that I get these papers to the right people. I don't want them to remain in the house overnight," he had told her. "Why don't you stay here at home? It isn't safe to venture out so late."

Father was nervous, but he always seemed so when working for the bank. She often wished he didn't have such an important job, for she knew it placed him in harm's way. She had begged him to leave it, but the money had been too good.

"One of these days we'll move away from Denver," he said as they walked. "We'll go somewhere warm. Somewhere special. A place where you can find yourself a good husband, and perhaps I'll even find a new . . ." He didn't finish his sentence, and Alice wondered if he might have been thinking of remarriage.

Father was never one to speak about such things. He wouldn't even discuss Alice's mother and the good memories . . . but why should he? He and Alice felt the same sense of betrayal.

The hair on her neck bristled at the sight of three men stepping out of the shadows to block their way. The largest one demanded Father's satchel.

"It contains nothing but papers," her father declared. "Now be gone with you."

"Give me the satchel, old man." The stranger moved closer, and Alice's father stepped to one side—away from Alice.

"You can look for yourself." He opened the case. "It's just paper."

"I don't care what it is. Hand it over."

"No." Her father was adamant.

Alice started to move away, thinking she might run for help. Her father's assaulter motioned to his companions, however, and they took hold of her. One man pulled her against him and held her in an iron-like grip, while the other pulled a large knife.

The man who faced her father smiled. It was a heartless and terrifying smile. "I think you'd better do what I say. Otherwise the boys might be inclined to persuade you."

"Don't hurt her!"

The man with the knife grabbed her by the hair and yanked her head back. The knife cut into her flesh without warning.

"Too late, old man. How much I cut her, however, will depend on you."

Alice was too stunned at first to even feel the pain. That moment, however, was short-lived and she cried out. Her father charged at the man in front of him, but the larger brute was able to easily push him aside.

"Here, take it. Take the satchel, but leave my girl alone," Father pleaded.

Her attacker breathed heavily against her face. He smelled of tobacco.

"I skinned me a rabbit with this knife earlier today, and now I'm skinnin' me a little gal."

Alice, dizzy with pain, felt blood flow down her face. The warmth seemed strange against the cold night air. The man released her and stepped back as if to assess his handiwork. Alice's father took the opportunity to once again rush his assaulter. This time the man sent him flying backward.

Alice screamed as her father's head made contact with the edge of the brick building. She heard a terrible thud and watched her father crumple into the mud. It was the last thing Alice remembered before fainting.

"Wake up," Mrs. Landry said, shaking Alice by the shoulders. "Wake up, it's just a nightmare."

Alice opened her eyes, blinking against the light. "What . . . what's happened?"

"You were screaming," Mrs. Landry explained. "I came as soon as I could. Goodness, but you gave me a fright. Are you all right?"

Panting for air, Alice struggled to sit up. "I . . . I'm fine. I'm so sorry to have disturbed you."

"It's quite all right, dear. You seemed terribly fearful of something. Would you like to talk about it?"

Alice looked at the disheveled woman. Mrs. Landry's robe was open and her nightcap askew. Obviously the woman had made a mad dash for Alice's room without concern for her own well-being.

"I'm fine, Mrs. Landry. Truly. I was just remembering . . . that night."

"When your father died?"

She nodded. Mrs. Landry sat down beside her on the bed. "I suppose that night will always haunt you, but you can rest assured that God will never leave you or forsake you."

The words offered comfort. "I'm glad that you believe that. Mrs. Wythe doesn't, you know."

Mrs. Landry smiled. "Mrs. Wythe is dealing with her own demons. In time, I believe she'll come around, but we must make a special effort to pray for her. For Mr. Wythe, as well."

Alice agreed. "They both seem to bear heavy burdens."

"They do," Mrs. Landry said. "I don't know exactly what it is that causes them each such pain, but Jesus does . . . and He's the only one who can heal them of their hurt."

"I agree."

"So you'll join me in praying for them?"

"Of course," Alice replied. "I've already been praying for Mrs. Wythe."

Mrs. Landry nodded and got to her feet. "Good. Then we shall both continue in that way and add Mr. Wythe, as well."

Chapter 12

Supper that Friday night proved to be a bigger event than Marty had first anticipated. Word came earlier in the day that several of the board members would accompany Mr. Morgan and Mr. Keystone for the meal so that they might discuss business afterward. Mrs. Landry passed the information on to Mrs. Standish, who seemingly performed the miracle of the loaves and fishes and served a meal fit for a king.

Marty wondered at the audacity of people to just force themselves on an employee and his family in this unannounced manner. For all the rules of social etiquette, it seemed there ought to be one that precluded such impositions.

For a time, all the niceties were observed. Marty listened in relative silence as the men spoke of various happenings in the city.

"They are planning to dig up City Cemetery and relocate it," Mr. Morgan declared. "Plans are already in the works, and families have been asked by the city to cooperate and arrange to move their loved ones."

"Seems kind of odd that they would disturb a cemetery that way. What's the purpose?" Jake asked.

"Progress." This came from Josiah Keystone. "Progress, my boy. That area is prime real estate—much too close to the city and growing neighborhoods. They will move out the graves and expand the park. Some of the land will probably be developed, as well."

"There's really no doubt on that count," another of the men added.

Marty thought it appalling. How would she feel if they came to her with plans to dig up her Thomas's coffin? She would hate it. It would be like reliving his death all over again. She shook her head and decided to change the subject.

"Are you men aware that George Chesterfield, your deceased employee, has a seventeen-year-old daughter?" Marty interjected.

Everyone looked at her for a moment before Mr. Morgan replied. "I suppose I do remember something of that nature. It's been a while now since George passed on. You remember him, don't you, Josiah?"

"Of course I do. He was your bank manager before Mr. Wythe. He was murdered, wasn't he?"

Morgan cut into his roast. "Yes. He was murdered and bank papers were stolen. Caused me no end of grief, I assure you."

Marty despised his calloused response. "They severely wounded the man's daughter. She bears a scar along the right side of her face and will for the rest of her life."

"And how did you come by this knowledge, Mrs. Wythe?" Morgan's tone almost suggested he didn't believe her.

"Because she is my personal maid. Alice is a wonderful girl, but she was completely devastated at the loss of her father—both emotionally and financially. I wondered why the bank hadn't offered her some sort of support or assistance since her father died in the line of duty."

Morgan shrugged. "We can hardly be in the business of compensating every family member who loses someone in my employ. I'm sure relatives must have come alongside her in her hour of need."

"No, there were no other relatives. Her father was the only one she had," Marty replied. "I believe friends who attended church services with Alice provided her some short-term help, but they moved from the area, and the girl was again left with nothing."

"That is a sad story, Mrs. Wythe," one of the board members agreed. "So much violence and loss goes on all around us. In fact, I heard there was to be a new orphanage erected next year because of such sorrows. The girl was most fortunate to obtain employment with you."

Everyone murmured an awkward agreement and continued eating.

Marty could see nothing more would be said or done about the matter and fell silent. These men had no idea how difficult Alice's life might have been if she hadn't obtained decent work. Or maybe they did know and simply didn't care.

Marty continued to listen to the discussions about new industry that would soon arrive to make Denver ever more successful. Apparently there were ongoing plans for everything from additional rail lines to a new mint.

"The mint is in desperate disrepair," Keystone told them. "Of course, they don't create coins there, but even for a glorified assay office taking in silver and gold from the local mines, it deserves better and safer quarters."

"I thought coins were minted there," Jake threw out. He hadn't said much that evening, and Marty couldn't help but wonder if this was a calculated move on his part. Jake was a smart man and probably knew well enough to listen much and speak little.

"Coins were only minted there for one year, although some $600,000 worth of gold coins were the result," Morgan explained. "I believe it was during the war, however, and they decided to forgo the expenses involved in continuing that project. We are hopeful that once we get Congress to agree to funds for a new building, they will also see the benefit of expanding operations to include minting coins."

Mr. Keystone hurried to add, "One would contend that with nearly six million in gold and silver passing through those doors, Congress would see the immediate need for better provisions."

The topic continued through dessert. Marty sampled the chocolate torte. It was delicious, but much too sweet. She pushed it aside and instead sipped her creamed coffee and waited for an appropriate time for her to leave.

"I suppose we have bored you with our discussions of civic plans and politics," Mr. Morgan said upon finishing his torte. "I do apologize if we made ourselves poor company."

"Not at all," Marty replied. This was the opening she'd been waiting for. "However, I am rather tired this evening, and if you do not mind, I would like to excuse myself." She got to her feet, and all of the men stood, as well. "Please, gentlemen, take your seats and enjoy your evening. I'm sure we will all meet again very soon."

"Good night, Mrs. Wythe," Mr. Morgan said, with the others following suit.

Jake came to her side with a smile. "Good night, my dear." He pressed a kiss upon her cheek.

Marty made her way upstairs as the men returned to their discussions of banking and the economy. She couldn't help but wonder if she should be more concerned about the state of the country. Earlier during the meal, Mr. Morgan had commented on several banks that might be forced to close. Nothing more was discussed on the subject, however. Surely if these titans were expecting Congress to hand over funding for a new mint, they couldn't be too concerned about local banks folding.

She decided it wasn't worth worrying about, but perhaps she would start reading the newspaper for more information. Maybe it would give her something more to talk about with Jake when they shared evenings together.

Later, after Marty had read for a time in front of her cozy fireplace, Alice helped her into her nightclothes. The beautiful white silk gown slid against Marty's body—a cold kiss against her warm skin. Alice then brought out a majestic white silk wrap. The set had been created with the new bride in mind. The shoulders were overlaid with a wide lace ruffle that cascaded down the right front side of the robe. There were buttons that lined the left side, but Marty waved Alice away from doing these up and chose instead to simply belt the garment closed. She sat at the vanity and toyed with the lace cuffs while Alice unbraided her long blond hair and began brushing it.

"Did I receive any mail today?" Marty asked.

"Not that I'm aware of, ma'am."

"Please, Alice, don't call me ma'am. At least not in private. Here we can just be informal. You call me Marty and I'll call you Alice and we shall be the best of friends."

Alice smiled at her in the mirror. "Mrs. Landry would have kittens."

Marty laughed. "Well, I happen to like cats."

"The book she gave me to read about being a proper lady's maid would also warn against it. Apparently it's a grievous error to allow employees and employers to have anything but a professional relationship."

"Yes, I'm sure that's how society sees it. But in the privacy of my dressing room, I don't see any reason for pretense. When I was growing up, we had a wonderful woman at our house who cooked and helped my sister. They were the best of friends, and she was quite dear to me. Goodness, she even prayed with us and told us stories about her life in Mexico. It never caused any problems, and I'd like to think it could be the same way for us. I want to be able to speak my mind, and I want you to do likewise."

"Truly?" Alice asked, continuing to work the brush.

"Truly. Why do you ask?"

"I just wondered . . . I wondered if you would tell me why you're so angry at God."

The question caught Marty completely off-guard. "I blame Him for not keeping my husband from death." Her answer was out of her mouth before she'd given it any real thought.

"What happened to your husband?"

"He was a rancher, and he had a longhorn bull that had been injured. Thomas nursed the animal back to health and was attempting to check the wound when the bull got spooked and went wild. Thomas was gored by the horns and died a short time later. On Christmas Eve."

"That must have been awful." Alice continued the rhythmic strokes.

"It was."

"And do you have any children?"

"No." Marty hoped that would be the end of it, but Alice wasn't through.

"And you blame God for letting your husband die." It wasn't really a question, but more an observation.

"For letting him die. For letting him get hurt. For letting us both down."

When Alice said nothing, Marty felt compelled to explain further. "You see, I was raised to put my trust in God. I went to church and learned the Scriptures. I knew what was expected of me by God, but I thought I could count on certain things from Him, as well. When that didn't prove true and Thomas died, I lost heart."

"How was it that you couldn't count on God?" Alice asked softly.

Marty shrugged. "I prayed for my husband's safety, and it didn't work. I prayed to have a child, and that didn't come about, either. I prayed for rain for the ranch, and we suffered on with drought. I prayed for so many things over the years, and so many things were denied me. It didn't seem that my faith was worth the effort."

"I'm sorry."

Despite the attack she'd suffered, Alice was still so innocent—naïve, really. Marty could see that she was genuine in her feelings, but it didn't help. In fact, Marty could see no purpose in continuing the discussion.

"Can I ask you something else?"

"Of course," Marty agreed, happy to move the conversation in a different direction.

"Did your husband Thomas hate God, too?"

"Hate God? I don't hate God. I would never do that." Marty turned around abruptly. "Thomas loved God." She smiled at the memory of him puzzling over passages in the Bible. "He used to sit in the evening and read the Bible to me. There would be times when he felt confused by something, and he'd continue to study and ponder it for days. He'd pray for understanding, and after a while he'd tell me he'd gotten some great epiphany." Marty met Alice's gaze. "Why do you think I hate God?"

"Well, I suppose because you're so angry with Him. Anger never seems to hold any love—at least not to my way of thinking. And . . . well, I just thought maybe in the absence of love, that anger had created hate."

"No," Marty said, shaking her head. "It's not created anything. It's left a void."

★

Jake was glad that Morgan concluded their business quickly. They had reached quick decisions on several pressing issues and agreed to proceed on Monday and spend no further time that evening on the matter. Jake bid the men good evening.

"Please give our best to Mrs. Wythe," Mr. Morgan said before climbing into his carriage.

"I will," Jake promised.

As he made his way up the grand staircase, the clock struck nine. The chime echoed through the large house and left Jake feeling rather lonely. He felt a sudden desire for Marty's company, and he wondered if she might still be awake.

He entered his bedroom and walked straight to the door that adjoined her dressing room, knocking loudly. The door opened almost immediately, and Alice jumped back in surprise.

"Mr. Wythe!"

Marty quickly stood up from where she was seated at the vanity. Her long blond hair hung loose to her waist—something Jake had never seen before that moment.

"I'm glad to see you're still up. I wondered if we might have a conversation." He looked at Alice with a smile and added, "In private."

"Of course," Marty replied. She moved across the room in a swirl of white, leaving Jake to feel rather breathless at her beauty. The gown was the kind any man might desire his wife to wear.

"Alice, I can see myself to bed. Why don't you go ahead and turn in?"

"Thank you, ma'am," Alice said, giving a little curtsy. She hurried out of the room through the opposite door.

"What did you want to discuss? Should we go and sit in my room?"

"No, this is fine," Jake replied. "I was just curious as to why you brought Alice's situation into the conversation tonight."

"Was that wrong of me?" she asked plainly.

"No. It wasn't a matter of right or wrong. I was just surprised."

Marty shrugged. "I suppose I thought it intolerable that a man should be killed working for another and yet no one saw fit to see after his family. After all, these are men of means."

"That doesn't make them charitable."

"No, I suppose not, but it seems like common sense would place a reasonable obligation at their doorstep. Even on the ranch when a family man was killed or injured, we took care of the family. Even the single men were given proper care, and if they died, we helped arrange the burial and saw to it that their remains and final payment went to their folks."

"That was because you and your family are good people," Jake said.

"The world, unfortunately, isn't populated with only good people. Many are self-centered and focused solely on what profits them most."

"Like Mr. Morgan and his friends?"

"I suppose so. But don't worry. Alice is welcome to work here as long as she likes. I'll even increase her pay if you tell me to."

Marty smiled, and the warmth of her expression caused Jake to feel weak in the knees. She inspired emotions in him that he had believed long dead. He hadn't expected to have these kind of feelings for . . . his wife.

Jake looked at her for a long moment. She was far more beautiful than he'd allowed himself to realize. The delicate design of her face was like that of a Grecian goddess—at least the statues he'd seen of the same. But instead of cold marble, Marty was all flesh and blood. Jake reached out and touched Marty's long hair.

He grinned. "It's like silk."

Marty said nothing, but her eyes widened, and Jake worried he'd gone too far. She didn't move, however, and this only seemed to entice him more. Reaching up, he put his hand against her cheek.

"Soft."

Still she didn't speak or move. A million thoughts cut loose in Jake's mind, and there was no way to make sense of any of them. He wanted more than anything to kiss her, but something warned him that this would only cause rejection on her part. He had made her a promise. They had agreed to a marriage of convenience, and now he was threatening the security of that agreement. Forcing himself to step back, Jake took a deep breath.

"I just wanted you to know that I'll see to it that Alice is taken care of." With that, he hurried back through the passageway to his room and closed the door behind him. Leaning hard against the wall, Jake berated himself for his lack of good sense.

"She didn't marry me for romance," he whispered aloud. "I need to keep that in mind and not allow my heart to get broken . . . again."

Chapter 13

Movement outside the window caught Marty's attention. She'd just bent down to retrieve her book when she spied someone hurrying away from the house. Alice had mentioned someone sneaking around the stable—could this be the same man? She strained to catch another glimpse in the fading light, but the man was gone.

A glance at the clock showed it was nearly time for Jake to return from work. Marty determined to speak with him on the matter to see what he thought.

Jake . . . The thought of Jake and what had happened last Friday evening between them had plagued Marty for nearly a week. She could still feel his warm hand against her cheek. Still see the desire in his eyes. She had never expected to have a man look at her like that again. Furthermore, she hadn't wanted one to. Until now.

"I'm being silly," she said aloud, straightening a piece of bric-a-brac on the nearest table. "We went into this arrangement fully aware that neither of us wanted a real marriage."

But Jake's touch had made her remember how Thomas would reach for her, and Marty found that she ached for someone to hold her—to offer a hug and the reassurance that she was loved. She frowned. Love had only served to deepen her pain. Why would she want to experience that again?

Taking up her book, Marty snuggled into her favorite chair by the fire and began reading. She had to keep her mind occupied with something other than the way Jake had looked at her. The way she longed to have him look at her again.

★

Jake climbed down from the carriage, anxious to see Marty. She'd been on his mind all day. In fact, she had been in most of his thoughts all week. Ever since he'd caressed her hair and cheek, Jake had found it impossible to forget the way she'd made him feel.

She doesn't know she made me feel that way. She would no doubt be upset to learn the truth, so there's no use in bringing it up. But maybe if I brought it up . . . things might change.

Change wasn't likely, however. They had both agreed to the parameters of their arrangement, with no provision for change. Despite this, Jake bounded into the house with no other desire than to see his wife and hear about her day.

Maybe I'm a hopeless romantic. Maybe I will always have a penchant for falling in love with any woman with whom I have more than a casual conversation.

"Mr. Wythe," Brighton said, receiving him in the entryway. "Let me take your coat." He helped Jake out of his overcoat and took his hat. "There is a small matter that I should speak to you about. It can wait until after supper if you wish."

"No, that's all right. What's the problem?"

Brighton nodded. "It would seem that the new groomsman found boot tracks in areas where no one should have been. He spied them coming from around the stable, which was the only reason he was intrigued to follow them. They led, I'm afraid, to the house windows on the south side."

Jake considered the matter a moment. "And everyone is certain the tracks did not belong to any of the servants?"

"Yes, sir. The tracks were made by a man's very large boot. The print was even larger than Samson's."

Rubbing his chin, Jake wondered what was to be done. "Does my wife know about this?"

"Yes, sir. It would seem she observed someone running away from the house. She couldn't get a good look, however. Also, she tells me that Miss Alice noted someone moving about the grounds the other day. It was thought that she was mistaken and that it was either myself or Samson, but that was not the case."

"I'll talk to Marty about this," Jake said. "Thank you for telling me. Keep your eyes open for anything unusual. I would guess it's probably someone looking for a house to rob. We need to be on guard."

"Yes, sir." Brighton moved toward the sitting room and pushed back the doors. "I believe you will find Mrs. Wythe in here."

Jake left the foyer and crossed the sitting room to find Marty comfortably ensconced before the fire. She was wearing a tawny gold-and-cream-checked gown with brown trim. She looked up and set aside the book she'd been reading.

"I see you're hard at it again," he said, pointing to the book. "What are you reading?"

"*The Picture of Dorian Gray*," she replied. "It's quite unusual. It's about a man who sells his soul to retain his youth, while his picture ages instead."

"Sounds intriguing. If I had the time, I would definitely give the book a try." He rubbed his eyes.

"Yes. I'm used to having more to do," she told him, sounding sad. "Sometimes I think I'm growing fat and lazy with all this idle time."

Jake gave her a smile. "Well, you look quite lovely being idle, and you'll be well-read." He plopped down on a red velvet chair near the fire. "Brighton tells me that someone has been sneaking about the grounds."

Marty's blue-eyed gaze never left his face. "Yes, that's right. I saw a man, but I cannot give you much of a description. The groomsman saw tracks, as well." Her voice lowered. "Alice saw someone a few days back, but I thought it was nothing. Now I'm not so sure."

Stretching out his legs, Jake sighed. "We are people of means, and as things continue to worsen financially, there will no doubt be those who will seek to take what they can from our blessings."

"Is it truly all that bad?"

"Worse every day, I'm afraid." Jake felt weary from the long day and suppressed a yawn. *She'll think I'm bored with her, but nothing could be further from the truth.*

"There are dozens of railroads in trouble—some have already folded, while others are trying their best to find a way to regain their profitability. And there's the second term of Grover Cleveland to face, as well as the aftermath of so many labor strikes last year. It's all bound to catch up and take its toll."

"So you figure that whoever was outside the window was looking to rob us?"

"That's my guess. I suppose I should hire someone to walk the grounds from time to time. Perhaps I could get a man who would be responsible for the gardens, and he could act as a guard. I hadn't figured to hire one until spring since Samson has been able to handle the snow removal."

"No need to rush it," Marty said. "Just buy me a double-barrel shotgun and I'll discourage window peepers."

He chuckled at this but could tell by her expression that she was serious. "I would happily buy you most anything your heart desired."

"Then a double-barrel shotgun is what I desire."

"What about your revolver?" His grin broadened at the thought of her wielding the weapon. "Wouldn't that be good enough?"

Marty shrugged. "It does its job, but I find men to be far more intimidated when staring down the barrels of a loaded shotgun. Perhaps it's realizing that even a poor shot has difficulty missing with that kind of weapon. Tends to make men rethink their choices."

Jake shook his head. "You amaze me. Just when I think I've come to know all there is about you, you surprise me. You are such a strong and capable woman—exactly the kind of Lone Star bride I'd hoped you'd be. You don't need anyone or anything."

"I need that double barrel," she replied with a hint of a smile.

He roared in laughter. "Then you shall have it. Goodness, Marty, your reputation has already survived the stage rescue. I'm sure that being known for walking armed around the grounds of your fine Capitol Hill home won't damage your social standing a bit."

Marty couldn't resist joining his laughter. "I honestly don't care what society thinks. I know full well how to protect what is mine. I won't have Alice worrying about another attack or Mrs. Landry wondering if someone is going to steal her linens when they're hanging out to dry."

"You're a good mistress of the house, Marty, and you genuinely care about our staff. I think so many people treat their servants as unimportant. . . . I suppose that's why I enjoy the banter between Brighton and Mrs. Landry. I feel like they're just a part of my family."

Marty grew thoughtful. "When I was growing up, we always had help around the house, but Juanita and Berto were also our friends—we even ate together. Will and Hannah didn't hesitate to seek their opinion or advice. I suppose our isolation and dependence on one another made a difference, but even here I have difficulty considering the staff nothing more than servants."

Jake couldn't agree more. "We were the same. Our ranch had a great many people who worked in various jobs. My mother had a housekeeper and two maids, and it wasn't unusual at all for the four of them to quilt together or work in the garden side by side. They were more like sisters to her than employees. It's a different world in large cities and upper-class society. I saw it in California to be certain, and it's most likely no different back east. In fact, I think the folks living here are just doing their best to mimic those people."

"Frankly, I don't believe their way of living is anything to emulate. Don't get me wrong—I am greatly enjoying the luxury here." She smiled and ran her hand down the front of her checked gown. "I've never had so many beautiful clothes, and my hands have never been this soft. Mrs. Landry and Alice have pampered and spoiled me. . . . But as I said earlier, I've become quite idle. And as my sister would contend, idle hands often lead to trouble."

"Perhaps you could involve yourself in some of the local charities. Maybe ask Mrs. Morgan about it. Which reminds me: Despite concerns about the economy, Mr. Morgan is giving me a bonus. I can't say anything about it, however. The board is afraid if it comes to light, the other branch managers will be upset because they didn't receive one, as well."

"That's wonderful news . . . I think. I know you've been working hard."

"It puts me that much closer to one day having my own ranch."

Marty frowned and looked away. "Was there a particular reason for your reward?"

Jake pushed back his dark blond hair and gazed upward at the ornate crown molding. "I have reviewed the bank books for the last three years and uncovered a number of problems. Most were poor bookkeeping and management mistakes, but there's also an amount of money that is missing. Strangely enough, it seems to change from time to time."

"Change? What do you mean?"

He was touched that she genuinely seemed to care. He appreciated having someone intelligent to converse with—someone not related to the banking business. "The amount of the missing money is never the same. It changes. Sometimes it's one amount, and then the next time I check, it might be higher or lower. I keep thinking it must have been a posting or accounting error, but I can't find it."

"Perhaps someone is taking money and putting it back," she said in a casual manner. "Then when they need more, they take it out again."

Jake straightened and looked at his wife. "You know, you may be right. I've never heard of an embezzler who puts money back, but . . ." He fell silent. Nearly a year ago there had been a substantial amount of money missing—several hundred dollars. Then a few months later the balance was only off by ten or twenty. In fact, when the bank audit took place, the amount was so small that Morgan himself agreed that it was a simple error and made the books right and the auditor a little richer to look the other way. So maybe it was Morgan who'd borrowed the funds? But why would he need to?

★

Alice had just finished doing up the buttons on the back of Marty's shirtwaist when a knock sounded on the dressing room door. Alice hurried to answer it and found Mr. Wythe holding a long wooden box.

"Good morning, Alice." He moved right past her without waiting for an invitation. "And how have you enjoyed your Saturday, wife?"

"We've been ever so busy," Marty declared. "I've changed into my second ensemble and am ready to face another few hours of boredom before lunch is served. What about you?"

"I was out shopping first thing this morning and brought you a gift."

Alice decided now would be a good time to see to the ironing that needed her attention. She walked to the far end of the room to gather the necessary articles of clothing.

"I think you'll like what I have here," Jake told Marty.

Alice heard Mrs. Wythe respond, but couldn't make out the words. How wonderful to have a husband who surprised you with gifts. *Mr. Wythe certainly loves her a great deal. His entire face lights up when he sees her. How I long for someone to love me like that.*

Touching her hand to her cheek, Alice couldn't help but be reminded that she was forever marred. The scar would fade a bit, the doctor said, but she would always bear the reminder. He had told her she was fortunate that the damage had been mostly superficial. Apparently the attacker knew exactly how deep to cut without causing greater damage to the nerves and muscle beneath.

"It's perfect!" Marty squealed in delight.

Alice turned to find her hoisting a shotgun out of the wooden box. She found it strange that her mistress should get so excited about a weapon. Trying not to eavesdrop, Alice focused her attention on the clothes, only to hear something that made her blood run cold.

"If that window peeper decides to return," Marty told her husband, "I'll brandish this in his face and see if he's still inclined to steal from us."

"I figure he'll forget about us mighty quick," he said, his southern drawl becoming more pronounced. "Once he sees that my little Texas wife can shoot, well, he'll mosey along and leave my womenfolk alone." They laughed together over this.

Alice froze at Mr. Wythe's comment. So the man had returned. Icy fingers went up her spine. They were looking for her, no doubt. But why? They'd taken the satchel from her father. What else were they looking for?

Her mind scrambled for an answer as fear welled within her. These men seemed unwilling to leave her alone. They had come to the hospital asking after her. They had eventually located her with church friends.

In fact, their threats were the biggest reason her hosts had left Denver. They had wanted Alice to come with them, but she knew the men would only follow. But why? What did they want?

"I couldn't help but pick this up for you, as well," Mr. Wythe announced. He drew out a small jewelry box and opened the lid. Alice couldn't see what it was, but from Marty's reaction, it apparently met with her approval.

"You shouldn't have. The shotgun was more than enough. It's not like it's my birthday," Marty declared.

"Speaking of which, I don't even know when that is."

Alice frowned. How could he not know when she was born? They were married, after all. Hadn't they shared all of these kinds of things with each other prior to the wedding? She couldn't imagine that two people would wed without knowing such details.

"It's in January," Marty admitted.

"Then I missed it. Good thing I bought the brooch." Alice thought he looked more than a little pleased with himself. Mr. Wythe continued. "I know you love just sitting around the house, but I thought we might take a carriage ride after lunch. You haven't seen much of the city, and since the streets are fairly dry, I thought it would be a good time to show you around."

"Oh, I'd love that," Marty replied. "And it will give me a good excuse to change my clothes again." She laughed and looked to Alice. "After we eat, I shall need an appropriate outfit for sight-seeing."

Chapter 14

"It's been a wonderful afternoon," Mrs. Cooper said, nodding to each of the women in her opulent sitting room.

"I should say so," Mrs. Morgan replied. "And I've decided that this new mauve color is lovely. Not really a pink and certainly not a true purple." She reached over to gently finger the damask draperies. "Very lovely."

"I knew when I first saw it featured in Byrant's store that I must have it for my sitting room. I'm quite pleased."

Marty tried to appear interested. The women had been good to include her, and she wanted to show them as much kindness and attention as she could. Unfortunately, there was little in their lives that appealed to her.

"So have you begun to redecorate your home?" Mrs. Morgan asked her.

Thinking of the house and how she could find little fault with the design, Marty shook her head. "I'm not entirely sure I will."

The other two women exchanged a look. Marty could see the hint of disapproval in their expressions. "I suppose," she continued, "that I'm still trying to adjust to living here and being married again. Besides, you arranged for it to be done so beautifully, Mrs. Morgan."

The women seemed to accept this as a valid excuse. Mrs. Morgan smiled and asked, "How long were you married before, Mrs. Wythe?"

"Ten years. Thomas was a rancher, and he was killed when a longhorn gored him." She added the latter, anticipating the women's curiosity regarding her husband's means of death.

"I'm sure that living as a rancher's wife in Texas was quite different from what you know today. Still, you were mistress of your ranch. Was it large?"

"The ranch?" Marty questioned, but continued before either could answer. "Yes. It was a decent size. My brother-in-law and sister gave large pieces of land to both my brother and me. By the time I returned from finishing school, my brother had already established himself on his portion and had purchased a homestead that abutted the property, as well. So my acreage isn't quite as large, but large enough."

"You attended finishing school?" Mrs. Cooper said, brightening. "Where, if I might ask?"

"In Georgia. Atlanta, to be exact. I have relatives there, and Hannah, my sister, thought it would do me good to get away from my primarily male world and engage with other young ladies and learn social etiquette."

"How wise of her," Mrs. Cooper said, looking to Mrs. Morgan for approval.

"Yes," Imogene Morgan agreed. "I knew there was a great deal of gentility to you, and now it's obvious as to why. Breeding always shows. In fact, when Mr. Morgan mentioned sponsoring you and Mr. Wythe in society, I was skeptical. I'm pleased that you have proven yourself to be a refined young lady."

Marty wanted to make a snide comment but held her tongue. What had the woman expected—savage behavior and unsavory conversation? Did she believe Texans to be social clods incapable of mingling among society's elite?

The footman arrived to clear away their dishes, and Marty took the opportunity to excuse herself. "I want to thank you for such a lovely time, but I really must be going. I have become interested of late in one of the local orphanages, and I want to stop there on my way home to see what I might be able to do to help."

Mrs. Morgan smiled in her tolerant way. "I'm certain a small donation would benefit them. I have several charitable organizations that provide assistance to such places. Perhaps you would care to join me for one of our meetings?"

Marty nodded. "I'd enjoy that very much. I'd like to be doing something more than holding teas and reading every book in my husband's library." She smiled and couldn't resist adding, "One day you and Mrs. Cooper must tell me how you endure this idle life."

She quickly got to her feet and the butler escorted her and helped her with her coat. Once Marty was in the carriage and headed down the street, she couldn't help but giggle. Those women were skilled in holding long conversations about nothing of importance—while believing themselves full of valuable information—and she couldn't help but feel bored in their presence.

Samson brought the carriage to a halt outside a three-story redbrick building in a poorer part of the city. Marty glanced around the neighborhood, noting the startling contrast to that of Capitol Hill. Spring weather was doing its best to brighten things up; the grass had begun to green rather nicely and the trees were leafing out. But where Capitol Hill prided itself on well-manicured lawns, it seemed this area of Denver did well to keep glass in the windows of its buildings.

She made her way to the door and noted a sign that read *Auraria Orphanage*. Before she could knock, a young man of about twelve opened the door. "Good afternoon," he said, sounding very formal.

Marty handed him her calling card. "I wonder if I might see the person in charge."

The boy took her card and nodded. "Mr. Brentwood is in his office." He knocked and opened the door to reveal a stern-faced man sitting behind a desk.

"Mr. Brentwood, this lady wants to see you," the boy said, some of his formality reverting to a more youthful tone.

The man stood and took hold of the calling card the boy extended. "Very good, Adam. Now return to your post." The boy nodded and scurried past Marty, pausing only long enough to give her a slight bow.

"I'm afraid Adam tends to forget his manners, Mrs. . . . ." He glanced down at the card for a moment. "Wythe. Mrs. Wythe. Won't you be seated?"

Marty smiled and did as he bid. Already she felt the edges of her boredom give way. She was about to embark on a worthy project. At least she prayed it would be such.

★

"And he said that I might come and read to the children," Marty told Alice as she helped dress her mistress for dinner. "They are also in need of funds. The children seem to wear out their clothing so fast that I thought I might actually take up sewing for them."

"What will Mr. Wythe say?" Alice questioned. "That's hardly the kind of thing a lady in your position would normally do."

"I don't care," Marty replied. "I'm bored out of my mind most days. I'm not supposed to garden or make my own clothes. I'm not responsible for laundry or cooking because you and the other staff handle all of that. I can't care for the animals because that's not fitting. Honestly, I don't know how these ladies of leisure endure their existence."

Alice couldn't help but giggle. "Most women would love to be in your shoes, Mrs. . . . Marty."

Marty slipped her arms into the sleeves of her silk evening gown and smiled. "Well, I'm glad to be in my own shoes tonight. Mr. Wythe is taking me out for what he promises will be a lovely dinner and time of music. It's been quite a while since I've heard a concert. My sister and brother-in-law took Thomas and me to a wonderful performance in Dallas many years ago. Before that . . . well, when I was little, my sister, Hannah, always tried to expose Andy and me to music and art whenever possible. It just wasn't always available or timely. Ranch life is hard work and requires constant attention."

"I can only imagine," Alice said, doing up the back of the gown.

"I suppose that's why it's hard for me to sit and do nothing," Marty continued. "I'm used to pulling my weight. Seeing you and Mrs. Landry and the others work so hard . . . well, it makes me uncomfortable. Hannah said my mother was a fine lady, but she was always seeking to do good for others."

"My mother seemed to care about the good of others at one time," Alice admitted, not really wanting to allow the memories to resurface.

"You seem very bitter toward your mother. Are you angry because she died?"

Alice looked at the back of Marty's head as though carefully scrutinizing her coiffure. She thought about the question and then finally spoke. "My mother left me and my father when I was thirteen. She took my five-year-old brother and deserted us."

Marty turned to face her. "She deserted you? I thought she died."

"She did, but not until some months after she'd taken my brother and ran away with him. My father was devastated, as was I. I couldn't believe she'd just up and leave like that . . . no good-bye . . . nothing. She didn't even ask me if I wanted to go with her. Which I wouldn't have," Alice said in a tone that almost convinced her own heart.

"Did your father mistreat her?"

"No . . . at least I don't think he did. They did have some ugly arguments, but I never saw him hit her. My father could be rather indifferent at times, and he worked really hard to keep us in a lovely home. I think perhaps my mother felt his neglect, but that's certainly no reason to tear apart your family."

"I'm truly sorry, Alice. I didn't have any idea."

"Maybe I should have told you sooner." Alice shrugged. "I used to spend long hours trying to figure out why she left me. Right after it happened I would cry myself to sleep every night. I would ask my father every morning if they'd returned. Finally after several long months of this—maybe even a year—my father told me he'd received word that they had died in an epidemic back east."

"That must have been hard." Marty's words were soothing and kind. "I know what it's like to grow up without a mother."

Alice went to the dressing table for the gown's sash. She returned and fitted it to Marty's waist and artfully tied it in a large bow. "I got very angry. Father would speak ill of Mother and I suppose that birthed anger in me—anger at her and even anger at him. I'm still trying to overcome it."

"I can imagine your hurt."

"I remember one of the first times Father and I attended church after learning that Mother had died. The pastor spoke about forgiving

132

people the wrong they'd done you. He said that often the hardest thing to let go of was our disappointment in others, including God. That spoke straight to my heart. I'd like to say that I immediately forgave my mother and no longer felt anger toward her, but that wasn't the case. Forgiving Father was less difficult—after all, no matter his role in her desertion, at least he stayed."

"So you still battle your wounded heart?"

"Yes." Alice stepped back and admired her mistress. "You look so beautiful. That color of blue makes your eyes seem even brighter."

Marty didn't appear to hear her, however. The older woman had drawn her brows together, as if thinking hard on something Alice had said.

"Are you all right?" Alice asked.

Her mistress nodded. "I think part of my own trouble has to do with my anger at God. Maybe even anger at Thomas for getting himself killed. It's hard to accept that God could have stopped a bad thing from happening but didn't. I'm just not sure what to do with that knowledge."

"It isn't easy, I'll admit. I'm still struggling to forgive my mother, but every morning I wake up and tell myself that today will be the day— even if for just a few hours. Maybe you could try that, too, to help you forgive Thomas for dying and accept that God is good, even when He doesn't ward off the bad."

"Maybe," Marty said, not sounding at all convinced.

★

Jake stepped into one of the handsomely appointed lounges of the exclusive Denver Club. Mr. Morgan beckoned to him immediately and one of the footmen escorted Jake to where he sat. Men all around the room were puffing away on fat cigars, chatting about the day's events. Jake wasn't sure why Morgan had sent word for him to join him there. It was going to make Jake extremely late getting home, and he'd forgotten to send word to Marty.

"I received your note, Mr. Morgan."

"Good to have you join me, Mr. Wythe. Have you been here before?"

Jake shook his head. "No. I'm afraid this club has always been too elite for me."

"Nonsense. This is exactly where you need to be. If you want to get ahead in the banking industry, this is where business is done."

Jake didn't wish to tell him he had no desire to get ahead in the banking industry, so he simply gave a curt nod and took an offered chair.

"Cigar?" Morgan asked, holding one out.

"No, thank you." Jake noticed another footman had arrived.

"Would you care for something to drink, sir?"

Jake could see that other men in the room, including Morgan, were imbibing liquor. Since he'd made a fool of himself in Texas at the house of the Vandermarks, Jake had sworn off all alcohol. "No. I'm fine, thank you."

"My boy, you need to learn the importance of relaxing." Morgan smiled. "Business and pleasure are more easily enjoyed when a man is calm and not so anxious."

He wished Morgan would get to the point of this meeting. Jake had picked up a bouquet of flowers for Marty, which the doorman was now watching over. Jake didn't trust the man to watch them indefinitely, and besides, he was anxious to give them to Marty and see her reaction.

"So, what kind of business are we about today?" Jake asked.

Morgan laughed. "The business of getting your membership arranged in the Denver Club."

"That's hardly necessary," Jake answered. "The cost alone is rather prohibitive."

"Nonsense. It's a part of your duty as bank manager, and therefore the bank will pay your dues. Of course, I don't want that to get around to any of my other employees." He slid an envelope across the table. "I will sponsor your membership, and the board will also act as references. This will take care of your dues."

"But, Mr. Morgan, I assure you it's not necessary."

"But I say it is. I intend to see you in the position of vice-president by summer's end. That will only be accomplished by your working hard to bring in new accounts and see to it that this financial wrinkle doesn't cause us any setbacks."

"Vice-president?" Jake shook his head in surprise. "But what of Mr. Keystone?"

"He will assume the role of president for a time. Eventually, I intend to see you in that position, when he retires. But one step at a time. Keystone will be much too busy to tend to the daily operations of business. That's why you need to have a membership in this austere club. The wealthy men you need to entice to my banking organization will frequent this place. I'm counting on you, Wythe. I expect to get a strong return for my investment." Morgan gave him a pointed look.

"And I always get what I expect and then some," Morgan added, then lifted his glass in a salute to Jake.

Chapter 15

April arrived, and with it a growing concern in the financial world. Many people were now convinced that the problems were only going to get worse and because of that, were starting to pull back on investing. Jake had witnessed several customers, mostly those with smaller savings accounts, pull their money from the bank. They were inclined to trust their mattresses or other hiding places more than the bank's questionable future.

Jake had tried to assure each man that the bank was sound, but as he continued to look into the monetary backing of their branch, he felt less and less certain. Josiah Keystone only added to his concern on that early Friday morning.

"Wythe, good of you to see me," Keystone announced, entering the office. "I realize it wasn't in the best taste to send you a message so early in the morning. I appreciate your meeting me here."

"You said it was urgent."

"And so it is," Keystone said. "I won't take up much time, but I wanted to ask you to personally handle a matter for a friend of mine."

"I'll do what I can," Jake replied, still not knowing what Keystone needed.

"It would need to be kept quiet. I don't want Morgan hearing about it. He'll feel offended by our friend taking this path."

"What path is that?"

"He wants to trade in his gold certificates for gold. He's fretful about the economy, as are many. I tried to convince him otherwise, but he's convinced that this is what he must do. He said he'd rather have the gold itself on hand rather than a marker from the bank. I told him we would try to handle it with as little fanfare as possible. Not to mention we don't want to give the public any reason to make a run on the bank."

"Mr. Keystone, you know that this can't be kept from Mr. Morgan. All redemptions of gold certificates must have his approval. Besides, it will all depend on how much this man intends to cash in. You know as well as I do that the bank doesn't keep large amounts on hand and that the ratio of deposits to currency is severely declined."

"Surely this can be dealt with," Keystone all but growled. He clenched his jaw and pursed his lips as if trying to rid himself of a bad taste.

Jake hesitated, unsure of what to say. "I'll do what I can, Mr. Keystone. But again, it's all going to depend on the amount of withdrawal."

"Where is Morgan? I suppose I'll have to speak to him on this matter."

"I would imagine that he's still at home," Jake said, glancing at his pocket watch. "Perhaps you could catch him there."

"No, I don't want to make a scene."

"Well, he intends to be at the Denver Club around three. I'm to meet him there."

"I suppose it will have to wait until then." Tension laced his words, and he stormed from the office, leaving Jake to stare after him.

It seemed anyone with something to lose walked a narrow line these days, and there was an overwhelming sense that the financial world was holding its breath. Unfortunately, the daily newspapers were doing nothing to help the matter. Every time Jake picked up the paper, he read another story about a railroad facing bankruptcy or the rising unemployment. Such widespread problems, stated in the most alarming ways possible, served only to cause mass hysteria. It was a wonder they hadn't had a full run on the bank.

"Sir, this letter arrived for you," Arnold announced from the still open doorway. "It's notification of our upcoming audit."

Jake rolled his eyes. "Why not?"

137

★

Marty awoke after a restless night's sleep. Alice hadn't opened the drapes, yet there were hints of light playing at the corners. Silence cloaked the house in a sort of surreal, almost dreamlike state.

Getting out of the bed, Marty yawned and tried to ignore the fact that she was still exhausted. Glancing at her writing desk in the muted light, she could see the reason for her inability to sleep.

Hannah had written her a letter. Her unhappiness at Marty's last missive was quite clear. Hannah didn't try to hide her disappointment or pretend to understand Marty's desire to remain in Colorado for an extended visit. She wanted to know why Marty was being so vague with her information and when she intended to return.

There was more—comments about the ranch and Hannah's worry that Marty would get herself into trouble.

"If she only knew," Marty said, walking across the chilly hardwood floor. She picked up Hannah's letter and wondered how she could best reply.

Marty's first thought had been to just tell the truth—it would be the simplest way. But since when had she ever taken the simple way out? Her stomach growled. Perhaps a little milk and maybe one of Cook's good biscuits would stave off her hunger until a later breakfast.

Marty put the letter down and took up her robe. It was still early enough that she thought perhaps she could sneak down to the kitchen without notice. Cook was usually quite occupied first thing, and she and her assistant, Willa, would most likely be in the pantry or perhaps busy elsewhere.

Well, even if they're right there in plain sight, I am mistress of the house, and I have a right to the food that's in it.

Her reasoning did little to still the unease within. It wasn't the early morning raid on the larder, however, that had Marty tied in knots. It was knowing that she had to answer Hannah's letter and tell her about Jake.

Deciding to slip down the servants' stairs, which would lead her directly into the kitchen's back entry, Marty did her best to descend quietly. She was on the next to the last step when she heard a woman speak.

"Why don't we end our study with prayer," Mrs. Landry announced.

Marty frowned and halted, remaining still as one woman after another asked for God's provision and offered thanks for His blessings already received. It wasn't until Marty heard Alice in prayer that she felt a strange sense of guilt mixed with irritation.

"And Lord," Alice prayed, "please help Mrs. Wythe. She has a wounded heart and needs to see that you love her and that you are there to comfort her. Help her with the decisions she needs to make."

Marty stepped back, shaking her head. She didn't want to listen to another word. She hurried back to her room, hoping that no one had known of her presence. She didn't know why the prayer had bothered her so much. She knew that Hannah prayed for her every day, but there was something about these women—her servants—praying for her that was unsettling.

Returning to bed, Marty tried her best to go back to sleep and forget about the letter from her sister and the women's prayers. But her mind kept returning to Hannah's missive, Alice's words. When Alice came into the room to pull back the drapes an hour later, Marty reluctantly gave up the battle.

"Good morning," Alice said with a bright smile. "Did you sleep well?"

"Not exactly." She slipped her legs over the side of the bed and stretched.

Alice went about the room attending to her daily chores until she came to the desk. "I see you had a letter from your sister. Have you told her yet about your marriage to Mr. Wythe?"

"That's none of your business," Marty snapped and immediately regretted it. "I'm sorry, Alice. Like I said, I didn't sleep very well. I'm afraid I'm acting like those snooty society women. I hope you'll forgive me."

Alice's expression changed from surprise to warmth. "Of course. Everyone has a bad day now and then. I'm sure this matter has weighed on you heavily."

"It has," Marty admitted. "I'm certain that's why I couldn't sleep. I don't know how to break the news to her without it hurting or alarming Hannah. She worries about me more than she should, and if I tell her what I've done, I know she'll probably load up and come here demanding to meet Jake and know everything about him."

"Would that be so bad?"

Marty grimaced at the thought. If Hannah came here, then the knowledge of Marty's ranch would be revealed. "I don't know," she lied. "I just don't know."

Alice moved into the dressing room. "I know you plan to go to tea this afternoon at Mrs. Keystone's. Would your lavender striped gown suit you?"

"As well as anything," Marty replied. "I have no desire to go to tea. No desire to make small talk with women of society. Perhaps I'll send my regrets and tell her I'm feeling unwell."

"Lie to Mrs. Keystone? Over tea?" Alice asked, popping back into the doorway. "Why ever would you sin in order to get out of tea? Just send her a note that says you won't be there and leave it at that."

Marty smiled. Alice really had gotten over her fear of talking back and offering her opinion. "I suppose I could, but you know how these society women are. They take offense at the smallest thing."

"So let them," Alice countered. "If not over this thing, then it will be another. No sense in being miserable over it. It seems to me that being firm in your convictions is something these women understand."

"It's just that every time I meet with them, they have yet another restraint or rule for me. Do you know that Mrs. Morgan was actually appalled by my idea to read to the orphans? She said it wouldn't be fitting. She used excuses like how it would be unfair to the destitute motherless and fatherless children to see such obvious examples of money and know that they would never have such things. I told her I could dress very simply and have the carriage leave me off a block away, and that upset the poor woman further. I thought she might actually faint."

Alice smiled. "You have a good heart. I don't know those women, but it doesn't sound as if they value the same things. Now, I'm not judging them, mind you—I couldn't begin to say what's in their hearts. But their actions will speak for them."

Marty followed Alice into the dressing room and considered her maid's words. She'd never considered herself good or selfless. Alice's comment only served to vex Marty all the more. A good and selfless woman wouldn't treat her sister as Marty had. She wouldn't feel the need to lie and hide the details of her life—and she certainly wouldn't have gone into an arranged marriage and kept it a secret from the people she loved.

★

Jake smiled as he came into the house an hour earlier than usual. Despite the rainy weather, Jake felt more than a little excited. He had a surprise for Marty, and he could hardly wait to tell her about it. Brighton greeted him at the door as usual and asked after his day.

"It started much too early, as you will recall," Jake told his man. "I must say I'm glad that it's Friday." He handed Brighton his umbrella and outer coat.

"Yes, sir."

Just then Mrs. Landry appeared. "Goodness! Don't let that umbrella drip all over my freshly polished floor. There's a porch for such things."

"I apologize, Mrs. Landry," Jake declared before Brighton could speak. "It's all my fault. I was in such a hurry to get inside and see my wife, that it totally slipped my mind."

She gave an exasperated sigh. "It's not your fault at all, Mr. Wythe. If Mr. Brighton knew his job properly, he would have been waiting for you on the porch."

"But I came home early. Hardly his fault."

Brighton looked at Mrs. Landry with a rather smug expression. She jerked her chin high. Jake wanted to laugh out loud at the twosome, but knew better.

"A good servant anticipates his master's every move. If Mr. Brighton were American trained, he would know that. I seriously doubt the English ever do anything without a fixed schedule in place. Americans are far more spontaneous."

"I will admit the truth of being spontaneous, Mrs. Landry. However, I couldn't say if that is the case or not for the English. I've never been abroad."

"Mrs. Landry is rather ignorant of how a gentleman's manservant performs his duties." Brighton looked at the woman in a matter-of-fact manner. "The truth is, Mrs. Landry is woefully uninformed when it comes to understanding gentlemen."

"Ha! I know well enough, you rapscallion. You would think that the only people in the world who know how to keep order in a house are the English! I can tell you this much: I've been overseeing households for more years than I care to admit. I know perfectly well how to keep a house and how to keep the folks in it. And you still haven't removed that umbrella. I'm going to have to redo this entire foyer."

To Jake's surprise, she got down on her knees and pulled a cloth from her pocket. Wiping at the water, she shook her head and muttered about Brighton's inadequacies. Jake smiled at Brighton, who only gazed toward the ceiling and sighed.

"Do you know where Mrs. Wythe might be found?" he asked no one in particular.

"I believe she's reading in the small sitting room," Brighton replied.

"Of course she is," Mrs. Landry muttered from the floor. "Just as she is every afternoon at this time."

"Thank you." Jake headed off to find Marty just as Mrs. Landry started in once again on Brighton's failings.

"Marty?" he called, entering the sitting room. He looked around the room and thought perhaps she'd retired. Instead, he found her dozing by the fire. How pretty she looked, curled up with her feet under her. She was dressed simply but looked as fresh and beautiful as any grand dame of society.

"Marty?" he said again, not wanting to startle her.

She opened her eyes slowly and looked up. Obviously still drowsy, she smiled and closed her eyes again. Jake touched her cheek and at this, Marty's eyes flew open and she was fully awake.

"What's wrong?"

He laughed and took a seat. "Nothing. In fact, I have a surprise for you."

"A surprise? Goodness, you've done nothing but bestow presents and lovely things upon me since I arrived. I honestly feel spoiled." She straightened in her chair and the book she'd been reading dropped to the floor.

Jake picked it up and looked at the title. "*The Adventures of Sherlock Holmes?*"

She shrugged. "I found it in the library. It's really quite entertaining. Written by an Englishman named Sir Arthur Conan Doyle."

"Actually, as I recall from my days at school," Jake said, "he's Scottish. He just lives in England now."

"Ah, I see. Well, I enjoy his writing." Marty set the book aside. The clock chimed and she glanced at it as if something were wrong. Looking back at Jake she shook her head. "You're home very early."

"I went to work very early. I'd received a note from Mr. Keystone requesting we meet prior to the bank opening for the day. Therefore, I took it upon myself to close up shop early and come home with a marvelous surprise."

This made her smile. "Do tell?"

He leaned forward on the edge of his chair. "Well, it has come to my attention that you've not yet attended our new opera house. I was fortunate enough to secure tickets to tonight's performance of *Cavalleria Rusticana*. I thought I might entice you to spend the evening with me."

Marty's face brightened. "I would love to. Oh, what a treat. Thank you!" She jumped up and without warning leaned over and kissed Jake on the cheek. "I've been so bored. You have no idea."

Jake watched her for a moment, wondering if she would spoil the moment by apologizing. To his relief, however, she smiled. "I should go get ready." She paused at the doorway. "Will we dine in or out?"

"Why don't we make a complete evening of it. I'll take you to one of the best restaurants in town."

"That sounds wonderful. I'll let Mrs. Landry know so she can tell Cook."

He watched her leave and couldn't contain his smile. Not only was she pleased at the thought of an evening out with him—even if it was based on her boredom—but she'd kissed him. Never before had she originated such a sign of affection. His grin broadened. Tonight might very well be the start of something entirely new.

★

"I wondered if you'd like to go to church with me tonight," Mrs. Landry said to Alice. "Since the master and mistress are out until late,

I thought you might enjoy it. I know it's not your regular church, but we're having a ladies gathering. There will be a speaker and good food. I'd love for you to join me."

Alice looked up from her ironing, pleased. "I'd be happy for the diversion. Do you suppose Mr. and Mrs. Wythe would mind?"

"Not at all. I will arrange it with them so you needn't worry." Mrs. Landry touched her hand to her graying hair. "I should go fix myself. It's been a very busy day, and I'm sure I look a fright."

Alice shook her head. "Not at all. You look fine."

"Beauty is in the eye of the beholder," Brighton murmured from where he sat polishing a teapot.

"What was that?" Mrs. Landry questioned. "Did I just hear a dog yammering?"

Alice smiled and turned back to her ironing.

Later that evening as they walked to Mrs. Landry's church, Alice couldn't help but ask the housekeeper about her deceased husband and whether she'd considered remarrying.

"Oh goodness, no. Not truly. I mean, there have been thoughts, of course, but nothing of any substance," Mrs. Landry answered quickly, then fell silent. "Mr. Landry was quite a handful, let me tell you. That man was always in need of something. I wore myself out just trying to anticipate him. No, I don't think I'll marry again." She walked in silence a little longer before adding, "Of course, it would depend on the man."

"Of course," Alice replied, hiding her smile.

They continued their journey in silence. The chilly night air caused Alice to pull her shawl close, and she couldn't shake the feeling that someone was watching them. She glanced around, trying to be as inconspicuous as possible.

I'm being silly. I'm just remembering that night.

Of course. That was all it was. This night was so similar to the evening she'd been injured and her father killed.

"You remind me of my daughter, Meg," Mrs. Landry stated without warning. "She's a sweet girl like you. She's in her thirties now, but when she was younger, she could have been your sister in appearance."

"Except for the scar, I'm sure," Alice said.

"Alice, we all have our scars. Some are visible and others aren't, but they are there all the same. Your scar makes you no less worthy."

"I'm afraid it will make me less worthy of a man's love."

"Bah! If he's worth his salt, it won't matter to him," Mrs. Landry said. "You wait and see, Alice. You're but seventeen. In a short time, the right man will find you, and you will lose your heart to him and he will lose his to you. It will be just as it should be, and the scar will not matter."

"I hope you're right," Alice replied, not really convinced. Though she'd prayed for just such a thing, her heart doubted.

"Here we are," Mrs. Landry said, leading the way toward the large oak doors of the church. "Let's get in out of the damp night air."

Alice hurried to follow her, but just as she reached the door, she stumbled and dropped her small purse. Pausing to pick it up, Alice noticed movement across the street and straightened. She could see the outline of a man. The cherry-colored glow of a cigarette at his lips left her feeling shaken. The man who'd cut her had reeked of cigarette smoke.

The man didn't move, even though Alice was sure he knew she'd seen him. What was he doing there? Why was he following them? Or was he? Maybe this man was simply out for an evening stroll.

Swallowing back her fear, Alice picked up her purse and hurried after Mrs. Landry, whispering a prayer as she went.

Chapter 16

The following Monday morning, Marty looked at the paper on her desk. The blank page intimidated her in a way she didn't like to admit. Dipping her pen in the inkwell, she began to write a greeting to her sister.

> *Dearest Hannah,*
>
> *I hope this letter finds all of you well. The weather is quite lovely here. I find it very different from Texas. The mountains are still covered with snow, which sends chilled air down over the city each evening after the sun goes down. The air is also much dryer. That, perhaps, is one thing I'm not certain of getting used to. My skin is always in need of lotions.*

She put the pen aside and tried to think of what to say next. She had thought to speak about the new fashions she now possessed, but that would only cause Hannah to question how she could afford such luxuries—she knew that Marty hadn't taken much with her. No, there was little Marty could write about, if she was determined to keep her secret.

She thought again of her life in Denver and of Jake. The opera had been so enjoyable. Even now she found herself humming the intermezzo. The music had been glorious, and Marty found that it touched her soul like nothing she'd ever known. Perhaps it was because the story was one of love gone terribly wrong—of sacrifice and death.

Or maybe it was nothing more than the evening itself. She and Jake had shared a wonderful dinner together. He had been in such a happy mood, regaling her with stories of his youth. She could see the passion he had for returning to Texas, and though it concerned her, she couldn't help but recall her own fond memories of that state. More troubling, however, was that she was starting to feel things for Jake that she had only experienced with Thomas. And always, it came in unexpected ways. The touch of his hand on her arm. His hand at the small of her back. The way he looked at her.

She picked up the pen again and tapped it against her head. The time had come. She needed to tell Hannah about Jake. Perhaps she should ease into it, tell Hannah she had met someone and found him to be of great interest. Then again . . . maybe not. She dipped into the inkwell again.

I find Denver to be a marvelous place to live. In fact, I am giving strong consideration to making this my permanent home.

Marty frowned. *That alone is enough to send Hannah here. She'll wonder if I've lost my mind.* She sighed.

I know that might seem strange to you, given that I have no family here. But I very much enjoy the climate and the people. I have made good friends who are kind to me and have

She paused, wondering how much to put into detail.

taken me under their wings. They are well placed in society, and I find their lives to be quite interesting. The grandeur and opulence is unlike anything I've ever known.

She reread the last few lines. Hannah would know that Marty's simple taste would not be drawn to such finery. How could she make it sound more like her old self? A thought came to mind, and she smiled.

I find myself wondering just how much better the money might be spent on helping the poor or attending to the needs of orphans.

147

Speaking of which, I have arranged to spend some time at a local orphanage reading to the children there. I've even decided I might take up sewing for them, as well.

Marty bit her lip and whispered the next words aloud before she wrote them. "Of course, the pay would not be much, but with my wealthy guardians insisting that I need not concern myself with the financial aspects of life, it will give me a small amount of spending money for extras."

It was a perfect way to ease any worries Hannah might have about Marty's well-being. She wrote the words, then wondered if she should go forward with her plan to mention Jake.

"Mrs. Wythe?" Alice called from the doorway.

Marty looked up to find the young woman with Kate, the household maid. "What is it?"

"Mrs. Landry would like to have Kate scrub the floors in here. Would that be acceptable?"

Marty nodded. "Yes, I need time to think about what else I want to say in this letter." She put the pen down and got to her feet. "I'll be downstairs if you need me."

Her mind overflowed with scenarios she could make up—stories that would sound completely plausible. She could mention meeting Jake at church her first week there. That would have an element of truth, but it would cause more questions, since Hannah knew she'd not attended church after Thomas's death. She could just say that she'd fallen head over heels and they'd gotten married. Or she could tell Hannah the truth . . . but she doubted her sister would take very kindly to having been duped.

No sooner had Marty stepped onto the first floor, however, when she noticed someone looking into the foyer from the porch window. She pretended nothing was amiss but went quickly to where she kept the shotgun.

"It might be nothing," she told herself as she moved back to the foyer. "But I'd rather not take a chance." Opening the front door, she peered out but didn't see anyone. She walked to the railing and looked out on the yard. Apparently whomever she'd seen was gone now.

A shiver went up her spine. She didn't like the idea of people sneaking around the house. But she also didn't want to jump to conclusions. She needed to make sure she hadn't mistaken one of their own workers for this mystery man. Marty made her way down the porch stairs and around to the back of the house, crossing to the stable.

"Samson?" she called, pausing just inside the doorway.

"Mr. Samson is fetching supplies for Mrs. Landry," Obed, the young groomsman, replied. He beamed a broad smile. "Can I help you?" His eyes widened at the sight of the shotgun. "You gonna go huntin', Miz Wythe?"

Marty smiled and shook her head. "Have you seen anything of Mr. Lawrence . . . the gardener?"

"No, ma'am. He ain't been here today. Leastwise not yet."

Marty nodded. It answered her question. She turned to go, but the boy called after her. "You want that I should have Mr. Lawrence come to you when he gets here?"

"No. That won't be necessary."

★

"It was good of you to come today, Mrs. Wythe," Mr. Brentwood said, leading her down the hall of the orphanage. "As I mentioned to you when we first met, we have only been open a month and already we have fifty children."

"Goodness. I had no idea there were that many orphans in the area," Marty replied.

Mr. Brentwood gave her a sympathetic look. "My dear Mrs. Wythe, these are but a handful of those out there. Denver has many orphanages. Some are run by churches, and others like ours are helped by the city or are funded by private individuals. Unfortunately, there are hundreds if not thousands of motherless and fatherless children in Colorado."

Marty couldn't begin to comprehend. "Where do they all come from?"

"A great many have come to us from the mining towns to the west. Parents left their homes in the East and came to find gold or silver. Unfortunately, most found starvation and death. Rather than see their

children die, they leave them with us or one of the other institutions."
He paused at a classroom door.

"This is where we school grades one through three. Miss Vernon is
the teacher here."

Marty looked into the classroom and found a dozen or more children.
It appeared the tall, willowy Miss Vernon held their attention as she
showed them pictures of animals and asked the children to identify them.

"Then down the hall here, we have Mr. Cabot's classroom. He handles
the fourth through sixth graders."

Marty followed him down the hall, noting the extreme cleanliness.
From what she'd been told, each of the children helped in the upkeep of
the house, as well as learned to handle laundry duties and other skills.

They paused a moment at Mr. Cabot's room, and Marty looked
in. There were a couple dozen children—mostly boys. Mr. Cabot was
directing their attention to a map of the United States. The children
looked clean and well groomed, and most appeared content enough.

"You will do a great service to the teachers by offering the children
your services. I know you had only in mind to read to the little ones,
but since you are an educated woman, I wonder if you might also be
willing to offer some tutoring. Some of our older children could benefit
from having someone take a little extra time with them."

"I'll do whatever I can," Marty replied. "I want to be useful."

"Well, you are an answer to prayer for us. We don't get a great many
volunteers—not like the church-sponsored orphanages that have pastors and priests to request help from the pulpit." He smiled. "I hope
this doesn't sound too forward, but I will admit I'm surprised that a
woman of your social standing would even take the time."

"Social standings mean very little to me. I am where I am because
of my husband's placement in Denver society. In Texas, I was a simple
rancher's wife. I know, however, what it is to grow up without your
parents. My sister and her husband were good to my brother and me,
however. We were very loved."

"So many of these children will never experience the love of a family. We're the only family they have, and we do our best to encourage
them, but it isn't the same."

He continued their tour. Climbing the stairs to the second floor, they looked in on the boys' dormitory first. Row after row of iron-framed beds lined the walls.

"We have more boys than girls at this point."

"And do you only have the younger ones—up to grade six, I believe you mentioned?"

The man shook his head. "We also have some older children. They attend the public school. We believe that will better prepare them for their life ahead. We're trying to find apprenticeships for them, as well. They very much need to learn job skills in order to support themselves as adults."

"And what do most of them desire to do?" Marty inquired.

The man chuckled. "Well, right now I have a great many would-be cowboys and a few who would like to attend military school. The girls mostly want to be nurses or teachers, wives and mothers, that kind of thing. Although I will admit we have one young lady who desires to be a suffragette."

Marty smiled. She thought of all the young men they had employed on the Barnett Ranch. Perhaps in time she could recommend some of these youngsters to Will and Hannah. They often hired boys as young as fifteen. Maybe with a little bit of information on the plight of these children, they would agree to take them on at an even younger age.

"I must say I'm very impressed with the organization and cleanliness of your orphanage," Marty told Mr. Brentwood. "I suppose I had in mind a gloomy place where the rats ran free. Forgive me." She offered him a smile. "I'm glad to be wrong."

"There are such places, of course," the older man replied, directing Marty to the girls' dormitory. "We strive here to teach the children pride in their surroundings. We do not seek to make it all about work, however. You will note out back we have a very nice play area."

He drew Marty's attention to the window, and she followed him and peered out. There was, just as he said, a nice area for the children to play, complete with swings and a seesaw.

"There is a movement," he told her, "that has been encouraging schools and public facilities such as city parks to provide a variety of equipment to encourage physical activities. Fresh air is good for one's health."

Marty again thought of ranch life. Ninety percent of her day had been spent outdoors during the warm months. She couldn't imagine growing up in a city and having only limited sessions of outdoor play.

She finished the tour and returned home more determined than ever to do what she could to better the lives of the orphans. It grieved her to imagine thousands of children without the love of a mother and father. Perhaps she would consider adoption one day.

Later that afternoon, Marty picked up her letter and read the lines she'd penned. She hoped that Hannah wouldn't overreact to her confession.

"It's silly. There's nothing wrong with the choices I've made. Jake's a good man." She looked over the final lines of the letter.

I have delayed far too long in finishing this letter. I wanted to share some news with you, however, and I hope you won't think me silly. I know this will come as a shock, but I have remarried. I have married a wonderful man, a Colorado banker named Jacob Wythe. Jake is a fine, upstanding man who has shown me great affection and consideration. He has generously provided an opulent home for me and has gifted me with more than you could imagine. We attend a wonderful church every Sunday.

She smiled to herself. That alone would entice Hannah to think twice before reprimanding.

I do hope you will be delighted for me and not angry. I didn't mean to be so covert. Well, I suppose I did, but not for the purpose of hurting anyone. Please be happy for me, because I'm happy.

Love,
Marty

"Would you like me to post your letter for you?" Alice asked.

Marty turned, surprised to find the young woman there. The blond-haired girl smiled. "I hope I didn't startle you."

"Only a bit. And, yes, I suppose you can go ahead and post this letter."

"Did you tell your sister . . . about . . . Mr. Wythe?" Alice asked.

This time Marty didn't chide her for the personal question. "Yes."

"Do you think she'll be angry about your marriage?"

"I honestly don't know what Hannah will think or feel. She's always been very protective of me, but I know she would want me to be happy."

"And are you happy?"

Alice was the only one with whom Marty had shared the truth about her arrangement with Jake. As her personal maid, Alice was already well aware that the couple never shared the same bedroom.

"I'm content," Marty finally added. At least that much was true. "I prefer it here to Texas, and I find it's better for me to pretend there is no Texas and no family living there worrying after me."

Alice shook her head. "Pretending doesn't make it so."

Marty gave a heavy sigh. "No, but it does give me a little peace of mind. Very little, I'll admit, but enough for now. Hopefully Hannah and Will can accept my choices and will forgive me for my secrecy. Then there will be nothing more to worry about."

She met Alice's doubtful expression and knew the young woman didn't believe a word.

★

Jake put aside the newspaper and turned his attention back to the ledgers he'd been working on. It seemed that the missing money he'd been tracking had been returned very nearly in full. He frowned. How could this be happening under his nose?

Arnold came in with a stack of papers. "These letters will need your signature before they can go out."

"What are they?"

"Mostly notifications. The usual. Mortgage payments that are behind, loans that have been in arrears. We're calling in the notes on most."

"Foreclosing on the mortgages?" Jake asked. "Who arranged that?"

"Mr. Morgan himself. He brought this list in when you were at the Denver Club. You can review it to make sure there are no mistakes."

Jake nodded and took the papers. Looking through them, he frowned.

Most of the notices were to homeowners who were behind on their mortgage payments. The addresses listed revealed homes from modest to lower income areas, suggesting the common man and his family.

"How can we foreclose on these people?" Jake asked aloud. He glanced up to find Arnold giving him a confused look. He shook his head and placed the papers on the desk. "I suppose the bank must have its money, but it seems heartless to put families out on the street."

"Indeed," Arnold agreed. "However, Mr. Morgan seemed to think it important for the health of his banks."

"I suppose." Jake drew a deep breath and blew it out. "Seems mighty unneighborly," he drawled.

This didn't sit right—but neither did the direction of his own life, especially in these uncertain times. Mr. Morgan was constantly speaking to him about promotion and an increased salary. He liked the way Jake handled himself and the bank and had even commented that he would like to put Jake in a position to oversee all of the branches. It sounded quite daunting to a man who longed only to be back in the saddle.

Arnold turned to go. "Please close the door on your way out," Jake called after him. The younger man did as instructed, leaving Jake to the quiet of his office.

"I'm not where I want to be," he whispered and glanced upward. His first love, Deborah Vandermark, would have told him he should pray on the matter. It had been a long time, however, since Jake had done any real talking to the Lord. He touched the scar on his right hand. He'd cut it while working for Deborah's family. She had been training to become a physician and had sewed it up for him. Whenever he saw the scar, he thought of her kindness to him and her faith. She was a strong woman of God. . . . How different from Marty, who obviously struggled when it came to the Almighty. He smiled. Hadn't he had his own issues? He couldn't fault Marty for feeling untrusting when he had some of the same problems.

"I suppose it wouldn't hurt to mention a few things to you, Lord." Jake got up and walked to the window. He couldn't help but wonder what Marty would think if she knew that he was beginning to wish for more in their marriage. More in his life.

Taking it to God in prayer was something his mother had always encouraged. He knew a Christian was supposed to pray, read his Bible, live a life pleasing to God. Jake knew, too, that he'd been focused only on survival—doing whatever it took to get one step closer to Texas.

Marty had been an important part of that, but the more time they spent together, the less inclined she seemed to be toward the idea of returning. He wasn't entirely sure why she held Texas a grudge. Maybe it had to do with the death of her first husband. She had loved him a great deal; that much was evident. No one had ever loved Jake that way, and it made him just a little bit jealous.

Pray about it.

The words seemed to burn deep into his heart.

"I wanna go home, Lord," he finally prayed. "I wanna go back to Texas."

Chapter 17

"The Morgans do love to entertain," Marty declared as they made their way home in the carriage. "And how interesting to have a May Day party complete with a Maypole. I have to admit I've never seen the dance involved, but it was quite lovely with all those ribbons."

Jake nodded but said very little. He seemed glum and restless, and Marty couldn't help but wonder what had been said or done to bring about such a mood.

"Did you have a bad time?" she dared to question.

He looked at her from across the carriage, but the dim street lighting did little to reveal his expression. Who was this man she'd married, and why couldn't she better understand him?

"I didn't have either a bad or good time," he answered her. "It was just one more party—one more meaningless day." The weariness in his voice rang clear.

Marty tried not to panic at his comment. Lately Jake was given to speaking more and more of his longing for Texas and the ranch life that he loved. "There are days here when I just want to pack up and walk away. I'm tired of bank ledgers and businessmen more concerned with their vast wealth than the condition of the people around them. I want more than this, but . . ."

He fell silent for a few moments, and then started in again. "You know how I feel about owning my own spread one day."

"I do," Marty said, keeping her tone neutral. She deeply feared what he might say next.

"I was speaking with Dennis Sheedy tonight. You'll remember he used to ranch a great deal."

"Yes."

"Well, he advised against any ranching or farming venture at this point. He said the markets weren't good for either. He said it would be a waste of time and money, and I would soon find myself in the same position my father was a few years ago."

Marty's heart skipped a beat. *God bless you, Mr. Sheedy.* She remained silent, hoping that Jake would tell her he was giving up on his dreams.

"I reminded him that folks will always need to eat, but he said there was already a glut of ranches and farms and that with the economy as it is, there have been a great many foreclosures, as well. I thought that would make it more reasonable for me to be able to buy in. After all, the places will sell dirt cheap."

"But you would be benefiting from another's loss. That doesn't seem like something you'd be comfortable with."

"I wouldn't like it, but better that someone continue the dream— don't you think?"

"I don't know," Marty said, though she had her own opinion about such dreams. "I do know that ranching is a dangerous business. There are things there that can take your life in a moment's notice."

"And there aren't here?"

She shrugged. "It's hardly the same. On the ranch a man can die from his horse taking a misstep or crossing the path of a rattler."

"And that can't happen here—to a banker?" He sounded irritated. "You weren't that far away from Denver when your stage was attacked. Someone's been creeping around the house, probably looking to steal us blind. There's always something or someone looking to do evil."

Marty knew she needed to rein back her negativity toward ranching. Perhaps changing the subject would help. "Oh, let's not dwell on the sad and bad. I very nearly forgot to tell you about my experience at the orphanage today. I was able to spend some time helping the little ones with their reading. It reminded me of how Hannah used to teach us when we were little." She paused and noticed Jake was lost in thought.

"There are a great many children in this city who have no one. Did you realize that? There are a dozen or more orphanages and all of them full," she rambled.

Jake, however, remained silent the entire journey home. She worried that her comments had left him overly discouraged.

"I'm sorry, Jake. I'm sorry if I sounded unfeeling in regard to your dreams," she said as they approached the house. Marty turned to find they were only inches from each other. The glow of the porch light made it easy to see the sadness in his eyes.

"I truly don't wish to see you hurt. I don't want to lose another husband the way I lost Thomas."

Jake's head cocked slightly. "Sounds as though you've come to care about me."

Marty trembled—grateful that Jake wasn't holding on to her arm or he might have felt it and wondered why. "Of course I care about you. We've been together now for more than three months. I've come to enjoy your company and thought you felt likewise."

"I do," he whispered.

She smiled. "Then surely you can understand why I don't want to see you hurt. I want to have you around for a good long time. I want to enjoy our life together."

"And you're content with this and nothing more?"

Marty hesitated, not sure of his meaning. They were so very close, and for just a heartbeat, Marty thought Jake might kiss her. Worse still, she wanted him to. When she said nothing, however, Jake apparently took this as a dismissal.

"I'm sorry. I shouldn't have said that. I appreciate that you care. I'm sorry if I've been poor company."

Disappointment flooded Marty's soul as Jake moved to the open front door, where Brighton awaited them. Why did she feel so out of sorts? Was she losing her heart to this man?

I swore never again. I never wanted to love another person like I loved Thomas—especially not a rancher.

She vowed then and there to guard her heart more carefully. She couldn't risk allowing Jake to make her care about him the way she would a husband. Theirs was a sensible arrangement—nothing more.

★

Brighton followed Jake to his bedroom and helped him with his clothes. "Will you need anything else this evening, sir?"

Jake shook his head. "Please feel free to retire. I will be fine."

"Very good, sir." Brighton moved toward the door with Jake's coat in hand. "I'll give this a good brushing and return it in the morning. Good night, sir."

"Yes, good night," Jake replied and all but closed the door in Brighton's face.

Pacing the room in his trousers and shirt, Jake couldn't stop thinking about Marty. She had looked so beautiful tonight. When they'd arrived home, she had mentioned caring about him and Jake had been certain she would have allowed him to kiss her.

So why didn't I?

He stopped and stared at the door that adjoined their rooms. It would be easy enough to open it and pass through to her dressing room. He could hear her in there. Alice was no doubt readying her mistress for bed, combing out her silky blond hair and braiding it for sleep. He could go to them on some pretense.

But why bother? Even if she has come to care about me, it doesn't mean she wants anything more.

Jake began pacing again. There had to be something more, however. He was so discontent with the way things were. He felt that life held no meaning. He had married because the bank had insisted he have a wife, but now he found himself feeling something more for his wife . . . and it stood to ruin everything.

Am I in love with her?

The question seemed simple enough, but Jake struggled to even allow the thought. He had been so certain that he would never love

159

again. Of course, he'd been just as certain that he would never marry again, yet here he was . . . a husband.

At least there were no children to worry about. But that thought caused just as much anguish. He had wanted children, had always seen himself as fathering a large family. A family who could help him run the ranch and inherit the fruits of his labors.

Brighton had laid a small fire in the hearth—just enough to ward off the chill of the evening, but Jake couldn't help but feel cold. He was cold from the inside out. It was like sinking in quicksand and knowing you weren't going to get out.

Maybe it had been a mistake to marry Marty. He frowned. "But I can't imagine my life without her now."

He heard laughter from the room next door and longed to be a part of it. He went to the door and put his hand out to touch the polished wood.

If only you knew how I felt. If only I could help you see that we could have something more—something deeper—richer.

Jake spent the rest of the night in a restless sleep. He dreamed of Marty and how their marriage might be. He awakened several times almost sensing her nearness, only to realize it had been nothing more than his imagination at work.

He heard the clock chime four and wondered if he would ever again be able to enjoy a restful night. With that beautiful wife of his so close, yet so far away, it seemed doubtful.

I could woo her.

The thought seemed reasonable enough. Jake rubbed his jaw. *I could court my wife and show her that there could be a great romance between us.*

But what if that wasn't what she wanted? What if Jake put his heart and soul into winning Marty's affection, and she turned out to despise him for it? She might accuse him of altering their marriage agreement. She might even decide to have the marriage annulled, and he certainly didn't want that.

She said she cared about me. Jake wrestled with that thought. Wasn't that enough to build on? He'd never claimed to know much about courting and wooing, but he felt confident that the friendship they shared was a good foundation for something more.

We enjoy each other's company. We have a great deal in common.

Thoughts poured through his mind—all the reasons why this courtship should work. Jake grinned in the dark. He felt a surge of excitement and a rush of energy that made him feel like a youth again. He could be charming. He could make Marty fall in love with him. He was convinced of it.

He put his hands under his head and his smile broadened. "She thinks ranch life has its hidden dangers," he whispered to the night. "Wait until she sees what we Colorado bankers are capable of."

★

Trinity Methodist Church was beginning to grow on Marty. Or at least the music was. The organ's four thousand pipes were not to be ignored when sounding a hymn. Jake had once commented that this church made you *feel* the music deep within your soul. Marty agreed.

She listened only halfheartedly to the sermon. The minister was teaching from the book of Genesis, about Isaac and Rebekah. Abraham had arranged for his servant to go back to the country of his origin and get Isaac a wife. It was a story Marty remembered well from childhood.

Rebekah was rather like the original mail-order bride, Marty reasoned.

She listened momentarily as the Word was read. "'And they called Rebekah, and said unto her, Wilt thou go with this man? And she said, I will go.'"

Marty gave a quick side glance at Jake, who seemed completely caught up in the sermon. He was such a handsome man—more handsome than she'd even noticed when she'd first married him. And he was kind and generous. She couldn't fault him for much of anything. If only he would put aside his desire to return to Texas.

I can't go back there. There's nothing there for me—just memories. Even if she gave Jake the ranch and they started their life together there, the ghost of Thomas would always be between them. It wouldn't be a real marriage at all.

It isn't a real marriage, she reminded herself.

A longing stirred deep within her, and Marty did her best to squelch it. Desires, however, came unbidden, as they were known to do. She wanted a real marriage with Jacob Wythe. She wanted a lifetime of love and laughter—of children and growing old together. The thought brought tears to her eyes.

Why must I feel these things now?

"'And Isaac brought her into his mother Sarah's tent—'" the minister's voice broke through her thoughts—"'and took Rebekah, and she became his wife; and he loved her.'"

And he loved her.

The words echoed in her ears. Isaac and Rebekah were strangers to one another—arranged in a marriage not of their own doing—yet Isaac loved her.

Could Jake love me?

And what if he did? Could she set aside her fears and share the truth with him? Could she tell him about the ranch and give him the choice of having his dream or remaining in Colorado?

I can't. I already know what he would choose.

She bit her lip and stared down at her gloved hands. If not for that stupid ranch, she wouldn't have to feel all this guilt. There would be no chance of love between them until she was free of that ranch. A thought came to mind: She didn't necessarily need to sell the place. She could just deed it over to William and Hannah. It had been their land to begin with.

She relaxed a bit. She could tell Jake the property reverted back to them—that she'd felt honor bound to return it after Thomas died. But how would she explain the delay? Maybe she could tell him that she hadn't been ready to move forward with her life, and they had been gracious enough to let her remain on the ranch. That made perfect sense. They were that kind of people.

Realizing she was once again spinning lies to save herself, Marty pushed the thoughts aside. There would be plenty of time to figure out the details later. No sense in using God's house for such underhanded purposes. She looked at Jake, and he turned to her and smiled.

She smiled in return. Maybe they *could* have a real marriage.

Chapter 18

"I heard someone at the door," Marty mentioned to Brighton as he entered the dining room.

"Yes, madam. A gentleman arrived to speak with Miss Chesterfield."

"Alice?" Marty put down her coffee. "Did he say why?" Alice had told Marty that she had no friends in the area—that she had led a very reclusive life after her mother had gone. Perhaps the bank had sent someone to offer her compensation.

"No, madam. He only said it was of some urgency."

Marty pushed away from the table, and Brighton hurried to assist her from the chair. "I think I'd better check on her. Where are they now?"

"I put them in the formal sitting room."

Marty nodded. "Thank you."

She made her way to the pocket doors of the front sitting room in time to hear the man speak. "You'd better figure out where they are—unless you want a scar on the other cheek."

Marty's blood ran cold. She hurried from the hall and went to where she had hidden her shotgun. Cocking it open, she checked the load. Both barrels were loaded and ready. She started to snap it closed, then thought better of it. With a smile, she draped the open barrel over her arm, hoping to look casual but ready for action. The man might find it easy to intimidate Alice, but let him mess with a Texan and see what he thought.

Walking on tiptoes toward the large sitting room, Marty listened for the sound of conversation. Voices could be heard in muffled tones, though she couldn't quite make out what was being said.

She eased herself into position by the open pocket doors and waited for a moment.

"I told you," Alice said, sounding terrified, "I have no idea what you're talking about. My father was robbed that night and everything was taken. Everything he had from the bank was in that satchel."

"I don't believe you. See, I happen to know what was in that satchel. Or rather, what was supposed to be in there."

Alice gasped. "So you were one of the men who attacked us?"

"Not exactly." He laughed, and the sound made Marty's blood boil. "I'm the one who hired them. I happen to know that your father should have been carrying a large envelope that night. It would have had the bank's seal on it."

"I never saw anything like that. My father never included me in his business. He worked at the bank and that's all I ever knew." She sounded terror-stricken.

Marty could stand it no longer. "Oh! Excuse me," she said, entering the room. "I heard voices and couldn't imagine who it could be." She watched as the man darted a glance at the shotgun and then back to her face. He smiled as if knowing full well what Marty was up to.

"Ma'am." He nodded his head.

Marty looked to Alice. "You have a job to do. Don't let me catch you in such idleness again." She turned away from the man and gave Alice a wink. "You don't want to lose your position, do you?"

"No, Mrs. Wythe." Alice gave a curtsy and hurried from the room. "I'm sorry, Mrs. Wythe."

Marty snapped the shotgun closed and looked back at the man with a smile. "I do hope you will forgive me, but we have a busy schedule today. My maid isn't able to receive visitors on working days, Mr. . . . ?"

He gave her a smile that suggested he was less than impressed with her game. "Call me Smith. Mr. Smith."

"Of course," Marty said, not trying to hide the sarcasm from her tone. "Well, Mr. Smith, unless there's something I can help you with, I'll show you out. . . ." She let her words trail.

The man looked at her cradling the shotgun and nodded. "I suppose it can wait. I can catch up with her another time."

"I think not," Marty said, the smile never leaving her face. "I'm rather possessive of my help. I think it might be better if you were to leave Alice alone. Otherwise . . ."

"Are you threatening me if I don't?" he asked, narrowing his eyes.

"Did I say something threatening?" She batted her eyes in the same southern flirtatious style she'd been taught in finishing school. "Goodness, but I can't think of why you should feel threatened by little ol' me." She let her drawl thicken. "Why, I just never meant to suggest anything of the kind."

He laughed, but his eyes remained fixed and then they narrowed. "Of course not."

Marty sobered and pointed toward the door with the shotgun. "I'm glad we understand each other. Now if you'll be so kind as to leave."

"You might as well know, Mrs. Wythe, that this isn't the end of it. I intend to speak to Miss Chesterfield again. I've looked long and hard for her. Sent my men around to watch your place and her comings and goings. She has something that belongs to me."

"Alice is my employee, and she came here with nothing but the clothes on her back. If I see you or your men on my property again, I'll arrange a reception for you." She glanced at the shotgun. "And that isn't a threat—it's a promise. See, I'm not easily intimidated—unlike Alice."

"She knows what I'm after," he said, taking a step toward Marty. "And I will have it."

She raised the shotgun just enough to remind him of its presence. For just a moment, Marty thought he might charge her—and if that happened, she knew she'd have to make good her threat. But just then another voice called out.

"Miz Wythe, Mr. Brighton said you needed to see me."

It was Samson. For all the time she'd been married to Jake, Marty had never once seen Samson inside the house.

The stranger stopped midstep. His gaze traveled the full length of the hulking man. He looked back to Marty and gave her a knowing nod. "Good day, Mrs. Wythe. I will speak to you again . . . no doubt."

Marty didn't relax until the man was out of her house and on the back of his horse. From the porch, she watched him trot the mount down the street and wondered silently whether she'd handled things poorly. She had wanted the man to feel threatened, but she certainly hadn't wanted to stir him to take further action. In any case, the man was clearly an enemy now.

She went back into the house and found Samson gone but Alice waiting for her. One look at the girl told Marty she'd overheard the entire exchange between herself and Mr. Smith.

"I'm so sorry, Mrs. Wythe. I'm so sorry. I had Mr. Brighton fetch Samson. I hope it was the right thing to do."

Marty shook her head and lowered the shotgun. "It was exactly right, but never mind that. What in the world was he after?"

"Some papers—papers that apparently weren't in my father's satchel when we were robbed. He admitted to sending the men to attack us." Tears welled in the younger woman's eyes. "I'm so afraid. I don't know what he's talking about. When I recovered from my wounds, everything we owned was auctioned off to pay for my father's burial and my hospital fees. I was still in the hospital when they sold the house. There were only a few things that I even managed to hang on to, thanks to my friends, and nothing I have was of any value. Certainly there was no envelope of papers like he's after."

"Well, from now on, you stay close to me. I don't want you going out alone. If you need to go somewhere, I'll send Samson along with you. Folks will think twice about bothering you with him at your side."

"Thank you, Mrs. Wythe." Alice looked around the foyer and whispered, "Marty."

Marty embraced the girl, letting the shotgun dangle at her side. "I won't see you intimidated by him or anyone else."

"I should have told you." Alice moved away from Marty and shook her head. "I'm sorry."

"Told me what?" Marty asked.

Alice wrung her hands. "I . . . well . . . there's been someone trying to get to me since the attack. They told me at the hospital that someone had come there searching for me, but the doctors wouldn't allow them to see me—especially since when they first arrived I was still unconscious. Then later, when I was staying with friends, they told me someone had come there looking for me. It just so happened that I was gone that day, but . . . well . . . the men who showed up threatened my friends. It frightened them so bad that they decided to leave Denver altogether rather than deal with that again. They figured I would go with them, but I reminded them that whoever it was would just follow, so I figured it was best to stay and let them escape."

"Well, Mr. Smith is going to find himself outnumbered here. You're safe with us. I grew up fending off Comanche and other marauders. You learn to be tough when you live out in the open range. In Texas you often have to be on your guard. That man doesn't worry me," she said gruffly. But truth be told, Marty had seen an evil glint in his eye that suggested he wasn't easily deterred from his plans.

"Will you tell Mr. Wythe?"

Marty nodded. "I think that would be best. He should know that the folks sneaking around the place were looking for you rather than stuff to steal."

Alice nodded. "I hope he won't be mad at me. I don't want to lose my position here."

"You won't. I believe he'll be just as protective of you as I am."

★

"He what?" Jake asked, his eyes narrowed.

"He threatened Alice . . . and in a way, me," Marty told her husband later that day. "He told me he would get what he wanted."

"I don't like this one bit. I wish you knew where he came from. I'd like to pay him a visit." Jake looked at Alice. "Do you have any idea who he is?"

Alice shook her head. "He didn't give me a name, sir."

"He told me his name was Smith, but I think that's just made up," Marty added.

Alice stood visibly trembling. "He just started in on me. Kept saying how the punishment I'd already been dealt would be nothing compared to what was coming if I didn't cooperate."

"And you know nothing about what he's after?"

Again Alice shook her head. "He said it was a large envelope with papers, and that it had been sealed by the bank. I know from things my father told me that they only did that on very important dealings. If it was something that needed to go from the bank to the person involved without anyone else seeing the material, it would be sealed."

Jake nodded, already familiar with the process. He ran a hand through his hair. The thought of someone coming around with malicious intent caused him to feel more than a little agitation. The very idea that someone would send men to scout out his house and threaten his staff and wife . . . "I'll speak to the police about this. Perhaps they can help."

"They weren't of any help to my friends," Alice said bitterly. "I doubt they'd be any more help now."

"Well, you didn't have the backing of people like Morgan and Keystone. I do," Jake assured her. "We'll get to the bottom of this. I will personally go and speak with Mr. Morgan and find out what was in that envelope your father should have been carrying."

★

Two days later, Jake had his opportunity when Morgan appeared at the bank with an invitation for the Wythes to join the Morgans and others for a celebration.

"Mrs. Morgan delights in throwing me birthday parties, and she wanted to make certain you and Mrs. Wythe could attend. Now, there aren't to be any gifts, of course. Just the company of good friends for a nice lawn party."

"We'd be honored to attend," Jake said, having little interest yet knowing that if he accommodated the man he would be more likely to get some reasonable response to his questions. "I wonder, though, before you leave, could I have a word?"

Mr. Morgan nodded and took a seat. "If this is about your vice-presidency, be assured it is moving ever closer to fruition."

Jake moved to close his office door. "No, it's not about that at all." He came back to his desk and sat. "As you know, my wife's maid was the daughter of your former bank manager, Mr. Chesterfield."

"Yes. Yes, I know that. Is your wife pestering you again to have the bank offer the girl some form of reparation?"

"Not at all. Marty understands the situation. Unfortunately, however, we had a bit of an incident the other day. A man came to the house and threatened Miss Chesterfield in order to learn the whereabouts of a packet of papers her father should have been carrying the night of his death."

Morgan frowned. "What papers?"

"I was hoping you could tell me."

"The man didn't say what he wanted?"

Jake shook his head. "Only that they were in a bank-sealed envelope. A large envelope. It should have been in the satchel that was in Mr. Chesterfield's possession, and apparently this man knew that it was missing. I wondered if you might know what was in that envelope that made it worth killing for."

For several moments Morgan said nothing. He looked as if he were trying to remember. Finally he shook his head. "I'm really not at liberty to tell you the details."

"So you do know what was in it?"

"I do, but very few others have been told." He looked at Jake and seemed reluctant to share the information. "We were afraid of making a public scene. We didn't need negative stories to spread regarding the bank's security."

Jake could understand that, given the problems the economy was already starting to see in 1892. "So might you enlighten me? After all, my family and home seem to be under some threat."

"And your maid has no idea of what the man was talking about?" Morgan asked.

"None. She came to our employ with virtually nothing. If there were an envelope amidst the things she and her father owned, it was either destroyed or lost. All of their things were auctioned off to pay for the funeral and her medical expenses. Now, I'd like to know what this man is after."

"I suppose you're entitled." Morgan drew a deep breath and laced his fingers together. "It was full of gold certificates—worth a small fortune."

Jake startled at this news. "Why in the world was he carrying something as valuable as that?"

Morgan shrugged. "It was the way we handled it. We put on a fussy show of guarded couriers for those who might think to rob us, while sending the real goods with no escort whatsoever. It worked quite well, and we shipped money, certificates, stocks, and even some jewelry that way. In fact, Chesterfield was the first man we've ever lost."

"Let me get this straight: You gave Chesterfield an envelope with a fortune in gold certificates to be delivered as if it were nothing more important than business correspondence?"

"Exactly."

"And did he know what he was carrying?"

"Not to my knowledge. Oh, I mean he would have known there was value to the papers. He always knew that any delivery we entrusted to him was of vital importance. He was paid well, however. As for his knowing the contents . . . well . . . I can't imagine that he did. I certainly wouldn't have told him. There was no need."

"But gold certificates were included in his satchel that night, and someone knew they were supposed to be there."

"I don't know how they could have." Morgan shook his head. "There were only a couple of us privy to the information."

"Well, somebody talked," Jake said.

★

Marty dreaded opening the letter in her hand. Either Hannah had mailed it before Marty's missive arrived telling her about Jake and the marriage, or she'd hastily posted it after hearing the news. Either way, Marty wasn't in any hurry to discover what was within.

She thought to distract herself with a nice quiet lunch alone, but after studying the thin slices of rare roast beef on her plate, she sighed. "I might as well read it. My mind won't rest until I do."

Pulling the envelope from her pocket, Marty ran her dinner knife under the seal along the top to open it. The missive was short—one page. Marty drew a deep breath and perused the lines.

My dear sister,

How wonderful for you to have found love again. I'm surprised that you worried I would think badly of your choice. I've long hoped that you could find another man to love. You are much too young to be a widow. Perhaps now you will have a family of your own and know the happiness of motherhood, as well.

Please know that William and I are praying for you and that we are so very happy for you and Jake. You have made him sound like such a wonderful man, and I look forward to the day we can meet face-to-face. William said we could use a banker in the family.

I know that you never planned to remarry after Thomas, but now that you have, I pray you will be happy. I was delighted to read that you are attending church once again, and I pray, too, that this new adventure in life will allow you to once again draw close to God.

Faithfully yours,
Hannah

Marty let out the breath she'd been holding. Hannah didn't mind, didn't protest the matter in the least. It was a surprise—her sister had carefully tried to manage Marty's choices for most of her life. The announcement of her traveling to Colorado had completely upset that tradition, and Marty had been certain her news would cause Hannah a fit of apoplexy.

"Thank goodness that's done with." Marty folded the letter and put it back in her pocket.

She tried to think of what she should do next. She wanted to get the ranch matter settled and figured the best thing to do would be to write immediately to her sister and suggest that Will have the papers drawn up for her to deed the place back to him. Of course, Marty was married now and had no way of knowing if she'd need her husband's permission to conduct business. Laws were often funny about that, and married women didn't have the same rights that widowed women did. Perhaps she should seek the advice of a lawyer.

"But how do I go about that without Jake knowing what I'm doing?"

★

Jake noticed Marty's good mood that evening. She seemed more carefree and lighthearted than he'd ever known her to be. He had no idea what had caused the change, but he was glad for it. He thought back to his conversation with Mr. Morgan and wondered if he should spoil her happiness with the details of what he'd learned. Deciding against it for the time being, Jake chose instead to enjoy a quiet evening reading while Marty worked on some project of her own.

The clock chimed the hour, and Jake yawned. He stole a glance at his wife, who'd been quietly sewing. With her head bent over the garment, she looked completely content. Marty loved keeping busy, and he understood that.

She seemed to sense his gaze and looked up. Smiling, she rolled her shoulders. "I suppose it's time for bed. I tend to get caught up in what I'm doing."

"What exactly are you doing?"

"Making a pinafore. It's for one of the orphans. I wanted to do something more for them, and I figured I could sew as well as the next woman."

"Probably better, given your new circle of friends." He watched her carefully tuck the sewing back into a basket by the chair. "You truly enjoy working with the orphans, don't you?"

"I do," Marty replied. "They are so . . . well . . . they seem to thrive on my affection and attention. God knows they don't get much. The workers do their best, but it isn't the same as having a family."

"No, I'm sure it isn't."

"Speaking of family, I had a very nice letter from my sister." Marty reached into her pocket and handed it over to him. "I finally told her about us."

"You did?" Jake opened the letter and scanned the lines. He felt

172

his chest tighten at the comment about Marty becoming a mother. The idea of having children with Marty had started to consume his thoughts more often than he liked to admit.

"She says you made me sound like a wonderful man," Jake commented, concluding the letter. "Whatever did you say to cause that kind of response?"

Marty gave a light laugh and got to her feet. Jake quickly followed suit. He handed her back the letter and waited for her to respond. For a very long moment all they did was gaze into each other's eyes, however. Jake longed to take her in his arms, but he forced himself to stand completely still.

Finally Marty replied. "I told her you were good to me—that you were generous and kind. I told her that I was happy and wanted her to be happy for me."

"And are you happy, Marty?" He was barely able to voice the words.

She smiled, and it warmed his heart in a way he'd never known. Neither Josephine nor Deborah had made him feel this way.

"Of course I'm happy. Especially now that my sister knows about our marriage and approves."

"Her approval was that important?"

She shrugged. "I suppose it was. Family has always been important to me. I guess I didn't make it seem that way, running off as I did without letting them know. I just wanted to make my own choices and be responsible for my life."

Her gaze held his. Jake wanted so much to tell her how he felt—how she had changed his mind about love. How he longed to alter their arrangement and start anew with a real marriage.

"I want to make you happy, Marty. I guess I want your approval, as well," he finally managed to whisper.

She surprised him by reaching up to touch his cheek. "You are an amazing man, Jake, and you do have my approval. I think together . . . we can be very happy."

He put his hand over hers. "I think so, too."

Chapter 19

Marty finished making her second pinafore when Brighton appeared with a large box. "This just arrived for you, madam," he announced.

"Goodness, what is it?"

"I do not know." He placed the box on a small table. "Would you like me to open it?"

Putting her sewing aside, Marty nodded. "Please." She got to her feet and joined him.

Brighton opened the box, revealing a dozen red roses. The fragrance wafted through the air, and Marty inhaled the sweet aroma. She hadn't been given roses since long before Thomas's death.

"They're beautiful," she murmured, gently touching one of the blossoms.

"There is a card, madam." Brighton reached in and pulled it from among the flowers. He handed it to Marty.

Marty opened the card. *To my wife. Thank you for the trust you've placed in me. You make my life so much better. Affectionately, your husband.*

The sentiment surprised and disturbed Marty. Already uncertain and confused by her own feelings for Jake, she didn't need this to further complicate matters.

But it's not such a complication if he feels the same way, is it? Should

I be afraid of falling in love with a man who clearly feels something for me?

"Would you like me to have Mrs. Landry arrange them in a vase?" Brighton asked.

Marty nodded. "Yes, please do."

"Very good, madam." He took up the box, leaving Marty with the note.

In the hallway he apparently ran into Mrs. Landry, because Marty could hear the two begin to pick at each other.

Mrs. Landry commented in a rather loud voice, "I know very well how to arrange flowers, you ninny. Don't be trying to tell me how to do my job."

Marty looked down at the card again and frowned. Why was this happening now? And why did it bother her as much as it did? Surely she should feel a sense of relief that the man she'd married was a good match—that they both enjoyed each other's company and had found some semblance of happiness in the aftermath of losing their prior mates.

So why do I feel so uncomfortable?

Marty tucked the card into her sewing box and moved back to her work. She tried to calm her mind, telling herself it was a kind gesture, nothing more. But there had been moments of tenderness lately that stirred her heart. . . .

Jake had made it clear in his letters prior to their marriage that he didn't want a romance. Had he changed his mind? Had she changed hers?

Marty had to admit the aching in her heart was evidence that something was afoot. She had thought herself incapable of loving again— Thomas had been the love of her life. Wouldn't it be a betrayal to his memory if she were to give her heart to another?

Folding the pinafore carefully, Marty tried to reason through her feelings. Thomas was dead. There was no one who could bring him back. Thomas himself would have been the first one to tell her to be happy—to find something in life she could enjoy and live for. He would have wanted her to remarry and have children.

"I saw the flowers," Alice said, entering the small sitting room. "They're beautiful."

"Jake . . . Mr. Wythe sent them," Marty replied.

Alice looked at her for a moment. "Is that a bad thing?"

"Why do you ask?"

"You seem troubled. I just wondered, given your . . . arrangement . . . if it made matters difficult for you."

Marty shrugged. "I've been asking myself the same thing, to tell you the truth." She put the pinafore into her sewing basket and frowned. "I never figured to have these feelings again, and now that I do, I have to say they're making me most uncomfortable."

"What feelings are those?" Alice asked in her innocent way.

Marty met her maid's gaze. The girl was young enough to have been Marty's daughter. Her blond hair even resembled Marty's own thick tresses. For reasons Marty couldn't even begin to put into words, Alice touched a special place in her heart.

"I suppose . . . love," Marty finally answered. "I'd hardened my heart against it until I came here. Then I found myself moved by you and your plight, touched by the orphans and theirs, and . . ."

"And you're falling in love with your husband?" Alice dared to ask.

Marty wasn't yet ready to admit that idea aloud. "I don't know."

Alice smiled. "I think you do, and that's the problem. You just don't know how to face the truth."

Marty heard male voices coming from the hallway and glanced at the clock. It was only half past two. Had Alice's tormenter returned? She looked to Alice, who seemed to wonder the same thing—if the look on her face was any indication.

"Don't worry," Marty said. "You're safe."

Jake marched into the room with an expression of grave concern. "There's been an unexpected board meeting called at the bank this afternoon, and I've been asked to attend. I expect it will run well into the evening, and I wanted to let you know."

"What's wrong?" Marty questioned. The tone of his voice and his countenance were most severe.

"The president has called for an emergency session of Congress. He hopes to repeal the Sherman Silver Purchase Act. It won't bode well for anyone, but especially not this state. We rely heavily on silver holding its value, and this will change everything."

"Is it really that bad?" Just last week she'd dined at one of Denver's finest homes, and the wealth there flowed like an undammed river.

He stopped in front of Marty. "It is. Colorado is responsible for over 60 percent of this country's silver. It's not right that the president should imagine silver is the culprit for all our financial woes, but apparently he does. This is only going to make matters worse, the way I see it."

Marty longed to offer him comfort. "I'll wait up to talk with you. Perhaps once you know more about it, things won't seem so bad."

"It'll probably be late. You might as well go to bed."

"I don't mind waiting," she said softly. "I'm sure it will be important for our future."

He nodded. "I'm afraid it's going to completely alter the future of a great many folks."

Marty had never heard him sound so grave. She knew at one time she would have encouraged solace with prayer. A sparking in her heart told her she should again suggest such recourse, but bitterness quickly snuffed out the ember. Why ask God for help? If He cared, wouldn't He have already offered His protection?

Another thought came to mind. "Should I send someone with a meal for you and the others?"

Jake smiled. "I doubt anyone else has thought of that."

"I could have Cook put together some sandwiches and cookies. Food that would be easy to eat without benefit of table service."

"That sounds like a grand idea, Marty. Thank you. Why don't you send Samson over with it at about six?"

"That will give us plenty of time to arrange it," Marty replied, smiling. She was glad to be able to do something to make things easier for him. "Try not to worry," she added. "These things have a way of working out."

"I hope so. God knows this isn't going to be pleasant for anyone. We may well watch the collapse of our entire country's financial foundation."

The evening passed in relative silence. Alice helped Marty dress for bed early.

"Are you sure you don't want me to keep you company for a while?" Alice asked.

Marty shook her head. "No, go enjoy an evening to yourself. You work hard, and I appreciate all that you do. Besides, I'm just going to sit here and read."

"I think I'll do the same," Alice told her. "It'll be nice to just have the time to myself." She picked up the rest of Marty's clothes and smiled. "I'll take these to the laundry first. Good night."

"Good night."

The day had been warm, so Marty opened one of her bedroom windows and breathed deeply of the night air. She could smell the scent of flowering trees and marveled at the slight chill to the air. The weather here was so different. The day could be hot and dry, then often in the afternoon a brief rain would come down from the mountains and by night the air would be cool. She marveled at the glow of electric lighting coming from the neighboring houses. Folks in this elite community wouldn't know how to function without their wealth. If things were as bad as Jake thought, Marty couldn't help but wonder what would happen to these people.

Of course, she knew that the rich usually had contingencies for such things. They wouldn't suffer as much as those poor souls who relied on the generosity of the wealthy.

Rubbing her arms, Marty closed the window again and took up her book. She heard the large grandfather clock chime the hour. Nine o'clock. And still there was no sign of Jake. Marty wondered how the meeting was going—what it would mean for them.

She couldn't help but think of the ranch. She knew that Jake had put aside money for what he hoped would be his future purchase of a spread in Texas. She knew that this tragedy could prevent that from ever happening. Maybe that was the answer to her problems.

Am I hopelessly greedy in wanting things my own way? Is it wrong to hope that the financial situation will keep us right here in Denver?

Marty had read nearly half of her book by the time she heard someone at the door to Jake's bedroom. She listened and waited. She'd left both of her dressing room doors open wide in hopes that he would come and tell her all about the meeting. Voices were soon evident.

"I won't need anything, Brighton. Go ahead and retire. I'm sure that anything I have to see to can wait until morning."

"Very good, sir."

Marty heard the exchange and noted the weariness in her husband's voice. Maybe it would be better if they didn't speak. Maybe the news would be so bad that she'd be unable to sleep.

But maybe if I share the load with him, Jake will rest better. Given her guilt over the ranch, Marty wanted to push aside her own selfish needs and reach out to Jake.

"Marty?" Jake called from the dressing room.

"I'm in here. Please join me," she called back. She put the book away, then adjusted her robe to make certain she wasn't being immodest.

Jake entered the room in a state of undress. His tie was gone and shirt unbuttoned partway but still tucked into his trousers. He'd shed his shoes, coat, and vest and looked more tired than Marty had ever seen him. It gave Marty a start. He looked far more like a Texas cowboy than a Colorado banker.

He plopped into one of the wingback chairs by the fireplace and began to rub his neck.

"Let me," Marty said, pushing his hands aside. "I'm pretty good at this. Years of milking and toting gave me strong hands." She began to knead his tight muscles.

"Oh, that feels so good. Thank you." For several minutes he said nothing more. Marty remained silent, as well. It was one of the most intimate moments she could recall having with him. They were like an old married couple at the end of a busy day. The thought made her smile.

Finally, after nearly ten minutes had passed, Jake stilled her hands and motioned her to sit. "The news is better taken sitting down."

"That bad—already?"

He nodded. "They fully expect that hundreds of banks will close almost overnight in anticipation of what's to come. Ours isn't one of them—at least not yet. We're strong enough to survive for a time, but there's no way of knowing how long that will last. Morgan has in mind to close a couple of the branches and consolidate all his efforts into just a few banks. Ours would be one of them, and he wants me to oversee the reorganization."

"So you won't lose your position?"

"Not yet. But who knows what will happen in the months to come. There's no way of estimating just how bad this is going to get, Marty. Most of the silver mines are going to close. The value of silver has dropped already. This will send property values sliding. I feel bad because I promised you pleasantries and a life of ease, and now this is going to change everything. We're going to have to let some of the staff go and tighten our belts."

"That's all right. We can manage." She tried to not think of what Alice might do. The poor girl needed protection, as well as a job. Perhaps she could send her to Hannah.

"I figure we'll keep Samson, Brighton, Mrs. Landry, and Alice for now. Oh, and Mrs. Standish. Unfortunately, the others will have to go."

"If need be, Jake, I'm a pretty fair cook and I know perfectly well how to care for horses and hitch my own carriage, although I'd hate to lose Samson. I can also wash clothes and clean house. I am, as you have always said, quite capable."

Jake nodded. "You've proven that again and again. You know how to handle yourself and you don't need anyone."

"I wouldn't say that." Marty's voice dropped to almost a whisper. "I'm becoming rather dependent on you. I rather like our time together."

He gave her a weary smile and his drawl thickened. "Yup. I do, too." A sigh escaped his lips. "I just don't know how bad this is gonna get. I figure we should know better in a few weeks, but for now it's a mystery."

"Then we hunker down and ride out the storm," Marty replied. "We're young and strong. I've even got a few things—things I left in Texas that I can sell."

"No, I don't want you doing that. At least not yet. There's no need. I have money set aside—at least as long as the bank is solvent."

"Is there a chance it won't remain so?"

"There's no way of knowing, and I can't very well pull my money out. Even though I might want to." He laughed. "Imagine that—the bank manager, soon to be vice-president, pulling his savings out for fear that the bank will collapse. That wouldn't go over well."

"I suppose not," Marty agreed. In the back of her mind she thought again of the ranch. She could sell it and give the money over to Jake or at least use it for their day-to-day expenses. That would resolve several problems at once. Maybe Will would buy it from her rather than just take it back. She could ask him for a pittance of what it was worth.

"I'm gonna need you to watch your spending—not that you've ever given me reason to worry. Seems like the only time you have spent money has been for someone else—like the orphans."

"That won't be a problem. I already have a good bolt of broadcloth for the projects I'm working on. Otherwise, I don't need anything."

"I'll speak to Mrs. Landry about the household budget, as well."

"We can certainly eat in a simpler manner. Unless you need to entertain, I can do quite well on beans and tortillas." She grinned. "Of course, I doubt Mrs. Standish knows how to make tortillas, but I could teach her."

Jake nodded. "I would enjoy some tortillas myself. It's been a long time."

She leaned forward. "Seriously, we can weather this together. I'm not worried about social status or fancy baubles. Although I will say the roses you sent today were beautiful and most appreciated."

"You deserved them. That and much more. You've been a good wife and done everything you agreed to. You even go to church with me, and I know you've had a difficult time with that."

Marty felt her heart squeeze at his words. "Maybe it's time to stop having such a hard time of it." She got up and walked to the fireplace. "I know my anger at God needs to end. I know the truth, and I can't just go on ignoring it."

"I feel the same way, Marty. Maybe it's time we repented and let the past go."

She met his eyes. Such wonderful eyes.

Getting to his feet, Jake came to where she stood. "There's been a lot of things I've done wrong in life, Martha Wythe, but you aren't one of those things. I think you're probably the best thing that's ever happened to me."

Marty didn't know what to say. She was touched at his declaration and hoped with all her heart that Jake might seal his statement with a kiss. She offered what she hoped was an inviting smile. Jake just held her gaze for a few silent moments, then let go his hold.

"I'm gonna get some sleep before I fall down. You'd better do the same. No tellin' what tomorrow's gonna bring."

★

Marty slept restlessly, and by the time dawn cracked the horizon, she was up and pacing. A thought had come to her: Alice said she read her Bible and prayed every morning before work. Would she be doing just that at this hour?

Making her way to the third floor, Marty crept along the hallway to the room Mrs. Landry had assigned Alice. There was light coming from beneath the door, so Marty gave a light knock.

Alice opened the door, her eyes widening in surprise. "Marty, is something wrong?"

"May I come in?"

"Of course. It's your house." Alice backed up and pulled the door open.

Marty went into the simple room and noted the furnishings. The bed had already been made and the side table revealed an open Bible. "I remember you said that you spent this time in prayer and reading the Word of God."

"I do. I was just getting ready to pray when you knocked."

"I . . . well . . . I've not been right with God for a very long while now, as you know," Marty began. "I blamed God for taking Thomas from me, and I know it was wrong. It just hurt so much to lose him. Seemed easy to blame God for most of my miseries."

Alice nodded. "I know how much it hurt to lose my father and mother. I can only imagine the pain of losing a husband."

"My sister, Hannah, shared the plan of salvation with me when I was just a little girl. It seemed so easy then to accept that Jesus would

182

come to earth and give His life to bring us into right accord with His Father—God. I remember Hannah telling me that Jesus loved me so much that He would rather die a horrible death on a cross than spend eternity without me." She smiled. "Isn't that a sweet way of putting it?"

Again Alice nodded, but this time she said nothing, as if sensing that Marty needed to get something off her chest.

"I asked Jesus to forgive me my sins, just like Hannah told me to do. I was a terrible liar at that time . . . I still have trouble with lies." She frowned. "Hannah told me lying was a sin just as much as killing was—that sin was sin in the eyes of God. All sin would keep us from Him."

Marty toyed with the belt of her robe. "I know the truth, and I've ignored it these last four years. Well, maybe not in whole, but in every way that mattered. I put a wall between me and God, and frankly . . . I'm tired, and I think it's time for that wall to come down."

Alice smiled and nodded. "Would you like to pray . . . with me?"

Marty felt a sense of relief and warmth of comfort pour over her. "I would like that very much."

Alice took hold of her hand. "I think God would like it, too."

Chapter 20

The weeks slipped by in a nightmarish sort of madness. Marty continued her work with the orphans, feeling that it offered her some semblance of order. But in truth, life in Denver verged on chaotic.

Daily the papers told of the financial collapse and all the problems that the state was bound to face. Women's suffrage was mentioned in the background, with some people claiming it would pass on the ballot come November. Marty had never concerned herself much with politics or the idea of voting, but given the state of the country, perhaps women did need to have a voice.

She considered the day laid out for her that June morning, and while the morning's activities were to her liking, the afternoon's were less favorable. She would first go to the orphanage; Marty loved getting to know the children, and today she planned to take pinafores for all the girls. Samson had already loaded them in the carriage. And, lest the boys feel left out, Marty had managed, with the help of Mrs. Landry, to secure a good number of donated shirts. She figured the sizes would be questionable, but since there hadn't been time to measure and sew for each boy, this would have to do. Those, too, awaited her in the carriage.

She ate breakfast alone that morning, as she often did of late. Jake had been forced to arrive at the bank earlier and earlier. Just as Jake had predicted, many banks were folding, though Mr. Morgan's banks seemed to be managing. Jake served faithfully to see that they continued to keep their place in the business world, but who could say where it would all end. Often he was gone until late at night, and Marty noticed that he'd begun to lose weight.

Soon after Jake had mentioned his concerns for both the banks and the silver market, Marty had written to Hannah. In the letter she had requested that Will sell her ranch. She told Hannah that she would prefer they buy the land so it would remain in the family.

Marty was anxious to hear what her sister would have to say, but feared Hannah would brush aside her concerns for the banks and her husband's job and instead chide Marty for not simply returning to Texas. But for Marty, Texas was still a thorn in her side.

The children at the orphanage welcomed Marty with open arms that morning. The kids had come to recognize her carriage and would eagerly await her arrival. Since it was summer, school was concluded for the time, and Marty had taken the opportunity to volunteer her time to read with them more often.

"Children, Mrs. Wythe has come with gifts this morning," Mrs. Staples announced. She was one of the caretakers of the children and although strict, was quite pleasant. "You will have a chance to receive a present later—if you listen well to the story and do not give Mrs. Wythe any trouble."

"What's the present?" one of the boys asked.

Mrs. Staples smiled. "Robert, you will have to wait with everyone else until after story time. Mrs. Wythe cannot spend all day with us. She has other appointments to tend to after this."

Marty waited until some of the other children posed their questions before pulling out her book. This signaled the children to take their seats on the floor around her. She waited patiently until everyone was positioned where they wanted to be.

"Good morning, children," she said, smiling. "I've brought a new book today, just as I promised. This one is called *The Adventures of Tom Sawyer*."

"Who's that?" a boy named Clyde asked.

"He's an energetic young boy who has many great adventures along the Mississippi River," Marty replied.

"Is he a big boy?" one of the little girls asked.

Someone else called out, "Does he swim in the river?"

Marty laughed. "Why don't I read the book, and then you'll see for yourself what kind of boy our Tom is and how he lives his life."

She opened the book and thumbed to the beginning. "Chapter one."

The children settled in and Marty, in her animated way, began to read.

After entertaining the children for over an hour—without a single one wanting to leave or do something else—Marty had to bid the children good-bye. She didn't want to leave. Leaving meant she would have to attend the luncheon being hosted by Mrs. Carmichael. The pretentious rich woman gave Marty a case of hives. Well, very nearly.

Samson waited faithfully to help her into the carriage. "There's lots of folks out today," he told her. "Might be late."

"That would be fine with me," Marty murmured. "I wouldn't even be attending if it wasn't important to keep up appearances."

"Yes'm."

She settled against the leather upholstery and sighed as Samson merged into traffic. Marty couldn't help but feel like she'd left a part of her heart behind. A half dozen of the youngest had given her hugs before she'd departed. It made her want to load them all into her carriage and take them home. The children gave meaning and purpose to her life, and she was starting to consider speaking to Jake about adoption.

Of course, the timing wasn't exactly ideal; it might be difficult to care for children in an uncertain future. Still, Marty knew that the children needed love and attention whether the economy fell apart or not. They couldn't comprehend the devaluation of silver or the insolvency of banks. Nor should they have to. Children were to be loved and protected, and Marty found herself stirred to do both.

Mrs. Carmichael's butler met Marty at the door with a curt nod. He ushered her to the garden, where tables had been laid for their luncheon. Mrs. Carmichael greeted Marty in her cool and composed manner. She always had a way of making Marty feel substandard, no matter the gathering.

"Mrs. Wythe." She peered at Marty as if she were something the cat had dragged in. "We feared you weren't coming."

"Mrs. Carmichael. It was kind of you to invite me." Marty smiled and nodded her head toward a group of society matrons seated around a table.

"Please have a seat. I believe we can finally get started."

Marty nodded and hurried to take an empty chair. She felt overly conspicuous with everyone else so carefully assembled. She had clearly committed a grave error in her late arrival. She had thought to offer an excuse and tell the women about the traffic, but they'd only want to know where she'd been. Marty knew they'd never approve of her work with the orphans.

"Ladies, as you know, our city is in peril," Mrs. Carmichael began. "Our very society has been altered in the wake of this new economic injustice." The women seemed fixed on her every word, while Marty wished they'd get to serving the food. She was starved.

"I wanted to host this luncheon in order to review the situation and to determine what, if anything, is to be managed by our number. I believe Mrs. Morgan would like to speak first."

Mrs. Morgan stood. "As you know, I am not one to frequent these occasions. However, I felt that the circumstances of our dear city necessitated my presence. Several of our former friends have found themselves completely stripped of their financial status. Thankfully, they have taken their families and left the city, so there is no need to feel uncomfortable in their presence."

Marty tried not to roll her eyes. These women—these so-called dear friends—were as fickle as they came.

"In addition to that, we are faced with a grave concern. There are a great many homeless arriving into Denver on a daily basis. As you know, a good number of the silver mines have closed, and this has put many men out of work and onto the streets. I believe this situation will only worsen as time goes on. In turn, it will cause many dangers for the people of our town."

Marty listened with only halfhearted interest. The women who inevitably attended these affairs bored her. Unlike some of the women she'd befriended in Texas, these women seemed to have no real understanding of or concern for humanity. They were wealthy and spoiled, and the only thing that seemed to concern them was remaining exactly so.

"I have spoken to Mr. Morgan on this matter and have suggested that these unemployed men be sent elsewhere to look for work. Obviously, the city cannot accommodate them, and their presence will only lead to a sullying of our environment."

Marty frowned and couldn't help but interject. "Where would you have them go? As I understand it, the entire country is struggling with this financial crisis." The women at her table looked aghast that she had dared to interrupt.

Mrs. Morgan smiled tolerantly. "That's true, but the rest of the country isn't my concern. Denver is. I would have them go anywhere but here."

The other women nodded and murmured their approval. Marty knew she should just keep quiet, but she couldn't help herself. "Seems rather selfish. What if we were to figure out ways to help those poor folks instead?"

"There are institutions and churches for such things, and the larger eastern cities would be better suited to see to their needs," Mrs. Morgan replied. "I'm sure that given your background, it's difficult to understand our position. However, people of means are the guardians of their surroundings. That instills in us a responsibility to oversee the welfare of our people and properties. Our men rely on us to practice wisdom in this matter, and this city is dependent upon such sacrifice."

"I understand that. And, given my background," Marty said in a somewhat sarcastic tone, "I know what it is to help the needy. I'm suggesting that rather than try to rid ourselves of them, we give assistance— perhaps offering shelter and teaching them new trades. After all, if their work as silver miners is over, they will need to be reeducated to work in another field."

There were gasps from several women, but Mrs. Morgan was patient. She gave Marty a look, however, that left the younger woman cold.

"It is not the responsibility of our society to provide such things."

"Maybe it should be," Marty replied. She could see she was alienating every woman at the luncheon, but she didn't care.

"Such matters are better left to the churches," Mrs. Morgan insisted.

"Are we not the church?" Marty could have heard a pin drop. "Does the Bible not show that it is our responsibility to care for the body? I'm not suggesting mere handouts. I'm not even saying that we need deplete all our wealth. I'm merely stating that sending these people away isn't going to solve anything."

"Well, you are entitled to your opinion, Mrs. Wythe. However, my husband would disagree with you. When I mentioned that these homeless and jobless people should be sent elsewhere, he agreed. He and some of our other good men are making plans to arrange for just that."

The other women nodded their approval. "Do tell," Mrs. Keystone called out. "Let us know how this is to be accomplished and what role we are to play."

Mrs. Morgan turned away from Marty to smile at her friend. "I suggested that these people be given a train ticket to leave the city. Let them go to friends and family elsewhere." She glanced back at Marty. "After all, we are not without heart. If they have no one to go to, then let us send them to one of the larger cities where help might be more readily available. Chicago, Kansas City, New York, and so on. All of those places would be better suited to assist the downtrodden than Denver."

"But Denver *is* a large city," Marty protested. "Maybe we should focus on making it a better city by incorporating ideas to help the downtrodden, as you put it."

"Mrs. Wythe, I believe your country manners might well be acceptable in some settings, such as the wilds of Texas," Mrs. Carmichael interjected. "But here, we rely on a better society—a way that affords us a protected life. I think perhaps you believe your Texas ways better than ours, and if that is the case, then might I suggest . . . you return to Texas."

"Hear, hear," many of the women called out. Mrs. Morgan nodded her agreement.

The women who had pretended to be Marty's friends had now made their true feelings clear. Marty stood and shook her head.

"I feel sorry for you. I thought you were women of means, but instead I find that you're simply mean women. You have, but you've no

189

desire to share. You know comfort and full bellies, but you would send others away hungry. I would remind you that it was Jesus himself who said that whatever we do unto the least of these . . . we do unto Him."

With that, she left the murmuring dissension and made her way back through the house and out the front door. Samson looked up in surprise as she stormed to the carriage.

"Get me out of here, please. Those women have seen the last of me."

He grinned, seeming happy for the news. "Yes'm."

★

Marty fretted the rest of the day, worrying about what Jake would say when he heard what she'd done. She feared she'd be the reason he'd fall from the good graces of his employer. She agonized over whether they'd be put out on the street for her behavior.

Perhaps I should send a letter of apology to Mrs. Morgan. I shouldn't have been so cantankerous, I suppose. I could have handled the situation with better judgment.

But the women had been so calloused and unfeeling. Maybe it was their fear of change that made them so, but to Marty, they bordered on cruel. She thought of all the orphans in the city—would the elite put them on a train and rid their precious Denver of their presence, as well?

I won't apologize. For once I did speak the truth, and they didn't want to hear it. They were much too worried about their town being dirtied with the poor and needy. And they call themselves Christians! How she seethed. It made her want to march right over to the Morgans and give them both a piece of her mind.

It was past eight before she heard the carriage arrive with Jake. She panicked. What if he was livid over her actions? What if she'd ruined everything? Marty began to pace in the sitting room. Jake cared for her, but he also cared about keeping his position at the bank.

It wasn't long before she heard Brighton greet her husband at the front door. There was a quick exchange that she couldn't quite hear, and then footsteps sounded on the hardwood floor outside the sitting room pocket doors.

The doors slid back, and Jake walked wearily into the room. Marty could see he was exhausted. She had arranged a very simple dinner for them that evening and hoped he wouldn't even feel the need to change his clothes.

"You look spent," she said. "Why don't you sit here and I'll rub your shoulders."

He shook his head. "I'd rather eat. I'm famished."

"I waited dinner for you. It's simple fare, so you needn't redress. It's just you and me and we could even take it upstairs if you'd like."

"No, that's all right. We can eat in the dining room, but I will take you up on the suggestion of not changing. I doubt I'd have the energy to return if I climbed those stairs."

She smiled. "I'll let Mrs. Landry know." She pulled the cord and waited until the housekeeper appeared. "Mrs. Landry, we'll have dinner in the dining room—right away, please."

The housekeeper smiled. "I figured as much. Well, not the exact location, but I had Cook get to it when I heard Mr. Wythe's carriage."

"Thank you. We'll be right in," Marty said. "Oh, and please have Brighton ready a hot bath for my husband. I'm sure he'll need to soak a bit after he eats." She looked to Jake, who smiled in spite of his exhaustion. "What are you smiling about?"

"You. The way you're taking care of me. Feels good. You're a real asset, Marty."

She thought of the way she'd acted at the garden party. "You might not be inclined to say so after you hear about my day," she said in as nonchalant a manner as she could manage. "But that can wait. Let's eat first."

Chapter 21

Jake awaited Marty's arrival at breakfast the next morning. She had told him of her falling-out with the society women, and he wanted to assure her that she needn't fear—at least not on his part—any repercussions. He couldn't care less about the social side of life. At one time it had seemed important, but financial crashes had a way of leveling the playing field, and Jake was beginning to see what a fool he'd been to even worry about such matters. Just looking back on the choices he'd made to please Morgan almost made him feel sick.

It seems all my life I've been trying to please someone rather than figure out what God desired for me in the first place.

"I didn't expect to find you still here," Marty said as she entered the dining room. "I was so glad you sent Alice for me."

"I thought you deserved to see your husband in a rested state." He held out her chair and helped seat her at the table. "Not only that, but I wanted to reassure you."

Marty's expression changed to one of confusion. "Reassure me?"

"Marty, I haven't wanted to say anything, but I think our days in Denver are numbered anyway. Your falling-out with Mrs. Morgan and the other great ladies of society may simply coincide with a progression of changes that cannot be stopped."

"What do you mean?"

"I mean that I feel confident, given the problems going on in the country, that it will only be a matter of time until our bank collapses. There are all manner of problems at our institution, and I cannot begin to figure them all out. I can say without a doubt, however, that changes are upon us."

"It can't be that bad," Marty declared. She shook her head when Brighton offered to pour her a cup of coffee. He retreated to Jake's side of the table and refilled his cup instead.

"I'm afraid it is. What you experienced at the garden party is just the tip of the iceberg, I'm afraid. The few ladies that were mentioned as having left the city with their families are only the start of what may well become a mass exodus."

"But things aren't any better anywhere else, are they? I mean, my sister has even talked about how awful things are in Texas. Cotton prices have dropped so low that farmers aren't even considering replanting another crop."

"I know, but it would seem that folks of means are tightening their belts just as we are. Instead of having three or four homes at their disposal, they're consolidating and selling off some of their holdings and real estate. At the very least they are closing the houses in an effort to save money. I heard Mr. Morgan speak of selling his seaside place in California. He may move back east if he finds it necessary to close down the banks here. All I'm saying is that I didn't want you to fret over what happened with the ladies. You aren't to blame. You've a kind heart, Marty. That's something most of them can't understand."

"And you believe we'll need to move, as well?"

Jake nodded. "I never wanted this house in the first place. For now, Mr. Morgan told me to sit tight. He's not even requiring I make the mortgage payment on it since he's had to cut back on my salary."

"I didn't know that he'd done that," Marty said, the worry in her tone obvious.

"I didn't want to scare you."

"What will we do if you lose your position?" she asked.

He shook his head. "I don't know. I do know, however, that there's little we can accomplish by being afraid. We'll take this one step at a time."

Marty looked unconvinced but said nothing more on the subject. They made small talk over a light breakfast of eggs and toast, but Jake could tell her heart wasn't in it. He finally pushed back from the table.

"I'd best get down to the bank." He moved to where Marty sat and gave her a kiss on the cheek. In the past he'd only done this for show, but now he felt his heart beat a little faster at the mere touch of his lips to her face.

"Will you be late?" she asked. Her gaze lifted to meet his.

"Probably. But don't worry about me, Marty. You need to take care of yourself."

He rode in silence to the bank and arrived twenty minutes before the doors were to be opened to the public. Jake tensed at the sight of Mr. Morgan's fine carriage. There was another carriage parked in front of Morgan's, and Jake guessed it belonged to Mr. Keystone.

Making his way into the bank, Jake spotted the men waiting for him in his office. "Good morning, gentlemen," he said, walking to his desk. "Did we have a meeting this morning?"

"No," Morgan replied. "But we need one. I've been going over the papers you sent me. It would appear there are problems with some of the numbers being duplicated, just as you stated."

Jake felt a sense of relief. He'd almost worried that the men were there because of what Marty had said and done at the garden party. "Yes, it's clear that there are duplicated numbers and a lack of inventory to back up what's been declared."

Morgan smiled and lit a cigar. "Well, I know we'll get to the bottom of it in time. I just wanted to tell you that you've done a fine job here. I'm going to turn it all over to Mr. Keystone, and he will take care of it."

"I'm glad to hear that. I've enough on my agenda to keep me busy. Is there any other news out of Washington?" Jake asked.

"Not per se," Morgan replied. "Although I read this morning that Lizzie Borden will most likely be acquitted of murdering her parents."

Jake had read about the Massachusetts woman who had been accused of killing her parents with an ax. He nodded but had no desire to discuss it. "I thought maybe something related to the economy and the well-being of the American people."

Morgan gave a laugh. "Oh, there is news out of Washington, but it's from last month. However, it continues to amuse me. It would seem the Supreme Court has finally ruled that a tomato is a vegetable."

"Well, that's a relief," Keystone said sarcastically. "At least now waiters will know the proper place setting for it." He and Morgan roared with laughter, and even Jake couldn't help but chuckle. The world was falling down around them, but at least they now knew that a tomato was officially a vegetable. And because the Supreme Court had declared it such—it must be so.

★

"Mrs. Wythe?" a little boy said in a questioning tone.

Marty looked to her left and found the little waif looking at her with great expectation. "What is it, Wyatt?"

"Do you have children of your own?"

The seven-year-old's question threw her for a moment. Marty finally shook her head. By now several other children had gathered at her side. "No, I don't have any . . . yet."

"Maybe I could be your little boy." His eyes were filled with hope, and it made Marty want to snatch him up and pledge her undying love.

"Well, right now all of you are my children," Marty replied. "I so enjoy getting to be with you and share our stories together."

"But it ain't the same as havin' a real ma and pa," one of the older boys stated.

Marty caught his look. She saw betrayal and hurt in his eyes. This was a child who had been gravely wounded. "You're Adam, aren't you?" The boy nodded. Marty wondered how best to answer the lad. "You know, when I was a newborn baby my mother died. My father died when I was five, and my sister raised me. I know it's not the same as having to live in an orphanage, but I think it's important to find love wherever we are."

"Do you love us?" a little girl Marty knew as Nettie asked.

Marty smiled. "I do indeed. I love each and every one of you. You make my day brighter."

"So couldn't you 'dopt us?" Wyatt asked.

How she wanted to tell him yes. She knew these children were afraid of their future. They only had the employees of the orphanage to show them affection and love. She hated that she couldn't just tell them to line up—that she'd take them all.

"Children, it's time for lunch," Mrs. Staples called from the door. Most of the children made a mad dash for the dining room.

Wyatt gave Marty one last hopeful look, then ran after his friends. Marty knew that as long as she lived, she would never forget that face.

"Are you all right, Mrs. Wythe?" Mrs. Staples asked.

Marty looked up and met the woman's questioning gaze. "I suppose so. I . . . well . . . what are the chances these children will find homes?"

Mrs. Staples shook her head. "Not good. Especially now. The wealthy have never been inclined to take in poor children—except as servants, of course. The families who would be likely to adopt are now doing without daily provisions for themselves. So many are out of work and can't feed the folks already reliant upon them. And of course the poor are the ones who brought us most of these youngsters to begin with. They found themselves unable to raise children even when the economy was booming."

The woman gave a sigh. "I'm afraid in the very near future, most of the older children will simply be put out from the orphanage in order to have enough money to tend to the younger ones."

"Put out . . . where?"

"On the streets." Mrs. Staples shook her head again. "It isn't what any of us want, but there aren't very many options. We encourage the children to seek out the churches for help. We encourage them to find places where they can work for room and board. Sadly, it's only going to get worse before it gets better." She glanced over her shoulder and then back to Marty. "I'd best get in there. Miss Hayden has a difficult time handling the older boys."

Marty let the woman go without another comment. Her heart ached at the thought of Adam being turned out of the orphanage. She had no idea what age classified a child as "older," but surely it wouldn't be that long before Adam would be on that list.

Gathering her things, Marty walked to Mr. Brentwood's office and knocked on the door.

"Come in," he called, and Marty opened the door.

"I was about to leave but wondered if I could speak to you."

"Of course," he replied, standing. "Won't you have a seat?"

"Thank you. I heard today that you will have to release some of the older orphans."

He frowned. "I'm sorry to say that is true. Given that our support comes from private funds and donations, I'm afraid we can no longer afford to keep everyone. In order to see to it that the little ones have a minimal amount of care, we have no choice."

"I wonder if you could delay long enough for me to contact my sister in Texas. She and her husband own a ranch. They might be able to provide work for some of the children. I know you said that there were several who wanted to work with cattle."

He looked at her for a moment and rubbed his chin. "How long would this delay take?"

"Only as long as it takes to get a telegraph off to Texas and receive an answer," Marty replied. "A letter would be better, as I could explain in more detail, but I think I can get my sister to understand the situation with a telegram."

He nodded. "I don't know why it couldn't wait a day or two—maybe a week at most. We haven't yet spoken to the children."

"Good," Marty said, getting to her feet. "Don't. I will check with my sister and see what she can offer. Perhaps there will be other ranches in the area who can take on a boy or two."

Mr. Brentwood stood. "Mrs. Wythe, you are a saint. I know that God sent you to us in our hour of need. No one else has posed any kind of solution for helping these children—just you."

"Well, I don't know how much of a solution it will prove to be, but I'll do what I can."

As she made her way to her carriage, a heaviness settled on her heart. Marty wanted to make life better for the children, but she was just one woman. What could she do? Save Adam? Wyatt? But what of the others? John and Tim were in their teens, nearly adults. Nettie and Willen were each twelve. Would that be enough to send them from the safety of the orphanage? There didn't seem to be any reasonable answer. Even if Hannah and Will could take a good number of them—there were hundreds left.

"Samson, I need to stop by a telegraph office."

"Yes'm." He helped her into the carriage and by the time Marty had settled in, Samson had the horses in motion.

She mentally composed the message she would send. *Numerous orphans to be turned out on the street. Can you take some for ranch work? Need answer immediately. More to follow in letter.*

With the telegram on its way, Marty felt that she had done at least a small thing for the welfare of the orphans. Of course, Hannah and Will might say no. But she doubted it. They were just as concerned about assisting the helpless as she was. Maybe even more. It saddened her to imagine children trying to live on their own, begging passersby for food.

Upon arriving home, Samson helped Marty from the carriage. He beamed a smile, but it didn't change Marty's mood.

"Thank you, Samson." She didn't even try to hide her sorrow.

"Them children are mighty lucky to have you come there to read to 'em," Samson said. "Mighty lucky."

Marty wanted to contradict him, but thought better of it. Samson was just trying to help. She approached the front door, and Brighton, ever vigilant, opened it before she could even reach the handle.

"You have company, Mrs. Wythe."

"Company?" She looked at the grandfather clock. "I don't recall having extended an invitation."

"No, madam. Mrs. Davies, the dressmaker, arrived unexpectedly. I put her in the formal sitting room."

Marty nodded. "Thank you, Brighton."

She made her way to Mrs. Davies and could see that the woman looked quite upset. "Mrs. Davies, what a pleasant surprise."

As Marty got closer, she could see the woman had been crying. "Whatever is wrong?" she asked.

"Mrs. Wythe, I'm not usually one to gossip, but truth be told I don't see it as such since it involves you."

Marty's eyes narrowed. "What involves me?"

Mrs. Davies dabbed her eyes with a handkerchief. "The reason I'm here."

Taking a seat, Marty hoped her silence would encourage the woman to continue. It was obvious that the older woman didn't like what she had come to say.

"It would seem that certain . . . ladies . . . have informed me that they will no longer bring me their business . . . if . . . if . . . I'm also doing business . . ." She couldn't seem to finish the sentence.

Marty immediately understood. It was her punishment for speaking out at the garden party. "If you're also doing business with me? Is that it?"

Mrs. Davies broke into tears anew. "I didn't know what else to do. I didn't want to offend you, nor did I want to lose their patronage. There are so many of them . . . and . . . I need the income."

"Don't worry," Marty said, hoping to ease the woman's conscience. "I have no need for new gowns anyway." She smiled. "Would you like refreshments? I could have tea brought in or perhaps a small lunch?"

"No." Mrs. Davies got to her feet. "I only stopped by to tell you in person. I felt it was only right. You've been a wonderful customer and a good woman. You've always treated my staff so well. I'm sorry that it's come to this."

"Please don't fret over it, Mrs. Davies. Denver's well-to-do have spoken, and we mustn't defy them." She gave a harsh laugh. "Otherwise, we'll both pay for our indiscretion instead of just me."

★

That evening Marty ate alone in her room. She thought about the troubling day and all she had encountered. The children were still uppermost on her mind, and she wished she would hear back from Hannah. Then a thought came. Even if Hannah and Will would take them, how would she get them to Texas?

Perhaps Mrs. Morgan could give them all a free train ticket. She calmed a bit. *Why not? Why not get the woman to put her money behind her mouth. She's so anxious that the poor should leave the state—so let her pay to transport the orphans.*

Alice entered the room as silent as a mouse. She came to collect Marty's tray, but stopped. "You've hardly eaten anything. Would you like me to leave it?"

"No. I'm not hungry. It's been a difficult week." She sighed. "You see, I have been ejected from the elite society of Denver's wealthy matrons. I said some things the other day when we were together, and it didn't set well."

"And that troubles you?"

"No, not exactly. I think what troubles me is that for the longest time, I actually thought I could be happy in their world. Now I know better. They don't even approve of my work at the orphanage."

"Of course not. They don't understand it."

Marty nodded. "I suppose that's true enough, but they should. What's so hard to understand about children needing someone to love them?"

"For some people," Alice replied, "love is the one thing they never understand."

Chapter 22

"You've had a ranch all this time, and you didn't tell me?" Jake questioned. "How could you do this? How could you betray my trust like this?"

Marty felt her blood run cold. "I couldn't tell you. You would have insisted we move there, and I didn't want to be a rancher's wife. Thomas was killed working with cattle—do you suppose I want to be a widow a second time?"

"You lied to me. You are nothing but a lying, scheming woman. I've nothing more to say to you. You ruined my life, Marty. Ruined it and all my dreams." Jake turned to leave.

Marty called after him, begging him to come back. "Please don't leave me—I love you! I can't lose another husband." Then all at once the scene began to shift and Jake was in the middle of a cattle pen—with an angry bull charging at him.

"No!" she screamed over and over. "No, Jake—watch out!"

"Marty, wake up! Marty!"

She opened her eyes and realized it had all just been a nightmare. Jake sat beside her on the bed, his hand casually resting on her shoulder. Without thinking, Marty threw herself into his arms. She was so glad to see that he was there—that nothing had changed. He was safe and her secret was, too.

Sobbing, Marty clung to Jake as though she might be pulled back into the dream should he let go. She drenched his bare chest with her tears.

"It's all right, Marty. You're safe and nothing can hurt you," he whispered. Stroking her hair, he held her close. "It was just a bad dream. Nobody can harm you. I won't let them."

Marty felt terrible. The entire nightmare was because she'd refused to tell Jake the truth about the ranch. It was time to just face her demons. She pulled back just a bit. "Oh, Jake. I . . . I . . . should tell you . . ."

"Shhh, there's no need to go relivin' the dream. You just take it easy and get yourself calmed down." His lazy drawl filled the night air and her heart.

Jake hadn't bothered to turn the lights on, and Marty couldn't see the details of his face, but she felt the wonderful warmth of his arms about her. Cheek against his chest, Marty focused on the steady beat of his heart. It comforted her. She could remember a time so long ago when she had laid her head upon Thomas's chest and listened to his heartbeat.

I cannot lose another husband. The thought was the same as the words she'd spoken in the dream. The idea of Jake dying sent a shiver through her. The trembling only caused Jake to tighten his hold on her.

Marty calmed but refused to leave his embrace. She loved this man. She'd told him so in her dream, and now she could admit to herself that it was true. She loved him most dearly, but her lies stood between them. She felt tears come anew. How could she ever make this right?

"I figure we'll be all right, Marty. No matter what happens. I'll take good care of you. Whatever happens, we have each other."

Marty raised her head again. She could feel Jake's warm breath against her face and knew his lips were only a few inches away. She ached for him to kiss her. "I'm glad we have each other," she whispered, wanting to speak of her love. Instead, she could only bring herself to add, "I need you."

Jake said nothing for a moment, and Marty couldn't help but worry she'd said the wrong thing. He hadn't pulled away, but neither had he replied. Could it be that her words had made him rethink his feelings for her?

She felt his hand at the back of her head before realizing that he was guiding her into a gentle kiss. Their lips met and Marty wanted the moment to go on forever. Then as quickly as it had started, Jake put an end to it. He dropped his hold on her and got to his feet.

"I'm sorry, Marty. I'm so sorry."

"Don't . . . don't . . . be."

"It wasn't right. You've been so good to honor our arrangement. You've demanded nothing of me, and you've been content to do all that I've asked of you—and this is how I reward you. I'm such a dolt. I was never the kind of man to take advantage of a woman's emotions, yet here I am. Please forgive me."

He stalked from the room, leaving Marty stunned. She wanted to call to him—beg him to return—but something told her it would do little good. She heard him slam her bedroom door closed behind him, then the dressing room doors and the one to his own bedroom followed in rapid pace.

A part of her wanted to run after him—tell him that he'd done nothing wrong. That she loved him and wanted to be a real wife to him. Another part warned her that it would only serve to ruin everything. They had both gone into this marriage of convenience knowing the truth—at least most of the truth.

I should have told him about the ranch, and every day that goes by makes it just that much harder to be honest. Oh, God, please help me. I don't know what to say or do to make this right. I keep thinking if only Hannah will just write to tell me the ranch has been sold or that William has reclaimed it, then it wouldn't be so bad.

But wouldn't that just be another lie?

She pounded her fists against her pillow. *Why do I always choose a lie to get me out of trouble?*

Lies had always come easily to her, and if not lies, then omissions of truth or exaggerations. These had always been Marty's downfall. She could remember Hannah praying that she not give in to such temptation, but Marty didn't see it as a truly sinful thing. At least not until now. Now she could see the full implications of this sin. She could see the potential damage and pain it would cause.

"I want to do the right thing," she said. "I want to tell Jake the truth." She buried her face in the pillow. *Please, God, show me what's right and give me the strength to do it.*

---★---

Jake leaned out his open bedroom window and drew in deep breaths of night air. How could he have been so stupid? He should never have gone to Marty's room. He should have just left well enough alone.

"But she was scared. She was screaming and crying out. What kind of husband would I be to ignore that?"

The kind of husband I signed on to be.

He wrestled with his conscience. He should never have married Marty. It wasn't right that they had pledged faithfulness to each other and to God. Jake had even promised to love Marty. Was this his punishment for such blasphemy?

"God, I never meant for this to happen. I never meant to lie to you. It seemed reasonable to marry and pledge to love and honor. Without a real wedding it didn't seem wrong—it felt like just a bunch of words." He pulled back into his room and buried his face in his hands.

He tried to figure out how to fix the mess he'd made. It would be best to just come clean and tell Marty the truth. Tell her that he'd fallen in love with her, that he wanted her to be his wife for real. If he just told her the truth, they could work through it. She might get angry about it, but Jake could promise to just love her from afar. Love her until she was ready to love him back.

"But what if that never comes?"

He lifted his face and stared across the darkened room. What good was any of this now? He'd thought to make a new life. Thought he could actually endure this life and be happy until he had enough money to return to Texas. Now, even Texas seemed a foolish desire compared to wanting Marty to return his love.

---★---

By six in the morning, dawn was starting to brighten the horizon and Marty gave up trying to sleep. She could still smell Jake's cologne in her hair. She could still feel his arms around her. The rest of the night she had done battle with her conscience, and now she was completely exhausted. No answers offered comfort.

"If I tell him the truth," she whispered, "he will never come to care for me. I would be effectually ending our marriage."

The truth shall make you free.

The Bible verse seemed to ring like a bell in the air. It was one Hannah had quoted to her on many occasions. That and the commandment about not bearing false witness.

"But I'm so afraid." She looked toward the ceiling as if she might see the face of God in the ornate plaster. "I'm afraid that you aren't listening. I'm afraid I've strayed too far and you can't . . . won't reach out to me."

The truth shall make you free.

Ye shall know the truth, and the truth shall make you free.

Marty remembered that this was the day Alice and the others would be having their Bible study in the kitchen. She could join them and ask them to pray for her. *I'm not strong enough to face this on my own.*

Pulling on her robe, Marty wondered if the women would be offended by her presence. After all, she was the mistress of the house. Maybe they wouldn't want her to be a part of their gathering.

She paused at the door and swallowed hard. What if they refused to let her join them? What would she do?

None of her worries stopped her, however. Marty knew she needed someone to reassure her—to help her with the truth. She made her way down the back stairs, not even trying to be quiet. When she entered the kitchen, Mrs. Standish, Mrs. Landry, and Alice were all anticipating her entry.

"Are you all right, Mrs. Wythe?" Mrs. Landry asked. "Are you ill?"

Marty shook her head. "I'm just . . . I'm . . ." She paused to gather her courage. "I wonder if I might join you. I know you don't approve of the help mingling with their employers, Mrs. Landry, but we are all equal in the sight of the Lord."

Alice smiled. "Of course we are, and of course you can join us. We're studying the life of Abraham."

205

Mrs. Landry got up and retrieved another chair. "Sit right here. You are quite right—spiritually we are equal."

The housekeeper sounded hesitant, but Marty sank into the ladder-back chair with a sigh. "Thank you. You don't know what this means to me. I've been tossing all night."

"Can you speak to what is troubling your heart?" Mrs. Standish asked.

Not knowing how much to say, Marty shrugged. "Everything. The world is in such a fix right now, and so am I."

"Then perhaps we should spend time in prayer," Mrs. Landry suggested.

Alice nodded. "I think that's the perfect place to start."

★

With the afternoon post came Marty's answer to prayer. A letter from Hannah informed Marty that William was happy to take back the ranch. He would weigh out the situation—the assets would be assessed, and he would send her a fair price for the entire property.

"Well, that's that," Marty said, feeling a little of the pressure ease from her heart. "I have no need to ever return to Texas, and if Jake insists we leave Denver, then I will suggest we look elsewhere for our new home. I can mention the ranch sometime if it comes up and explain that the land reverted to Will. I'll tell Hannah not to mention otherwise." No, that would never do. Hannah would see that as evading the truth.

Must I tell him? Must I admit to having the ranch all this time? He'll hate me, just like in the dream. Because the truth is that I have wronged him. I have lied and kept from him the only thing in life he really wants.

She caught a glimpse of herself in the foyer mirror. Marty thought she looked tired—not even the least bit pretty. The lies and worries had taken their toll. She wished fervently she could start anew . . . and perhaps that's exactly what was happening. Maybe she could just explain to Jake that she had once owned land and now it was held by her brother-in-law. Maybe if Jake demanded they return to Texas, he could go as a banker or bookkeeper. That was a nice safe job. But could she live again in Texas?

It's not Texas, she told herself. It's the ranch and the dangers there. It's all the terrible things that happen. She remembered her brother and

Will suffering broken bones and nearly losing their lives in multiple incidents. They had lost ranch hands to kicking horses, stampeding cattle, and even one to snakebite. Life on a ranch was an unforgiving world. She could never risk living—and loving someone—in such a place.

Why did I even think of sending children there? As if in answer to her thoughts, a knock sounded at the front door. Disregarding Brighton's duties, Marty opened it to find a young man.

"Telegram for Mrs. Martha Wythe."

"That's me." Marty pulled some coins from her chatelaine bag and handed them to the boy. "Thank you."

The boy handed her the telegram, then turned to run back down the porch steps. Marty immediately opened the reply from her sister.

Happy to have them. Send as soon as you like. Look forward to hearing more. Hannah.

There it was. Only now Marty felt guilty. What if she was only sending these children to their deaths? She heaved a sigh. Leaving them to face an uncertain life here was no better. At least under Hannah and Will's care they wouldn't go hungry.

"Madam, I heard someone at the door," Brighton said.

Marty hid the telegram behind her back and smiled. "It was nothing."

She closed the door and made her way to the kitchen, leaving Brighton to stare after her. She knew most likely he hadn't believed her, but his manners wouldn't allow him to challenge her.

Marty checked for Mrs. Standish. Seeing that the cook had gone out back to the small herb garden, Marty hastily tossed the letter and telegram from Hannah into the stove and watched a moment while they burned. She couldn't risk keeping either one. If Jake saw the telegram he'd know that things were apparently going well enough for Hannah and Will that they could take on a bunch of children. And if he saw the letter . . . well . . . he mustn't ever see the letter.

When the papers were nothing more than ash, Marty closed the door and stepped back from the stove. Just then, Mrs. Standish returned and upon seeing Marty held a wide smile.

"You don't look nearly so tired as you did this morning. I hope you had a bit of a rest."

"I did," Marty replied. "Now I find myself in need of tea. I just thought I would make it myself rather than disturb you or Mrs. Landry."

"Nonsense. 'Tis my job," the older woman declared. "You go right on to your sitting room, and I'll bring you a good hot cup in three shakes of a lamb's tail."

Marty smiled. "I've seen lambs shake their tails, Mrs. Standish, and it's quite speedy. You needn't rush that much."

The woman chuckled, and Marty made her way to the sitting room she'd come to love. But upon entering, she was surprised to come upon her butler and housekeeper in each other's arms.

"I'm so . . . sorry," Marty declared. "I was only passing through."

"Nonsense, Mrs. Wythe," Brighton replied, dropping his hold on the older woman. "Mrs. Landry learned this morning that her sister has died."

Mrs. Landry looked up, and her tear-stained face revealed her grief. Marty embraced her. "I'm so sorry. What happened?"

"She's been ill for some time." Mrs. Landry sniffed and stepped away. "Even so, it comes as a shock."

"Of course it would," Marty agreed. "I want you to take the rest of the day and weekend off to rest. Where does your sister live? Will you need time to travel there for the funeral?"

"No. She lived in Michigan. I won't be attending the funeral. It's too far and too much expense."

"I'm certain that we can find the funds if you desire to be there," Marty insisted.

"No. I'd rather remain here. We weren't all that close . . . it's just . . . well, I thought we'd have time to settle our past."

"I'm sorry, Mrs. Landry. I didn't realize there were problems."

The housekeeper nodded. "That's why Mr. Brighton was so good to console me. I felt I had failed as a good Christian woman to help my sister see the truth about God. She called herself an atheist, and we had many a fight over it. Funny, isn't it, that something as wondrous as God's love should cause families to fight?"

It was difficult to see the pain in the woman's eyes and not feel moved. Marty reached out and touched her housekeeper's shoulder. "I still want you to take some time to yourself. I want you to know how very sorry I am, but that I'm certain you planted seeds in the life of your sister. Maybe one of them took root. You can never tell."

Mrs. Landry nodded. "It's my fondest wish that she would have accepted the Lord. I don't know why people reject Him—the truth seems so evident to me."

Marty knew why people rejected Him. From her own personal experience, she knew that often they did so for no other reason than to harden their hearts from the possibility of more pain in their life.

She looked to Brighton and smiled. "I'm so glad you were here to comfort Mrs. Landry. She's fortunate to have a good friend like you."

Brighton flushed red and looked away. "Thank you, madam."

Marty couldn't help but think of Jake holding her in the night. That comfort had meant more to her than anything he could have bought her or done for her. The troubles of the world were upon them, but in his arms she felt completely safe—at ease. Somehow, she had to convince him that this was where she belonged.

Chapter 23

Alice hated waiting outside alone for Mrs. Landry, but neither did she want to frighten or upset the children inside the church. She'd been the recipient of too many ugly comments about her face; she couldn't bear to see the repulsion and hear the whispers from the little ones. Mrs. Landry had scoffed and insisted Alice come inside, but Alice simply shook her head.

"I'll take this bundle of cookies in and then come back for yours," Mrs. Landry said in exasperation. They'd baked cookies for the children's fair that the church was sponsoring, and Mrs. Landry had needed Alice to help carry the cookies because the carriage was in use. Samson had taken Mrs. Wythe to the orphanage.

A few minutes later, Mrs. Landry returned and took the bundle from Alice. "I don't know why you worry so much about your face. That scar isn't as noticeable as you think."

She touched the scar on her cheek and tried to forget how a child had once screamed in terror at her face. Of course, that had not been long after the attack, when Alice was barely up and around the hospital grounds. The scar didn't look as bad now as it had then, but it was still puckerish and very evident.

"With adults it's not so bad, but it scares the children," Alice whispered.

Mrs. Landry gave a heavy sigh. "Very well. I'll try to hurry, but I have to speak with the pastor." The older woman disappeared inside the church, leaving Alice alone once again.

Pacing the small walkway, Alice glanced at the door of the church and tried to calm her nerves. It was broad daylight and no one would—

"Well, I see you're finally alone."

She whirled around to find the man she feared most in the world. "What do you want?" She moved toward the church, but the man reached out and held her fast.

Smith gripped her arm in a painful manner. "You know very well what I want."

"I told you before and I'm telling you now: I don't know anything about a bank envelope. I told you that. I had very little left me after I got out of the hospital. My friends had to sell off our things to pay for my hospital bills and Father's funeral." She pulled against his hold. "Not only that, but you and your thugs frightened them so much, they left town without a chance to even tell me all that had transpired while I'd been in the hospital."

"They were only questioned about the envelope. If they were afraid, that was their problem."

"No, it was your fault. Your friends threatened them. They told me how awful it was."

He shook his head. "Not nearly as awful as it's gonna get if I don't get that envelope." Alice tried again to move away from him.

"You're a fool if you think you can escape me." He grinned, forcing her closer. "That scar does mar your face, but it doesn't steal all your beauty. I might have use for you. I have gals uglier than you making me a good living."

"Leave me alone!" Alice pulled even harder.

Smith slapped her across the face, and Alice fell backward from the blow and crumpled onto the ground. She had hoped he would leave her there, but instead he reached down and yanked her back to her feet.

"That's just a sample of the kind of pain I can cause you. You have something that belongs to me, and I intend to have it back. I'm watching you all the time, Miss Chesterfield. There's no place you can hide and nothing you can do to escape my reach." He let go his hold. "Even if you think you can. Now, I suggest you write a letter to your friends and find out what they did with your father's personal papers. That ain't something you can sell."

Alice frowned. She'd not really given that much thought in the aftermath of the attack. Her father hadn't had many personal business dealings, and he wasn't one for corresponding with anyone. Alice did recall there were a few personal things he kept in a box—among them her mother's wedding ring, which she had left behind. He'd once showed it to Alice and told her it was a reminder to him of how the devil can appear as an angel to fool man. Alice had never thought about what might have happened to that box.

"It's been nearly a year. I honestly have no memory of him keeping any personal papers." Alice was silent a moment. "I suppose there might have been things that wouldn't have been sold. . . ." She shook her head and let the words trail off.

The man loosened his hold, to her surprise. "Write to your friends. I'll be in touch." He hurried down the road and had already turned a corner by the time Mrs. Landry appeared.

"They were ever so glad for the refreshments. Thank you for helping me get them here." She stopped and looked at Alice oddly. "What happened?"

Alice shook her head and struggled to keep her hand from covering the cheek where Smith had hit her. "What are you talking about?"

"Your cheek, it's red—and there are grass stains on the sleeve of your blouse."

She swallowed hard. "I fell, that's all."

"Alice, don't lie to me. You have the perfect imprint of a hand on your face."

Alice lowered her gaze. "That Mr. Smith showed up."

"Here? Why didn't you scream for help?"

"I was too surprised. I never imagined anyone would attack me outside a church in the middle of the day."

Mrs. Landry frowned. "We must tell Mr. and Mrs. Wythe immediately. That man is a menace."

Alice nodded and felt her every hope dissolve.

212

★

"You must know this is an answer to prayer, Mrs. Wythe." Mr. Brentwood slapped his hands atop his desk. "An answer to prayer."

"My sister and her husband are quite generous. I know they will see that the children are well provided for. There may be other ranchers and farmers in the area who could take a few on, as well. I will write to her and let her know your situation. There are some very good people in our circle of friends."

He let out a heavy sigh. "This has weighed so heavily on my heart. I immediately went to prayer and fasting after you mentioned the possibility. So now my question is, how do we arrange for their travel?"

Marty smiled. "I've already thought of that. You see, I happen to know that Mrs. Morgan has petitioned her husband and his friends to provide free rail passage to the poor in order to rid our precious city of their presence. She is no longer receiving me, because of my response to her ideas."

Mr. Brentwood frowned. "I am sorry, Mrs. Wythe. I don't see how this will help us."

"She won't see me, but she would no doubt see you. I think you have only to go to her and request train passage for the orphans. Tell her you thought you would have to put these children on the streets, but instead you have found a location for them in Texas—if only you can transport them there."

He smiled. "I think I understand. She would rather get her husband to pay the passage than to have additional homeless milling about her fair city."

Marty nodded. "Exactly."

"I don't think that will be a problem," Brentwood replied. "I will go and see her this afternoon. I won't ask for an appointment ahead of time, lest she refuse me. I'll simply show up and explain our plight."

"I think that's best." Marty felt a deep sense of satisfaction. "If my time spent with her has taught me anything, it's that surprise will work to your advantage. When anything threatens their way of life, they can't help but respond quickly."

———————————— ★ ————————————

Jake thought so often of Marty and their kiss that he had to refigure a column of numbers four times to get it right. Everything balanced. The money that had been missing, though comparatively small, was now all accounted for.

When Jake had repeatedly mentioned the missing money to Mr. Morgan, the bank owner had been unconcerned. And now that it appeared the matter had resolved itself, Morgan felt certain the money had just been mislaid or accounted improperly. At least that's what he'd told Jake earlier that morning.

Still uncomfortable about the matter, Jake closed the ledger and stretched. He felt weariness settle over him. He thought again of Marty and the way she'd felt in his arms.

He grinned. She didn't seem to hate the kiss so much herself. Maybe, just maybe, she had wanted it as much as he had. After all, she did call out to him and ask him not to leave.

But that could just have been the fact that she was afraid. Something had caused her great worry in her sleep.

"Sir, Mr. Keystone is here to see you," Arnold announced.

Jake nodded and straightened his tie. "Send him in."

Arnold gave a nod and left the doorway. Keystone quickly entered and Jake got to his feet. "Mr. Keystone, this is an unexpected surprise."

"Yes, well, it would seem a most necessary one." He seemed bothered by something, so Jake only motioned to the chair and said nothing more.

Taking the seat, Keystone wasted no time. "Our funds are short. The banks are not doing at all well here in Colorado. We held a board meeting just a short time ago. I'm here to report on our decision."

"Decision about what?" Jake could only pray they hadn't decided to close the bank.

"We're going to start refusing to cash depositors' checks. Instead, we will issue them bank checks that they can use in lieu of money."

"Won't that signal a problem and cause a run on the bank?" Jake asked.

"Not if it's handled properly," Keystone replied. "We must assure

214

the depositor that this is merely a safety precaution and point out that we've remained solvent while other banks have collapsed—but only because of implementing such measures. If we focus on the fact that their money is still safely available to them in this form, I believe they'll understand."

Jake was less inclined to think so. "I've seen these people daily," he began. "I'm not convinced it will work. After all, we're talking about the life savings of some of these folks."

"I'm well aware of that, Wythe," Keystone said, clearly irritated. "It's a sound measure and we're not the only bank doing this. If folks want to be able to access their funds, they'll do it through a bank check or not at all."

"And what of the larger depositors? The businesses?"

"It will work well for everyone. You'll see. We have this all figured out. I only stopped here to let you know what was decided. You needn't approve or disapprove. It's done."

Jake nodded. "Well, I thank you for letting me know."

"Honestly, Wythe, the customers will be glad just to have the ability to purchase goods and pay their mortgages. You'll see. This is the only way it can work right now."

"I suppose so." Jake thought to change the subject. "What of the gold certificates being duplicated? Did you get to the bottom of that?"

"I'm still working on it," he assured Jake. "It won't be an easy matter to resolve. After all, each of the gold certificates is backed by gold marked with the same identifying number. With the banking system in the mess it is now, we will be hard-pressed to get anywhere with this investigation for some time. It falls low on the priorities we have."

"And if those people come to get their gold?"

"That's exactly why we are resolving matters this way with the bank checks. There's obviously been a moratorium placed on cashing out for gold. Hopefully the bank checks will ease the worries of those who had thought to redeem their silver certificates."

"I hope you're right," Jake said, still uncertain it would satisfy the customers.

On his way home from work that night he very nearly had Samson stop by the florist's shop. Though he wanted to bring Marty flowers again, he put aside the idea, when considering the cost. He knew they would have to be very careful with their limited funds. He was thankful that Morgan continued to waive their mortgage payments, but that was only a short-term solution.

Samson slowed the carriage to round a street corner, and Jake heard a young boy calling out with the new edition of the *Evening Post*. Jake tapped on the roof of the carriage. "Samson, would you stop so I can buy a paper?"

"Yes, sir," the man called back, drawing the carriage to a halt. Jake jumped out and went to where the boy was announcing the headlines and waving a newspaper in each hand.

"I'll take one," Jake said. The boy exchanged the paper for coin and continued hawking the news.

Jake returned to the carriage and read the paper as Samson headed for home. One headline caught his attention: *Big Failure in America*. He read the first paragraph.

The Chamberlain Investment Company, of Denver, the largest real estate company in Western America, has suspended payment. The liabilities exceed $2,250,000.00.

Neither Morgan nor Keystone had said anything about this, but Jake knew it had been anticipated and would send the city spiraling further into fear. He blew out a heavy breath and continued to read the article. Elsewhere in the paper, Jake read of hundreds of people demanding the governor grant them audience to discuss what was to be done about Colorado's severe depression.

Samson opened the door to the carriage before Jake even realized they had stopped. He looked out at the tall man and shook his head. "The times are truly getting worse, Samson. I wonder, do you have family somewhere?"

"I gots me a sister in Kansas City."

Jake climbed down and looked up to meet the man's questioning look. "I may very well need to let you go, and if so, I want to be able to send you to family if need be."

Samson smiled. "Don't you go worrying about me none. The good Lord done already took care of my needs."

Jake looked at the man. He seemed genuinely unconcerned. "Aren't you worried?"

"Sakes, no. What good would that do me? Been without money all my life and don't 'spect this time around gonna make a bit o' difference. I'll jes go on like before."

"But what will you do if I have to let you go?"

Samson shrugged. "Good Lord ain't told me that yet, 'cause you ain't let me go."

Jake smiled. "I suppose that makes sense. I have to say, I wish I had more of your faith in the matter."

"You don't go gettin' faith by wishin' it, if you pardon my saying so, sir. The Good Book say that 'Faith cometh by hearing, and hearing by the word of God.'" He smiled again.

"Thank you, Samson. I think I needed to hear that. It's easy enough to hear the world crying out its problems." He held up the newspaper. "People are only too happy to bemoan all that's going on these days. I guess I need to put that aside and put my mind on the Bible."

"Yes, sir," Samson said, climbing back atop the carriage. "You can't go wrong by lookin' to the good Lord."

Jake knew the man was wiser than he'd ever given him credit for. Oh, to have faith like Samson—not to worry about the future or where he'd get the money to feed and care for his people. To stop fretting over whether he'd ever get back to Texas. If God wanted him there, then surely God would make a way for it to happen.

I want to leave it all in your hands, Lord. Jake looked heavenward. "Help me to have faith—to trust you more."

Chapter 24

"I've asked Morgan to meet us here," Mr. Keystone told Jake. "I had the opportunity to do some further digging on your discovery of the duplicated gold certificates. Unfortunately, what I've found leads us to a major betrayal."

Jake frowned, his brows knitting together. "What do you mean . . . betrayal?"

Keystone shook his head. "I mean that there was a great deal more to this than you can imagine. By my own calculations, it must have been going on for several years, and there is no way of knowing to what extent it will affect this banking institution. Or for that matter, our country."

"I don't exactly follow you. What did you find?"

"Counterfeiting," Keystone replied.

For a moment Jake said nothing. He sat down at his desk and considered the full implications. "Counterfeit gold certificates? It wasn't just an error."

Keystone nodded. "I can't even begin to tell how far-reaching it is or who all might be involved. I met with Morgan and filled him in on everything I knew—that's why he's coming here today."

"I don't understand." Jake leaned back in his chair. "It would have to be an awfully large group of folks to pull something like this off—

wouldn't it?" His drawl thickened. "Seems to me that it couldn't be handled by just a man or two."

"Exactly." Keystone pounded the arm of the chair. "That's why this is a betrayal of the most serious sort. This would have to involve not only men on the outside, but obviously men on the inside."

"And the only inside man who could have been responsible," Mr. Morgan said, entering the office unannounced, "was George Chesterfield."

Jake rose, but Morgan waved him to return to his seat. Taking the chair beside Keystone, Morgan sat stiffly. "Chesterfield," Morgan continued, "is the only one who would have had access to the original gold certificates—besides me, of course."

"You mentioned that the night he was killed, he was supposed to be transporting certificates, didn't you?" Jake asked.

"Yes. It was presumed they were lost in the robbery. But now, according to what you've told me, it would seem they weren't in the satchel, which leads us to this question: Where are those gold certificates?"

Keystone nodded. "And how many counterfeits were created?"

"And how much of the original gold has been redeemed without the actual owner realizing the loss?" Jake threw in. The entire matter was a colossal mess. It would most certainly ruin Morgan Bank.

"We must handle this discreetly," Mr. Morgan continued. "I can tell by the look on your face, Mr. Wythe, that you've already come to realize the ramifications. We cannot, under any circumstances, let this become public knowledge."

"But how will we keep it quiet?" Jake asked. "People are already clamoring to redeem as much as they can for gold. No one believes in paper or silver—it's all about the gold."

"Granted, but we have put an end to that. We must have some measures in place to keep the country from falling into bankruptcy. And now, with this matter of counterfeit gold certificates, I hesitate to even stir the pot for fear of what might rise to the surface."

Jake looked at the newspaper on his desk. "What will happen once the Senate finally approves the repeal of the Sherman Silver Purchase Act?"

"Mass chaos. The panic will only deepen," Morgan promised. "The stock exchange crashes back in May and June will pale to the problems we will see. Already thousands of businesses have collapsed and banks have closed. It's only the beginning, Mr. Wythe. Mark my words."

Jake nodded. The hopelessness of the future was made all the more clear with each conversation he had with Morgan. He seriously considered cashing out what he could of his savings, letting the house go back to the bank, and hightailing it back to Texas. Of course, what would they do there? People were hurting in Texas just as they were everywhere else—though maybe not as much as Colorado, which had come to depend on silver as a standard.

"I'm here today because we have no choice, Mr. Wythe. There is to be absolutely no cash given out—no silver exchanged for gold. Nothing but loan certificates that can be used in lieu of cash. If the people ask why this is happening, remind them the president has caused this fuss and nonsense. The collapse of this country rests on his shoulders."

Jake considered the matter another moment before speaking. "And what of you gentlemen? What will you do to weather this storm?"

Morgan looked at Keystone, then back to Jake. "I can't speak for Josiah, but for myself, I took measures long ago when I saw the problems that were upon us. I would imagine most sensible men did."

"At least if they were wealthy enough to have something set aside," Keystone countered.

"But most of the savings in this bank were put here by men who were poorer than you two," Jake replied. "Like myself. They put their savings here, hoping for a future."

"Your future is safe enough, Mr. Wythe," Morgan declared. "Have I not taken good care of you, my boy? I can see that this situation might seem overwhelming to you, but I assure you that so long as you are in my employ, you needn't worry."

Jake nodded. "And I appreciate all you've done. But what happens when this bank folds and you no longer need my services? My savings are here just like every other depositor, and now you're telling me I can't have it."

Morgan smiled, but it didn't quite reach his eyes. "I suppose for the time, you are dependent upon me."

★

Marty and Alice sat discussing the latest visit of Mr. Smith. "Will you write to your friends?" Marty asked.

"I suppose I must. After all, Mr. Smith brought up a good point. Where did my father's personal things go after the sale of the house? I don't know why it never occurred to me to question it."

"Shock and loss will do that to a mind," Marty declared. "I know from personal experience. After Thomas died, I couldn't have managed such matters on my own. Hannah was the one who helped me and she made a very neat and orderly inventory of the things she packed away. It was a godsend, but I don't suppose everyone is quite as well organized as my sister." She heaved a sigh. "Jake . . . Mr. Wythe believes that we should speak to the authorities about this."

"But what can they do?" Alice questioned. "The man has threatened me—even struck me—but I don't know who he really is, nor can I tell them where to find him. We are at his mercy.

"If I just knew where that envelope was," Alice said, "I would hand it over to him in a heartbeat—even knowing that it doesn't belong to him. I'm weary of the entire matter and desire only that this madness end. It took the life of my father and left me . . . like this. What more will it demand before it's settled?"

Marty wasn't used to seeing this side of Alice. For all the time she'd known the young woman, she'd been reserved but joyful. Now her fear and frustration were overriding any potential for happiness.

The sound of the clock chiming altered Marty's train of thought. It was nearly time for supper. Jake had plans to stay late at the bank, so Marty had already decided to take her meal upstairs.

"I'll leave you now," Alice said. "I need to spend some time praying on this, and I know Mrs. Landry will be coming with your tray. She said she wanted to speak to you about something, so I don't want to be here and make her uncomfortable."

"Oh dear, that sounds most grave."

Alice shrugged. "I really don't know what she wants to discuss, but she didn't seem upset. But happy or sad, I just don't feel up to answering her questions. She's as worried about this as you are, and I don't think talking about it more is going to help at this point."

Marty nodded. She could understand Alice's desire to sequester herself away, but in the girl's departure, Marty felt all the more lonely. Ever since Jake had kissed her, she'd not been the same. Everything had changed with that kiss. It had awakened in Marty a desire and hope for a future she had never thought possible.

The day had been unbearably warm, but thankfully a nice breeze blew in through the open window now. Marty relished the fresh air and prayed that the evening would cool off considerably. Just then she heard a knock on the bedroom door, and Mrs. Landry entered with supper.

"Mrs. Wythe, I hope you have had a pleasant afternoon," Mrs. Landry stated, placing the tray on the small table beside Marty.

"I have, and you?"

Mrs. Landry smiled and reached for the teapot. "I have enjoyed a very fine day, thank you, ma'am." The housekeeper appeared quite content, even joyful. Perhaps she'd come to discuss something good, rather than bad, as Marty had worried.

"Alice tells me that you wish to speak to me about something."

Mrs. Landry poured the tea and replaced the pot before straightening. "Yes, there is an important matter I wish to discuss. I came to make an announcement and offer a request."

"I see." Marty nodded. "Continue."

"Well, you see . . . Mr. Brighton and I . . . we . . ."

"Would like to marry?" Marty interjected.

Mrs. Landry's face flushed. She gave a little nod and smiled. "We would, Mrs. Wythe. He asked me just this morning. I've been fit to be tied waiting to discuss it with you."

"What is there to discuss?" Marty asked, laughing in relief. "I'm delighted, and Mr. Wythe will be, as well. We've long thought the two of you belonged together."

The housekeeper smiled but appeared completely flustered. "We plan to marry early next week, and that brings me to my request."

"Please, whatever I can do to help make this happy occasion happen, I am very glad to assist."

"Oh, there isn't anything you need to do, Mrs. Wythe. We simply . . . well . . . we wanted permission to . . . uh, share the same room once we are wed."

Marty couldn't help but giggle. "Of course you may share the same room. Goodness, I would never keep two people in love from being together as they should be. Do you anticipate how this might work?"

Mrs. Wythe nodded. "Neither of our rooms is very large; however, there is a more spacious room that was designed to house four servants. It's at the far end of the third floor. I wondered if we might take that room."

"Of course. I'm certain Mr. Wythe would approve. If I see him tonight, I will insist upon it, so feel free to start arranging it as you'd like."

"Oh, thank you, ma'am. You have no idea how happy this has made me."

Marty got to her feet and surprised the older woman by embracing her. "I think I do, and I'm glad to be a part of it. Please give Mr. Brighton my congratulations."

"Oh, I will, Mrs. Wythe. I will." Mrs. Landry started to hurry from the room, then halted. "I apologize, ma'am. I didn't uncover your supper." She started back for the tray, but Marty waved her away.

"Never mind. I will see to it myself. You go and speak to Brighton now. Let him know how much we approve." She smiled broadly and motioned the housekeeper to leave.

Once Mrs. Landry had gone, Marty pulled the cover from her supper plate. There rested a simple but adequate meal of roasted meat and potatoes. Mrs. Landry had included a thick slice of homemade bread, as well as a fruit tart that Mrs. Standish delighted in making.

Marty settled in to enjoy her meal, but all the while her thoughts wandered back to Mrs. Landry's announcement and Jake's kiss. It would seem the house was full of romantic hearts. She longed for Jake to throw off his fears as Brighton had. She longed for him to come home and tell her how much he wanted them to enjoy a real marriage—a true love.

Nibbling at the bread, Marty couldn't help but consider the older couple's future. There would no doubt be the same good-natured quibbling, but now they could kiss and make up at the end of every day. With a sigh, Marty wondered if it might ever be the same for her.

Tell him the truth. Set yourself free.

The words echoed in her heart, and whether they were simply remnants of Marty's guilty conscience or the Lord himself speaking to her, she didn't know. She did know beyond a doubt that until the truth of the ranch was disclosed, there would be no hope of a real marriage.

"But what do I do, Lord?" she asked, putting the bread aside to take up the teacup. "He's already so deeply distressed by the bank and all the problems they are facing. I can't bear for him to be disappointed—betrayed, angry—with me, as well." She didn't know if he'd be able to trust and forgive her after hiding the truth for so long.

Marty knew that the only place she could go was to prayer and the Scriptures. She'd avoided both for such a time that now it felt like she was learning to walk all over again.

With the meal concluded, Marty picked up her Bible. Hannah had sent Marty to the Scriptures whenever a lie had been revealed. Marty was pretty sure she knew every verse in the Bible that dealt with truth or lies.

Proverbs 12:19 was one of the first that came to mind. *The lip of truth shall be established for ever: but a lying tongue is but for a moment.*

The lip of truth shall be established forever.

That's what I'm afraid of. If I tell the truth, it will forever be established and divide me from Jake.

She flipped to 3 John 1:4 and read aloud. "'I have no greater joy than to hear that my children walk in truth.'" She sighed.

I want to please you, Father. I truly do. I know that means I need to be honest. I know that you hate lies. Please help me. I want so much to make this right.

Marty fell to her knees and prayed in earnest. *Father, I love him. I love him so dearly, and I never thought I could love another. I know I've done wrong. I know I should have told him about the ranch the first time he mentioned his longing for Texas. Oh, Father, I just don't know if I can endure that again. I fear that Jake might be injured or killed if we take up ranching. And now that Hannah and Will are taking the ranch back—I know it's really too late.*

224

She paused and shook her head. *No, that isn't right. They would quickly return the ranch to me. It's not too late, and that's what makes this so hard. With everything falling down around us, Texas seems to be the answer to all our needs. But I don't want it to be the answer.*

Tears came to her eyes. Was a ranch in Texas the price for love?

Marty lost track of the time as she prayed and wept before God. She paused occasionally to pace the room or read the Scriptures, but she always ended up back on her knees. And that was where she was when Jake knocked on her open dressing room door.

"Marty?"

Without reserve, she rose and at the sight of him flew to his arms. Jake's surprised expression said it all, but Marty didn't let that stop her. "I love you, Jake, and I want to be your wife." She pressed her lips to his, not letting him respond.

But it was clear Jake didn't need words. He wrapped her in his arms and kissed her with all the pent-up passion they both felt. Marty melted against him, hoping the moment might never end. She knew she still needed to tell Jake the truth, however.

Pulling back, she met his gaze. "I need to tell you . . ."

He put his finger to her lips. "Tell me later." He lifted her in his arms. "Much later."

Chapter 25

Jake looked at the woman sleeping by his side and smiled. Marty loved him. It was amazing that he should know the love of such a woman. She had given him a new reason to face the day, and despite all the problems that awaited him at work, Jake was inspired to forge ahead.

Careful not to wake her as he slipped from the bed, Jake couldn't keep himself from gazing at his wife for just a moment longer. He was in love and nothing else mattered. He would have whistled a tune if not for disturbing her peaceful slumber. Without waiting for Brighton, he gathered his things and dressed by himself. He was halfway downstairs when Brighton met him on the landing.

"Good morning, sir. You are up very early. I'm sorry to not have been ready to assist you."

"No problem." Jake glanced back at the upstairs hall. "Uh, you might want to wait to make up my room until later. Mrs. Wythe is still sleeping."

Brighton glanced upward but said nothing. He gave a professional nod and continued as if nothing were amiss. "Sir, I wonder if I might have a word with you."

"Of course. Let's do it while I eat, however. I'm pert near starved to death."

In the dining room, Jake was pleased to see breakfast already waiting on the sideboard. He helped himself to scrambled eggs, which Cook had blended with green peppers, ham, and onion. It was one of his favorites. The day was looking better all the time.

By the time he sat down, Brighton had toast and coffee waiting for him. Jake offered a quick silent blessing. *Father, I don't know quite what to say or how to thank you, but . . . thanks a lot. Amen.*

He looked up to find Brighton waiting. "So, my good man, what can I do for you?" Jake asked in an animated tone. He dug into the egg concoction.

"I wanted your . . . permission to marry Mrs. Landry."

Jake nearly dropped the forkful of food. He couldn't contain his grin at the stately announcement. "I'd give you a good ol' Texas whoop, but I'm afraid it might wake up Marty. That's wonderful news, Brighton, and of course you don't need my permission."

The man gave a small smile. "Thank you, sir. Mrs. Landry spoke to Mrs. Wythe last night and I thought perhaps you two had discussed the matter already."

"No," Jake said, lowering his face so that Brighton couldn't see his grin. "We didn't have much of a chance to . . . talk last night."

"Mrs. Landry, it would seem, has asked Mrs. Wythe's permission to claim the larger room on the servants' floor for us to use after our vows are said. Would that be acceptable to you, as well?"

"Of course. If Marty said it was all right, it's fine by me. When will you two marry?"

"I believe next week, sir. So long as we can put everything in order."

"I would love to be there," Jake said, finally feeling able to meet Brighton's gaze. He smiled. "I know Mrs. Wythe would want to, as well."

"We thought only to see a justice of the peace, sir."

"That's fine. Marty and I would be happy to stand as your witnesses."

"Very good, sir. I would like that."

Jake could see a twinkle in the older man's eyes. "I can't tell you how happy I am for you both. It's been a time in coming, but I'm happier than a dog with a new bone."

Brighton covered what sounded to be an amused chuckle with a cough. When he'd cleared his throat a couple of times, he excused himself.

Jake finished his breakfast and was out the door before anyone else appeared to speak with him. The joy of the night and morning fled, however, as Samson pulled up to the bank. There were people lining the walkway outside the bank and the line stretched clear around to the side of the building. Jake waited for Samson to open the carriage door, wondering if he might need the man to assist in making a way through the crowd.

As he stepped out, a chorus of cries erupted. "We want our money!" "Let us have our money—it belongs to us!" "You thieves aren't gonna take my savings!"

Jake looked to Samson, who seemed to understand. The big man stepped forward and the people parted like the Red Sea for Moses and the children of Israel. When Jake reached the locked bank door, he paused and turned. Raising his hands, he called to the crowd.

"Folks, if you'll quiet down, I'll hear you out. But not if everyone just keeps talking over the other."

"This bank is failing," a man close to him said. "We know it, and we want our money. I heard you folks weren't of a mind to let us have it."

Jake shook his head. "I've not heard anything of the kind. However, I am to attend a meeting this morning. Most likely they are awaiting me now. I would very much appreciate it if you'd give me time to speak to my board, and then I can better understand what's going on."

This did little to calm the crowd, but there was nothing else Jake could do. With Samson at his back, he turned and unlocked the bank's front door. "Thank you, Samson. Come for me at five. I'm not staying late tonight."

"Yes, sir."

With that, Jake closed and relocked the door behind him. He turned and found a wide-eyed Arnold standing near his office door.

"They started coming at eight. I've never seen the likes."

Jake nodded and noted the time was half past. "Quite a crowd for just half an hour."

"Yes, sir. And they aren't at all happy. They've been out there yelling and demanding they be let in here the entire time."

"I can well imagine. Tell me, have the board members arrived?"

228

Arnold nodded. "They're assembled in the back room away from the noise. They weren't any happier than you are about the scene."

Jake handed Arnold his hat and made his way to the back of the bank, where the board had assembled. He opened the door hesitantly and peered inside. Already the men were arguing and pointing fingers.

He slipped in and found an empty seat at the table just as Morgan slammed his fists down on the hard oak wood. "I won't have this kind of insubordination. You may be the bank's board of directors, but I'm its owner and you will listen to me."

"Those people indicate otherwise," Mr. Cooper declared. "It would seem we will have to keep the bank closed or face a riot."

"We'll face a riot if we keep the bank closed," Keystone threw out.

"I've telephoned for the police," Morgan replied. "I didn't build up this business just to watch a bunch of dim-witted fools tear it apart."

"They've cause to be worried," one of the other board members declared. "I can't say that I don't have my own concerns. Especially given that we're facing the complete devaluation of silver. Most of those people know the truth, and they aren't going to be easily reassured."

Morgan eyed Jake as if just realizing he had joined them. "What say you, Mr. Wythe? I realize you are only the branch manager, but I'm sure you have dealt with these customers."

"I have," Jake replied. "My guess is that they won't be put off. You have a lot of folks out there who live nickel to nickel. Now that they know you aren't planning to let them have their cash, but instead are giving them bank checks, I think they're going to panic. They'll figure the money could be lost to them."

"That's my take, as well," Keystone agreed. "They are like children. It only takes one to start raising a ruckus until all of them join in."

A knock sounded on the door. It was Arnold. "Mr. Morgan, sir, the police have arrived. They are working to disperse the crowd. However, they want a word with you."

Morgan got to his feet. "Very well. Keystone, carry on."

Josiah Keystone didn't look excited to take the helm of this sinking ship, but he did nevertheless. "We will suspend all cash transactions, as Mr. Morgan has explained. Instead, we will be issuing bank checks.

If this is not agreeable, the people will either need to await further notice to get their money in cash, or they will have to do without it altogether."

Jake listened to the discussion of the members, with talk centered on the fall of stocks and gold reserves and the role of the government.

"The president of the United States will get his repeal—of this we can be sure. The House has already passed it, and the Senate is just concluding their discussion on the matter. By summer's end we will face a devastating situation in this city. The western states' economy will collapse like dominoes," Mr. Cooper declared. "There will be no stopping it. We might as well close our doors now and keep them closed."

And that was the way the rest of the meeting continued. Finally Jake had stomached all he could. When Morgan returned, he asked if he could be excused to attend to daily business, and Morgan quickly agreed.

Jake slipped from the room and made his way to the solace of his office. Unfortunately, he was not to find peace of mind there, either.

Jake had barely sat at his desk when Winfield Mays appeared in his doorway. The older man, a longtime teller at the bank, looked almost sick. "Mr. Wythe, I must speak with you." He twisted his hands and looked to the floor. "It's important, Mr. Wythe, or I wouldn't have bothered you."

Jake nodded. "Come in and take a seat, Mr. Mays. What can I do for you?"

Mays closed the door, then walked slowly to the desk. He didn't sit, but instead continued to twist his hands as he glanced up a bit. "I've wronged you, Mr. Wythe. I've wronged the bank, but I tried to make it right."

Jake couldn't imagine what the old man was talking about. "Go on."

Mays nodded. "You see, Martha—she's my wife—has been very sick."

Jake immediately thought of Marty and smiled. "I didn't realize you were married, Mays. I am very sorry to hear that she's been sick."

"It's been going on over a year now—closer to two. The doctors have tried all sorts of things, but nothing much has worked. It's been hard on me to pay all those bills, and some of those newfangled medical procedures . . . well . . . they are expensive."

230

"I can imagine," Jake replied. "But what does this have to do with me or the bank?"

The old man cleared his throat. "I know you've studied the books. I know you saw the discrepancies in the bank's listed assets. It's my fault, Mr. Wythe, and if you want to put me in jail, I ask only that you wait until my Martha passes. It shouldn't be long now."

Jake finally understood the direction the conversation was taking. "You took the money?"

"I did. Put it back, too. See, I knew I couldn't get a loan with the bank. I didn't have any assets to put up as collateral. One day when the doctor told me he had a new procedure that he thought would save Martha's life, I just lost all sense. I took the money that I needed. Only for the procedure, mind you. I knew in time I could pay it back, and I did."

"So why are you telling me this now? Surely you know that Mr. Morgan told me to just consider it a fluke—money mislaid and refound."

"I know that, sir, but I also know that things aren't going well for the bank. I've found it hard to live with myself. . . . Now that my Martha is passing on, I don't much care to live in this world without her."

"I'm sure her loss will be difficult," Jake replied. "Even so, you can't give up on life, Mr. Mays. The good Lord will let you know when your time has come.

"As for the money," Jake said, shaking his head, "I am sorry you felt that you had to take it in such a manner. There should have been a provision for a bank employee to receive a loan against his wages. However, it was a crime, and your confession puts me in a difficult position."

"I know that, sir. Like I said, my Martha won't be here more than another day or two."

"Then why are you here?" Jake asked, moved by the man's situation and need to come clean.

"I have to keep my position for as long as possible," the old man replied. "I . . . have a funeral to pay for."

Jake got to his feet and pulled out his wallet. There wasn't a great amount inside, but definitely as much as the old man made in two days' time. He handed the cash to him. "Take this and go home to your wife. Be at her side. That's where you belong. The bank will most likely not even open today."

"I can't take your money, sir. It wouldn't be right—especially now." The old man had tears in his eyes as he tried to push the cash back into Jake's hands.

"Mr. Mays, I am your superior here, am I not?" Jake asked with a gentle smile. "I have told you to take this money and not return to work for at least two days. You take all the time you need. For as long as this bank is solvent, you will have a job. I will fight Mr. Morgan and anyone else to see to it."

"But after what I did—"

"You've confessed your sins and made restitution. Now I ask that you say nothing more about the matter. That's the end of it. Even Mr. Morgan declared it so, and I see no reason to contradict him."

Mays looked at the cash in his hands and then back to Jake. Without another word, he simply nodded and left the office. Jake sighed and reclaimed his chair. At least now he understood what was going on with the missing and replaced money.

At five o'clock Samson picked Jake up at the bank. They had kept the doors closed and the crowd had finally given up and gone home. Jake knew they'd be back on Monday morning, however. What he didn't know for sure was how Morgan intended to handle it. Josiah Keystone had come to see him after their meeting concluded and indicated they would open as usual on Monday at nine, but Jake feared the crowd would no doubt storm the place without regard to anyone's safety or well-being. It would be mass chaos.

Despite this, Jake couldn't keep a smile from his face as he approached home. Marty would be there waiting for him. He knew it would be a little awkward to face each other after last night, but he was eager to see her again. He wanted to tell her how much he loved her—how glad he was that God had put them together. It seemed that his prayers had mattered to God after all.

Brighton met him at the door. "Welcome home, sir."

"Brighton," Jake said, barely taking time to hand the man his hat.

232

"Don't worry about helping me with my clothes. I'll manage for myself. Where's Mrs. Wythe?"

"She's in her room, sir. I believe she's been unwell."

Jake frowned. "I'm sorry to hear that. I'll go to her right away."

He bounded up the stairs, taking them two at a time. He hated to think of Marty sick and prayed silently that it wasn't anything serious. He knocked on her dressing room door but didn't receive a response. Opening it just a crack, he could see that no one was in the room. He quickly made his way to her bedroom door and knocked again.

"Come in," she said in a voice that suggested she'd been crying.

Jake entered and noted that only a sliver of light from the window penetrated the darkness of the room. He reached for the lamp, but Marty halted him.

"Please don't. I have a terrible headache."

"I'm so sorry. Brighton told me you were sick."

"I'm not really so much sick—I'm . . . I'm worried."

Jake crossed the room and pulled up a chair to where she was sitting. "What's wrong?" Fear edged his soul. "Is this about last night?" He closed his eyes, dreading her response.

"In a way," she whispered. "I shouldn't have let it happen. I should have . . . I needed to tell you something first. Something that may alter . . . no, I'm sure it will alter your feelings for me."

His eyes snapped open. "That's impossible. I love you. I've loved you for some time, but I couldn't bring myself to tell you for fear of your rejection."

"Just as I fear yours now," Marty said. She turned her face to his, and he could see that her eyes were swollen from crying.

"You don't need to fear me, Marty. You can tell me anything. I love you."

"I hope you'll feel that way after you hear what I have to say."

***

Marty hesitated a moment before continuing. She could see that Jake was surprised by her statement. "I want you to know that I've tried several times to tell you the truth. But for one reason or another, I've always backed down. Mostly because I'm a coward. But I cannot live with this lie between us. Not now. Not when I know I love you more than I ever dreamed possible."

Jake reached out and took hold of her hand. "Marty, there's nothing you can say that will make me love you less."

She wanted to believe him. She had spent the day in tears and prayers, and now that her moment of confession had come, she felt unable to continue. Her lies had finally caught up with her . . . and she feared the cost would be more than she could bear.

"Jake, I've kept something from you. Something that I knew would have pleased you. Something that you had hoped for."

He looked at her, puzzled. "What are you saying?"

"I own a ranch, Jake. That is, I owned a ranch until a short time ago. My brother-in-law has reclaimed it, as it was his gift to me to begin with. I gave it back to him, however, because I couldn't bear the idea of returning to ranch life. I couldn't bear the thought—no matter how much it meant to you—of losing you as I lost Thomas."

Jake looked at her without saying a word. The light seemed to go out of his eyes, and he released her hand. Marty knew the impact of her confession was only now starting to hit him. She hurried to continue, praying he would understand her pain.

"I'm so sorry. I know I should have told you the first time you mentioned your dream of returning to ranching. Each time you talked about it, however, I felt my fears get the better of me. I answered your ad for a wife mainly to get away from Texas and all that it stood for, yet you wanted to take me back to that life. I just couldn't bear the thought of it."

"So you lied to me? You lied about something that you knew was important to me—was my very heart and soul?"

She bit her lower lip and nodded. "Yes."

He rubbed his hand over his mouth, staring straight ahead at the cold fireplace. For several minutes he said nothing at all. Marty wished he would speak. She'd rather have his rage or even his sorrow rather than this silence.

When he got to his feet, Marty jumped to hers as well and took hold of his arm. "Jake, I'm so very sorry. I don't know what else to say. I want our marriage more than you'll ever know, but if you feel you . . .

have to . . . to . . . send me away . . ." She gave a heavy sigh. "I'll understand." She bit her tongue knowing that, too, was just one more lie. She wouldn't understand.

He looked at her for a long time, his face betraying his anguish. "I can't talk to you about this right now. You've near broken my heart, and all I can think about is getting away from you." He turned and left without another word.

Marty collapsed on the floor and sobbed. Once again she'd lost a man she loved more than life itself. Why couldn't God just end her life now and be done with it? Why wouldn't He just show mercy and put her out of her misery?

Chapter 26

Alice found Marty on the floor, weeping as if her life were over. She knew of her mistress's plans to tell Jake everything, and apparently it hadn't gone well. With a gentle hand, Alice helped Marty up from the floor and directed her to the bed. Marty stared aimlessly at the wall as Alice undressed her and replaced her tear-soaked dress with a white lawn nightgown. She helped Marty into bed, then surprised herself by sitting down beside her.

Taking up Marty's hand, Alice told her, "The truth will set you free. You may not believe that, but you've done the right thing, and God will bless it."

"He said that all he could think of was getting away from me," Marty said in a hushed, weak voice.

Alice patted her hand. "He's shocked and hurting. Give him some time to pray through this—to think on it."

"I crushed his spirit, Alice. I wounded him more deeply than he could bear." Marty shook her head slowly, her blond hair spilling out across the pillow. "I never thought a lie could hurt anyone that much. It seemed such a simple thing—an easy thing."

"But a very harmful thing," Alice added.

Marty continued to look away. "I can't bear the way he looked at me. He knew I'd betrayed him in the worst possible way. He could have forgiven me had I been unfaithful in our sensible arrangement, but not this. Not keeping him from his dream of ranching. Not keeping him from his beloved Texas."

She turned to Alice and gripped her hand tightly. "I've lost him. The truth set him free from me, and now I'm alone again."

"No," Alice said, shaking her head. "You are never alone with God."

"Why would He do this to me?"

"Marty, listen to yourself. God didn't lie, nor did He make you lie. You made that decision. I don't say this to hurt you, but you have to see the truth of it. God loves you, Marty, and He wants you to give Him your life—your love—your all. You had to tell the truth, otherwise things would never be right between you and God or you and Jake."

"I know," Marty whispered. She closed her eyes. "I can't bear who I am—what I've done. I'm a wretched creature. A sinful, wretched creature."

Alice smiled. "Well, now that you realize what you are . . . maybe you can let God show you what you can be. I'm going to pray for you, Marty. Just as I have been doing for the entire time I've worked for you. I'm going to pray that you and Jake will both seek God's healing in this and trust Him to help you both know what to do about it."

She released Marty's hand and stood. "I'm going to get you some hot tea and lemon—maybe some headache powders, too. I'll be back shortly."

After she got Marty settled, Alice went to her room and sank to her knees. "Oh, Father," she began to pray, "please hear my prayers."

★

Marty lay awake throughout the night waiting and listening for some sound that might indicate that Jake had returned home. Alice had checked on Jake's whereabouts several times, only to have Brighton tell her that he had stormed from the house, not even stopping to take up his hat.

Tossing and turning in her bed, Marty did her best to pray, but the words seemed stuck in her throat. She had no desire to go back to being the woman she'd been before—bitter and angry at God. She desperately needed God's love at this moment, probably more so than any other time in her life.

Even in losing Thomas, Marty had not felt so alone. Back in Texas she'd had Hannah and Will at her side. Hannah had stood by Marty and cared for her. Marty had known that her family loved her and that love would get her through the loss. Now, however, she had betrayed everyone—even her family.

She knew that in the days to come, she would write to tell Hannah everything. If Jake insisted she leave—if he annulled their marriage—Marty had already decided to remain in Colorado. She would ask Alice to be her friend, to find a place where they could live together. She would get a job.

I know how to work hard. I can do any number of jobs. If Jake won't have me anymore . . . I'll find a way to live my life.

But she doubted the truth of that. She might be able to survive the blow, but she seriously doubted life would be worth living.

Closing her eyes, Marty imagined life without Jake and tears formed anew. It wasn't a life she desired—at all. When sleep finally came, Marty endured one nightmare after another. She relived her confession to Jake and felt the cut of his rejection over and over.

She dreamed about Thomas at one point, and instead of seeing him attacked by the longhorn, he stood in accusation, telling Marty that she had disappointed him. That was worse, in some ways, than watching him die.

Waking, Marty brought a hand to her forehead and noted it was beaded with sweat. She felt the damp perspiration all over her body and longed for a cool bath. She got up and sponged off with the water that Alice had left in her room. It helped a little, but not enough. She went to the window and leaned out as far as she dared. The cooler night air hit her damp skin. It felt good, and Marty lingered there for some time.

She noticed a hint of the darkness lessening. *It must be close to dawn. In a few hours I'll have to face another day. But how?*

For a moment she gave serious consideration to just packing up the things she'd brought to Colorado and leaving. She could stay with her brother, Andy, in Wyoming for a time. Maybe that was the answer she sought. If she left and gave Jake time to consider the situation, it might do them both good.

Oh, Jake. I'm so sorry.

Marty turned toward her closed bedroom door and wondered if Jake had ever come home. Without much thought she opened the door and passed through the dressing room. She hesitated a moment at the passageway that would take her to Jake's bedroom. Dare she continue? If he wasn't there, she would worry all the more. If he was there, he might be awake and waiting to speak with her.

She opened the first door and tiptoed through the hall to the second door. Opening it just enough to glance inside, Marty could see that the room was dark. Even so, she could hear Jake's even breathing. He'd come home. Relief and dread washed over her in equal parts.

Entering the room, Marty made her way to the bed. She could see his outline in the darkness, but little more. The urge to pray overcame her and Marty knelt beside the bed. At first she prayed silently, but then her heart grew much too heavy, and the words just seemed to pour from her mouth.

"Oh, God, please help Jake not to hate me. Please let him know how sorry I am. I never knew my lies could cause such pain. It wasn't my desire to hurt him like I did—I was just a coward. I kept thinking of how Thomas had died, and it was more than I could bear. Forgive me, God. Please forgive me, and help Jake to forgive me, too. I promise I won't lie again . . . leastwise, I promise to do my best to never lie again."

"Do you mean that, Marty?" Jake asked, rolling to his side.

Marty nearly jumped from the floor at the sound of his clear voice. Obviously, he hadn't been sleeping. "I do," she said, barely able to speak. Her heart pounded so hard she could hardly hear his voice. For several long moments Jake simply stared at her. When he did finally speak, it pierced Marty to the heart.

"You know, I couldn't believe you would do such a thing. I didn't see how you could say you loved me and yet lie like that. Josephine betrayed me like that. I loved her and thought she loved me, but she didn't. She was a liar and betrayed my trust. And then you went and did the same thing."

"I know. What I did was horrible, and I have no right to ask your forgiveness. I've spent a lifetime lying to get myself out of uncomfortable situations and never thinking of the cost. It was only my love for you that made me tell the truth." Marty knew he probably couldn't see the details of her face, but she hoped he could hear the sincerity in her voice. "I didn't want to tell you. I thought after . . . after . . . our night together, that maybe I didn't need to tell you. But my conscience wouldn't leave me be. I knew I had to tell you, but I also knew it was going to destroy any affection you had for me. All I ask is that you give me a chance to make it up—to prove my love."

Jake sat up and reached out to take hold of Marty's hands. He pulled her to her feet and had her sit on the side of the bed. "And there will be no more lies between us?"

"No more. I know it's in my nature, but I'm sick of my nature—and I want to be a good wife to you, Jake. Please forgive me. Please. I never meant to hurt you, but I know I did and for that I'm so very sorry."

"I love you, Marty, but your lie really tore me apart."

"I know. Please forgive me."

"I wanted nothing more than to return to Texas and own my own spread again. I wanted to be back in the saddle rather than in a bank office."

"I know. Please . . . forgive me."

Jake drew a deep breath and let it out slowly. "But mostly I want a wife I can trust. A wife I can plan a future with—have a family with."

Marty felt a pang of sorrow and drew in a deep breath. "I don't think I can have children, Jake. Thomas and I tried for ten years, and they all ended in miscarriages." Silence hung heavy between them, and Marty thought she might burst into tears anew.

"There's always your orphans."

Marty laughed and cried at the same time. She fell into his arms and sobbed again. "Please forgive me, Jake. I can't bear one more minute if you don't."

With a tenderness she had never known, Jake pulled her close and kissed her wet cheek. "Ah, Marty, God knows I've needed enough forgivin' in my life. I love you, and love sometimes comes in pain as well as joy. I forgive you, Marty. I forgive you."

★

Standing before the justice of the peace, Marty and Jake held hands as Mrs. Landry and Mr. Brighton exchanged their vows. Alice and Mrs. Standish had also come to witness the marriage, while Samson waited patiently at the back of the church. His smile clearly showed his approval, and Marty couldn't help but glance back at him from time to time.

"I now pronounce you man and wife," the justice declared. "Groom, you may kiss your bride."

Brighton's face turned several shades of red, but Mrs. Landry was not nearly so embarrassed. She took hold of the man's face and planted her lips on his. Marty couldn't help but giggle and ducked her head to try and disguise her glee.

Jake didn't bother. He laughed out loud at the scene and squeezed Marty's hand. "He said we could kiss."

She looked up in surprise. "He said that the groom could kiss his bride."

"Well, I'm a groom, and I want to kiss my bride." He leaned over and placed a very chaste kiss upon her lips. Marty didn't even have time to close her eyes, but rather met his blue-eyed gaze. They were the same color as a Texas summer sky.

Marty congratulated the new couple, and Alice and Mrs. Standish did likewise. Brighton had arranged a private carriage for them and soon swept his new bride off for some mysterious honeymoon that he'd not shared the details of—not even with Jake.

Outside the day was perfect and bright, a bit warm but not unbearably so. Marty thought of humid summer days on the ranch and smiled. The dry Denver air was so very different.

"You seem very pleased with yourself, Mrs. Wythe," Jake whispered in her ear.

"I'm just happy that things could work out for Brighton and Mrs. Landry. I know they'll probably bicker and pick at each other the entire time they're away, but I'm also certain they'll forgive each other and go on."

"As am I," Jake said, heading toward the open carriage where Alice and Mrs. Standish were already waiting.

"It was a lovely ceremony," Mrs. Standish declared. "Made me think I might one day find another husband for myself."

"Why, Mrs. Standish," Marty said, "I didn't know you were of a mind to remarry."

The older woman shrugged. "Didn't know I was, either, but it doesn't seem like a half bad idea. Mrs. Landry certainly looked happy."

Jake nodded and gave Marty's hand a squeeze. "Indeed she did. Brighton looked rather pleased with himself, as well."

They shared a chuckle and gazed at the city as Samson drove them home. Marty thought Denver a wonderful mixture of elegant town, cowboy respite, and miner's playground. It intrigued her, but there was a small part of her that longed for the open spaces she'd left behind.

"Extra! Extra! Read all about it! Silver prices fall by half!" a newsboy called out. "Extra! Extra!"

Marty stiffened and looked at Jake. She could see the worry in his eyes and though Alice and Mrs. Standish chattered on as if nothing were amiss, Marty knew that somehow their world had just crumbled around them.

Jake patted her hand, then held it tight. "We're in for a bit of a Texas twister, I think."

Marty nodded. "I'm sure you're right."

Mrs. Standish heard the exchange and exclaimed, "Why, there's not a cloud in the sky! And besides, we don't get cyclones up here. The mountains don't allow for it."

Jake and Marty smiled and looked back to the older woman. "I'm sure you know the place better than I do," Jake replied.

★

"Do you suppose the bank will close right away?" Marty asked Jake later that evening. They had decided to take a stroll in City Park to enjoy the beautiful weather. Samson kept the horses and carriage at a distance, ever ready to pick them up when they tired of their walking adventure.

"I don't know. I don't know what's going to happen. Thousands are out of work and more businesses are folding by the day. The closing of banks is just a natural progression of this mess, and no one will feel it more than Colorado. I doubt there's a single silver mine still producing."

Marty tightened her hold on his arm. "I know we'll be all right no matter what. We have each other and for me . . . that's everything."

Jake stopped, and in the fading light he beheld his wife as if seeing her for the first time. Her delicate beauty never failed to stir his heart. "It's everything for me, as well. I have my Lone Star bride and nothin' else matters."

She laughed lightly and kissed his cheek. "And I have my Lone Star man—troublesome though he may be."

"Troublesome?" he questioned. "If you wanna know about troublesome, let me tell you a story. It starts with a little gal who shot at bandits on her way into Denver, then hoisted herself up to the driver's seat and took the reins of a team of half-crazed stage horses and brought the wounded driver and passengers to safety. You, Marty Wythe, are the very picture of trouble itself."

She laughed and put her arms around his neck. "I concur, Mr. Wythe, and don't you forget it."

"Mrs. Wythe . . . you forget who you are. You are making a spectacle of yourself. What will the Morgans and the Keystones say if they see us?"

Marty grinned. "I don't reckon I much care what they say."

Jake shook his head. "Neither do I, little gal. Neither do I."

A MOMENT
IN TIME

Chapter 1

DENVER, COLORADO
NOVEMBER 1893

Alice Chesterfield could feel the intensity of the man watching her. Not just any man. She knew very well who it was and why he continued to hound her steps. Gathering her brown wool skirt in hand, Alice did her best to avoid the muddier spots in the road as she crossed to the small fabric store on the opposite side. Her heart pounded wildly. Her breathing seemed to catch in her throat.

Would he follow her there? Would he dare? She had been plagued by this stranger—this man who'd been responsible for upending her world—for over a year now. The wind picked up just as she reached the door of the establishment and chilled her to the bone. At least she told herself it was the wind that caused her shivers. Forcing herself not to look back, Alice raised her chin and slipped inside.

Stay calm. Don't let this disturb you any more than it already has.

A small bell over the door heralded her entrance. The warmth of the room was welcome, but it did little to help the icy fingers that seemed to run down Alice's spine. Reaching her gloved hand out to touch a bolt of blue cotton broadcloth, she closed her eyes and drew a deep breath.

"May I help you?"

Alice jumped at the voice and opened her eyes to find a matronly woman standing at her right.

"We don't have much in stock, as we're closing our doors on Friday."

Alice nodded. So many of the smaller businesses had folded since the banking crisis struck earlier in the year. "I'm looking for needles. The mercantile was out and suggested you might have some."

The woman shook her head. "Sold the last of them on Monday. I have some pins and plenty of thread, but as you can see for yourself, my shelves of fabric are pretty much exhausted. I can give you a good price on this broadcloth."

"Yes, well . . . thank you. I don't really need any fabric." Alice steadied her voice as she glanced out the window to see if the man was still there. He was.

"I haven't seen you in here before." The woman frowned. "I would have remembered you . . . your scar."

Alice put her gloved hand to the scar that ran from ear to chin on the right side of her face. "I . . . well . . ." She didn't know quite what to say to the woman's open rudeness.

"Such a pity it should have happened. Your old man do that?" She watched Alice carefully. "I used to be married to a man who carried a knife. Thought nothin' of threatening me with it from time to time. Eventually he threatened the wrong man, and now I'm a widow."

"No," Alice said, shaking her head. "I'm not married." She glanced over her shoulder at the man who continued to wait for her on the other side of the street. "I was attacked—a year ago."

The woman didn't miss a thing. "That the man?" she asked, nodding her head toward the stranger.

Alice realized this woman might well be her salvation. "Yes. At least he was responsible. He calls himself Mr. Smith, and he's been following me since I left home."

"Well, I won't brook any nonsense," the woman stated, moving back behind the counter. She pulled up a shotgun. "Like I said, I was married to a man who got his way at the end of a knife. I just won't have it."

"I wonder," Alice said, moving toward the counter, "is there another way out of here?"

"Of course there is." The woman pointed. "You go ahead through that curtain over there, and it will take you through the storeroom and into the alley behind my store. I'll keep an eye on the no-account, and you get on home."

Alice looked at the older woman with gratitude. "You are a blessing from the Lord."

"Bah, I don't know about that," she said, squinting her eyes to study the stranger. "I do know about mean-tempered men, however. Now, get on with yourself."

"Thank you." Alice hurried through the curtain and made her way to the back door. The alley was a muddy mess, but she didn't care. Picking her way through the ruts left by numerous delivery wagons, Alice slipped between buildings and disappeared.

She all but ran the rest of the way home. It wasn't that Mr. Smith didn't know where she lived, but she would feel a lot better once she was safely behind the locked doors of the Wythe house.

Hard times in the financial world had altered the stately beauty of the upper-class estates that lined the road. Many of the wealthier Capitol Hill residents had closed their houses and moved away. With silver devalued and the mines shut until further notice, Denver had suffered a tremendous blow to its economy. No one knew that better than the stuffed shirts of this elite neighborhood.

Reaching the red stone and brick house she'd come to call home, Alice hurried up the back steps and burst into the kitchen, not even bothering to remove her muddy boots. Thankfully, there was no one there to chide her. The housekeeper and butler had resigned their positions the month before, and due to the financial situation, Mr. Wythe had not seen it possible to fill their jobs.

Alice didn't really mind. At eighteen, she was willing to work to get what she needed. She'd certainly never had a maid to wait on her hand and foot, even when her father was alive. Instead, she was the one required to work. Mrs. Wythe—Marty—had been kind enough to let Alice stay on with them. She'd hired Alice, without references, as her personal maid, and over time the relationship had developed into something more. Now, despite Marty's being able to pay only a small pittance, Alice remained for the comfort and assurance that she was cared for by someone.

"I thought I heard you in here," Marty declared, coming into the kitchen. "Were you able to . . ." Her words trailed. "What happened? Was it Smith again?"

Alice knew it would be impossible to hide her fear. "He fell in step behind me almost from the start. I tried to lose him in the shops, but he watched me too carefully. Finally, I just accepted that he would trail me wherever I went and pretended not to care. With the help of a woman at Bennett's Fabrics, I managed to get away unseen."

Marty crossed her arms in contemplation. "Of course it won't stop him. I think it's time we speak with the authorities."

"But what will we tell them that I haven't already explained?" Alice asked. "They know all about him but don't care. They said they were much too busy with the increase in crimes. People are desperate."

Marty narrowed her eyes. "That's no excuse. Of course crime is increasing with so many people suffering financial ruin. Even so, it's not right that a young woman can't feel free to walk down the street without being accosted. Next time, I'll drive you myself, and we'll see if Mr. Smith is inclined to reacquaint himself with my shotgun."

With her muddy boots discarded, Alice put them on the back porch and then hurried to clean up the mess she'd made on the floor. Marty had already retrieved the mop and pail. Alice took them from her and smiled. "I'm supposed to be the hired help."

Marty laughed. "Those days are long gone, as you well know. I can't help but wonder when Jake will walk through the door and tell me the bank has closed its doors. He knows his job there hangs by a thread. Mr. Morgan told him the banks were falling into failure like dominoes lined up in child's play." She shrugged. "I don't know what to expect from one day to the next. But then, I suppose no one does."

Alice nodded and worked to clean the floor. "I know I've said it before, but I think it's time you stop worrying about giving me any money for pay. I'm blessed just to get to eat and have a bed to sleep in. You should just put that money aside for emergencies. That's what I've been trying to do."

"Yes, well, I was going to address that subject with you. My money is pretty well dried up. I could write to my sister and brother-in-law in Texas. They still haven't paid me for the ranch, but I know they're most likely hurting, too."

Shaking her head, Alice opened the door and emptied the bucket outside. There was an icy bite to the air and she shivered. Looking quickly around, she saw the unmistakable outline of a man near the stable. She hurried back into the house and slammed the door closed. Locking it, she looked to Marty. "He's out there."

"Not for long." Marty took off and returned momentarily with her shotgun. "I think I should have a little talk with him."

"But it's nearly dark," Alice protested, "and Jake, I mean Mr. Wythe, isn't home yet. What if Mr. Smith decides to call your bluff?"

Marty smiled. "Who said I'm bluffing?"

Alice put her hand on Marty's arm. "Let's just pray instead. He'll leave soon enough, and if you threaten him, he'll just come back later."

"I don't appreciate being made a prisoner in my own home," Marty replied. "Even if you could give him what he wants, he needs to know he can't push people around."

Alice thought back to the man's demands. The night he'd sent his men to waylay her father, it had seemed they were to be victims of a simple robbery. But the attack turned out to be more than expected. One man had sliced Alice's face to motivate her father, and when her father protested, he was shoved to the ground, hitting his head and dying almost immediately. Alice was hospitalized and was sick for weeks afterwards with a fierce infection. When she regained consciousness and eventually her health, Alice prayed that would be the end of the ordeal. Mr. Smith, however, had appeared not long after the incident to ask about an envelope that should have been in her father's satchel.

"I wish I had what he wanted. I wish I could find a way to rid us both of his threatening presence."

"Men like that are never satisfied. Your father was delivering gold certificates for the bank. Mr. Smith believes they should be his, but we know that isn't the case. However, since no one knows where those certificates got off to or even where the envelope might be, Mr. Smith will have to accept his plight. You can't get blood from a turnip."

Alice put her hand again to her face. "But you can get it out of people. I would never forgive myself if harm should come to you or Mr. Wythe."

Marty placed the shotgun on the top of the wooden worktable. "No harm is going to come to anyone. Not if I can help it. Now, as you pointed out, it's getting late. Let's get the stew from yesterday heating. When Jake gets home we're bound to hear all the worrisome news, and Mr. Smith will be nothing more than a minor thorn in our flesh."

★

Jake ate like a starved man and Marty once again felt guilty that they were still in Colorado instead of Texas, where Jake would rather be. Her husband longed to return to ranch life, but Marty stood in the way of that happening. Though they both had been born and raised on Texas ranches, Marty and Jake had opposite feelings toward those settings. Jake's parents had been forced to sell off the family ranch when the drought of the '80s had caught up with them. It had ripped a part of Jake's heart away, and he had mourned the loss ever since.

While I couldn't leave Texas quick enough.

Marty toyed with her bowl of stew. She had been widowed in Texas, and although she once owned a ranch and could have made all of Jake's desires a reality, she'd kept the truth from him—until recently. Even now when he talked of returning to Texas so he could get work with friends or maybe even at her brother-in-law's ranch, Marty cringed and changed the subject. She had hoped that in selling her ranch to her brother-in-law, the matter would be closed for good.

She smiled at her husband, pretending her past mistakes didn't haunt her. She had asked for his forgiveness and the Lord's, as well. But she just couldn't seem to forgive herself. Especially now.

"Has Mr. Morgan said anything more about closing the bank?" Marty asked.

Jake looked up from the piece of bread he'd been about to break in half. "No. He's hangin' on like a man breakin' in a new bronc." His Southern drawl rang clear, as it often did when Jake let down his guard.

"There's a chance he might be able to pull through?" she asked, trying not to sound too desperate.

"There's always a chance," Jake said with a look of seeming indifference. Then he offered her a smile.

It was one of the first she'd seen in days. "You seem hopeful."

He shrugged. "I guess there's not much else we can be. I figure we have to have hope. I know God hasn't forgotten us down here. Someone reminded me today about the depression of '73. Things were bad then, too, and we fought our way outta that one."

"Mr. Brentwood at the orphanage mentioned that, as well," Marty countered. "Apparently his father was some type of investor back then and lost most everything. He managed to rebuild his business, however, and that was what gave Mr. Brentwood the money to start the orphanage." Marty had taken to volunteering at the orphanage frequently, especially since the economical problems had forced Brentwood to let go of so many workers. "He also reminded me that God sometimes allows things to happen that we can't begin to understand in order to benefit us later."

"We can be assured that God will never forget us," Alice agreed, "although sometimes it does seem He's distracted."

After losing the butler and housekeeper, Marty had insisted Alice join them for meals and be an extended member of the family. At first the girl had been uncomfortable with the idea, but she was gradually getting used to it.

For several minutes the conversation waned. Marty finished her bowl of stew, and though she could easily have eaten more, she settled for what she'd eaten. Jake would need another serving, and there wasn't much left.

"I hope you won't mind," Jake said, putting his spoon in the empty bowl, "but I arranged with a man today to take some of the furniture from the house. He'll be by tomorrow to crate it off."

"Let me refill that for you, Mr. Wythe," Alice said, jumping up.

"Thanks. I have to say it makes a mighty fine meal on a cold night." He smiled at the younger woman and then looked back to Marty. "Anyway, like I was sayin', he'll be here tomorrow."

Marty tried to hide her frown. She knew this was probably a sign of things to come and didn't like it. If Jake felt it necessary to sell furnishings, he'd probably had his salary reduced once again. She tried to force a smile. "I think that sounds wise. We certainly don't need so much stuff. With winter nearly upon us I thought perhaps we should close off the third floor all together. Alice can sleep in one of the second-floor bedrooms. It should help dramatically with the heating."

"I agree," Jake replied as Alice placed the bowl of stew in front of him. "Thank you, Alice. Next time, though, I can just fetch it myself."

Marty turned to Alice. "Jake and I were just talking about closing off the third floor. It's hard enough to heat the downstairs bedrooms, and we figure it will save on the overall heating of the house. You can take one of the second-floor bedrooms in the same wing as ours. That way we can also close off the other unused rooms."

Alice nodded. "That's perfectly acceptable to me. I'll arrange it tonight. Did I also understand that Mr. Wythe is selling off furniture?"

"Yes." Marty looked to her husband. "Just some of the things we don't really need."

It wasn't the first time Jake had sold something from the house. In the beginning he'd only handed off his own meager possessions for cash. Now he was actually going to sell things that could be considered as belonging to the bank.

Paul Morgan, the bank president and distant relative of J. P. Morgan, had presented the furnished house and mortgage to Jake, along with a promotion to bank manager. He had been carefully schooling Jake to eventually take a position of higher regard and wanted the Wythe family to be part of the socially elite. Marty couldn't help but wonder whether the man would be accepting of Jake's present plans, especially knowing they were months in arrears with the mortgage payment.

Jake had assured her that with his cut in salary, Morgan had promised that the mortgage would be covered by the bank as part of his pay. Marty didn't say so at the time, but she'd never had a good feeling about this arrangement, since there was nothing in writing.

"Thanksgiving and Christmas are nearly upon us," Jake declared. "It would be nice to have a little money so we can at least celebrate with a nice meal." He once again smiled. "Not that this stew and bread isn't just as satisfying. Even Cook didn't make anything that tasted this good, but I thought maybe we could buy a ham or turkey."

Marty remembered some of the outrageously rich meals they'd shared in the early days of her marriage to Jake. They weren't even to their first anniversary, yet they'd gone from feast to famine. Marty's sister, Hannah, had taught her that money would always be fleeting and a person shouldn't ever put their trust in such a temporal thing. Even so, it was a very necessary thing, and Marty had to admit, she missed it.

"Can we sell the house?" Marty asked without thinking.

Jake said nothing for what seemed an awfully long time. "I've asked around, but no one is buying. No one wants a house that's clearly above the normal man's means."

His serious expression gave Marty cause to wonder if there was more to it than Jake was letting on. "I didn't know you'd asked around."

"I was plannin' on tellin' you about it," he admitted, "but only if it looked like a real possibility. I didn't want to get your hopes up."

"I see." Marty looked to Alice and then back to her husband. She offered him a smile. "I guess that isn't what God wants for us then. If He had plans for us to sell this place, then He'd also send a buyer our way. We'll just have to trust that He has something else in mind."

"I agree," Jake said with a tired sigh. "In the meantime we'll just sell what we have to and get by the best we can."

"Living frugally is something I know very well," Marty assured him.

"Me too," Alice agreed.

Jake nodded. "I know. But . . . I . . . well, it's not what I wanted for any of us." He looked as if he might say something more but got to his feet instead and once again smiled. "I sure didn't mean to put a damper on supper. I'll stoke up the fire in the sitting room and maybe we can retire there. Then I'll read the Scriptures before we head upstairs."

Marty said nothing to Jake, but once he left the room, she turned to Alice. "Something's not right. There's more to this than he's saying."

"Maybe he'll tell you later tonight . . . in private," Alice replied, gathering up the dishes.

"I'd just as soon he tell me now instead of letting me wonder about it."

"Something else you might consider," Alice said with a pause. "We could move our bedrooms to the first floor and close both the second and third floors."

"There aren't any bedrooms down here," Marty said, and then it dawned on her what Alice was getting at. "But we have the two sitting rooms, the library, and the music room. We could certainly convert two of those into bedrooms. It's not like we need them for entertaining."

"Exactly."

"I'll mention it to Jake. I think he'll go along with it, as well. We'll have to figure out how to get things moved around. I wish Samson were still with us." Samson was the former stableman and driver, and Marty missed his presence when it came to moving furniture . . . and to intimidating the irritating Mr. Smith.

Marty helped Alice with the cleanup, but all the while her mind raced with thoughts of what was going on inside her husband's head. It was only as they put away the last of the clean dishes that Marty realized she'd said nothing to Jake about the reappearance of Mr. Smith.

I don't suppose now would be a good time to tell him.

She looked at Alice and forced a smile. "Well, we might as well join Jake." She pulled off her apron and hung it on a nail by the door.

"I'll be there shortly," Alice replied. "Let me put water on for tea."

Marty met Alice's gaze. The young woman clearly felt the tension. She had become Marty's dearest friend, and yet there was still so much the two women kept hidden away. Maybe it was better that way. Maybe if the worst came about and they had to part company it would be easier to bear.

"I doubt it," Marty muttered.

"What?" Alice asked.

Marty shook her head and turned for the door. "It wasn't important. Just me grumbling. Tea sounds wonderful."

She hurried away before Alice could press for more details. Sometimes life here was like juggling balls at a circus. Keeping everything in motion required not only skill but complete concentration. Unfortunately, Marty wasn't at all certain that she had enough of either one to get through this crisis.

Chapter 2

"What exactly are you saying?" Marty asked her husband. Just days earlier he had assured her there was hope for the bank and his position, but now everything had changed.

"I'm saying that as of today, I'm no longer employed. Morgan closed the bank. He's taking what he can and reinvesting elsewhere."

"But what does that have to do with us living here?"

Jake looked her in the eye. "The house is in foreclosure. The bank owns it now. There's nothing left for us to do but leave. I figure we can take what's ours and head to Texas."

"No! I'm not moving to Texas," Marty said, a little angrier than she'd intended. "I don't understand any of this. Mr. Morgan didn't even give us a warning. He said that everything was fine, that the house was included as part of your salary. How can that be changed now?"

"Sweetheart, I wish I had better news. Truly I do. But you can't make something outta nothin', and that's all that's left."

"But it's not right." Marty began to pace. Surely this was nothing more than another nightmare. She would wake up any moment now.

"Nothing about this financial mess is right," Jake replied. "The government has devalued silver, the railroads are almost all in receivership, and the only man in the country with any ability to dig the government out of its grave is J. P. Morgan. I was told in strictest confidence that

J. P. Morgan will most likely end up loaning the government money to continue running its day-to-day operations."

"How can any one man be that rich?" Marty asked, sitting down rather hard. The news regarding the bank's situation wasn't unexpected, but she'd never anticipated that they would have to make an immediate move. Where could they go?

"I guess he played his cards right," Jake replied with a shrug. "Mr. Morgan at the bank said J. P. Morgan is a financial genius."

"Then perhaps he should share some of that genius with everyone else," Marty said, shaking her head.

"It's to his benefit to share his money and get some hefty interest payments on it," Jake said. "But be that as it may, we have to make plans, Marty. I know life isn't what you wanted it to be, but I have to go where there's work. I have friends in eastern Texas, and you have family near Dallas. Between the two places, I ought to be able to find something."

Marty felt discomfort in the pit of her stomach. Why was this happening? Why couldn't they just go on living in Denver? Maybe she could get a job . . . and Alice, too. Alice would be happy to help, just to have a place to stay.

"We can get jobs here," she told him, jumping to her feet again. "I'm sure there is something Alice and I can do. After all, we aren't helpless socialites." She walked back and forth as she thought. "I can sew, cook, clean, take care of children. I'm sure to find something."

"Well there isn't much here for *me*," Jake said. "I only know two things—banking and ranching." He laughed. "Who would have thought a man could have two such opposite skills. My life ain't exactly predictable."

Marty stopped in midstep. "Jake, I know you understand my feelings about Texas. They haven't changed." She didn't want to make him feel guilty for his plans, but she had to make him choose another path. "Why don't you get in touch with my brother Andy? He's ranching in Wyoming. You could write to him and see if he needs some help."

Her mind whirled with thoughts. She didn't want Jake to go back to ranching. The dangers were too high and the payoff too minimal. Even so, if she talked him into writing to her brother, that would at least give her a little time in which she and Alice might be able to secure jobs. If they were both working, maybe Jake could relax a bit and find some menial task to put his hand to. It was worth a try.

"I don't know anything about ranching in Wyoming," Jake replied. "I know Texas."

"But ranching is ranching, isn't it?"

He shook his head. "You know as well as I do that the elements are completely different. Now, stop with this nonsense." He sounded firmer than he had earlier. "I'm gonna do what I can to support you. I figure you and Alice can stay here in Denver while I go to Texas. Once I get established I'll send for you both."

She looked at him in surprise. "And where do you propose we stay? You've already told us we have to vacate the house. I don't see that affording us many choices."

"Well, that's what I really wanted to talk to you about. See, I spoke with Mr. Brentwood at that orphanage you like so much. I happened to see him on my way home and told him what had happened. He suggested you and Alice could come stay at the orphanage and help out there in exchange for room and board. I told him I thought that would work well."

"You decided that without even talking to me first?" she asked in a rage. She wasn't really mad about the prospects of living at the orphanage. God knew she loved the children and was completely devoted to helping them through this bad time. She'd been sharing whatever she could with them ever since the country's crisis began. What angered her most was that everything was spinning out of control, and she had no say in it.

"Marty, listen to me," Jake said, coming to put his hands on her shoulders. She tried to move away, but he'd have no part of it and held her fast. "Marty, we aren't the only ones sufferin' here. The rest of the country is hurtin', too. We knew it was only a matter of time."

"For you to lose your job and the bank to close, yes. To lose our home and have to relocate to Texas, no. I didn't bargain for that."

He gave her a lopsided smile, which only served to irritate Marty all the more.

"None of us exactly bargained for any of this." He sobered. "Now listen to me, please. I've been looking around the city for work since this summer. I knew there'd come a time when my job would be no more. There's nothing here. There are hundreds—no, thousands of men without work. Denver doesn't offer a whole lot of opportunities just now."

Marty relaxed just a bit. "I know that. I'm not naïve."

He nodded. "No you aren't. You're a reasonable woman when you want to be, and I need you to be that now. My friends, the Vandermarks, live in eastern Texas and have a logging business. I figure they can hire me on for a time."

"Logging? But that's just as dangerous as ranching, maybe more so," Marty countered.

Jake shook his head. "You can't keep me from harm by hiding me from danger, Martha Wythe. I'm a man and I have to do what is right for me. I know you're afraid. I know you hate Texas, although I don't pretend to understand why."

"But you've gone to college. You have an education. You should be one of the men helping to change this country and solve the problems we're in. You don't need to go back to branding and driving cattle to market. You're worth more than that."

"Now, wait just a minute, Marty. Are you suggesting that ranching is less important work than sittin' behind a desk? 'Cause if you are, then I must disagree. You know full well that ranching is an honorable and necessary way to make a living. Some of the finest and smartest men I've known were ranchers. You're just worked up because of the news, but I won't have you talkin' like ranching is somehow demeaning. You grew up with it, and it benefited you nicely. Kept you fed and clothed and in some ways brought us together."

She started to speak, but he put his finger to her lips. "I know. You lost one husband to a ranching accident in Texas and you fear losin' another. But, Marty, we both know that's not the way things work. God is either gonna take me home or leave me here to work out livin' my life. We've gotta trust Him for the answer."

"I do trust Him," Marty declared. "But I don't trust that this is the right decision."

"Because you don't trust me?" he asked. His voice was full of sorrow.

Marty considered the question. Was that the problem? Did she lack the ability to trust Jake? To trust him to do the right thing for both of them? Jake had never done one thing to break the trust between them, while Marty on the other hand had lied about owning the ranch in Texas, about selling it back to her brother-in-law, about so much. Certainly she'd done her best to make up for it. She'd finally told the truth, and Jake had forgiven her and trusted her. Didn't she owe him the same?

"I trust you," she said, nearly choking from the emotions rising up in her. "It's not about trust."

"Isn't it?" He studied her for a moment. "I love you, Marty. You know that. I wouldn't do anything to hurt you, but you have got to let me be the man of this family and make decisions that I think are best."

"But you don't care about my desires," she said. "If you did, you wouldn't talk about Texas."

"Texas isn't the problem, Marty, and we both know it."

She stiffened. "Meaning what? That I'm the problem?"

He shrugged. "As my grandmother used to say, 'If the shoe fits, you might as well kick yourself with it.' You know as well as I do that your brother-in-law and sister would have us back on the ranch in a heartbeat."

"They've never said any such thing." She pulled away. "You're just assuming on their good nature."

"I'm not assuming anything. I know from the way you've talked about them that they're God-fearing people. They wouldn't see you go in need, and because we're married, they wouldn't see me go in need, either. And I'm not talkin' about a handout. I could work for them, Marty. I would work hard, and you could be back amongst your family again."

Marty searched her mind desperately for some excuse to reject such a resolution. "And what . . . what of Alice?"

"She could come, too. You know that I care about what happens to her. She's too young to be on her own. And that Smith character is just a step away from causin' her harm. Think about that, Marty. Put your selfish desires aside and think about Alice. Texas could mean freedom for her. Freedom from the fear of Smith and his cronies."

Marty hated being made to feel guilty for her fears. She bristled and narrowed her eyes. "Go then. Go to Texas or wherever else you choose. Just don't expect me to follow."

She left him staring after her and fled for the quiet of the kitchen. Shaking from head to toe, Marty hovered near the stove for comfort. But the heat hardly seemed to permeate her body. The cold she felt came from the inside and nothing could warm it.

★

The following day Marty allowed Mr. Brentwood to show her and Alice to a large room with two single beds.

"This used to be one of the rooms for the older children," he told the ladies. "Of course those orphans are gone now. Some, as you know, to your sister's place in Texas, and others . . . well, they were dispersed to the streets or wherever we could find temporary homes. Anyway, there used to be eight beds in here, but I had to sell some of those. Didn't even get a pittance of what they were worth."

Marty knew very well about the hardships Mr. Brentwood faced. The orphanage had once housed over fifty children and now maintained no more than fifteen. Even that number taxed Mr. Brentwood's meager funds.

"I strung a rope in the corner from one wall to the other. It's good and secure. I figured you could hang clothes from it or make a curtain for changing behind."

"This looks fine," Alice said, pulling Marty from her thoughts. "I'm sure we will be quite comfortable."

Marty met the man's worried look. "Yes. It will be fine." She wanted to give him a smile of reassurance but had none to offer. Just that morning she had told her husband good-bye. She'd offered him neither her encouragement nor her love, and only now was beginning to feel guilty for her actions.

"Frankly, I'm glad to have your help," Brentwood admitted. "I have plenty of room for you here. Even the food will stretch to include two more mouths. What I don't have is time for all the needs of the children or money for staff. You will both be very valuable to me in that sense.

With you here, I can leave you in charge while I go appeal in person to some of the churches and charities that have helped us in the past. There may not be much to be had in the way of donations, but anything is better than nothing."

Alice stepped forward. "I have managed to secure a job waiting tables. It's only part-time work and won't pay very much. I'm happy, however, to contribute what I can to help with the food purchases for Marty and me."

"That's most generous, Miss Chesterfield." Mr. Brentwood offered her a warm smile. "Now if you'll excuse me, I'll let you two get settled in while I return to the classroom."

Marty nodded but said nothing more. She looked around the stark room that would become her home for no one knew how long. Without thought, she plopped down on one of the beds. It wasn't anywhere near as comfortable as the goose down mattress she'd shared with Jake.

"I suppose we could have it much worse."

Alice turned and met her gaze. "Much worse . . . believe me. This is truly an answer to prayer, Marty. I know you aren't happy about it, but at least we're safe here. Mr. Brentwood and the children will help keep us from being so easily accessible to Mr. Smith. With Mr. Wythe gone, we were bound to be vulnerable to Smith's attacks."

Marty knew the truth of it, but she didn't want to admit it. Admitting it gave credence to Jake's choice, and that was something she couldn't do. He hadn't cared about her feelings. He hadn't listened to her pleadings or even taken into consideration her ideas for alternatives. It caused her great pain to know that her desires weren't important to him.

★

Robert Barnett settled back in the saddle and waited for his father to catch up. The day was chilly but otherwise not too uncomfortable for working out on the range. He and his father had just finished checking on the herd in the north pastures and knew it wouldn't be long until they'd have a great many new calves. New calves equaled more stock, and more stock meant more financial security—at least eventually. With the country suffering a depression right now, Robert knew they might well have to sit on the herd for a long time before being able to sell at a reasonable price.

Of course, profit wasn't everything, and Robert knew his father to donate animals to some of the charities and poorhouses. Kindness and concern for his fellowman was something Robert's parents had instilled in him from the time he was a little boy.

"There will always be someone less fortunate than you," his mother had told him on many occasions, *"and you must remember that what you do for them is serving the Lord himself."* Robert always took that to heart—maybe too much so. He was always finding some poor soul to take on as what his mother fondly called his "special project."

His father's bay made good time closing the distance between them. William Barnett rode a horse as if born to it and had made certain his son could do the same. Robert couldn't help but admire his father's daring as he put the horse into a fast gallop and jumped the narrow ravine that divided the two sections of the north range.

"Ma would have your hide if she saw you do that," he said as the bay came to an abrupt halt about ten feet away.

"Your mother isn't out here, and I'll have *your* hide if you say anything to her about it," his father replied.

Robert grinned. "Yeah, well, I'd just as soon not have a tanning from either of you. So I guess I'll keep my mouth closed. What'd you find?"

"Most of the herd has stayed together on this side," he said. "There's a good mix of brands—Atherton's, Watson's, and ours for a good start. I saw a few head that belong to some of the smaller outfits, as well. We'll get 'em all sorted out at roundup."

Nodding, Robert turned his horse toward the south. "The cows seem to be in good shape. Most look to be expecting. Hopefully the weather will hold and we'll have a mild winter."

Father drew up alongside as they made their way back toward the ranch. "The talk at the Grange was that it would be."

"You been hangin' out at the Farmer's Association again?" he asked with a grin. "What will the other ranchers think?"

His father laughed. "My guess is they're listenin' to whoever will help them keep their stock alive and well fed.

"Plenty of good feed out here." Robert scanned the open grasslands. A carpet of brown and gold had replaced the rich greens of summer. He breathed in the surprisingly dry air and smiled. This was his home, his land. His parents had long ago told him of their plan to pass it on to him, and in turn he had developed a deep love of all that he could see.

"That smile on account of the party tonight?" his father asked.

The comment pulled Robert's thoughts back to the immediate. "Not exactly."

"I thought maybe you were thinking of a particular young lady. You know the holiday season is a good time to propose."

"I know that everyone figures that's where my mind is most of the time," Robert replied.

"Well, it's long been figured that you and Jessica Atherton would marry. Now that she's just had her nineteenth birthday, I thought maybe you two would be makin' an announcement." His father threw him a wry smile.

"Yeah, well, folks have been figurin' a lot of things that aren't necessarily so," Robert countered. "As far as I'm concerned, Jessica is too young and too spoiled."

"She'll grow up fast enough. Besides, you're twenty-seven. You ought to settle down and start a family. You're gonna need a good number of sons to help you keep up with this spread."

Robert considered the comment. It wasn't that he didn't want to have a family, especially a wife. He'd long been desirous of that very thing, but he loved Jessica Atherton like a sister, not a woman to marry.

"Pa, I . . . well . . . Jess and I don't have a lot in common. I care about her, don't get me wrong."

He shifted his weight in the saddle and realized his back and shoulders were weary of the ride. By the look of the sun's position he'd been in the saddle for nearly eight hours without many breaks.

"What are you sayin', son?"

"I'm sayin' that I don't know that I can marry her. She doesn't want a ranching life. She's told me over and over that she wants to live in a big city with loads of servants and free time." He shook his head. It was hard to even imagine such a life and how a man might fit into the scheme of things. "I know some people expect us to marry. Mostly her ma and mine, but honestly, I don't know that I want to spend the rest of my life with her."

"Marriage is a real important thing, son. You don't want to be toying with the girl's affections if you don't intend to do the honorable thing." His father's weathered face bore considerable concern.

"I've never toyed with her affections, Pa. I haven't even kissed her." He felt his face grow hot. The topic had suddenly become embarrassing. Truth was he'd not kissed any girl other than his mother and sisters. He'd had plenty of chances, but his mother and father had always put into his heart the need for chastity and caution when it came to stirring up romantic feelings.

"I didn't mean to suggest you hadn't treated her right. I just want you to be sure that you don't lead her on."

"I don't think Jessica loves me any more than I love her. We're just like brother and sister or good friends. And I hope we will always be that—after all, we grew up knowing each other's families. We're all close, and I don't want to lose that."

His father nodded. "Well, make sure of your heart. I know you've long taken up the affairs of the broken and wounded. Don't let your heart be swayed by guilt or worry over what folks will think. She'll recover a lot faster if you just lay it on the line with her. I don't want to see either of you compromising or giving in just to keep the other from feeling bad."

"I just don't know for sure what I'm supposed to do."

"Have you prayed on it?" his father asked.

"I have. I still am."

William Barnett smiled. "Good. I'm glad to hear it. Maybe tonight at the party you'll get a feel for what you're supposed to do."

"Christmas seems a bad time of year to tell someone you aren't gonna marry them, especially when everyone figures you will."

"Christmas is still two weeks away, and the truth is never something to be delayed. Think about it, son. You may have more feelings for her than you realize. Might be that the expectations are what's clouding your heart. Give it to the Lord and see where He wants to take you."

Father was right, of course. He always offered wise counsel, and Robert would do well to heed it. Still, he hated to hurt Jessica. She might be a pampered child, but she was still deserving of genteel consideration, and he did care about her. Putting the matter to the back of his mind, Robert gave his father a grin and touched his spurs to his mount.

"Right now He wants to take me home to some of Ma's great cooking. Race you back!" His sorrel gelding shot forward in a streak of red.

Chapter 3

Alice gave a quick glance in the mirror to check her blond hair before heading out to wait tables at the Denver Daily Diner. She'd been blessed to get a job so quickly, despite her scarred face. The owner, Frank Bellows, told her that it didn't matter to him. The clients he catered to were mostly rough and rugged railroad men whose aim was to eat quickly and get back to work. She could still hear the words of Mr. Bellows: *"You're still kind of pretty—enough to entice them to buy an extra piece of pie. Just keep your face turned to the right and maybe they won't notice the scar."*

But Alice knew that wasn't enough. The scar was still noticeable, although after a year it was finally starting to fade. Marty's idea to use whale oil on the scar had helped in a most remarkable way.

Touching her fingers to the line that ran from just below her earlobe to her chin, Alice couldn't help but relive the horrible moment. Memories of the night her attacker cut her flooded her mind. She could almost smell his putrid breath and the stench of cigarettes.

"Place is filling up, Miss Chesterfield. Best get out there," Bellows said as he passed her on his way to the storeroom.

"Yes, sir." Alice pulled on a pinafore-style apron and tied it securely. She was grateful the man had been willing to take a chance on her, and she didn't want to let him down.

In the dining room the counter was already full. Some of the men had been waited on by Mr. Bellows and were happily focused on their meals, but others were waiting for attention.

She smiled and approached the counter. "Who's first?"

"Me," a burly man in oily denim announced. "I'll take the beef sandwich special—three of 'em." He drew out a large handkerchief from his pocket. Wiping his face, he quickly added, "Cup of coffee, too."

"Sure thing," Alice said.

"I'm next," a skinny but equally dirty man said, motioning Alice to the far end of the counter. "Give me a bowl of gravy and biscuits, a ham steak, and a glass of milk."

Alice jotted down the order and hurried to the next man. She took five orders in all before turning them over to the cook. By this time even more men had crowded into the small diner. It looked to be a very busy day.

Without regard for her aching back or sore feet, Alice maneuvered amidst the hungry men, dealing out menus and coffee like a gambler might deal cards. She smiled and for a time forgot about her scarred face. The men were hungry and didn't seem to care all that much that she was damaged. They were mainly interested in filling their empty bellies and getting back to work before the lunch whistle blew. No one wanted to risk losing a job in this economy.

"Order for four more beef sandwiches," she announced, putting two tickets on the cook's counter.

The man glared at her. He wasn't at all the pleasant sort. "I only got two hands," he told her.

Alice didn't wait to comment. She had a half dozen pie orders to deliver, and since desserts were something she had sole responsibility for, she didn't want to take time out for conversation.

By the end of the lunch rush, Alice felt like she had barely managed to meet the demands of the men. There was a great deal of improvement needed before things would run smoothly.

Hurrying to gather the dirty dishes and clear the tables, Alice nearly ran over Mr. Bellows. He reached out to steady her. "Whoa there, li'l gal."

"Sorry. I should have been looking where I was going."

He nodded toward the now-empty dining room. "You did a good job there. I have to say you surprised me."

She smiled. "Thank you. I know I'll get better with time."

"Tell Joe I said to get right on those dishes after he puts another batch of roasts in the oven."

Alice nodded and hurried with an armful of plates and cups to the kitchen sink. Joe, the cook and dishwasher, stood to one side of the room picking his teeth. He noticed her and frowned.

"Ain't no end to it."

Feeling self-conscious as he continued to stare at her face, Alice motioned toward the dishes. "Mr. Bellows asked me to tell you he needs those dishes done as soon as you get the roasts in the oven."

"I know my job. Nobody's gotta tell me." He pushed his hand back through his greasy hair. The man's slovenly appearance was only worse after working the noon rush.

Alice didn't like him, nor did she like the way he always seemed to be watching her. She didn't mean to be so judgmental, especially at their first meeting, but the way he watched her reminded her of Mr. Smith—almost as if he were studying her for some troublesome purpose.

Alice thought to apologize for offending the man, but she didn't want to encourage conversation, so she simply deposited the dishes on the counter and returned to the dining room for more.

With the tables finally clean, Alice set to sweeping the floors. She was just finishing when Mr. Bellows appeared in his coat and hat. "I'm taking the noon monies to the bank. We did good today. I'm sure you made some decent tips."

There hadn't been time to check, but Alice did feel the considerable weight of change in her skirt pockets. Mostly it was pennies, but even those added up. "I suppose so," she murmured.

"Good. I hope so. This job don't pay much, so those tips are gonna make all the difference. That'll encourage you to be extra nice to the fellows."

"Is it always this busy at noon?"

Bellows shrugged. "Not always. A lot of the married workers bring their own lunches and might stop by for hot coffee. Others are single

270

and don't have anyone to look after them. Many who used to work for the railroad shops here are out of work now. It's anybody's guess as to when things will turn around. I figure the word got spread about you being here and most came out of curiosity. With any luck, they'll be back.

"When you've finished cleaning up in the front, you can head out. Tell Joe I'll be right back to handle any customers."

Alice nodded and watched Mr. Bellows leave. She was weary to the bone but glad to have a chance to earn a little money. She hurried to finish wiping down the counters and was just about ready to leave when she noticed Joe watching her again. Remembering Mr. Bellows's comment, Alice cleared her throat.

"Mr. Bellows said he'd be right back and will handle any customers once he returns." The man gave a brief nod but said nothing. He kept watching her with his piercing gaze, leaving Alice most uncomfortable.

A sense of dread crept up her spine. She hesitated a moment. "Is something wrong?"

He smiled. "Just wondered if you'd like to step out with me tonight. There's a good place a few blocks away where we could hear some music and maybe dance. Good food, too. I know you made some tips today, so maybe you could treat me to a cold beer or two."

The man's comment left Alice confused. "You . . . you want me to buy you a beer? Or two?"

"Sure and maybe some supper." He laughed. "I can't leave until after the roasts and pies finish baking, but I figure we could have ourselves a little fun."

Regaining her composure, Alice undid the ties of her apron. "I don't think so. I have responsibilities."

"You ain't married. I heard you tell that to Bellows. So you can't have that much to be responsible for." He once again pushed back his oily hair, as if it were the only thing out of place on his person. "I know how to show a gal a good time, and I can clean up good."

"I'm sorry. No." Alice hung her apron and went to retrieve her coat. "I'm expected at home." She pulled the coat on and hurriedly buttoned it. Then, retrieving her bonnet and securing it over her hair, she made her way toward the back of the kitchen.

Joe deliberately blocked her path to the door. "You're kind of uppity for a gal who's all marked up like that. Ain't like you can rely on your looks to get yourself hitched. You be nice to me, and I might even think about lettin' you be my steady gal. I don't much mind the scar, since you got a fetchin' backside."

Alice couldn't keep the surprise from her face. Her eyes widened and she stammered for words. "I . . . you can't be . . . Oh my . . ." She stopped attempting to make sense. "I have to go." She looked past him to the door, wishing she could somehow will herself outside. For a moment she feared he might try to force her to stay.

However, with a grunt, Joe shrugged and stepped away. "You'll change your tune soon enough. Ain't gonna be just any man who'll want you around—leastwise not the marryin' kind. No one's gonna want a wife lookin' like that."

Alice hurried past him and out the back door before he could say another word. The man was abominably rude, but she knew he was right. No decent man would want a disfigured woman. Tears came to her eyes, stinging as the December wind hit her face. She did her best to control her emotions, but this time of year was especially hard. It was only the second time she'd faced Christmas without any family of her own.

Pulling her coat tight, Alice fought to regain control of her thoughts. Joe was just one of those unpleasant sort of men who preyed on vulnerable women. His nonsense needn't upset her any more than it had. Alice was fully capable of taking care of the matter, and if he got out of hand, she would tell Mr. Bellows. Hopefully the proprietor would be so pleased with her service that he wouldn't brook such nonsense from his cook.

With her emotions back in check as she approached the orphanage, Alice vowed to put the matter behind her. It was just one incident, and now that Joe knew how she felt . . . well . . . they could put the discomfort aside and do their jobs.

Inside the orphanage Alice caught the aroma of freshly baked bread. It gave her a sense of security and welcome. Marty was a marvel at baking. Her biscuits were always light as a feather and her cinnamon rolls the best Alice had ever tasted. Making her way to the kitchen, Alice paused in the doorway to breathe in the scent as Marty peeked into the oven.

"Ah, you're here at last," Marty said as she pulled several loaves of bread from the oven.

"Yes, it was a busy lunch, and it took time to clean up afterward."

"I can well imagine. The railroads might be suffering, but life goes on, eh?" Marty put a pan of biscuits into the oven. "Supper will be in an hour. You probably want to go freshen up."

Alice nodded. "I do. I'm worn to the core. The job is much more difficult than being a maid for you." She gave a laugh. "I'm afraid Mrs. Landry was right—you spoiled me for proper work."

Marty joined in the chuckle. "She's Mrs. Brighton now, as you will recall, but I believe she was wrong. There isn't a spoiled bone in your body. Now take this kettle of hot water and go give your feet a good soaking." Marty wrapped a towel around the handle and pulled it from the stove. "You'll feel better in twenty minutes. Oh, and don't forget to add some peppermint oil to the water."

Alice took hold of the kettle. "I don't have to do that, Marty. I can stay here and help you prepare supper."

"I insist. There will be plenty of work for you to help with another day, but tonight you need to take it easy. Now go."

She didn't have the strength to argue. Instead, Alice made her way to the bedroom and did as Marty had suggested. The hot water was soothing to her aching feet, and she eased back into the chair and closed her eyes. The scent of peppermint wafted up from the steam, reminding her of her childhood.

"*Can I have some candy?*" she had asked her mother once when they'd been shopping. Alice couldn't have been more than five or six, but the memory was quite clear.

"*Of course,*" her mother had answered, reaching for three peppermint sticks. "*You are my little princess, and you can have most anything your heart desires.*"

Alice couldn't remember the details of her mother's face, but the scent and sweet taste of peppermint always reminded her of her mother. Pity the woman hadn't truly cared for her daughter. The last time Alice had seen her mother and little brother was now just a dim memory.

Since she was young, Alice had been told she favored her mother considerably. They both had blond hair and blue eyes, while Alice's younger brother, Simon, favored their father, with brown hair and blue eyes.

Alice had thought there'd been a special bond between mother and daughter. But since her mother seemed to have little difficulty deserting their home in the middle of the night with Simon in tow, Alice knew she couldn't have felt very strongly about her daughter.

How could a mother just walk away from her child? How could she leave Alice to fend for herself? To face abandonment and bitterness? Alice's, father had been a bear to live with in the early days after Mother left. He'd raged against her mother, declaring her a heartless woman who had no concern for the pain she'd caused Alice. Father had lectured Alice daily about all of her mother's shortcomings. Little was mentioned about Simon, yet Alice missed him with all her heart. He had been her only sibling, and though he was eight years her junior, she had loved him dearly.

After a few months, Alice's father seemed to settle into their new life. He kept guarded watch over Alice, even hiring a woman to walk her to and from school. He gave strict orders that Alice never go outside without him. She wasn't sure why he demanded this but eventually decided he was afraid something might happen to her and then he'd be alone.

Alice continued to watch and hope that her mother and brother would return to them. She spoke of them whenever her father appeared to be in a good mood and often asked if he thought they'd ever come home. He always told her it was a hopeless desire.

In spite of her father's negative thinking, Alice would hurry home from school and ask if there'd been any word from Mother. She saw a mixture of pain and resentment cross his expression as he replied that there wasn't. Alice had longed to comfort him, but it seemed the only way to do that was to say nothing at all—to pretend Mother and Simon had never existed. It wasn't something she could easily do. She wanted them to come home. She wanted her father to go out and find them.

"Do you think maybe the sheriff could find them?" she had innocently asked her father one morning nearly a year after her mother's disappearance.

"No," her father had said adamantly. "He won't be of any help to us now. I've had word about them."

"You've heard from Mother?" Alice could still remember the feeling of hope. Her heart had been wrung like a wet towel, squeezing out the pain of loss and betrayal of abandonment until all that remained was the desperate desire of a child to see her mother again.

"I'm sorry, Alice. Your mother and brother are dead."

He said the words so matter-of-factly that for a moment they didn't even register. Alice forced meaning into the words, however, and her eyes filled with tears. "Dead? How? When?"

She thought her heart might actually stop beating. "Dead?"

"It was some sort of epidemic. I'm sorry. They died quickly and the authorities sent me word. That's all I intend to stay about the subject."

And that was all he would say. No matter Alice's pleading to know more, her father was determined that they put the matter behind them. To his dying day, he refused to ever allow Alice to mention her mother or brother again. It was as if they had simply been eradicated.

Chapter 4

Christmas morning found the orphans awake before dawn. Marty could hear them whispering and giggling from their separate dorm rooms. The boys were especially noisy in their space. Since there were ten boys and only five girls, it made sense they would be louder.

"I think we'd better hurry," Marty said, tucking her blouse into her skirt. "They don't sound any too patient."

"Given the promise of presents and goodies, you can hardly blame them," Alice replied. She finished braiding her hair and tied it off with a ribbon.

"Church comes first, though, and they know that full well."

Marty took up a jacket to match her dark blue wool skirt. Slipping her arms into the added warmth, she couldn't help but wonder if it had snowed again in the night. She could still remember her first Colorado snow and how she and Jake had thrown snowballs at each other. The memory caused her heart to ache. How she missed him.

But she didn't want to miss him. She wanted not to care that he was gone. God had been her mainstay through these difficult weeks, but Jake was never far from her thoughts. Now she would face Christmas without him. Without any word from him. Marty frowned.

"Is something wrong?" Alice asked.

"Nothing that hasn't been wrong for a while now."

"Mr. Wythe?"

"Jake. Just call him Jake," Marty insisted. "And yes, I suppose there's no sense in pretending otherwise."

Alice smiled. "It's only because you love him so dearly."

Marty buttoned her jacket and turned away to take up a handkerchief. "My love means very little to him. But let's not fret over things we cannot change. It's time to ready the children for the morning service. Hopefully they've managed to start dressing themselves."

She headed out of the room, hoping Alice would let the matter drop. She didn't want to talk about Jake and how much it hurt to be without him.

Mr. Brentwood was already busy with the boys. "We were out early to clear the walkways of snow," he told her. He had most of the ten wearing their clean Sunday clothes and was working to get everyone to comb their hair. Marty had to smile at the question posed by seven-year-old Wyatt.

"Why do we have to wear our Sunday clothes again today? It's Monday."

"But," Mr. Brentwood replied with infinite patience, "we are going to church again to celebrate the birth of our Lord Jesus. Remember what we talked about yesterday?"

Wyatt looked at the other boys, ranging in age from four to eleven, and nodded with a sigh. "We gotta go to church two times 'cause it's Christmas."

Marty smiled. "And you want to look your best."

"Can God see us even when we're not wearin' our best?" ten-year-old Thad asked.

Mr. Brentwood straightened from combing the hair of a rather rambunctious four-year-old named Benjamin. "God can see us everywhere—all the time."

Thad shrugged. "Then why does He care which clothes I wear? He's already seen the others."

Marty ducked her face to avoid the gaze of the children. She thought she might well burst into laughter at any moment and pretended instead to fuss with her buttons. How the children lightened her weary heart.

"God doesn't really care which clothes we wear. We're doing this to honor Him—to show Him that we're willing to take extra care to clean up and look our best for Him." Mr. Brentwood cleared his throat. "Now, remember what I said. We will eat our breakfast and open gifts when we return. If you misbehave in church, you will miss out on the fun. So remember the rules about being in God's house: No talking. No running. No fussing or fighting. We owe God our respect."

This sobered all ten of the boys in the wink of an eye. They nodded, assuring their compliance. Marty raised her gaze and nodded, as well. "You all look very nice. I think we should make our way downstairs and get our coats."

The boys hurried to line up. Wyatt came to tug on Marty's jacket. "Can I walk with you?"

Marty smiled. The boy had become one of her favorites. "Of course."

"Me too?" six-year-old Sam asked. His little brother, Benjamin, nodded rapidly in agreement. They had been in the orphanage for about five months, dropped off by their father after the death of their mother. They always seemed to crave Marty's attention.

"You too. In fact, I'll be right there with all of you," Marty declared. "I love to celebrate Christmas and sing carols. You know, we could probably sing a Christmas carol on the way to church."

"I think that's a splendid idea," Mr. Brentwood said, beaming Marty a smile. "Let's sing 'Silent Night.'"

They were joined downstairs by the girls and Alice. When everyone had their coats and hats on, Mr. Brentwood led the way. Marty mused that the children were rather like a group of little ducks waddling after their father.

The children sang at the tops of their lungs, a little off-key but nevertheless filled with joy. Marty couldn't remember when she'd enjoyed Christmas so much. Indeed, she'd nearly forgotten that just five years earlier she'd been made a widow when her first husband, Thomas, died on Christmas Eve.

How did the day get past me?

Marty fell silent as she considered the matter. The last year had been such a busy time. It wasn't that she hadn't contemplated her years with

Thomas or the tragic accident that claimed his life, but her marriage to Jake had changed her focus. Jake's kindness and gentle nature had eased her pain and filled some of the empty holes. Not all of them, of course. She would always remember Thomas. Her love for him was something special. But so, too, was her love for Jake. Maybe that's why it bothered her so much to imagine that he didn't care about her feelings.

She had hoped to hear something from him by now. Especially since it was Christmas. But there hadn't been any word at all. Marty found herself regretting the harsh words she'd spoken to him before their parting. She wished she could take back the ones spoken in anger—in fear, really.

What am I afraid of?

She almost laughed out loud at the question. The answer wasn't at all difficult. *I'm afraid of losing Jake like I lost Thomas.*

But haven't I already lost him?

The question haunted her throughout the church service, and the joy she'd originally felt for the celebration waned. She was at war with herself. She hadn't really lost him. But she had refused his solution. What obedient wife would do such a thing?

But he knows how I feel about Texas. And now it's more important than ever before.

"Wise men from the east followed the star," the minister declared. "They followed it because they knew what they would find at the end of their search. They knew they would find the Christ child."

The children fidgeted but didn't make a sound. All the normal problems of sitting too close to each other or of needing to share a comment were banished at the thought of missing out on the Christmas festivities.

"So what is it that *you* are searching for?" the minister asked.

Marty felt the question prick her conscience. *What am I searching for?* The uneasiness that had threatened to engulf her since Jake's departure reared its ugly head as if to answer.

You want everything your own way, a voice seemed to accuse. *You are so unworthy of anyone's love. You are selfish—a liar—a schemer. Even God has cast you aside.*

Marty frowned and lowered her head. She felt tears come to her eyes.

Was it the devil who tormented her? Had God given up on her? She hadn't been willing to see Jake's side of the disagreement. Certainly he could have sought ranch work in Colorado, but there was something to be said for returning to those who already knew you and knew your abilities.

"Sometimes we search for what has been lost," the minister continued. "But sometimes it is we who are lost and who are searching to be found. Maybe you have lost your way today. I want to encourage you to remember that it was through the birth of Jesus that we were given hope. It is through Jesus that we are found. Believe in Him and be saved. Believe that Jesus came as a babe in a manger, innocent and pure. Believe that He grew into a man who took on the guilt and filth of your sins and mine and died upon a cross. Believe!"

The choir stood to sing, and Marty silently prayed that God would help her to make better choices—to be obedient to both Jake and to God. It was a prayer she had prayed many times before. *I want to do what's right, Father. I want to live in a way that would be pleasing to you. Help me, please. I know I can't face the future without you.*

★

The children were happily stuffing themselves with sweets and playing with their Christmas gifts when Mr. Brentwood approached Marty and Alice.

"I believe the wooden blocks and dolls were a success," Marty said, smiling. She and Alice had worked to create five rag dolls for the girls, and Mr. Brentwood had arranged for the wooden building blocks to be cut and sanded. Painting them had been a time-consuming project, but Marty and Alice had mastered the task in love.

"I believe you are right. That is the joy of having nothing—even something small seems a great treasure. Speaking of which, I have something for you," he said, smiling at Marty in particular.

"For me?"

He nodded and handed Marty a neatly folded shawl. "I couldn't afford wrapping for it, but I knew you'd understand."

Marty unfolded the material to reveal a beautifully crafted piece.

"This is lovely, Mr. Brentwood, but I don't understand." She looked to him and saw his eyes light up and his smile broaden.

"It was knit by a poor Irish woman. She was selling her wares near the capitol, and I thought, well, I thought the color would be wonderful for your . . . eyes."

Marty looked at the light blue yarn and nodded. "I love it." She glanced at Alice. "The workmanship is quite impressive."

As if remembering that they weren't alone, Mr. Brentwood handed Alice something. "I purchased this for you."

Alice smiled at the dark green scarf. "How lovely. You are too kind. I have nothing to exchange, I'm afraid."

"I wouldn't expect a gift from either of you. Your presence here has been a wonderful gift for me. I don't know what we would have done without you," he said, looking at Marty. Then he quickly added, "Both of you."

"We feel the same way about you and the orphanage," Alice replied before Marty could find her tongue. "Being allowed to stay here has been quite beneficial."

"Indeed it has," Marty said, growing a little uncomfortable. She hadn't thought about it before, but now she couldn't help but wonder if Mr. Brentwood was coming to depend on them too much. After all, as soon as she and Alice could figure out what their future held, they would need to be on their way.

"I'm quite blessed," the man said as he rubbed his hands together. "With you here, I can take a little time to solicit funds for the orphanage. I plan to do so immediately after today. People tend to be in a giving mood around Christmas. If I can secure pledges of monthly support, I can rehire at least one worker. For instance, I could offer you a salary, Mrs. Wythe."

"Nonsense," Marty replied. "I am working for room and board. That's more than fair. What you need is your former staff. They are better trained at the workings of an orphanage."

"But the children clearly love you," Mr. Brentwood said, glancing over his shoulder. He looked back at Marty and Alice. "You have made them feel loved and cared for."

Marty didn't want to ruin the day so she let the matter drop. In time, she would remind Mr. Brentwood that her presence at the orphanage was only temporary.

"Now, if you'll excuse me," Marty said, "I have work to do. The children need something other than sweets and sandwiches and it will soon be time for supper." She made her way to the kitchen, still clutching the shawl. Alice was right behind her.

"Is something wrong?" the younger woman asked once they were alone.

"I can't really say." Marty carefully placed her gift on a chair and went to put on her apron. "I suddenly felt uneasy. I'm worried that Mr. Brentwood is coming to depend on us too much. I fear he will expect us to remain here forever."

"At least you," Alice said, raising a brow. "He cares for you."

"He cares for us both," Marty protested. She took down a mixing bowl. "Would you retrieve the chicken and broth we put in the icebox and get it warming on the stove? I'm going to make dumplings."

Alice hesitated. "Marty, you do realize that his feelings for you are different than they are for me. I might only be eighteen, but I can see that the man adores you."

Marty laughed. "You're being silly, Alice. He's just grateful for the help. I gave money and time to his cause. That's what he loves."

Alice took hold of Marty's arm but then just as quickly let go. "I suppose I could be wrong, but I've seen the way he looks at you. He doesn't look at anyone else that way. I think he's fallen in love with you."

"He's knows full well I'm a married woman. Goodness, he made these arrangements with Jake. Mr. Brentwood is an honorable man—a godly man. He wouldn't dream of defiling me that way."

Alice shrugged. "I don't think he has defiling in mind, but I do think he has deep feelings for you."

Marty turned away and placed the bowl on the counter. Alice was young and impressionable. No doubt her girlish ideals saw romance at every turn. Opening the flour bin, Marty retrieved a large sifter full of flour. She hoped that Alice would put the silly notions from her mind and realize that Mr. Brentwood held nothing more than respect for her.

———————————— ★ ————————————

Alice decided to leave well enough alone. She had planted thoughts in Marty's mind, and now she would pray that Marty would understand the truth before it was too late. Alice had no doubt that Mr. Brentwood was relying on Marty to ease the pain of having lost his wife not so very long ago. Perhaps he wasn't even conscious of what he was doing.

Supper passed by easily with the weary children almost happy to head for bed when the hour finally came. Mr. Brentwood gathered everyone together for prayer, and afterward Alice and Marty got the children tucked in for the night. With their work done, the women settled down before the fireplace in their room and breathed a collective sigh.

Marty quickly picked up a shirt to mend, while Alice took up her crocheting. Outside, the wind had picked up and chilled the drafty room. Alice paused in her work to add another log to the fire. She thought of Christmases when she was little. She'd been happy then with both mother and father to offer love and care.

I miss them both—so much. Walking to the window, Alice pulled back the curtain and looked out into the night. There was a slight glow coming from the windows of the house next door. It offered enough light to reveal it was snowing again.

"The first Christmas I can remember was right after my father went away," Marty said, as if Alice had asked a question. "We didn't yet know that he was dead. I was five years old and my sister Hannah—she was much older than I—she raised me after my mother died. . . ." Marty paused.

Alice returned to her chair by the fire. "Yes, I remember. I've always thought that a tremendous blessing."

"It was." Marty smiled. "That year she made clothes for my doll, and one of the dresses was an exact match for a dress she made for me. I thought it was the most wonderful thing in the world. That is, until I saw my brother's present." She shook her head. "Andy got a horse and saddle. I was so jealous. Especially when he commented that he was a real rancher now. I declared to everyone that I was a real rancher, too. I told them I had a horse and could rope. I was always given to lies and exaggerations."

"What did your sister do?"

"She reminded me that I was being untruthful. I remember telling her that I had spied a horse in the pen that I liked a lot and decided that one was mine. She told me that the horses belonged to Will, and I couldn't just go picking one out and deciding it was mine." She smiled, remembering. "That Christmas was very special, in spite of Pa's absence. I felt safe and happy. Maybe Pa's being gone was part of the reason. He wasn't a very happy man. Hannah told me that after Mama died he changed completely."

"My father changed after my mother went away, too," Alice remembered. "He had always been a very strong man—focused on his work and dedicated to whatever task was before him. He was sometimes rather stern with us, and I remember he could be quite angry at times."

"Even before your mother left?"

"Yes." Alice closed her eyes for a moment. "But I remember Christmases before my mother went away. A special one was when my brother Simon was just three or four. We weren't rich, by any means, but we had plenty. That year mother bought Simon a wooden train set. He loved it and scooted it across the floor for hours on end." She laughed lightly. "He would make chugging noises and toot like a train whistle."

Marty put one shirt aside and picked up another. "Boys make a lot more noise than girls do. Or rather, I suppose I should say *different* noises than girls do."

"Yes." Alice felt the memory fading.

"What did you receive for Christmas that year?"

Marty's question brought back the images. "I got a new china doll with the most beautiful satin gown and a wonderful bonnet trimmed with feathers and lace. She had long brown ringlets that spilled down her back. She made me wish I had brown hair." Alice met Marty's gaze. "I don't know what ever happened to her. I suppose she might have been sold with most of our other things after the attack."

"I'm sorry. I can't imagine how hard that must have been for you."

Marty's words betrayed her affection for Alice and it made the younger woman smile.

"It would have been awful enough to have suffered such a heinous

284

attack, but to wake up in the hospital and realize all that you'd known was gone . . . I can't imagine how hard that would be."

"It was difficult," Alice admitted. "I felt so ill from the infection and was very weak. The doctor wasn't certain I would recover. My friends from church were good to visit and to encourage me to keep fighting. But I knew Father was dead, and since Mother and Simon were, too, I figured the best thing for me would be to die, as well. I knew there was nothing to go home to. Later, when I found out there wasn't even a home left, I was truly lost in despair."

"I can only imagine the nightmare of losing everything."

Alice shook off the thoughts. "It's Christmas, and we really shouldn't be sad. We've a warm place to sleep, food in our stomachs, and despite the crisis going on all around the country, we are safe. If not for the threat of Mr. Smith's constant harangues, it would be nearly perfect."

"Yes, well, hopefully with the new year, Mr. Smith will lose track of you entirely. He hasn't come to the diner, has he?"

"No. Not yet, but I have to admit I am in constant expectation."

"At least then you won't be surprised by his appearance," Marty offered.

"I suppose I'm more surprised when each day passes and I don't see him lingering off in the shadows somewhere."

Marty reached over and patted Alice's still hands. "God will see us through. He will protect you. I feel confident of His watchful eye on you and me."

Alice nodded and gave a sigh. "I just wish God would remove Mr. Smith from our lives completely. I have nothing to give him. No possible means of helping him find what he feels is his." Alice thought of the things Jake had told her. "I can't imagine my father as being corrupted enough to forge gold certificates. Someone must have threatened him to make him choose such a path."

"Well, given Mr. Smith's threats to you, do you doubt that might be the case?"

Alice shook her head. "My memories of those days seem even more blurred than those of long ago. It's as if the accident robbed me of thought. Even so, I remember my father's nervousness at the time—and his fearfulness. It wasn't like him at all."

"Men often do things they don't want to do . . ." Marty started and then fell silent.

"You're thinking of Mr. Wythe . . . of Jake."

Marty nodded. "Yes, I suppose I am. He never wanted to be a banker. His father pressured him to finish his university studies and make a different plan for his life. Jake, however, wanted nothing more than to be a rancher."

"And return to Texas," Alice said more than questioned.

"Yes."

Alice offered Marty a look of sympathy. "God will provide the answers and direction. We have to remember that, whether it's in our dealings with Mr. Smith or with Jake."

"Or with Texas," Marty murmured.

"Yes," Alice agreed. "Or Texas."

Chapter 5

Marty decided that the time had come to part with the last of her finer clothes. She had tucked away her two last gowns in a trunk, hoping to somehow hang on to them. They were her favorites, but with a new year upon them, there were new needs.

Sickness abounded and medicines were necessary to help the children recover. The doctor's expenses alone ate away at the monies Mr. Brentwood had budgeted for the month of January. Marty felt it was her duty to sacrifice these last treasures. What good were two gowns packed away in a trunk to neither be worn nor displayed?

With Mr. Brentwood busy teaching the children, Marty and Alice each took one of the luxurious gowns in a folded bundle and headed to the dressmaker's store near the Capitol Hill neighborhood. There was a small shop at the front of an establishment where the woman often advertised remade clothing as well as new pieces. It was here Marty had sold her other gowns and hoped the woman might take these, as well.

Snow covered the lawns and walkways like icing on a cake. The sun on the vast white sea caused the snow to sparkle and gleam. It was almost painful to the eye.

"I certainly never knew anything like this in Texas," she said, her warm breath making clouds in the cold air.

"I like to imagine the warmth," Alice said amidst the chattering of her teeth.

"Everything looks so clean, so untouched." Marty marveled at the landscape. "And isn't it something how the snow muffles the city sounds?" They had just reached the shop and, anxious to leave the cold behind, hurried inside.

"I didn't think to see you again," the middle-aged matron declared. She wore her hair in a tight bun and looked quite severe, yet Marty knew her to be very friendly.

"I don't imagine I will be back after this. I have brought you my last two gowns. They were my favorites," Marty declared, placing one of the gowns on the counter.

The woman eyed the silk material and lace and smiled. "It is most beautiful. I know a woman who would pay very well for this piece. She has purchased several of your gowns."

Alice put the other dress on the counter, as well. "How can anyone afford such opulence at a time like this?"

The woman made a *tsk*ing sound. "Remember, not everyone was solely dependent upon silver. There are a good many folks who put their money into more profitable situations." The woman unfolded the dusty rose gown that Alice had brought.

"The workmanship is so perfect. I remember Mrs. Davies very well. Pity she took ill and died. Her talent will be sorely missed."

Marty nodded. "Yes."

The woman continued to look over the pieces. She finally drew her glasses down on her nose. "I will give you five dollars for both."

"Ten," Marty countered. This was their routine, and she wasn't afraid to barter.

"Seven," the woman replied.

"Eight." Marty smiled. "I must help buy medicine for the orphans. You wouldn't want to deny them, would you?"

"Ah, you will be the end of me. If I weren't confident of reselling these to my client, I would show you the door." Nevertheless, she smiled. "Eight it is."

Marty collected the money and let her hand trail one last time along the rose-colored silk. "Those were interesting and glorious times, but I shan't miss them. Not really."

Alice followed her outside. "Not even a little?"

Marty laughed. "It was quite amazing to try my hand at living the life of ease and opulence, but it wasn't for me. I need to keep busy. I was always kept busy as a child—probably to keep me out of trouble more than the true need of having me work."

"It served you well," Alice said. "Look at all you are capable of doing. You sew and cook, you can handle reading and writing. My handwriting is terrible, but I do love to read."

"I can also handle a team of horses, brand, and rope, and ride as well as any man," Marty declared. "And that isn't exaggerating." She gave a laugh. "I was determined to match my brother, Andy, at anything. Even so, women on our ranch worked just as hard as the men. We kept massive gardens and canned and smoked food. We had chickens and milk cows, even a few of our own pigs, although the men preferred wild boar and would go east to hunt them every fall."

"It sounds like a very fulfilling life. I think I would like the wide open spaces." She glanced westward toward the Rockies. "I find the mountains beautiful but foreboding. I've never cared much for the cold weather and snow." She shivered. "I think I would like your Texas."

"It's not mine," Marty snapped. She gave Alice an apologetic look. "I'm sorry. For all the good I knew in Texas, I knew equal parts of sorrow and heartache."

"Losing your husband when that bull gored him must have been the worst."

"It was one of the worst," Marty admitted. "The miscarriages of my unborn children were equally sorrowful. I always wanted a big family—Thomas did, as well."

"I'm sorry, Marty." Alice touched her arm, and Marty stopped walking. "I know losing your babies must have been a terrible thing. Maybe one day God will give you and Jake children. You mustn't let the past keep you from being hopeful for the future."

The icy cold wind whipped at their long wool coats, but still Marty did not move. She looked Alice in the eye. "I'm pregnant."

"What?" Alice's eyes widened at the news. "Truly?"

Marty nodded. "I spoke with the doctor when he came to care for the children."

"Does Jake . . . does Jake know?"

Marty swallowed a feeling of guilt. "No. I thought there was a possibility before he left, but I didn't want that to be the reason he stayed. I plan to tell him, but since we've had no word . . . well . . . I don't have any way to get in touch."

Alice's surprise seemed to leave her speechless. Marty knew the young woman couldn't possibly understand the fears that filled Marty's soul.

"Well, it seems to me," Alice finally began, "that maybe you should go live with your sister. You don't want to be doing a lot of heavy work while you're carrying the baby."

"I also don't know about risking travel and the problems that living in the South can bring."

"What do you mean?"

"It is said that the further south you live the greater the chance you have of miscarriage," Marty replied. "The doctor told me he believed such things were 'Pure hogwash,' to quote him, but there are those in the South who believe that the closer one lives to the equator, the stronger the pull of gravity. They believe it can pull a child right from the womb. I lost several babies in Texas. I don't think I can risk another."

"Oh, Marty, I'm so sorry. I know this is hard for you, but it's also such a happy thing."

Marty looked away and fixed her gaze down the snowy street. "I want to be happy, but I'm so afraid. I want this child very much."

"Then we will do what we can to ensure you remain healthy. Did the doctor offer any advice?"

"Nothing beyond the normal things: no heavy lifting, caution when walking in the snow and ice, eat beneficially and regularly."

"Have you told Mr. Brentwood yet?"

"No, I don't plan to tell anyone. At least not for a while. Honestly, Alice, I don't want anyone to know. I'm not that far along—not even starting to show. I'd rather just wait and see what happens. If I get past the next month, then perhaps I'll say something."

"But what about Jake? You will tell him, won't you?"

Marty bit her lower lip and said nothing. Alice took hold of both arms and turned Marty to face her. "You have to tell Jake. He's your husband—the father. He has a right to know."

She was right. There would be no avoiding the subject if Marty proved capable of carrying the child to delivery. But so many miscarriages, so many disappointments stood between her and the ability to share this news.

"When the time is right," Marty finally whispered. "Then I'll tell him. For now, you must swear to me that you'll say nothing."

Alice hesitated a moment but then finally gave a nod. "I'll say nothing . . . for now."

★

Alice couldn't help but dwell on the news throughout the rest of the day. Marty was going to have a baby. The thought delighted and terrified her. She had to find a way to get Marty and Jake back together. A woman in such a condition needed her man, and Marty definitely needed Jake.

Not only that, but Alice feared the emotions that were growing in Mr. Brentwood. Marty might be blind to his devotion, but Alice could see that he had lost his heart to Marty. She knew him to be an honorable man, just as Marty had said, but she also knew that honor could give way under the pressures of life. Wasn't that what had happened to her mother and father? Honor certainly hadn't kept them together.

Alice walked in silence alongside Marty as they made their way down Fourteenth Street to catch the tram. As they approached the corner of Sherman Street, however, Marty took a turn.

"Where are you going?" Alice asked.

"I thought it might be nice to walk through the old neighborhood. Just to see what's what and whether anyone is still there," Marty replied. "I heard that the Tabors lost all of their money in the panic."

"Everything has changed in such a short time," Alice said, shaking her head. Many of the grand homes were deserted—their wrought-iron gates locked tight. Gone were the bustling activities of visiting and sharing in one another's luxuries. The Queen City of the Plains had sadly succumbed to the devastating financial epidemic sweeping the country. Poverty was an infectious disease.

"Do you suppose the people will ever come back?"

Marty shrugged. "Jake said these things always seem to run in cycles. Those who were diverse in their investments will ride this out like they have before. Others will be destroyed."

A carriage approached from the opposite direction, and Alice recognized one of the city's socialites, Mrs. Kountze, staring out her carriage window. Their opulent mansion at Sixteenth Avenue and Grant Street was said to be the most ostentatious and grand of all Denver homes. Alice knew Marty had attended several affairs at the Kountze estate, yet the occupants of the carriage did not so much as signal the driver to slow.

"Glory is fleeting, but obscurity is forever," Marty murmured.

"What does that mean?" Alice questioned.

Marty smiled. "It means that we are once again nothing more to the Kountzes than the dust beneath their feet." She smiled. "Napoleon Bonaparte once said it. He had his glory and fame, his wealth and successes, but also his failings and defeats. I suppose that is a part of everyone's life in one degree or another."

Alice nodded. "It certainly was so in my life. I always fancied I would marry a man who was amply positioned—perhaps a bank employee like my father. I thought I would be a wife and mother and live in relative comfort." A tiny laugh escaped. "Guess it was only one of my many mistaken assumptions."

"We have all had them," Marty admitted. "Some of us more than others."

Alice took hold of her arm. "Come on. Let's get out of here and catch the tram home. I'm freezing and you need to take better care of yourself now that you're to be a mother."

Marty gave Alice a look that suggested being a mother might well be yet another mistaken assumption. Alice refused to let Marty's worries control the moment, however. "When we get back to the orphanage I will make you some hot tea."

Marty smiled. "Or I will make you a cup. We are equals now—sisters really. No longer employee and employer."

Alice smiled. "Sisters? I like that idea. I've always wanted a sister."

★

That evening, Marty sat watching flames dance in the bedroom hearth. She absentmindedly placed her hand over her stomach and pondered the possibilities. Would God allow her to carry this child to term? She was already further along than the previous times.

She thought of Jake and wondered if he would be happy at the news. No doubt he would be delighted. He had once mentioned wanting children. It was strange how their marriage had come about from a simple newspaper advertisement, but now it was more precious to Marty than she could have ever imagined.

We were only going to be good friends, she remembered. Companions who would ease the loneliness of having lost their spouses. Companions who would say and do all the proper things expected of them by society.

Marty remembered the snubbing she'd received by the Kountzes earlier in the day. It wasn't the first. There had been several occasions when she'd been downtown and her former so-called friends had turned away as if ashamed. Marty was not from a famous family or a well-moneyed background. Her Texas family was better off than many, but only because they had worked long and hard at ranching.

Thoughts of Hannah and Will came to mind. She knew she owed her sister a letter. Hannah had written the week before to beg Marty to come back to Texas. Marty had told her of Jake's decision to head to Texas for work while she remained behind in Denver with Alice. Hannah didn't like the idea and thought it much too dangerous. She even said that Will had a position for Jake and that Marty should tell him right away.

"But I can't tell him if I don't know how to reach him."

It was over a month since he'd gone and still she had no word. Perhaps he had been killed or wounded. Maybe he had given up on Marty and simply disappeared.

"And if he has, what will I do then?" she whispered to no one.

The thought of being alone—truly alone—frightened her. Here at the orphanage in the company of so many, Marty was too busy to feel lonely. But what would happen when she began showing? Would people assume a dalliance with Mr. Brentwood? Even Alice thought there were feelings on his part, though Marty was certain she was wrong. Still, two women living at the orphanage with a widower was hardly the best of circumstances.

Time was slipping away, and Marty knew it wouldn't be long before she would be forced to make a decision. Why did these things have to be so hard? Why did she always have to face the worst of it alone?

But you aren't alone. The whispered words fell across her heart like balm.

She smiled and drew in a long deep breath. "No, I'm not alone. I have the Lord. I have Alice." She gently rubbed her stomach. "And for now . . . I have you."

Chapter 6

Robert Barnett always enjoyed the ride over Fort Worth way. Today was no exception. The weather was beautiful and the humidity low. He preferred Fort Worth to Dallas, even though the ride was longer. Fort Worth was like wearing a pair of comfortable boots and old jeans, while Dallas felt more like donning your Sunday best. It was all a matter of preference, he supposed. As Robert recalled, his younger sisters preferred Dallas.

"Looks to be a good turnout for the sale," his father said, interrupting Robert's thoughts.

Robert had also noticed the swelling crowd. "You gonna buy some of those Aberdeen Angus this time around?"

"I'd sure like to. I've heard great things about them. They're a hardy bunch, and the calves are thicker, heavier at weaning time. Seems we ought to at least give it a try. Wanna stay away from those Durhams, though. I read in the *Journal* there are too many birth defects with them. Last thing we want is to put a bunch of calves down."

"I'm guessin' we'll find both here at the sale." Robert had been attending cattle sales with his father for as long as he could remember. Sometimes his mother even came along and enjoyed a day of shopping, but not this time. "I have to say I'm partial to the flavor the Angus-longhorn crossbred gives. I think we'd do well to incorporate the breed into our herds."

"Seems most folks here agree with you." A number of men were already gathered around the Black Angus sale pen. "Guess I'd better be ready to part with a good bit of money."

A year ago the Stock Raisers Association had changed their name to the Cattle Raisers Association of Texas and headquartered themselves in Fort Worth. Robert was glad to hear about the change now that they were able to participate with the group on a regular basis. Such associations were beneficial and made ranchers stronger as they stood together. This association had seen them through the closed-range issues, the drought of the '80s, and the recent economic failures and drought of the '90s. Issues of disease, the introduction of new breeds, and innovations for raising profitability were also addressed. Robert found the information of great use, as did his father.

"Where'd Mr. Atherton and Mr. Reid get off to?" Robert asked after his father finished the business of registering with the salespeople.

"Lookin' at horses. Brandon Reid is always lookin' to improve his herd. The man's gained himself a reputation as an expert on horseflesh."

Robert nodded. The mount he rode today was sired by a Reid stallion. The sorrel stood sixteen hands high and was a mix of Thoroughbred and American Paint. Robert had never known a cow horse with better instinct. The gait was easy, too. Robert could sit for hours in the saddle. He'd owned the horse since it was a colt and had been the only one to break and ride him. Aunt Marty had teased him about the horse he affectionately called Rojoe, a play on the Spanish word *rojo*—meaning red. When Robert had first learned to read Spanish, he had insisted the word was pronounced with a strong J sound instead of the H the Spanish used. Marty had given him such a hard time about it that it had become a running joke.

"We'll all meet up for the discussion on increasing profits. I can't say there's much hope during this panic, but you never know," Robert's father said, moving to remount his black. "Meanwhile, I'd like to take a look at some of those Angus."

The day passed in a flurry of activities. Robert went with his father to consider the Angus, after which the older man was determined to buy a young bull and three breeder cows. They looked into some of the other breeds, listened to the lectures on how to survive the lack of water and decent range grass, saw some of the new barbed wire available for fencing, and heard a highly regarded veterinarian speak on a new dip to eradicate Texas tick fever.

Robert listened as his father made deals on new watering tanks and lumber for building another barn and pen, as well as other supplies. Sometimes William Barnett allowed his son to barter for some of the ranch needs, but most often Robert simply accompanied his father. He had learned a great deal by keeping his mouth closed and his eyes and ears open. It was to his benefit that his father handled business and helped Robert establish relationships and connections in the industry.

Of course the Cattle Raisers Association was in and of itself a school of training for the men who sought to make a living raising Texas cattle. The state's weather could be ruthless and unforgiving—sending droughts, floods, tornadoes, and even blizzards. The ranchers had endured a great deal over the years, and only by helping one another learn from their mistakes, banding together in difficult times, and making changes to how operations were managed had they thrived.

"Ready to grab something to eat?" Tyler Atherton asked Will.

Robert felt a little uneasy around the man many presumed would one day become his father-in-law. He'd grown up as just another one of the Barnett children, but as his mother conspired with Tyler's wife, Carissa, to put Jessica and Robert together, Robert felt Mr. Atherton watched him with an especially critical eye.

"I'm starved," Robert's father said. "Where's Brandon?"

"Tied up right now with some horse trading. Said he'd join us across the street." Atherton motioned to one of the larger restaurants set up to accommodate the cowboys and ranchers.

Will nodded and the threesome headed out. Robert couldn't help but wonder if the topic of his marrying Jessica would come up. Mr. Atherton and his father weren't usually given to such conversational issues, but Robert couldn't be sure.

They placed their orders for fried chicken dinners, which came complete with biscuits, gravy, and grits. Robert hadn't realized how hungry he'd gotten until the serving woman placed a huge platter of chicken and one of biscuits in front of them. She quickly followed with bowls of gravy, grits, and another platter of biscuits.

Robert's father paid the woman and then turned to Tyler. "You wanna offer grace, or are we gonna wait for Bran?"

Tyler grinned. "If he don't know when to come to dinner, that ain't my problem. Let's pray."

Will offered a short blessing before the trio dug in. Robert sank his teeth into a crispy chicken breast and smiled at the most satisfactory flavor. He was on his second piece when Brandon Reid finally showed up. Brandon eyed the diminished platter of chicken.

"Looks like I barely made it in time."

"You know how it is," Tyler teased. "A man's gotta do what a man's gotta do."

"And we had to eat," Will added with a grin.

Brandon wasted no time in gathering food to his plate. "Well, while you three were sitting here stuffing your faces, I made a great deal for some new horseflesh. Craziest animals you've ever seen—got a curly coat."

"Why'd you want to go with that?" Tyler asked.

The question seemed to take Brandon by surprise. "Well, I figured if it was smart to diversify your cattle breeds to make them stronger and fatter, maybe I could come up with a new hardy breed of horse. These curlies are stout but have really great spirits. They aren't afraid of anything. Could come in mighty handy in a cow horse."

"Gotta give you that," Will said, grabbing up another biscuit. He immediately sopped it in gravy and bit off a huge chunk.

Robert listened to his elders talk about their purchases and endeavors until the conversation turned to him.

"So what about you, Robert? You find anything worth buyin'?" Tyler asked.

Robert looked up from his plate. "Saw some great Angus with Pa. Should be interesting to see how they do, although they don't seem much suited to our climate. From what the man said, they have a hard time with the heat."

Tyler nodded. "But Angus have a good reputation for cross-breeding

298

with the longhorns. Should improve the stock. Instead of twelve hundred pounders we'll get upwards to two thousand."

"Well, given the talk we just heard," Robert's father began, "I'm beginning to wonder if we shouldn't consider opportunities to invest in slaughterhouses back east. Seems Texas cattle are getting noticed, and it might be one way to diversify our investments. Law allows for Texas cattle to be shipped by rail and immediately slaughtered. They aren't seeing any spread of tick fever that way. So what if we were to set up our own slaughterhouse on the rail line, say in one of the eastern cities?"

The older men got caught up in the positives and negatives of such endeavors while Robert got lost in his own thoughts. He would be twenty-eight come April. It was time to settle down and establish his own ranch. His father had said it more than once. He needed to get serious about marrying and starting his own life. Pa had even commented that maybe Robert would like to buy his aunt Marty's ranch. It wasn't real big, but it did abut the land Will had already given him. Robert had even been checking in on Marty's place in her absence.

It would be a good idea, he supposed. After all, Marty's land already had a house and outbuildings. Robert's land had nothing. He would have to start from scratch—build his own home, barns, pens. On the other hand, if he made a deal with his father for Marty's place, he would immediately be in debt. Both situations had their drawbacks.

"You seem mighty deep in thought, son." Robert looked up to find his father watching him. "You got something on your mind?"

Robert gave a chuckle and pushed back his empty plate, as if he'd been contemplating nothing more important than a game of cards. "Nothing worthy of our discussing. Guess now that my belly's full I wouldn't mind a nap." The older men laughed.

"You're startin' to sound like us," Tyler declared, "and you're way too young for that."

"I reckon so," Pa threw in. "Besides you don't even have a wife and children to wear you out like we do."

Robert shifted uncomfortably. "Maybe that's 'cause I'm smarter than you guys." He grinned and tucked his thumbs in his belted waistband.

"Or just a coward," Brandon Reid said in a good-natured manner.

He returned Robert's grin and then looked to Tyler. "That little gal of yours has scared him to death."

"Jessica can do that to a man, for sure," Tyler replied. "The good Lord knows she keeps me awake nights worryin' about her."

Robert feared the conversation was going to turn to him and Jessica. He was squirming in his seat when a very tall, broad-shouldered man approached their table with hat in hand. "Mr. Barnett?"

"William or Robert?" Pa questioned.

"William," the man answered.

"That's me," Robert's father said, getting to his feet.

"I'm Austin Todd, field cattle inspector."

William Barnett extended his hand. "Glad to meet you. These are some of my associates—Tyler Atherton and Brandon Reid. And this is my son, Robert."

Austin tipped his head. "Pleasure."

"Mr. Todd." Tyler stood. Brandon did likewise and Robert followed suit.

"Is there a problem?"

"Not at all," Austin replied with a smile. "Mr. Nystrom over at the sale barn told me I could find you here. He described you right down to your boots. I was hoping I could talk to you for a minute. He said you might have some land for sale."

★

Alice handed Marty two letters. "He's written," she said, pointing to the top letter.

Marty glanced down. "I'm almost afraid to see what he has to say."

Uncertain if Marty wanted to be alone, Alice said nothing for a moment. Finally she started for the door to their room, but Marty called her back.

"Don't go. This will no doubt affect you as well as me." She drew a deep breath and opened the letter. A five-dollar bill with President James Garfield's profile fell to the floor.

Alice bent to retrieve it and handed the money to Marty. "Jacob sent you money. Must mean he's found work."

Marty took the bill and scanned the letter. "He's working for his friends the Vandermarks, but they can't keep him. There isn't enough work to go around because lumber sales are in a slump. He plans to leave there at the end of the month and go to my sister and brother-in-law's ranch." She looked up from the letter. "He hopes they can hire him, and he wants us to join him there."

Alice smiled. "We've talked about doing just that. But you don't have to include me. Mr. Brentwood would probably let me stay here if I would work full time for room and board."

"I don't know what to do," Marty said, looking at the money and then back to the letter. "He says he misses me and loves me more than life. He plans to send me more money in his next letter. If William will hire him, he's going to ask them to advance enough money so that we can buy train tickets."

Alice could see that Marty was anything but comforted by the news. She wished she could still Marty's fears, but she had nothing in the way of words that might assuage her friend's concerns.

"At least you've had word," she said, taking the chair beside Marty. "And he loves you despite how you parted. You both miss each other so much, Marty. It seems reasonable that you would join him."

"I . . . I know."

"But you're afraid," Alice said, knowing the truth. "For the baby."

"Yes." Marty raised her gaze to Alice. "I'm terrified. I don't want to miscarry."

"I wish I could promise that you wouldn't, but of course I can't," Alice admitted. "I do know what fear is like, though. I live with it every day. Mr. Smith seems to delight in frightening me. But that's fear for myself and not for an unborn child."

"My fear is for myself, too," Marty said, shaking her head. "I just don't know if I can handle this, Alice. I don't know if I can go back to Texas. I know that I miss Jake. I know that I want us to be together. I even want to see my sister and Will again."

"But you don't want to see Texas."

"It's not even that. I found myself wishing I could enjoy the warmth of Texas again when the room turned so cold the other day." She smiled. "I guess I don't hate Texas as much as I hate what I've experienced there."

Alice took hold of her hand. "We need to pray about this, Marty. There isn't anything we can't ask God about."

"But I already know that God expects me to honor my wedding vows and be with my husband. I know God wouldn't have a child be without his or her father. I know what's expected of me. Praying about it won't change that."

"Maybe not, but perhaps it will change your heart." Alice patted her hand. "Marty, you have done nothing but care for me since we first met. You have shown me grace and love. Despite Mr. Smith's threats, you've stood by me, and because of that my heart has changed and I have new hope. You've proven to me that a person's heart can change and life can be better, even when circumstances do not change. I think God can do the same thing for you."

Marty seemed to consider Alice's words, and Alice found herself praying that God would give the older woman peace about the situation. She wanted Marty to be at peace, and she also hoped that if they left Denver for good Alice could once and for all be rid of Mr. Smith.

"I will pray about it, Alice. I know what you're saying, and I want to accept that truth." She looked at the other envelope in her hand. "No doubt Hannah will be advising the same thing. I told her in my last letter that Jake had gone to Texas. She'll be beside herself that I'm alone in Denver."

Alice shook her head. "You're *not* alone, Marty. Whether you stay here or go there, you're not alone. I'll stay with you—if you'll let me. We're sisters now, remember?"

The two women shared a glance and then a smile. Marty nodded. "Yes. Sisters."

Chapter 7

Alice hung her apron on the peg by the kitchen and rolled her aching neck to ease the pain. She had been busy at the diner since arriving that morning, and now, to her relief, it was time to head back to the orphanage.

Joe hadn't said much to her since she'd refused his proposition that they spend time together. Alice was glad that he hadn't challenged her on the matter. He seemed a bit standoffish, but otherwise cooked the orders and performed his other kitchen duties without further complicating her life.

Mr. Bellows complimented Alice daily on her hard work and serving abilities with the customers. Alice knew the diner's business had increased and hoped it was because of her good service. In the throes of a busy day she had little time to think about her scar, Mr. Smith, or even her concerns about Marty. But when the day concluded and she began her long walk home, those thoughts always returned.

Bundling up in her coat and wool bonnet, Alice headed out onto the snowy street. Overhead the skies threatened to deliver even more of the wet, white annoyance. She tried not to let the cold discourage her, however. She'd made nearly a dollar in tips that day and felt on top of the world. She had been able to set aside a little bit of change here and there after tithing and hoped that eventually the money would help get her and Marty to Texas. The rest of her earnings went to help defray expenses at the orphanage.

Mr. Brentwood always seemed grateful for the assistance, but Alice knew he was gravely worried about the situation. While he'd managed to secure some funds, he was unable to solicit the amount needed. It seemed the winter of 1893 to 1894 would go down as one of deep poverty and hopelessness in Colorado.

Alice was only halfway home when the hair on the back of her neck prickled. She felt an icy sensation run down her spine and knew without looking that Mr. Smith had somehow found her. She could feel his gaze and wondered where he was. Looking around as casually as she could, she pretended to notice a book in the window of one of the general stores. She thought about going inside and seeing if she might escape out the back as she had done that day in the fabric store but knew it was fruitless. Smith had a way of always finding her.

For a moment Alice considered confronting him. She thought of telling him that she would go to the police and have him arrested. Maybe the threat would dissuade him from his constant haunting. But that would require her to be close enough for conversation. And Alice wanted no part of that.

She picked up her pace just a bit. It would do her little good to appear to be running from the man. No, it seemed to her that if she pretended not to notice him, he might keep his distance. Perhaps he didn't know exactly where she lived. Maybe he'd found her completely by accident. But she doubted it.

Maybe heading to Texas wouldn't help. Maybe he'd follow me there, as well.

Yet Texas held great appeal to Alice. She reasoned it to be a calmer setting, for cattle and crops, rather than silver, seemed to hold court there—at least according to Marty. Surely life in the South would be better than here.

Keeping her focus on the path before her, Alice prayed that Smith would keep his distance. Lost in her prayers, she nearly jumped out of her skin when a man called her name. She steadied herself and drew in a deep breath before turning.

"Mr. Brentwood!" She let out a sigh. "You startled me." She put her hand to her breast as if to slow her racing heart.

"I apologize for that, Miss Chesterfield. I saw you heading home and wondered if you would like to ride. I have my carriage just around the corner."

"Thank you. That would be wonderful."

He led her to the single-horse conveyance and helped her up. Alice settled in as Mr. Brentwood climbed in beside her and pulled a woolen warmer from beside him. "Here, this will help with the cold."

She smiled and spread the blanket over her lap. "Did you have business in town today?"

"I did," he said, snapping the reins. "I am happy to say I procured a charitable donation to help with the rent on the orphanage. We will be secure for another three months."

"That's wonderful news."

"Indeed. I'm also given hope that there will be an offering from one of the churches to help with the cost of coal and electricity."

"That's good to hear. I don't suppose it's easy to get assistance these days."

"No, not at all. Although I have appealed to several of the women's organizations and hope to offer a small program to encourage donations. I thought we might have the children learn a song or two that they could perform. Maybe even have an affair at the orphanage itself to encourage godly people to come and share anything extra that they might have."

Alice considered this a moment. "Such as food and clothing?"

"Exactly. Or perhaps kerosene and candles. After all, electricity is certainly not a necessity. I've long thought to eliminate it—at least temporarily."

"Is it less expensive to run on kerosene?"

"Yes, but also more dangerous. Children aren't always cautious of fire hazards. I suppose that's why I've delayed in giving up electricity."

"So you plan to ask people to donate everyday items that will allow for the running of the orphanage. I think that's wise. Then if people can't afford to give money, they might give something else useful."

"They could even donate items we might be able to fix and sell. I have long considered the possibility of training the boys to make repairs to various items and resell them. Perhaps I could have a shop right there at the orphanage. The older children are certainly capable of helping."

"I think that's a wonderful idea. Marty and I could help with mending old items for resale. The shop would be a wonderful way to help support the orphanage and the community—especially if you weren't to charge outrageous prices like most of the town businesses."

"Do you think Marty—Mrs. Wythe—would approve?" he asked with a quick glance at Alice.

She heard the hope in his voice. "I think she would, for as long as we are here. Her husband has asked us to join him in Texas."

"But you're needed here," he said, sounding most desperate. "Mrs. Wythe has said nothing of leaving."

"I know. She is waiting for the money her husband plans to send, and then we will purchase train tickets."

Mr. Brentwood frowned. He seemed to consider the matter for several blocks before changing the subject entirely. "How do you like working at the diner? I have to say I was quite impressed with your donations to our food budget."

"I don't always care for it, but it does allow me a means of helping. I know the money is much needed and I don't mind the hard work." They turned a corner and the orphanage came into view. "I keep praying that the economy will improve, but it would seem that most of the men believe this is only the beginning."

Mr. Brentwood nodded. "I fear they are correct. I also fear for the children. I've been asked to take on more orphans but have had to refuse. I know the state orphanage is overflowing, as are many of the other church-run houses. Every day I see children, as well as adults, begging on the street. Some of the children are much too young to forage for themselves."

"It's sad that people feel they can cast their children aside like unwanted trash."

"Many of the parents are dead, and there's no one to take the little ones."

"Dead? I thought most of the children were abandoned."

"Some are, but sadly suicide is on the rise. One of the ministers was just telling me today that many people have given up. Of course winter brings with it more sickness, and some have succumbed to that. But winter and despair also increase those feelings of hopelessness. Some folks aren't strong enough to endure the pain." He pulled the buggy around to the back and came to a stop. He jumped down and helped Alice from her seat. "I'll be in directly after I see to the horse. You might tell Mrs. Wythe that I'd like to speak to her in my office. I'd like to know how soon she might . . . when you two plan to leave us."

"I'll tell her," Alice replied. She wanted to say something more. Something regarding his obvious feelings for Marty, but she held her tongue. It was probably best that she not assert her opinion just yet. Marty was a grown woman and fully capable of taking care of the matter herself.

★

Robert glanced up from the repairs he was making to espy a rider heading toward the house. The man rode well and looked to be completely at ease with the day. Dusting off his gloved hands, Robert straightened and made his way to the front yard in order to greet the man.

"Howdy," he called as the rider came to a stop.

"Howdy yourself," the man greeted with a smile. "I was wondering if Mr. Barnett was around."

"I'm Robert Barnett."

The man dismounted and extended his hand. "Jake Wythe. I'm married to Marty."

Robert couldn't help but smile. "She's my aunt. I've heard a great deal about you. Pleased to meet you." They shook hands. "Ma told me you might be headed our way. She had a letter from Marty sayin' as much. I know she'll be glad to meet you—Pa, too."

"I hope they'll still be glad when they hear why I've come. I'm in need of work." His frank admission seemed almost apologetic.

"They already know about that. I believe Pa has been planning to hire you on since Aunt Marty wrote and told him you needed work. Come on with me and I'll introduce you. Pa's just out back of the barn plotting out an additional building for hay. You can tie your horse off over here. We'll tend him after the introductions."

Jake tied the animal to the fence. Robert led the way around the pen and to the back of the barn. "Ma said that you'd been in the East working."

"Sure have. I got friends over near Perkinsville. They own Vandermark Logging and I worked for them a spell. But with all the changes goin' on over that way, they weren't even sure how long they'd be in business. A fella named Temple has bought up some seven thousand acres of timber and plans to start up his own sawmill. Might just put the Vandermarks in a bad way."

"Do you prefer loggin' to ranchin'?" Robert asked.

"No." Jake was matter-of-fact and to the point. "I grew up third-generation Texas rancher. We had a place just south of here, but Pa had to sell it during the drought. Didn't set well with me losing my inheritance, but I learned to give it over to the Lord."

"It's best that way." Robert noticed his father and called to him. "Pa, look who's come. It's Aunt Marty's husband, Mr. Wythe."

"Jake," the man interjected. "Just call me Jake."

William Barnett came forward and extended a hand. "It's good to finally meet you. I have to say when Marty told us she'd remarried, I was skeptical." He gave Jake a head-to-toe assessment before smiling. "Looks like she chose a good Texas man."

"I am a Texan, to be sure, and me and the Lord try our best to keep me on the good side." He grinned. "I've heard a lot of great things about you and Mrs. Barnett."

"You can call me Will. I'm sure my wife will want you to call her Hannah. Come on to the house. Speaking of my wife, I'll never hear the end of it if I don't get you two introduced right away."

Jake nodded. "I'm hoping you might be able to put me to work. I know ranchin' like the back of my hand. I grew up workin' every aspect."

"I heard you were a banker," Will said with a grin. "A banker rancher."

Jake laughed. "Guess you could call me that. My pa insisted I finish my education after he sold off the ranch. I worked a time in eastern Texas loggin', then joined my folks out in California. Got my education and went to work as a teller and then moved on to Denver, where I was promoted and eventually managed a branch for Paul Morgan. When the bank failed, I thought only of returning to ranch work."

"I can't imagine that set well with Aunt Marty," Robert threw in. He knew his aunt had soured on ranch life after losing Uncle Thomas.

"No, it didn't, but your aunt is a practical woman. I'm hopin' I can get some work here and send her money to come."

"We'd like nothin' better," Robert's father admitted. "We've been hopin' you'd show up sooner rather than later. Hannah's been half beside herself to get Marty out of Denver and back down here. We don't much like her livin' there alone."

"I don't either. There didn't seem to be a whole lot of choices, though. She wouldn't come and I couldn't stay."

Robert thought there was a hint of regret in the man's voice but said nothing. They entered the house through the back porch. Robert saw his mother look up from the table where she was kneading bread. Her face lit up at the sight of his father. Even after all these years Robert could see that his parents were still very much in love.

"Well, who have you there?" she asked. Wiping her hands on her apron, Robert's mother came from around the table to greet them.

"Hannah, this is Marty's husband, Jake."

Robert watched his mother assess the man only a moment before smiling. She stepped forward and embraced Jake, much to his surprise.

"You are a sight for sore eyes. So glad you finally came our way. You know you should have come here first."

Jake nodded as she let him go and stepped back. "I know I should have, but I didn't want to impose."

"Nonsense. You're family. Now, you come with me, and I'll show you your room."

"I left my things outside with my mount."

Robert noted his mother's nod in his direction. "I'll take care of it," he volunteered, knowing full well what his mother expected. Once Jake and his mother had disappeared, Robert turned back to his father.

"Seems like a nice fellow."

"He does. Can't imagine Marty marryin' a foul-tempered one."

Robert nodded. "You suppose she'll come home now?"

"I don't see why not. She can't hardly live separate from her husband, and now that he's here, she knows her place is here, as well."

"You figure they'll take back her ranch?"

"I hope so. I never wanted her to give it up in the first place, and since her husband is a Texas rancher by birth, it seems only right."

Robert didn't mention that he'd actually had hopes of buying Marty's ranch for himself. After all, he had his own land and his folks certainly didn't mind him staying on with them. Fact was, he preferred the idea of his aunt returning. It was good to have family close by, and he had always liked the idea of them working the land as one.

"It'd be good to have her home," Robert admitted. "Then if we could just get Uncle Andy back with his family, it'd be perfect."

"I hear you, son, but your Uncle Andy seems to be content to ranch in Wyoming with his wife's family. He wrote just the other day, and I've been meanin' to tell you about it. He wants to sell off his land here, and I thought maybe you'd like to have his acreage. He plans to stay in the north."

Robert considered the land that lay to the north of his own. "That would be good."

"There's no house or buildings for you, but it will give you an even better setup. Good water there, and Andy already cleared one area for building on. I figure you could put up a small place of your own when you had a mind to do so. It'll put you in a good position—closer to the Athertons."

He suppressed a negative comment and turned away. "Guess I'd better fetch Jake's things and get his horse put away. Feels like temperatures are droppin'."

His father said nothing, but Robert knew he probably wondered at the way he avoided discussing the future. No doubt he would bring the matter up in time. And when he did, Robert couldn't help but wonder what he'd say.

Chapter 8

Alice loved Sunday afternoons. They were a time for rest and relaxation. The children were given time off from chores and schoolwork, and Alice wasn't required to go to the diner for work. She and Marty always managed to start the day off with a nice breakfast and then Mr. Brentwood would share his thoughts on a Scripture passage, as he did every morning.

When everyone was dressed and hair combed, they would head off to church as a group and return afterwards to eat a lunch of leftovers from the day before. Everyone was then encouraged to have a time of rest. The little ones always protested, declaring they weren't tired and didn't need to sleep. They were always, amusingly enough, the first to fall asleep. Alice thought it comical to watch the way they fought napping. It reminded her of how she often fought against the rest that God offered her. So many times she had declared her ability to bear up under the load, to keep pressing forward, when all God wanted for her was rest.

"Have you seen Rusty?" Marty asked, coming into the kitchen.

Alice was just taking the last batch of sugar cookies from the oven. They were to be a surprise for the children when they awoke.

"I thought he was taking a nap."

Marty shook her head. "I thought so, too, but he's not there."

"Perhaps he needed to relieve himself."

"Maybe, but he usually comes and gets me to go with him to the outhouse." Marty frowned. "This isn't like him. He's generally too afraid of his own shadow to wander off very far."

"Maybe since the day was so nice, he snuck out to play," Alice suggested. "After all, this is the warmest day we've had in some time. To a four-year-old it probably seemed like summer."

"I suppose I should go speak with Mr. Brentwood."

"Speak with me about what? Umm, cookies." He winked and looked beyond Marty. "Perhaps I might sample them for you?"

Alice laughed. "There's a plate of them on the counter that have already cooled."

Mr. Brentwood crossed the room and helped himself. "Now, what was it you wanted to talk to me about?" He took a bite and smiled in satisfaction.

"I can't find Rusty," Marty declared. "I thought all the boys were in bed, but when I went to check, Rusty's bed was empty."

"That is strange. I remember him enjoying his lunch. Cabbage soup is a favorite of his."

"Yes, and he had two bowls," Marty replied. "Then we noticed he had muddy boots, and you told him to go clean them and leave them by the back door."

Mr. Brentwood nodded. Alice tried to recall if she'd seen the boy after he'd cleaned his boots, but nothing came to mind.

"I'll start looking for him. You're sure he didn't climb into bed with one of the other boys? He sometimes does that when he has a bad dream."

"No. He's not there. I made sure of it before I started searching for him." Marty looked quite worried.

Alice pulled off her apron. "I'll check out back. Could be he woke up and slipped out without anyone noticing."

"I'll check in my office and the classroom," Mr. Brentwood said, taking another cookie with him. "Although once he gets a whiff of these cookies, I doubt he'll be in hiding much longer."

Alice took up her shawl and headed outside. Most of the snow had melted due to the warm Chinook winds. The January day was deceptively enticing, but Alice knew from experience not to trust the moment. By nightfall it would no doubt be freezing cold, and by tomorrow they could once again find themselves buried in snow.

"Rusty! Rusty, are you out here?" she called. She looked around the play area, bending to inspect the old crates Mr. Brentwood had arranged for the children to use for play. There was no sign of the boy.

She went to search in and behind the outhouse but again found nothing. Looking back at the orphanage, she tried to imagine where she might hide if she were a four-year-old boy. Just then, however, she heard a giggle coming from behind her. She turned and saw the bushes move.

"Rusty, is that you? Come here this minute."

The boy peeked out from behind the seemingly dead brush. "We're playin' hide-and-seek."

"It's naptime and you were supposed to be in the house asleep," Alice chided.

"I waked up," Rusty said, holding up his hands in surrender.

"You need to go find Mr. Brentwood and Mrs. Wythe and let them know that you're all right." Alice took hold of the boy's shoulders and turned him toward the back door.

"Can Mr. Smith come, too?" the boy asked.

Alice froze. "Mr. Smith?"

A low chuckle chilled her to the bone. She turned to find her enemy watching her with a leering stare. He tipped his hat. "One and the same. Me and the boy, well, we had us a nice time together, didn't we, Rusty?"

The child grinned. "Mr. Smith said he can come back and play with us anytime he wants."

"Rusty, go inside and let them know you're all right." Alice's knees wanted to give way, but she forced herself to remain strong for the child's sake. She stared hard at Smith, hoping—praying—he might feel some sort of intimidation.

"I don't have anything for you," she said. Anger stirred inside and she clenched her jaw tight.

"I know that envelope has to be somewhere," he said. "Something that valuable ain't gonna just disappear."

"Well, it has. You have no choice but to stop this madness. I can't give you what I do not have." She put her hands on her hips. "You have followed me all over this city, and I'm sick of it."

He laughed again. "Then find my envelope. I have a feeling you know exactly where it is. I think you're keeping it for yourself."

Alice narrowed her eyes. "I know why you want it. I know about the counterfeit gold certificates. Mr. Wythe explained what he could find out about it. I wouldn't give them to you even if I could find them."

Smith crossed the distance between them and grabbed hold of Alice so quickly she didn't have time to react. His iron-like fingers dug into her tender arms. "You'll find them and you'll give them over or . . ." He let his words trail and nodded toward the door where Rusty had just gone. "Or next time it might not be hide-and-seek I play with that boy."

"You're a monster. I'll warn all of the children to be on the lookout for you. Not only that, I'll go to the police!"

His grip tightened. "You do and there will be blood on your hands."

Alice could imagine him stealing one of the children and hurting them. "I don't know what you expect me to do. I've told you before, everything my father owned, everything that you didn't take that night, has been sold. The house was sold before I even got out of the hospital. It was handled by friends and colleagues of my father in order to pay for his funeral and my hospital expenses. Whatever was in the house, with exception to a few of my personal items, was sold, as well. There's nothing left. Threaten all you like, but there's nothing!" She was nearly hysterical and knew she had to get a hold of herself. Forcing air into her lungs, Alice lifted her chin in a defiant pose.

It seemed that perhaps Smith finally believed her. He loosened his hold but didn't let go. "What about the house? Maybe your pa had a secret compartment where he hid such things."

Alice shook her head. "If he did, I didn't know anything about it."

"Well, maybe you need to find out." His expression once again became fierce. "You go there. Go to the house and find out if your pa hid anything away."

"The house sold. Other people are living there. I can hardly just show up at their doorstep and demand entry."

"You'd better do just that," Smith replied, finally letting go of her arms. "In fact, you'd better go and do that today if you know what's good for you. I'll come see you at the diner in the morning."

He left so quickly that Alice was still trying to think of what to say to him when she realized he was gone. For several minutes she stood frozen in place. The man was clearly insane. Perhaps the desperate times had done this to him; then again, maybe he had always been this way.

Gathering her skirts in her hand, Alice wondered how in the world she could heed his demand. The house she had shared with her father was on the other side of town. She couldn't hope to walk there, visit the people, and walk back before nightfall. Yet if she did nothing, Smith would come back and hurt one of the children.

Perhaps Mr. Brentwood would loan her his carriage and horse. She bit her lower lip and entered the back of the orphanage, wishing she had a better plan. How could she explain the situation to Mr. Brentwood? It would be hard enough to tell Marty what had just happened. Marty would want to go after Smith with her shotgun, which would be quite impossible since the shotgun had been sold off with most everything else.

"Where is he?" Marty asked when Alice stepped into the kitchen.

Alice noted Marty had a cast-iron skillet in her hand and had been headed toward the door. "Rusty told you about Mr. Smith?"

"Yes, and I intend to put this skillet up against his head. How dare he involve a child in his schemes."

"I know. And that's not the half of it."

Marty frowned. "What else is there?"

"He plans to be back—to cause harm if I don't do what he's commanded."

"Which is what?

Alice squared her shoulders. "He wants me to go back to the house I shared with my father and look for hiding places where Father might have put the envelope and gold certificates."

"The man is crazy," Marty said, lowering the pan. "How can he imagine there would be anything there after all this time? If someone found those certificates, they would endeavor to use them for their own survival."

"I don't know of any place where Father could have hidden them, but I am determined to go and put this thing to rest once and for all.

I'm going to go to the house right now if Mr. Brentwood will lend me his horse and carriage." She lowered her voice and stepped closer to Marty. "I just don't know what excuse to use or if he'd allow for it."

Marty nodded. "Leave that to me. We'll go together. Mr. Brentwood will let me have use of the carriage. He's offered it to me many times."

"I don't want to drag you into this, Marty." Alice felt her eyes dampen. "You've already gone through too much, and now you have the baby to consider."

"Shh. Say nothing. There's no reason to worry. We will go to the house and speak to the new owners. I'll simply tell Mr. Brentwood that it's come to my attention that a friend of mine is in need. That much is true." She put the skillet on the stove. "I'll tell him we have need of the carriage and that we will be absent from the orphanage for a time. There are plenty of leftovers for their evening meal."

Within a matter of minutes Alice was in the carriage house with Marty. She felt helpless to assist Marty with the harnessing of the horse and feared for the mother-to-be.

"I wish I could handle that for you. I couldn't live with myself if anything happened to the baby."

"I'll be fine," Marty assured her. "Women in my condition have been harnessing and unhitching wagons, handling horses, and doing much more for centuries. I'm sure it will be all right. Besides, this old nag barely has enough energy to pull the buggy. She's not going to be any trouble to me."

They made their way across town with Alice directing Marty to the old neighborhood. The houses there were far less opulent than those on Capitol Hill, but clearly nicer than those in some of the poorer parts of town. When Alice saw her childhood home, she felt something akin to sorrow rush through her. She hadn't been back there since the night of the attack.

"That's it—right there. The one with the pine tree on the side." She swallowed hard and silently prayed for strength.

"It looks like a lovely place to grow up," Marty said, pulling back on the reins. "Whoa." The mare complied without protest. Marty got down and tied off the reins. "Do you want me to come with you?"

"Yes. Please. I'm . . . I don't know what to say or to do."

"We'll just have to wait and see," Marty said, pulling Alice up the walkway. "Do you know the people who bought the house?"

"No." Alice had never asked, nor had anyone bothered to tell her. Having been desperately ill for so many weeks after the attack, she had hardly cared what happened to the house or her things.

They knocked on the door and waited. Alice imagined her mother opening the door to them with a warm smile and a loving embrace. Many had been the time Alice had returned from school to find her mother awaiting her arrival in just such a manner.

"Hello?" A woman looking to be in her midforties greeted them.

"I . . . ah . . . well," Alice stammered and looked to Marty.

"This is probably going to sound strange to you, but I'm Mrs. Martha Wythe and this is Alice Chesterfield. Alice used to live here."

"Oh," the woman said, seeming to notice Alice's scar at the same time. "Your father was killed, wasn't he? You were injured, but we never knew what became of you." The woman's expression became quite sympathetic. "I remember being told all about it from the owner."

"The owner?" Marty asked. "Don't you own this house?"

"No," the woman said. "I rent it. My mother and I live here. Won't you come in?"

Marty and Alice stepped into the house. For a moment Alice gazed around the room and let the memories wash over her. The front room looked much the same, although there was now a piano by the front window.

"So what can I do for you, Miss Chesterfield, Mrs. Wythe? Oh goodness, where are my manners. I'm Sylvia Ingram. My mother, Matilda, is napping just now or I would introduce you."

"That's really all right, Mrs. Ingram," Marty said, much to Alice's relief. "Our visit here will seem rather . . . strange, but I beg your indulgence."

The woman's expression changed to one of concern. "I hope I can help."

"As you probably know, Alice was severely wounded in the attack that killed her father."

The woman nodded and glanced at her cheek. "Such a pity."

Marty quickly continued. "The house was sold while she was still in the hospital, and Alice never knew what happened to their things or this place."

"Poor girl. I'm so sorry you had to endure such a terrible tragedy."

"We were wondering," Marty said, glancing at Alice, "if there was anything left behind. Something perhaps that had been hidden away and not sold."

"Particularly papers," Alice said, finally finding her voice. Mrs. Ingram seemed so calm and kind that she lost some of her fear. "It's most important I find my father's papers—his personal effects."

"Oh, my dear child, there was a box of personal items. They were upstairs in the attic, tucked back in an alcove."

Alice looked to Marty with hope of what they might find. "And do you have them still?"

The woman frowned. "I'm sorry. No. I sent them on to a relative whose address was amidst the papers. I didn't realize you were still in town."

"A relative?" Alice questioned, feeling her heart sink. "I don't know of any relatives—not still living."

The woman shook her head. "I can't remember the name. It was unusual, but I'm certain the last name was the same as yours." She thought for a moment and then raised her finger toward the ceiling. "Aha. I have a letter. After I sent the box, the recipient responded to thank me. Oh, wait. I remember now. It was from your mother. I have it still."

Mrs. Ingram hurried from the room without further ado, leaving Alice to stare openmouthed after her. She felt as if someone had hit her hard in the stomach. Her mother was dead.

"What in the world is going on?" Alice whispered and looked to Marty for encouragement. "My mother is dead. This can't be."

"We should know soon enough, Alice. Don't worry. At least we know now that there were some papers and personal effects that have been sent on to someone. We will find out to whom they were delivered and see about retrieving them."

Mrs. Ingram was gone for nearly ten minutes before reappearing, waving the letter in hand. "Here it is. I knew I'd kept it. It's from Ravinia Chesterfield—your mother, I believe."

Alice nodded slowly and took the letter Mrs. Ingram offered.

"Goodness, but it seems like forever since that letter arrived. You can read it for yourself. Of course, you may have it. I don't even know why I hung on to it. She wrote me to thank me for the box of things and for telling her about your father's death. She asks about you and your whereabouts in the letter. Seems your father wouldn't let her have anything to do with returning home."

Alice removed the letter from the envelope and began to read.

Dear Mrs. Ingram,

Thank you for informing me about my husband's demise and sending me his personal papers. We have been estranged now for many years, and much to my heartache, Mr. Chesterfield would not send me word of himself or our daughter, Alice, and neither would he allow for my return. If you know of her whereabouts, I would be much obliged if you would share the information. She is very dear to me, and I hope to be reunited with her.

Sincerely,
Ravinia Chesterfield

Alice handed the paper to Marty. "My mother . . . my mother is alive!"

Marty glanced at the paper and then back to Mrs. Ingram. "When did you receive this letter?"

"Oh my, it's probably been a year now—maybe not quite. I wrote her back to say that I didn't know anything about her daughter. I told her that I knew her husband had been murdered and that her daughter had been injured, and I thought . . . well . . . I was almost certain you had died." The woman gave her an apologetic look. "I do hope I didn't cause your poor mother undue heartache. Perhaps you can write her yourself and let her know that you're alive and well."

Alice felt the room begin to spin. She couldn't breathe and the world was going black. The last words she heard were Mrs. Ingram's.

"I'm certain your mother will be delighted to know you are safe."

Chapter 9

"Don't you think you should write to her?" Marty questioned Alice later that night after everyone had gone to bed.

In the darkness she couldn't see her friend's face, but she knew it was no doubt still twisted in an expression of confusion and pain. Poor Alice. The girl had taken quite a shock at the news that her mother was still alive.

"I don't know." Alice's simple statement echoed in the silence of the room.

"Well, it seems to me that there is far more to this than either of us understands. It would seem that your mother wanted to be in touch with you, wanted to see you, but your father—"

"My father loved me!" Alice interrupted. "He was a good father."

"I . . . I'm sure he was, Alice." Marty tried to choose her words carefully. "But obviously there were issues, problems that perhaps kept him from being a good husband."

For several minutes neither said anything. Marty wondered if she'd overstepped her bounds with the younger woman. Alice was only eighteen and she hardly understood the problems that could exist between a husband and wife. Marty thought of Jake and the issues they were struggling with.

I miss him so much. How I wish you were here, Jake. I wish I could tell you about our baby and about my fears.

"I don't know what to do," Alice finally whispered. "It was so hard to accept her leaving and then hearing that she and Simon had died." She gasped. "Do you suppose my brother is alive, too?"

"Quite possibly," Marty replied. "How old would he be now?"

"Ten. He probably doesn't even remember me."

Alice's tone was so forlorn that Marty spoke quickly to assure her. "Oh, I'll bet he remembers you very well. That was only five years ago. I have vivid memories from when I was five."

Marty waited for Alice to say something more and when she didn't, Marty decided to make some suggestions. "If you're worried about it, I could help you by writing to your mother first. I could explain what has happened—even ask her about the gold certificates. We have her address on the envelope of the letter."

"She lives in Chicago."

Rolling to her side and pulling her blankets close, Marty considered the matter for a moment. "That's not that far by train."

"This is like some kind of nightmare and good dream all in one," Alice said. "I always prayed that my father was wrong and my mother and brother hadn't died. Now that I know they are alive, I also know that my father lied to me. He betrayed my trust in him and purpose-fully lied."

"He must have thought he was protecting you."

"From my mother? My little brother?"

Marty tucked her hand under her head. "Alice, why did your mother leave your father?"

"I don't know. Father always said it was because she wearied of being a faithful wife."

"Did they fight?"

Alice said nothing for several long minutes. Finally she whispered her reply. "Yes. But never violently. I mean, my father could say some really horrible things, but he always . . . usually . . ." She fell silent as if remembering something important. "Sometimes he apologized afterwards."

"Sometimes apologies aren't enough to diminish the pain," Marty replied and thought of ways she had hurt others or been hurt herself. She had always been taught to forgive, but it was sometimes hard to do so and to heal from the pain. "Do you suppose . . . I mean . . . is it possible he was violent when no one could see him?"

"I don't know. I feel like I don't know anything anymore. I thought he loved me. I thought he wanted good things for me, but instead my whole life has been built on a lie. Everyone lied."

"But your mother said she was stopped from seeing you. That suggests to me that she never wanted to end the relationship. It seems to me that she didn't lie but was forced out of your life. Maybe she didn't leave of her own accord."

"She snuck out in the night and took my brother with her. My father didn't know about it, because the next day when we learned the truth, he was half crazy with anger and grief. I remember that morning very well."

"Why didn't she take you?" Marty asked without thinking.

"That is the question that has haunted me all of my life. Perhaps it was because my room was upstairs and she was afraid of waking my father. Maybe it was because I was my father's favorite, and she knew I'd be safe in his care. Or maybe she didn't love me as much as she did my brother."

"Or perhaps she feared she couldn't get away if she took you both. It's really hard to say what her reasons were, but now you have a chance to find out."

"I'm not sure I want to know anymore."

"Alice, I'm so sorry. I'm sorry for the shock this is to you. I'm sorry for the bad memories it's stirred up and the problems it's created. I want you to know that I am here for you in any way I can be. I will do whatever you need me to do."

"Thank you. Right now . . . I just want to think on it. I'm sorry, Marty. I can't talk about this anymore."

"That's all right, Alice. I understand."

And she did. She knew what it was to have a burden so complicated that it couldn't be shared with another person. But it could be shared with God. Marty hadn't always thought that to be true, but she did now and started to pray in earnest for her friend.

★

The next day after Alice left for her job at the diner and the children were settled in with their studies, Marty took the opportunity to speak with Mr. Brentwood in his office.

"Willeen is looking after the classroom," Marty announced. "I wondered if we might talk a moment." She knew the twelve-year-old would be able to manage the children should they have any questions, and this would give her a chance to explain Alice's situation—and maybe her own.

"Of course." Mr. Brentwood jumped to his feet with a beaming smile. "I've always got time for you. Please come in and have a seat."

Marty nodded. "I wanted to let you know about yesterday."

"Your friend in trouble?"

She smiled. "It was Alice, actually. I want to explain it, although I'm not sure Alice would want me to say much about it. I feel you deserve an explanation, however."

"Go on," he said, closing the ledger in front of him.

Marty took a chair and settled in. "You know that Alice was wounded the night her father was killed. I believe we told you that much."

He nodded and sank back into his chair. "I heard her telling the children about it, as well. Such a horrible thing for one to experience."

"Yes, well, a man has been threatening her ever since. We don't know the man's true identity, but he calls himself Mr. Smith."

"The same Mr. Smith that Rusty spoke of yesterday?"

Marty gave a slow nod. "I wanted to tell you about it then, but we had to hurry in order to . . . well . . . let me back up."

She did her best to explain the past and all that Smith had put them through. Marty tried to carefully weigh the details in her mind before she spoke. There was no sense in telling him everything.

"So we went to the house where Alice grew up and found a very kind woman living there. She shared with us that she had found a box of personal items in the attic and had mailed them to a woman in Chicago. The woman in Chicago had responded with a letter of thanks, which she gave to Alice yesterday. She was shocked to learn that that woman is her mother—who is alive, or at least was alive a year ago."

"How shocking it must have been for her," Mr. Brentwood replied. "I thought she looked unwell when you returned."

"She's struggling to know what she should do. I suppose we both are, actually."

He shook his head. "What do you mean?"

"My husband has written to me. He wants me to join him in Texas. My sister and her husband want that, as well."

"Alice mentioned as much, but you're needed here. I couldn't run the orphanage without your help." He got up and came around the desk, leaning against it, directly in front of Marty.

She thought for a moment he might take hold of her hands and pressed back further in the chair.

"The children adore you and I know you love them, too."

"I do," Marty replied. "Especially little Wyatt and of course the brothers, Sam and Benjamin. They are so needy and in want of love." Marty stopped short of adding that she knew what that felt like.

As if reading her mind, however, Brentwood confessed his own thoughts. "I think we all are. Orphans suffer such great sorrow in their abandoned lives. When they lose someone precious to them, the loss is overwhelming, and they seek to fill that hole with something or someone who can make it better."

Marty knew he was speaking of himself. She hadn't wanted to believe Alice's comments on Mr. Brentwood's feelings for her, but it was clear the younger woman had been right. Marty knew she had to be forthright with Brentwood. She had to make certain he knew there were boundaries that had to be observed.

However, before she could speak, he did the unthinkable and knelt beside her chair. "I know this isn't at all what you expected, but Mrs. Wythe—Martha—I need you. Since losing my wife, this orphanage has been a daunting task. With you and Miss Chesterfield here, it has taken on new meaning."

Marty shook her head. "I'm a married woman."

He nodded. "I know that. I honor that. I'd never try to compromise your union. It's just that your husband . . . well, he's deserted you. He chose to leave for Texas."

"Because he knew he could find work there," Marty defended. "Mr. Brentwood—"

"Please call me Kenneth." His tone was pleading as his eyes sought hers. "I promise you that I am not suggesting anything untoward. I would never want to hurt you like that. I care about you and your reputation. I can offer you a good home here and only ask in return that you would remain and help me with the orphans. And be my friend."

Marty shook her head. "I will always be your friend, Mr. Brentwood, but I'm Jake Wythe's wife, and we both know that will always come first. Especially given my condition."

He startled and jumped to his feet. "You're with child?"

"Yes." She nodded to emphasize her words.

"He left you here to bear his baby alone?"

"He doesn't know. I didn't know for sure until he was already gone. That's why I can't stay."

It was as if in that moment her decision had been made for her. Marty knew the truth of her own words. She couldn't stay. She needed to be with Jake. Their baby needed its father. Whether Texas claimed another child from her or not, she had no choice.

"I just wanted to let you know what had happened yesterday, and what is going to happen in the near future. Alice and I are going to Texas as soon as my husband sends us the money. I think we both know that it's for the best." She got to her feet. "Now that we've spoken here . . . well . . . everything has changed."

"No, not at all," Brentwood declared, taking hold of her arm. "I'm sorry for my forward suggestions. I truly know the limits of our relationship. It's just that you've come to mean so much to me. You've helped me in so many ways. I swear to you, you're safe here. You don't have to flee me. I won't put myself upon you in a compromising manner."

Marty patted his hand and pulled away. "I know you won't. You're a good and godly man. I don't say these things because I feel threatened by you. I say them because I love my husband. I want to be with him—even if that means going back to Texas. Now if you'll excuse me, I need to get back to the children. It's almost time for their lunch, and then you'll need to take over the classroom."

She walked to the door and paused. Turning there, Marty saw the look of anguish in his expression. "God will make provision for you and the orphanage. He has always done so in the past and will continue to. You just need to trust Him for the answers."

★

Alice found Marty rocking Benjamin in the front room when she returned from her shift at the diner. The little boy slept while Marty hummed quietly. She was the picture of radiant motherhood, and Alice couldn't help but remember her own mother rocking Simon. How she wished she could remember being rocked in her mother's arms.

"He seems quite at home with you," Alice whispered.

"Yes," Marty replied. "I'm going to miss him."

Alice narrowed her gaze in a look of curiosity. "What do you mean?"

"I mean when we go, when we leave here."

"And are you planning to do so?" Alice came further into the room and took a seat in one of the other rockers. "Have you decided to join Jake in Texas?"

"Yes. I told Mr. Brentwood today."

Alice hadn't expected this news. "And what did he say?"

Marty pushed back a curl on the boy's forehead. "You were right. He has feelings for me. Feelings much deeper than he should. He wanted— begged me to stay. Promised he would never compromise my reputation. I told him about the baby, and even that didn't seem a deterrent."

"I'm sorry, Marty. Sorry that it happened and sorry to have been right. I had hoped that perhaps my thoughts were skewed by my own romantic notions." Alice smiled. "I can be quite the dreamer."

"No, you saw quite clearly and now I must go, even if I hadn't already decided it was the thing to do."

"And when did you decide that?"

Marty shrugged ever so slightly. "I suppose I've known it all along. I've simply delayed acceptance." She smiled. "I'm terrified, but I'm also deeply in love with my husband. I hate that we are separated. I never thought I could feel that way about any man but Thomas, and now here I am hopelessly devoted to another."

"But that's good," Alice replied. "I know he feels the same way about you."

"I hope he still does."

Alice laughed lightly. "Of course he does, silly. He wouldn't be working to send you money for train tickets if he didn't."

For several minutes nothing more was said. Finally Alice glanced over her shoulder and then back to Marty. "Did you tell Mr. Brentwood about me?"

Marty nodded. "I did. I hope you don't mind. I felt we owed him some sort of explanation about yesterday." She frowned. "Did Mr. Smith come to see you today?"

Alice nodded and smiled. "I told Joe and Mr. Bellows that he was giving me a hard time and I feared him. They both acted as my protectors." She giggled. "When Mr. Smith came in, I told Mr. Bellows who he was, and he immediately intercepted the man. I took to the kitchen and told Joe what was going on. He wasn't about to let Mr. Bellows have all the honor. He quickly joined him and then I followed suit. Because no one else was around, I told Mr. Smith quite plainly that I visited my old home and there was nothing to be found."

"You didn't tell him about the box that had been sent to your mother?"

"No. Nor will I. That would only encourage the man further. I did lie to him and I feel rather guilty for it."

"What did you say?"

Alice gazed toward the ceiling. "I told him that everything had been sold or destroyed—burned. I told him that the woman did remember there being some personal papers, but that they had been gotten rid of, as well."

"And what did he say?"

"It's more what he did," Alice countered, lowering her gaze. "He threw a table across the room. I was glad no one else was in the diner. Joe and Mr. Bellows demanded he leave, and Mr. Bellows drove me home tonight. I thanked him and told him I wouldn't be back."

Marty nodded. "It would seem we are committed to leaving for Texas as soon as possible."

"It would seem that way."

Chapter 10

"I can see why Marty is so fond of you," Hannah told Jake. She served him an extra portion of flapjacks and then took her seat opposite him at the table. "You have certainly brightened our days with your stories."

Jake smiled. "I loved my life on the ranch, and the stories are all that keep me going sometimes. I've always known I would one day return to Texas and to ranching. I want to say how much I appreciate that you folks would take me in and give me work."

"You're definitely earning your keep," Will told him. "I could use a dozen men like you."

"It's true," Robert added. "I know you've lightened my workload considerably. Especially since Pa is insistent on overseein' the building of the new hay barn."

"Not just overseein'," Will corrected. "I'm doin' plenty of the buildin'."

"Well, I'm glad to oblige." Jake looked up at the family—his family. Marty's sister and brother-in-law were easy to talk to and work for. He poured a generous amount of syrup over his flapjacks. "You've got a pretty amazing spread here. I have to say it's exactly as I'd have a place."

"We've definitely put a lot of hard work into it," Will replied. "I know your pa put a lot of work into your family's ranch. From what you told me about the location, I figure it to be the ranch owned by the Andersons."

Jake nodded. "Yes, that was their names. I couldn't remember it until you mentioned them. Anderson was a fairly young man. Made a lot of money after the war. Seemed he was from down Houston way."

"Well, I'm sure you could make your way over and meet them if you were of a mind to do so."

He considered it for a moment. "I suppose in time I will. I'd like to know if there's a chance of buying the place back. Not that I'm in any position to do that right now. But maybe one day."

"I know that would mean a lot to you," Hannah said, smiling. "I'll commit it to prayer."

"As will I," Will said before taking a long swallow of coffee.

"You never know how God might provide," Robert added with a grin. "I've seen some miracles around here that had to be His hand."

"Robert's right," Will agreed. "There have been some stretches when we wondered if we'd get through the hard times, but God has always provided a way."

"And He always will," Hannah said.

Jake liked the positive spirit of Marty's older sister. They looked a great deal alike with their blond hair and blue eyes, although Hannah's hair showed definite signs of gray. Being with Hannah made Jake miss Marty all the more. He feared at times he might never see his wife again, but Hannah assured him that Marty would never make light of her marriage vows. Jake said very little in response. He wasn't sure exactly what Marty had told her sister about their marriage. Did Hannah and Will realize Marty had answered his ad in the paper? Did they know she had thrown caution to the wind to marry a stranger—a stranger she didn't love?

"Well, as soon as I can, I plan to send Marty and Alice train tickets to join us here," Jake said between bites. "I appreciate that you would open your home to us . . . and to Alice, too. She's young but very capable. Life's not been any too kind to her."

"You said she was alone in the world," Hannah said, passing Jake a platter of crisp bacon. He took the plate as she continued. "We would never allow for her to be left to the whims of that madman you said was tormenting her."

"I know Marty wouldn't leave her behind, either," Will said. "Between her and Robert, we were always takin' in strays and wounded animals.

They both have a heart for helping mend the broken." Will took a sip of coffee. "Besides, my little sister-in-law is even more stubborn than my wife." He motioned toward Hannah, adding, "And I didn't think that was possible."

"Oh, it's true enough," Jake said, laughing. "Marty is more stubborn than a longhorn momma tryin' to get to her calf. I can't say that I've ever met anyone quite as headstrong."

Robert chuckled. "Aunt Marty says it's just a matter of her stickin' to her guns. She thinks if more people would stick to what they say, the world would be a better place."

"I can just hear her sayin' that," Jake agreed.

"I wish she would have come with you to Texas. I hate that she's unprotected in a city like Denver," Hannah interjected.

Jake remembered Marty standing with her shotgun in hand. Then a flash of memory came back regarding her entry into Denver. "Did Marty ever tell you about holding off bandits on her stage trip into Denver? In fact, she had to drive the stage partway to the next stop because the driver and shotgun had been wounded."

Hannah's eyes widened. "She what?"

Jake laughed. "Well, I could have guessed she didn't share all the details."

"I remember her saying there had been some problems that delayed her trip into Denver," Hannah said, looking to her husband.

Will and Robert both looked more than a little interested and encouraged Jake to continue with his story.

"As I recall, Marty was on a special stagecoach for women only, so the only men around were the driver and his shotgun rider. When they were still a ways out of Denver, some bandits attacked and started firing at them. Well, Marty pulled a revolver from her handbag and started firing back. The shotgun said they probably wouldn't have made it if not for her good shootin'."

Robert laughed. "She can put a hole through a silver dollar at a distance farther than any man I know."

"Well, when the bandits fled and the shotgun got the stage stopped, Marty got out to check on everyone. That's when she found out the driver was unconscious and the shotgun was pert near the same. She hoisted herself up into the driver's seat and drove the team of six on into the next stage stop. She was a heroine, and the papers wrote it all up for everyone to read."

"Sounds like our Marty." Will grinned. Hannah looked less than happy about the news, but said nothing.

Jake shrugged. "I knew then and there I'd found me a proper Lone Star bride."

"But I thought you two had never met before Marty got to Denver," Hannah said, looking at him oddly.

Will laughed. "Sometimes a fellow can take one look at a gal and know he's gonna marry her. I felt that way about you."

Hannah eyed him with a look that suggested he was crazy. "You hated me when we first met."

"Nope, you hated me," Will declared. "You thought I was gonna kick you and your family off the ranch."

Jake was glad for the turn the conversation had taken. He hadn't meant to give away any of Marty's secrets. He'd have to be careful what he said in the future. As talk turned back to Marty and her abilities, Jake decided to refocus the conversation.

"That woman can do just about anything, so I wasn't afraid to leave her behind while I figured things out down here. Besides, she wasn't exactly eager to return. She has a bad taste in her mouth when it comes to Texas."

"She made that clear enough in her letters," Hannah said. "I don't know why she holds such contempt for Texas. The state has been good to all of us."

Shaking his head, Jake considered the matter for a moment. "I know she figures ranchin' to be too dangerous. She doesn't want to lose another husband—she told me that much."

"But fighting off stage robbers isn't exactly safe," Robert said. "Marty doesn't always think about things like that. Life's full of trials and hardships, and they aren't limited to Texas."

"That's for sure. I saw just as many threats in California. Denver wasn't exactly minus hard times, either. Alice's situation was proof of that. I reminded Marty that Alice's father had been killed just carrying papers for the bank, so injury and death wasn't limited to ranch work."

"Oh, and she knows that full well," Hannah said. "My little sister has always been given to exaggerating. She'll endure something and build it up to be ten times bigger than it actually is. As a child she often told lies—sometimes just for the fun of it. I liked to never broke her of it."

"She did confess that much," Jake admitted. "We had a few go-rounds because of it, but I know she's a good woman and she's trying to start fresh. I won't hold the past against her."

"Nor will I," Hannah agreed. "I just hope she won't hold it against Texas."

"I guess we'll know soon enough," Will said, putting a stack of bills on the table. "I want you to take this money, Jake. You and Robert ride into town and purchase train tickets and get them mailed off to Marty."

Jake looked at the money. "I . . . won't . . . won't take charity. I mean to pay this back in work."

"Nonsense," Hannah declared. "She's my little sister, and I want her here as much as you do. Let this be our gift—to Alice, too. Now finish up your breakfast. Robert, I want you to pick up some things for me while you're in town, so you might as well take the wagon."

The matter was settled and Jake knew there'd be no chance of changing Hannah's mind. He hid his smile and finished off his flapjacks. She was just as stubborn as Marty.

------------------------ ★ ------------------------

"And Ruth told her mother-in-law that she would follow her wherever she went—that her people would be Ruth's people and her God would be Ruth's God," the minister declared from the pulpit.

For Marty, the words seemed to hit particularly close to her heart. Jake wanted her to share in his love of Texas, to follow him wherever he went. He was now with her people, and it was all the more important that she join him. They needed to be a family.

She thought of her expanding abdomen. Few knew of her condition, and she intended to keep it that way. Sam snuggled close to her on one side, and Wyatt edged closer on the other, while four-year-old Benjamin had claimed her lap. Marty couldn't help but wish she could take them with her. When the time came for her to leave, it would be especially hard to leave her three little shadows. The boys were bonded to her, and she to them. She couldn't help but wonder what Jake would do if she showed up in Texas with three additional family members.

A week later, the pastor spoke from the book of Genesis and told of Jacob's leaving his uncle's land to head back to his home. He was afraid of what he would face. He had duped Esau, his brother, out of his birthright and blessing. Now he wanted to return home to be with his family—God wanted him to return home.

Just as you apparently want me to return home.

Marty thought of the train tickets they had received only two days earlier. She and Alice were set to leave for Texas on the morrow, yet Marty still felt apprehensive.

Jacob, in Genesis, wanted to return home and feared the consequences. Marty wanted to be returned to Jake—her Jacob.

Why does this have to be so hard?

Images of Thomas's lifeless body came to mind. He had died with Marty at his side, clinging to his hand, begging him to stay. Marty closed her eyes and other tragedies clouded her thoughts. There had been times when Andy had gotten hurt, when Will had nearly died from pneumonia after riding for days on end in an icy rain. Hannah had known her share of problems, too. She'd nearly died when her youngest daughter had been born breach. There was always a chance of death and dying in life, and Marty knew there was no avoiding it. Not by staying in Colorado. Not by avoiding the ranch.

I'm so afraid, Lord. So afraid. I know trials and problems are everywhere. I look at Alice and I know it could just as easily have been Jake and me getting held up. I don't want to let fear steal my joy, Lord, but . . . well . . . it is, and I don't know how to change it.

"Sometimes God's directions to us seem impossible. Think of Abraham being told to leave his country and his people for an unknown land. Think of Noah being given the order to build an ark—a protection against something no one had ever seen or experienced. Throughout the Bible there

333

are examples of God calling His children to difficult and arduous tasks with seemingly impossible odds. But with God . . . all things are possible."

It seemed with every word the minister spoke, confirmation was at hand that Marty and Alice were doing the right thing.

"Let me say that again," the minister asserted, emphasizing his words. Marty opened her eyes to find him looking directly at her. "With God . . . all things are possible."

She smiled. *Even Texas?*

After the service she and Alice gathered the children around the dinner table, and Mr. Brentwood offered a blessing on the meal. Once everyone was seated, Marty took that moment to make her announcement.

"You heard the story this morning about Jacob returning to his homeland," she began. The children nodded and she smiled. "My husband's name is Jacob and he, too, returned to his homeland—my homeland in Texas."

"Texas is far away," Wyatt declared.

Marty nodded. "It's quite a ways." She paused and looked at Mr. Brentwood. She could see the sorrow in his eyes. Soon she would have to endure the sadness of the children, as well. She steadied herself. "Well, just like Jacob, I need to return to my homeland. My husband has sent train tickets for me and for Miss Alice. We will leave tomorrow."

"You can't go," Wyatt said, reaching out to take hold of her hand. "We need you to cook for us."

The other children nodded and Benjamin looked at Marty with tear-filled eyes. "I wanna go with you. Can I come, too?"

Sam nodded. "Me too. Please let us go with you."

"Me too," Wyatt pleaded. Some of the other children joined in.

Marty felt her heart nearly break at their sweet voices. She held up her hands to still them. "I'm afraid I can't take anyone with me. I haven't the money. I wouldn't be able to go myself if not for others sending the tickets. Alice and I will write to you, however. We won't go away without sending back word. We want to know how you're doing in school and what you're learning. We want to know who Mr. Brentwood gets to cook for you." She smiled, hoping to dispel their fears. "I told him he needed to get someone who makes really good cookies."

Some of the children clapped their hands at this idea, but Wyatt buried his face against Marty's skirt and began to cry in earnest. This caused Sam and Benjamin to do likewise. How could she leave them? Yet there was no choice.

Marty hated the pain she was causing. A part of her wished she'd never agreed to stay on at the orphanage. She had known the day would come when she'd have to go. She had only pretended to believe Jake would give up Texas and return to Denver. Now she had to deal with the devastation their choices had caused to these little ones. Taking her seat in utter defeat, Marty prayed God might ease the children's misery.

"Let us pray and ask a blessing on our meal," Mr. Brentwood said. He began to pray, but Marty didn't hear his words. She had her own prayer to offer.

It's not their fault, Lord. The children have done nothing wrong. They've needed love, and I've given what I had to share. Now I'm taking it away, and they will bear the pain. Oh, Father, it seems so unfair, so wrong. Please help us.

The meal passed in questions about Texas from some of the children who seemed more intrigued by the place than troubled by Marty and Alice's departure. Marty answered the questions and explained to the children about life on a ranch. The girls all envied her ability to have a horse of her own and go riding.

"I'd never want to stop riding," Willeen declared. "I love horses."

"I love them, too," ten-year-old Edith joined in. "When I was little, I used to ride my brother's pony."

There was a great deal of discussion about horses and ponies, riding and being a real cowboy, before the meal ended. The children all helped to clear the table. They each took their own dishes to the kitchen and deposited them in a tub of soapy water before heading off to wash up before their nap.

Wyatt, Sam, and Benjamin lingered in the kitchen for as long as Mr. Brentwood would allow and then tearfully let the man lead them out.

"You'll still be here when we wake up, won't you?" Wyatt asked, pausing at the door. Tears streamed down his face.

Marty nodded. "I'll be here, Wyatt. In fact, I'm gonna spend the day making ya'll a whole bunch of cookies." Her Texas drawl thickened with her emotions. "That way you can eat them and think of Alice and me." Usually the mention of cookies would instantly bring a smile to the boy's face, but not this time.

"I want you to be my mama," he said sadly.

Marty crossed the room and knelt beside him. "I would have loved to be your mama." Wyatt wrapped his arms around her neck and hugged her tight.

"Come on, Wyatt," Mr. Brentwood ordered, pulling the boy away. His expression looked nearly as sad as the boy's.

Marty felt as if a part of her heart went with Wyatt. She got to her feet and wiped her eyes. Just then, Alice put her arm around Marty's shoulders. "I didn't think this would be so hard," she said at Alice's gentle touch. "I love them so much."

"You could adopt them," Alice told her. "You've always talked about doing such a thing."

"I know, but there's no money for it. We wouldn't even be heading to Texas yet except that Will and Hannah insisted on paying for the tickets. And then there's the matter of the baby. I don't know if Jake would consider adopting others now that we're expecting our own. I mean, he was always very positive about adoption before, but he might feel different now."

"You have no way of knowing unless you ask him. Maybe Mr. Brentwood could take Wyatt, Sam, and Benjamin off the list of those children available to adopt. You know, just in case someone comes and wants to take them on."

"I suppose I could speak to him about it. I can't promise anything, but maybe since I'm giving in to what Jake wants, he'll give me what I want in return." But even as she said it, Marty knew that was no way to handle the matter. Marriage was, of course, full of give and take, but it wasn't right to put expectations—demands really—on each other for something that involved the life and happiness of so many.

Turning, Marty broke into sobs and cried against Alice's shoulder. There was no possible way to make this parting easy. Her heart was being torn in two. Without a doubt she would leave a part of herself behind at this orphanage.

Chapter 11

FEBRUARY 1894

Alice dozed to the rhythmic sway of the train car. She couldn't help but feel a sense of relief as the train put first one mile and then several hundred between her and Mr. Smith in Denver. She looked at this as her own independence day. Despite it being a cold February morning and the poor heating in the train, Alice was happier than she'd been in years.

Of course, with one issue behind her, there were others Alice knew she'd have to face. Her mother was alive. That alone caused disturbance to her peace of mind. Not that a part of her wasn't excited to find out if her mother still lived in Chicago and if her brother Simon was alive. Ever since learning about the letter her mother had sent, Alice had looked at the orphanage children with new eyes. Her own brother would be the same age as several of the children.

Does he resemble me? Is he blond and blue eyed? Does he remember me?

She opened her eyes and stared out the sooty window. The vast open lands stretched for as far as the eye could see. Gone were the snow-covered Rockies. Now scrub and twisted mesquite dotted the sandy landscape. Western Texas looked much as Marty had said it would. Desolate. Dry. Deserted. Marty had also told her that the scenery would change drastically. Texas, Alice had been informed, was such a huge state that it was very much like several smaller states rolled into one. In the east there was an abundance of forest and water. To the south the Mexican and seaside influences were evident. Central Texas held vast farmlands and cattle ranches, as did the north. Western Texas had its share of ranches, as well, with a bit of desert flare in some areas. Alice found it all truly amazing. Marty had been all over the state, traveling with her sister and brother-in-law to purchase cattle or other supplies, while Alice had never been anywhere outside of Colorado.

Glancing at the woman across from her, Alice wondered if Marty had finally found relief in sleep. Marty was so afraid of what Texas would bring.

Please give her peace, Lord. Help her to carry this baby in health and to deliver it in the same. Oh, Father, she needs your comfort. Alice bit her lip and looked back out the window. *And so do I.*

Alice watched the miles race by and thought again of her mother and brother. Marty had wanted her to write immediately to her mother, but Alice hadn't been able to bring herself to the task. Whenever she gave it serious consideration, doubts crept in. Her mother had deserted her. Her mother had taken Simon and left Alice behind. How much could her mother possibly care about her? And if she didn't care, why had she asked after her in the letter to Mrs. Ingram? Why had she written those haunting words?

She is very dear to me, and I hope to be reunited with her.

Could Alice trust that her mother was being honest? Had she only written that in order to sound the part of the caring mother? But what purpose would that serve? These questions and a hundred just like them raced through Alice's mind.

Marty thought she was being immature in her delay to write. She had chided Alice and even threatened to write to Mrs. Chesterfield herself, but Alice had made her promise she'd not interfere.

"This has to be my decision," she had told Marty. "She's my mother—not yours."

Alice looked again at Marty. She felt a sense of security with the older woman. She was like the big sister Alice had never had. Marty had cared for her from the time of their first meeting. She hadn't been concerned with the scar on Alice's face or her lack of references when she'd showed up begging for the job of personal maid to Marty. Instead, Martha Wythe had offered Alice a home and employment.

More than that. She gave me an advocate—a protector—a friend.

Alice knew that no matter what, she would always have the deepest love and respect for Marty because of her willingness to extend grace and kindness to a scarred young woman with no other future.

And now here she was—in Texas. Alice couldn't help but wonder what would happen once they reached Marty's family. She didn't know if she'd return to being Marty's personal maid or if she'd be needed to work elsewhere, but either was acceptable. She felt blessed that the Wythes hadn't just abandoned her in Denver.

"Did you get any sleep?" Marty asked.

Alice was surprised to find Marty watching her. "I slept off and on throughout the night. I can't say that I'm truly rested, but I know it's been much worse for you."

Marty sighed and straightened in the hard leather-wrapped seat. "I'll be glad to put this trip behind us and sleep in a real bed again."

"Happy, too, to see your family and Jake?" Alice asked with a smile.

Marty nodded. "It's been over a year since I saw my sister. Feels just as long since I saw Jake. I suppose because we parted on such poor terms, the time seems longer than it has been."

"I know he'll be happy to see you again. I've always envied the love he holds for you."

Marty raised a brow. "We fight like cats and dogs despite that love. I wouldn't be envying it if I were you."

Alice glanced around the train car. There weren't too many people sharing the space, but she lowered her voice just the same. "If I could know a love like yours, I would be the happiest woman in the world."

Marty sighed. "I hope I still have Jake's love."

"You know you do. He wouldn't have sent for you otherwise."

"He sent for me because my sister probably made him do so." Marty didn't try to hide her smile. "My sister Hannah is . . . well . . . quite determined when it comes to having things her way."

Alice giggled. "And you aren't?"

A slight chuckle escaped Marty. "I suppose I might as well tell you—

she and I, well we don't always see eye to eye. In fact, most of the time we tend to be at odds. It's all in good sport, though. We love each other dearly. Hannah has always been one of the most important people in my life. I suppose I've always wanted her approval, and so I challenge her."

"How is challenging her going to get you her approval?" Alice asked, rather confused by this comment.

Marty shrugged and reached up to straighten her hat. "I suppose it's a sort of game we play. I want Hannah to realize that I'm smart and self-sufficient. Hannah has always held the highest regard for strength and capability. She has no use for women who consider themselves to be too good to work—too refined to lend a hand. She calls them 'fancy window dressings.' Pretty enough to look at but without any other purpose.

"Maybe it's because Hannah had to grow up so quickly. She was supposed to marry when I was born. But her fiancé died in the war, and our father demanded she care for me after our mother died giving birth to me. Our brother, Andy, was just a few years older, so Hannah became mother to us both. She needed strength for that, and she needed us to be strong, as well."

"And was your father also demanding of you?" Alice asked, thinking back on her own father. George Chesterfield had always been a man of purpose, driven to accomplish, less than forgiving of error. She hadn't really thought about the latter until now, but there were many examples that came to mind to prove such ideals.

"My father lost his will to live after losing Mama. Hannah said it started even before that. He was devastated when Hannah's mama died. I think of Hannah as my sister, but she's really my stepsister." Marty paused and watched the dry landscape. "Papa also lost my older brother to the war. Hannah said the war took what little life was left in Papa, and after that he was more reserved. I remember only little bits of him," Marty recalled. "I was sad when I learned he was dead, but I knew it would have been far worse if it had been Hannah who had died."

Alice nodded. "Sometimes I wonder about my father. I know he was deeply injured when my mother left. I remember times when they would argue and he would call her names and make her cry. Usually I went to my room or outdoors and avoided the conflict. I knew no other

340

way, of course. We didn't have relatives or close friends to give me other examples of married life."

She looked out the window. The sun was now bearing down in a crispness that only came with winter days. "Living with my friends after the attack showed me how different life could be. I never heard a mean-spirited word given or names called. Even so, I found it in my heart to make my father's behavior acceptable. I suppose no one ever wants to think badly of their parent—especially when that parent was the only one remaining in their life. Now, knowing that my mother is alive, I have to confess I would like to hear her side of the story."

"I think it would do you good to hear it," Marty said. "At least then you can judge the matter for yourself."

"I think it's possible I've been a fool, Marty." She frowned and twisted her gloved hands. "My father lied to me. He knew my mother was alive. He had her letters. Mrs. Ingram told me there had been a dozen or more that had been kept in his things. How could he lie to me like that?"

"Men do what they think they have to in order to get by. Your father obviously felt it was best to keep your mother from you. Whether that decision was made because he was selfish or trying to punish her, or even if it was because he knew your mother could cause you real harm, I'm sure he acted on the belief that he was doing good for you."

"Good? How could he think it was good to lie?"

Marty shrugged. "Folks lie for a lot of reasons—I ought to know. But even when I've lied in the past, even when I knew what I was doing would end up causing me trouble in the long run, I always had the best of intentions." She shook her head. "I could always rationalize my decisions."

"I'm so afraid." She sighed and met Marty's gaze. "I'm afraid of what the truth will reveal."

Marty gave her a knowing nod. The expression on her face was almost pained. "I know just how you feel."

★

"So this was Marty's place," Jake stated more than questioned. He and Will had ridden over to the ranch after breakfast, and Jake couldn't help but feel a sense of unease.

"As far as I'm concerned," Will said, "it still is Marty's place. Oh, I told her I'd buy it back, but I didn't actually do the paper work on it. I sent her some money to help out with her needs, but I figured she'd come back one day." He eased back in the saddle a bit and rested his hands on the horn. "Texas is in Marty's blood. She might as well have been born here. I can't imagine she'll truly be happy anyplace else."

"She holds Texas a grudge. And it runs pretty deep." Jake looked at the small ranch house. "She and her man build this?"

Will nodded. "We all did. It was a community effort—a wedding gift. Thomas added to the place a few years after they wed. He built the barn and pens, the outbuildings and such. He was a hardworkin' man—like yourself."

Jake could see the place was sadly neglected. The house needed a coat of paint, as did the barn. Some of the fencing sections had been allowed to give way, and weeds rose up in place of well-groomed flower beds and vegetable gardens.

"I figure you'll want to take it back over. Marty may hold Texas a grudge, but she's never been one to stay mad for long." He grinned. "As I'm sure you know."

"She endured a powerful hurt here," Jake said, shaking his head. "I wouldn't want her to think she had to live here. Not if it makes her uncomfortable."

"Why don't you just plan to stay on with us for a time," Will suggested. "At least until we're able to mother-up the calves and get 'em branded. Once we have the cows paired with their babies, we can see exactly which belong where. Marty's herd did well last year, and I expect this year will be the same. Last time I checked, most of the cows had delivered and the calves all seemed healthy.

"Anyway, you and Marty can live at our place for the time bein'. Miss Chesterfield, too. The house is more than big enough for all of us. That'll give Marty a chance to ease back in, and I'll have you to help me with roundup."

Jake met the older man's intense gaze. "Thank you, Will. I appreciate what you're doing for me, for us. I don't take any of this lightly. I want to do a good job—to be a good husband to Marty. I know she's

342

worried I'll get myself killed like her other husband, but I don't intend that to happen."

Will chuckled. "Can't say anyone ever intends it to happen, son. However, troubles will come. We've seen it over the years, as I'm sure your family did. Death is a part of life that we have to accept. No sense in frettin' and fearin' it if a fellow knows what lies beyond this world."

"I agree," Jake replied. "I have to say I haven't always lived a life that I'm proud of, but God did get a hold of me and put me back in line."

"You wear His brand," Will said, nodding in approval. "That's clear enough to see. I watched you studying the Bible the other morning, and I've seen you at prayer. We all made mistakes in the past—me included. Or maybe I should say, me especially. God had His hands full with my sorry spirit. But thankfully, He didn't let me go."

"Yeah, I feel the same way. Don't know where I'd be if He had." Jake looked back at the ranch one more time and then turned his horse toward the road they'd come up earlier. "But I know I wouldn't have Marty, and if that were the case, my life wouldn't be worth livin' anyway."

Chapter 12

Robert waited by the buggy while his mother finished saying her good-byes to Carissa Atherton and Jessica. He had agreed to drive Mother over that Sunday afternoon because she'd been worried when the family hadn't shown up for church that morning.

"I hope that you'll let us know if you need anything," Robert's mother told Mrs. Atherton.

"Oh, we're just fine. Tyler's been sicker than this before. I think it's a bad chest cold, but I told him if it worsens he's going to the doctor."

Mother nodded. "This is a bad time of year for it. Just make sure you don't let old Doc Sutton give him calomel. I know the old man is fond of it as a cure-all, but I've read some disheartening things that suggest it's not as good a cure as was once thought."

Mrs. Atherton smiled. "'The doctor comes with free goodwill, but ne'er forgets his calomel.'" She chuckled. "I remember hearing that when I was growing up. Never liked the stuff."

"Dr. Sutton is nearly eighty, and his notions are so outdated. I heard it said that he still bleeds people on occasion."

"I remember him telling me that I'd miscarried a baby because of the gravitational pull of the earth or the moon or some such nonsense."

Mother nodded. "Yes, I've heard others say the same. Frankly, we need to encourage him to retire and get a younger doctor to take over his practice. I know there are plenty of good doctors closer to Dallas, but we need someone who would be willing to come farther out."

"Well, Tyler won't be getting calomel from me. I can promise you that," Mrs. Atherton said.

"I think it does little good and a lot of harm."

Robert knew his mother had been something of a local healer for years, and people often sought her advice before going elsewhere. He wasn't at all surprised when she told Jessica's mother that she would be happy to help in the matter.

"I have remedies that I know will suit better than that," Mother told the ladies. "Just let me know if you need something."

"I will." Mrs. Atherton's expression suddenly changed. "Oh, I almost forgot. I have that lard I promised you." She turned to Jessica. "Take Robert to the springhouse and show him where that lard is. It's near to fifty pounds," she said rather apologetically. "I hope you don't mind. I put it in one tub."

Robert pushed off the side of the carriage. "It's not a problem."

Jessica turned up her nose. "I find it appalling. Smelly stuff." She led the way to the springhouse but turned and stopped when they were out of sight. "Still, it gives us a few minutes to be alone." She smiled and let her shawl fall away. "Do you like my new gown? I had it made in Dallas. Isn't it just about the most beautiful color you've ever seen? They called it *Samson* and it came all the way from London."

"Looks like green to me," Robert replied with a shrug. "Nice enough. You always fill out a dress real well."

She looked at him and frowned. "You are such a . . . a . . . cowboy."

He laughed. "Well, I reckon I should be insulted, but I'm not. Years of ranching have made that the case. But I still know that green is green, and Samson's a fellow in the Bible."

Jessica stamped her foot. "You can be such a bubbleheaded philistine."

Robert shrugged thoughtfully. "Samson had a bad time of it with the Philistines. Guess it fits that you are, too."

She shook her finger at him. "You know very well that I am only trying to bring a little beauty and culture into your life and into the world around me. Goodness, but you'd think we were at the beginning of the 1800s instead of approaching the end. The 1900s are soon to be here and with it a new modern world."

Sobering, Robert looked at the young woman. So many people expected the couple to marry, yet Robert knew they had little in common.

"Jess, you can have your new modern world. Just leave me Texas."

"But once we're married," she said, giving him a knowing nod, "you'll change your tune. I intend for us to live abroad for a least part of our lives."

"Abroad? And what would I do abroad? I'm a Texas cattleman." Robert shook his head. "Sometimes I don't think you know anything about me at all."

She came and took hold of his arm and tucked it close to her side. "Now, Robert, don't be such a bore. Of course I know you. I know all about you, and that's why I want to show you what you're missing."

"But that's just it, Jess. I don't feel like I'm missin' a thing."

She pulled back just a bit. "But you've never been out of Texas. I have. I've traveled with my grandparents, and there's so much more to the world than just Texas."

Robert liked the way the sun glinted on her honey-brown hair. She was a striking woman, to be sure, but he wasn't in love with her.

They resumed their walk toward the springhouse. Robert ignored the annoyance in Jessica's tone as she continued to belabor her point. She told him about the glorious big cities she'd visited and all the wonders she had yet to see.

"I know you'll love seeing the world once you're actually doing it," she said, stopping at the door to the springhouse. "You just need to trust me on this."

"Maybe you just need to hear what I'm sayin'." Robert pulled his arm away. "I don't intend to travel abroad or anywhere else, for that matter. I'm happy here, Jess. I love the land and the animals. I love what I do. This is my life."

"But it's not what I want," Jessica said.

"Which is why we aren't married," Robert countered.

She frowned at this and began to pout as she pushed back the door. "You're such a mean person sometimes."

"It's not meanness, Jess. It's the truth. I think we've been going two different directions for a long time. I know folks figure we ought to marry each other, but honestly, we don't see eye to eye on much at all."

"You're just scared."

"I'm not scared. I'm tryin' to be honest with you. I don't want anyone sayin' I duped you. I don't plan to live in a grand house and wear fancy duds. I don't plan to travel or buy priceless bits of junk to put in my house. I just wanna run my ranch and raise a family."

"Well, you'll need a wife to raise a family, and in order to get one, you're going to have to learn to compromise. My mother says that marriage is one big compromise."

"So where does that figure in for you compromising on all these big schemes?" Robert asked.

She looked as if his question confused her. "I'll have children."

"And that's a compromise?" Her comment left him feeling even sadder than when they'd started this conversation.

"Well, children require a great deal of care and attention. It's difficult to travel with them and harder still to have nice things. The compromise will be that I will bear children and endure the consequences."

"Maybe we could just have a houseful of servants to watch over them while we make our way around the world," he replied in a sarcastic tone.

She didn't hear it that way. Instead, she smiled and nodded. "Exactly. That's what I think. A good governess or two and a nurse can take care of the children. Of course, I'll still have to compromise in bearing them."

"You can have that compromise without me. I want to be a father, and when I have children, I want them to be with me."

"You are so difficult." Jessica's words echoed a bit from the interior of the springhouse. She pointed to the large tub of lard. "Take it and go. I hardly think we need to belabor this subject further. You'll understand my point of view in time."

"I don't think time will help me one bit." He hoisted up the lard. "I think you should probably just look to workin' over some other fella. There's bound to be one out there who wants to wear a fancy top hat and cavort with you all over the world—without children. But it ain't me."

She turned and beamed him a smile that he completely did not expect.

"Oh, Robert. You do say the funniest things. You know I couldn't be untrue to you."

Robert stopped and put the tub down momentarily. "Jessica, I'm serious. I don't want to lead you on. I'm not the man you want me to be."

She put her hand on his arm once again and leaned close. "But you could be . . . if you wanted to be."

He shook his head. "But that's just it. I don't want to change. We've been good friends since we were little. You followed me around like some kind of lost puppy. I thought you were a sweet little girl, like my sisters. But I wouldn't marry my sister."

Jessica frowned. "So you don't care for me?"

"You know that's not true. I do care for you. That's why I'm not sure—"

She put her finger to his lips. "I'm sorry, Robert. I was too pushy and too insensitive to your feelings. Forgive me." She stepped back and pulled her shawl close. "Now, we'd better get back before our mothers believe us to be up to no good."

Robert felt the muscles in his face tighten. He wanted to say something more. He wanted to tell Jessica that they needed to just forget about marrying and let everyone know they weren't suited to a life together. So why couldn't he seem to get the words out?

He lifted the tub again and followed after her, trying to figure out how he could make Jessica understand without crushing her spirit and causing problems between the families. He didn't want to hurt or disappoint anyone.

Back at the buggy Robert could see that his mother had already settled in for the ride home. He put the tub at the back and strapped it down.

"You be careful now," Mrs. Atherton said. "Looks like we could get a good rain out of those clouds to the west."

Robert gave the sky a glance. "I'm sure we'll be home before then." He tipped his hat at Mrs. Atherton and Jessica before releasing the brake.

They were well down the road for home before Robert's mother questioned him. "What's wrong? Did you and Jessica have a spat?"

He gave his mother a side glance. "Why did you marry Pa?"

She laughed. "Well, I wasn't expecting that question, but the answer

348

is simple. I was crazy with love for him. I couldn't imagine my life without him in it."

Shaking his head, Robert sighed. "I don't feel that way about Jess, and I don't think I ever will."

"What do you mean? I know you care about her. You've been her hero since she was a little girl."

"Maybe so, but Ma, I don't love her like that. It's really startin' to bother me, too. Everyone figures we'll marry. Everyone calls us engaged, and God knows I've never done anything to change their minds."

"Of course not. Why should you? Goodness, Robert, I think sometimes young folks expect some sort of freight train to run them over when they fall in love. But sometimes love just comes along in a quiet and gentle fashion. Sometimes love is born from a lifetime of knowin' each other, and other times from just a few hours. Pray about it, son. You might just be feelin' the pressures of the season. We've got a lot of work to do, and I know you've had a lot on your mind. Don't make rash decisions."

Robert blew out an exasperated breath. *I doubt anyone's gonna let me make any of my own decisions—rash or otherwise.*

★

Marty checked her reflection in the small mirror one more time before deciding there was no way to improve her tired-looking face. She felt exhausted from the long hours on the train. She frankly didn't care to ever set foot on another—at least not for a very long time.

Her stomach growled in hunger, reminding her that it had been over twelve hours since they'd eaten anything. All the food they'd brought with them was gone, and with no money to spare, buying more was out of the question. Jake and the others would probably be there to greet them. Perhaps they would bring sandwiches. Marty certainly hoped so.

"Are you eager to see everyone again?" Alice asked. "I have to say I'm excited to be a part of this adventure."

Marty smiled. "I have to admit I am looking forward to seeing my husband and my family. I'm nervous, too. I want very much for everything to be good. There's no telling how things have gone for Jake since he wrote. He might not get along with my family. They may have even had a falling-out by now."

"Oh, that's silly." Alice shook her head. "I don't think that would ever happen. Jake is a good-natured man. And from what you've told me about your family, well, I think we will all get along just fine. It was so kind of them to include bringing me here."

"My sister is especially fond of helping those in need. She's a good Christian woman. I sometimes wish I could be more like her. I'm afraid I don't have her sensitivity to the needs of people around me. I figure it's because I'm far too self-centered." Marty sighed. "I've tried to be a good person. I really have."

"You have a good heart," Alice said, taking hold of Marty's gloved hand. "You need to stop fretting. No one is perfect, nor will they ever be. The only good thing about us is Jesus. Don't you think He will forgive you for whatever flaws you have?"

"Of course," Marty agreed. "But I know He also wants us to become more like Him. I want that, too, but sometimes I fail so miserably. I can't help but worry about things that seem important to me and don't know how to stop being like that. You'd think for a woman who just turned thirty-six, I would be making some progress."

Alice chuckled and patted Marty's hand. Just then the conductor swung through the car. "We'll be in the station in less than five minutes. Remember, this is just a brief stop, so be ready to disembark. We have a schedule to keep."

The women nodded and Marty could feel the train begin to slow. The grinding sound of metal on metal, coupled with the blasts of the train's whistle, permeated her ears. Her heart began to beat faster. Jake would be there waiting for her. If the rest of the world forgot all about her or was otherwise occupied, Marty knew without a doubt that Jake would still be there. The thought made her smile, and she lovingly put her hand to her waist.

I know he'll be happy about you, too. She bit her lower lip. *But we'll wait just a little longer before we tell him the news. Just in case . . . just on the chance that . . . that you can't stay.*

The train came to a halt and Marty noticed the depot sign. *Cedar*

Springs. Back where I started. Back in Texas, where I'd hoped never to return. She grimaced and got to her feet as Alice moved to collect their smaller bags. Her back ached from the long hours of travel. She prayed that was all it was. She'd had a backache the last time she'd lost a baby. She frowned. What if . . .

Marty knew she had to get her heart and mind under control. They seemed to be warring with each other at the moment, and that would never do. She needed to put aside her fears and be strong.

I'm being fretful and silly. I'm just sore from travel, and I needn't create a problem where there isn't one. I'm going to be happy. I want to see Jake, and that's the most important reason for being here.

Jake would know how hard this was on her. Of that Marty had no doubt. But he wouldn't know the full reason for her fears.

"Careful now, ma'am," the porter said as he helped Marty down the train steps.

She glanced for some sign of her family. No one seemed to be around. The entire platform was nearly deserted.

Alice looked toward the baggage car. "I'll see to our things." She smiled at the baggage man, who stood not far from his cart. "Would you assist me, please?"

"Yes'm," the man said, giving her a brief nod. "Pleasure be mine."

Marty tried not to fret at the absence of her family. She knew that any number of things could have happened to delay their arrival. Her stomach growled again.

"Well, whether they get here or not, I'm going to have something to eat."

"Talking to yourself, Mrs. Wythe?"

She turned to find Jake standing only a few feet behind her. Without giving any thought to the public display, Marty threw herself into his arms. "I'm so sorry," she said, breaking into tears. "I'm so sorry for the way I acted. I've missed you so much."

He wrapped his arms around her and pulled her close. "There now, don't cry, Marty. You're here and that's all that matters." He lifted her chin and kissed her tenderly. "I missed you, too."

"I know I'm making a spectacle of myself," she said, meeting his gaze, "but I don't care. I don't like the idea of living in Texas, but I hate the idea of living without you even more. I don't want to ever be apart again."

He grinned. "Me either." He hugged her close and Marty felt her fears give way. Surely God would keep Jake safe. Surely He wouldn't demand another husband from her—or another child.

★

Robert had heard a great deal about Alice Chesterfield. He knew about the attack that had taken the life of her father and left her scarred. Jake had told them about the situation and of the man who tormented Alice for property she no longer had in her possession. But now sitting across the table from the blond-haired woman, Robert felt completely captivated by her.

Alice smiled and answered all the questions his mother had for her. She seemed as patient and relaxed as if they'd all been old friends reunited after a brief separation.

"And is the room to your liking?" Mother asked.

"Oh, it's beautiful and so big. You really didn't need to give me such a large room," Alice answered.

Robert's mother smiled and passed a plate of corn bread in Alice's direction. "Nonsense. It was one of our daughters' rooms, and it wants for someone to enjoy it. This house seems so empty sometimes. I'd love to fill it with people again."

"Well, we're off to a good start with Jake and Marty and Alice," Robert's father interjected. "Marty, I can't tell you how good it is to see you again. And you look quite fit. Colorado must have agreed with you."

"It did," Marty said. "It's very beautiful there, and the air is dry and fresh."

"And it snows . . . a lot," Jake added.

"That's true," Marty agreed. "I have to admit I'm no lover of the cold."

"I'm so amazed at how things are already greening up down here," Alice commented. "February in Denver is never anything but cold, snow, and ice."

"Well, we've had a mild winter—drier than most, but before you came we had a couple of rains. It did wonders for the land," Pa told her. "But you wait. In another few weeks we'll be full of blossoms and greenery."

"And we'll be very busy planting gardens," Robert's mother announced. "I'm so glad you'll both be here to help."

Alice nodded. "I don't know much about gardening, but I'm happy to learn."

"Then we'll have you ridin' and ropin' before you know it," Pa said with a smile.

"I think I'd like that, too," Alice replied, giggling.

Her amusement only served to make Robert all the more fond of her. She was lighthearted, yet there was something very serious about her spirit.

"Don't do it," Marty whispered in his ear.

Robert startled and looked to his aunt for an explanation. She smiled in her knowing way. At the other end of the table the family was already busy chatting about teaching Alice to brand calves, so Robert leaned close to ask. "Do what?"

"Don't make her your new project. She might bear life's wounds, but she's not one of your injured animals, and I don't want to see her hurt."

"Aunt Marty, I have no idea of hurting anyone," Robert replied quietly and leaned back in his chair with a smile. "You should know me better than that."

"I do know you," Marty whispered. "And I recognize that smile on your face. You think you've got me fooled, but I can see in your eyes that you're already making plans."

Robert said nothing but turned his attention back on the meal. He was making plans, but Aunt Marty didn't need to know anything about them.

Chapter 13

"I usually plant corn over here," Hannah told Alice as she and Marty followed her from one plot of ground to another. "I've had some of the orphan boys you sent us last year work on turning up the dirt for me and getting it ready for planting."

"I can't wait to see them again," Marty said, glancing around. "Where are they?"

"Out on the range. We only have two of them with us now. The rest have found homes elsewhere. Hiram and Nate are working with the cattle. They ride like they were born to it and have taken to their duties with ease. They remind me of Andy when he was first learning to rope and ride."

"I'm so glad," Marty replied. She barely remembered the older boys. Her mind however went to thoughts of Wyatt, Sam, and Benjamin. "Those children are so precious. They deserve much more than what they've been given."

"We very much enjoyed working with the orphans in Denver," Alice added. "And the children were quite fond of Marty."

"They just loved me for my cookies," Marty said and laughed. She pulled at the cuff of her sleeve. "I think they'd be glad for anyone who would give them some attention. After all, they're hardly more than babies. They are frightened and so alone. The folks who should be in their lives are either dead or gone. I just wanted to show love to each of them."

"It must have been hard to leave," Hannah said, looking at her sister with great compassion. "I know how attached a person can get to children. Had anyone tried to take you or Andy from my care, I would have protested loudly."

"As I recall, there was that horrible Mr. Lockhart who wanted to send me and Andy to the far reaches so he could have you to himself."

Hannah shuddered. "I try to forget about that man." She turned to Alice. "You aren't the only one to have tragedy and evil men in your past. Mr. Lockhart was the one responsible for killing our father. He caused this family a great deal of harm."

"That's terrible," Alice said. "I hate to hear that anyone else should have to endure the things I've gone through." The look on her face betrayed her fears.

Hannah reached out and touched the younger woman's shoulder. "You are among friends here, and those people can't hurt you anymore. We'll see to that."

Alice looked into Hannah's eyes, and Marty could see that she very much wanted to believe those words. "I feel as if I'm on the run and always will be."

Hannah hugged her close and then stepped back. "You can let that thought go. You are home now. At least for as long as you want to call it home."

Home. Marty looked around her. There wasn't an inch of this place that she didn't know like the back of her hand. She'd had a wonderful childhood on this ranch. Oh, it hadn't been without its problems and lean years, but they'd had one another, and that had made it all bearable.

Can I learn to be happy here? Can I call this home and know in my heart the kind of contentment that should come from such a place?

She thought of the ranch she'd shared with Thomas. She'd loved her little house. Maybe it would be wise to talk to Will about taking the ranch back. He'd bought it from her—well, he'd agreed to. The paper work hadn't been finalized, though he had sent her a down payment on the purchase. Perhaps she could work something out with him. She knew that Jake would find the spread she and Thomas had worked ideal—just as Thomas had.

"I don't think you've heard a word we said."

Marty looked up to find Hannah and Alice watching her. "I'm sorry. I was off in my own thoughts."

Hannah smiled. "I'm sure it's a challenge to be back and take it all in at once. Jake seems like a very good man. I've enjoyed getting to know him. I was just telling Alice that although you have your own place, I selfishly would like you to stick around for a while."

Marty was surprised by this turn of events. "Stay here? With you and Will?"

"Yes. What's so strange about that?"

"Nothing, Hannah. I suppose I hadn't really thought about it."

"You should. It's been over a year since anyone lived at your place. It's gonna need some attention before anyone lives there again."

Alice gave her a knowing look. "Maybe it would be a good idea, considering."

Marty realized what Alice was getting at. She supposed she should come clean and admit her condition to Hannah. After all, her sister had borne three children and had also acted as midwife for a great many women.

"Considering what?" Hannah asked. She looked from Alice to Marty. "What should be considered?"

"I'm going to have a baby," Marty replied, watching for her sister's reaction.

Hannah's face lit up and her smile stretched from ear to ear. She rushed to take hold of Marty and all but gave a yell of approval. "That's wonderful news! When?"

"Shh," Marty said with her finger to her lips. "Jake doesn't know yet."

"What? But why not?"

Marty shrugged. "I haven't had a chance to tell him. I was too tired last night. Right after supper I fell asleep. I don't even remember getting into bed. I think I fell asleep in the wing-backed chair by our fireplace. Jake must have carried me to bed. When I finally woke up this morning, he was already gone."

"Well, you need to tell him right away. A fella needs to hear that kind of news."

"But . . . well . . ." Marty heaved a sigh. "I'm afraid to get his hopes up."

"Why?" Hannah looked at her oddly.

Marty bit her lip and turned away. "It's hard to get excited when . . . well . . . I could lose the baby. I did before."

Hannah forced Marty to face her. "You never told me."

"I know." Marty shook her head. "I thought it better if you just figured I couldn't get pregnant. Thomas and I were so saddened by the losses."

"More than one?"

Marty nodded. "I don't want Jake to have to go through that. That's one of the biggest reasons I didn't want to come back to Texas."

"I don't understand," Hannah said. "Why would that be a problem?"

"Dr. Sutton told me that miscarriage is common here because we're closer to the equator."

Hannah rolled her eyes. "That old man needs to retire. I was just talking with Carissa about this. It's nonsense. There's no such thing as a gravity pull that causes miscarriage. That's old superstition and nonsense. Women miscarry in the North as well as the South. Some babies just don't get to be born. It's sad but true. We have no way of knowin' why. But I can tell you this, Marty, it has nothin' to do with Texas."

"How can you be so sure?" Marty wanted to believe her sister. She knew the doctor in Denver had told her much the same thing, but it seemed that men of science often told people whatever was the most popular theory of the day. "How can you know that I won't lose this baby, too?"

"I can't know that, Marty. But I do know that only God can create or take a life and that we have to trust Him. It's hard, to be sure, but you won't benefit yourself or the child by worrying and fretting."

"I want to believe that."

Hannah smiled. "Then do. This is a time of joy. You need to let Jake know as soon as possible. I won't stand for you keeping it from him any longer. By the way, when should we expect this little one?"

Marty put her hand to her stomach. "August. Or maybe July. I'm really not sure."

Hannah nodded. "Good summer months for birthing. And I'll help you through it all. Alice and I will help you make baby clothes, and we'll fix up a nursery, and you can just stay here with us. I don't want you to overdo it."

Hannah directed them to start back toward the house. "Now, I want to know everything about your miscarriages. How far along were you? What were you doing when the pain started?"

Marty couldn't get a word in edgewise as they went back into the kitchen. Alice threw Marty a smile but said nothing. There was simply no chance of it with Hannah's animated chatter.

Later that day, Jake invited Marty to go riding with him. She asked Hannah if she thought it would be all right, given her condition, and her sister assured her that many women rode well into their pregnancy.

Marty changed into a split skirt for the occasion and made her way to where Jake already had the horses saddled and ready. She'd grown up riding astride, as many women in Texas did, and was pleased to see that Jake hadn't prepared the feminine sidesaddle.

He helped her into the stirrup and up atop the gentle brown mare before heading over to his own mount.

"I bought this chestnut gelding in Lufkin after getting my first pay. The Vandermarks had some friends who made me a good deal, other-wise I'd still be afoot." He climbed atop the tall horse and smiled. "His name is Bobbin. Not sure why, but the woman who had him told me he knows his name, and she begged me not to even think of changin' it."

Marty couldn't help but smile. "Bobbin isn't such a bad name."

They moved the horses down the lane and headed out toward Marty's ranch. She had been the one to suggest the destination, and Jake seemed pleased with the idea. She didn't know if anyone had bothered to show him the spread or not, but she wanted to talk to him about the baby and about her fears before any more time could slip away.

The ranch house was nearly five miles away, but the day was beauti-ful, with blue skies that didn't even hint at rain. They talked about the work Jake had been doing, and Marty could hear in his voice a kind of joy she'd never known him to have when they were in Denver.

"So I suppose you don't want to ever consider banking again?"

"Banking?" he asked, looking over from his mount. "Seriously?"

"Sure. Texas has banks, too." She tucked an errant strand of hair back under her hat. "And things won't be bad forever."

"My heart isn't in banking, Marty. I thought you'd understand that by now."

She did understand it, but that didn't mean she didn't hope to change his mind. "You know, the older you get, the harder ranch work is going to be. I look at Will and he's aged a lot just in the last year." Marty didn't bother to add that her brother-in-law only looked better for it.

"I'm trying to keep my focus on what God wants for me," Jake told her. "I feel His presence in my ranch work. That never happened with banking."

"Well, one can hardly argue with the presence of God," Marty muttered.

"Look, I know you worry about my safety, but I've been careful. I never was one for takin' undue risks, anyway," he said with a grin. "That's for your brother. Given the stories your sister and Will told about him, I'm surprised he lived to be grown."

Marty laughed at this. "Andy was always daring. He said taking risks made him feel alive. He never wanted to be one to die with his boots off."

"And you can laugh about that in a brother but not in a husband?" he asked good-naturedly. "Honestly, Marty, you gotta let me be a man. One day, who knows, we might have sons, and you'll have to let them be men, too."

Marty swallowed hard. They had just reached the ranch, and he'd given her the perfect opportunity to tell Jake the truth about the baby.

"Hmm, would you mind helping me down?" Marty asked. "I'd like to walk the rest of the way."

Jake quickly complied and all but lifted Marty off the horse. He let her slowly sink to the ground and gave her a quick peck on the nose. "You are a beauty, Mrs. Wythe." He went to tie the horses off in a grassy patch and then returned to Marty and offered her his arm. "I do need to confess, I came out here with your brother-in-law."

"I thought Will might have brought you here." She took hold of his arm and began to walk. "He is usually a very thorough man. However, I'd like to return to something you said earlier."

"What's that?" He looked at her with one brow raised.

"You said that I have to let you be a man, and that I would have to let our sons be men."

"Well, you sure don't wanna turn boys into sissies. I wouldn't stand for that. It seems to me that there are already a lot of sissified men—"

"Jake, I'm gonna have a baby," she interrupted.

He immediately shut up and turned to face her. His expression changed almost immediately from shock to sheer joy. He gave a yell loud enough to be heard in Dallas and lifted Marty in his arms.

"Why didn't you say so sooner! Wahoooo! This is the best news ever!" He whirled around with Marty in his arms then set her back on the ground. "When?"

"August. Or maybe as early as July. I can't be sure."

"But that's only about five or six more months. Why didn't you tell me sooner?"

"I only found out for sure after you'd gone. Then there were other things . . . fears that kept me from saying anything—especially in a letter."

He looked at her oddly. "What kinds of things?"

"I couldn't help remembering the times Thomas and I thought we were going to have a little one. I miscarried and lost those babies. I feared the same might come true this time around. Of course, I also thought a lot of it had to do with living in Texas. The doctor here told me that there were a lot more miscarriages due to the heavier gravity because we're closer to the equator."

"That sounds like hogwash," Jake replied.

"That's what my sister and the doctor in Denver said, too. But I couldn't help worry, because the doctor here said otherwise." She shook her head and raised her hands in surrender. "Call me silly or dim-witted. I'm still not sure what to believe, although this is the longest I've managed to carry a child."

"Oh, darlin', you aren't silly or dim-witted. Stubborn, yes. Given to exaggeration? Hmm, on occasion." He laughed. "You don't need to be afraid that Texas is gonna cause you to lose the baby, Marty. Lots of women have babies in Texas." He grinned and the delight was reflected in his eyes. "I can't believe I'm a papa."

"We still have six months to get through," Marty declared.

Jake shook his head. "Nope, I'm already Papa to this little one." He put his hand to Marty's waist. "I can hardly wait. Marty, you've made me the happiest man in the world."

"But you'd be even happier if I said yes to moving back here to the ranch, wouldn't you?"

He withdrew his touch. "Marty, I can't lie and say that ranching isn't what I wanna do. But, I will say this. If livin' here where you made a home with your first husband makes you uncomfortable, we'll live elsewhere."

Marty sighed. There was no possibility of changing her destiny. Texas and ranching were always going to be a part of her life. She gave Jake a smile. "This place is nice," she told him. "The trees provide cool shade in the summertime. There's a river that flows across the property, and while it gets low in times of drought, it doesn't usually run dry." She choked a bit on the words. "It's a good house, too. Will and most of the men in the community came and helped Thomas build it. It's sturdy. Oh, and there's a wonderful root cellar that's good for storms as well as food storage."

Jake took her in his arms. "You're a good woman, Marty. I promise to do everything I can to make you happy. I love you."

She fought back tears. "I love you, Jake. I was so unhappy with you gone. I'm sorry that I'm so afraid. I don't mean to be. I wanna trust this to God, but sometimes I just remember seein' Thomas lying there . . . the blood . . . the—"

"Shh, let it go. You don't need to be dwellin' on such things, especially now that you have our little one to think on." He smoothed back a lock of hair. "I want you to be happy, Marty. We don't have to live here."

She nodded and reached up to touch his face. "Hannah would like us to stay on with them a while. I told her about losing the other babies, and she wants to take care of me."

"I'd like that, too. It'll be a sight easier to go off and work away from the ranch if I know you're being looked after. Between her and Alice, you'll be in good hands. I'm happy for us to stay put. I just hope one day you'll be ready for us to run our own ranch."

Marty let out a ragged breath. "One day, I will be. I promise."

Chapter 14

"You seem mighty deep in thought," Robert said, coming to sit at the small table by the fireplace.

Alice had positioned herself there to gain a little warmth from the hearth. The evening had turned cool, and the chill seemed to cut clear to the bone. She tugged at the edges of her shawl, feeling rather nervous in the presence of Robert Barnett. "I suppose I have a great deal on my mind," she answered.

"Would you like to play a game of checkers?" He motioned to the board on the table.

"Why not?" She shrugged. "It won't interfere with anything I have planned."

He laughed. "You know, for someone who's just eighteen, you have an old spirit."

Alice looked at him quizzically for a moment. "What makes you say that?"

Please don't make this about my injury and how brave I am to live my life.

Robert shook his head and arranged the checkers on the board. "I don't know. It's just something about you. You've been through a lot, so I suppose that has something to do with it. It just seems that other ladies your age are flighty and immature. They seem a whole lot more

363

interested in the next party or a new dress." He gave a chuckle and added, "And most are completely obsessed with tryin' to find a husband."

Alice couldn't hide her frown, nor did she try to. "Well, it goes without saying, but I'm certainly not doing that."

He cocked his head to one side. "And why not? You're a lovely woman." He smiled. "And just because you're a deep thinker doesn't mean you can't marry."

Alice didn't want to talk about such things. Still careful to keep her face turned to the right so that her scar was less visible, she asked, "What makes you so sure my thoughts are all that deep?"

He chose a red checker and made his first move. "Well, you sure don't talk much, and for a female I find that interesting in itself. Havin' grown up with sisters and a ma who all speak their mind, finding someone like you is a real treat." He nodded toward the game. "So why don't you take a turn at the board and tell me what deep thoughts you were thinkin'."

Alice felt her face grow warm under his scrutiny. She moved her black checker. "I was thinking about my mother, if you must know."

He moved again. "I heard Aunt Marty say you thought she was dead but recently found out otherwise."

"Yes." Alice selected another checker without thought. "That's it exactly. Marty's been after me to send my mother a letter and let her know where I am."

"But you don't want to?" He continued to stare at the board, seeming to ponder his choices.

"I don't know. It might just tip over a big can of worms if I do."

He looked up and smiled. He had the most beautiful eyes, and his face was like a fine sculpture, chiseled in warm flesh tones instead of cold marble. He was the kind of man she'd always dreamed of—before the accident. Alice felt her heart skip a beat.

I've never felt this way about anyone before. Why am I so consumed by this man all of the sudden? Am I falling in love?

The idea startled her. She would never have admitted her thoughts to anyone, not even Marty.

"Might not," Robert said and slid a checker into place.

"Might not what?" Alice asked, forcing the confusion from her mind.

"Knock over a can of worms. It might be a real good thing."

Alice looked at the board for a moment and then glanced to where Hannah was showing Marty some kind of crocheting stitch at the other end of the room. William Barnett had settled in a large chair near them and was reading a book. Even so, it was as if Alice and Robert were the only people in the room. She felt self-conscious and again tugged at her shawl.

"I suppose it just comes down to me being afraid," she admitted. Alice stopped and shook her head. "I really don't know why I'm telling you all of this. I hardly know you."

"Does that matter?" He looked at her as if her words had somehow hurt him. "I wasn't tryin' to pry."

"I realize that," Alice said, softening her tone. "I hope I didn't offend you."

"Not at all. I guess I just find your story to be . . . well . . . interesting. But more than that. It's like a puzzle to be solved. I guess I like to see things put in order."

"So you think I should write to her?"

"Does it matter what I think?"

Alice stopped trying to figure out her next move and folded her arms. "I wouldn't ask if I didn't want your answer."

He chuckled and leaned back in the chair. "Then yes, I think you should write to her. I think you should ask her all those troubling questions and demand answers."

A smile touched the corners of Alice's lips. "Demand answers? Is that what you would do?"

"I'm a man who likes to get right down to the point."

"I don't know if the address I have for her is any good. And she might very well be dead."

"And you'll never know either way unless you write to her."

Alice nodded, knowing he was right. "I have been thinking that same thing. I asked your mother if I could borrow some writing paper. I just haven't been able to make up my mind."

"I can't tell you why, but I don't think you'll be sorry . . . Alice." He paused. "It is all right if I call you Alice, isn't it? We tend to be pretty informal out here."

"Of course." Losing herself for a moment in his blue eyes, she paused. Here was a man with whom she could talk, share her heart, and not feel uncomfortable. She straightened up, no longer trying to hide her face. He didn't look away. "I'd like for you to call me Alice."

"Good. And you call me Robert. We'll be the best of friends, and tomorrow I will take you out riding after I finish my work. *If* I finish. Pa has a way of finding new tasks for me all the time."

She stiffened. "I don't know how to ride."

He gave a low chuckle. "Good thing I do, then. Your lessons will start tomorrow." He moved his checker over one of hers and grinned. "Better get your mind back on the game. I've just taken one of your pieces."

More than that, she thought, *you may well have taken a piece of my heart.*

★

Alice looked over the words she'd just written, spending some time on the chilly February morning in her room. She'd thought long about what she would say to her mother, and even then the letter had been hard to write.

What will you think when you get this? How can we possibly put aside all the years lost and all the pain?

She held up the sheet of writing paper and began to read aloud.

> *"Dear Mama,*
>
> *"I can't believe you are still alive. When Mrs. Ingram told me the truth, I didn't know quite what to think. About a year after you'd gone away, Father told me you and Simon had died. It's been over a year since you wrote to Mrs. Ingram, but I decided to try this address and let you know that I am alive and well.*
>
> *"I moved recently to Texas with a dear woman named Martha Wythe—Marty. We are staying with her brother-in-law and sister, Mr. and Mrs. William Barnett. They own a large ranch not far from Dallas, near a town called Cedar Springs. I find it peaceful. Having never been outside of Denver, I also find the warmer climate quite agreeable."*

Alice paused and drew a deep breath before continuing.

"I don't know how to say the things that are on my heart. I was so hurt when you left, and I've never known what to do with that pain. How does a mother leave her child without any warning, without any word? How you must have hated me. The very thought of that causes me to want to forget about sending this letter, but Marty tells me I must."

That sounds so harsh. Perhaps I should rewrite it.

She looked at several wadded-up pieces of paper and knew she shouldn't waste yet another piece of Hannah's good writing paper. Maybe letting her mother see the pain was a good thing.

"I won't lie and pretend the past doesn't matter. I won't try to sugar this up so that it goes down easier. Nobody did that for me."

Alice's anger stirred and she fought to push it back down.

"If you desire to correspond with me, you may feel free to do so at the address you'll find at the bottom of this letter. I would particularly like to know why you left and whether my brother Simon is still alive.

"Yours truly,
"Alice"

Taking up the pen, she wrote the mailing instructions and set the letter aside to let the ink dry. A part of her felt good for what she'd accomplished, while another part felt sick. Marty had been after her to write ever since they'd learned the truth in Denver, and Alice knew she would never stop hounding her about it.

She knew Marty was right. It needed to be done. Whether her mother had a proper explanation or even cared, Alice knew she had to have at least this small contact. She could only pray that her mother was still alive and residing at the same place.

Her thoughts quickly passed from the letter to Robert's promise of riding lessons that afternoon. He was a most incredible man, nearly ten years her senior, as Alice understood from Marty. He was the only son and heir to the Barnett ranching empire, but even if he'd been poor, Alice would have found herself drawn to him.

There was something about the casual way he interacted with her. He didn't seem to care about her appearance. He had never commented on the scar once. No doubt Marty had filled everyone in on her situation prior to their arrival. And if she hadn't, now that they were in residence the story would surely have been told. Even so, Robert made no mention of it.

Perhaps it truly doesn't bother him. Maybe he doesn't care that I'm less than perfect.

A knock on her door brought Alice to her feet. She crossed and opened to find Marty standing there. "We have guests and I thought you should come meet them."

"Let me get my shawl." She picked up a dark blue shawl and wrapped it around her shoulders before joining Marty in the hall. "Do I look presentable?"

"Very much so. You know, I think that scar is fading even faster now that Hannah has you using that special salve she made."

Alice put her hand to her jaw. "Do you really?"

"I do. My sister is a wonder. She knows about all sorts of things like that. You'll like getting to know her better."

"I'm sure I will," Alice said, letting Marty lead her down the hall.

In the large front room, Alice saw two women sitting and speaking with Hannah. She offered a smile but again kept her face to the right. It was a habit she found hard to break.

"Alice, this is Mrs. Carissa Atherton and her daughter Jessica. You and Jessica are about the same age," Marty declared.

Alice looked first to the older woman. Mrs. Atherton's honey-colored hair was neatly tucked and curled into place beneath a lovely hat of plum velvet and black ribbon. Alice thought her one of the most beautiful women she'd ever met.

"It's a pleasure to meet you, ma'am," Alice said, giving a little nod.

She turned next to the younger woman, who seemed rather indifferent to the introduction. "Miss Atherton, I'm pleased to make your acquaintance."

Jessica looked her over for a moment. "Mother tells me you are Marty's maid."

"Not anymore," Marty replied before Alice could say a word. "Alice and I are just dear friends now."

Alice heard Jessica give a little sniff, as if disapproving. She wondered if the young woman had been raised to look down on those of less fortune. Alice waited a moment longer and then felt a sense of relief when Marty motioned her to sit.

"We were just having a nice visit," Hannah said, "and I wanted you to join us. We've been discussing plans for several events that will take place in the next few weeks, and I want you to be a part of it."

Marty seemed quite eager to share the details. "One of those events will be Jake's and Hannah's birthdays. Hannah's is on the fifth of March and Jake's is the seventh. We want to have a big party."

"*They* want to have a big party," Hannah corrected.

"And of course Robert has a birthday on the second of April," Jessica said, smiling. "I do hope we can have a party for him, as well."

"First things first," Mrs. Atherton interjected. "The men won't have time for much of anything until after roundup. We need to think on how we're going to handle that. I was speaking with my sister, Laura, a couple of days ago, and we thought it might be nice to host the roundup at my place. It's pretty centrally located to all the participants, since we'll have the Harpers and Watsons joining us."

"I think that sounds fine," Hannah replied.

Alice had no idea what they were talking about, but it sounded like quite the occasion. She looked to Marty for clarification, but her friend didn't seem to notice.

"So there will be eight ranches involved all together?" Marty questioned.

Hannah and Carissa Atherton nodded in unison, but it was the latter who spoke. "The Reids will be there, the Harpers, Watsons, Barnetts." She paused a moment to count on her fingers.

Marty used that opportunity to explain to Alice, "The Reids are Carissa's sister and brother-in-law and their sons, of course. They have a horse farm with some of the finest quality animals to be had."

Carissa seemed to regain her thoughts. "Of course our family will be there. Then there's the Palmers, the Kirbys, and the Armstrongs. Yes, eight ranches in total."

"Speaking of the Armstrongs." Marty paused and looked to Alice. "Mrs. Atherton's oldest daughter married the Armstrongs' youngest son, Elliot." She returned her gaze to Carissa. "How is Gloria doing? Are they still in North Dakota?"

"No, they were reassigned last year to Fort Assiniboine," Carissa said. "It's located way to the north in Montana. It just so happens that the black Tenth Cavalry was also moved north from its duties west of here. We just had a letter telling us all about it. Elliot was promoted to captain and has very much enjoyed getting to know some of the buffalo soldiers and hearing their stories. Gloria finds life there to be quite taxing, but she has her friends."

"And what about children?" Marty asked.

Carissa shook her head. "She lost two and I think she'd just as soon not have any more, at least for the time. It's such a hard life there. I honestly don't know how she bears it."

Hannah looked to Marty and smiled. "Are you going to share your news?"

Alice saw Marty blush as she nodded. "I'm going to have a baby. It's due in August or perhaps July."

"Oh, that's wonderful news," Carissa said. "I was just telling Jess that we needed some little ones around here. All the children are grown."

"I know just what you mean," Hannah agreed. "I keep trying to convince my daughter Sarah that she and her family should move here. Goodness, I try to talk my brother, Andy, into it, as well. I suppose we shall just have to wait to spoil Marty's baby."

"What of your younger daughter?" Carissa asked.

Hannah shrugged. "Ellie will probably never marry, or if she does, her husband will have to be a very strong man. Ellie is far too caught up in women's rights. She wants education and the ability to vote for every woman. I admire her passion, but I'd just as soon have a houseful of grandchildren." A soft laugh escaped her lips. "I think babies make a house more cheerful."

The topic of babies quickly overtook the conversation, and Alice sat patiently listening as the women planned and plotted regarding Marty's summer delivery. She lost track of the conversation and reflected once again on her letter. If Simon were alive he'd be ten.

I wonder what kind of boy you are. Are you sweet and scholarly? Are you strong and well-mannered? Visions of her brother at the age of five flickered through her mind for just a moment and then were gone. She could barely remember how he looked.

The memory of Robert's face came to mind. Alice loved his strong jaw and full lips. She wanted very much to reach out and touch his cheek and feel the stubble of his beard, the warmth of his skin. Was it possible to fall in love with a man based purely on his appearance? And if one did, was there any sense in it?

I don't even know him. He could be a lazy good-for-nothing. The thought made her smile. Of course he was neither of those things. His family had raised him to be God-fearing and responsible. He was kind and gentle in his nature and very generous with his time.

Otherwise he would never have offered to take me riding.

The Athertons left before lunch, despite Hannah's encouraging them to stay. It seemed Jessica had a dress fitting or some other appointment in town, and they needed to push on. Alice put aside her reflections on the handsome Robert Barnett. She had just begun to help with the cleanup when Marty posed a question Alice hadn't expected. A question that left her feeling sick.

"So, Hannah, when do Robert and Jessica plan to marry?"

Chapter 15

"Are you comfortable?" Robert asked, looking up into Alice's pale, anxious face.

"It seems awfully high up here," she replied from the horse's back.

He chuckled. "I suppose it would, since you aren't used to ridin'." He handed her the reins. "Now take these and hold them firm in your left hand but not tight. Your hand will cramp up on you if you clench the reins."

She took the straps in her gloved hands, as if she were handling a rattlesnake. Robert knew she was terrified and longed to find a way to reassure her. He knew the only way for her to get comfortable, however, was to actually ride the animal, so he quickly mounted his own horse.

"Betsey, there, is a good old gal. She won't go runnin' off with you, so try to relax." He motioned toward the open range. "Let's go up this way and let you get a feel for the saddle."

Alice said nothing. The set of her jaw and her stiff posture told Robert she was focusing completely on her position. No doubt she was terrified of falling off and equally certain that Betsey could feel her tension. This might require a little more work than he'd originally thought. Reaching out, he took hold of the bridle. "Come on, Betsey. Let's show her how it's done."

The horses moved forward and Alice reached for the horn with her right hand. Robert smiled but said nothing. She still held on to the reins, so he didn't want to discourage her.

"I know a lot of gals ride sidesaddle, but Ma suggested I train you on the regular saddle instead. Riding astride isn't always looked favorably upon for women, but I think it offers you more security, and out here with the snakes and holes and such, I think you need that extra help. This way if something spooks your horse and she rears, you have the added advantage of holding on with your . . . uh . . . legs."

"I'm sure you know better than I would," Alice replied in a tight, clipped tone.

Robert let go of Betsey's bridle and allowed Rojoe to fall back even with the mare. "The important thing is to keep yourself balanced and centered. The horse will do the work if you just keep a few things like that in mind. A horse needs to know who's in charge, for one."

"He is," Alice said. "Or, I should say, she is."

Robert chuckled. "No. You are. You need to establish that with the animal as soon as you make contact. Betsey, here, has been a good horse to train children on, so I have the utmost confidence she'll be easy for you."

Alice gave a hint of a smile. "I don't think any part of this will be easy."

"Remember what I told you about holdin' your legs tight. If you tighten up too much you're gonna wear both of you out." He thought Alice relaxed the tiniest bit. "Now I'm gonna show you how to stop her. I want you to gently pull back on the reins."

Alice did so, but as her right hand was still firmly on the horn, she pulled with her left, and Betsey veered toward the left and headed straight into Rojoe.

Robert corrected his mount. "No, you need to pull them straight back toward your waist. You pulled left, so Betsey thought you wanted to turn. Straighten up and loosen the reins again." He watched and waited. "Now, pull straight back and say, 'Whoa.'"

"Whoa!" Alice called out a little too enthusiastically.

Robert smiled. She was such a petite thing, and her nervousness on the back of the fourteen-hand-high mare made him want to just pull her over onto his lap and comfort her like he might a child. Of course, he wasn't thinking about Alice as a child. She was a beautiful young woman, and he had meant what he'd said about her maturity and old spirit. Compared to Jessica Atherton, Alice was far more astute and sensitive. She showed genuine concern for the people around her, and despite her fears and ordeals in life, she had the gumption to get up and try again.

"There now," Robert said, looking at Alice's tight hold, "ease up on the reins a little but keep control."

He heard Alice let out a heavy breath. She looked at him as if to question what was next. He smiled. "All right, now you get us started again."

"Me? I don't know what to do."

"Remember what I told you. Give her a little nudge with your heels. Keep your feet in the stirrups and mostly squeeze with your legs. I'm sorry if this sounds too forward talkin' about legs and such," he said, realizing he was speaking in a most familiar manner with a woman he hardly knew. "If you're too uncomfortable I could just have Aunt Marty or my mother teach you."

"No, I'm not offended."

"But you are very tense. Relax, and don't forget to draw a good deep breath. Sometimes folks forget to breathe while riding and faint off the back of the horse."

Alice grimaced. "I certainly wouldn't want to fall off Betsey. It's a long ways down."

Robert chuckled. "Now, just squeeze with your legs and give a little click with your tongue. She's leg trained so she'll respond to the pressure, but the clicking just lets her know you mean business."

Alice did as he instructed and the mare began to move. "Oh my," Alice said, again going rigid in the saddle.

"Relax. You're gonna be sore when we get done if you don't learn to ease into it."

He had to give her credit. She was trying hard not to be afraid. Alice obeyed his every order and after half an hour, Robert decided she'd had enough.

"Let's walk 'em back. It's not that far. Stop your horse."

Alice pulled back on the reins. "Whoa!" Betsey halted instantly.

"Good. You learn quick." He jumped off Rojoe's back in an effortless manner. Having been riding since before he could walk, Robert felt as if the horse was a mere extension of his own limbs.

Still holding on to the reins of his horse, he went to Alice. Rojoe seemed more interested in the new spring grass than his master, but he quickly complied and followed.

"Now you are going to dismount," Robert told Alice. "It's not all that difficult. Coming down is always easier than getting up there."

"That's what I'm afraid of," she said, looking down.

"Don't be afraid, Alice. I have you."

She frowned and looked back at the neck of her mount. "What do I need to do?"

"Keep the reins in your left hand and slip your boots out of the stirrups," he instructed. She did as he said, looking only a little bit frightened. "Now lean forward, and with your right hand you can grip the saddle or the horn. While you do this, I want you to swing your right leg back over the horse. You're gonna lean against her and then push off to slide down Betsey's side."

He heard Alice's heavy sigh and stood ready to help in case she lost her balance. To the surprise of both of them, however, she managed a perfect dismount the first time.

Robert grinned and patted her on the back. "See? You're a natural."

She shivered. "I wouldn't go so far as to say that."

"Let's walk. It'll warm you up and get your nerves untangled."

He showed her how to lead Betsey, and the two began to move back down the trail toward home. Robert couldn't help but admire the young woman at his side. He wanted more than anything to know everything about her. He wanted her to talk about her mother and brother, to tell him about the night she was knifed. Instead, he said the first thing that came to mind.

"I hear you're gonna help with the roundup cookin'."

Alice didn't look at him but nodded. "I want to be useful. I don't know anything about roundups, but I'm willing to learn."

"This will probably be our last open-range roundup," Robert said, feeling a certain sorrow. "Everyone is fencing these days. Farmers say the open range causes their crops to be ruined and thieves will drive off portions of the herd if you don't keep them under watch. Times are especially hard for folks, so stealing seems like an acceptable way to feed the family."

"Do you lose a lot of your stock?"

"No. We're in a pretty good position. We have good neighbors and we work together. We've always helped one another at roundup, but I know the time is coming when we'll be handlin' these things separately." He shrugged. "'Course that doesn't mean we won't still help one another. I know Pa will always be willing to lend a hand to anyone who needs it, and so will I."

"So you plan to remain in the area?"

Robert grinned. "I do. I have land Pa deeded me when I turned twenty-one. Five hundred acres. I have my own cattle, too. I guess now all I need is a wife and children to make my life complete."

"I understand you are engaged to Jessica Atherton."

It was Robert's turn to be uncomfortable. He hadn't wanted to talk about Jessica. "Not exactly. Folks around here think we ought to be engaged. They've expected us to marry for the last ten years, but there's never been a formal agreement."

"Ten years? But I thought Miss Atherton was my age."

"She is. She's been followin' me around like a puppy since she was little. I think it had to do with her brothers never havin' time for her. They were only a few years older than Jessica, while I was almost ten years her senior. And . . . well . . . I was nice to her."

"Well, you are fortunate to have someone who cares about you," Alice murmured.

For several minutes she said nothing, and Robert was hard-pressed as to how he should respond. Before he could speak, however, Alice continued. "I wrote to my mother. Marty was going to have the letter posted for me today, along with her letter back to the orphanage in Denver."

"I'm glad you decided to write to her," Robert said, feeling much easier about this subject. "I don't think you'll be sorry."

"I hope not. I find myself completely at odds with the decision. I pray in time God will make all things clear."

"He's good to do that. My ma always told me that when I found things were too hard to figure out, I could probably bet that I hadn't prayed on it first."

Alice nodded but said nothing more. They were nearly back to the pens, so Robert decided not to press her further. He reached out and took Betsey's reins. "I'll put her away for you, but next time you're gonna learn to saddle and unsaddle her yourself." He threw her a wink. "I know you'll be just as good at that as you were riding."

★

The weeks passed, pushing the calendar into the first of March, and with it came roundup. Alice learned there was a great deal that happened at such times. She had figured it would primarily be the job of the men, since they would be the ones roping and riding. It seemed, however, that the ranch wives and daughters had just as much to do in order for the event to be successful. Alice found herself cooking and baking days in advance of the actual roundup. There wouldn't be time for lengthy processes while seeing to the cattle, so some foods were prepared and stored ahead of time to make the workload more manageable. When the time arrived to move everything to the Atherton ranch, Alice found herself busy with toting and fetching alongside the other women. Later, she was assigned to cooking beans and helping with the washing up afterwards.

The work was arduous. The men had rounded up cattle from every point of their open ranges. They had a process for what they called mothering-up the calves. This allowed the men to separate out the pairs from the non-producing cows. The cows that were barren would be sold to the feedlot. After the animals were separated, the cowboys would start the process of dividing them up again—this time by brands.

They'd hired extra men to help with the additional tasks of branding, castrating, and treating injuries and diseases, as well as separating out those animals that would be taken to market. Alice had never seen anything like it in all her days. Having grown up in a city, her knowledge of such affairs was completely void. Meat was something to be purchased at the butcher's, and she'd never given thought to exactly what had happened to get it there.

Cooking and cleaning, however, were things Alice was well acquainted with. She found herself amazed at the fast pace of the day. She rose early in the morning, before it was light, and helped Hannah and some of the other women prepare breakfast for the cattlemen and wranglers. The menu was simple but filling. Biscuits and ham steaks, with gallons and gallons of hot, strong coffee to wash them down. The noon meal was usually ham and beans, corn bread, and some kind of sweet treat—cookies, cake, or cobbler. The evening meal was a little more relaxed and spread out. It was during the evening that the men were able to settle in and discuss the day.

Alice liked the suppertime gatherings. There were usually a few of the men who came together and played music. Some of the fellas sang, and on occasion one or two of the wives would join in, as well. Evening meals were the only time Hannah allowed Marty to join them. One of the older hands who'd been left to oversee the Barnett ranch would drive Marty over in the buggy.

Jake always seemed happy to see her, and the two would usually slip off to a spot where they'd share supper alone. Alice was delighted that they were growing closer together. Their start had been rough—there was no doubt about it. Being a mail-order couple was never an easy situation, but they had made good on their commitment, and Alice could only esteem them for it. The key to it all had been their willingness to look to God for help.

"I almost forgot," Marty said, approaching Alice that evening. "This came for you."

Alice looked at the letter Marty held. There was only one person who would be writing to her here in Texas. With shaking hands, Alice took the envelope. It was from her mother.

"She's alive."

Marty nodded. "Read it and see what she has to say."

"Read it here?" Alice asked.

With a shrug, Marty looked around the camp. "Why wait? Nobody here will mind. There is still a little light, and if it's not enough my sister hung lanterns by the cook wagon."

Alice moved toward the wagon. "What if it's . . . well . . . what if the news is bad?"

Marty was right beside her. "Then you'll have friends to stand beside you. Now open it and read it or I will." Marty's determined look told Alice that she wasn't joking.

Alice opened the letter and silently read the few words penned by her mother.

Dearest Alice,

I cannot tell you how happy I was to hear from you and know that you are alive and well. Simon and I are packing to come immediately and be with you. We should arrive no later than the tenth of the month.

With greatest affection,
Mother

"She's . . . she's coming here." Alice looked to Marty. "She's coming with my brother."

"That's wonderful news! I know Hannah will be delighted to have them."

Alice shook her head. "I . . . can't . . . I don't know why she's doing this." She dropped the letter and hurried away from Marty and the gathering of ranch workers. She had to be alone.

Moving just far enough away to be out of the main circle of light and noise, Alice dropped to her knees in the twilight shadows. The news had left her all but faint. She found it hard to breathe, and her vision seemed to swim.

"Are you all right?"

She looked up and found that Robert Barnett had followed her. She wanted to tell him to go away, but the words wouldn't form in her mouth. Instead, she shook her head slowly.

He knelt down beside her. "What's wrong, Alice?"

For several very long minutes she tried to think of what to say. She should be happy for the news, but instead she felt a sense of fear that she'd not known since dealing with Mr. Smith in Denver. Why should she be so unnerved?

"Alice, what is it? Talk to me."

"Marty brought me a letter. My mother . . . she's . . . alive."

"Oh, that's wonderful news." He looked at her. "Isn't it?"

The shadows fell across his face, and in the growing darkness, Alice could barely make out his features. She knew instinctively, however, that his expression would be one of great compassion.

"I . . . think so. Yes." She nodded. "But . . . well . . . she's coming here."

"Does that worry you?"

Tears formed in Alice's eyes and blurred her vision even more. "I . . . I . . . don't know." She broke down and sobbed with her face in her hands. It was such a relief to know that her mother was alive—her brother, too.

Why am I acting like this? Why this sudden sense of fear?

She didn't look up when Robert moved closer and drew her into his arms. She continued to cry quietly against his shoulder. She could feel his gentle touch and the way he stroked her head like a parent might do for a small child.

"It's the shock of the thing," he whispered. "Shock and relief."

"Well, what in the world is all this about?" The curt, suspicious words of Jessica Atherton caused Alice to snap to attention and all but jump to her feet. She struggled to put as much distance between her and Robert as she could, wiping furiously at her eyes. Tripping over her gown, she struggled to stand.

Robert seemed unfazed. He got to his feet and threw Alice a sad smile before giving Jessica a reply. "Alice had a letter about her mother and brother. You knew she thought they were dead, didn't you? Well, they're both alive and coming here to be with her."

Jessica folded her arms, not looking at all convinced. "A letter? And just how does a person get a letter in the middle of roundup?"

Alice could hear the suspicion in Jessica's voice. She felt bad that she had somehow caused this turn of events. Robert had assured her the couple's engagement wasn't official, but still she didn't like to come between sweethearts.

"Jess, if you must know, Aunt Marty brought it. If you need further proof, Alice would probably show it to you."

"I'm sorry for breaking down," Alice said before Jessica could reply. "I'm not usually given over to crying and such. If you'll excuse me, I need to get back to work."

She didn't want to hear any further exchange between Robert and Jessica. She felt terrible for what had happened. She hoped Robert would be able to set things right with Jessica and the two could go on being as close as ever.

Drying her eyes again on the hem of her apron, Alice went directly to the tubs of hot water and began washing dishes. Roundup would last only another few days, and then they'd return to the Barnett Ranch, and she'd be able to think more clearly about what was to be done.

Chapter 16

Robert had always liked his father's brand. The Bar NT was one folks in the area recognized. The small line over the letters *NT* had been his grandfather's idea—a casual way of putting the Barnett name on each head. For Robert's cattle they had added a small pigtail onto the *T*. It wasn't much, but it definitely distinguished between his head and those belonging to his father.

"Looks like you've got a good increase, son," his father said as they turned the last of the cattle out to pasture.

"I'm pleased," Robert said. "How about you? You gonna get that Angus bull out there breeding right away?"

"That's the plan. Of course our biggest task is going to be working with the other ranchers to get fencing up."

"If Mr. Terry were still alive, he'd tell you it was all a lot of bother for no good reason," Robert said, remembering their former neighbor. His father had bought the Terry ranch when Ted had passed away. Mrs. Terry had moved east to be with her children, but she had died shortly thereafter. Folks had always said the two couldn't be separated for long.

"He would," Pa said, nodding. "I doubt he'd much like the way things have changed. Fencing, registrations, and restrictions—it'd be enough to make him swear, and I never heard that man ever utter a single bad word."

"So I guess you know about Alice's ma and brother comin'," Robert threw out casually.

"Sure. Your ma told me right after the letter came. I'm glad for the gal. It's only right that she have a chance to be with her family. Hannah told her they could stay in the Montoyas' old house for as long as they needed. The gals are all over there cleanin' today."

The Montoyas had been a part of the ranch since the beginning. As his father's foreman and mother's housekeeper, the Montoyas were considered to be a part of the family. His mother and father had always treated them with respect and kindness and taught Robert to never look down on a workingman—no matter his station. When they made the decision to move back to Mexico to be near family, it had nearly broken Robert's mother's heart.

"That's generous of you. I know Alice appreciates your kindness."

His father eyed him curiously. "You and Alice seem to be gettin' along well."

He wasn't sure if his father approved or disapproved by his tone. "Well, I've been teachin' her to ride and showin' her some of the duties I have here at the ranch. Thought I'd ride her over to my land and show her where I hope to build a house."

"And what does Jessica think about that?"

Robert shrugged. "I don't know that Jess thinks anything about it. Why should she?"

Will Barnett's eyes narrowed. "Robert, you aren't toyin' with those two gals, are you? I raised you better than that."

"I'm not toyin' with anybody. Jess is my friend and so is Alice. I can't help it if everybody has a notion that Jess and I are supposed to marry. I've never proposed."

"Maybe not, but neither have you really denied the possibility. I think you'd better be decidin' what it is you want before someone gets hurt."

Robert knew his father to be a man of wisdom. "Well, I've been prayin' about it, Pa. I just don't know exactly what I'm supposed to do. Like I've said before, I love Jess like a little sister. I know her as well as I know my own sisters. But there's something about Alice that intrigues me. I want to know everything about her. I want to spend all my free time with her."

Pa smiled and looked out across the field where the longhorn were happily grazing. "That's how I feel about your ma."

"So what do I do?"

His father took a long moment before answering. "I think you have to let Jessica know that you aren't going to marry her. Then you'll be free to actually court Alice and see if this is the woman God has for you."

★

Alice waited nervously with Marty and Jake at the train station. They had decided just the three of them would come to welcome Ravinia Chesterfield and her son, Simon. As Marty had put it, "There's no sense scarin' 'em off with a herd of folks piling in around them."

The comment made Alice smile even now as she watched for her mother and brother to disembark the train. Marty squeezed her arm in support, but Alice found herself feeling strangely displaced. No doubt Marty knew that a part of Alice's thoughts were back in Denver on that horrible morning when she'd learned her mother had taken Simon and gone.

Can I forgive her? Can I put aside my own pain to give true understanding to her reasons for leaving?

"Is that them?" Marty asked. "It must be," she quickly continued. "There aren't any other women and young boys getting off the train."

Alice looked ahead and saw her mother. She recognized her immediately, despite her memories being so foggy over the long years.

Ravinia Chesterfield was a small woman with hair just a little darker than Alice's blond. The boy at her side had thick, fairly long hair the same shade as his sister's, but it was the blue eyes that Alice recognized. It was rather like looking into a mirror.

"Alice!" the boy yelled and disengaged himself from his mother's side. He came running down the wooden platform and threw himself into Alice's arms. "Alice! It's me, Simon. I'm your brother. Do you remember me?" He hugged her close and then pulled back to look her in the eye as if for an answer.

Tears came to Alice's eyes. "I do now."

"Mama told me all about you, and we have your picture. You don't look so different now," he said. "Do I look different?"

Alice nodded. "All grown up." She looked past Simon to her mother.

Ravinia Chesterfield stood in uncertain hesitation. Despite the questions and pain of the past, Alice longed to hold her mother close once again. She moved from Simon and went to her mother's open arms. For several minutes the two women embraced, weeping softly and saying nothing. Finally Alice's mother stepped back and took a closer look at Alice. She ran her gloved finger along the line of Alice's scarred face.

"Oh, my poor sweet child. What did they do to you?"

Alice hadn't thought of what a shock her face might be. She bit her lip and tucked her right cheek to her shoulder, as she often did. Her mother would have no part of that, however. She lifted Alice's face very gently.

"You have nothing to be ashamed of. Hold your head high."

Alice met her mother's gaze and felt a rush of emotions. Pushing them aside, Alice dried her eyes and motioned to Marty and Jake. "These are the Wythes, the people who took me in and gave me work after I got out of the hospital."

"But now we're all just good friends," Marty said, stepping forward. "I'm Martha Wythe, but folks call me Marty. This is my husband, Jake."

The older woman nodded. "Thank you for being so good to my daughter."

"I'm Simon," the boy announced, positioning himself between Marty and his mother.

Marty smiled. "I suspected as much. You look just like your sister."

The boy's eyes widened. "But she's a girl."

Marty chuckled at this, as did Jake. Alice remained sober, studying her little brother's features. Simon did look just like her. The same cheekbones and nose. Definitely the same eyes. Alice bent down. "They don't mean you look like a girl, Simon. They mean we have similarities in our appearance—our eyes and mouth and so forth."

The boy reached up a hand to feel his face. "But I don't got a scar."

Alice knew he meant no harm by the comment, but it hurt nevertheless. She reached out to touch his face. "And I pray you never will."

"Does it hurt?" he asked her.

"Not anymore," Alice replied. "It was very painful at first—something I'll never forget."

"Did the police kill the bad guys who did it—the ones who killed our pa?"

Alice shook her head. "No."

"Why not?"

Looking around her at the questioning faces, Alice straightened. "I don't know, Simon. I guess because they never found out exactly who they were."

"That's enough talk about it, Simon," their mother interjected. "I'm sure your sister would rather not speak on something so sad just now. Why don't you go see if you can find our bags?"

"I'll go with you," Jake said, and he and the boy headed off toward the baggage car.

"Are you and Simon hungry?" Marty asked, taking charge.

"No, we ate the food we'd brought along," Mother replied. "Of course Simon thinks he's always hungry."

"I spent time working at an orphanage in Denver, and I know exactly how little boys can think themselves starving to death." The two exchanged a smile at this.

Marty motioned the women toward the depot. "Well then, we have a carriage waiting and a bit of a drive to get to the ranch. At least you picked a pretty day, although my brother-in-law has some concerns about the weather turning bad. Feels it in his bones." She smiled and spoke as if she and Alice's mother were old friends.

Alice felt slightly jealous at their ease. Already she was thinking of the things she would discuss with her mother—things that had to be said and questions she desperately needed answered.

Marty crossed the depot and led them out the other side to the Barnett carriage. "Why don't we go ahead and settle in while the fellas collect your things."

Alice followed in silence. She wasn't exactly sure what to say or feel. It all seemed very strange. That morning she'd had a million questions to ask, but at the moment not one came to mind. She waited as her mother settled into the backseat while Marty took her place in front. Her mother smiled and scooted to the far side of the carriage.

"There's plenty of room," Mother said, patting the leather upholstered seat. "We'll just squeeze Simon in between us."

Reluctantly, Alice climbed into the back with her mother. She wasn't sure why, but she suddenly felt very awkward and out of place. There was no good reason for it, but the discomfort continued.

"So you live in Chicago?" Marty asked Ravinia.

Alice's mother nodded. "We have two small rooms at a boardinghouse. It's just across the street from where Simon attends school, so I don't have to worry about his having a long walk."

"And how does he like school?" Marty asked. "Is he a good student?"

Alice saw her mother's hesitation. "Well, I can't say that he really enjoys it. He hasn't made good friends in our time there. Most of the neighborhood boys tend to bully him because he's small."

The thought of her little brother being hurt caused Alice anger. Why was it the big and mean folks of the world thought they had a right to cause the smaller, gentler people trouble? Was there no justice in this life at all?

"As for studies, I don't think Simon has a head for it." Mother looked to Alice and smiled. "Don't get me wrong. He's no dummy, that brother of yours. Rather, he's a hard and cautious worker. He'll do whatever I need him to, but book learning hasn't ever appealed."

She turned her attention back to Marty. "Not like it did with Alice."

Marty had turned sidewise in the seat in order to talk to the women behind her. "I found school to be a bore, myself, but my sister insisted it was necessary. I know now that she was right."

Alice's mother gave her a sidelong glance. "I'm sure you continued your studies, didn't you?"

Alice shook her head. "I finished eighth grade and . . . and . . ." She drew a deep breath. "I finished eighth grade. It was enough." There was no sense in telling her mother that in her absence, Alice had felt it necessary to quit school and take care of the house and her father.

Mother seemed to understand her discomfort and changed the subject. "I had always thought Denver a large and dirty town, but Chicago exceeds her greatly. There is so much more activity there, and they are in a constant state of building something new—even with the country in such monetary hardship. The railroads coming through the city and the Great Lakes shipping traffic give Chicago a great many people and problems to handle."

"I've never been to Chicago," Marty said, glancing out the window.

"Then you were only one of a few who didn't make it to the World's Fair last year." Mother clasped her gloved hands together. "It's believed that nearly 27 million people came during the six months the fair was in operation."

"We read all about the fair while in Denver," Alice murmured.

Marty nodded. "Yes, we enjoyed the coverage given it by the newspapers. It sounded quite unusual."

"Oh, it was. They built an entire city—the White City, they called it. A separate area for amusement provided rides and games and sideshows. Goodness, it was quite amazing."

Marty seemed to consider this for a moment. "I take it you and Simon attended the fair?"

"I actually had a job helping to serve food. Simon was allowed to help me with cleanup when he wasn't in school. It earned us a little extra money and allowed me to take Simon on the Ferris wheel. He didn't stop talking about it for months afterward."

Alice smiled at the thought of her little brother's pleasure. She was glad he'd had the opportunity to do something so fun. He would never have known such a thing had he remained in Denver.

Marty motioned back toward the building. "Here they come."

Jake carried a small trunk while Simon managed a large carpetbag. Alice smiled as the boy struggled to hoist the bag up to the carriage. She quickly leaned forward to help.

"That looks heavy," she said, giving him a smile of approval. "Good thing you're so strong."

Simon nodded and climbed up behind the bag as Alice pulled it inside. "I can carry a lot when I'm not wearing this coat." He pulled at the traveling jacket in discomfort. "Mama said I had to wear it on the train, 'cause that's what a gentleman does."

"Well, you'll be happy to know that gentlemen out on the ranch dress a little different," Marty told him. She gave him a wink and Simon smiled.

"Can I ride a horse?"

"Of course you can," Marty declared. "The question is, do you know how?"

Simon frowned and plopped down between his mother and sister. "No. I never got to ride."

Marty reached over the seat and chucked him on the chin. "Don't pout. We have people aplenty to teach you. You'll be a natural in the saddle before you know it. Your sister is even learning to ride."

The boy grinned, and it warmed Alice's heart to see how naturally he related to Marty. She could only hope that somehow, some way, she might find the same openness with him. Of course, he had been the one to initiate their embrace, and he mentioned they had her picture and Mother had told him about her. Had Mama kept Alice a part of their family all these years? It gave Alice a great deal to ponder.

It wasn't long before Jake had the trunk secured and had reclaimed the driver's seat. "Are we set for home?" he asked, calling over his shoulder. Everyone nodded their approval.

"Good. Then we're off," he said and snapped the reins.

Alice sank back into the leather upholstery and said very little. Marty and her mother chatted as if they'd known each other for a long time, while Simon was intent on watching the sights and people around them.

I don't really know either of you. You are flesh of my flesh but complete strangers. How could that have happened in such a short time?

The thought really bothered Alice. Then doubts crept in. She had never really known her mother. At least not in the way she thought she had. The woman Alice knew would never have gone away and left her daughter behind. It was a stone in her shoe to be sure, and like a pilgrim set upon a hundred-mile journey, the rock only served to rub a wound deep and painful.

★

Robert gave the expectant mare a pat on the rump. "You'll be a mama soon." He left the stall and had just grabbed up some oats when Marty located him. "We've got Alice's family settled in the Montoya house," she declared. "Hannah said to tell you supper will be in an hour."

"Sounds good. I just wanted to check the paint. She's due to foal most anytime." The brown-and-white-blotched horse whinnied softly as if to agree with his comment. He poured the oats into a small feeding trough and then returned the bucket to the wall.

Marty put her hand to her belly. "I wish I were." She laughed. "I know I still have months to go, but I would be a whole lot happier to have my baby here safe and sound."

Robert put his arm around Marty's shoulder. "Ma says the baby will be here before you know it. She's lookin' forward to spoilin' him, too."

"Oh, has she decided it's a boy?"

He chuckled. "I don't think so. I recollect her calling him a her a time or two."

They walked together toward the house, but Marty stopped without warning. "I wanted to talk to you—alone."

"Me? Why?" Robert was surprised by the sudden change in his aunt's tone.

"I guess I'm sticking my nose in where it doesn't belong, but I wanted to ask you about your plans to marry Jessica."

"I don't have plans to marry Jessica."

She looked at him with a stern expression. "That's not what I've been told."

"Me either, but it's the truth," he said, trying to make light of the situation. "Folks have been sayin' that for years, but it don't make it so."

"And does Jessica know this?"

He shrugged and stuffed his hands into his pockets. "I've tried to tell her."

"And what does she say?"

"She changes the subject or makes like it's not a problem. But it is."

Marty's expression softened. Her head cocked to one side. "And why is that?"

"Because I have feelings for someone else."

He wasn't sure it was the right time to share that information, but if anyone would understand, it would be Marty. His aunt had always had a way of making him feel at ease, and Robert realized he probably should have talked to her about Alice a while ago.

"Alice?" Marty questioned, as if reading his mind.

Robert nodded and glanced overhead at the thick white clouds. "She's got to me, and I don't know what to do about it."

"You always have been one to take up for the disadvantaged. Are you sure this isn't just another case of your wanting to fix an injured critter?" She smiled and crossed her arms. "'Cause a woman is a whole lot more complex than a cat with a broken foot."

Robert chuckled. "You still remember that?"

"How could I forget? You were only six and so very worried about that animal. I didn't think you'd ever let it walk on its own again. Just kept carryin' it around with you all the time. And, as I recall, the cat wasn't any too pleased about it."

"I suppose it had something to do with being confined in that crate," he replied. "But I know Alice isn't a cat. She's a beautiful woman, and yes, she has been hurt, but I . . . well . . . I love her."

Marty shook her head. "Then heaven help you."

"What would you do if you were me, Aunt Marty? Everyone knows about Jess, and I don't want to hurt her."

"It'll only hurt her more if you don't put an end to it. Being in love with someone else while you're expected to marry another is never a good foot to start out on."

"Sometimes I just want to sweep Alice up and run off with her."

"Then do it. But set things straight with Jessica first, or you'll always regret it."

Chapter 17

With breakfast over and the men off to their chores, the women of the house began their routine. Alice had taken to helping with the ironing and was busy at work in the kitchen when her mother decided to join her.

"You seem happy here," Mother said, taking hold of a nearby chair. She studied the ladder back of the simple piece for a moment. Running her hands along the top rung, she cleared her throat. "I hoped maybe we could talk now."

Alice knew that Hannah and Marty were busy outside and wouldn't be back in for a while. "That would be fine." She put the iron back on the stove. "Would you like to sit?"

"Yes." Mother took a seat without further prompting. "I find that I'm quite exhausted."

Alice noticed that her appearance was that of a woman who'd been days without sleep. Her color was pale and her eyes seemed more sunken today. "Did you not rest well?"

"Well enough." Her mother smiled. "I think the weight of everything is just coming to rest on me."

Alice took a seat across from her mother and folded her arms against her body. Suddenly she felt very vulnerable and wasn't at all certain she could say the things that had been on her mind.

"Alice, I know I hurt you in leaving. But you need to understand why I had to go."

"I'm listening."

Mother looked up and met her gaze. "It wasn't ideally what I wanted. I had hoped that things could be worked out another way." She twisted her hands together. "I don't know where to start, but it's important you understand that I always loved you, and I wanted you with me."

"But not enough to take me with you when you snuck out that night." Alice hadn't meant to reply in such a manner, but now that it was out there she didn't try to take it back.

"You're right to be angry with me. I was angry with myself." She gave a heavy sigh. "I knew you were the light of your father's eye, and he would always treat you well. Unfortunately, that couldn't be said about me or even Simon. You see, your father was a very jealous man. He always seemed to fear someone would come and steal me away from him." She smiled sadly.

"I suppose it was because I was very popular when we courted. I had many suitors, and your father had little patience for his rivals. When you were born nine months after we married, I thought he would finally realize there was nothing to fear, that I was his and we were a family. But, Alice, that wasn't how it was."

Alice frowned. She knew her parents were given to arguments but had never understood why. Now she tried not to form any opinion on the matter before her mother could share her story.

"Your father was involved in some underhanded illegal affairs. I think you know that now, given the things Marty said to me about the envelope you were looking for and the missing gold certificates."

"I know that he was used by someone to deliver forged certificates."

Mother shook her head. "He was the one forging them, Alice. He was in the middle of everything that was going on. He had cohorts, to be sure, but your father was nobody's fool."

"You're saying he willingly did wrong?" Alice leaned forward. "I find that hard to believe."

"I know you do. You always loved him so dearly."

"I loved you, too," Alice threw back. "I thought you loved me."

"I do love you, Alice. I do." Her mother reached out to touch her daughter's hands, but Alice quickly pulled away.

"How can you say that after what you did? You left without warning, and I never heard from you again."

A heavy sadness seemed to wash over the older woman. "I wrote you letters. I wrote a great many. Your father wouldn't let you see them or even acknowledge them, from what I know now. He wrote to me and threatened me—he threatened to see me jailed if I so much as tried to come back and take you away. I felt so bad that I even offered to return to our marriage, knowing that it would be a living hell. But he told me no. He didn't want me back."

"I can't believe that," Alice said, shaking her head. "Papa loved you and Simon. Simon was the son he wanted."

"As I said earlier, your father was a very jealous man."

"What does that have to do with anything?" Alice knew she was letting her temper get control of her. She tried to calm down, but with her mother's next words there was no hope of that.

"Your father didn't believe Simon was his son. He thought I had betrayed him with a business associate."

Alice felt sickened and wasn't sure what to say. Her mother seemed sincere in what she was saying, but this just couldn't be the truth.

"I don't . . . I don't believe you."

Tears formed in her mother's eyes. "That's exactly what your father said to me when I told him that I had never been with anyone but him, that Simon was his son. He knocked me to the ground and walked away, never willing to discuss the matter again."

Alice wanted to scream that it was all lies, but in the recesses of her memories she recalled her father's indifferent treatment of Simon. She had always believed that it was nothing more than favoritism, and since it benefited her, she had given it no other consideration. Especially in light of the way her mother always seemed to compensate and show Simon extra attention.

"Your father wasn't the man you think he was. He was tied up in all sorts of deals and had all manner of evil friends. I feared for our safety, but even more so, I feared your father and what he might do. That's why I had to go. I had to protect Simon from your father's wrath."

"But you didn't see fit to protect me."

"Alice, I knew he would never hurt you. He lived for you. He adored you. There was no question in his mind as to your heritage. But you need to know that I never intended to leave you behind. I had planned to come back for you the next day. I thought I could go to the school and take you from your classroom. I planned for the three of us to board a train for Chicago and stay with a distant cousin there. By putting miles between us and your father, I hoped he would see the error of his ways and make changes. I never intended for it to be the end of our family."

Unable to hear another word against the man she loved, Alice jumped to her feet. The chair spilled over backward and made a loud clatter against the floor.

"I don't believe you. This isn't true. It can't be! You would have me believe my father was some sort of criminal, but he wasn't!"

She left the room without waiting to hear her mother's reply. The things her mother said rang over and over in her ears. And though she longed to refuse them, they burrowed deep into her mind and taunted her.

Mindless of where she walked, Alice crossed the barnyard and made her way down the long drive toward the main road. She fought to control her emotions, but tears began to fall.

I can't believe my father would be so cruel. I can't believe he was so devious and . . . so evil. Surely she's just making this up to make herself look better. After all, Papa can't defend himself.

But even as she considered this, Alice remembered that he had lied to her about her mother and Simon being dead. She glanced heavenward with a single word on her lips.

"Why?"

* * * * *

"Looks like it'll be anytime now," Brandon Reid told Robert as they considered the laboring mare. "Legs are out and well positioned. Front legs are white."

"I hope the foal will be a beauty like her mama."

Brandon eyed the horse. "She is a fine animal. One of the best paint quarter horses I've ever bred. She comes from good stock. I'm sure you'll be pleased with her offspring."

Robert gave the mare another look and then smiled. "You know, I'm gonna go get Alice. She's never seen anything like this, and I know she'd enjoy it."

"You know how persnickety horses can be in giving birth. You get an audience in here and she may hold off for hours."

"I know, but . . . well . . . Alice will just sit back quiet. She's not like some women who'd be all fussy and chatty." Robert headed out of the barn toward the house. He knew Alice had planned to iron that morning and would be set up in the kitchen, so he came in through the back entrance.

"Alice?"

"She's . . . not here," Mrs. Chesterfield replied.

Robert found the older woman at the table. She'd been crying. "What's wrong? Is Alice all right?"

She shook her head. "She's upset with me. She stormed out of here about twenty minutes ago."

"Did she say where she was going?"

The woman again shook her head. "I don't imagine she had any particular place in mind so long as it was away from me."

Robert wanted to say something comforting to the woman, but he was more concerned with Alice's welfare. "I'll find her. If she does come back, let her know I'm looking for her. We have a mare about to foal, and I thought she'd like to see it." He didn't know why he felt the need to give her the details of what was happening. Somehow, he hoped it might soften her discomfort to focus on something else.

He left the house and looked around the yard for some sign of Alice. He noted his mother and Marty working in the garden, but Alice wasn't with them. Rounding the barn, he glanced out across the front grasslands and spied Alice walking up the long lane to the house.

Mrs. Chesterfield had said Alice was upset with her. Robert couldn't help but wonder what had been said in their exchange that would send the normally even-tempered young woman off alone. He decided he'd say nothing about it. In time, maybe she'd tell him.

"Alice!" he called, giving her a wave as he made his way down the drive. "I've been lookin' for you. Belleza is about to foal, and I thought you might like to witness it."

She picked up her pace and made her way toward him. Robert could see that her eyes were red-rimmed, but he said nothing. "It might take a while or it might be quick. With a mare you can never tell." He held out his hand.

Alice looked at him oddly for a moment. "I would like to see the new baby, but I have a lot of work to do."

"Ma and Marty will understand." He didn't wait for her to take his hand, but took hold of her arm. "Come on."

They made their way back to the barn, and Robert tried to figure a way to get Alice to talk to him about what had happened. "That little brother of yours sure has taken to Will. He's followin' him all over the place."

"He seems to enjoy the ranch setting," Alice said after a few seconds.

"And what about your ma?"

She shrugged. "I guess so."

They reached the barn and Robert knew there'd be nothing else said on the matter. "Mr. Reid is here. You met him at the roundup, remember?"

Alice nodded. Brandon approached them. "She's just dropped the foal." He looked worried and Robert couldn't help but tense.

"What's wrong?"

Alice looked at him in confusion, but he didn't take time to explain. Instead, Robert made his way alone to the stall. There in the hay was a most incredible sight. A pure white foal. Belleza was working to lick the baby's face. Everything seemed perfectly fine.

He turned in confusion. "What's wrong, Mr. Reid? Your voice sounded . . . well . . . you look like there's something to worry about."

Alice and Brandon joined him at the stall. "I don't wanna buy trouble," Reid began, "but I've seen this kind of thing before, so I have my concerns."

"What kind of thing?"

"White foal. You can see the skin is pinkish and the eyes are blue."

"I don't understand." Robert looked again at the foal and shook his head. "Looks like they're gettin' on just fine."

"I've seen this a couple of times before. There's no way of tellin' right away," Reid answered, "but usually this doesn't bode well for the foal.

Somethin' happens with the paints deliverin' whites. Not sure why, but we'll know soon enough."

"Know what?" Alice asked before Robert could.

"If we need to put it down."

"Kill it? A newborn?" Robert looked at the man in confusion. He completely respected Brandon Reid's knowledge of horses and knew that he wouldn't say such a thing lightly.

"The next twenty-four hours will tell us what we have to do. Most of the time, though, it seems these paints have problems with white foals not bein' able to digest and pass waste." He watched the baby try to get to its feet. "We'll just have to wait it out."

Alice didn't like Mr. Reid's prognosis of the foal's situation. She knew nothing about horses, but it seemed horrible to imagine that a newborn might be killed. She reached out and touched Robert's sleeve.

"Don't let him harm the foal." Her pleading tone was barely audible.

"I wouldn't do anything to hurt that animal," Mr. Reid replied. "However, if the foal can't process food, it'll be in a lot of pain. The waste will just pack up inside, and then it will die a slow and painful death. I won't have that."

"Neither will I," Robert said, patting Alice's hand. "You wouldn't want that, either."

"Of course not. But . . . I mean . . . isn't there something we can do?"

"Pray," Mr. Reid suggested. "Pray for a miracle."

And that's exactly what they did. First Robert suggested they pray together. Mr. Reid offered up a prayer asking for wisdom and God's will to be done. Robert added that he hoped that will would include the foal being healthy. Alice silently prayed that the baby would live and that God would somehow help her to deal with the information her mother had given her earlier.

She waited in the barn with Robert for the next hour. It was discovered that the baby was a male. A darling little colt that Alice instantly lost her heart to.

Poor baby. I don't even know if you will get to live, and you have no way of knowing, either.

The foal nursed while the couple watched in silence. This was a good sign, Robert had told her, but she knew it wasn't the sign they needed. Robert suggested they go about their business and meet back after lunch. Alice went to her ironing, glad to find her mother had gone to tend to something else. She attacked the baskets of clothes and sheets as if they were enemies to be conquered. By the time Marty and Hannah showed up to start the noon meal, she had things well in hand and was just finishing with a pillowcase.

"Goodness, but I thought that would take you most of the day," Hannah said, noting the freshly ironed pieces.

"I suppose I found it better to focus on this than that poor little colt."

Marty smiled. "Robert told us what Mr. Reid said about it. I hope that he's wrong."

"He could be, couldn't he?" Alice asked hopefully.

Hannah patted her back. "Of course he could. There's always exceptions to every situation. I've seen plenty of pretty white horses in my day."

"Mr. Reid said it was something that happened at times with the paints," Alice relayed.

"He can still be wrong. We have a mighty God who answers prayers, and I'm praying that colt will live."

"Me too," Alice said.

"I think we all are," Marty agreed.

After lunch Alice went to the barn with Robert. The baby seemed to be doing well. He nursed without seeming to notice them, although Belleza was very aware of them. They agreed to come back just before supper and see how things were going.

Alice continued to pray, even as she worked on the evening meal with Hannah. Alice's mother wasn't feeling well and had taken a nap. Marty had gone to rest, as well, and that left the two women alone.

"You seem awfully quiet," Hannah said, interrupting Alice's thoughts. "Is it just the horse or is something else bothering you?"

Alice looked at the older woman and found only compassion in her expression. "I had words with my mother. I'm afraid I wasn't very kind."

"Ah, I see," Hannah replied and picked up a carving knife. "Sometimes that happens. If you care to talk about it, I'm willing to listen."

For some reason, Alice didn't even consider remaining silent. "She told me my father was a bad man. He did bad things—illegal things. That's why she had to leave. I can't believe it. He was always so good to me. Sure, he lost his temper at times, but . . . well . . . she said he was cruel toward her and Simon."

"That had to be hard to hear." Hannah busied herself with slicing up a large roast.

"It was horrible. My father isn't here to defend himself, and I suppose I felt as though I should. Now I find myself so confused. I was only thirteen when Mother left. I loved them both so much, but I thought my father was very nearly perfect. I knew I was his favorite, and I thought there was nothing wrong with that because I figured Simon was Mama's favorite."

"Favoritism never leads to anything good. We can see that in our Bible stories about Jacob and Esau, and of course the ordeals of Joseph and his many brothers."

"I know, but when I was younger, it didn't seem to be a bad thing. My mama said it was a big problem because . . . well . . . my father . . ." She fell silent and tried to think how to express the delicate matter. "He thought my mother had been unfaithful."

Hannah looked up. "He didn't believe the boy to be his son?"

Alice nodded. "Mama said he wouldn't believe her. He was jealous of everyone. I don't know what to think. She said he was involved in illegal activities and he had evil people for friends. That doesn't fit my memories of him."

Smiling, Hannah continued to slice the meat. "I think we often create our own image of people, especially after they've passed on. Remember, if your father favored you, then most likely you benefited from his good nature and kindness. If he didn't extend the same to your mother and brother, it wasn't your fault. You mustn't carry any of the blame. Obviously there were circumstances that made the situation unbearable, or your mother would never have made such a daring choice."

Alice considered that for a moment. It was true that it must have been quite perilous to sneak out in the middle of the night—to leave with a small child and no one to help her. She mulled these things over in her mind as everyone was called to supper and Will offered the blessing.

Hannah's words stayed with Alice throughout the meal, even while her brother detailed his day with Will.

"I got to ride on a horse, and it was really big. Mr. Barnett showed me how to put the saddle away and how to brush the horse. It almost stepped on my foot, and Mr. Barnett said if we stayed very long I was going to need a pair of boots." He paused with a big grin. "When Mama's feeling better, I'm going to ask her if we can stay for a long time."

Alice loved the excitement in his voice. She felt a bond with him that she couldn't explain. He was so like her in appearance that she found it hard to believe her father could have ever doubted Simon's paternity. Perhaps jealousy could make a person blind.

After dinner, Marty and Hannah urged Alice to go ahead with Robert to check on the foal. "Don't worry about a thing," Hannah ordered. "I'm going to pop in on your mother and see that she eats something. You go on and see how that baby is doing. Let us know."

Walking alone with Robert, Alice tried not to think about her mother or father. Instead, she focused on the colt and the man at her side. In the distance she heard a rumble of thunder and noticed dark clouds moving in.

"It's gonna storm," Robert declared. "Hope we get some decent rain with it." He opened the barn door and reached for a lantern that hung on the wall. Nearby a metal box of matches had been nailed to the wall to allow for quick lighting. He struck a match and lit the lantern. Light spilled out across the barn, and Alice made the mistake of looking up to find Robert watching her with a strange look on his face.

"What's wrong?" she asked, putting her hand up to cover her scar.

"Nothing. I was just noticing how beautiful you are."

She shivered and tried to make light of the moment. "Not nearly as pretty as your fiancée."

He shook his head. "She's not my fiancée." The tenderness of his expression hardened, and the magic of the moment passed. "Come on. Let's see how they're doing."

Alice followed Robert to the stall. He hung the lantern on the post and opened the gate. "You stay here."

She nodded and leaned against the stall rail. The little foal seemed quite interested to find Robert in the stall with them. He danced around a bit and backed off behind his mother as Robert approached. Belleza seemed unfazed, however. She knew Robert and it was evident she felt safe with him there. Alice had to admit that she did, too.

"Is he doing all right?" she asked softly.

"I think so. He's frisky and doesn't look to be in any discomfort." Robert worked his way around the mare to better see the colt. The animal did its best to avoid him, and made Robert work to get to him. After maneuvering around the mare, Robert stopped.

Alice couldn't see much of Robert behind the large animal, but just then he started laughing.

"Why are you laughing?" she asked. In such a grave situation, laughter seemed quite foreign.

Robert came around to the front of the mare and gave her face a nuzzle with his own. "It's gonna be all right, Mama," he told the animal. He glanced back over at Alice with a grin. "The little guy is making a mess back there, and I stepped right in it. Best thing I've ever seen."

Alice felt a surge of joy. "You mean he'll be all right? He won't die or need to be killed?"

"No, ma'am," Robert said, coming to where she stood. "We got our miracle."

Relief flooded her and Alice couldn't help but laugh. "That's what you should name him. Miracle." She didn't attempt to turn away when Robert hugged her. The fence between them seemed to make it all very innocent and proper.

"I'll give him the name in Spanish," Robert said. "Milagro."

She fixed her eyes on the white colt. "I think that's beautiful."

Robert smiled and whispered against her ear. "And I think you are."

Chapter 18

Alice sat listening to the preacher share his thoughts on Jesus' teachings on the Beatitudes. She was well familiar with the Scriptures taken from the fifth chapter of Matthew, but her heart wasn't at all on the topic. At least not until the man spoke out on verse nine.

" 'Blessed are the peacemakers: for they shall be called the children of God.' "

She didn't hear much else the man said. She pondered the word *peacemaker* and wondered if that included being the kind of person who put aside old issues and focused on the ones at hand.

Forgiving her mother for leaving her was something that Alice had complete control over. No one could force it from her or keep her from giving it. The past could not be altered, not even in part. If her father was the man her mother declared him to be, Alice could not change that by denying it.

You were good to me, Papa. Why not to them?

Her mother had been sickly that morning, and Hannah insisted she remain behind. No one seemed to question Mrs. Barnett's commands. Even Will just nodded and told everyone he'd have the carriage ready by eight. Hannah remained with Mother, and for this Alice had been grateful. She wasn't yet ready to sit at her mother's side and hear further discussion on her father's failings. Alice had questioned Hannah about her mother's condition—seeking to learn the extent of her ailment. Hannah told her that most likely she was just overly exhausted from the trip to Texas. But Alice thought Hannah had seemed guarded in her response.

Simon fidgeted beside her. It was clear the boy found confinement in his suit coat to be a misery unlike any other. He looked downcast and continued to glance toward the windows. Alice thought to take him out of the service and let him walk a bit, but she didn't want to draw attention to them. She'd never thought to ask if her brother was used to attending church. They weren't an overly religious family when they'd all been together years ago.

After the service concluded, Alice whispered in his ear. "Why don't you go outside with the other children and see if you can make friends."

She didn't have to suggest it twice. Simon darted away like a startled fawn. She smiled and watched him weave his way through the mass of people. Alice stayed by Marty's side, uncertain of what she should do. Her scar made her feel quite self-conscious as she noted several people seeming to study her face.

"When is the birthday party, Mrs. Wythe?" a young woman asked Marty. "I thought it was gonna be right after the roundup."

"We had to postpone it a week, but it'll be next Friday evening," she assured her. "Have you met Miss Chesterfield, Miriam?"

The young woman shook her head. She was a pretty redhead with a simple taste in her fashion. She looked to be Alice's age.

"Miriam, this is my dear friend Alice Chesterfield. Alice, this is Miriam Palmer. She's the daughter of Mr. Palmer, who participated in the roundup with his sons. Miriam remained at home to help her mother."

"She'd just given birth to my little sister," Miriam announced proudly. "I liked to thought we'd never get us another girl after five boys."

Alice smiled. "I'm pleased to meet you."

"What did your folks name the little one?" Marty asked.

"Edith," Miriam replied. She returned her gaze to Marty. "After my grandmother."

"It's a good name." Marty put her hand to her growing waistline. "We haven't yet thought up names for our baby. Hopefully by the time he or she arrives, we will have sorted it out."

Alice couldn't help but smile. Marty was finally starting to act and think like this pregnancy was something she could carry through to completion. It did Alice's heart good to see her friend brighten at discussions of the baby and plans for the future.

Jake joined them just then. "Will said he needed to help the preacher with something, so we'll be a little delayed in returning home. You feeling all right?"

"I'm fine," Marty said. She smiled at her husband as he put his hand on her arm.

Alice excused herself. "I'm going to go look for Simon."

She exited the church and exchanged greetings with various people, keeping her head down to avoid their stares. She walked along the front of the church and spied Simon, now jacket free, playing with a couple of the other boys. He seemed content and so she continued her walk toward the cemetery yard.

Reflecting on the pastor's words, Alice strolled among the headstones and thought of her father. How could he have done the things her mother said he'd done? How could he have put Alice in such a precarious position? If what her mother said was true, then he was as much to blame for the attack as the men who carried it out. If the company he kept was corrupt and evil, how could he expect their actions to be otherwise?

She frowned and touched one of the more ornate marble statues. The angel form seemed to glare at her in disapproval. Alice quickly pulled her hand away and looked heavenward.

Why? Why is this happening, Lord? I don't know what to think or to do. I want to be a peacemaker, but I don't understand what that means. Do I just forget that my mother left me? Do I accept that my father was truly evil?

Alice couldn't help but remember the nights she had cried herself to sleep, wishing and praying that her mother and brother would come home. When Papa told her of their deaths a year after their departure, Alice wanted to die, as well. She had been so certain they would return. Father had been very angry about her concerns for them, and at the time Alice thought it was because of her nagging. Now she wondered if it was for the very reasons Mother had stated.

Alice continued to walk amongst the dead and ponder the living. There had to be answers if she was just brave enough to find them.

"You look awfully deep in thought," Robert said, coming upon Alice in the graveyard.

She seemed not to mind his interruption. "I was contemplating."

"Would you care to share what you were thinking about?"

Alice shrugged. "My life. My father's death. My mother and brother being alive. I suppose the quiet of the place led me to such reflections."

He nodded. "I've always liked cemeteries myself. They are, as you say, quiet and good for thinking. I can leave you alone if you'd like."

"That isn't necessary." She gave him a brief smile and glanced all around the yard. "Did you know most of these people?"

"Most," he admitted and came closer to where she stood. "Some not so much as others. Why?"

"I don't know. I suppose because I've always wanted to feel connected, a part of something or someone. My family was torn apart when I was thirteen, and my father kept to himself. He insisted I do the same."

"Didn't you have friends?"

"At school I had a couple of friends, but because of my mother's desertion, I quit school after eighth grade. Most figured that to be an adequate education for a young woman, but I wanted more."

"I think times are changing," Robert said. "Used to be most children ended their education about that time. Boys were needed to help with the work, and girls married or helped their mothers. These days I know there's more of a push to get a full education. I don't mind at all that my folks insisted I stay in school. I went away to college for a year, but found it wasn't for me." He smiled. "My heart is out there on the range, not in a classroom."

"I can understand that. It's beautiful here." She turned to walk away and stumbled.

Robert reached out and caught her before she could fall. To his complete frustration that was the moment Jessica Atherton chose to appear.

"Robert Barnett, I've been looking for you." She eyed him with a raised brow and then turned her attention to Alice. "Miss Chesterfield." Her look was one of contempt.

"I should get back to Simon," Alice said in a most uncomfortable manner. She pulled away from Robert's hold and hurried past Jessica.

Robert waited for whatever assault Jessica might release. She looked madder than a wet cat, and he knew she could be twice as dangerous.

"What are you doing with her? All throughout church I saw you watching her."

"Jess, you need to calm down. Alice and I have become good friends."

"We used to be good friends, but now you avoid me like I should be in quarantine. What is it that's happened between us?" She came to stand directly in front of him, blocking his way to leave.

"Jess, I've told you before, we are friends. You're like a little sister to me. I'd do whatever I could to help you or protect you. You mean the world to me."

Her eyes narrowed. "Then stay away from Miss Chesterfield. I know you feel sorry for her, but you belong to me."

"I don't belong to anyone," Robert countered, "save God. I keep tellin' folks that, but nobody seems to believe me. Furthermore, Alice is staying at our ranch. I can't ignore her or stay away from her any more than I can my folks. Nor do I want to."

"She's an unsightly woman with troubles brewing. I know, because I heard Mama talking to Marty about it just a few minutes ago. Marty said that Alice has had trouble most of her life and now with her mother and brother here, things might even get worse."

"Then I want to be here for her."

"You need to be here for me," Jessica said, sounding childish. She stamped her foot. "We were doing just fine until she came here. Now everywhere I go, folks are talking about her. It's Alice this and Miss Chesterfield that. I'm sick of it. You've always cared about broken things, but that damaged woman doesn't need to be one of your projects, Robert Barnett!"

"I never knew you to be so heartless and meanspirited." He pushed her aside gently and left her to contemplate her words. It was all he could do to keep from slapping her for what she'd said. He didn't like anyone talking mean about someone he loved—especially not this time.

★

Back on the ranch, Alice quietly changed from her Sunday clothes and put on a simple cotton blouse and skirt. She and Marty had rid themselves of most of their surplus clothing and now maintained only a few pieces. It sometimes amazed Alice that she had come full circle from a time of well-being with her father to poverty after his death, then to wealth and opulence at the Wythe mansion and finally to this. Life had a way of changing the scenery without a person even realizing what was happening.

A light rap at the door grew her attention. "Come in."

Hannah Barnett opened the door. "I hoped to find you here. May I speak to you for a moment?"

"Of course. What is it?"

"It's about your mother."

"Is she worse? Do we need a doctor?"

"No. I think her condition is mostly one of the heart."

Alice felt herself stiffen. "Why do you say that?"

Hannah sat on the bed and patted the pretty quilt that covered it. "Come sit with me for a minute."

Alice did as instructed but already felt more than a little guarded.

Hannah quickly got to the heart of the matter. "Your mother is discouraged and downtrodden over all that has happened between you two. She wants so much to renew her relationship with you."

"I know, but she said so many things that I just don't understand."

Hannah took Alice's hand in her own. "I know you're hurt and maybe even afraid. Afraid that if you believe your mother, you are somehow betraying your father. Alice, your father is dead. You can't help or hurt him anymore, but you can do both to your mother. She needs you to forgive her. . . . Otherwise . . ."

"Otherwise what?" Alice asked.

"Otherwise, I'm not sure that she'll ever forgive herself."

"So it's my responsibility to make her feel better for her mistakes?"

Alice asked in a snide voice. She immediately hated herself for having those feelings. "I'm sorry. That wasn't kind. But sometimes I feel so frustrated by it all. I was a child. I was deserted by the one person I thought would never leave me. I trusted her to always be there." Tears spilled down her cheeks. "I needed her, and she left me to face life all alone."

Hannah pulled Alice into her arms and hugged her close. "She didn't want to. She loved you. She loves you now. Yes, she hurt you and she made a terrible mistake in leaving you. But your father made mistakes, too, and you will, as well. We all make bad choices—decisions that would better be left to rot in the bottom of the barrel. But we can't undo them. We can only move forward."

"I want to," Alice said, trying to regain control. Hannah's warm embrace was like that of a comforting mother, and Alice couldn't help but remember the way she and her mother had held each other at the train station. "I love her so much."

"Then tell her. Tell her that you love her and forgive her. She needs to hear it from you, and Alice, you need to hear it, as well." Hannah let her go and got to her feet. "I'm gonna get the noon meal on the table. Why don't you go spend some time with your mother? I had the men bring her here so I could keep an eye on her. She's in the room at the end of the hall. I'll bring you two a tray to share."

Alice nodded. She wasn't sure how things would go with her mother, but it was worth a try. Escaping the past was one of the reasons she'd come to Texas with Marty. There was no sense in letting part of it go and not all.

She made her way to the bedroom. Mama was resting on the bed, but her eyes were open and she gave the slightest smile as Alice entered the room.

"I was hoping I might see you today."

Alice pulled up a chair close to the small bed. "I'm sorry I didn't come before church."

"That's all right."

Mother looked so small and helpless. Even though the bed was narrow, it seemed to swallow her up. Alice drew a deep breath to steady herself and prayed for strength.

"You look tired," her mother said.

"I was worried about you," Alice admitted.

Her mother seemed surprised by this confession. "You don't need to. I'm just weary."

"I probably added to that weariness." Alice stared at her hands and folded them in her lap. "Mama, I'm sorry that things weren't good between you and Papa. I didn't know. I thought that was just the way husbands and wives treated each other. I had no way of knowing otherwise. We didn't socialize, so I didn't have other families to learn from."

"I know," her mother said in a barely audible voice. "I'm so sorry that you didn't have those people in your life. Given your father's choices, we stayed mostly to ourselves to avoid problems. I always wanted better for you and Simon."

"I think I know that," Alice admitted, "but you have to know how much it hurt when you went away. I thought . . . I thought it was my fault."

"Oh, Alice, no. It was never your fault." Her mother reached out to touch Alice's knee. "Children are never to blame for the mistakes of their parents. I kept hoping that things could be different, hoping that your father would accept Simon and realize I had never betrayed him. I kept hoping . . . until my hope was all used up."

Alice nodded. "I know how that feels. I kept hoping you and Simon would come home, and when Papa told me you were dead, my hope was used up, too."

"I'm so very sorry, Alice. Please know that I always loved you, and I love you still. Please forgive me for not being a better mother."

Something inside Alice yielded to the sincerity in her mother's voice. She reached out and took hold of her mother's hand. "I forgive you. I love you, Mama." Her voice broke and despite her resolve, Alice buried her face in her hands and sobbed.

She felt her mother's engulfing arms. Mama sat up to take hold of her, and Alice had never been happier. She held tightly to her mother's small frame. It was a moment in time that Alice longed to hold on to forever. After a long while, Alice straightened and met her mother's tear-filled eyes.

"I want to know more." She hesitated. "I want to know what was in the box Mrs. Ingram sent you. I want to know more . . . about Papa."

Her mother smiled. "And I want to tell you." She motioned to a bag beside the bed. "I brought most of what she sent. I thought you might want to see it. I also brought your father's letters to me." She licked her lips, and Alice could see that they were dry.

"Would you like a drink?" Alice reached for the glass of water on the nightstand. She wanted more than anything to see the letters and the other things in the bag, but they could wait. Alice handed her mother the glass and waited for her to drink. Once done, Alice returned the water to the table and picked up the bag.

"Is this the bag you were talking about?" Alice asked, knowing it was but suddenly feeling uncomfortable.

"Yes. Everything is in there. I want you to have it."

For a moment Alice only looked at the small cloth bag. She wasn't sure what to say. "I'm sorry for being so upset when you tried to talk to me," Alice began. "It was wrong of me."

"You were hurt—you still are. I can see that in your eyes, and I wish I could take it from you. The scar you bear on your face is only one of many that you have from the past. Deep within you are many reminders."

Alice met her mother's sad eyes and nodded. "It's . . . it's just so hard to think of Papa the way you described. I don't want to think badly of him."

"Then don't. He was a good father in many ways to you. No one can take that from you."

"But he wasn't good to Simon? Or to you?"

Her mother shook her head. "Not at the end. There was a time when I was very happy with him despite his jealous rages. I felt cared for and safe. As the years went by and his suspicions grew, however, it was no longer the same. I felt as if I were in a prison, locked and guarded in my cell. I could have endured that if not for the way he treated Simon."

"Why did you choose to go when you did?"

"Simon had started asking questions, and he didn't understand some of the painful things he heard your father and me say to each other. Remember, you were at school during the day, and Simon was home with me. With your father's growing suspicions that I was being unfaithful, he had taken to coming home without warning. I think he figured to catch me with some lover."

Alice frowned. "I'm sorry."

"Your father was often harsh with Simon. Your brother tried so hard to win his affection, and George would have no part of it. He even started hitting the boy—not for the purpose of correction but out of his hatred."

"That's the part I find so hard to believe."

"You can ask Simon if you'd like. He remembers it well. He still holds his own sorrow for the fact that his father never loved him."

"Just like I bore the sorrow thinking you didn't love me." Alice bit her lip. She hadn't meant to say it aloud.

"But I always loved you, Alice. Always. If you read through those letters, I think you'll see the truth for yourself. It will be painful, but I want you to know the truth."

Alice looked at the bag and nodded. "I'll read them." And even as she said the words, Alice knew the letters would forever change everything. Without reading a single one, she knew that the things her mother had spoken were no doubt true.

Chapter 19

"Did you speak with the doctor?" Hannah asked Marty. She had just finished washing the breakfast dishes while Marty gathered the ingredients to bake bread.

Marty nodded and placed a canister of flour near a large mixing bowl. "He's the same old doctor he's always been—full of admonitions and cautionary tales."

"He's much too old, and his medicine is outdated," Hannah replied. "You'd do best to rely on me. I don't say that as a matter of pride, but I know how obsolete some of his philosophies can be."

"It would be nice to have a younger doctor come to the community." Marty remembered something her husband had said. "You know, Jake has good friends in the Lufkin area—a married couple and both are doctors."

"A woman doctor—imagine that," Hannah said, drying her hands. "It would be so nice to have a doctor who understands a lady's body. Of course, just having a younger, more up-to-date physician would be wonderful. We had a couple of younger doctors here last year, but they were encouraged to move their practice closer to Dallas.

"Will says with the number of ranches having grown in the area, he hopes to entice the railroad to build a spur out this way. Once in place, he feels certain we can encourage a little community of our own to spring up. It would make it a whole lot easier to get provisions that way."

Marty tried to imagine the expansion of the area and smiled. "We're definitely civilizing Texas."

Laughing, Hannah handed her a dish towel. "I'm glad to have you home, Marty. Not just for the added help." She grew thoughtful for a moment. "It was kind of lonely around here. Once the Montoyas decided to move back to Mexico, well, I didn't have the heart to hire on new staff. I doubt I could find anyone to get along with me as well as they did."

Marty smiled and began drying the dishes. "I remember how she taught me to make tortillas."

"She taught me so much," Hannah admitted. "And I suppose I taught her a thing or two." She gave a chuckle. "We were definitely more like sisters than employer and employee."

"That's how it is for Alice and me. I guess that's why I'm so grateful you allowed her to come with me and to stay here. I appreciate what you've done for her mother and brother, too."

"Family is important. Staying close, whether in distance or just in heart, is something that will see you through the worst of life. It's important to remember that, Marty."

"I will," she promised. Marty hesitated a moment and then decided to move the topic in a different direction. "I wonder if you would give me your opinion on something."

Hannah looked surprised. It wasn't often that Marty asked for anyone's opinion, so her sister was bound to be rather taken aback. She waited a moment for Hannah to regain her composure. "I've been thinking about something for a long time now. I discussed it with Jake back in Denver, but, since I learned about the baby I haven't said anything more to him."

"What are you talking about?"

"You know that I helped out at one of the orphanages in Denver?"

"Yes, I remember."

Marty looked away, bit her lower lip for a moment, and tried to figure out how best to share her thoughts. "Well . . . you see . . . there are these three boys." She turned back to find her sister watching her.

"I want to adopt them." There, it was out. Marty waited for her sister to condemn her desires or at best chide her for her foolish thoughts. When she remained silent, Marty found the courage to continue. "I fell in love with them. Wyatt, Samuel, and Benjamin are their names."

"How old are they?" Hannah began to busy herself with sifting flour.

"Wyatt is going to be eight in July. Sam and Benjamin are natural brothers. Sam is older—he'll be seven in May. Benjamin's just four. His birthday isn't until September."

"Sounds like quite a handful."

Marty smiled at the memory of trying to teach Sam how to tie his shoes. Benjamin had felt the need to learn, too, and Wyatt came along to help instruct. It had turned into a catastrophe. "They can be. But they are precious to me, and I want very much to be their mother."

"How does Jake feel about it?"

"Well, as I said, when I first wrote to you about the older orphans coming here to Texas, I also spoke to Jake about adopting. However, I'm sure he thought I meant to take only one—two at the most. We were financially well-off at that time, and that's not the case anymore. And, of course, I wasn't expecting a child of our own."

"And you're afraid now he won't want to adopt?"

"That and the fact that I had a letter from Mr. Brentwood, the director of the orphanage. Money has been very tight for them. Donations are way down, and all of Colorado is in a horrible state of depression. He's closing the orphanage."

"Where will the children go?" Hannah asked, her look revealing grave concern.

"To other orphanages, I suppose. The state runs several, and there are some churches that have their own organizations. But I don't want that to happen to these boys. I want them to be with me—always. Is that wrong?"

Hannah shook her head. "Love is never wrong. It is often misplaced or premature, but I think there is always an element of good and right in it." She smiled. "I think you should talk to your husband about this. Personally, I would love to have children around the ranch. You know that."

Marty had heard her sister express this on more than one occasion. Maybe that was why she had decided to discuss the matter with Hannah first. She needed to see her sister's reaction before speaking to Jake.

"I'll talk to him tonight." Marty felt a sense of relief in making the decision. Hopefully Jake would understand her heart.

A commotion outside drew their attention from the kitchen, and Hannah and Marty went to investigate. Several men were carrying another man, and when Marty saw that it was Jake, her heart all but stopped.

"What happened to him?" Marty heard Hannah ask.

"Horse got spooked and threw him. He would have been all right, but then the horse kicked and caught him square in the head." That accounted for the blood running down his face.

"Bring him in and put him on the dining room table," Hannah instructed. She held the screen door open for the men while Marty tried to regain her breath. It was as if Thomas's accident were happening all over again.

She thought for a moment she might faint. Her vision swam before her and her face felt hot. But even as Marty considered giving in to the sensation, Hannah shook her hard.

"Come on, I said. I need your help."

Marty wasn't sure how, but she managed to follow her sister into the house. The men had positioned the unconscious Jake on the table, and Hannah was already examining him when Marty finally felt her senses return.

"Is he . . . ?" She found it impossible to ask the question on her mind.

Hannah wiped some of the blood from Jake's wound with her apron and surveyed the situation. She opened each of his eyes and then closed them again. Next she listened to his heart, putting her ear against his chest.

Meanwhile, Marty stood helpless. Just as she had all those years ago with Thomas. She could almost see Thomas on the table in Jake's place, only instead of a head wound it was a horrible gash in his abdomen.

"Marty, fetch me some hot water and clean dish towels. Let's get him cleaned up and see if he's gonna need stitching."

For a moment Marty didn't move. She wanted to—meant to—but her feet were fixed in place. She couldn't tear her gaze from Jake's lifeless body.

"Marty! Get me water now!" Hannah demanded.

Hearing her sister's authoritative command shook Marty out of her haze. She hurried to the kitchen and dipped a small pan into the water reservoir. She poured the hot water into a bowl, took up a dozen dish towels, and hurried back to the dining room.

Hannah motioned her to wet some of the towels. "Hand me one after you wring it out."

Marty did as instructed and waited for her sister's next command. When Hannah finally had the wound cleaned, Marty could see that it wasn't all that deep.

"Head wounds always bleed bad, but I don't think he's gonna need stitches," Hannah said. She looked to the men who were standing around waiting. "Looks to me that horse just grazed him. Let me bandage his head, and then you can take him to his room. Marty, go turn down the bed for them. Joe, Bert, remove his boots. Davis, help me get his bloody shirt off after I get the wound covered."

Everyone worked together like a well-oiled machine. Hannah was quite adept at running the household and the men who worked for her. Marty seriously wondered if she could ever be that competent.

Readying the bed, Marty tried not to fear the worst. She prayed, just as she had prayed for Thomas. But this time, she didn't feel quite as afraid. Maybe she was getting numb to all of this. Ranch accidents were everyday events. Maybe in her heart she'd given up hope that the cattle business could ever be safe.

Why would I want to bring children into this?

It was only a matter of a few minutes when the men showed up carrying Jake. Marty got out of the way so they could put him on the bed. Once he was deposited, the boys left to get back to work. It was their way of life, and they seemed to accept it as part of the job.

Marty waited as Hannah checked Jake once again. He moaned softly. "I don't think it's all that bad, Marty. He's already showing signs of coming around. You stay here with him while I mix some salve for his head and get him something for the pain. When he wakes up, he's going to have a doozy of a headache."

Sitting on the bed beside her husband, Marty lifted his hand. She bent her cheek to it and remembered that she'd done the same with Thomas. She shook her head and closed her eyes. "Oh, God, please don't take him from me. I love him so much. I need him so much." She couldn't stop her tears from falling. "Father, I have fought returning to Texas and the ranch for this very reason. I can't bear to lose another husband. I can't lose the father of my baby. Please don't take him away."

"Take who?"

Marty opened her eyes to see Jake looking at her in confusion. "Jake!"

He gave her a lopsided smile. "What's all the fuss about? Who's gettin' taken away?"

Her chest felt tight and Marty gasped for air. "Oh, Jake." She fell against his chest and wept.

Jake put his arm around her. "What's all this? Why are you cryin'?"

"I thought . . . I couldn't bear . . ." She couldn't speak for the catch in her throat. Marty straightened and tried to regain control of her emotions. She replaced worry with anger, something she'd learned long ago helped her to compose herself after a shock. "You scared the life outta me, Jacob Wythe! I thought you were gonna die and leave me here in Texas."

He smiled and shook his head. It was evident that he was in pain as he grimaced, but the smile returned and he put his hand up to her face. "Marty, you worry too much. I'm not going anywhere. At least not until I see if I've got a son or a daughter."

"You better not plan to go anywhere after that, either," Marty scolded. "Here I wanted to talk to you about adopting three little boys, and instead you go get yourself hurt. I don't know what I was thinking, but I think you were mighty inconsiderate, Mr. Wythe. Sometimes I don't think you care for me like you claim."

Jake gave a small chuckle. "Like I said, Mrs. Wythe, you worry too much."

"What's all the shouting about?" Hannah asked as she rushed into the bedroom with a small tray.

"My wife is giving me a mouth-whoopin' for gettin' hurt," Jake replied in a lazy drawl.

Marty got to her feet. "Well, he deserves it. He knows how much something like this scares me. I think it's mighty inconsiderate, given my condition."

Hannah grinned and put the tray on the stand beside the bed. "Sounds like you're being inconsiderate of *his* condition."

"I haven't got a condition," Jake declared. He tried to sit up but fell back. "Well, at least not much of one." He closed his eyes. "Think I'll just rest a bit."

"You've got that right," Hannah said. "I'll tie you to that bed if you don't cooperate."

"You won't have to," Marty said, coming alongside her sister. "If he thinks he's gonna set foot out of that bed, he's got another think coming. I'll sit on him if I have to."

Jake opened his eyes and gave her a half-cocked smile. "I just might test you out, Mrs. Wythe. Sounds like I could be in for a world of fun."

"You'll be in for a world of hurt if you don't do exactly what my sister tells you to do," Marty said.

Hannah shook her head and reached for the salve she'd brought. "I've dealt with children less troublesome than you two. Now, settle down while I redress this wound. I've brought you something to help with the pain, Jake, and don't go tellin' me that you haven't got any. I know that head of yours is hard, but you're gonna hurt for at least the rest of the day. I want you to promise me you'll stay in bed—flat in bed and rest. Hear me?"

"Yes, ma'am," he replied with a wink at Marty. "Can Marty stay with me—maybe read to me?"

"Ha!" Marty declared, hands on hips. "You scare me nearly to death and then you want me to read to you?" All of the sudden she stopped and her hand went to her belly.

"What's wrong?" Jake asked, looking concerned.

Hannah turned to her sister. "What is it, Marty? Are you in pain?"

Marty shook her head. "It's been ongoing. The baby moves all the time."

"That's unusual," Hannah said and looked at her oddly. "You're hardly far enough along to have that kind of movement."

Worry crept up Marty's spine like a tingling snake. "Does this mean something's wrong?"

"Not at all. But my guess is you're further along than you realize. You said you weren't sure if the baby was due in July or August. Maybe it's coming sooner than that. Is it possible?"

Marty considered the matter for a moment. "I suppose so. There was such upheaval what with losing the house and Jake's leaving."

"My guess is this baby may come a month or two sooner than you think."

She glanced over at Jake, who was watching her in wonder. "A month or two sooner?"

"Can I feel it?" he asked.

Marty sat back on the edge of the bed and positioned his hand on her stomach. Just then the baby shifted again, and Jake's eye widened.

"Feisty little fella," he declared.

"Could be a little filly," Hannah said, smiling. "Either way, I think we'd better speed up our work on clothes for the baby."

★

Alice read the last of her mother's letters and sat back in her chair to take it all in. The truth was there on the pages. Her mother had loved her most dearly, had pleaded with Alice's father to be allowed to come back into her daughter's life—only to be rejected.

The letters written by Alice's father had been brief and to the point. They were also ugly and heartless. He had threatened his wife with arrest and ruin if she so much as showed her face in Denver again. He threatened to take Simon from her and have the boy sent far away. He threatened to disappear with Alice so that she might never find either of them again. The words were heartbreaking. He even threatened her mother's life.

Alice could scarcely believe her father's cruel nature. How could he have been so loving toward her and so hateful toward them?

She decided to look through the rest of the papers and items in the bag. There was very little left to her. A small framed picture of Alice, a letter opener, and a pipe were all that remained of her father's personal effects. The other papers proved to be notes he had made for himself and half-written letters that were never finished. Then Alice spied the large envelope at the bottom of the bag. She took it up and wondered if the gold certificates were inside. Opening it, she found a single sheet of paper.

NEVER AGAIN were the only words written.

She had no way of knowing if it was her father's writing or someone else's. The large block letters could have belonged to anyone. It was a mystery that would most likely go unresolved. One thing was quite clear, however. There were no gold certificates, plates, or other counterfeit materials. If there had been, they were long gone. Mr. Smith would never have what he sought, and hopefully that would include Alice's whereabouts.

Chapter 20

The night was perfect for a party. To celebrate Jake's and Hannah's birthdays they had cleared the Barnetts' yard of obstructions, set up a half dozen tables, and made an area for dancing. Hannah and Alice had worked hard to place dozens of lanterns around the area. Some hung from the large cottonwoods, while others were affixed to the fence posts or positioned on creative stands. It definitely lent an air of something special to the party. Parties like this were always a time of great joy. Local ranchers gathered together and discussed the cattle business while their wives swapped recipes and gossip. And, of course, the children entertained one another with games of hide-and-seek and tag.

These are the best folks in the world. Not one of them needs to be cut from the herd. Robert smiled and nodded greetings to the various people who caught his gaze. He loved it here. The heavy humidity of the day had lifted a bit, and now in the cool of the evening, these Texans were ready for a hoedown.

Robert's stomach growled, and he had to admit that most of his excitement centered around the food. His father and Tyler Atherton had decided to roast a pig, and the aroma of cooking meat had plagued him since yesterday. Not only that, but the tables were all but bowing from a bevy of dishes his mother, Marty, and Alice had worked to prepare. All of his favorites were present: cheesy grits, jalapeño corn bread, corn salad, and molasses baked beans, just to name a few. There were also at least a dozen pies of varying kinds and a chocolate pecan cake. Robert had eaten various renditions of the latter on many occasions and always found he could put away a good portion of the cake by himself.

Then there was the food other folks had brought to share. People had been gathering since early afternoon, and now there were probably eighty or so spread out across the yard, dancing to the tunes the musicians were playing. Inevitably when there was a party, those who were musically inclined knew to bring their instruments without being asked. Tonight they had three guitars and two fiddles. They made for a nice little band and as soon as the skies had grown dark and the lanterns had been lit, they'd begun to play.

Someone took the opportunity to call a square dance, and the crowd split up into paired couples and then squares of eight. Robert decided to take that opportunity to help himself to the food table.

"I don't suppose you've had a chance to speak to Jess yet, have you?" Robert looked up to find Tyler Atherton with plate in hand.

"No, sir. Not yet, but I will." Robert helped himself to a large slice of the roasted pig. "I figure to get her alone tonight and explain it. That way she can have friends around to take her mind off of the matter."

"Could be she'll be all the more embarrassed for it," Mr. Atherton replied, "but I trust you to be as easy on her as possible."

"Absolutely. I care very much for her." Robert continued heaping food on his plate as Tyler dug into the roasted pig.

Earlier that day he'd managed to speak to Mr. Atherton by himself. Pulling him away from the roasting pig, Robert had spoken his mind. Tyler Atherton had listened without interruption.

"I love Jess," he'd said, "but not in a way that would lead us to marriage. She's like a little sister to me. I would do anything to keep her safe and protected. I would give my life for her, Mr. Atherton, but I cannot marry her."

Mr. Atherton hadn't seemed at all surprised. Robert had always known the man to be rather casual in the way he dealt with life, but he was, in fact, quite astute.

"You're in love with the Chesterfield gal, aren't you?" he'd asked.

Robert couldn't deny it and Atherton nodded. "I could see it in your eyes—the way you look at her. Reminded me of how I felt about Carissa. You know, I want exactly that for my Jessica, and if it's not to be with you, then I want her set free to find that person."

Now all Robert had left to do was break the news to Jessica.

The opportunity to do just that came some time later, after Robert's second plate of food. Eating with some of the older ranchers, Robert enjoyed their stories of cattle drives to Kansas and the hardships of days gone by. Reluctantly, he got to his feet and searched the dancers for Jessica. She didn't seem to be among them. He was about to take his search to where the other women had gathered when Jessica approached him to ask for a dance.

"They're playing a waltz," she said with a coy smile. "Wouldn't you like to dance with me?"

All evening Robert had avoided Alice, but now with Jessica standing before him, it was Alice that he longed to dance with. He took hold of Jess and led her toward a quiet spot under a tall sugarberry tree. "We need to talk."

Jessica looked up at him. "Talk?" She gave a tug and broke free of his hold. With great flourish, Jessica whirled in a circle, her skirt splaying out around her. "Isn't this the most beautiful gown? It's perfect for dancing, and I want to dance."

"I know, but this can't wait." Robert knew what needed to be said, but finding a way to do it gently was harder than he'd thought. "Jess, I've been trying to talk to you for a long while now, but you won't hear me out. I talked to your pa this morning—"

Her face lit up. "To ask for my hand? How wonderful!" She looped her arm through his. "And now you've brought me away from the crowd to propose. This is perfect. We can announce it tonight."

He pulled free and took hold of her shoulders. "No! Listen to me, Jessica. I am not going to marry you." He hadn't meant for the words to come out so harsh. He softened his tone. "I will always care about you. Like I told your pa, I would even give my life for you. You're like a member of my family—a little sister who I dearly love. But, Jess, I'm not in love with you."

424

"But you love me, and out of that a deeper love can grow," she said, smiling.

Robert shook his head. "No, Jess. It's not going to grow deeper."

Jessica lost her smile and fixed him with a stare. "You love her—that scar-faced mousy blonde. You love her, don't you?"

"It's not like you to belittle those less fortunate than you," he reprimanded.

"You love her, don't you?" she pressed.

For a moment Robert didn't say anything. He didn't want to declare his love of Alice to Jessica. What he felt was private and personal. He needed to speak with Alice and share his thoughts with her—not Jess.

"Answer me, Robert. You love Alice Chesterfield."

"I do," he said, blowing out a heavy breath. "I didn't start out to fall in love with her. I wanted to be her friend and help her adjust to life in Texas. I had no notion of anything else. The love just happened."

"But not for me," she said, her voice cracking slightly. "Why can you love her . . . and not me?" A single tear slid from her eye, and Robert reached out to touch it. In the lantern light it glistened for a moment and then faded. She bit her lower lip and said nothing more.

"But I do love you, Jess. Just not that way. Falling in love is a matter of the heart. You can't force it."

"I didn't think you'd have to," Jessica replied. "I thought . . . well . . . I'm pretty."

"Jess, it has nothing to do with looks. You're a beautiful woman. You're smart and talented—everything that a man could want."

"But not for you."

He shook his head. "I'm sorry, Jess."

She lifted her chin, appearing to regain some of her steam. "Not as sorry as you're gonna be." She sniffed. "You'll see. I'll make someone a wonderful wife, and we will travel and be wealthy. I'll be the most beautiful woman in Texas, and he will be the handsomest man."

Instead of making Robert jealous, as he was sure she was trying to do, he smiled and nodded. "I bet you will be. I hope that for you and so much more. I still want us to be friends, Jess. We're practically family."

She started to walk away but then turned back. In her expression

Robert saw hurt mingled with anger. "I don't want to be friends with you, Robert Barnett. I'd rather have a rattlesnake for a friend." She stormed off in a huff.

Robert might have chuckled at her reference to the snake if it hadn't been such a serious moment. He watched Jessica approach one of the local rancher's sons. Apparently she asked him to dance, because he willingly followed her to the area where other couples were doing a reel.

"She'll be all right," Tyler Atherton said, coming up behind Robert.

"I hope so. I sure don't like lettin' her down, hurtin' her."

"I heard everything you said, Robert. It takes a big man to be honest in the face of such a thing. I'm proud of you for treatin' her with respect."

Robert looked at the older man. "Thanks. That means a lot comin' from you. My pa says he doesn't respect anybody's opinion more than yours."

Atherton smiled. "We've been friends a long time—gone through a lot together. I feel the same way about your pa." He slapped Robert's back. "And I have a feeling I will always think highly of you, as well. I would have liked havin' you for a son-in-law." The older man squared his shoulders. "Now, come on back to the party. There's still more cake, and I have a mind to get me another piece."

Robert laughed. "I can definitely see the benefit of that."

★

"How are you feelin'?" Jake asked Marty. He knew she'd been worried about him ever since he'd been kicked. He knew that it compounded her worries that he would die like her first husband. "You know I'm concerned that you aren't takin' it easy enough. I know you're thinkin' you gotta get things done because the baby will probably come sooner than August, but you can't do everything."

"I know," Marty replied. "I'm trying to be cautious and take things slow, but there is a great deal to oversee. As for how I feel, I'm a little tired, but otherwise fine. The real question is how do you feel? You know I think it's much too early for you to be out here carrying on with the others."

"Even your sister said I was doin' fine, and it's not like I'm up there square dancin'. Marty, you gotta stop worryin' about everythin'." He put his hand on her stomach. "For the sake of our children, if not for yourself."

"I can't help it. I love you so very much. I don't want to lose you." She stared off at the dancers and musicians. "I know that you're in God's hands, but—"

"But?" Jake interrupted. "But God isn't big enough to handle this? But God won't give you your own way all the time? Grief, Marty, you either trust Him or you don't. I'm not sayin' that we won't have doubts about Him, but I am sayin' that we don't need to. We know He's faithful." He turned her to face him. "Marty, if I drop over dead tomorrow, will you stop lovin' God again?"

She still wouldn't meet his eyes. "I . . . don't know. I don't like to think I would." She shook her head. "I'd like to say my faith is strong enough to get me through anything, but I know better." Finally she raised her gaze to his. "I'm a coward."

Jake chuckled. "Marty, there's no one less cowardly in the world. You are a strong woman, but unfortunately, you think it's your own strength that makes you so. It isn't. We don't do a thang in our own strength, Marty."

"You're sounding more and more like a Texan and less and less like a banker," she told him.

He nodded. "That's who I am, Marty. You gotta let me be who I am. And, you're gonna have to let our boys be who they are."

"Our boys?" She smiled. "So you already plan for a houseful of boys?"

"Didn't you want to adopt three of 'em?"

Recognition dawned on her. "You mean you'd be willing?"

"I love children, Marty. I love the idea of helpin' those needy ones. If you love those children, then I know I'll love 'em, too. I want you to wire Mr. Brentwood and have them sent down on the train."

She threw her arms around Jake's neck. "Oh, thank you. Thank you so much! I've missed those boys more than I can say. I really want them to be a part of our family."

Jake kissed her soundly on the mouth and smiled. "Then that's what I want, too."

Marty reached up and touched the smaller bandage Hannah had put on Jake's wound. "I'll try to be accepting and understanding. I really want to trust God more."

"Then do it, Marty. You've always been a woman who went after what she wanted."

★

Alice found herself watching Robert for most of the evening. She'd been unable to take her gaze from him when he led Jessica Atherton away from the party. However, once she saw him tenderly touch her cheek, Alice knew she had to stop fooling herself. She had fallen in love with another woman's man. The idea sickened her.

"This is such a wonderful place," her mother said, coming to stand beside her. "I can see why you love it so. I have to say it's nothing like Chicago."

Alice turned toward her mother. "Speaking of Chicago, Mama, I wonder if I might go with you when you return."

Her mother seemed surprised but pleased. "I would love for you to come visit Simon and me in our home."

"No, I meant . . . would you let me come live with you?"

"Well of course," her mother said, taking hold of her arm. "But I thought you preferred it here."

Alice shrugged. "There's nothing to keep me here. I do enjoy it and I love Marty like a sister, but honestly, it would probably be better for all concerned if I were to leave."

Just then Simon barreled into Alice. "This is the best time I've ever had," he said, wrapping his arms around her waist.

Alice smiled down at her brother. "Well, do you suppose you could show me a time like this in Chicago?"

The boy straightened and dropped his hold. "There's nothing like this in Chicago. I want us to move here."

Alice looked to her mother, hoping she would set Simon straight. "Why don't you go on and have some more fun," Mother told him. "We are talking about something serious just now."

"But this is a party," he reminded them. "You don't talk about serious things at a party."

428

Alice felt bad and nodded. "Perhaps he's right. I probably shouldn't have brought it up just now; you should be out there with the others."

"Go on, Simon. I want you to go play," Mama encouraged. She turned back to Alice and smiled. "It's all right, Alice. We can talk about anything you want—anytime you want. I am so glad to have you back in my life that I could easily spend all of my time with you and Simon and never speak to another soul." Mother seemed to scrutinize Alice for several moments before continuing.

"Alice, you seem troubled about something. What is it?"

"I . . . well. . . ." Alice paused, not wanting to lie to her mother. "Marty and Jake were so kind to take me in when I had nothing—not even references for the job they hired me to do. When the banks fell apart and they lost everything, they still allowed me to stay on with them. I knew it was difficult for them, but they insisted. Now I find myself again having the benefit of someone else's generosity. I guess I just feel that I've overstayed my welcome. I don't want to be a burden to anyone."

"I've seen the way you help out around here. You aren't a burden. I think you more than earn your keep. And they all seem to very much enjoy your company."

"Which is why this is so hard." Alice glanced at the revelers and saw Robert kiss his mother's cheek. How she longed for him to kiss her. "I think we should go before we are no longer enjoyed and useful." She looked at her mother. "But I don't think we should say anything about our plans. At least not until we're ready to leave. Otherwise Mrs. Barnett might feel slighted or believe us to be ungrateful."

"I don't know why she would. She knows I have a home in Chicago."

"I know, but she also said we could use the Montoya house for as long as we liked. Mrs. Barnett is generous to a fault. I don't want to hurt her feelings."

Her mother remained silent for several minutes and then nodded. "If you think that's best, Alice, then I will go along with you. However, have you considered the matter of your train fare? I was under the impression that you had no money."

"I don't," Alice said realizing the problem. "But I'll get it. I'll figure a way." She didn't know how she could possibly make it work, but she was determined to try.

"I wonder if I might have this dance."

Alice turned to find Robert Barnett standing directly behind her. She wanted to refuse him, but instead she found herself nodding in agreement. She let Robert take her to where a dozen or so couples were waltzing.

She looked at him and shook her head. "I don't know how."

He smiled that lazy smile of his and her heart melted. "Then it's time you learned. We enjoy having our get-togethers, and you'll just have to get used to dancin' if you're gonna be around here."

But I'm not going to be around here. I have to leave before you realize that I've lost my heart to you. I have to go before anyone knows how I feel.

"I have to go," she said suddenly and pulled away. She heard Robert call after her, but Alice continued to make her way with great haste to the solitude of the house. It wasn't until she was behind the closed door of her room, however, that she felt she could finally let down her guard. The pain of losing something she didn't really have seemed such a contradiction, but there was no other way to look at it.

I've lost him, but I never had him. So why does it hurt so much?

Chapter 21

For weeks the men planned their trip to Fort Worth and the cattle sale. Knowing they'd be gone for several days, Alice decided it would be the perfect opportunity to leave without any uncomfortable good-byes.

She had been plotting and planning for their escape, but when the time came, she still felt uncertain. She and her mother had spoken several times, but Alice knew her mother wasn't convinced she was doing the right thing. For Alice, however, there was no other choice.

Robert had tried his best to get Alice alone. He continually nagged her to go riding with him or to sit and talk with him in the evening. It was getting harder and harder to avoid him. Alice had even given up going to church, because twice Robert had cornered her after services to speak to her. She felt almost certain that he'd figured out or been told of her feelings for him.

The second night after the men's departure, Alice knew she'd never have a better chance. "We'll leave tomorrow, no matter what," Alice had told her mother. Even now the look of shock on her mother's face was imprinted in Alice's mind.

"Are you sure that's wise? What about money?"

Alice had talked Marty into lending her some money. It wasn't a lot, but it would be enough for train tickets and maybe some food.

The problem, however, was getting away from Marty and Hannah.

She knew if either of them caught wind of her plans, they would do their best to put an end to them.

When Marty and Hannah announced they would be heading out just after lunch to work on Marty's place, Alice felt confident God had intervened to help her leave. Watching at the window, Alice jumped into action once the buggy pulled away. That would leave the large carriage, which was exactly what they'd need.

"We must work fast," Alice told her mother. "I don't want any teary good-byes. I've written letters for Hannah and Marty explaining our leaving this way."

"It hardly seems good manners to sneak out," her mother replied.

"We're not sneaking. We're avoiding a scene. I know these people better than you do. They will fuss and fret and nag us to stay."

"Your brother isn't going to like this one bit. He's quite happy here."

Alice looked at her mother in confusion. "Did you come here meaning to make Texas your home?"

"No, I bought round-trip tickets. But seeing how Simon has thrived, I've begun to think about the possibility. Simon has blossomed while here. You have no idea how it was for him in Chicago. He was so unhappy."

"Perhaps with me there, we can find a way to better his life. I'll get a job, and maybe I can earn enough to lavish him with special gifts. Papa used to do that for me."

"And did it make everything seem right?" her mother asked, giving her a look that suggested she already knew the answer.

Alice looked away. "No. I suppose not."

"Alice, why are we really leaving this way? I'm your mother, and I want you to be honest with me."

A lie was on her lips, but one look back at her mother and Alice knew she had to confess her reasons. "I'm in love."

"With?"

"With Robert." She reached up and felt the scar on her face. "He has been so kind to me and never made me feel ugly. When I'm with him, I forget I even have this reminder of the attack." She shook her head, feeling the weight of the world on her shoulders. "I let my heart get carried away."

"And how does he feel about you?" Mother asked.

"I'm sure he feels nothing but friendship." Alice paused, wondering if her mother hadn't yet heard that he was engaged to Jessica Atherton. "He's to be married. Do you remember at the birthday party that one girl about my age, very pretty, and most every man there sought to dance with her?"

"The Atherton girl?" Mother questioned.

"Yes. Jessica Atherton."

"And Robert is supposed to marry her?"

Alice sighed and stopped rubbing her scar. "Yes. They've been promised to each other since they were young. Mama, I don't want to do anything to come between them. I would feel terrible if I caused Robert and Jessica pain. They've been nothing but good to me."

Mother took a seat on the side of the bed. "I see."

"And I couldn't explain that to Hannah and Will. They've taken me in and treated me like family, just as Marty and Jake have. I couldn't tell any of them the real reason, because I'm ashamed of having let things get out of hand."

Mother nodded. "I suppose you're right."

Alice went to the dresser and pulled out the last of her things. "Hannah and Marty will be busy most of the afternoon. They're going to measure for new curtains and figure out how they want to arrange things when the boys come from Denver. That should give us plenty of time to get to town before the train pulls out of Cedar Springs."

"But how are we to get there?"

"I will ask one of the men to take us. There's always a hand or two around here. I'll tell them that something has happened and you need to return to Chicago immediately. I'm sure it will all work out."

But she wasn't. There were a great many things that could go wrong. The men could change their mind and come home early. Hannah and Marty might have forgotten something and need to return to the house.

I might not even be able to find someone to drive us to the train station. And then what?

The thoughts worried her, but Alice was determined to make things work.

———————— ★ ————————

"I'm glad we're finished here," Robert told his father. They walked past several Fort Worth storefronts and made their way to the jewelry store at the corner. Robert had already mentioned his plan.

"I'm gonna find the perfect ring for my bride." Robert's grin stretched almost from ear to ear.

"I think I just might pick out a little somethin' for your mama. I didn't have anything special for her birthday, and this will more than make up for that."

"I'm glad Jake was willing to stay with the others and start the cows for home. I need the time," he said as they approached the brick building, "to have a word or two with you in private."

Robert paused before the jewelry store door. "You and Ma love each other a great deal. I've always admired that. Even when you argue, I can see the respect you hold for each other. It's like you two were always meant to be together."

Father laughed. "You wouldn't have thought so in our early years. Your mama was the most stubborn woman I'd ever met. She would stand her ground over the silliest things."

"Like when she went to help the Comanches?"

The older man nodded. "Took nearly ten years off my life. I thought for sure she'd get us both killed, but your mama has a way with folks— even Comanches. She's stubborn, but she's also the bravest woman I've ever known. Saw her crawl out on a tree limb to rescue a cat for Marty. And it wasn't on some low-hangin' branch, either. I've seen her kill rattlers with a hoe and face down tornadoes and wildfires like she already knew the outcome."

Robert had seen it, too. He saw that same kind of bravery in Alice. Maybe that's why he loved her so much. Despite the attack and all she'd lost, Alice faced life with great determination and strength.

"Alice is like that," Robert said, meeting his father's eyes. "I wanna do right by her, Pa. I wanna give her the things she deserves. I was hopin' you could help me get to work building a house."

"You wanna build right away? You know you two are welcome to live at the house as long as you like. In fact, I had thought about discussin' a change of plans with you."

Robert cocked his head to one side, looking at his father. "Change of plans?"

"Your ma was the one who got me to thinkin'."

Robert almost hated to ask. His mother was well known for coming up with some of the zaniest ideas. "And what did she get you thinkin' about?"

"Well, she reminded me that the ranch will one day be yours. Sooner, rather than later, since we're both gettin' older every day. It seems kind of senseless for you to build a new house elsewhere. She suggested that you two could take the whole east wing for yourselves—that would afford you some privacy. We could tear down a couple of walls in that wing to open things up a bit, remake it with your own sitting room and such."

"But *your* rooms are in the east wing," Robert said, as if his father didn't already know this.

"Yup, but that's where your mama has her plan. Since Marty and Jake will be heading back to Marty's place and Alice's ma will most likely head home before long, the house will be empty again. But you know your ma. She's convinced there will be an abundance of little ones once you and Alice marry. So she thinks it's time to add on again. I thought on it and I like the idea. I can put an addition on the west end of the house for us."

Robert didn't know what to say. He'd never really thought of his parents getting old and settling into an easier life.

"Cat got your tongue?" his father asked.

"I can't imagine you and Ma not livin' in the east wing. I mean, that's all I've ever known. And I sure haven't thought much about the two of you gettin' old."

"Well, it's time you did. I'll be fifty-nine come June. You know as well as I do that I'm slowin' down. I can't ride as long as I used to without causin' my back a world of hurt. The time is comin', maybe earlier than either of us would like to see, when you'll be takin' over."

It took some joy out of the moment to consider his parents unable to do the things they loved. He couldn't imagine his father not sitting on a horse or his mother not gardening.

"Well, we gonna just stand here?" Father asked.

"No, sir." He reached for the door handle, and Father put his hand on Robert's arm.

"Don't go broodin' over this. Your mama and I like to plan ahead. You talk to your little gal about it, and then we can all sit down and have a discussion."

Robert nodded. "I will, Pa. I'll do that first thing."

Just then gunshots rang out. Robert and his father glanced up to see an armed man on horseback holding two other mounts. The man had his neckerchief tied around his face.

The bank's being held up.

Robert looked around to see people scurrying out of the way, taking cover wherever they could.

"Get back," his father said, pushing him around the side of the building. "Stay down. We need to figure out what we can do."

"We don't have any weapons," Robert said. "Our rifles are back with the horses."

"I know." Father looked more than a little irritated at the reminder.

Another gunshot sounded, and shortly after that came the bellowing voice of one of the robbers. "Let's get outta here!"

The man on horseback waited with rifle cocked as his two confederates mounted. Robert could see his father edging closer to the front of the building.

"Pa, we can't do anything." The helplessness of the moment only served to make both men more determined.

But from out of nowhere came rifle fire. Three shots in a row, fast and precise. Each one hit its mark and the men fell from their horses like leaves from a tree. Seeing that, Robert's father bounded out into the street and took hold of one of the thieves' guns before he could shoulder it.

"Thanks for the help," a familiar voice called out.

Austin Todd, the field inspector they'd spent time with earlier in the day, came striding up the street. He wore a determined look and quickly disarmed the other men, who were no match for him. Several armed police officers arrived just then, guns drawn and pointed at Austin.

"Texas Ranger," he told the first officer. The man seemed to relax at this.

"What happened?" the officer asked, looking at the three who were roiling in pain on the street.

"Bank robbery. I think you'll find the money in that bag over there." Austin pointed to the farthest man. Beside him was what looked to be a pillowcase with something in it.

"Anyone else involved?" the man asked.

"I'm guessing the bank personnel. You take over here, and I'll go check out the bank." Austin headed for the building, Robert and his father following after him.

"We saw them but had no weapons. Felt like a fool just crouchin' down there in the alleyway," Robert's father told the ranger.

"It was the right thing to do. If you'd been out there, you could've been shot."

"How did you come to be here?" Robert asked, remembering something Austin had said earlier. "I thought you were headin' to the railroad station, and by the way, when did you become a Texas Ranger?"

"Last year. They incorporated all of us field inspectors into the Rangers. Makes it a whole lot easier." Austin paused at the door.

Robert figured he was making sure there was no one pointing a gun at them.

"Texas Ranger!" he called out. "I'm comin' in, so if you have weapons, put 'em down."

There was no response. The trio made their way into the bank only to find the bodies of the bank manager and his teller on the floor. They were both dead.

"I was headed for my train," Austin said, "then I realized I had forgotten to tend to some other business. Guess God just put me in the right place at the right time." He shook his head at the bloody scene. The look on his face suggested an anger that burned deep and hot. "I should have aimed to kill those murderers."

Two hours later the Barnett men rejoined Jake and the cowhands as they made their way back to the ranch. Jake threw Robert a grin and moved his mount closer.

"Did you get it?"

With the ruckus of the bank robbery, Robert had nearly forgotten what he'd come to town for in the first place. New cows weren't the only thing they had on hand.

"I did," he admitted.

"Then you can 'I do' right away," Jake teased. "I can't tell you how happy I am to see you and Alice gettin' married."

"Well, she has to say yes first."

Robert kept reaching inside his vest pocket to feel for the box. He'd spent a pretty penny on the ring, but he knew Alice would love it, and she was certainly worth it. He smiled to himself and made his plans.

When we get back, I'm gonna find her and tell her that we need to talk. I'll make it sound all serious. Then once we're alone, I'll tell her how much she means to me. I'll get down on one knee and hold up the ring in the box. No, maybe I'll just hold up the ring.

Thankful for the time to figure it all out, Robert said very little as his father related the events at the bank.

Jake seemed more than a little disturbed by the turn of events. "And Marty worries about me ranchin'. I don't suppose she ever thought that bankin' could be just as dangerous. I hope you tell her about the robbery when we get home. Maybe it'll settle her down a bit."

Robert's father shook his head. "There's danger all around us. Marty knows that full well. She always blamed the ranch and Texas for killin' Thomas, but the hard truth of it is that a man could die sittin' at his desk or at the dinner table. Robert and I could have just as easily caught one of those stray bullets. Or the lookout man could have thought us a threat and shot us as a matter of business." He paused.

"Apparently God's not through with us just yet, eh Robert? One thing I know: When I get home I'm gonna kiss my wife for a good long time and then . . . I think I'll clean my guns."

Chapter 22

"What are you saying?" Alice asked the stationmaster at the train depot in Cedar Springs.

"I'm sayin' there's trouble on the line, and there won't be any passenger service out today." He gave her a sympathetic smile. "However, there are other railroads. You could head on to Dallas and catch one of those."

"We've hardly got the money for additional tickets," Alice stated in worry. Biting her lip, she tried to figure out what they should do. By now Marty and Hannah might have returned to the house. She couldn't very well go back to the ranch without creating an uproar.

"Well, I can refund the return passage cost on your mother and brother's tickets. That should allow you to cover costs on another line."

With a sigh, Alice realized this nightmare wasn't going to go away. "All right. But how are we supposed to get to Dallas?"

The man grinned. "That one's easy enough. One of the Dallas freighters arrived earlier. He won't be takin' anything much back with him. I'm thinkin' you could hitch a ride for free."

She thought about it for a moment. She certainly had no way to get the Barnett carriage to take them. The driver had been hard enough to convince to bring them here in the first place. "Very well. Where can we find the driver?"

After getting instructions on where to locate the man, Alice returned to where her mother and brother waited. Simon was in an ill temper. He was decidedly upset that they were leaving Texas. He had whined and complained all the way to the train station, reminding Alice that she couldn't take her colt with her on the train nor could she take any more riding lessons from Robert. Now played out, Simon sulked beside their mother.

"There's a problem, but I believe we have a solution." Alice told them what had transpired. Her mother turned over the train tickets and received the money due her before they went in search of the freight man.

The trio approached just as the driver was ready to pull out. He was an older gentleman with gray at the temples. Alice summoned up her courage. "Excuse me."

The man looked down from his seat and smiled. "What can I do for you, little gal?"

"Our train has been canceled because of problems on the line. The stationmaster said you might be willing to take us to the Dallas station. However, we don't have any money."

"Oh, that's quite all right." He set the brake and climbed down. "I'll take you just for the company. Been a long time since I talked to a couple of pretty ladies." He gave Alice's mother a nod. "I'm Roy James—no relation to Jesse James." He guffawed as if it were the most priceless of jokes.

"Mr. James, this is my mother, Mrs. Chesterfield, and my brother, Simon."

He again nodded toward Alice's mother and smiled. "You can call me Roy, ma'am. Let me help you up. You can sit with me while you young'uns ride in the back."

Alice's mother looked hesitant, but Alice gave her arm a pat. "That will work just fine for us." Her only concern was managing to get out of Cedar Springs before someone from the Barnett ranch showed up to stop them.

Once they were settled, Mr. James put his team in motion. He smiled over at Alice's mother. "So, headin' home or goin' to visit?"

"Home," Mother replied.

The man looked straight ahead. "Got your man waitin' for you to return, eh?"

"No. I'm widowed."

Roy James beamed her a smile that could have brightened a dark room. "Widowed. That's quite a coincidence. I'm a widower myself."

And with that Mr. James began a nonstop conversation with Mother that made Alice smile, in spite of her worry. It seemed the man had taken an instant liking to her.

★

Robert didn't like the way his mother looked when she greeted him at the door. He knew immediately that something was wrong.

"What's going on?"

She glanced at his father before saying, "The Chesterfields have gone."

"That must have been difficult for Alice. Is she all right? Should I go talk to her?"

"She's gone, Robert. All of the Chesterfields have gone."

He shook his head. "Why? When?"

His mother sighed. "Marty and I went over to her place after lunch to measure for curtains. While we were gone, they left. Joe said Alice came and got him and said it was imperative that they get to Cedar Springs right away."

"But that doesn't make sense. Why would they just leave like that without a word?"

Mother held out a folded piece of paper. "Alice left a letter for me and Marty and one for you."

Robert took the paper with trembling hands. This couldn't be happening. Not now. Not when he'd put everything right and even bought the ring.

He unfolded the note and read the lines to himself.

Robert,

By the time you read this letter I will be on a train to Chicago. I am sorry that I wasn't able to say good-bye in person, but I couldn't bear the thought. You see, I've fallen in love with you. I know that probably comes as a shock, and believe me I didn't set out to do so. I wouldn't come between you and Jessica for all the world, which is why I have to go. I'm so sorry. I feel just horrible about it all.

You are by far and away the best man I've ever known. You made me feel as if I weren't damaged goods, and for that I thank you. I hope you will be happy in your marriage to Jessica. She's a beautiful woman with much to give.

Yours,
Alice

He looked up and fixed his mother with a stern look. "She says she had to go because she loves me. That doesn't make any sense at all. She doesn't want to come between me and Jess, but I've told her more than once that we aren't engaged."

Mother reached out and touched his face, as she often did when she wanted to calm him. "She probably felt guilty. In her letter to me, she mentioned feeling that she had disrupted our family and changed our plans. She felt that she and her family had become a burden."

"But they hadn't!" He crumpled up the letter. "I'm going after her."

"Son, she probably caught the evening train. It's too late for you to stop her now."

Robert hadn't considered that. "Did she ever tell you what her mother's address is in Chicago? I could go there and bring her back."

"I don't have it. Perhaps Marty does," his mother suggested.

He didn't wait to hear more. "Aunt Marty!" he yelled at the top of his lungs.

Stomping through the house, he continued his search. "Aunt Marty!"

Marty poked her head out of her bedroom. "Goodness. What is all the yelling about?"

"Alice is gone."

"I know. She left me a letter and her Bible." Marty shrugged. "I can't tell you how sorry I am."

"Sorry isn't what I came for. I want her mother's address in Chicago."

"I don't have it. I don't recall ever even seeing it. When Alice learned the truth about her mother and sent her a letter . . . well, I never asked." She pushed open the bedroom door. "Jake, did you ever see an address for Mrs. Chesterfield?"

442

Jake was sitting at the end of the bed and pulling off his boots. "No, can't say that I did."

"That's just great. Now I'm gonna have to go to Chicago and scour a city bigger than Dallas to find her."

Marty took hold of his arm. "Robert, what did Alice say in her letter to you?"

"That she had to go because she loved me and didn't want to come between me and Jess." He gave the door a fisted punch. "But she didn't come between us. There was no 'us.'"

"Alice was always very sensitive about hurting people. She couldn't bear the thought that she might cause someone pain. I'm sure she felt any delay or doubts you might have in marrying Jessica were her fault."

"But they weren't, and she didn't even give me a chance to tell her that. I can't help what folks assumed, including Jessica. I never proposed to that girl, and I told her weeks ago that I couldn't marry her."

Marty looked perplexed. "Why didn't you tell Alice?"

"I tried, but there was never a chance. I'd ask her to go for a walk with me or go ridin', but she always refused and kept her brother or mother with her so we couldn't be alone. I figured when I got back from Fort Worth, I'd show her the ring I got her and propose—even if I had to do so at the dinner table."

"That would have been something," Marty said with a hint of smile. "Well, what are we to do? We don't have any way of finding her mother, short of perhaps hiring someone in Chicago. There's no sense in your going up there blind. We could send a wire and have them intercepted on the way."

"That's a good idea." He turned on his heel and headed back through the house. Despite the late hour, he was determined to go to Cedar Springs and start the process.

"But it's so late," his mother said. "Why don't you wait until morning? That train won't get to Chicago for at least a couple of days."

"Your mother's right," Father agreed. "The stationmaster will have closed things down, and you won't be able to find out exactly what connections the Chesterfields will be making."

"I could go to his house." Robert didn't like the idea of delaying.

"It's not like hundreds of people catch the train here. He's bound to remember what their plans are."

"Robert, listen to reason. Get cleaned up and have yourself something to eat." His mother motioned to the stove. "We kept food warm for you. Eat and then get a good night's sleep and head out early in the morning."

He knew she was right but hated to admit defeat. To delay his search made him feel that Alice was slipping beyond his reach. He started to refuse her suggestion but finally agreed. "I guess morning will be soon enough."

Mother smiled. "Of course it will be. You'll see."

★

Alice swallowed back an angry retort as the stationmaster in Dallas explained that the train had pulled out only minutes ago.

"When is the next train?"

"Headin' north? Tomorrow," the man informed her. "Best if you take a room for the night."

"I can't afford that," Alice declared. "I have just enough money for our tickets."

"One of the pastors here takes in folks from time to time. He and his wife have spare rooms." The man smiled. "They'd most likely put you up for the night. You could leave most of your things here if you like. I can lock 'em in the office and then you wouldn't have to carry them all over town."

Alice knew there was no other choice. She took the name and address of the parsonage and asked for directions. The stationmaster cheerfully related the information, which further frustrated Alice. How could anyone be so happy in the face of her sorrow? How dare the world go on turning when her heart was clearly breaking?

"We will take only what we need for the night," she told her mother. "Pack it all here in my bag, and I'll carry it. We have a bit of a walk."

"Pity that Roy didn't stick around," Mother replied. "I know he would have driven us. Do you know he asked to call on me?" She gave a laugh. "I would have said yes if I lived here."

"We can move here, Mama," Simon insisted.

"Well, either way," Alice said, taking a few things from her bag to make room for her mother's and brother's articles, "we have to go to

444

Chicago and get your things." She knew full well that once they were in Chicago there wouldn't be money enough to return to Dallas.

The reverend Goodman and his wife, Ophelia, were an older couple who lived not far from the station. They were kind and easygoing and instantly welcomed the sad trio into their house.

"We've got a couple of extra rooms," the pastor told them. "And we believe it a part of our ministry to offer them to folks in need."

"We thank you for that," Alice's mother said. "We were to have taken the train from Cedar Springs to Chicago, but apparently there was some sort of trouble on the line. The stationmaster sent us here to Dallas, but the train we might have taken had already departed. So we find ourselves rather abandoned."

"Well, you are no longer orphaned," the man declared. "Ophelia and I are happy to help. Now, are you hungry?"

"I am," Simon said. His misery had only deepened with each new problem.

"We could all stand a meal, if it's no trouble," Alice replied. "We have no money, however."

"Nor would we take any." Mrs. Goodman *tsk*ed. She moved to take the single bag that Alice had brought. "Let me show you where your rooms are. You can wash up, and by the time you return, I'll have supper for all of you."

With a weariness that seemed to grow by the minute, Alice followed the woman. She longed to be back at the Barnett ranch, enjoying an evening of checkers with Robert and some of Hannah's tasty cinnamon rolls.

I can't let my thoughts take over like that. I have to put Robert from my mind.

Though it seemed an easy enough task, Alice knew it wouldn't be as simple to put him from her heart.

Later, as she shared a bed with her mother, Alice stared in the darkness at the ceiling. She couldn't sleep in spite of being exhausted.

"Why don't you share your heart with me," Mother told her. "It might help."

"I'm sorry," Alice said. "Did I wake you?"

"No. I've been awake and praying for you. I know you're deeply troubled. Are you sure this is the right thing to do? Leaving, I mean."

"I'm only certain of one thing, and that's that I love Robert more than life."

"Then perhaps you should return and give him a chance to speak his mind. Seems to me he cares for you, as well."

"But if he does, it would mean I came between him and his intended." Alice contemplated the matter further before speaking. "It would mean . . . well . . ."

"It would only mean that you fell in love with him without any thought to hurting anyone else. I know you wouldn't have set out to cause harm. You were never that kind of a child, and I can't believe for one minute that you've become that kind of woman."

"I'm not, but I can't help thinking how messed up everything has become. Why would God let me fall in love with someone—someone who doesn't care about how hideous I look—and then take him away?"

"First of all," Mother said, rolling to her side to face Alice. "You aren't hideous looking. You are a beautiful young woman with a scar. But that scar does not define you. Everyone has scars to bear. I have mine. And your father left me with a great many. Although you can't see them.

"And second, I'm not convinced that running away from a problem is the proper way to resolve it. I felt at first, selfishly I must say, that you should return with us to Chicago. But upon reflection, I'm not at all convinced. I can't help but think God has put these delays in our path to give you time to reconsider."

"But I can't stay and watch him marry another," Alice replied.

"Who says you will? What if Robert feels exactly the same way about you that you feel about him? Wouldn't it be better for him to end his engagement to someone he doesn't love and marry the woman he really loves? How fair would it be to Jessica Atherton if he married her only because he could not have you for his wife?"

"I don't know, Mother. I have no answers, only questions. I don't know anything anymore."

Her mother reached out and pulled her close, as she had done when

Alice was a child. The warmth of her mother's arms gave Alice a moment of comfort.

"Then pray about it, Alice. Pray and ask God to show you the answer. He has already seen tomorrow, and He knows exactly what you need and to whom you should be wed. Pray on it tonight and see if you have an answer in the morning."

★

Robert tossed and turned in his bed all night long until finally he pushed back the covers and got up. There was no sense in pretending he could sleep. By the time the tiniest hint of light showed on the horizon, he was saddled and ready to ride.

"I'll be back as soon as possible," he told his father and Jake before putting his heels to Rojoe's flank.

All the way to Cedar Springs, Robert kept thinking about the wasted time. *If the bank robbery hadn't taken place, we would have been home much sooner. I might have been here to stop her—to show her the ring and convince her of my love.*

The miles seemed endless, but it gave him more than ample time to pray. He'd tried to pray during the night. Every time he woke up, he issued another plea to God. But he didn't feel as though his prayers went any higher than the ceiling.

"I know you're with me," Robert said aloud, glancing heavenward, "and I know you hear me. So why do I feel alone in this?"

The cloudless sky offered no reply, and even Rojoe seemed to ignore him. Why was it that God let people find each other and fall in love, only to separate them again?

"Why, Lord?"

There was still no answer, no comfort, no understanding. Robert tightened his grip on the reins. He had to find her. She was already such a part of him that Robert felt as if he'd lost a limb.

"I need your help, Lord. I need to find Alice. I need to tell her that I love her."

Chapter 23

"So there we were," Will related at the breakfast table, "about to go into the jewelry store, when shots sounded from the bank across the street. Robert and I ducked into the alleyway to figure out what we might do to help, but we had no weapons."

"And I'm certain that wouldn't have stopped you," Hannah said, shaking her head.

"Well, we were tryin' to figure things out when two of the robbers ran out from the bank to the man holdin' the horses. They mounted and just then three shots rang out, and they dropped like dead weight."

"Were they dead?" Marty asked. The thought of such a thing gave her the shivers.

"No, they'd only been wounded. A Texas Ranger we know got 'em."

"All three of them taken down by one man?" Hannah asked in amazement. "He must have been a very good shot."

"His name is Austin Todd, and he plans to pay us a visit this fall," Will interjected. "He's interested in buying a small piece of land so he can build a house. He doesn't want to ranch or farm but also doesn't want to live in the confines of a town. Thought I'd take him around to some of the various ranches and see if anyone wanted to sell him some acreage. He's going to look at a parcel we have, as well."

Marty tried to ignore the conversation but found herself hopelessly drawn in once again when Will mentioned the bank manager.

"He and the teller had been shot and killed by the two bandits who robbed them. They both had families."

Hannah passed her husband a platter of ham steaks. "That's so sad. Such a violent end to a person's life."

Marty grimaced. The uneasiness she'd felt at the start of the conversation was magnified by the comment regarding the bank employees. She pushed the eggs and grits around her plate but had completely lost her appetite.

"I don't care to ever endure such a thing again," Will admitted.

"I'm with you," Jake agreed. "When you told us the story on the trip home, it made me glad we don't live in a city. I doubt I could ever live there again. Too many people and too much noise. Not to mention all the added dangers."

Hannah raised her coffee cup and took a sip before responding. "I lived in a city once. Nothing good came from it. I prefer the life we have here."

Marty thought about Denver and all that she had known there. If a person had plenty of money to spend, the city could be quite entertaining. On the other hand, the poverty she'd known in the months before leaving convinced her that without adequate funds it was sheer misery.

She hadn't really considered the problems of the city in comparison to her life here in Texas. Marty had to admit there was a peacefulness here that spoke to her spirit. Perhaps Texas wasn't to blame for her sorrows. Just then the baby moved as if in agreement.

"Seems with the economy continuin' to be bad," Will continued, "folks are gettin' more and more desperate. I imagine there will be quite a few more bank robberies before it's all said and done."

"I have to admit," Jake threw in, "there were several times in Denver when I had grave concern about our little bank. Anywhere you have money, you'll also find someone who wants to take it away. When everything started fallin' apart financially, we had so many angry customers that we all feared for our lives."

Marty's head snapped up at this. "You never told me that."

"I didn't want to worry you." Jake gave a shrug. "There wasn't anything you could do to help."

"But I should have known about the danger." She pushed back her plate and got to her feet. "I'm not hungry. Please excuse me."

Marty moved as quickly as her expanding figure would allow. She departed through the kitchen and out the back of the house with no real destination in mind. All she knew was that she had to get away from the conversation and the idea that Jake's life could have been taken at any moment during his bank work.

I was so sure banking was safer than ranching and now this. Why does life have to constantly threaten us with death?

"I'm sorry, Marty."

She turned to find Jake had followed her. Looking at him as if truly understanding him for the first time, Marty drew a heavy breath and let it out. "I never realized. I've been such a fool."

"I didn't want to frighten you. You were already so much against ranchin' because of the dangers. I figured you'd have a real hard time of it if I told you about the bank's situation."

"I should have known. I knew that things were bad, that men were rioting because they couldn't get their money. Grief, I knew people were abandoning their children, so why wouldn't they also kill and rob?"

Jake reached out and touched Marty's cheek. "Danger is everywhere. It's a reality we have to face no matter where we live or work. I don't want you livin' in fear, Marty. The Bible says that perfect love does away with fear. I know my love isn't perfect, but God's love is, and He's the only one who can do away with your fears."

"I know," Marty said, shaking her head. "But it's so hard. I love you and I love our child. I love Wyatt and Samuel and little Benjamin and can't wait until they are with us. I love my family. I can't bear the thought of losing any of them."

"Marty, folks die every day. Family and friends aren't immune to death just because we love them. But we know that death can't hold us. By givin' our hearts to Jesus, we have eternal life with Him. He's the door into heaven. If we don't go through Him, we can't get in. But you and I, we've already been accepted. There's a place for us up there." He glanced at the cloud-strewn skies. "It might take a little while before we can join up with our loved ones, but it won't be forever."

Marty nodded, knowing he was right. "I suppose death has always seemed like . . . well . . . the end. My mother died when I was born, and I never knew her. When I lost my father, I never thought about seeing him again. I just knew he was gone, and that seemed final."

"But you will see them again one day. They loved Jesus just as you do, just as I do. Death isn't the end of anything. Instead, it's a beginning."

She gave Jake a smile. "You always seem to know just what to say to make me feel better."

He pulled her into his arms. "That's my job." He kissed her lightly and then put his hand on her stomach. "Baby's gettin' mighty big. Sure lookin' forward to this little one."

Marty marveled at the love he clearly held for their unborn child. "Me too."

"Have you been thinkin' on names?"

She nodded. "I have a name in mind for a girl. Johanna—after my father John and sister Hannah. Then maybe Frances for a second name—after your mother."

"I'd like that name very much. You know my middle name is Frances—after her." He smiled and tried the name out. "Johanna Frances. Has a good strong sound to it. But what if this is a son?"

Marty considered the matter for a moment. "I still wouldn't mind using the name John."

"I wouldn't, either," Jake replied. "I was thinkin' maybe we could call him John Jacob."

"That's a perfect name. John Jacob Wythe." Marty leaned forward and kissed Jake. "That way he would be named after you, as well."

"I was thinkin' more of him bein' named for my grandfather and father, but you're right."

"I usually am," Marty countered.

He chuckled and finally released his hold on her. "I don't know about that, Mrs. Wythe. I seem to recall several occasions when you were dead wrong."

Marty's gaze traveled across the distant pasture land. "I can't imagine what you're talking about, Mr. Wythe."

★

"Are you sure they haven't been here?" Robert asked the young man at the ticket counter.

"I haven't seen anyone like that around here. Stationmaster might have seen them earlier, but he had to leave. Word came that there was a death in the family. Closed the window down until I could take over. Had a bunch of angry folks, even though it wasn't much more than ten minutes."

"I am sorry about that, but I'm desperate to find my friends." Robert looked around the Cedar Springs depot. The place bustled with activity, but there was no sign of Alice or her mother and brother.

He turned back to the ticket window. "They were headin' to Chicago."

The man nodded. "Well, they could get there any number of ways. There's still one train due out late this afternoon that's headed north. They might be taking that one."

"What time does it depart?"

"At 5:45. Heads north to Kansas City. They might take it and change trains there. Why don't you come back then. Maybe they'll be here, waiting to board."

There was really nothing else he could do. If he left to go in search of them, Robert had no idea where he would start. There were numerous hotels and restaurants. He didn't have time to visit them all.

"I think I'll just stick around here until then," he said. "Thank you for your time."

Robert crossed to the waiting area and took a seat. The gentleman across from him offered a newspaper.

"I've already read this, if you'd like to take a look," the older man declared.

Robert took the paper. "Thank you. I'm much obliged."

He looked through the pages, trying to focus on anything but the worry in his mind. What if they'd arrived in time to take the train out the night before? The stationmaster didn't think that possible, but what if they had?

The minutes ticked by as slowly as any he'd ever known. People came and went, seemingly with no cares at all. A group of gentlemen stood at one end of the room smoking cigars and discussing something that seemed of great importance. A woman with a brood of children took a seat not far from the ticket window and immediately began to share food from a basket. It reminded Robert that he'd not eaten since the night before.

He checked the clock. Still another hour to go. He tried to relax and refocus on the newspaper, but it was no use. He didn't care about the local happenings or comments on the ongoing financial troubles. He had no interest in various sales offered by Dallas merchants, and he certainly didn't care about the opinion of the editor. Folding the paper, he handed it back to its owner.

"Thank you."

The man nodded and smiled. "Where are you headed?"

"I'm not," Robert replied. "I'm waiting for someone."

"Ah, I'm Kansas City bound myself."

Robert nodded, but had no desire to keep up with the small talk. "If you'll excuse me." He got to his feet and headed outside for a breath of fresh air.

Clouds had begun to build. It looked like they might be in for a storm before nightfall. Robert didn't like the idea of having to return to the ranch in the rain. If he managed to find Alice and her family, he'd suggest they wait it out until morning. It was getting much too late to travel all the way home.

Pacing the depot platform, Robert tried to think of what he'd say to Alice. It was important that she understand his heart. He didn't want her thinking she'd done anything to come between him and Jess.

As if anyone could come between two people who truly loved each other.

A whistle sounded from one of the locomotives several tracks away. A freight train moved forward ever so slowly. The rail yards seemed just as busy as the depot. Robert looked at his pocket watch. Half an hour. In half an hour he would be with Alice again. In thirty minutes he would propose to the woman he loved. At least he hoped as much.

But what if she isn't taking this train? What will I do then? No one has the address for her mother's place in Chicago. I don't even know what train she might be on so I could wire ahead and have her return to Texas.

There was no sense borrowing trouble. If they didn't show up, Robert knew he would figure something out. He wasn't going to lose Alice—not if he had anything to say about it.

I'm just gonna keep a positive attitude. I'm gonna expect the best.

But in thirty minutes nothing had changed. Robert returned to the waiting area to search for Alice, but she wasn't there. More passengers arrived by the minute to board the train, but none of them were Alice. By the time the 5:45 pulled out, Robert felt his hopes drain away.

There was nothing left to do but head back home. Dejected, Robert exited the depot to find it had begun to sprinkle. His stomach growled. The hollow feeling seemed appropriate.

Chapter 24

"I wrote my friends in Diboll," Jake announced. "The two docs I was tellin' you about. One's a lady doctor."

Hannah smiled. "Good. It's about time we had a few of those."

"Well, since you talked about the old doc in Cedar Springs, I thought I'd put out the word that we could use a couple of younger doctors. I don't know if they'd ever consider leavin' Diboll, but I figured it was worth a try. I don't want Marty to be without a good doctor."

"Oh, you shouldn't fret, Jake. Women have been having babies without doctors for centuries. I've even known doctors to refuse deliveries because that's something a midwife could handle. If I were you, I'd just relax. I've delivered babies before, and I'm sure I can deliver this one just as well."

Jake hated that he sounded ungrateful for the care Hannah had given her sister. "Oh, I know you're well trained. I've been real impressed with the way you take care of everybody around here. I hope you'll forgive me for implying otherwise."

Hannah handed him one of the freshly baked cookies she'd just taken from the pan. "Jake, there's nothing to forgive. You're just being mindful of your wife's needs. I admire that. And frankly, I would like to have a lady doctor around."

Marty entered the room with her nose up in the air. "Do I smell your cinnamon sugar cookies?" She spied the pan and gave a squeal of delight. "Oh, I did. You have no idea how much I've craved those."

"You should have said something," Hannah chided. "I would have made you a batch every day."

"And I'd be four times this size," Marty replied, patting her abdomen.

"You're a perfect size, and cravings are natural for expectant mothers. Here, have a cookie. They still need to cool, but I'll put a stack of them on a plate for you, and you can eat to your heart's delight."

Marty took the cookie and bit into it. A look of satisfaction and pleasure filled her face. "Mmm, just as I remembered."

Jake had already devoured his cookie and was hopeful that Hannah would hand out more right away. She seemed to read his mind and did just that. Jake offered no resistance.

"So when should we expect the boys?" Hannah asked Marty.

"Almost anytime. We sent the money. In fact, we sent extra to make sure the boys had what they needed. Mr. Brentwood is making arrangements for them. He doesn't want them to travel by themselves, so he's trying to find someone to accompany them. He said he might be able to secure a chaperone within the week."

"That's wonderful. We should have your place completely ready for their arrival. Although I do wish you'd stay here until the baby is born."

"It's not like you're that far away," Marty replied. "You told me first babies are usually long in coming, so I should have plenty of time to send Jake or someone else to fetch you."

Jake knew that Marty had her heart set on moving the boys right into their new home. "I think I'd best get back to work. I promised Will that I'd have that new pen built by the time they came back from the Reids' with those new geldings."

He cast a glance at Marty. "You doin' all right?"

She smiled. "I'm doing just fine. Stop worrying."

He nodded and made his exit without another word. Approaching the new pen, he could see that the other men had been hard at work. It was nearly complete. The worst job had been digging postholes. After that, the rest almost seemed easy.

"You fellas made good progress," he said.

"Had to, since you ran off," an older man named Bert declared. He threw Jake a grin. "But I guess if I had a pretty wife about to have a baby, I'd wanna check up on her, too."

Jake knew that Bert had once worked for Marty and went to work for William when she moved to Colorado. He rather hoped the man might want to return with them to Marty's ranch. He was going to need all the help he could get, and Bert knew the ranch better than anyone else.

"Say, Bert, you ever think about leavin' this place?"

Bert straightened from his work. "Leave the Barnetts'? What'd you have in mind?"

"I know you worked the Olson ranch after Marty was widowed. I wondered if you'd like to come back and work for me. I don't have much money just yet, but your room and board would definitely be covered. Marty and I plan to sell off a few head this fall, so I could give you part of that in wages owed."

Bert took off his hat and wiped his brow. "I reckon I'd be right honored to come back. Always enjoyed the work there. How quick were you two plannin' to return?"

"Soon. We want to get settled in before the orphans we're adopting arrive."

Nate, one of the boys who'd come to live with the Barnetts the year before, perked up at this. "Who's coming—if you don't mind my asking?"

"Not at all," Jake replied. "There are three of 'em. Wyatt is the oldest. Then there's Samuel and Benjamin."

"I remember Wyatt but not the other two. I know they're going to love it here. I never had a real home until the Barnetts took me in."

Jake couldn't imagine not having a close family connection. "What happened to your folks?"

The sixteen-year-old shrugged. "My mom died when I was young, and my pa just sort of drifted. I was passed around from one family to another. We didn't have no other folks. Finally one of the families learned that my pa had died of typhoid fever. They decided enough was enough and turned me over to the orphanage."

Jake thought it sad to have been so unwanted. "How old were you?"

"Eleven."

"Most folks would have found a boy like you to be an asset. You could have easily helped out with the workload, if nothing else." Jake realized that sounded as though the boy were only good for labor.

Nate didn't seem to notice. "There wasn't much for me to do in the city. I was in school during the day, and when I came home there were chores to do, but not like here. Most of the folks who took me in were poor as church mice, and I was just another mouth to feed."

"Well, I'm sure glad you came to Texas. Down here folks know the value of a young man like you. I'm sure you've more than earned your keep. I heard Hannah say that you two were a real pleasure to have around."

Bert joined in at this. "Him and Hiram are two of the best greenhorns I ever had to train. He learned quick and that's always good."

"I'm glad you and the missus are adopting those boys. It'll be good for them to have a real home and somebody who cares about them." Nate picked up a long rail. "I'm gonna need help attaching this to the corner post."

Jake pulled on his gloves and followed the boy to where the rail would be secured. Listening to Nate's story had touched him in an unexpected way. Marty had told him stories about the children, but they remained just that . . . stories. Now it all became much more.

Jake hadn't really considered how adoption might affect the lives of those children. He'd only considered how it might affect his life and Marty's. It shamed him to think that he'd not even thought to find out the story of each of the boys. Where had they come from? Who were their people, and how could they just abandon their children?

★

The sound of a wagon drew Marty's attention to the front window. The large freight wagon pulled to a stop out in the drive, and Marty could see that Mrs. Chesterfield was sitting atop with the driver.

"Goodness, Mrs. Chesterfield is back," she announced when Hannah came to investigate.

"Are Alice and Simon with her?" Her voice betrayed hopefulness.

Marty could see the two climbing down from the wagon. "Yes! I'm so glad. This will mean the world to Robert." She flung open the door and made her way outside.

"Alice!" Marty went to the younger woman and embraced her. "I thought I might never see you again."

The driver helped Mrs. Chesterfield from the wagon. She seemed quite pleased with herself, and Marty wasn't sure if it was the fact that they'd returned to the ranch or the company of the driver.

"Roy James, ma'am," the man announced, tipping his hat as Hannah came alongside. "No relation to Jesse." He chuckled heartily, and Marty found that she instantly liked the man. "I drive freight outta Dallas to Cedar Springs and beyond. Headin' up Denton way today."

Hannah extended her hand. "I'm pleased to meet you. I'm Hannah Barnett. Why don't we go inside and I'll prepare some refreshments."

"I'd be pleased to do so," he declared.

Marty remained with Alice as the others made their way into the house. "What in the world were you thinking?"

"You got my letter, didn't you?"

"Yes, and your Bible. Grief, Alice, you nearly sent me into labor," Marty said in a stern reprimand. "Don't ever do that again."

"I don't know that I can remain here," Alice answered, "but I knew I had to come back and try to explain my heart to Robert."

"You won't have to explain much. The poor man went half mad when he learned you were gone. He took one look at your letter to him and was ready to charge off in search. We finally convinced him to wait until morning. He hasn't returned yet."

"He came looking for me?" Alice asked in disbelief.

"Yes, silly. He's half over the moon in love with you."

Alice's mouth dropped open and her eyes widened. "He is?"

Marty laughed. "I guess love truly is blind, but the answer is yes. He had fully planned for the two of you to talk things out when he returned from Fort Worth with . . ." Marty decided against mentioning the ring Robert had purchased. "With the others," she finally added.

"That means I destroyed his chance for a life with Miss Atherton." She shook her head. "I never meant for that to happen. I didn't set out to fall in love. It just happened."

"There was never going to be happiness for Robert if he married Jess. He knew that, and so did she. They ended any possibility of that weeks ago."

"But he said nothing."

"You weren't listening," Marty insisted. "He tried on more than one occasion to get you alone. He said you went out of your way to avoid him."

Alice nodded and dropped her gaze to the ground. "I did. I thought if I stayed out of his way, kept myself from any hint of intimacy, that we'd both be better off for it."

"And were you?"

Alice let out a heavy breath and raised her head. "No."

"Well, you're back now and that's all that matters. I don't know when Robert will return, but when he does, I hope I'm around to see the reunion. It's gonna be a doozy."

With Alice at her side, Marty made her way into the house. Hannah had already seen to it that a plate of her cookies was positioned on a side table and was just returning with a tray holding tall glasses of sweet tea.

"Mr. James, will you drive all the way back to Dallas tonight?" Hannah asked. "You don't have to, you know. We can put you up." She offered him tea and he took a glass.

"No, ma'am, that won't be necessary. Like I said earlier, I've gotta make my way up to Denton. I've got friends up that way, and I'll spend the night with them."

Hannah nodded and served the others. When everyone was settled with a glass and cookies, she finally took a seat. "Well, I'm glad you were available to bring our friends home."

"I had the pleasure of their company on the way to Dallas, and when they looked me up this morning, I couldn't help but assist them in returning. The company is the best I've had in years." He turned to Mrs. Chesterfield and winked. The woman blushed and looked at her hands as the man added, "I hope to share it again."

Hannah looked at Marty and smiled. It was easy enough to see that the older couple was already sweet on each other.

"I'm gonna go out and see your horse, Alice," Simon announced. He held a cookie in each hand. "I'll bet he's gotten bigger."

"Simon, we've only been gone a day." Alice sat down beside Marty on the couch and sighed. "You'd think we'd been away for weeks."

The boy shrugged. "Well, I hope we aren't gonna leave again. I want to stay here forever."

Mrs. Chesterfield shook her head as Simon barreled out of the room. "I swear that boy has the energy of a wildcat. He wears me out, but it does me so much good to see him happy again." She looked to Hannah. "I was wondering if maybe you could use a housekeeper."

Hannah nodded. "I'm sure I could use the help. If Robert has his way, he'll marry Alice and start having a family before we know it, and I'll want all the free time I can get to spoil my grandchildren."

Marty looked at Alice. She was clearly embarrassed by the declaration but said nothing.

From her position by the window Marty could hear a rider approaching. She leaned forward to glance out and saw it was Robert. She couldn't help but grin. "Oh, this ought to be really good."

The others looked at her in confusion, but it was Hannah who posed the question. "What are you talking about?"

"Robert just rode in."

The room went silent. All gazes shifted to Alice. The younger woman was biting her lip and twisting her hands together. Marty reached over and stilled her hands.

"Remember, he's just as much in love with you as you are with him."

Alice said nothing and even the boisterous Mr. James remained quiet. It was as if the entire house held its breath in anticipation of Robert's arrival. They didn't have long to wait.

"Ma!" he called at the top of his lungs. He was coming in from the back of the house from the sound of it.

Marty squeezed Alice's hands and dropped her hold.

"Ma, are you sure you don't have Mrs. Chesterfield's address in Chicago? I couldn't find—" He fell silent the moment he stepped into the room.

Marty watched his face as he caught sight of the party gathered there. She might have laughed at her nephew's stunned expression, but without warning he crossed the room and pulled Alice up from the couch.

461

Then without so much as an explanation, Robert hoisted her over his shoulder like a sack of beans and headed for the door.

"We need to talk," he declared.

Once the couple was gone from sight, the entire room erupted in laughter. "She's in for it now," Mrs. Chesterfield said. "Did you see the look on her face?"

Hannah shook her head. "If I'm any judge of people, I'd say Robert is in for it, as well." She shrugged and held up her glass of tea in a toast. "I guess we're to be in-laws. Here's to us."

Ravinia Chesterfield raised her glass. "To Robert and Alice."

Chapter 25

Alice had the wind knocked from her when her body hit Robert's rock-hard shoulder. His strides only made matters worse as he stormed out of the house and across the yard. He headed in the direction of the river and ranted all the way.

"I can't believe you would go runnin' off like that. Scared a dozen years off my life. I never in my life seen a woman more stubborn and irritatin'. Here I was half sick with worry and wonderin' how in the world I was ever gonna find you in Chicago, and you just turn up here pretty as you please."

Alice tried to comment, but it was hard enough just to get her breath. "You . . . don't . . . have . . . to—"

"And how many times do I have to tell you that there's nothin' between Jessica and me. Just because folks expected us to marry didn't mean we were gonna marry. I tried to tell you that I felt nothin' for her except brotherly love. But you wouldn't listen."

Again Alice tried to speak. "Robert . . . you need . . . to . . . put me . . . down."

"You know, it just never fails to amaze me how folks can get their minds made up about a thing and not let it go. I put an end to any weddin' plans weeks ago. I wanted to tell you, but you kept avoiding me. I swear you were harder to corner than a badger."

He finally stopped, and Alice could see they were at the ravine above the river. Several cottonwoods shaded the sun and made a rather pleasant setting. Alice struggled against Robert's hold, and he finally put her down.

Fixing him with a stare, Alice gulped in air. However, he didn't give her time to comment. "I don't love Jessica Atherton. For your information, I've loved you since we first met. You did something to me deep in my heart." He thumped his hand against his chest. "I know Marty was worried that I only cared about you because you'd been hurt—" he paused, shaking his head—"but that wasn't the reason."

Alice decided it was better to remain silent and let him speak his mind. His face seemed to contort between expressions of love and anger. Alice thought him the handsomest man she'd ever known, even with the two-day growth of stubble on his face. Truth be told, she'd loved him from first sight.

"I love you because of who you are inside. You're thoughtful and kind, gentle and lovin'. I've watched you with your brother and seen how you came around to forgivin' your ma. You brood over Marty like a mother hen to her chicks. I've seen you work, too. You've helped my ma in more ways than one."

He began to pace before her. "When I found out you were gone, I thought I was gonna be sick. I read your letter, and when I saw that you loved me, too, it only made me all the more determined to find you and set things right. Instead, I chased all over the countryside only to lose any sign of you. Do you know how I felt when I realized you were probably already on your way to Chicago?"

Alice started to answer, but Robert continued his tirade. Turning, he pointed a finger at her. "Well, it wasn't good. I can tell you that. Fact is, it liked to have killed me. I hate big cities, but I hated more thinkin' that I'd never see you again."

With her hands on her hips and her brow raised in question, Alice finally had a chance to speak. "Are you done?"

Robert seemed surprised by this. He started to comment but then closed his mouth and knelt on one knee. "Not quite." He fumbled in

464

his pocket, and when he extended his hand toward her, Alice could see he was holding a ring.

"Will you marry me?"

A smile formed on her lips. He really was the man of her prayers. "I thought you'd never ask." She reached out to take the ring.

But instead of giving it to her, Robert rose and slipped it on her finger. He started to embrace her for a kiss, but Alice held him back. "I've never been kissed by a man, and I'd like to wait until we're married."

Robert studied her face for a moment, and Alice wasn't at all sure what was going through his mind. He reached up and tenderly ran his hand down her scarred face.

"I've held back from that kind of intimacy, as well. Never thought I'd meet up with someone who felt the same way. I'd be honored to wait." He took hold of her hand and kissed the back of it in genteel fashion. Lifting his head, he gave her a lopsided grin. "So long as you don't keep me waiting too long."

"How about a few weeks?" she asked. "We could marry in June."

"Why June?"

"That will give my mother time to collect her things in Chicago and get moved down here. She's going to work for your mother."

"Truly?" He chuckled. "Well, looks like we'll have all our family around us." He stopped and frowned. "You know I don't intend to live anywhere else, don't you? This is my home, and Pa told me that he wants to rearrange things right away so that we have the east wing of the main house to ourselves."

She smiled. "I wouldn't want to live anywhere else. Texas and this ranch suit me just fine." Now it was her turn to frown. "But what if Mr. Smith tracks me down here? There's still that complication to contend with. I don't trust him to give up just because we left Denver."

"If he shows his sorry face around here, I'll deal with him," Robert said in a most protective way.

His declaration warmed Alice's heart. She would finally truly be safe and happy. She gazed back across the field toward the house. "I suppose we should go tell them we plan to marry."

He took hold of her arm. "I think they probably already know, but it can't hurt to make it official."

Alice paused and looked at the man who would be her husband. "I love you, Robert."

He grinned. "And I love you, but if you keep lookin' at me that way I'm gonna haul you off to the justice of the peace right now."

★

That evening at the supper table the conversation was all about the changes that would be made to the main house.

"I think maybe we should keep Ravinia and Simon in the Montoya house," Robert's mother said. "Alice can live there, too, of course, until she and Robert marry." She glanced at her husband. "Couldn't we just build ourselves a little place—maybe over by the river?"

"I suppose we could."

Robert looked at his bride-to-be and then to his parents. "I don't want you to go to all that trouble and expense. Alice and I talked about it, and there's no reason we can't all live under one roof."

Marty put her fork down. "You know, he's right."

"Well, we wanted to afford them some privacy," Mother replied. "After all, they need time to get to know each other without a lot of folks hanging over them."

"Might I offer a solution?" Mrs. Chesterfield asked.

"Of course," Father said.

Robert winked at Simon, who was fidgeting in his seat, anxious for dessert. A tremendous feeling of relief washed over him as he realized everything would be exactly as he'd hoped. He offered a silent prayer of thanks.

"What do you think about that, Robert?"

He looked to his mother in confusion. "I'm sorry. I didn't hear what was said."

Father laughed. "Better get your head outta the clouds, son. There's a lot of work to be done before that weddin'."

"I was just prayin'. Thankin' God for His mercy . . . and for Alice."

She blushed at this and put her attention on the food. Mother quickly picked up the discussion. "Ravinia has suggested that she and Simon live here in the house for at least the first year, while you and Alice take the Montoya place."

Robert grinned. "I think that would work out well for all of us. Thank you, Mrs. Chesterfield."

"You can start calling me Mother Chesterfield, if you'd like."

"I'd like that very much." He glanced at Simon and smiled. "And you're gonna be my little brother. I always wanted a brother." Robert then took pity on the poor boy. "But, Ma, I think if you don't serve up that custard pie, Simon is gonna waste away." Everyone laughed except Simon, who was nodding most enthusiastically.

After dinner, while the women cleared the table, Robert and his father had a chance to talk. Robert relished these times. They'd always been close, and he couldn't imagine doing anything without his father's support.

"So, do you approve of my marryin' Alice?"

Father seemed surprised by this question and narrowed his eyes. "Haven't I made that clear? I think Alice is a fine woman. She's gonna fit into our family just right. Fact is, she's everything I ever prayed your wife would be."

"You prayed about my wife?"

"Don't sound so shocked," Father replied, easing down into his favorite leather chair.

Robert took a seat, as well. "I guess I never thought about it."

"Well, since you'll no doubt be a father one day, you ought to give it some thought. Prayin' for your children is something you do on a daily basis. You pray for their safety and health. You pray for their happiness. You pray they'll make good decisions. And you pray for the people who will touch their lives, especially when it comes to a spouse."

"And you've been prayin' about mine."

"Since the first day you were born."

Robert shook his head. "I never knew."

Father chuckled. "Son, you don't know the half of it, but one day you will."

"I know that I want to be as happy as you and Ma have been. I've

467

never seen two people more suited to each other. Folks are always sayin' it's like you were meant to be together from the beginnin' of time."

"I like to think so, too. Your mother completes me. I didn't even know that something was missin' until I met her. She's caused me no end of grief at times, but also no end of love." He paused and rubbed his chin. "You know, there will be times of grief and anger. You can't avoid those things in life."

"I do know. But I also remember your tellin' me that when we belong to God, we don't have to bear those things alone. I want to be a good husband to Alice."

"Then stay close to God, son. If you're right with the Lord, everything else will fall into place. It doesn't mean there won't be ups and downs, but He will be a strong support in times of need."

Robert knew that support already. His faith was a stronghold in which he found security and love.

Alice appeared at the opening to the dining room. "They've kicked me out of the kitchen and said I should spend some time with you, Robert."

He got to his feet and crossed the room to take hold of her arm. "Why, I'd be plumb pleased to spend the evenin' with you. Why don't we go on out to the barn and take a look at your colt?"

"I would enjoy that very much."

"Now, don't you two go gettin' carried away," Father warned. "I know a thing or two about rolls in the hay."

Robert looked at him in mock horror. "You and Ma—rollin' in the hay? And I thought my folks were respectable."

Father laughed. "Respectable, yes. But with a flood of feelin's for each other. Now, you two go on before I change my mind. I could always find a chore for you to do, Robert."

"Yes, sir!" He pushed Alice toward the door. "We're movin'."

The night skies held an abundance of stars. The earlier clouds had moved out, and now there was nothing to keep them from seeing the vast expanse of the heavens.

"It's so beautiful," Alice said, gazing upward. "I've never known anything like this."

"I never want to know anything else," Robert said softly. "Except for you."

She trembled slightly, and Robert worried that she would catch a chill. "Are you cold?"

"No," Alice whispered. "Just overcome by my heart and the way I feel about you. I never thought true love would come along for me after the attack. Oh, I hoped it would. Your aunt and I used to talk about there being a good man somewhere who wouldn't mind my scarred face."

Robert stopped and turned Alice to face him. "When I look into your eyes and see the love you have for me shinin' back, I don't see the scar. You are an incredible woman, Alice. I wanna have children with you and grow old with you. And when I die, I wanna be buried next to you."

"I feel the same way," she said in a barely audible voice. "I'll never want for anything more than that."

★

Jake and Marty retired to their bedroom. The day had been quite productive, and Marty was more than a little tired. She yawned and rolled her head to ease the tension in her neck. Jake led her to a chair and had her take a seat. He began kneading her sore muscles.

"The house is nearly ready," he told her. "Once I hang those curtains for you, we'll be ready for the boys. I hope goin' back there won't be too hard on you."

Marty shook her head. "I thought a great deal about that. When I went there with Hannah, I took some time to just walk around the place. I have to admit I was worried that I'd only be able to think of Thomas, but it wasn't that way.

"We had a good life there and I know you and I can have a good one there, too." She closed her eyes and enjoyed the feel of Jake's skillful hands. The tension drained away and made her all the more sleepy, but she wanted to assure Jake that all was well.

"I realized something as I walked around the yard."

"What was that?"

"I missed the place. I missed my flower beds and garden. I missed the trees we'd planted. I felt a sense of coming home. It took me completely by surprise, but it comforted me in a way I hadn't expected."

"That's how I felt in comin' back to Texas. At least in the beginning." He stopped and came around to the front to kneel down beside her chair. "Texas was my home, and I spent the last few years longing to return. When I got down here, I thought that I could finally be happy. But I wasn't."

Marty hadn't expected this declaration. "Why not?"

He gave her a hint of a smile. "Because you weren't here. That's when I realized that my home wasn't really Texas anymore—it is with you. I've given it a lot of thought, Marty, and if you don't want to stay here, we won't. After the boys and the baby come, if you're of a mind for us to move elsewhere, we will. But I wanna be ranchin' no matter where we go."

Marty touched his cheek, and love for her husband swelled within her heart. "You would do that for me?"

"Yes. That and so much more. I want you to be happy, Marty."

She pulled him close and hugged him as best she could. "I am happy, Jacob Wythe. I'm happy with you, and I'm happy to remain in Texas."

Chapter 26

JUNE 1894

"The train is late," Marty declared. She had argued with her sister and husband, insisting that she accompany them to Cedar Springs. Neither thought her in any condition to take the long ride, but Marty wouldn't hear of not going.

"Those are my boys, and I will be there to welcome them! If you won't take me with you, I'll saddle a horse and ride there." She had stood her ground, and finally everyone gave in and let her accompany them to town. Marty knew they understood she would do exactly as she had threatened.

Now, as she paced the depot waiting area, Marty could only focus on the clock. "Why are they late? You don't suppose there was trouble on the line, do you?" She looked to Jake for an answer. "Should we inquire?"

"Marty, you've got to settle down. You promised you'd take it easy," Jake reminded her.

"I'm just walking back and forth," she said. "It's warm in here. I think I'd be more comfortable out on the platform."

"So long as you stay out of the sun," Hannah commanded. "I won't have you overheating and getting sunstroke just as you're about to gain three sons."

Marty nodded and started toward the door. Jake was instantly at her side, helping her. "You really should have stayed home. I don't know what got into me lettin' you come along."

"Well, it's not like you could've stopped me," Marty said, giving him a stern look. "I still know how to hitch a buggy or ride a horse, and I truly would have done it."

Jake laughed. "I can just see you and your expanding middle up atop a horse. But I know how stubborn you can be, and I doubt it would surprise me if you tried it. But if you try it before you safely deliver my son or daughter, I'll put you over my knee."

It was Marty's turn to laugh. "With all this extra weight I'm carrying, you'd be sorry for it."

"You're still no bigger than a mite," he replied, shaking his head. "And I don't think I've ever seen you quite so beautiful."

Just then the train whistle could be heard off in the distance. Marty ran to the edge of the platform to look down the track. She might have fallen over if it hadn't been for Jake's quick thinking.

"Marty, you seem bound and determined to get yourself hurt. Now, step back here. The train will be here soon enough."

The air was heavy and damp with humidity, and the sun made everything seem unbearable. Marty wasn't about to say as much, however. The last thing she wanted was Jake ordering her back into the depot. She allowed her husband to lead her away from the edge of the platform.

"I hope they're all right. I hope the trip hasn't been too hard on them."

"I'm sure they're fine, Marty. Mr. Brentwood found that woman who was willing to travel with them, and I'm sure she managed quite well."

The locomotive engine came into view, chugging and puffing thick black smoke. The whistle sounded again, and Marty could barely keep herself standing still. She had thought constantly about the boys since Jake had agreed to adopt them. She knew the boys would be half out of their minds with excitement to take the trip and to gain a mother and a father.

The train approached the station. The engine and coal car passed by, as well as the mail car and several baggage cars. It seemed to take forever to stop the behemoth, but finally it came to a rest with the passenger cars neatly positioned beside the platform.

The conductor descended from the steps of the car and placed a little step stool on the ground. "All off for Cedar Springs. Next stop Dallas."

Marty pressed forward despite Jake's hold. "Do you see them?"

"Not yet," he replied.

She craned her neck to see around several people who had come to board the train. "I can't see anything. Maybe we should get closer." She knew that there would most likely be more passengers getting on the train than debarking, but even so, she wasn't about to be pushed aside.

"Excuse me," she told one stocky older man. "My children are coming off that train."

And then she finally saw them. Wyatt stepped down first, aided by a porter. Next came Samuel and finally Benjamin, who was being carried by a middle-aged woman.

Wyatt saw her first and came running. "Mama!"

That single word hit Marty like a ton of bricks. She was his mother now. Wrapping her arms around the little boy, Marty began to cry. "I'm so happy to see you."

Samuel and Benjamin followed suit until Marty was being hugged from every side. "I can't believe you're finally here. Oh, how I've missed you. And look, you've all grown so much since I left."

Wyatt patted her stomach. "You growed, too, Mama."

She laughed but tears welled in her eyes. "I'm going to have a baby."

"Do we really get to ride a horse?" Samuel asked, pulling away. He frowned. "Why are you crying?" Wyatt and Benjamin stepped back, as well, and awaited an answer.

Marty smiled. "These are tears of happiness."

"Are you really going to have a baby?" Wyatt asked.

She nodded. "I am, and it will be your little brother or sister. I'm going to depend on each of you to be good big brothers."

Benjamin hugged her again. "I'll be good," he promised.

"Ahem." Jake cleared his throat. "I'd kind of like to meet my sons."

Marty regained control and wiped her eyes. "Boys, this is your new papa. He's a good and fair man, and he already loves each of you dearly."

The boys were shy in meeting Jake. Wyatt was the first to step closer.

"I'm Wyatt," he told Jake. "I used to have another papa but not anymore."

Jake squatted down and offered Wyatt a smile. "I'm mighty glad to meet you, Wyatt. I've always wanted a son."

"I'm Sam, and this is my brother Benjamin," Samuel introduced.

Jake nodded to each of them. "I hope you all know how much we want you to be part of our family. You boys are mighty special, and I'm gonna do my best to be a good pa to all of you."

"I'm Sarah Mitchell," a woman declared from behind the boys. "Mr. Brentwood paid my way to Dallas if I would accompany the boys here." She smiled, and Marty went immediately to the woman.

"Thank you so much for bringing them. I've missed them more than I can even tell. Would you like to join us for lunch?"

"All aboard for Dallas," the conductor called.

The woman glanced over her shoulder. "I've got to return to the train. My mother lives in Dallas, and she's not been well. Mr. Brentwood's advertisement for a companion to these children was an answer to our prayers." She handed Marty a small traveling case. "This is all they have, but I'm sure you knew they'd arrive with very little."

Nodding, Marty took the case, only to have Jake quickly retrieve it from her. "Thank you, Miss Mitchell," he said.

"It was my pleasure. They were quite excited about the trip, but they are good children." She smiled at the trio. "Boys, I hope you enjoy your new home."

With a little wave she turned toward the train. Marty watched the woman climb the steps and disappear into the train car. How strange to be so grateful to a complete stranger who shared only a few moments in her life.

"Well, I'm bettin' you boys are hungry," Jake said. "We've got plans to have a meal at a little place around the corner. I'll put your case in the wagon, and then if you like, we can walk there while Marty and her sister, Hannah, bring the wagon."

This met with everyone's approval, and Jake led the way back through the depot and out a door on the opposite side. Marty followed close behind and saw her sister waiting near the exit. Jake paused and introduced the boys to their new aunt. Hannah embraced each of them. She didn't seem in the least concerned that her action would put anyone off.

"I'm very happy to meet all of you. I'm your aunt Hannah."

"Do you have horses?" Samuel asked.

Hannah laughed. "I do, and I'll be happy to show them to you when we get back to the ranch."

The warmth of the day started to overwhelm Marty. She felt flushed and then dizzy. "Jake, I think I need to sit down."

He handed the case over to Hannah and quickly took hold of Marty. "I told you comin' here was too much for you, but you wouldn't listen." He helped her to a chair. "Next time I'm not takin' no for an answer."

"Mama, are you sick?" Wyatt asked. The boys crowded around her in worry.

"Your mama is gonna be fine," Jake assured them. "She's too stubborn to be sick."

"Come on, boys, let's bring the wagon up close so your mama doesn't have far to walk." Marty was grateful that Hannah took charge. She hated that Jake was right and the trip had proved more than she should have undertaken. She knew it would only worry him if she mentioned the pains she had started to have.

★

Alice busied herself with laundry while awaiting the return of the others. Her mother was otherwise occupied with entertaining Mr. James, who had just stopped by on his way back to Dallas. He laughingly had told them it wasn't out of his way and seemed only right, but Alice knew better. She couldn't help but smile to herself. Her mother and Mr. James had become quite close, and even Simon seemed to like the man.

She may very well get hitched before I do. And wouldn't that be something?

Alice and Robert had set the date of their wedding for the twenty-third of June, and that day was fast approaching. Of course there had been so much work to do in preparation that Alice didn't have time to be bored and worry over such matters.

With Hannah and Marty's help, she and her mother had designed and sewn Alice's wedding dress. Being a practical woman, Alice hadn't wanted to worry about an elaborate white gown and instead settled on a sensible gown that could be used again and again.

After all, the country was still suffering, and even here at the ranch they needed to tighten the belt. Hannah and Marty had insisted there be a big wedding celebration at the ranch, but Alice would have been just as happy to marry Robert in a small family ceremony.

"Alice, come see what Robert's doing," Simon called from a pen near the barn.

"I'm busy hanging the laundry. Can't it wait?"

"Nope. He's riding one of those new horses, and it's throwing him all around."

Alice felt her heart jump to her throat. Leaving the basket of clothes, she hurried to where her brother waited. "Where?"

"Over behind the barn," he said, pointing. "In that big pen they use for working with the horses." He looked at her as if she should know this already. "He's just started riding the new bay."

She didn't wait to hear any more. Making her way to the pen, Alice whispered a silent prayer for Robert's safety. She didn't want to be a widow before she got the chance to be a bride.

Clasping her hand to her mouth, Alice caught sight of the event. Several of the ranch hands were standing at the sides of the pen. A few were sitting atop the fence, and all were cheering Robert on in his endeavors.

Alice could hardly bear to watch. The gelding was not happy to have a rider and was doing his best to eliminate him.

"Isn't it great!" Simon declared more than asked.

"I thought Robert said they were already saddle broke." Alice didn't see a thing about this horse that spoke of being trained in any way.

"Mr. Reid taught them to wear a saddle, and now Robert's going to teach them to allow a rider," Simon told her. "He said it's always hard to get horses used to having someone on their backs, and they have to do this to get them trained. Sometimes it takes a long time, and sometimes just a short time." Simon grinned up at his sister. "Robert's teaching me all about horses."

The bay bucked a few more times, but Robert held fast. Alice found it hard to breathe as she continued to watch. Was this what it would be like to be a rancher's wife—always worrying about the dangers her husband faced? No wonder Marty had been wary of returning.

Finally the horse seemed to realize who was in charge and settled down. Robert walked it around the pen several times and then encouraged it to speed up to a trot. The bay responded well, and the ranch hands nodded their approval as Robert passed by.

After another fifteen minutes of working with the animal, Robert finally halted the bay and climbed down. "He's a good one," he declared. "I think he's gonna make a fine cow horse. He learns fast." Robert relinquished the reins to Nate, who in turn led the horse off to another pen.

"Where's the roan?" Robert asked.

Alice swallowed the lump in her throat. Was he going to do this again? She shuddered and moved away from where she'd watched the affair. She didn't care to see it again.

She finished hanging the laundry, all the while thinking of the dangers her beloved had to face. Robert loved this life. She knew that full well, and it would not suit either of them if she were to voice a complaint.

"Lord, I don't mean to be afraid," she whispered as she headed into the house. "It's just that I'm not at all familiar with living on a ranch. Help me not to be afraid. Help me to leave Robert in your hands."

She felt tears come to her eyes and chided herself. "You're being silly, Alice. You don't want anyone to see you like this, so you have to get a hold of yourself."

Drawing in a deep breath, Alice paused at the back door and gazed around the yard. Despite the dry conditions, recent rains had caused most everything to green up. There was still a considerable amount of dry, brown vegetation strewn across the landscape, but it was the refreshed grass that caught her eye. She let out her breath in a slow steady manner and felt a sense of peace settle on her.

The thought of Robert getting hurt still troubled her, but Alice knew that as a rancher's wife she would have to be strong. Maybe stronger than she'd ever had to be before.

Inside the house, Mother was finishing up the final sweeping. The vision brought back memories of days long past when the older woman had done things in a similar fashion in their own home. For a moment, Alice could only watch. She thought of how hard it had been to accept her mother's still being alive and the deceit of her father. Now, however, Alice felt only joy at having her family back.

Mother spied her watching and halted her work. "Is something wrong?"

Alice smiled. "No, I was just remembering when I was a little girl and you would sweep our house. It seems like a thousand years ago instead of just a few."

"I remember teaching you to make strawberry jam," her mother said, leaning on the broom. "It is one of my favorite memories. You were only nine. Do you remember?"

She did. It had been such a wonderful experience. It was really the first time Alice had done much of anything in the kitchen. "I loved sampling the jam." She laughed. "I remember you worried that none of it would make it to the jars."

Mother chuckled. "I think you ate as much as you canned."

Alice sobered. "I'm sorry you were so unhappy, Mother. Those days seemed fairly pleasant to me. I knew you and Father argued from time to time, but I figured that was what married folks did. I'm sorry that I couldn't have somehow made it better for you and Simon."

Putting the broom aside, Mother came to take hold of Alice's arms. "That was never your job. Besides, it's in the past. We must let go of the awfulness of those ways in which we were wronged and look to a better future. If not, we are destined to bring even more sorrow upon ourselves."

"I'm glad you came here. I'm glad you're back in my life," Alice said and hugged her mother close.

The sound of an approaching wagon caused both women to end their reminiscing and instead head to the front door. Alice could see that it was Hannah and the others. She smiled at the sight of Wyatt, Samuel, and Benjamin hanging half out of the wagon in order to take in all the sights.

"Whoa." Jake stopped the team and set the brake.

"Is this going to be our new house?" Wyatt asked, standing in the back of the wagon.

"No," Hannah replied from the front seat. "This is my house, and you're going to rest up here a bit before heading to your home."

Alice came to the wagon as Jake helped Marty from the well-cushioned place he'd made for her in the back. Marty looked rather tired, and Alice hoped she would lie down before endeavoring anything else.

"Alice, would you help Jake put Marty to bed?" Hannah asked, as if reading her mind.

"I will. I was just about to suggest the same."

"I'm really all right. I just got a little warm. I'll be fine," Marty protested.

Jake would hear none of it. "You're gonna take a nap, or I'm gonna tie you to the bed until you do."

Alice put her hand over her mouth to suppress a giggle. Marty started to say something, but Jake held up his hand.

"Save it, Marty. You aren't gonna win this fight." Then without warning he lifted her in his arms and headed for the house.

Alice hurried on ahead to pull down the bedcovers. She barely managed the task before Jake placed Marty gently atop the clean sheets.

"Now, stay there while I go fetch you somethin' cold to drink. Your sister said there was sweet tea in the cellar." He looked to Alice. "Make sure she stays put."

Already Alice was removing Marty's shoes. "Don't worry. She's not going anywhere."

Marty gave an exasperated sigh and crossed her arms like a defiant child. "Now you have everyone against me."

Jake rolled his eyes and Alice couldn't help but smile. It wasn't going to be easy to keep Marty from overdoing it, and both of them knew it full well. Once Jake had gone, however, Marty surprised Alice by asking for help.

"Can you unbutton this blouse? I can't bear the heat of it anymore."

Alice quickly complied and soon had Marty undressed down to her lightweight shift. With Marty resting, Alice took up a cloth and dipped it into the water bowl atop the dresser. She came to the bed and began to wipe Marty's face and arms. The older woman offered no resistance and instead thanked Alice for her care.

"Jake worries too much. Hannah, too," Marty said and then closed her eyes. "But I think I will take just a little nap."

Alice smiled and finished her ministering. "I think that's a good idea."

★

Later that evening Marty climbed back into the wagon with Jake's help. The pains had stopped once she'd rested, and for that Marty was grateful. It worried her to think that her stubbornness might have brought the baby too early.

"When are you going to have the baby, Mama?" Wyatt asked.

"Oh, in another few weeks," Marty replied and reached out to ruffle his hair.

Benjamin curled up next to her as Jake moved the team out and headed for home. "Mama, will we have a big bed?"

"No," Marty told them. "Your papa made you each your very own bed."

"We don't have to share?" Samuel asked in amazement.

"Nope. You'll have a bed all your own. But you three will share a room. At least until we can afford to add on to the house."

"We can share," Wyatt declared. "We can share real good."

Samuel nodded in agreement. "We have to share. We're brothers now."

Marty chuckled and touched the boy's face. "That's right. You are brothers, and together we are a family."

Chapter 27

FRIDAY, JUNE 23, 1894

"You may now kiss your bride," the preacher announced.

Alice trembled as Robert took hold of her and pulled her close. She closed her eyes in anticipation and then felt his warm lips on hers. A spark of passion grew into a flame. She wanted the kiss to go on forever. She wanted always to remember this moment in time.

But as quickly as it started, it stopped and Robert pulled away. Alice could barely hear the crowd of onlookers cheering them. Her heart beat so loudly in her ears that it drowned out nearly everything else.

People soon began to surround them, offering congratulations and well-wishes. Alice found herself separated from Robert as the ladies moved in around her, commenting on her pale blue gown and her carefully styled hair.

"I think the lace trim on your bodice is perfect," Laura Reid said, reaching out to touch the modest neckline. "So fine and delicate."

"She looks like an angel," Hannah declared. "When she said she didn't need a fancy wedding dress, I wasn't sure I could approve. After all, it is the rage."

The ladies around her laughed. "Since when have we Texans worried about what the rest of the world thinks?" Carissa Atherton questioned.

"I like the pleating in the bodice," Hannah pointed out. "It took hours of tedious work, but it came out beautifully."

The others agreed while Alice craned her neck to find where Robert had gotten off to.

Since the wedding had taken place midmorning, everyone was now prepared to celebrate with a spread of food that Hannah and some of the other women had been busy making all week.

Alice wasn't a bit hungry, however. She wanted only to be left alone with Robert. She wanted to again feel his lips upon hers. She felt her cheeks grow hot and looked around, almost worried she'd spoken her desires aloud.

Little by little the crowd thinned, and Robert came to reclaim her. Alice allowed him to lead her to the head table. He helped her to take a seat before offering to get her food.

"You sit tight. I'll fetch a plate for both of us."

She nodded her approval and couldn't help but watch him as he walked away. He was her husband. They were really and truly married. Alice marveled at the thought and reached up to touch the scar along her jaw. It might have been her imagination, but the scar felt less prominent. Maybe it really was fading, as Marty had suggested.

The thought of Marty caused Alice to search for her dear friend. She finally spotted Marty standing away from the others near one of the cottonwood trees. The grimace on her face suggested she was in pain. For a moment it didn't register, and then all at once Alice feared the reason.

Leaving her place of honor, Alice hurried across the yard to where Marty stood. "Is it the baby?"

Marty looked up, her face pale and her mouth tightly clenched. She nodded, drew a deep breath, and then straightened. "It started just before the wedding. I didn't want to say anything. It's your day, after all." Her features relaxed. The pain had apparently passed.

"Is it too early?"

"I don't know. Hannah has insisted that I was further along than I originally thought." Marty gave her an apologetic smile. "I'm sorry to spoil things."

"You aren't spoiling anything. But you need to get to bed. Come, and I'll help you." Alice looked around for Hannah.

"Oh, don't make a fuss. I don't want everyone knowing. Jake will—" Marty gasped and bent over, clutching her stomach.

Alice couldn't take any more. "Someone, please come help me. Marty is going to have the baby!"

Jake was first to reach them, with Hannah close behind. Several other people followed until nearly everyone had gathered to see what assistance they might offer. Hannah ordered people around like a well-trained general.

"Jake, get her into the house and help her out of her gown. Ravinia, put more water on the stove and then get that stack of towels I set aside."

They quickly obeyed, and Alice could only stand helplessly watching as Jake carried Marty away. Robert seemed to understand and put his arm around her waist.

"Alice, she's in good hands. My ma is the best midwife around these parts."

"I believe you. I just wish there were something I could do to help."

"There is," Carissa Atherton announced. "You can go on with your wedding celebration. Marty would want you to do so. Now come. The birthing will probably take some time."

Reluctantly Alice allowed Robert to lead her back to the table. Carissa took over as hostess, and soon had everyone's focus back on the festivities. Alice found it almost impossible to eat despite the wonderful array of foods set before her. Robert didn't seem to have any problem at all, and after he'd cleared his plate, he started in on hers. He spoke casually with those who came to speak to them, while Alice's mind was on the delivery of Marty's baby.

"I can't stand not knowing what's happening," she whispered to Robert when they were finally alone.

"I understand, but this is our wedding day, and I'd really like for you to share it with me." He smiled and patted her hand. "You know Aunt Marty wouldn't like it if she knew you were neglecting me."

This made Alice smile. She could imagine Marty chiding her quite severely. Just then Simon came up to the table with Wyatt, Samuel, and Benjamin in tow.

"They're worried about their mama," Simon declared. "I told them she'd be done having the baby pretty soon. That's right, isn't it?"

Alice could see the hopefulness in the boys' eyes. She nodded. "That's right. Sometimes babies seem to take forever, but other times they come real quick. You boys just need to pray and ask God to watch over your mama." She gave them a smile. "Everything will be all right."

Two hours later, Alice's mother appeared at the door. It seemed that everyone noticed her at once, and silence blanketed the yard. She smiled and made her announcement.

"It's a girl."

Cheers erupted from the crowd, and several of the attendees rushed toward Ravinia Chesterfield to learn more. Robert, however, took the opportunity to slip away with Alice.

"Where are we going?" she asked as he led her away from the party.

"Anyplace where we can be alone," he said.

He pulled her behind the smokehouse and drew her into his arms. Without giving her a chance to protest, Robert pressed his mouth to hers. A charge like lightning shot through her, and Alice wrapped her arms around him as if she might otherwise drown.

The kiss seemed to go on forever, and Alice lost all thought of anyone but her husband. When he finally lifted his head, Alice found herself almost faint.

Robert grinned like a little boy who'd just gotten away with a prank. "And that, Mrs. Barnett, is how to properly kiss your husband."

Her senses returned and Alice smiled. "Behind the smokehouse?"

He laughed. "I hid here for many a questionable deed. I tried my first smoke here. I figured no one would know, 'cause the smokehouse was in use. My pa caught me just the same. I came here once when I stole cookies that my ma had forbidden me to eat. I don't know why I figured she'd not notice them missin' off the plate. She never said a word about it, however, but when I was half sick from havin' eaten too many, she just smiled and gave me castor oil."

"Goodness, I had no idea you were such a hooligan," Alice said, unable to hide her amusement. "I don't know if I would have married you had I known."

Robert nodded most soberly and tightened his hold on her. "That's why I didn't tell you." He kissed her again, but this time it was brief and left Alice longing for more.

"Come along, Mrs. Barnett. I'm sure we'll be missed if we don't return, and I, for one, don't want my pa comin' in search of me."

Alice quickly agreed. "Neither do I, Mr. Barnett. I wouldn't want to scandalize him."

Robert laughed heartily and drew her alongside him. "I don't know how I ever enjoyed life before you came here, but I have a feelin' it's only gonna get better. Ma once told me that Pa was a blessing from heaven, and that's how I feel about you. God knew the kind of wife I needed, and He brought you right to my doorstep."

Alice leaned closer and smiled. God had known her heart and her desires, too, and He had given not only her mother and brother back to her, but brought an entirely new family, as well. Most important, God had given her a man who would love her despite her scars.

"And just where have you two been?" Robert's father asked with a raised brow.

Robert gave him a sheepish grin. "I was just showin' Alice around—behind the smokehouse." His father roared with laughter, and Alice felt her cheeks burn with embarrassment. There would be no keeping secrets in this family, and maybe that was for the best. Secrets had a way of coming between folks, and Alice wanted nothing to ever come between her and her beloved. Smiling, she gave a sigh and prayed that this moment in time would last forever.

A MATTER
OF HEART

In memory of Ruth Seamands—
Mama Ruth to writers and believers near and far—
an incredible woman of God.
Can hardly wait to see you again!
Save me a chair.

Chapter 1

They're all talking about me.

Jessica Atherton could feel their furtive glances. *They have their husbands and children, and I'm still unmarried. Me, the one who was always the most beautiful, the most favored.* She frowned and looked back at the paper in her hands. Her thoughts betrayed an unappealing attitude, which Jessica was only beginning to recognize.

I am spoiled. Just as spoiled as everyone says. Shallow and selfish.

She raised her head and forced a smile as she met the gazes of several women. The women had gathered at her parents' home for a meeting of the Texas Cattle Women's Society, so there was no escaping their looks and comments.

They pity me.

The very thought annoyed and vexed Jessica in a way she couldn't ignore. At the age of twenty-one, Jessica had planned for her life to be much different. She'd imagined herself married and living a life of luxury in Houston or perhaps in some large city like Chicago, where she had often visited her grandparents. She had held great plans for her life—travel, wealth, opulence, and of course, a handsome man at her side, lavishing her with gifts and adoration.

"So, Jessica," Aunt Laura whispered, leaning close, "how are you holding up?"

Jessica knew her aunt was sympathetic to the situation. "I feel rather like an animal caught in a trap with no escape. My only choices are to gnaw off my own leg or await the kill."

Laura Reid smiled and patted her niece's hand. "They're soon to depart. With the business end of things complete, most will need to get back to their homes. It's not a good time of year for socializing—too much work needs their attention."

Unfortunately, Jessica knew these particular women were inclined to visit, even with work awaiting. Hannah Barnett was said to be arriving at any moment with her daughter-in-law, Alice, and new grandson. Jessica figured the women were there for the long haul, since this would be Alice's first social appearance since giving birth.

"You know they won't leave before they've seen the new baby," she replied.

A baby that might have been mine.

The very idea gave her a bevy of mixed emotions. On one hand, Jessica wasn't even sure that she wanted children. And on the other, she was still smarting from the fact that the scar-faced Alice Chesterfield had managed to steal away the only man Jessica had ever figured to marry—Robert Barnett. Of course, it hadn't been all that much of a theft. Robert and Jessica weren't in love, and it was only because of people's assumptions that they were linked as a couple. Their so-called romance was something created in the minds of their sentimental mothers, who saw their children as good choices for each other. Still, it bothered Jessica that Robert had so quickly cast her aside.

"Well, perhaps you can slip away," Aunt Laura suggested.

"If the moment presents itself, I will. Until then," Jessica conceded with a heavy sigh, "I must simply endure."

"Jessica, have you settled on any particular young man now that Robert has a wife and child?" Mrs. Pritchard asked from her other side. The woman was a notorious gossip and loved to get the inside scoop on everyone's life. Her husband owned one of the stores in Cedar Springs, and it gave her the perfect conduit for sharing information.

Jess looked to the gray-haired woman with a smile. "Goodness, no. I'm enjoying being able to come and go as I please. I'm not saddled down in any way, and if I want to travel or leave for an extended visit elsewhere, I have only to pack my bags."

"But you must be lonely at times," her friend Beth offered. Beth was Mrs. Pritchard's youngest daughter and Jessica's longtime chum from school. Beth had married at eighteen and already had two children, who were now being cared for with some of the other children in another part of the house. Earlier, she and two other young wives announced they were were having another baby.

Jessica knew that Beth was truly concerned for her well-being, but with all gazes now fixed upon her, Jessica felt completely out of sorts. "Of course I'm not lonely. Goodness, I have people around me all the time and plenty of suitors." She gave a light laugh, as if the entire world knelt at her feet. "I'm perfectly content."

But she could see in the eyes of the other women that they didn't believe her.

Another of her former schoolmates, Constance Watson, piped up. "I don't believe any woman can be completely content until she is wed. I know I wasn't." Several of the women nodded as she continued. "Life completely changes once you marry, and as Mother often says, it will change again when children come along—an event I hope soon to know." She smiled sweetly at Jessica. "I hope that you, too, will know those pleasures for yourself—both marriage and motherhood."

Jessica heard a hint of sarcasm in the woman's tone but smiled in return nevertheless. "Well, bless your heart for sayin' so."

Constance sat back in her chair and nodded soberly. "I will pray for you."

"Yes, we must all pray that God will send Jessica a husband," Mrs. Smith said, smiling at her daughter. "Constance is always so willing to pray for others."

Jessica wanted to flee the room but knew she couldn't without causing a scene. Instead, she folded her hands and thanked the ladies for their concern and prayers.

"I thought Hannah would be here by now," Aunt Laura commented to the group.

Jessica's mother nodded. "Should be anytime now. I can hardly wait to see the new baby."

"What was it they named him?" one of the older ranch wives asked.

"William Robert Barnett," Jessica's mother replied. "After his grandfather and father. Hannah tells me they intend to call him Wills, but her husband has nicknamed the baby Billy Bob."

The women smiled or chuckled and continued to ask questions about the baby and the mother's health. Jessica never thought she'd be glad for the topic to settle on Alice and her child, but at least it took the focus off of her own inadequacies.

Inadequacies. It seemed like such a harsh word, but Jessica could think of no other. These days she was her harshest critic. Others were always commenting on her charm, beauty, and accomplishments. She had finished out at one of the best schools for young ladies that Texas could boast, and she'd done well academically in her earlier school years. Some even commented on her being quite intelligent and in possession of a good wit. Surely a woman with such attributes could not be called lacking. In addition to these qualities, Jessica knew her waist was the smallest in the county, and her face had been compared to those of various Greek goddesses. She had always known of her appealing looks. Her mother, also a woman of great beauty, had warned that she could easily use her appearance to manipulate others. She urged Jessica to draw closer to God and forget about her loveliness.

"God doesn't consider a person's outward appearance, and neither should we," her mother had chided.

Jessica always thought that strange. Why would God have made some things beautiful and others ugly if He hadn't expected folks to notice?

"Oh, that must be them!" her mother announced at the sound of an approaching carriage. Having every window open to allow for the least hint of breeze on this stifling hot day caused the sound to echo throughout the house.

The gathering seemed to rise and move slowly en masse to greet the new arrivals. Happy to see them all exit the house, Jessica sprang to her feet. This made the perfect opportunity for her to slip away unseen. She hoped for at least a few quiet moments to herself and made her way out the back door, past the barn, and toward the horse pen, where her own mare, Peg, stood loyally waiting. The humidity and heat of the day made her feel even more miserable.

"Are you as unhappy as I am, Peg?" Jessica asked, reaching out to stroke the velvety muzzle of the dapple gray. The horse had been a gift from her father and mother six years earlier, along with a very smart sidesaddle. Jessica had been delighted at the time and remained so. She and Peg were the best of friends. "At least you have plenty of shade and water."

The mare lowered her head to search Jessica's hand. "I'm sorry, girl. I didn't think to bring you a treat." Jessica reached up and stroked the black mane. She was a true beauty, standing sixteen hands high. Her dappled body bore an intriguing pattern set against the black mane and tail. Peg was the perfect mount for Jessica. Both horse and owner were beautiful and unusual.

For a moment Jessica allowed the mare to nuzzle her, then stepped back. "Maybe we'll go for a ride later, when it cools down a bit."

"I could escort you" came a familiar voice.

Jessica turned to find Lee Skelly. Lee was shorter than most of the men, but quite muscular. He acted as her father's foreman and right-hand man when her brothers Howard and Isaac were otherwise occupied, as they were now.

"Have you had word from your brothers about when they're headin' home?" he asked, leaning back against the fence of the pen.

"Mother said they would be home by Christmas."

"They still buildin' new houses for colored people in Corpus Christi?"

Jessica nodded and pulled a handkerchief from her sleeve. Her mother's friends had written to encourage the mission. Howard and Isaac, true humanitarians that they were, eagerly gave up ranch work in favor of construction. Both had a mind for politics, and this was exactly the kind of thing that would speak of their giving characters.

"They are enjoying the change of pace, I think." She dabbed at the perspiration forming on her face and turned to leave.

"So what about that ride?" Lee asked, coming alongside her.

Jessica continued walking. "I don't think my father would approve. It isn't becoming for me to be out with a man my own age without a chaperone."

"I'm completely honorable," he protested. "We can even take old Osage with us."

Jessica thought of the older man who was once her father and grand-father's ranch foreman. Osage was nearing eighty now, but he hadn't slowed down much, despite her father's insistence that he retire. Having no part in lounging around, Osage kept an eye on things around the house and took time to oversee some of the younger cowboys in training.

"I won't make that kind of demand on Osage. He has enough to keep him busy."

"Ah, Jess, you could talk him into it. If not Osage, then maybe your pa would make an exception and let me escort you."

Jessica threw him a glance and shook her head. "He's not likely to agree."

"Why not? I'm a good fella, Jess. I think we could have a right good future together."

At this she stopped. "Are you proposing to me?"

He gave a sheepish grin. "Well, why not? I'm a fella of my word, and you're a beautiful woman. We could have a great life together."

"You don't even know what I want out of life."

"I figure you want the same things every girl wants: security, family, a home." He took on an air of confidence and asked, "Ain't that right?"

Jessica shrugged. "I couldn't say. I don't know what I want."

He laughed. "Jess, you don't need to want for anything if you agree to be my gal."

Turning, she looked hard at the man. "It would hardly be appropriate for me to be your gal. You're my father's foreman." The minute the words came out of her mouth, Jessica thought they sounded terrible. Lee frowned, and Jessica knew he'd taken offense. She hurried to cover her tracks.

"In your position here, the other men might think Father was giving you an unfair advantage if he allowed you to court me." *There. That doesn't sound quite so arrogant.* But from the continued scowl on Lee's face, Jessica wasn't sure he'd even heard her.

"You don't think I'm good enough for you?"

Jessica felt her cheeks warm at the question. "I have no thought of it either way," she lied. "I know it would not meet with my father's approval, and therefore have not contemplated the idea. I do know, however, that a simple thing like that could cause all sorts of problems among a group of men."

She shrugged. "Besides, Lee, I have no desire to marry anyone. I rather like having my freedom. I can come and go as I please. And I very well may do just that. I have cousins who live in Chicago. I got to know them when I spent time up there with my grandparents. They've been begging me to visit."

Lee shook his head. "You don't think I'm serious, do you?"

She put her hands on her hips. "And just what is that supposed to mean?"

It was Lee's turn to shrug. "Just that you don't think of me as a man, as a possible beau. You're the boss's daughter and deserve much better than the hired hand. And why not? Your pa owns this place. It's like he's king over this ranch, and that makes you his little princess. Can't have the princess marryin' the pauper."

Jessica hated his analogy. God had already been pricking her conscience about the way she acted and the times she'd made other people feel ill at ease. For a moment she felt completely defenseless.

"I'm . . . I don't know what to say." Jessica shook her head and fixed her gaze on his face. "I really wasn't thinking any of that, Lee. You're a fine man. My father thinks highly of you, and I don't have any reason to believe you wouldn't be a proper suitor."

"Then why won't you step out with me?"

She knew the reason but worried he would take it wrong. "I don't see a future in it." She held up her hand. "Before you go off thinking I'm being uppity or believe myself too good for you, let me tell you the exact opposite is true."

He frowned. "Whadd'ya mean?"

"It has nothing to do with whether you are good enough for me. It has to do with me." She shook her head. "This isn't coming out right. I don't mean it's all about me and what I want out of life . . . or need. It's about me . . . being . . . a mess."

He laughed. "Oh, Jess, you ain't no mess. You're the purtiest gal in these parts. Now, if you wanna see a mess, you ought to see my little sister. Grief, but that gal can't hardly turn around without breakin' something or causin' disaster. Ma says she puts her foot in her mouth more often than she puts on her shoes."

Jessica wanted to shout that he had no idea what she was saying, but she held her tongue. Maybe part of maturity was recognizing when to fight your battles.

Lee sobered, as if realizing he'd acted inappropriately. "Sorry, Jess. I didn't mean no disrespect."

"I know," she said, and the sadness in her voice hung in the air. She turned and made her way to the house, hoping Lee wouldn't follow her and press for more. He didn't, and Jessica let out the breath she'd been holding.

Poor Lee. He truly was a nice young man, but Jess had never seen him as anything more than one of the workers. Not because he was of a lower station, but because she simply only saw him in that capacity. She'd not dealt with him much at social events, and he wasn't really one to attend church.

"There you are," Beth said, thrusting a bundle at Jessica as soon as she entered the kitchen. "We're all taking turns holding little Wills. It's your turn."

Jessica looked down at the dark blue eyes of Robert's son. Something akin to deep regret washed over her.

He might have been mine. If I had been a different woman—with a different heart—I might be the one sharing my son with family and friends.

"He's beautiful," she whispered, almost afraid to say anything more.

"We all thought so," her mother said, coming alongside. "Hannah says he's the spitting image of Robert."

Jessica nodded. "Yes, I think she's right."

The baby started to fuss, and Jessica feared she'd done something wrong. She looked to her mother with a questioning expression. Alice stepped in just then and took Wills.

"He's just hungry. I hope you don't mind if I take a few moments to feed him." She said it more to the group than to Jessica.

Free of the baby, Jessica hurried away from the gathering and sought the solitude of her room. The women might talk about her abrupt departure, but unlike times before, Jessica didn't care.

"Let them talk," she said, pacing her bedroom floor. "Those old biddies are always gossiping about someone. It doesn't need to ruin my day. If they have nothing better to do than pick apart my actions, then so be it."

She plopped down on the carefully made bed and sighed. She didn't like people thinking poorly of her. She wanted them to like her, to desire her company. She wanted them to be impressed with her knowledge and abilities. Folks felt that way about her mother and her aunt, and it was only natural that Jessica should want the same.

"Is that just more of my self-centered ways?" she asked aloud. "Worrying about what people think of me?"

She looked around her room and couldn't help remembering Lee's earlier comment. This was the room of a princess. From her feather mattress and beautifully crafted canopy bed swathed in pink tulle to the wardrobe filled with expensive, intricately designed gowns, Jessica was living the life of royalty. At least Texas royalty.

"But does that have to be bad?" she asked the empty room. "Is it wrong to enjoy fine things?"

Getting to her feet, Jessica crossed to the window, where new drapes of the finest damask had been placed only the week before. She had told her mother how tiresome the other drapery had become, and her mother had arranged for replacements. Toying with the fringed edges of the cream-and-gold material, Jessica knew that it had been an additional expense that could have been better spent. There had been nothing wrong with the other curtains. In fact, Mother had placed them in one of the other bedrooms.

Jessica turned and spied her reflection in the mirror. Soft brown curls had been carefully arranged atop her head. They spilled down the back to just cover her neck. She wore a gown of sheer white muslin with a lining of pale pink silk. Six-inch-wide lace in a V shape gave the bodice a narrowing appearance and made Jessica's waist appear even smaller than it was. And with the full leg-o'-mutton lace sleeves, the gown seemed most ethereal—fairy-tale like. She always received compliments when she wore it.

Jessica touched a finger to the glass. Was that all there was to her? Was she just a pretty bauble designed to turn heads and fascinate suitors? Nothing more than a storybook princess?

She glanced back at the door to her room. Just on the other side and downstairs, a collection of women gathered. Women who had husbands and children, whose lives meant something, who had people who loved them.

"What do I have? What do I offer? Robert married Alice rather than be saddled with me."

Knowing in her heart that Robert and Alice genuinely loved each other didn't ease her momentary self-ridicule.

"Of course Robert would marry someone sweet and quiet like Alice. Even with her scarred face. I say what I think, and often I'm loud and insist on my own way. No one wants those qualities in a wife."

She sat down once again, this time at her dressing table. Yet another mirror reflected her pensive countenance. Picking up one of a dozen ornamental hatpins, she studied it a moment, then stuck it in a pin cushion. One by one she did the same for the others. The action seemed to calm her.

Maybe I should marry someone like Lee. Maybe that's what I deserve—a loveless marriage to a poor man.

A light knock sounded on her door. "Come in." She leaned back as her mother entered the room.

"Are you feeling all right?"

"Physically? Yes, I'm fine. Emotionally? I'm not sure."

Mother smiled sympathetically, and Jessica vacillated between wanting to scream at the implied pity and needing her mother's embrace.

"Is this about Alice and the baby?"

"I don't know. I think it's about everything. I'm starting to see some things about myself and my life that I don't really like. Things that need to be improved."

"Nonsense. You are perfect the way you are. Don't fret. One day the right man will come into your life, and he will sweep you off your feet and become the love of your life." Mother's expression became quite soft. "I know, because it happened that way for me. I thought I knew love with my first husband. Soon enough I learned there was no love between us. After he died, I was certain I would never find true love. Then your father came into my life, and everything changed."

Jessica knew her mother was trying to help, but her words rang hollow. "Everyone has things about them that need changing," she said in a barely audible voice.

"I suppose that's true; however, I know that you have a good heart and a wonderful nature. I don't want you thinking yourself hopeless or without value because Robert married another." Mother patted her shoulder. "You are my daughter, my baby. You have great value in my eyes and in those of your father. But more important, you have great value in the eyes of God. Remember that."

Jessica nodded, but the words didn't help. She hadn't been as focused on God and spiritual matters as she knew her parents wished. Religiosity and showing up for the Sunday pew warming seemed more hypocritical than spiritual, and Jessica found reading the Bible to be a bore. She looked in the mirror and found her mother looking at her with an expression that suggested she wanted to hear her daughter affirm her willingness.

"I'll try to remember it, Mother. I'll try."

"Good. Now why don't you come downstairs and rejoin us. There are only a few people still here, and Hannah has taken Alice and the baby home. It shouldn't be so painful for you now."

Jessica gave a heavy sigh. Mother simply didn't understand. Apparently, no one did.

Chapter 2

Sunday brought cooler temperatures, which was unusual for Texas at this time of the year. Nevertheless, Austin Todd had taken advantage of the less oppressive afternoon to snag a much-needed nap.

He'd barely closed his eyes, however, when he found himself caught up in the age-old nightmare. Why could he not lay the past to rest? Would he always be haunted by the ghosts of those he'd failed?

So many people had counted on him, and he'd let them down. The nightmare only served to remind him of their disappointment in him. Austin tossed restlessly atop his narrow bed as images of his brother, mother, and father passed before his eyes. His brother looked at him with the same stunned expression Austin had last seen on his face. Mother and Father fixed Austin with looks of disapproval and accusation.

And then there was Grace.

Austin awoke with a start. Soaked in sweat, he all but jumped from the bed as though it were afire. With hands trembling, he reached for the pitcher of water. He poured the tepid liquid onto a cloth and wiped his face. Why couldn't the past just die?

He replaced the pitcher and threw down the cloth, not caring where it landed. Stalking from the room, Austin fought against a lifetime of regret and unmistakable feelings of failure, especially when it came to family relationships.

Outside, Austin leaned his lanky frame against the house's front wall and breathed in deeply of the air. It was nearly evening and a new week would soon begin. He had obligations in Dallas on Monday and had no idea how long he would have to remain. As a cattle inspector—part of the Texas Rangers—Austin kept busy upholding law and order on the range.

It was a world of difference from his previous job in Washington, D.C., a job he'd shared with his brother, Houston, until that fateful night nearly six years ago. A picture of his brother's face came to mind. With laughing eyes, a strong jaw, and a perfect smile, Houston was three years Austin's junior. The brothers had been inseparable, even going into the same career of working for the Treasury Department's Secret Service.

They had worked side by side, feeling they knew each other's moods and moves better than anyone else ever would. Their job entailed ferreting out counterfeiters—something they did quite well. Austin had a keen nose for the business. Often with nothing more than the tiniest hunch, he had been able to expose criminals and put an end to their plots. Once, he'd even thwarted an attack on a top government official. Houston had teased him unmercifully when their boss had presented Austin with an award meriting his service.

"Your head will swell too big for you to get out the door," Houston had said. He joked about the matter but clearly was proud of his older brother. His parents had been proud, too. At least until that dreadful night when Austin killed his brother.

★

"Be sure and tell Austin that he can eat with us anytime he likes," Robert Barnett's mother announced as he made plans to ride over to the small cabin where the Texas Ranger lived. "He certainly doesn't need to wait for an invitation."

Robert glanced to where his mother sat happily holding his son. Alice was getting a much-needed rest while baby William's grandmother fussed over him. "I'll tell him again, Mother, but I can't force the man to eat with us."

"Well, at least take him some sugar cookies. Rosita made a fresh batch yesterday."

"I'll do that," Robert promised. He lost no time in getting to the kitchen, lest his mother stop him again. He wrapped a dozen or so cookies in a dish towel and made his way out the back door, munching on one of the treats as he went.

Manuel already had Robert's horse saddled and ready to go. The sorrel seemed happy to see his master and bobbed his head up and down at Robert's approach. As soon as the horse realized there was food involved, he made certain to get part of it. Robert allowed the animal a piece of cookie then finished it off himself. He tucked the bundled cookies into his saddlebag, then took the reins from Manuel and mounted.

"Gracias, Manuel."

The fourteen-year-old boy smiled and nodded. A younger brother to one of the ranch's cowboys, Manuel had proven himself a hard worker. Robert gave him a quick nod, then urged the horse into a trot.

The Barnett property had grown considerably over the years, and while it was no rival to the King Ranch in South Texas, it was garnering attention in its own right for quality livestock and trustworthy dealings. Robert was proud to bear the name Barnett. Prouder still that he could follow in his father's footsteps.

The ride to Austin Todd's cabin was several miles. Perched on the edge of what had formerly been Barnett land, the small house was perfectly suited for one man. Austin seemed to appreciate the solitude, but Robert wasn't sure that he would have much positive to say about the news he was bringing today.

When the cabin finally came in sight, Robert paused to wipe his brow and offer up a prayer. "Lord, you know what I'm here to say. Help me to say it right and for Austin to receive it well. Amen."

Robert caught sight of Austin chopping wood and gave a wave. Reaching the house, Robert quickly tied off his horse and made his way to where Austin continued to work.

"I see you're taking advantage of the cooler weather."

Austin looked up and gave a brief nod. "I figured it was a good time to stock up a little. I appreciated your pa havin' that dead tree dragged here for me. I've been whittling away on it." He motioned to the stack of leafless limbs. "I try to trim off a little every night I'm home."

"Sounds like a plan," Robert declared. "I was hopin', though, that we could have a little talk. My pa sent me."

"Problems?" Austin asked, setting the ax aside.

"No, not really. You're invited, in fact, to a gathering at our place. Night after next."

"Not sure I'll be back from Dallas. What's the occasion?"

Robert smiled. "Well, you know my pa wants to get a railroad spur built out here."

"He wants to start a whole town, as I recall."

"Well, he figures if there's a spur for the ranchers to use, the town will just form naturally. Because of that, he wants some say in how it comes about."

"You can't have any real control over that," Austin said, looking uncertain.

"Well, he figures he can control it to a point. After all, he owns the land he intends for the railroad to build on and where the spur will end. Of course, it crosses Atherton land, too, but they are supportive of the cause."

"Doesn't it seem kinda unnecessary to bring in the railroad? I mean, it isn't that far to drive the cattle over to Cedar Springs."

"It takes more time and manpower than you'd think. It's also getting harder to do, what with everyone fencing off. Pa thinks this is a good solution for several reasons. He wants to be able to get supplies quickly. If a store or two and maybe a bank could be situated in the new town, it would really benefit the community. Not to mention the idea of having a church and a school for the area people. It'd be real nice not to have to drive all the way into Cedar Springs for Sunday service."

"Won't it still take quite a bit of time for other folks anyway? After all, your pa owns a lot of acreage."

"Yes, but he's willing to allow others to cross his property. Not only that, but his plans for the town are on the main road, where his property abuts that of others. It'll be a good place for a town. There's water, the most important thing, and if the railroad will agree to Pa's terms, that will be the second most important accomplishment."

"I'm still not sure I'd like to see that happen. Towns always mean drinking and gambling. Pretty soon you have brothels and opium dens and folks getting killed or killing for what they want."

"That's why Pa wants to keep a tight rein on things. He wants to approve the businesses that go in. He doesn't intend for there to be any kind of opportunity for riffraff."

"It's been my experience," Austin mused, "that riffraff makes its own kind of opportunity."

Robert nodded. "I know you're right, but I also know my father's concept for this. He's always been a man of vision, and I think we can trust him to know best on this."

For a moment Austin said nothing, and Robert wondered if he'd pushed too hard. "Also, my mother wants you to know that there's no need to wait for an invitation to share our meals. You're always welcome, so don't go hungry."

Still Austin didn't reply. He stared out at the horizon as if contemplating what he would say. After another minute he turned back to Robert. "I like the solitude here. It's one of the reasons I bought the place. It's peaceful."

"Well, maybe it seems that way even more, given you're a lawman." Robert couldn't help but grin. "I have to say it's been a real comfort to Pa and me to know there's law close by."

Austin shrugged. "I'm a cattle inspector, not really a law officer. Not in the sense you mean."

"You're a Texas Ranger, and that makes you qualified in my eyes."

"Well, maybe that's why this whole thing bothers me. I know how it is when folks get together. There's always someone who wants to take what someone else has. I'm tellin' you from experience that it opens a whole new box of troubles."

"I understand your concerns. Have you always been a lawman?"

Austin gave a curt nod. "It's pretty much all I've ever known. Even before moving to Texas I was involved in . . . law enforcement."

"So what brought you to Texas?" Robert asked. "Where'd you come from?"

He saw Austin stiffen. "Not important. Heard this was a good place to live, so I came." He picked up the ax. "Tell your ma I said thanks for the invite. I'm sure to take her up on the offer, especially when it gets colder."

Robert thought it strange the way Austin had become almost uncomfortable. His stance suggested that he was keeping something hidden, but the rancher couldn't imagine what that would be or why Austin might feel the need.

Making his way back to the sorrel, Robert started to mount, then remembered the cookies. He pulled the bundle from his saddlebag and glanced back to where Austin was already hard at work swinging the ax.

"I almost forgot. Ma sent you some cookies." He held up the bundle as Austin took note. The latter crossed the yard to take the offering with a smile.

"Tell your mother I said thanks."

"I'll do that, but seems you could tell her yourself if you'd join us for dinner now and then. I know it would please her—she likes motherin' folks. Especially those who don't have any family around." Robert mounted his horse and could see that once again Austin had grown rather sullen. It seemed there was a lot about this man he didn't know. Maybe no one knew his secrets.

★

"A gathering for what purpose?" Jessica asked her parents over dinner.

"William Barnett and your father have been working with some of the other ranchers to bring in the railroad. Now that they have an idea of this happening, they want to discuss what is needed and how to go about setting up a community," Mother replied. She passed Jessica a bowl of ham and cabbage.

Taking a portion of the food, Jessica handed the bowl to her father before asking, "Why do I have to be there?"

"It's for the entire community," he said in a rather stern voice. "You're a part of that."

"But no one really cares what I think about the idea." Jessica picked up a cornmeal muffin and broke off a piece. "I'm not married, I don't own any land, and I'm a woman. So I have no say over what happens."

"Your father and Mr. Barnett are good to listen to the hearts of everyone—especially the womenfolk of this area. One of your father's thoughts is to get a doctor in this new community and pay him a regular stipend."

"How could they ever afford that? I know the world of finance has bettered itself, according to what I read in the papers, but we're still suffering the effects of a depression."

Tyler Atherton's expression softened, and Jessica saw a hint of amusement in his gaze.

"You always were the smart one. I appreciate you bein' up-to-date on current events. And you're right. We are still sufferin', but less so than other folks. Like your brothers said in their last letter, a lot of folk don't even have a house to call home.

"Will and I figure if we kick in enough money to keep the doctor satisfied with or without patients, sick folks will come around in time. After all, in this forty-mile radius there are over a hundred people. That doesn't include the folks who live in Cedar Springs, where there's several hundred. And when the railroad is established, more people will arrive to set up businesses. I figure we won't have to pay the doc forever—just long enough to get him on his feet."

"Your father and Mr. Barnett figure they can set the man up with a little house of his own, from which he can work and live," Mother said before sipping her tea.

"That's right," Father said. "If he lives rent free and we provide him with beef and canned goods from our gardens, then he'll have only a few expenses to meet. We'll probably look to get a preacher the same way. Of course, he'll have the tithes to help him out."

Jessica nodded and popped another piece of muffin into her mouth. She supposed they had reasoned out all the possibilities and problems.

"So the gathering is to be a picnic—a barbecue," her mother said, smiling. "Most everyone will be in attendance, so I would hate for people to say that our daughter didn't care enough to join her neighbors in discussion and celebration."

"Folks around here will look for any reason to have a party," Jessica said, toying with the cabbage and ham. "You hardly need my stamp of approval to draw in the crowds."

Her mother frowned. "Jessica, this really isn't like you. What's going on?"

Her accusing tone caused Jessica to sit up a little straighter. "Nothing. I just don't know that I want to be around a lot of people. We just had the cattle women here. It's not like I have no chance to socialize."

Her mother eyed her with suspicion. "You've never shied away from parties in the past. What is this really about?"

"Maybe I'm changing," Jessica replied with a frown. "Maybe I was too focused on parties before. Doesn't a person have a right to change?"

"Well, you don't need to go changing, darlin'," her father threw out. "You're practically perfect the way you are, just like your mama."

Her mother blushed, and Jessica bit her lip to keep from blurting out that she was nothing of the kind. But if she said anything at all, her mother would want to know more, and Jessica wasn't done wrestling with her conscience. She had no answers that would satisfy her mother's curiosity.

Chapter 3

It was a typical Barnett party with glowing lanterns hanging from lower tree branches and on well-positioned poles. Multitudes of quickly built tables and benches were set up for people to relax and enjoy the meal. Other food-laden tables were arranged in such a manner as to allow people to serve themselves from both sides. Jessica and her mother had helped to supply some of the meal, but most of it had come from Mrs. Barnett's kitchen.

Once everyone was filled up on smoked ham, green beans, potatoes, corn bread, cheesy grits, and baked beans, not to mention an array of desserts, Mr. Barnett began to discuss the plan he and others had been working on.

"Each of you men should have received a drawing of what we have in mind. My wife and daughter-in-law drew those up so you wouldn't have to suffer through my attempts to make sense." A chuckle ran through the gathering, and most of the men held up their maps as if in answer.

Mr. Barnett nodded his approval. "Now, if you'll look at the drawing, you'll see that we've tentatively called the town Terryton. This is in honor of Ted and Marietta Terry. Ted often joked that he'd been in Texas longer than mesquite, so we figured he deserved a town named for him." Again the crowd chuckled.

"I know everyone misses 'em, but bein' the godly folk they were, I know we'll see 'em again in heaven." A murmuring of "amen" went up throughout the crowd.

Everyone seemed to be in such a good mood. To Jessica's way of thinking, there was no reason for them to be anything else. They were full and safe and, for the most part, healthy. Indian problems were no longer an issue. There'd been no epidemics or storms of late to wreak havoc upon the people or the land. God was in His heaven, and all was right with the world. What better time to create an entirely new community?

"Tyler Atherton and I have talked with a lawyer. He plans to join us sometime in the near future. His name is Harrison Gable. He's from Dallas but will relocate if we all come together to set this thing in motion."

"What's required of us?" Mr. Palmer asked.

William Barnett smiled. "Patience, support—both financially and intellectually—and faith that together we can accomplish this."

"Pardon me for sayin' so," Mr. Harper, another area rancher, piped up, "but it seems to me we are still facin' perilous times. It's only been three years since this country fell flat on its face. I think we might be rushin' things a bit."

"But if I might interject," Jessica's uncle Brandon Reid said, moving closer to the front of the gathering, "three years has also seen us regain considerable ground. Industry is back on its feet, the solvent banks have rebounded, and the railroad has gone through rebuilding and in some cases a change of ownership. I think this is the perfect time for us to consider such an endeavor."

Jessica listened, only mildly interested, as the conversation continued. Most of the people seemed excited about the potential for a church and a school, not to mention an easier way to get to Dallas. She couldn't help but wonder what the changes might mean for her. She'd grown up with all of her needs met, but many of these folks had struggled. Some families had even sold out and moved away because they'd been unable to make a living in the intolerable conditions.

She toyed with a piece of pecan pie and continued to listen half-heartedly. She heard a man question something about law enforcement and wondered if it might be the Texas cattle inspector she'd heard her father talk about. Glancing around, she tried to see who was speaking but couldn't.

"Having law and order is always uppermost on the minds of the people," Mr. Barnett declared. "We have solid plans drawn up for a town marshal to be in place before the first locomotive arrives in Terryton."

"Will he be elected?" Mr. Harper questioned. "I don't want any appointed man."

"Yes, there will be an election," Barnett assured him, "but only of those who sign on to assist with this project. You see, until there's a true town and population to make decisions, we will need some sort of board or co-op to see to the running of this town. That will include the position of a mayor. This board will act as the counsel for the mayor and the marshal."

Jessica tired of the talk and her pie and got up from the table on the pretense of needing to refill her glass of lemonade. She made her way to the table where several pitchers of liquid stood waiting. The lemonade and iced sweet tea had been kept chilled in their springhouse, but having been out for several hours now, Jessica knew neither would be cold. Nevertheless she poured herself a glass of lemonade and began to slowly walk around the edge of the party.

Watching from a distance gave her more clarity. She studied with different eyes these people she'd known all her life. She could understand their fears of change. Change suggested a loss of control of the familiar. It could be a terrifying situation. But change could also be new and invigorating. Jessica had always relished change in that respect. Now, though, with everything going on in her life, she wasn't finding herself keen on the idea.

What's wrong with me? Is this what growing up is all about? Am I suddenly to become a fearful woman—afraid of my own shadow—unwilling to risk something different?

Jessica could see the hopeful expressions on the faces of mothers as Mr. Barnett spoke of a school and a church being their first building priorities. Such things equaled stability in the eyes of the gentler sex. But didn't they already have stability in the community? The area ranchers were good to help one another in times of need. The children already had a school and the people had a church to attend, although both were far enough away to discourage attendance. Why pull out of one town just to create another?

Without looking where she was going, Jessica backed away from the gathering. She turned abruptly and found herself face-to-face with a stranger. "Oh, excuse me." The glass of lemonade fell to the grass and spilled out across the man's boots.

"It was my fault," the man declared. "If I hadn't been hiding out over here, you wouldn't have had any trouble." He wiped his boot tops on the backs of his denim pants. "There. Now they're clean."

She smiled at the dark-eyed man and forgot about the glass. "I'm Jessica Atherton."

"Austin Todd," he replied. "I'm new to the area. I bought a small piece of land from Mr. Barnett."

"Oh, I know all about you. You've been the topic of conversation at many a meal or gathering."

He chuckled at this. "Really? And what are people saying about me?"

"That you're a cattle inspector who likes privacy."

"Is that all?"

"Well, no, but are you certain you want to know the truth?"

He frowned. "Is it that bad?"

Laughing, Jessica shook her head. "Not at all. Most of the women with single daughters are wondering if you're a good catch. Of course, for some of them, the only qualification a man need have is that he be breathing. And those single daughters are murmuring about you under their breath. They want to know what kind of provider you might be or how attentive you are to their gender. They have assessed you from head to toe and found you to be mysterious, handsome, and definitely of interest." She paused for a moment before adding, "Oh, and the men seem to admire you greatly. Probably because my father and Mr. Barnett have told everyone how you saved the day in Fort Worth when you shot down three bank robbers."

She looked at him with a raised brow. "I think that's about all."

"It's more than enough," he replied. "I appreciate the honesty. However, I had no idea I was being discussed in such detail."

Jessica shrugged. "I tend to speak my mind and that of other folks, as well. It's sort of a problem of mine."

"I don't see honesty as a problem."

She leaned back against an oak tree. "Neither do I, but I have learned that most people aren't that interested in the truth."

"Seriously?"

She shrugged again. "Well, it sure seems that way. Most people avoid hearing the truth—at least the way I see it. Sick folks don't want to know that they're dying. Spurned lovers don't want to know that it really was their own fault the relationship couldn't work out. Women don't want to know that their new dress is the most atrocious thing you've ever seen."

Austin let out a roar, and Jessica was glad the gathering had grown noisy, with numerous people all speaking at once. She pulled Austin back into the shadows. "You're going to have everyone wanting in on the joke."

"Sorry. I was just remembering a few atrocious dresses my mother owned. She was always asking my father how she looked, and of course, you are right. He couldn't really tell her."

Jessica nodded, imagining the situation. "It's really a kindness in some ways. Mother says it's still a lie and therefore a sin, but I know it's more often done out of good intentions than bad. Still, I prefer the truth."

"Always?"

She fixed him with a gaze. "Always."

"You're different from most women, then."

"I am. I make no claim to be otherwise. It's probably why I'm still unmarried and living with my parents. No one wants a blunt wife. Now, if you'll excuse me, I need to see if my mother wants help with the dishes."

"It was nice to make your acquaintance," Austin said. "And I *honestly* hope we can speak again sometime."

"I'm sure we will. After all, this town idea isn't going to just go away." Smiling, Jessica couldn't help but tease him. "I hope you won't worry overmuch about what people are saying about you."

"I make it a habit not to care what anyone thinks."

Jessica sobered. "I used to feel that way, but I've found it hasn't served me exactly as I'd hoped."

★

Austin thought about Jessica Atherton for a long time after she'd gone. He found her a refreshing change of pace, but at the same time her last comment confused him. Then he remember the glass she'd dropped and moved back to retrieve it. Luckily, it hadn't shattered. Making his way to where folks had been instructed to leave their dishes, Austin placed the glass on a tray alongside others.

"I hope you got enough to eat, Mr. Todd," Mrs. Barnett said, coming beside him with several more glasses.

"Yes, ma'am. I got plenty, and please call me Austin."

"I'd like that very much, and you can call me Hannah." She placed the glasses on the tray, then started to lift it.

Austin reached out to stop her. "Allow me." He picked up the tray and looked at her for further instruction.

"I was going to take them over to where we're washing dishes. It's that table just over there." She pointed to where several women, including Jessica Atherton, were working to clean up the numerous dishes and cups.

"Looks like folks are still grazin'," he said, glancing over his shoulder.

Hannah laughed. "They will be until they load up for home. Even so, it's best to keep on top of the dishes. Someone might need a clean plate, and I've exhausted all of mine."

"I thought most of them brought their own table settings. Robert said something about that earlier. I felt rather remiss, but in all honesty I don't have anything all that fine."

She leaned closer as if to tell him a secret. "Well, I've never yet expected a single man to show up with his dinnerware or food to contribute. Usually when we get together around these parts, we do it potluck style, and everyone brings food to eat and their own dishes to eat it on. This was just a little bit different because Will wanted to provide for everyone. I think it was his way of winning them over to agree to the building of Terryton."

"Well, you know, they say that the way to a man's heart is through his stomach."

"Yes, I know that full well. I also know you can get right through to his head with a piece of Rosita's Mexican chocolate cake."

"I'm not sure I had any of that."

She took the tray from him and motioned with her head. "Then you'd better try it. It's chocolaty and moist with a hint of cinnamon, and her buttercream frosting tops it off perfectly."

Austin nodded. "I think you've convinced me. I hope there's some left."

"Oh, there is," Mrs. Barnett assured him. "She made twelve of them."

Making his way to the dessert table, Austin spied the chocolate cake. He hurried to take up a dessert plate and sample the treat. It was just as Mrs. Barnett had said. It'd been a long time since Austin had enjoyed anything nearly as much.

"I see you found Rosita's prize-winning cake," Mr. Barnett said, joining him at the dessert table. "It's pretty amazing. I'm here for a second piece, but don't tell my wife. She thinks I'm getting pudgy in my old age."

"Your secret is safe with me."

Mr. Barnett secured his cake, then suggested Austin join him at an empty table. "So what did you think of our talk tonight?" He waited until Austin was seated before adding, "I want your honest opinion."

The comment reminded Austin of his earlier conversation with Jessica and made him smile. "Well, Mr. Barnett—"

"Call me Will," the older man interjected.

Austin nodded. "It sounds to me you've thought of everything. I couldn't really find fault with any of it, even if I do wish things could remain quiet and simple around here."

"I know. A lot of folks are against change, but I believe it's the way of the future. It's hard to imagine, but the way Dallas is growing, I expect one day all of this land will be a part of that city."

"Surely not," Austin countered. "That's a long way to come. Besides, I thought building up was the new style. What is it they call 'em—skyscrapers? There are a lot of them back east."

Chuckling, William cut into his cake. "Yeah, I read about some buildings going up in London, England. It said that Queen Victoria put a limit on how high they can build. I figure we're still a rebellious country, however, and we won't have any restrictions put on ours."

"So maybe Dallas can just build up and not out."

"I doubt it. Texas has a lot going for itself with all its resources. We've had to tighten our belts during this financial upheaval, but we definitely have known harder times. During the War Between the States, it was mighty difficult. Still, I think this state is probably one of the healthier ones."

"Or maybe it's just that you know how to get through a bad situation and still find the good," Austin suggested.

"Maybe."

Will turned his attention back to his cake, and for a moment nothing more was said. Austin wasn't sure if he'd offended the man or not, but it certainly hadn't been his desire. He wondered if he should apologize, but just then Barnett began talking.

"The way I see it, this is all gonna be prime real estate. Not that it isn't already a good investment, but I figure now's the time to build and invest in the property."

"What about the ranches? Do you think folks will just up and sell?" Austin asked.

The older man rubbed his chin. William Barnett was a man known for his thoughtful consideration, something Austin had witnessed many times.

"I reckon they'll have to," he finally replied. "I'm not a real visionary, but even I know that as the cities expand, there's gonna be less and less room for ranches and farms in this area."

"People are still going to need food," Austin said. "What then?"

"They'll move farther from the cities, I suppose. There's still good homesteading ground to be had. Folks will move and start over."

"And will you?"

Barnett shook his head. "I doubt I'll be around when it gets that far along." He refocused on the cake. "That's something for my children's children to figure out. For now, I was kind of hoping you might consider taking on the job of lawman for our town. It's not something we'll need for a while. There's a lot to put in motion before we need to worry about that."

Austin was surprised by Barnett's news. "I hadn't really thought about quitting what I'm doing."

"Well, like I said, there's no rush. Just keep it in mind and think on it a while. You can always get back to me." Will finished off his cake and got to his feet. "Guess I'd better see to my guests. It looks like several families are leavin'. Safety in numbers, you know."

Austin sat at the table for several minutes more. He'd long since finished his cake and was actually thinking of having a second piece. He was thinking about Jessica Atherton, too. She had been easy to talk to, and he missed the company of women.

A frown came to his lips. That was a dangerous thought to have. Hadn't he worked hard to keep himself from entanglements of the heart? After Grace died, he had determined never to love again.

Grace.

Just the thought of her troubled Austin's conscience in a way he prayed to forget. She had been so young, and she had loved him so completely. But just as he'd killed his brother, Austin had killed her, too.

Chapter 4

Having accompanied her mother to Cedar Springs on this fine September morning, Jessica found herself caught up in making the rounds. They generally started at the post office. After picking up the mail, they would go to the bank. Next they headed for the feedstore and put in any orders sent by Jessica's father. Then it was off to the general store for most of their shopping. When everything was complete, Jessica and her mother would usually have a bite to eat and then call on friends in the afternoon before heading home.

This morning, however, her mother had added an unscheduled visit to the pastor's wife, Mrs. Baker. Jessica sat with the two older women for as long as she could. She felt like a fidgety child, unable to focus on the conversation or find pleasure in the visit. Mostly the women talked about church affairs and the upcoming October harvest party, neither of which overly interested Jessica. Finally, she asked to be excused, commenting that she needed a bit of exercise. Mother had given her an odd look but nevertheless dismissed her. Now Jessica was free to wander.

Perhaps I'll see what's new at the jewelry store. Jessica headed in that direction, careful not to snag the hem of her gown on the boardwalk. She had almost reached the shop when she saw Marty Wythe coming her way.

Great, now I will have to visit with her. The idea didn't set well. No doubt she would want to talk about Robert and Alice and their baby.

"Why, good morning, Jessica. Are you here alone?" Marty asked.

"No. Mother is visiting Mrs. Baker, and I needed some air." She gave Marty a smile. "How about you?"

"I'm here with my sister. Hannah decided we needed more fabric. We've been sewing like crazy for the children. With the three boys we adopted and Johanna and the baby, I find my time quite valuable. Johanna is two now and seems to be everywhere at once. She grows almost faster than I can make clothes. Little John Jacob is in need of more diapers, and the older boys need clothes let out or down almost every other week."

Jessica nodded. "Did you bring the children with you?"

"Goodness, no. Alice is keeping the youngest two. She can nurse John Jacob, along with little Wills. I'm sure Rosita is also helping, as Johanna will be quite the handful. The boys are with Jake. He's teaching them about running the ranch. They love life in Texas."

"I suppose they feel safe and loved now," Jessica said, trying to speak as her mother might. "And what do you think of your brother-in-law's plans for a new town?"

Marty tucked an errant strand of hair back into her bonnet. "I think growth is inevitable, and since it can't be stopped, it should be managed. I think the idea is a good one. I know I much prefer sending my children only six or seven miles away to school rather than twenty-five and have them board with other folks. I was teaching the boys at home because of the distance. If we get things up and running, a school will be established, and I can take them in the carriage, or Jacob says they could ride together on one of the horses." She shrugged. "I think they're too young for that, but he swears they aren't. What about you? Are you excited about the new town?"

"I really haven't given it all that much consideration," Jessica replied honestly. "I don't intend to stay around, so it doesn't matter to me."

"Oh? And where are you planning on going?"

Jessica met Marty's quizzical gaze. "I'm not sure. I guess . . . anywhere but here."

Marty smiled. "I used to feel that way myself, and you can see where it took me."

"Yes. You met a wonderful man and lived an opulent life in Denver. That sounds perfect to me. Well, maybe minus the wonderful man."

"You mean you don't intend to marry?" Marty asked.

Jessica looked away momentarily. She didn't really want to share her heart with Marty. Word might get back to Robert and Alice, and she didn't want pity from either one. On the other hand, refusing to answer would look just as odd.

"I don't. Not now, anyway. When I realized that I didn't love Robert, yet had long planned a future with him, it caused me to think. I was comfortable with the plans everyone had for us, but I was foolish. Not only that, I was wronging us both by hanging on to those plans. Now I think that leaving this place and venturing out sounds more beneficial."

"Well, just be careful. As I said, I used to have that same attitude." Marty shook her head. "I set out to answer a mail-order bride request. You never know what desperation will make you do. Looking back, I see how tragic it might have been."

"I don't intend to let desperation make my decisions for me," Jessica replied, knowing her answer sounded rather clipped.

Marty looked away from her and frowned. Jessica worried that she'd offended the woman and started to offer an apology, but just then Marty's brows knit together, and her expression suggested she was perplexed.

"That man looked so familiar," Marty said, finally looking back at Jessica.

"What man?" Jessica turned to look behind her but saw no one.

"A tall, bearded man just turned down the alleyway. He looked familiar but disappeared too quickly." She shook her head. "I can't place him."

"If you'd like, we could go after him," Jessica suggested.

"No." Marty continued to ponder the matter for a moment. After several seconds of silence, she shrugged. "I'm probably mistaken. Given all the new people coming into this area, there are bound to be folks who remind me of others I know." But even as Marty stated this, Jessica could hear the wariness in her voice.

Just then Hannah Barnett came from a shop down the street. Spying the two women, she waved and made her way to join them. "Jessica, how nice to see you again. Is your mother with you?"

"Yes, ma'am. She should be finished visiting Mrs. Baker most any time."

"I don't know about you two, but I'm ready for something to eat. Do you suppose your mother would find that appealing?"

Jessica cast a quick glance toward the parsonage and was happy to see her mother leaving the Bakers' house. "I think she probably would, but you can ask her yourself. She's coming just now."

"Hannah. Marty," Mother declared as she joined them. The women embraced briefly. "Isn't it a pretty day?"

"Yes, and the temperatures are so much more tolerable than they were just a month ago. Although it's still plenty warm," Hannah replied. "I was just telling Jessica and Marty that I am ready for something to eat. How about you?"

"I'm famished," Jessica's mother admitted. "I planned to suggest the same thing to Jess."

"Good. Why don't we adjourn to the new café on Broadway Street and enjoy a meal together?"

"That sounds wonderful," Mother said, looking to Jessica. "Don't you agree?"

"Delightful," Jessica lied, knowing that no one really cared how she felt.

She followed the women to the café and took her appointed seat at the table. Blue-and-white checkered tablecloths adorned each table and a white linen napkin was set at each place. A small bouquet of flowers in an amber-colored fruit jar added a homey atmosphere.

"Ladies," the proprietor, Sylvia Baldwin, announced in greeting, "you are my very first customers of the day." She beamed them a smile. "Let me tell you what's available."

Jessica settled back as the woman recited the menu. "Today I have a wonderful vegetable and beef casserole, served with bread and butter. For dessert, the most delicious apple nut cake just came out of the oven, and it is drizzled with fresh cream. If the casserole doesn't appeal, I can fry you up a steak—ham or beef."

"I think the casserole sounds wonderful," Mrs. Barnett declared.

"It does," Mother agreed and looked to Jessica. "Don't you think?"

Jessica nodded and Marty did likewise. "It's agreed, then," Mrs. Barnett said. "Please bring four orders and some tea." The woman nodded and hurried from the room as Hannah Barnett unfolded her napkin and placed it on her lap.

It wasn't long before Sylvia returned with a full tea service on a cart. She poured tea for each woman, offered them lemon, sugar, or cream, then exited with the cart as quickly as she'd come. Jessica sipped the hot liquid, not really in the mood for tea. She would have much rather had something cold, but unless the café made its own ice or had refrigeration, it wasn't a possibility.

As if reading her mind, Marty sighed. "I wish this tea were iced."

"That would be nice," Mother agreed. She started to take a taste of her own tea when she seemed to remember something. "Tyler told me the other day that several homes in California now have air-cooled rooms."

"Air-cooled?" Mrs. Barnett asked.

"Yes, but I haven't any idea how it works. It's something based on the way commercial refrigerators work, I believe Tyler said. That and fans. Apparently they can cool an entire floor if the house isn't too big."

"That would certainly be welcome in the summertime," Marty said, pulling a fan from her reticule. She opened the lacy blue slats and began to wave it back and forth. "I know the weather is much cooler than last month, but I look forward to it cooling even more."

"You got used to snow in Colorado," her sister chided. "You know better than to expect such cold down here, although we have had our times, to be sure, and will again. In fact, William said it might be a cold winter."

"I would love a cold winter," Marty said with a sigh.

Jessica had very little to say during their luncheon. The food arrived and she immediately dug in, lest she be expected to talk. She had nothing to say that anyone would want to hear, and she feared these women might have questions for her that she didn't want to answer.

She had grown up knowing and loving these women as family—at least as much as she loved anyone—but she knew their penchant for wheedling information from unwilling victims. She frowned at this uncharitable thought.

How much of my life have I spent thinking unkind thoughts of others? I don't know their hearts and have never endeavored to do so.

That feeling of dread came once again and washed over Jessica like a wave. In her previous conversation with Marty she'd spoken of her desire to leave Texas. Such a plan would break her mother's heart—her father's, too.

It wasn't long before other folks arrived at the café. Jessica nodded at some of her friends as they took seats across the room. Mother spoke to several people, as did Mrs. Barnett and Marty, but Jessica felt void of words. She had no desire to make pleasantries when her heart was in such a state of confusion. Would the answer ever come?

★

Austin arrived at the Barnett Ranch a little after noon. On his way to Dallas he figured to stop by and see if the ladies needed anything from the big city. To his surprise, however, the womenfolk were gone or, in Alice Barnett's case, busy caring for two infants and a two-year-old.

Robert greeted him at the door. He seemed genuinely happy to usher Austin inside and immediately invited him to share their meal.

"I have beans and bacon, corn bread, and some of my mom's delicious cinnamon rolls."

"How could I refuse?" Austin said with a grin. "I have to admit I was hoping to make it in time for lunch."

Robert laughed. "As we've said on more than one occasion—you are always welcome to break bread with us." He led the way to the dining room. "Let me grab you some dishes and silver. Would you like a cup of coffee, too?"

Austin sank onto one of the chairs. "Sure. I make it a habit to never turn down a good cup of coffee."

It was only a matter of minutes before both men settled in to eat. Robert offered grace first. The prayer was simple, but it painfully reminded Austin of his upbringing. The family had always prayed over each meal.

Mother prayed with them at bedtime, and Father had devotions and prayer in the morning. Austin had taken some of those practices into his adult life, but after losing Grace, he'd fallen away. It wasn't that he didn't believe in God or know what it said about Him in the Bible. It was more a sense that while God did exist, He really didn't care.

"So why are you headed to Dallas?" Robert asked.

"I have a meeting tomorrow related to cattle inspections."

"Are there problems?"

Austin savored a large spoonful of beans before answering. "Rustling is on the increase. There've been some cases where thieves have cut big sections of fence and run out quite a few head."

Robert's expression changed to one of concern. "Around here?"

"I'm not sure. That's part of what the meeting is for. I think they also have plans to give out the latest brand books. It's important for us to memorize the brands and be able to identify each ranch's animals."

"That can't be an easy task. There are hundreds of ranches just in the Dallas area."

Austin nodded and continued to eat. He knew the task would be laborious, but that was what he'd signed on for. Besides, he'd been working at this for quite a while now and had most of the established ranch brands memorized.

"It's hard to believe we're this close to the twentieth century and folks are still stealin' cattle. You'd like to figure folks would just find an honest way to make a livin'."

"That'd be nice. But so long as there's something of value that someone wants, you're gonna have thieves and rustlers."

Robert pulled apart a piece of corn bread and buttered it. "I'll talk to Pa. It probably wouldn't hurt to ride the fence line and see for ourselves if there are any breaks. We are due to make that ride anyway." He smiled. "I'm glad you stopped by, though. We haven't seen you for a while."

"Hasn't been that long." Austin crumpled his corn bread and stirred it into the beans. "I thought I'd stop here on the way to Dallas and see if you folks need anything."

"Can't say that we do. My ma and Marty are over in Cedar Springs today, so I imagine they'll be able to get most anything we need. Alice is here. I could ask her. She's takin' care of Marty's two youngest, along with our son."

"She's a good woman," Austin replied, uncertain what else to say.

Robert smiled. "She is that. And to think I almost settled for second best."

"What do you mean?"

"Well, it's just that for the longest time folks expected me to marry Jessica Atherton."

"Really?" Austin questioned. "Why?"

Robert finished his corn bread before answering. "Our mothers kind of figured for us to marry. Mostly 'cause Jess followed me around like a puppy. Her brothers were too busy to give her much attention, and I made the mistake of feelin' sorry for her." He chuckled and pushed back his empty bowl. "I used to do rope tricks for her and make her little trinkets. I have to say I loved her like a little sister. I still do. But where marrying was concerned, she wasn't for me."

Austin wanted to know more but knew it wasn't smart to look too eager. He didn't want to give Robert Barnett the wrong idea. "So you married Alice instead."

"From the first moment I met her, I knew Alice was the one for me. Jessica couldn't understand it, even though I knew she didn't love me—not the way she needed to in order to marry. Jessica took it as somewhat of a personal blow, especially given that Alice has that scar on her face. I hardly even see the thing, but Jess seemed to think my choice was some sort of put-down on her. Like she was so bad that I'd choose anyone, even a scarred woman, rather than choose her. Nothin' could've been further from the truth."

"What do you mean?" Austin tried to sound only casually interested, but he couldn't hide his desire to know. He hadn't been able to put Jessica Atherton out of his mind since first meeting her at the Barnetts'.

"Well, Jessica is a beautiful woman—there's no denying that. She'll never suffer for beaus. But it wasn't mere physical beauty that drew me to Alice. She's like the other half of my soul. We see things pretty much eye to eye. I've never felt that kind of kindred spirit with anyone else, and now I know I never will."

Austin thought of his relationship with Grace. That was exactly how he'd felt about her. He knew he'd never again find a woman to love—one who would love him as Grace had. And that was all right by him. Austin had no intention of ever loving another woman. He might be fascinated with Jessica Atherton's boldness. He might even appreciate her fine form and pretty face, but that was it. He wasn't going to give his heart to anyone.

But still, there was that nagging vision of Jessica and her blatant honesty. Austin smiled. "I met Miss Atherton at your town planning party. She was full of information about the area."

"She can be very friendly," Robert said, getting to his feet. "But she can also be manipulative and selfish. She's been spoiled most of her life, and while she's got a good heart, Jessica is often only interested in what benefits Jessica." He moved toward the kitchen. "Now I'm gonna bring you some of my mother's cinnamon rolls. These rolls are famous around here. She even used them to appease the Comanche long ago."

Austin chuckled. "Then they must really be something."

Chapter 5

Jessica gave her hair a final touch before dabbing her earlobes with a tiny bit of perfume. She loved the flowery scent, so light and sweet, but she was going to the church social with Daniel Harper, so she used it sparingly. There was no sense in overdoing it. She liked Daniel well enough, but he wasn't exactly her ideal man. The son of one of the local ranchers, Daniel was handsome and could sing like nobody else, but he intended to remain a rancher, and that had never appealed to Jessica. Of course, right now, Jessica wasn't at all sure what appealed to her.

She made her way downstairs and paused momentarily at the drawing room door. She smoothed down the lace on her bodice and swept down the skirt of her gown to make sure everything was in place. The door was ajar, and Jessica could hear her father and Daniel talking inside the room.

"Well, you know our Jess," her father was saying. "If you're looking to win her heart, then you need to shower her with plenty of attention and an occasional bauble or two. She likes pretty things."

"Yes, sir. I know that's true."

Jessica frowned as the conversation continued. She knew she shouldn't be eavesdropping, but it was as if her feet were nailed to the floor.

"Jessica's always been different from her sister. She likes the best things in life. She's like a princess in a castle—spoiled, pampered, and beautiful."

"She's surely beautiful," Daniel declared. "She's the prettiest girl in the county, and I'd be proud to be her husband. With my inheritance, I could keep her in nice things."

"She'll want to take trips, as well. I've heard her say it many times. She has done a fair piece of traveling with her grandparents, but now they're gone and she has no one to take her abroad." Her father chuckled. "I swear that girl has covered more miles than my horse."

The men laughed and Jessica began to feel sick. *Is that all I am to Father? Ornamental and demanding?*

Tears came unbidden and she frowned. The painful words cut to the core of her being. She'd never thought her parents believed her so shallow and selfish. She backed away from the door and headed back upstairs. Her mind echoed with the reverberation of her father's comments.

"She's like a princess in a castle—spoiled, pampered, and beautiful."

What a horrible thing to say about her. Jessica plopped down on the bed and let the tears flow. It was horrible because it was true. She was spoiled and pampered. She'd never known real want. Oh, there had been lean years, but her father and Robert's father had wisely invested and were good to help others when times of trouble came.

"Jessica, Daniel is waiting for you," her mother called from the hallway. She tapped on the door, then opened it to find Jessica in distress. "What's wrong, darling?"

Unwilling to admit to her eavesdropping, Jessica went with the only thing she could think of. "I'm not feeling well. My stomach and head hurt something fierce." At least that wasn't a lie. "Please tell Daniel I can't attend the social with him. I'm sorry."

Mother came and felt her forehead. "Hmm, you seem warm but not feverish. I'll go tell your father and Daniel that you're indisposed. Oh, and I'll get some tea and crackers for you. That might help. Meanwhile, why don't you take your hair down and start undressing. I'll help you with the back buttons when I return."

Jess nodded and reached up to pull several pins from her hair as Mother disappeared from the room. She hated disappointing Daniel, but he would be seeking to get her to marry him, and she had no intention of doing so. Perhaps it was better this way. Was it wrong to step out with someone just for the fun of stepping out?

Pulling off her kid boots, Jessica continued to ponder the things she'd done when it came to beaus. She had never allowed for hand-holding or kissing, but she did flirt unmercifully. Was that a sin? Was it wrong to give false hope of marriage to a gentleman?

"I never meant it for harm," she murmured. "I only thought . . . of myself and having a wonderful time." Her conscience burned, and she knew in that moment that her intentions had been wrong, even if her actions could be excused.

Mother was gone for only minutes before she returned with a tray. On it was a cup of weak tea and a plate with several crackers. She placed the tray on the dresser and came to help Jessica with the buttons of her high-collared lacy bodice.

"I know you were looking forward to this social, but there will be others, and you certainly wouldn't want to go if you were coming down with something contagious."

Jessica sat at her dressing table and watched Mother's expression from the mirror's image. She was so kind and calm. She had no way of knowing the turmoil in Jessica's heart. Being freed from the gown and corset, Jessica rid herself of the petticoat and shift before donning a lightweight cotton nightgown.

Mother had her sit once again while she gently brushed Jessica's hair. "I remember doing this for you when you were little. Once you could braid your own hair, you didn't need me anymore."

Jessica frowned. "I'll always need you, Mother."

Her mother gave a light laugh. "Oh, my sweet girl, one day a young man will steal all of your interest. And that's the way it should be. But do know this: I will miss you."

Jessica turned abruptly. Her earlier thoughts haunted her. "Mother, do you think I'm a good person?"

"What?"

She sighed and tried again. "Do you think I have a good heart—that I'm a good person?"

"Of course." Her mother looked at her oddly. "Why would you ask a question like that?"

Jessica shrugged. "I don't know. I suppose I've just been thinking about too many things."

"Such as?"

"That I haven't always been kind to people or considerate of their desires and needs. I've been selfish at times and probably too concerned about things that don't really matter. I feel like I'm a rotten friend and daughter."

"Oh, sweetheart, just the fact that it bothers you proves that you're a good person. A bad person wouldn't care. If you were truly as awful as you seem to think, well, none of this would matter."

But it hasn't mattered . . . until now.

"I don't mean to be self-focused. I never meant to hurt anyone."

"Who have you hurt? Why all this remorse just now?" Mother tied a ribbon to Jessica's braid and stepped back. "Come on, let's get you lying down."

Jessica allowed Mother to lead her to bed. Once tucked in, Jessica posed another question. "Can a person truly change her ways?"

Mother brought the tray over to the bed. "The Bible says that with God all things are possible. I believe people can change." Jessica sat up halfway as Mother handed her the cup. The weak tea sounded more inviting than Jessica had originally thought. She sipped it carefully, mindful of the heat. It was perfect.

"However," Mother continued, putting the cup back on the saucer, "they have to want to change. My first husband wasn't of a mind to change. He didn't believe that his cruelty and ugliness were a problem. He thought he was doing a good thing overall."

"But how? How could a man who was trying to sabotage the Union soldiers as they slept consider that a good thing?"

"Because, despite the war being over, the Union was making the South feel abominable. Malcolm thought that since they felt the need to put soldiers of color in charge of Corpus Christi, it was his right to put an end to it. He wasn't doing it because he thought it was evil or wrong. He felt vindicated in his choices."

Jessica considered that for a moment. Hadn't she always felt justified about her choices? She was always quick with an answer when her conscience prodded her with guilt for something she'd said or done. She'd fought against that prodding voice in her heart, convincing herself that she was innocent of wrongdoing.

Biting her lip, Jessica wondered if there was any hope for her at all. She had said things to hurt people. She had done things to satisfy her desires, no matter the cost to others. Maybe worst of all, she had thought nothing of using people to her benefit.

"What's going on, Jessica?" Mother sat on the edge of the bed and studied her with a questioning expression. "This isn't like you."

"I know," Jessica replied sadly. "But it should be. I should care more about other people. I've been horrible about such things. I don't know what's going on in the lives of my old friends, or even if we are still friends. I'm ashamed of myself and frustrated by the turn my life has taken."

"But, Jessica, you aren't the only one to have ever felt that way, and you aren't entirely to blame for any distance you feel with your friends. After all, most have married and have or are about to have children. That takes them away from society for a time. They change with that, as well. No one is the same after marrying and having children. You take on new priorities."

"Yes, but I have neither husband nor child. I should be able to pay visits and see to the friendships. I should have gone calling and checked to see if my friends needed anything. I didn't. I didn't even think of it—I didn't care."

Mother shook her head. "I find that hard to believe. Folks show their concern in different ways. Now, drink some more tea. I put some headache powders in it. Nibble on the crackers, but don't overstress your stomach. I'm sure you'll feel better by morning."

Jessica took the tea and sipped the warm liquid. Mother nodded in approval, then got up and walked to the lamp by the door. "I'll come and check on you a little later and put this out for the night." She turned back toward Jessica. "Just pray about it, darling. God has a plan in all of this. He will show you the truth." She left then, pulling the door shut behind her.

"That's what I'm afraid of," Jessica whispered to no one. "That's what I fear the most—the truth."

★

Days after his trip to Dallas, Austin Todd sat trying his best to read a book on memory and determine whether it pertained to the spirit or to the brain. There was quite a wide field of thought on the subject. The book told of the powerful effect memories had on people—a topic that immediately drew his attention.

Memories had a debilitating effect on him. They haunted and tormented him daily. He had hoped the book might provide some guidance for putting painful memories away from the mind or spirit. Wherever they existed, Austin wished to exile them to some faraway place where they couldn't hurt him anymore.

He closed the book and gave a heavy sigh. Without meaning to, he thought of his brother Houston. His younger brother would no doubt make fun of the book and tease Austin about being too intellectual. The thought made Austin smile, just for a moment. He and Houston had always been so close. They liked many of the same activities, foods, clothes, and even careers.

Both had signed up to work for the Treasury Department and, after proving themselves worthy, had been promoted to the Secret Service as field agents. They were responsible for tracking down counterfeiters and those who committed fraud against the government. And the brothers were good at what they did.

Austin and Houston made the perfect team. They were able to complete more cases than some of their fellow agents had simply because they knew each other so well and could anticipate what the other would do.

Until the night Houston took a bullet that was never intended for him. Austin replayed the scene once again.

It was the middle of the night, but both Austin and Houston were enthusiastic about their situation. For months they had worked to break a conspiratorial ring of stamp counterfeiters. However, the deeper the brothers dug, the more people it exposed, and some were highly placed in society.

Their investigation had taken them to a warehouse on the outskirts of the capital. It was here that Austin's world began to collapse. He could still remember the stench of old fish. He could still see Houston leaping in front of him to save his life. . . .

"Hey, Austin, you to home?"

Austin roused from the memory, set the book aside, and opened the door. Much to his surprise he found Tyler Atherton and William Barnett waiting.

"Come in," Austin said, motioning to the men. Both did and Austin could see they were glancing around as if to inspect his living conditions. "I've tried to make the place as homey as possible, but I'm often gone." It sounded like an apology.

"It looks just right," Barnett said, smiling. Tyler nodded in agreement.

"It's kinda damp and chilly out there tonight. Would you like a cup of coffee?" Austin asked, heading to the stove in anticipation.

"No, we just wanted to talk to you for a little bit. We're on our way back from business in Cedar Springs. Talked with the lawyer who's helping us with the plans for Terryton."

"Well, I don't know what I can do for you, but have a seat at the table. It's really all I can offer." He looked to the two benches.

The two men settled themselves on one side, while Austin took a seat opposite them. He waited for someone to say something.

"You know we asked you to consider heading up law and order for us," Barnett began. Austin nodded. "Well, in our discussions with the railroad, they've made it clear that they would like to have the law in place prior to the railroad setting up a tent city for their workers. With that, it puts us in sort of a spot to get an answer from you."

Austin drew a deep breath and considered the situation. With his Ranger work he was often away from home, traveling from one place to another. Taking on the town marshal job would put him in one area and allow him to sleep in a bed every night. At least until some trouble broke out and he was needed.

"When would they want me to start? I don't want to leave the Rangers without some warning."

"I would expect nothing less from you," Barnett said. "The railroad won't begin building until January. And only then if we can get all the legal work taken care of. A lot of contract work goes into even the smallest spur line."

"January would work well," Austin said. That was little more than three months away. It would give the Rangers plenty of time to replace him. "I'll do it."

Mr. Atherton laughed. "Just like that? You didn't even ask what the salary was."

Austin shrugged. "I remember you talking about a few of those things at the meeting. I know you can't afford to pay much at the beginning. I figure as long as I have a roof over my head and food on the table, I won't have big expenses."

"Well, just the same, we will take good care of you. Rest assured." Barnett looked to his friend. "I don't know about you, Tyler, but I need to get on home. Hannah is going to start worrying if I don't show up soon. And knowing her, she'll set up a search party."

Barnett and Atherton got to their feet. Austin shook their hands and escorted them to the door. "I appreciate the confidence you have in me. You don't really know what kind of lawman I'll make, but you're taking a chance on me anyway."

Mr. Barnett turned and shook his head. "We aren't takin' a chance. I've seen you in action. I know everything I need to know. If you're good enough for the Rangers, you're good enough for me."

Austin closed the door once the men had remounted their horses. He felt almost deceptive. They didn't know everything about him. Maybe if they did, they wouldn't want him around at all, much less heading up the law for their new town.

★

Jessica appeared at the breakfast table prepared to take on the world. She was determined to make a change in her life and do something kind for someone. She had dressed neatly in a crisp white blouse and blue serge skirt. She had a little jacket that matched the material of the skirt and planned to wear that, too, but for now it hung on a peg by the front door.

"What has you up so early?" her father asked.

Jessica tried not to take offense at the comment. It was true she'd been lax in rising early. "I want to make some calls. I was hoping I could borrow the buggy."

"It's fine with me. You'll need to clear it with your ma."

"Clear what?" Mother asked, bringing in a platter stacked with griddle cakes.

"I want to make a couple of calls today. I asked if I could borrow the buggy. Osage said he could drive me."

"Well, that's fine with me, as well. I have plenty to keep me busy and won't be needing it. Just be home before it gets very late. Osage can't see all that well after dark. I don't want to be worrying about you."

Father smiled and put his hand to his face, as if to shield his words. "She'll worry about you anyway," he said in a low voice.

Jessica laughed and helped herself to a piece of bacon from the plate her mother passed. "Well, I don't want anyone fretting over me. I'm not waiting until regular calling hours, so I should be home by afternoon."

"Where are you headed?" her mother asked.

Jessica bit her lower lip and hesitated a moment. Finally she drew a deep breath. "To the Barnetts'. I want to speak with Alice."

Her mother exchanged a look with Father, then turned back to Jessica as if to question her with a gaze. Jessica had seen her mother act in this manner before. Her expression spoke volumes.

"I owe her an apology. I haven't been very nice to her since . . . well, since she got here. I want to set things straight."

Mother smiled. "I think that's admirable."

Jessica nodded and refocused on the food. *I think it's much overdue.*

Once breakfast concluded, Jessica arranged for the buggy. She had decided the night before that she hadn't shown Alice Barnett much charity or kindness. It was a hard pill to take, but Jessica felt she needed to set things right with Alice before attempting to address any of her other shortcomings. Of course, Alice might be unwilling to receive Jessica. She might have no desire to forgive. But from what Jessica had observed, Robert's wife was probably one of the sweetest people in the county and would no doubt be gracious and forgiving.

"You ready, Miss Jessica?" Osage asked, putting a hat atop his balding head.

"I am. I see we have some clouds overhead. I hope we won't have rain to worry about."

"No. These are fair weather clouds. They're movin' east and won't bring us a drop."

Osage held fast to her arm as Jessica climbed into the buggy. He wasn't too strong anymore, but she would never have suggested he not do as he had always done. Father had told her that Osage was a very proud man.

He seated himself and picked up the reins before asking, "Where to?"

"I want to start by going to the Barnetts'."

Osage smiled. "I'm mighty happy to do that. This is Mrs. Barnett's day to bake cinnamon rolls."

Jessica laughed and smoothed her skirt with her gloved hands. "Then we'd better hurry."

It was a pleasant ride to the Barnett Ranch. The sun wasn't nearly as fierce as it had been in the summer months, and there was a slight breeze blowing in from the west. The weather was nearly perfect.

Jessica watched as Osage handled the single horse with ease. She was quite comfortable driving her own conveyance—it gave her a sense of control and freedom—but her parents seldom allowed her to go alone. Yet even with Osage at her side, Jessica felt very much alone.

Maybe I'm destined to spend my life like this. Maybe being in charge of myself will be more fulfilling than tying myself to a husband and children. Maybe I'll live at home for the rest of my life and care for Mother and Father as they age.

But as she considered the possibilities, Jessica felt the same sense of loneliness that had tormented her before. She was so lost in her thoughts that she didn't hear the rider approaching until he was nearly even with the buggy.

Osage slowed the wagon and put his finger to the rim of his hat. "Mornin', Austin."

Austin gave his hat a slight tip. "Good morning, Mr. McElroy. Miss Atherton."

"Good morning, Mr. Todd. What are you about this fine day?"

"Headin' to the Barnetts', and you?"

"We're headed there, as well."

"Mind if I ride alongside?" Austin's horse gave a bit of a whinny, as though adding his thoughts on the question.

"I don't mind at all. It will give us a chance to get better acquainted."

She wasn't sure, but she thought Mr. Todd actually frowned. He turned away quickly. However, when he looked back, he offered her a pleasant smile. Jessica decided she'd been mistaken. It was probably nothing more than a trick of the sun.

Osage hummed softly to himself as he usually did when family members were having a conversation. It endeared him to both Jessica and her mother. They knew Osage could still hear every word, but also knew he would never dream of sharing that information elsewhere.

"From where do you hale, Mr. Todd?" she asked.

"Virginia, but my mother was born and raised in Texas. I suppose that's why I thought to come here."

"Was Virginia not to your liking?"

He hesitated. "Well . . . uh . . . it was just time for a change."

"I see." Jessica thought he sounded guarded and decided to change the subject. "I was born and raised here, but I've done quite a bit of traveling. My grandparents were good to take me along on many of their trips. I've been to Europe several times, as well as to England and Scotland and to several of the Caribbean islands. Grandfather had business down there, so we combined it with a pleasurable time, as well. How about you, Mr. Todd?"

He shrugged. "Well, I've been all over the eastern part of the country and up to Canada, but never abroad."

"Would you like to go one day?"

Austin shook his head. "I can't say that I've ever really considered it one way or the other. Though it could be exciting. When I was attending the university, I read about the Greeks and Romans. I thought it would be marvelous to journey to Italy and Greece someday."

"I think so, too," Jessica admitted. "We had plans to make a trip to that area when my grandfather fell ill. After he died, it wasn't long before Grandmother took a bad fall. She never recovered, and we lost her, as well."

"I'm sorry. Loss is never easy, even when it comes to those who are older."

Jessica arched a brow. "You speak as one who knows. Have you suffered much loss in your life?"

By this time they had arrived at the Barnetts'. Jessica awaited Mr. Todd's answer, but when he slid off his horse and thanked her for the company before walking toward the barn, she knew he wasn't going to give her one.

He is such a mysterious man. Sad too. It shows in his eyes. I'm sure he must know full well what it feels like to lose someone.

"I'm gonna go around back, Miss Jessica," Osage said with a wink. "I'll see if I can't sweet-talk a roll or two from Missus Barnett."

"I suppose I can take time for at least two rolls and a cup of coffee," Jessica said, amused by Osage's delight. She made her way to the front door and knocked. Her nerves returned, and for just a moment she thought of coming up with some other excuse for her appearance. But by the time Rosita answered the door, Jessica had regained her courage.

I'm more than ornamental and self-centered. I need to make a fresh start, and this is where I need to begin.

"I was hoping Alice might be here. I've come to call on her."

"Sí, she is here. You come in and sit. I will tell her you have come," Rosita replied. The small Mexican woman disappeared down the hall, and Jessica took a chair in the front room, where she knew the Barnetts usually received company. This was such a welcoming room. She studied the beautiful draperies and rugs. A fireplace adorned the middle of one wall. It was built from native rock and made a perfect contrast to the pine walls. Fancy work was displayed here and there. Someone had crocheted armrest covers for each of the chairs, as well as headrest guards. One could never tell when a visiting young man might have an overabundance of oil in his hair.

"Rosita said you'd come to see me," Alice said from the entryway. She held her small son and smiled. "Would you like some tea and rolls?"

Even though the aroma was tempting, Jessica declined. "No, I'd better not. It might distract me from my purpose in coming." Alice looked at her with a perplexed expression, and Jessica lost no time in adding, "I thought it was high time I apologized."

Alice looked at her strangely. "Apologize? To me?"

"Yes. I haven't been very kind to you. I was horrible to you, in fact."

Alice came and sat across from Jessica. She shifted the baby in her arms. "I'm not sure I understand."

"Well, when Robert chose you over me, I felt slighted. I wasn't in love with him, but it bothered me all the same. I know I said some things that weren't very nice." She bowed her head. "I made comments about your scar that I shouldn't have."

"Saying nothing about it wouldn't make it any less evident," Alice said with a smile. "I'm sorry that you felt slighted. I never intended to fall in love with Robert. I never planned for any of this life. I never figured I deserved anything more than servitude."

Jessica met her eyes. "But you do. You are the perfect example of a kind and gentle woman. You deserve to be happy, and I'm glad you have a wonderful man like Robert to see that you are. Robert was always good to me. He showed attention to me and made me feel special when I was a little girl."

"He certainly knows how to do that," Alice said, not sounding the least bit jealous.

Jessica was almost certain if the roles were reversed, she would be most unhappy. It only served to remind her of her failings. She sighed. "I hope you can forgive me, Alice. I'd like for us to be friends."

Alice's face seemed to light up. "But of course we're friends. As for forgiving you, well, I hold nothing against you. In my eyes there's no reason for forgiveness, but you have it just the same."

Jessica felt as if a small weight had been taken from her shoulders. "Thank you."

"Are you sure you wouldn't like some tea?"

Jessica shook her head. "No. I've already imposed long enough. One day soon, I will come to visit and spend more time." She looked at the baby in Alice's arms. "He's beautiful. I don't think I ever told you . . . congratulations."

Alice blushed and extended the sleeping child. "Would you like to hold him?"

Before Jessica realized it, Alice had placed the baby in her arms. She stared down at the infant and imagined he might have been her own. Hers and Robert's. The thought just wouldn't take shape, however. That was never meant to be.

She pressed the baby back toward Alice. The new mother quickly reclaimed her son. "Thank you," Jessica said. "He's quite a wonder."

"I think so, too. Sometimes I can scarcely believe I'm a mother."

Jessica didn't know what to say, so she said nothing for a moment. When she felt enough silence had passed between them, she began again for the door.

"Thank you for hearing me out." She stopped long enough to glance over her shoulder. "And for being so gracious in your forgiveness. Robert told me several times how wonderful you were. I guess I always knew that he was right."

"I'm glad you think so, but believe me, I have my moments, like everyone else." The baby stirred but didn't wake, and Alice continued in a softer voice. "I'm so glad you came today. I want very much for us to be the best of friends."

Her words drove away some of Jessica's sadness. "I know we will be."

Chapter 6

To further her plan for improving herself, Jessica arranged for Osage to drive her into Cedar Springs. This time they took the buckboard so that Osage could pick up supplies at the feedstore while Jessica attended to her plan.

The plan was simple. She wanted to check in with an old friend, Victoria Welch, now Victoria Branson. Victoria had married Marcus Branson, a man nearly twice her age, some three months earlier. Jessica hadn't approved the match and told her friend as much. She had begged Victoria to forget the man, but she'd insisted that she loved him. Jessica thought to put her foot down and prove just how disturbed she was by threatening not to attend the wedding. Then, before she knew it, Victoria had told her not to come. It had hurt Jessica deeply, but she'd never let on.

Around town, it was much talked about, since it had been thought that Jessica would be Victoria's maid of honor. Jessica cried on her mother's shoulder and was only comforted when her mother promised they would go spend a few days in Dallas. Particularly on the day of the wedding.

How could I have been so judgmental? Jessica felt consumed with guilt. It was as if the scales had fallen from her eyes, and now she could see the ugly truth about her soul. Was there even hope for her?

Jessica hoped to make amends. She wanted to see Victoria face-to-face and tell her how sorry she was. Not only that, but she wanted to honor the new bride and show her support. On her lap, Jessica held a belated wedding gift—a beautiful, expensive tablecloth of Brussels lace. She hoped the gift might smooth the way to her apology for missing the wedding.

"I have some calls to make while you attend to business for Father," Jessica told Osage as he helped her from the buggy. "Why don't you pick me up around three-thirty. That way we can get home before it's dark."

"Sounds good to me. I won't need any more time than that." He threw her a wink. "'Course it's been a lotta years since I had me a moonlight ride with a beautiful young lady."

Jessica laughed. "Why can't you be younger, Osage? I think you'd make a wonderful beau." The old man flushed red. She'd caused him to go speechless.

Smiling, Jessica patted his arm. "We can pick up the discussion on the way home."

His face remained red. "I think it might be better to find a new topic, Miss Jessica. I don't think your pa would approve of you and me sweet-talkin' our way home." He smiled and pointed toward the feedstore. "If you need me sooner, I'll be there playin' checkers with Charlie."

"Tell Charlie I said hello," Jessica replied. "Tell him I still remember coming to his feedstore with Papa when I was just a little girl." She hadn't thought about that in years. It had been a simple pleasure that she'd shared with her father and brothers. She paused and glanced toward Victoria's house. "Three-thirty, then. I'll be at Pritchard's store." Osage nodded and snapped the reins.

Jessica took the tablecloth and made her way up the path to Victoria's front door and knocked. Through the screened door she heard the sound of laughter. It would seem Victoria had guests. Jessica thought to leave, but it was too late. An older woman, wearing a starched white apron, approached the door.

"Welcome. The other ladies are in the parlor to the left. Would you like for me to take the gift?"

Jessica shook her head, uncertain what was happening. Apparently there was some sort of gathering that she had imposed herself upon.

"I didn't know she had company," Jessica whispered. "I only thought to see Victoria and give her a wedding gift."

The older woman seemed to consider this for a moment. "Well, she has some of the local ladies here for their regular sewing circle. However, the gals planned a surprise birthday party for her. Victoria had no idea and is now enjoying that celebration. I'm sure she wouldn't mind."

"Well, I wouldn't want to interfere."

"Who is it, Mrs. Humphrey?" Victoria asked, opening the parlor's pocket doors. She looked surprised to see her guest. "Jessica. It's . . . been . . . well, a long time."

Jessica nodded. "I know and I'm sorry. I came to apologize and bring you a belated wedding gift, but I see I've come at a bad time."

"No, no. That's all right," Victoria said, glancing hesitantly over her shoulder. "Some mutual friends decided to throw me a birthday party. I'd like for you to stay."

"Perhaps for a short time," Jessica agreed. She extended the table-cloth. "This is for you—that and a long overdue apology. I'm sorry for the things I said about your marriage. You were right to react as you did. I was thoughtless and judgmental. I never should have tried to stand between you and Marcus. I hope you'll forgive me." She prayed Victoria would hear the sincerity in her statement.

Victoria didn't acknowledge the request but took the tablecloth and ran her hand over the delicate piece. "This is beautiful. Thank you." She gave Jessica a wary smile. "Come inside and see the others."

Jessica followed Victoria into the room as Mrs. Humphrey pulled the doors shut behind them. Many of Jessica's former schoolmates and friends were gathered in the parlor for the party. She had obviously not been invited to attend, and it caused Jessica both pain and embarrassment to have invaded their celebration.

"Look, Jessica Atherton has come with a wedding gift. Isn't it beautiful?" Victoria asked, unfolding part of the tablecloth. "I've never seen anything quite so fine."

"Would have been nice if she'd given it to you at the wedding," someone behind Victoria murmured. Jessica couldn't tell for sure who had made the statement.

Beth Pritchard Englewood, daughter of the local mercantile owners Nelson and Dorothy Pritchard, got up and offered Jessica her chair. "Come sit, and I'll get you some cake and tea."

Jessica could see that the other women were just as surprised by her arrival as Victoria. They offered muffled greetings and then looked away, as if desperate to put some distance between them.

"How have you been, Jessica?" Karin Williams asked. Karin was married to one of her father's ranch hands and was just starting to show her pregnancy. "I saw you at church last week, but I didn't have a chance to speak with you."

I'm sure she didn't really want to speak to me. I spoke out against her marrying her father's hired man. The memory shamed Jessica. It was just one more example of her judgmental attitude.

"I'm sorry I missed you. I'm doing very well, thank you. How about you? Are you and Zeb settling into your new home?"

Karin gave her an enthusiastic nod. "We love our little house. Father says he'll help us add on to it later, when . . . we have more children." She blushed and lowered her head. "For now, it's big enough."

"I'm glad that you're happy," Jessica said. She looked around the room at the other women. "I'm sorry I've been so out of touch. I hope you'll forgive me for my lack of consideration. I haven't been a very good friend to any of you."

"Well, you're here now," Victoria said, rather uncomfortably. She smiled and looked to Beth. "You were just telling us about little Anna's teething troubles."

Beth handed Jessica a plate with a piece of cake and a cup of tea, which clattered a bit on the saucer as she handed it over. The tea sloshed, but Jessica said nothing. It wouldn't have been heard anyway as Beth began speaking of the woes her one-year-old daughter experienced as her teeth came in. Jessica listened, trying her best to be interested in the topic. As the other women commented and offered suggestions, Jessica felt more and more out of place. Everyone here was married.

"And Rusty is so very concerned about his little sister," Beth continued. "I told him she was getting new teeth, and he seemed completely in awe. Then he asked me why God hadn't given her any teeth before now." The other ladies laughed and Jessica forced a smile.

"Oh, did I tell you that Jason is now fully in charge of my parents' store?" Beth asked. "Father is also making him a full partner."

"That's wonderful news," Victoria said, clapping her hands. "I know you've wanted that for so long."

"We got word that Ollie's mother isn't doing well," Millie Stapleton piped up. Millie was a year older than the rest and as such was the unofficial head matron of their society. "Since his father passed on, his mother has been gradually declining. I fear we may have to bring her here to live with us."

"Oh, I'm sorry, Millie," Beth said, shaking her head. "I'm sure that would be difficult."

"Yes, with the children so young, it would be hard to care for a sickly old woman. But what can I do? She is family and is our obligation. Ollie would never forsake her." She glanced Jessica's way. "We simply do not forsake the ones we love." Jessica knew the comment was directed at her failure to have supported Victoria's choice of husband.

I don't fit in here. I don't belong. I really don't even know these women anymore.

Jessica thought back to their childhood days in school. They had all been quite close then. What had happened? Why had Jessica allowed them to slip away?

Because I was too worried about what I wanted for myself. I was too busy arranging my next grand affair, my next gown, my next trip.

Guilt washed over her. She took a bite of cake and felt it stick in her throat. Taking a quick sip of her tea, Jessica was able to avoid making a scene. She suddenly felt desperate to take her leave. That feeling grew stronger at the next question posed.

"So, Jessica, are you seeing anyone special?" one of the women asked.

Before she could answer, Millie spoke. "Jess is seeing a great many special people. I hear she goes out every week with a new beau." She looked at Jessica, as if daring her to refute the statement.

Jessica was floored by the comment, as well as the ensuing debate about her love life. She was mortified to find herself the center of this kind of attention.

"I think it positively risqué," Karin said. "A young lady ought to court only one man."

Jessica didn't think before answering. "If I were courting, then I would agree with you. I haven't chosen any one fellow, so I feel free to get to know each of them a little better. In this day and age a woman needn't feel it necessary to accept the first man who asks for her hand. I believe in taking my time and getting to know a fellow, learn what he stands for, what kind of husband and companion he'll make."

"But that's hardly a proper way to handle things!" Millie exclaimed. "It makes you seem . . . well . . . too forward."

The other ladies nodded. "You wouldn't want to get a bad reputation," one of them added, while another said, "It would shame your parents," making her angry.

"And how is it I would get a bad reputation and shame my mother and father?" Jessica asked, feeling defensive. "You all know my values and beliefs. You know I would never conduct myself in any way other than what was expected. Surely you would never speak out against me—slandering or gossiping about things that weren't true." The latter was issued as a challenge.

Her words hit the mark, and the women fell silent. Jessica sipped her tea and waited for their further attack. While it surprised her they would so openly show their disapproval, she was glad for it. It made her feel less guilty for having avoided them, and for a moment she forgot all about her campaign to make amends.

"Well, I believe a young lady of values should see only one man at a time, rather than stringing along several. It seems only proper," Millie finally said. "When I was courting Ollie, I never would have looked at another man. In fact, even before we were officially courting, I had eyes only for him. My heart knew from the time we were young that we were meant for each other."

"I envy you." Jessica drew in a calming breath. "I haven't had that experience."

"Well, you had Robert but then lost him to that woman from Colorado."

Jessica squared her shoulders. "I never really had Robert. We were good friends, and folks just assumed we would end up together."

"But you assumed it, too," Beth threw in. "I remember our discussions about how you would one day be Mrs. Robert Barnett. Of course, no one knew what was yet to come."

Jessica wanted to end the conversation but knew it was her own fault for allowing it to begin in the first place. "Robert and Alice are perfect for each other. They are well suited and love each other very much. I can't say that I ever felt that way about Robert. Frankly, I don't feel that way about anyone. Therefore, I believe I have the right to explore the possibilities of each single man."

"That sounds like a very modern way of thinking," Victoria murmured, sounding rather embarrassed. "Some of this new philosophy seems a bit scandalous to me." The other ladies nodded.

"Why, I was just reading the other day that in some places it's perfectly acceptable for women to go unescorted to dances and such. Can you imagine the commotion that must cause?"

To Jessica's relief, the woman began discussing social mores, leaving Jessica free to calm down. She knew if she didn't leave, she might very well say something she would regret. She supposed her old nature wasn't completely set aside.

Just then the clock chimed three. "Oh goodness. I didn't realize it was getting so late," she announced. "I have to meet my driver soon, and I still need to pick up some things." She put her teacup aside. "I do hope you'll excuse me." She turned to Victoria. "I wish you the best of birthdays and a very happy marriage. I wish all of you ladies well and hope you will come visiting soon."

The women seemed surprised by her sudden need to depart, but no one tried to stop her. Jessica knew they were just as glad to get rid of her as she was to go. No doubt they would spend the rest of the afternoon discussing her shortcomings.

She left Victoria's and made her way down to Main Street, where Pritchard's and other stores could be found. Jessica tried not to be bothered by the things the women had said, but she couldn't help it. Their comments had angered her. Did they truly believe her to be so scandalous? Was her love life really such a fascinating topic that they had nothing better on which to focus? Who were they to establish rules for her?

Glancing into the shop windows, Jessica tried to clear her mind. Changing her outlook on life and the driving forces of her internal nature was harder than Jessica had originally thought. There was so much to overcome—so much she hadn't even realized was at issue. Who knew that the women of Cedar Springs and the surrounding area were keeping track of how many different men with whom she stepped out?

Still, they were right. Reputations once lost were not easily regained. Jessica didn't want to cause her parents pain or disgrace. Perhaps she should find some charity and spend her time and efforts there. She thought of her sister, Gloria, and her generous nature and penchant for hard work. She was in Montana teaching Indian children to read and write English while her soldier husband worked to keep the area safe. Jessica's brothers, Isaac and Howard, were busy helping a local church join with other churches in building houses for the destitute in and around Corpus Christi. Her siblings were well known for their giving nature, their compassion for the less fortunate.

"What am I known for?" Jessica pondered. Sadly, she knew the answer. She was known for loving herself—for spending all of her time looking for ways to make herself happy.

For all my desire to do better, I find there are many hurdles to overcome. I wonder if I will ever be able to remake myself into a better person.

She browsed the aisles at Pritchard's. In days gone by she would have consoled herself with a new shawl or a pair of embroidered stockings, but now she had no interest. She knew they wouldn't help to ease her misery—they never really had. Jessica made her way outside to wait for Osage. She felt a sense of relief when she saw the heavily loaded buckboard pull up. All she really wanted was to go home—to get away from people and their condemning thoughts.

Thoughts that I no doubt deserve, Jessica realized. Again, she couldn't help but wonder if there was any hope for her to change. Transformations came with a price, she realized. Would she be able to afford the cost?

Chapter 7

"I'm certainly glad to see you," Jessica said as Osage pulled up alongside her.

He jumped down and helped Jessica. "Hee-hee! A fella likes to hear that a gal is anxious to be in his company."

Jessica shook her head and forgot her frustrations with the ladies. Osage never failed to improve her spirits. She folded her gloved hands and waited for him to climb into the driver's seat. After he settled in and snapped the reins, she jumped right into conversation.

"Did you get all the feed and supplies Pa needed?"

"Got 'em. I noticed the horse was walking funny, and when I took a look, I found he was about to throw a shoe. I went to the smithy."

"Good thing you caught it. Pa won't be happy that it happened. I suppose Manuel will get in trouble."

"Oh, your pa won't go too hard on him," Osage said.

For several minutes neither one spoke. Then, to her surprise, Jessica found herself asking Osage a rather personal question.

"Osage, did you get what you wanted out of life?"

"I did, for the most part. I found me a good job with your pa's pa, and then I found me a sweet gal to marry. We were happy and had a couple of boys. Had a good life those first few years. Then my wife died, and the boys were taken by their grandparents because I was about half outta my mind. When things settled down, I knew it was for the best. I couldn't have taken care of them. I would've liked my family to have stayed together, but otherwise, life has been good." He turned to look at her for a moment. "So, Miss Jessica, what is it you want out of life?"

Jessica searched her heart to give him an answer but couldn't find one. A month ago, she might have said she wanted travel and wealth and all manner of importance, even fame. Now, knowing how she'd presented herself throughout her life, Jessica was no longer sure what she wanted. Perhaps to clear her reputation and mend fences would be a good place to start. But she couldn't say that to Osage.

"I guess I'm still trying to figure that out."

Hours later at home, Jessica heard Osage's question posed again. This time it came from Lee Skelly. It was worded a little differently, but nevertheless pressed her for answers she didn't have.

Lee had ridden up while she was walking around the pasture just behind the house. Reining his horse to a stop, he'd looked at her in curiosity. "What are you lookin' for, Miss Jessica?"

She looked up to see Lee watching her closely. "I don't know. I'm just walking and thinking."

"Thinkin' about life and what you want out of it?" He didn't give her time to answer. "What do you want, Miss Jessica?"

"I want to be left to my thinking," she replied, irritated at the interruption.

"Thinkin' about me? About how you'd like to marry me?" He gave her a lopsided grin.

"To be quite honest, I don't know what I want."

"So then, you could be wantin' me and just not know it, right?" He jumped down from the back of his horse.

His determination fascinated her. Was he really that much in love with her? Did he actually pine for her? She had to ask. "Lee, are you in love with me?"

The question caused the young man to cough and then clear his throat rather noisily. "Miss Jessica, that's a silly question to ask. You know I worship the ground you walk on."

"But that's not the same." She looked out across the pastureland.

She knew it as well as she knew the back of her hand. What she didn't know was her own heart.

"You speak of marriage and a future with me, but you don't talk about the important things."

"Like love? Well, of course I love you, Miss Jessica. I've been sweet on you since you were fourteen."

Jessica looked at Lee and shook her head. "I didn't know that."

"Well, why would you? We don't exactly socialize in the same circles." He laughed. "I'm just the boss's hired hand. Still, I would feel mighty proud to capture the heart of the boss's daughter. I can just imagine how the other fellas would react. They'd see me in a whole new light."

"And that would be important to you?"

"Yes, ma'am," he said enthusiastically.

"But why?"

Lee's expression suggested she ought to know the answer. "Because it would prove my worth. I ain't never had nothing of value belong to me. If I was to marry you, it would show everyone that I was important, that I mattered."

"And you don't feel you matter otherwise?" Jessica hadn't expected this turn of conversation, but it fascinated her at the same time.

He shrugged. "I know I matter to me, but I want to matter to others. I want to be somebody. If I married the boss's daughter, that would make me special. The other fellas would look at me with respect. And more than a little envy," he added, laughing. "I guess I'd just like some say in my life, some control."

"I can tell you from my own experience that taking control of a situation isn't all it's thought to be. It requires a great deal of attention and work."

"Well, all I know is that you took control of my heart."

"Oh, stop it, Lee. I know what you want from me, but I can't give it. I don't love you."

He frowned. "I know that, but I'm willin' to take a chance on you learnin' to love me."

Jessica felt sorry for the man, but she couldn't give in. She shook her head. "Well, I'm not."

★

Austin thought long and hard about his decision to leave the Rangers as he rode home from Dallas. He'd told his superior of his plan, and the man hadn't tried to stop him. Instead, he'd congratulated Austin and said he thought he would make a fine town marshal. Some of the other men standing nearby had agreed.

The sun was near to setting, and it left a cold, empty feeling to the clouded sky. Twilight was not his favorite time. It always made him feel lonely. He couldn't help but think of Grace. They had married with only one thought—to spend the rest of their lives loving each other. They had planned for many children and a large house in which to put them. Austin smiled and then felt a sense of wonder. Thinking about Grace didn't seem to hurt like it had before. In fact, it was almost like a faint dream.

He allowed himself the memory of their wedding. She had been so radiant in her wedding silk. Her parents had died when she was little, and her grandmother had raised her. Having lived the life of a privileged only child, Grace's desires were surprisingly modest and simple. She had attracted Austin's attention from the first day he'd seen her walking along the street in Washington, D.C. Just a few short months later, she walked down the aisle to him.

Remembering her smile as he lifted the veil to kiss her, Austin had thought his life perfect. If he'd died in that moment, he would have died the happiest man in the world. Instead, she had died and he had killed her. Killed her by his absence. When she went into labor, no one had been there to help her, and both she and the baby had died.

He bore the responsibility like a heavy mantle. Austin was the one who had made her move to the country—away from her beloved grandmother and the city she so enjoyed. He had worried about her living in the city and being alone when he had to be gone on special assignments. Oh, certainly she had her grandmother, at least at first. They were still living in town when the old woman had taken ill and died only six days later. Even so, Grace loved to visit the cemetery, as if she could see her grandmother face-to-face. She loved to take flowers to the grave and spend time in reflection. She told Austin that she knew her grandmother was in heaven, safe and happy, but she felt certain God gave Grandmother the messages from Grace. And Austin had taken that away by insisting on the move.

Three months after her grandmother's death, Austin had found a place away from the city. He told Grace about it and about his desire to move. He could see the disappointment in her expression and knew she didn't approve.

"But she never complained," he murmured. He shook his head and gazed up at the darkening sky. It was starting to look like rain. "You never did complain."

When she'd told him they were going to have a baby, Austin had nearly fainted. It was the only time he'd felt so consumed by fear that he'd thought he might pass out. Even in all the close calls he'd had with his work, nothing had prepared him for the daunting task of fatherhood.

The thought of raising a child in a city the size of Washington gave Austin some concerns. It was a beautiful place, to be sure, and had much to recommend it. However, he had made enemies, and he knew there could be great danger for his family. He worried that even living ten miles away wouldn't be far enough. What if his enemies followed him and found Grace?

By August of 1890 they had settled into their country home. Grace was due to deliver in March, and despite her growing size, she'd made them a lovely home. Grace longed for the hustle and bustle of the city, but she assured Austin that she was happy. And he believed her. They truly had been happy there—at least for a short while.

When winter arrived travel became more difficult, and Austin insisted Grace do nothing to put herself in danger. He often had to leave her alone, and it worried him greatly. He managed to scrape together enough money to pay a housekeeper for the winter. The case Austin and Houston had worked for the past year was about to break wide open. They had been following stamp counterfeiters and felt certain they would have the entire ring rounded up by February.

Austin had figured after it was over, he would request cases that would keep him close to home. Close to Grace and his unborn child.

It seemed so reasonable that when everything fell apart, Austin only knew a deep and painful shock.

January 31 of 1891 had started out routine, but by the next day, Houston Todd was dead and Austin was explaining to his parents what had happened. The grief was overwhelming, but the blame was even worse. His parents had nothing kind to say about Austin's participation in the event.

He closed his eyes and saw their accusing faces. He felt betrayed and abandoned. He was grieving the loss of his brother, as well, and already felt so much guilt that it threatened to swallow him whole.

"It's your fault! You killed your brother!" His mother pointed her finger at Austin.

A rider approached from the north, and Austin quickly forced his thoughts from the past as Robert Barnett drew up and stopped his sorrel.

"I've been out checking the fence," Robert explained. "I'm headed home for supper. Why don't you join us?"

Austin felt half starved, but he was in no mood to be around people. "I'm tired and just gonna head home."

"You have to eat," Robert pressed. "Besides, my place is closer, and it looks like it might start raining any minute. I believe I'll have more light to see by, and it'll only get darker as you make your way home."

"I'll be fine. I'm not that far, and I have some of the food your mother sent over a couple of days ago."

Robert looked at him for a moment and then nodded. "I guess you do look worn down. I'll give Ma your regrets."

"Thanks." Austin turned his mount away from Robert.

"Hey, Austin—is there anything I can do?"

He glanced over his shoulder in the dimming light. "No. There's nothing anyone can do."

--- ★ ---

The skies were dark by the time Jessica and her family sat down to dinner. Father had been busy with one of his new foals and was late getting back to the house for supper. When he finally bounded through the door, he was ready to eat immediately.

Mother lit extra lamps and placed them around the house, but it didn't seem to dispel the gloom. Rain threatened at any moment, and flashes of lightning could be seen in the distance.

Father led them in grace, then dug into a bowl of jalapeños and corn. "Looks like we might actually get a good rain."

Mother nodded from her side of the table and extended a different bowl to Jessica. She took one of the smaller potatoes and passed the bowl to her father. While he continued to comment on the coming storm, Jessica mashed the potato on her plate and added butter, salt, and pepper. She couldn't help returning her thoughts to the events of her day and the way the women had treated her at Victoria's. It wasn't unkindness, she told herself, but rather disapproval. She realized that she cared quite deeply what those women thought, and it troubled her.

"Well, I have to say I'm surprised," Father said, turning to Jessica.

She startled and shook her head. "Why? What are you surprised about?"

"I went to help Osage with the feed, and when we finished I asked him where your parcels were. He told me you hadn't bought anything. I have to say, Jess, this is the first time you've come back from town without havin' a wagonful of purchases. I figured you'd be bringing home some new doodad or fancy dress."

Jessica frowned. "You know, there really is more to me than clothes and pretty things."

Father's expression turned troubled. "I know there's more to you, Jess. I didn't mean to hurt your feelings. I always kinda got a kick out of seeing how those things made you happy. It pleased me to give 'em to you."

Jessica knew that her tension from the day threatened to ruin the meal. "I'm sorry. I'm just feeling out of sorts."

Father laughed. "You got no need to be. The world is at your fingertips, and life is good." He put his fork down and smiled. "Tomorrow you'll be all sunshine and smiles. Just wait and see."

Her father's words seemed shallow and offered no comfort. Nevertheless, Jessica drew a deep breath and let it out slowly to calm her anger. "I'm sure you're right, Papa. Things are bound to be better tomorrow."

With that matter resolved in her parents' minds, they went back to discussing the ranch while Jessica ate in silence. Would things truly be better tomorrow?

Chapter 8

Austin pored over the new brand book provided to him by the Cattle Raisers Association of Texas. He was already familiar with a good many local brands, such as those that belonged to the Barnett, Wythe, Reid, and Atherton ranches. Those families represented a good portion of the area to the north and west of Dallas, but they were a small fraction of all the ranches he'd cover.

Thumbing through the book, Austin wasn't surprised to see that there were hundreds of brands listed. People took great pride in their own unique brands. It seemed a pity that others couldn't respect the marks as a "hands off" sign. Rustling was up from earlier in the decade, but the meeting with his fellow Rangers suggested that there were signs of it waning. He hoped that was true. It was one thing when people stole because their children were starving, and quite another when they stole just for the extra cash they could get. At least that was Austin's way of looking at it. Neither way was right, but it had more to do with a matter of heart. He found himself more forgiving of the man who stole out of desperation. Even so, he couldn't turn a blind eye.

Putting the book aside, Austin got up and poured himself a glass of buttermilk. Tyler Atherton had just brought it over an hour earlier, and it was still chilled from his springhouse. He let the tangy liquid slide down his throat and thought it about the best he'd ever had. He quickly finished off one glass and then poured another. At this rate the buttermilk would be gone by morning.

He marveled at the way these neighbors took care of one another. Everybody seemed to have one talent or another and shared the benefits of those talents. He'd seen Mrs. Barnett load him up with food, while Mrs. Atherton was quick to give him bedding and linens. Mrs. Reid had stopped by with her sister, Mrs. Atherton, and both women had brought him a whole carriage full of food, candles, and lamps and oil, not to mention several books. He was mighty grateful for their kindness, but it also made him feel uneasy. He'd never intended to get close to anyone ever again.

After losing his brother in January of 1891, he'd lost Grace and the baby the following month. By May his father had suffered a heart attack and passed, leaving only Austin and his mother to carry the grief. Mother wasn't able to bear up under the load, however, and she fell ill and died in June. Within less than six months, Austin had lost everyone he'd ever loved. It was a pain he never intended to repeat.

Still, visions of Jessica Atherton came to mind. She was feisty and high-spirited. Nothing like Grace had been. In fact, Miss Atherton might very well be the extreme opposite. While Grace hadn't quite come up to his shoulder, Jessica was taller. And while Grace probably weighed no more than ninety pounds, Jessica had a little more meat on her bones, and it curved in all the right places.

The real differences, however, were in their personalities and desires. He wasn't at all sure what Miss Atherton wanted out of life. It seemed the few times they had shared each other's company, she had been outspoken and independent. Grace had always been quiet and relied on him for everything.

He didn't know why he was comparing the two women. There was really no comparison. Grace had touched his heart and soul in a way that no other woman could. His biggest sorrow had been in losing her and the baby—a son.

Austin paced the small cabin, wishing he could drive Jessica's image from his thoughts. He wasn't about to let his heart get involved again. He'd made himself a pledge, and he would stick to it.

Miss Atherton probably has no idea that I'm even thinking of her, so it's best I not. Besides, I have plenty of other things to put my mind on.

He drew a deep breath and went back to the kitchen area, where a small wood-burning stove sat. He used it for cooking as well as for heating the cabin. He put a pot of coffee on to heat. It was left over from earlier and just needed some warming. Checking the stove's fuel, Austin added a few sticks of wood and let the fire build a little. After a few quick pokes with the wood tongs, the flames flared nicely.

It proved a good way to regroup his thoughts and put aside his sorrows. There was work to be done, and he couldn't waste time with memories.

Suppressing a yawn, Austin returned to the table and took a seat. He picked up the brand book and returned to memorizing.

★

The next morning Austin made his way into Cedar Springs. He wanted to make sure the local law understood what he had planned.

Greeting the town marshal, Austin showed him his brand book. "Marshal, I just wanted to tell you that I'll be traveling around to the various ranches to check brands against what's registered. I want to look over the cattle as best I can and hear any complaints the ranchers might have. I wanted you to know, so if anyone asked, you'd already have knowledge of my plans."

"I appreciate that, Austin. You're a good man."

The marshal's words made Austin wince. "I don't know about that, but it is a job."

"Rustlin' doesn't seem quite as bad as it did last spring. Still, I'm glad the Rangers are takin' this seriously." The older man smoothed back his graying hair. "Why don't you take a walk with me? I was just about to make my rounds. We could have a bite of something to eat before you head out."

"Sounds good," Austin admitted. He had already decided to make a visit to one of the cafés in town.

The marshal pulled on his Stetson. It was a "boss of the plains" style, with a flat brim and straight four-inch crown. The top was rounded, and it was unadorned except for a hatband that had been added. Austin knew the hat had cost him a pretty penny.

"I see you're admirin' my hat. My wife bought this for me as an anniversary present. Saved up her egg and sewin' money. Ain't it a dandy?"

"It is indeed." Austin's own hat had seen better days.

The two men left the jail and walked out into the late morning air. The temperature had risen considerably since Austin's morning ride into town. "Looks like it may be a hot one today."

"Yeah, I was thinkin' the same," the marshal answered. "Seems like it never can make up its mind this time of year." The marshal paused to tip his hat to a couple of ladies exiting one of the dry goods stores. Austin did the same.

"As a town marshal you have to get used to being the face of law and order, as well as a comfort to those in need," the marshal said.

Austin looked at him and shook his head. "What are you talking about?"

"Well, I heard about the plans for Terryton. I heard, too, that you'd been asked to take on the responsibility of law and order."

"That's true." Austin had no idea who had explained all of this to the marshal, but no doubt he needed to be told. "But it won't be for a while yet."

The marshal nodded, then gave a wave to a man sweeping his portion of the boardwalk across the street. "Matt, you're gonna wear that broom out."

The man laughed, waving the broom. "Already did. This is my third one in a month's time." The men shared a laugh.

Austin felt a little out of place. He didn't know many of the people in town. He seldom came to Cedar Springs unless it was to catch the train to Dallas or to pick up canned goods. The way the nearby families had taken care of him, he hadn't needed to do that very often.

"It's not always peaceful around these parts. We've had killers and thieves just like in the big city."

"I'm sure you speak the truth. Criminals scarcely stay within boundaries."

"That's true. If they did, they'd be a whole lot easier to catch," the marshal said.

They came to the bank and the marshal peeked inside. "Things runnin' okay today?" he called out.

Austin heard someone answer, "We're doing quite well. Off to a good start."

"Glad to hear it." He closed the door and motioned for Austin to follow him. "Got to make sure the Bisby Mercantile is locked up tight. They had to go east for the burial of her mother. Didn't know enough about the folks here to get someone to cover the store." They crossed the dirt street and made their way to the building. After a quick check of the front door, the marshal went around back. Satisfied that all was well, he nodded to Austin. "Now we can go have that bite to eat. I'll check the other half of town afterward."

"How many times a day do you do this?" Austin asked.

"Well, it depends. If we have a bunch of rowdy cowboys in town, I check a lot more often. And, of course, we check more at night than durin' the daylight hours."

"Makes sense."

The marshal kept glancing around as they walked. Austin could tell that he wasn't missing much. The man seemed concise and to the point in his conversation and attentive to everything that went on around him. Austin liked that about him.

"I do the town walk during the day. My deputies do the night hours unless they're sick or otherwise occupied. I usually walk the town first thing in the morning when the stores are opening. Then I check again around the noon hour and again at closin' time. During the evening the checks run every hour or two. It's a good way to make your presence known. But don't go at the same time each night and don't go exactly on the hour. You don't want folks ever believin' you have a set pattern. It'll get you in trouble every time."

Austin already knew that was true. He'd been warned of that on many of his Secret Service cases. Diversity was a good way to stay alive.

"Keep track of the troublemakers," the marshal offered. "Just because they aren't doing anything in particular doesn't mean they aren't up to somethin'."

With a smile, Austin turned toward the man. "You've no doubt seen it all."

"That I have. I used to be a deputy and then a marshal up north. I've seen men run stark naked down the middle of the street in winter because they were too intoxicated to know better. I've seen women, young and old, create scenes that would curl your hair. One woman was so angry about her husband spending all his pay each week at the saloon that she came to town with her double-barreled shotgun and blew a hole in the wall above her husband's head. He and his cronies looked pert near scared to death. When she told him to git . . . well . . . he got, and quick. You never know what you'll get yourself into."

"Maybe I should stick to inspecting cattle," Austin said, still smiling.

"Nah," the man replied. "What fun would that be?"

They shared a pleasant lunch together and then made the rounds for the rest of the small town. There was a busyness to the town, with folks making their way from business to business. Yet, even amongst the chaos there was a kind of order to everything.

"At night we check all the doors and windows. We look for any sign of forced entry. We check the water troughs to make sure nobody drowned themselves." He stopped and looked at Austin. "Had that happen to a drunk once, up north. Don't wanna ever see it happen again."

Austin nodded. "I wouldn't want to see such a thing, either." They were nearly back to the jail when Austin asked, "What else do you do?"

"Well, come with me and I'll show you. There's some paper work I sometimes have to see to. I keep track of the hours my deputies work and their pay. I sometimes have to go to the town council and ask for things we need at the jail. Then, of course, there are the wanted posters that I receive and the folks who amble in off the street for one reason or another. Some just wanna ask questions about the law, and other times they use me as a deterrent. Had a mother a couple of weeks ago come here with her eight-year-old son. Apparently he'd been stealin' from her milk money. She wanted him to know what it was like to sit in jail. So we put him in a cell while she went off shoppin'. The boy was mighty glad when she returned. I doubt she'll have too much trouble with him in the future."

They reentered the jail and the marshal was just showing Austin a logbook when a stranger entered.

"Good afternoon, Marshal. I wonder if you might lend me some assistance."

The man was well dressed in a brown suit, complete with a crisp white shirt, vest, and tie. He was older—probably in his fifties or sixties, Austin guessed. At least his well-trimmed beard and hair showed signs of graying.

"Could be, stranger. Why don't you tell me what you're needin'," the marshal replied.

"Thank you. I'm looking for the Wythes' ranch. I thought perhaps you could direct me."

At the mention of the name, Austin took more interest.

"Well, that depends." The marshal eyed him carefully. "Who are you and what do you want with the Wythes?"

The man smiled. "I do apologize. I'm Randolph Cuker. I was a good friend of the Wythes in Denver, when Jacob worked for one of the banks. They encouraged me to stop by their ranch anytime I was in the area. They assured me that just about anyone in town could direct me, but they particularly mentioned you. I had business that brought me to Dallas and thought I would pay them a visit."

"I see. Well, I suppose that's a good enough reason," the marshal declared. "There's a main road north of here that heads out and turns to the west. You follow that about twenty miles. You'll pass several farms and a couple of small ranches. Then you'll come up on a long stretch of land that belongs to the Athertons. The road will curve again and take you past the Barnett place. They have a big spread and the main entry to the property has a sign bearing their brand—looks like this." The marshal drew a line and put the letters NT beneath. "Just keep goin' another five miles or so to the Wythe place. Marty Wythe is sister to Mrs. Barnett and has the property that adjoins theirs. The Wythe place sits back off the road a ways, so just take the turnoff on the road to the right, and you'll find your way."

"Thank you. That was most thorough. I'm sure to find them." The man stretched out his hand. The marshal took hold and shook it. "I am very much in your debt, Marshal."

"Are you stayin' in town, Mr. Cuker?" Austin asked. He leaned casually back against the wall, as if only mildly interested.

"I have taken a room at the hotel. I'm not here for long, but it seemed prudent." The man pulled a watch from his vest pocket. "Now, if you'll excuse me, I must see about renting a horse and buggy."

He left without further comment, but Austin felt an uneasiness that made him want to follow the man. He went to the window and watched him cross the street.

"I'm not sure about him," Austin finally said.

"He seemed likable enough. He didn't shy away from coming in here. Most men who are trouble would avoid the jail like a dull knife."

Austin didn't want to stir up trouble. He gave the marshal a nod. "I'm sure you're right. Now, I better head out to start inspecting brands. Thanks for the company and the lessons in marshaling."

The older man gave a chuckle and took a seat behind his desk. "I was happy to help. Come back anytime."

★

"Manuel brought us the mail from town," Hannah declared as she joined Alice in the front room. "There's a letter here for you."

Alice frowned. "Who would write to me? I don't have any family or friends except those who live right here, and I just had a letter from Mother."

Hannah smiled. "Maybe it's from an old friend."

"I don't have any," Alice replied. She took the letter and studied the script. It was flowery and full of loops. The kind of writing a woman might make.

"Well, I don't suppose you'll know unless you open it," Hannah said, thumbing through the rest of the mail. "Mostly payments due. I had hoped Eleanor would write. I'm afraid my daughter is rather caught up in the women's movement for the right to vote. Writing to her mother to let her know how she's doing might delay the cause."

Alice smiled at her mother-in-law. She liked Hannah Barnett very much. The older woman was motherly and attentive—more so than Marty had been—although she never tried to impose herself on Alice.

Alice gave a brief nod, then carefully opened the letter. A single piece of paper was inside. Unfolding it, Alice read the brief message. She gasped before she could hide her fear.

"What is it?" Hannah asked and then apologized. "If you don't mind telling me."

Alice shook her head slowly and held the letter up to her mother-in-law. Hannah took it and read it aloud.

"Congratulations on your new baby. There are just some things money can't buy."

She looked back to Alice with a puzzled expression. "What an interesting message, but it's not signed."

"I don't have anyone who would write to me here. At least no one that I would *want* writing to me." Alice turned the envelope over. "It has a back stamp marked Dallas. I don't know anyone in Dallas except my mother, and this isn't her handwriting." She gave a shiver, but the older woman was already looking again at the letter.

"It's not really bad tidings," Hannah said, shaking her head. "But it *is* a mystery."

"A mystery I could do without," Alice said, afraid of what the letter might well mean to her family's safety.

Chapter 9

The skies opened up and poured rain just as church services began that September morning. Jessica tried to focus on the words of the hymn, rather than the sound of rain on the roof, but at one point she worried that the gully washer might cause damage. The land was still pretty dry, and if the rain came too suddenly, there would be flooding.

The congregation was just starting the second hymn when Jessica heard a disturbance at the back of the church. Apparently some poor soul had come into the service late. She didn't bother to look around from her family's pew in the front.

The congregation continued singing, drowning out the rain somewhat. Jessica had never been much for singing. She didn't find it all that appealing and had difficulty carrying a tune. For all her talents, singing wasn't one of them. Even so, she mouthed the words and tried to look involved.

There was a rustling sound to her right, and without so much as a whispered hello, Austin Todd slipped into the row right beside her. He was dripping wet and held his hat in his hands. Jessica knew she looked at him in surprise, but she couldn't help herself. When the song concluded, she took her seat and threw Austin a quick smile. His presence, even though he was dripping water everywhere, was pleasing to her.

The service lasted another hour, with the preacher teaching on the story of Daniel in the lions' den.

"Daniel's faith, much like that of Abraham and Joseph, whom we studied in the weeks past, saw him through much adversity—even in a dark lonely pit with man-eating lions."

Jessica was familiar with the story. She rather enjoyed all of the Bible stories she'd been taught in her youth. They spoke of great adventures and of people who left all they knew and traveled to make a new start for themselves in unknown lands. Such ideas had always appealed to her. Perhaps that was why she'd enjoyed traveling with her grandparents, while her siblings preferred to remain at home.

Maybe that's what I need to do.

Here in Cedar Springs, Jessica knew her reputation was that of a spoiled little girl. Maybe a new start in a city far away would suit her.

I could start over somewhere else. I could be my own woman, just as the women's movement encourages. Who knows, I could even join Eleanor Barnett in her cause. Jessica almost giggled aloud at the thought.

It might suit me, but Mama and Papa would have kittens.

She continued smiling at the thought only to find that Austin was watching her. He seemed neither disturbed by her amusement nor supportive. She felt her cheeks grow hot and lowered her head. It was then that she noticed Austin was dripping water onto the skirt of her gown. She frowned, then chided herself mentally. *It's only a dress and it will dry out.*

Lifting her head to look to the front of the church, Jessica tried to focus on the lesson. She stared at the pulpit with its handmade wooden cross nailed to the front while the pastor continued his sermon.

"When morning came and they opened that pit up, the king was mighty worried about his friend Daniel. You see, he hadn't wanted to put Daniel to death—not really. But sometimes folks in authority don't lead properly. They get impressed by the folks around them, and they're afraid to make the right decision. The king knew what was right but didn't choose to follow through, because the law at that time didn't leave room for changing.

"Now, you can find yourself relating to Daniel or to the king, but the important thing is this: God was faithful and trustworthy. The king halfway believed that Daniel's God would save him. But Daniel knew that his God was the true God, and He would take care of the details, whether Daniel lived or died. We must all strive for faith like that."

But how does one get faith like that? It's hard enough to trust the people you spend every day with. It's much harder to trust God, whom you can't see.

Jessica pondered the subject even while the pastor began to pray. She'd attended church all of her life. She'd accepted that she was a sinner and without Jesus she would be forever separated from God. When her Sunday school teacher had told her class that it wasn't hard to get saved, Jessica had listened closely. She could still hear old Mrs. Rogers explaining salvation. She had stretched out her arms and demonstrated that in this position her body formed a cross. She then said that Jesus had died on the cross to take away our sins. The cross was a bridge that allowed us to get to God.

"Anyone who would like to get saved has only to ask God to forgive their sins through the blood of Jesus, and then they need to walk in repentance and stop doing the bad things they did before."

Those words had greatly affected Jessica. And she had prayed silently as the teacher led the children in prayer. Jessica's parents had instilled in her respect for God and for her teachers, but this experience seemed different . . . more personal. When she told her mother about it later that evening, Mama had wept with joy and told Jessica they would arrange for her to be baptized. She was proud that her little daughter had made such a grown-up decision.

The congregation now rose to sing a final hymn, and Jessica got to her feet, as well. She put aside thoughts of her childhood and considered instead the man beside her. She'd never before encountered Austin at church and wondered if he was a new convert. He was certainly handsome, and his hands bore the rugged, tanned look of one who was used to working hard.

He extended the hymnal to share with her. She took hold of the book, but neither of them sang. The moment seemed to connect them in a way that startled Jessica. She couldn't help finding Austin fascinating.

She'd heard so much about him from others, yet now that she had met him face-to-face, none of those assessments seemed complete.

To Jessica's disappointment the song ended, and with one final prayer, the service was over. Austin took the hymnal and put it back while Jessica glanced around at various people shaking hands and greeting one another. The sanctuary hummed with voices. Jessica had started to follow her mother and father from the pew when she felt a slight touch on her arm. Turning back, she found Austin looking at her with an apologetic expression.

"I'm sorry for getting your skirt wet," he said, nodding to the damp spot. "Guess I pretty well washed my portion of the pew, as well." They looked in unison at the pew.

"It's wood," Jessica replied. "So as long as we dry it off, it won't suffer much." She took the dry edge of her skirt and gave the seat a quick wipe. She knew her action was rather scandalous, but it happened so quickly she didn't think to stop herself.

"That won't help your skirt any," Austin murmured, seeming just as surprised by Jessica as she felt.

"My skirt will dry and be just fine. It's only water." She met his eyes and fell silent. For a moment they stood staring at each other, neither one seeming to know what to say.

"Jessica, I want to introduce you to someone," her mother said from behind. "This is Harrison Gable."

She reluctantly turned. To her surprise she found a handsome man, probably in his midthirties, staring with a grin. Jessica smiled. "I'm pleased to meet you."

"The pleasure is definitely mine, Miss Atherton," Mr. Gable replied. "I've had the privilege of working with your father and Mr. Barnett on the plans for Terryton."

Jessica nodded. "You must be the lawyer from Dallas."

"Not anymore. I just moved here," he told her, looking quite pleased. "And I must say I'm not disappointed with the . . . area."

He looked her over from head to toe, making Jessica feel self-conscious. This man's confidence suggested he was someone used to getting what he wanted. She did her best to appear unaffected.

"This is a wonderful area," she countered with a coy smile. "We have many beauties."

"I noticed only one," he said, glancing over his shoulder.

He was flirting with her, but Jessica found that she enjoyed the attention. Still, she couldn't help worrying what Mother might think. Jessica's concern was for naught, as she found her mother was already busy speaking with Hannah Barnett. For a moment there was an awkward silence between Jessica and Mr. Gable. She wasn't at all sure what to say. Just then she remembered Austin and turned to introduce him. He was gone.

Jessica frowned and looked back to Harrison Gable. "I had thought to introduce you to Austin Todd, but it seems he has already departed. Mr. Todd works with the Texas Rangers to inspect cattle."

"Mr. Gable," Mother interrupted, "I understand you plan to have a late afternoon meeting with Mr. Barnett and my husband. I wonder if you might like to join us for the noon meal. Our place is right on the way to the Barnetts'. This way you can eat and rest before you and Tyler head over to your meeting."

Mr. Gable smiled, and for a moment Jessica felt her breath catch. "I would love to," he said.

Jittery and rather weak in the knees, Jessica tried to appear unmoved. She didn't know why she was acting like a silly schoolgirl with a crush.

"Wonderful. You can follow us home if you'd like, or we've plenty of room in the carriage. You could ride up front with Tyler as he drives. I'll ride in the second seat with Jessica."

"Oh no. I can't take your place beside your husband," he said, shocking Jessica by throwing her a quick wink.

Mother didn't seem to notice and continued. "It will be quite all right. That will give you two an opportunity to discuss any business that hasn't yet been tended. Come along. We're nearly ready to depart."

"I have my horse," Harrison Gable said, as if only then remembering.

"That's not a problem," Mother replied. "You can tie him to the back of our carriage." She left to join Father, who was already near the back of the church.

To her surprise, Harrison Gable leaned closer. "I would much rather sit beside you for the journey." His warm breath on her ear caused Jessica to jump back. Her eyes widened momentarily, but she straightened and feigned a reserve she didn't feel. Mr. Gable gave a low, almost inaudible chuckle.

★

Harrison Gable enjoyed the meal offered him by Carissa Atherton. She was a beautiful woman with impeccable manners, as was her daughter Jessica. He found he rather enjoyed the effect he seemed to have on the young woman. She'd been watching him with furtive glances from her seat across the table. Her interest pleased him, and he was equally attracted to her.

They settled in the drawing room after lunch, and Tyler asked him a few personal questions.

"You have family in the area, Mr. Gable?"

Harrison shook his head. "My kin are all in Alabama. I came west to explore the possibilities. I have to say, I'm truly more of a big city man. I prefer legal cases and the complicated practice of government law. In fact, I would like to one day work in Washington, D.C., or New York City."

He saw the way Jessica seemed to take note. Perhaps city life appealed to her, too. Before he could comment, however, Tyler Atherton asked yet another question.

"What about a wife and children?"

"Neither one," Harrison admitted. "Never seemed to have the time while studying to become a lawyer, and then I focused on actually practicing law. It's been an uphill battle, but I finally feel ready to consider marriage." He glanced at Jessica and added, "It would seem the possibilities are quite promising."

Tyler laughed, but it was Mrs. Atherton who commented. "I think you'll find some very nice young ladies in this area of Texas."

Harrison nodded, most serious. "I'm sure I will."

The conversation carried on in a casual, slow manner that put Gable at ease. He'd always had difficulty relaxing and enjoying people. Trained to listen to the details of client conversation and actions, Harrison usually found himself playing the lawyer even in his private life. Today, however, he felt as though he'd been accepted into a close group of people.

I think I'm going to enjoy this job. Maybe living out here in the sticks won't be so bad after all.

"I'm glad we can ride to the Barnetts' together," Tyler told him. "It's not hard to find, but we can discuss some of the other area ranches and farms on the way."

"I'm going to need to speak with all of the families," he replied. "Perhaps someone could accompany me as I make my rounds."

Jessica seemed to perk up at this. He watched as she leaned forward and opened her mouth to speak. Harrison smiled, sure that she would volunteer for the job, as he had hoped. Instead, Tyler spoke up.

"I'd be happy to show you around and introduce you. Why don't you plan to stop by here tomorrow?"

"Oh, I wasn't trying to impose myself upon you. I know you're a busy man."

"Bah," Tyler said, shaking his head. "I can take the time. This is important—not just to me, but to everyone in the area."

Jessica eased back against the chair and folded her hands. She looked disappointed but bowed her head. Harrison felt a sense of pleasure at her response, because he felt the same regret. It would have been wonderful to get to know her better. Especially away from others who might interrupt or interfere.

He scowled, thinking of the rain-soaked cowboy sitting beside Miss Atherton in church. He didn't know who the fella was, but he could very well be a rival.

★

"Well, I've stayed long enough," Austin declared, getting to his feet. He'd enjoyed a wonderful Sunday meal with the Barnetts and Wythes.

"I'm sorry you have to leave," William said, also standing. "Come back as soon as you can. You're always welcome here."

Austin nodded and looked to where the three ladies sat. "Thank you again, Mrs. Barnett."

"Please call me Hannah," she said, for what Austin figured was about the tenth time.

"I'll try, ma'am, but I wasn't raised to speak so casually to a lady."

William and Jake walked out with him, but Robert remained inside, seeming enamored with his young son and wife. A twinge of regret ran through Austin's heart, but again it didn't hurt nearly as bad as it once had. Maybe time was truly easing his misery.

"I'm meeting with Tyler and our lawyer here in a couple of hours," Will said as they walked to where Austin's horse had been tied to graze.

"I hope everything goes well."

"I plan to tell him that you've agreed to be our lawman in Terryton. That way he can get back to the railroad authorities and assure them that we have law and order in place."

"It's going to be interestin' to watch all of this fall in place," Jake interjected. "With the way Dallas is spreadin' out, I can't help but think our little town will suit the needs of folks who'd rather live in a smaller place."

"And it seems there are plenty of new folks," William added.

"Speaking of new folks," Austin said, turning to Jake, "did your friend find the place all right?"

"What friend?" Jake asked.

Austin looked from the younger man to the older. Returning his gaze to Jake, he spoke. "While I was visiting with the marshal in Cedar Springs, a fella stopped by the jail asking how to find your place. Said he was a friend from your banking days in Denver. He said you'd told him to stop by if he was in the area. Marshal told him how to find you."

"I don't have anyone from Denver who knows about me livin' here." His brow knit as he narrowed his eyes.

Just then Jake and Marty's three oldest boys came flying out the front door and disappeared in a flash around the house. That seemed to give Jake an idea. "There was the orphanage director. Maybe it was him bringin' more children to the ranch. You know he had the Barnetts take some older boys for local ranch help."

"He didn't appear to have anyone with him," Austin replied. "Said his name was Cuker. Randolph Cuker."

"I don't know any Cuker. What'd he look like?"

Austin could easily remember the man. "He was tall, lean, and had brown hair and a beard, although both were graying. He was well dressed and probably somewhere in his fifties, as far as age goes."

"I don't know anyone like that," Jake said with a frown.

"That's mighty strange," William said, his voice edged with concern.

"Seems to me," Jake began, "there have been a lot of strange things happening around here. Marty felt certain someone was watching her hang clothes the other day. Said she felt it more than saw anything, but it made her uncomfortable just the same. And then there's that note Alice received."

"What note?" Austin asked.

"It was one congratulating her on the baby, but it wasn't signed, and given her past, that doesn't bode well."

Austin felt perplexed. "What past?"

Jake looked to Will and received a nod before continuing. "In Denver some men killed Alice's father over some forged gold certificates. That's how Alice got the scar on her face. They held a knife to her and cut her when her father wouldn't give them what they wanted. He tried to interfere and they pushed him away. He fell and hit his head and died almost instantly. Alice passed out. Some folks found her and hauled her off to the hospital. After she recovered, one of the men followed her around and tried to bully her into finding the missing certificates. Then he started threatening her and Marty. When it got to be really bad, Marty and Alice decided it was time to join me here in Texas."

"I've worked around counterfeiters before," Austin admitted, without thinking. "I worked in the Secret Service for the Treasury Department. Counterfeit and fraud were my areas of work."

"Then maybe you'll have some insight to offer us. If this stranger is someone from Alice's past who's come to seek those certificates, we may all need to lend a hand," Barnett said. "All I know for certain is the letter scared my daughter-in-law to such a state that she's scarcely slept or eaten since it came."

"I can well imagine," Austin said, remembering the way the man at the jail had seemed most eager to find the Wythes. "I'll keep an ear out.

574

If I hear anything, I'll let you know. I've got friends back in Washington. I can let them know about the situation."

William nodded. "Maybe you should. If you want, you can come by tomorrow for breakfast, and I'll fill you in on more details. I'll let you know what we figure out tonight, too."

Austin agreed, but there was a heightened sense of concern that he'd not felt since working for the Secret Service. Counterfeiters could be quite ruthless, as those men in Denver had proven to Alice and her father. They would stop at nothing until they got what they wanted, and Austin had no plans to see these people hurt.

Chapter 10

With the harvest party only a week away, Jessica began to worry that she'd made a mistake in turning down the beaus who'd asked her to accompany them. She had hoped that perhaps Harrison Gable or Austin Todd might ask her, so she had refused the others. Now, with the festival nearly upon them, Jessica wasn't sure what to do. She supposed she could just attend with her parents. Or perhaps on her own.

She'd helped her mother can pumpkin all day. It was a tedious job, and it heated the house something awful. Mother had planned to do all of the cooking and canning outside, but then changed her mind. Now Jessica longed for cooler air. She was grateful the kitchen help had already cleaned out the insides of the pumpkins and had cut the edible parts from the thick orange skin. This shortened their work considerably. After that, it was easy enough to cook the pumpkin and jar it up. It was just far too hot.

"You certainly seem quiet today," Mother said, handing Jessica a cooled jar to label.

"I suppose I'm just thinking about things."

"Things?"

Jessica grimaced. She didn't want to admit her worry to Mother. "Just life, Mother. I'm just thinking about my life."

"And did you come to any conclusions?"

A loud knock sounded at the front of the house. "Who could that be?" Mother wore a puzzled look. "It never fails that when we get caught up in something like this, someone shows up to visit." She laughed and quickly washed up, dried her hands on a towel, and pulled off her apron. "I'll see who it is. You get the rest of these sealed jars off the stove. Let them cool before you try to label them."

Jessica nodded and lifted the heavy kettle off the stove. She'd barely made it to the wooden table before the weight and steam threatened her hold.

Her mother appeared at the door. "Jess, take off your apron and come. Mr. Gable is here."

Excitement flooded Jessica. She dabbed her forehead with a towel, then tossed her apron aside. Hurrying down the hall, she touched a hand to her hair, hoping she didn't look a fright. Everything felt in place, however, so she entered the front room with a smile.

Harrison Gable gave her a look that Jessica found almost invasive. He seemed to study her with great interest. "Miss Atherton, what a pleasure to see you again." Gable took hold of her hand and pressed a light kiss on the back.

Jessica trembled and pulled her hand away more quickly than she'd intended. "It's nice to see you again." Why did this man affect her so?

"Since it is Saturday, I thought I might have better luck seeing some of the local ranchers in the area. Your father suggested Saturday afternoon and evening might be best."

"I'm sure he's right," Mother said before Jessica could respond. "Most will be at home getting ready for the Sabbath. Tyler is out in the barn. I'll go ask him to join us."

"Thank you, Mrs. Atherton," Harrison said with a slight bow.

Once Jessica's mother left the room, Harrison moved closer. "I was hoping I might see you today. And here you are."

Jessica worried about her appearance and felt an explanation was in order. "I've been helping my mother to can pumpkin. I'm afraid I didn't have time to arrange myself."

"You look lovely." His gaze swept over her again. "Quite lovely."

"Thank you." She couldn't help but feel the intensity of his compliment.

For a moment neither said a word. When Jessica heard voices coming from the kitchen, she knew her time alone with Harrison was over.

Father bounded into the room with his hand extended. "Good to see you again, Harrison. I hope you'll stay till supper."

"I can't. I need to speak with some of the ranchers who border your property and Mr. Barnett on the north. I know there's just a couple, but it is important I get their signatures."

"Of course. That would be the Harper and Watson places. Let me get my coat, and I'll go with you."

"Thank you. I'd be much obliged." Tyler started to go, but Gable cleared his throat. "I wondered, too, if I might ask permission to escort your daughter to the upcoming harvest party."

Tyler smiled. "Well, it's good with me if Jessica gives her approval. I can have Osage bring her to town, and the two of you can meet up there."

Everyone looked to Jessica. Without hesitation she said, "Of course. I would like that very much."

Gable grinned. "Then this has been a most productive day. Shall we meet around ten that morning? I understand there is to be a bountiful noon meal and thought we might partake of that, not to mention the other activities."

"Of course. There's a dance later in the evening," Jessica offered.

"We plan to attend, as well," Mother said. "So it's no trouble for us to stick around for the dance. That way Osage won't have to wait in town until late."

Harrison looked to Mother. "Thank you, ma'am. That is quite considerate. I'd very much enjoy sharing a dance or two with Miss Atherton."

Jessica enjoyed his charm. There was something engaging about the man. She tried not to show her delight in his asking her to the party, for she didn't want to appear too eager, and she certainly didn't want him to know how he made her feel. That might truly cause embarrassment, since she didn't really know him.

"Well, if you're ready," Tyler said, "we might as well head out."

"Don't you want to eat something first?" Mother asked. "You might be gone a good while."

"No. I'll just see Harrison to the Harpers' and eat when I get back. I'm sure Hank Harper will show him how to get to the Watsons'. They'll probably offer you a room for the night," he said, looking to Harrison.

"Folks around here are certainly accommodating," Gable commented.

"Not like folks in the city, eh?" Father questioned.

"Indeed, they are nothing like the guarded and cautious folks who cross your path there. However, they guard themselves with good reason. Life in the larger cities can be quite difficult and even dangerous."

"Well, I wouldn't want it," Father said. He leaned over and kissed Mother. "I'll be back soon."

"We'll wait dinner for you, sweetheart," Mother said, embracing Jessica's father.

Jessica watched her father gave Mother another quick kiss, then he slapped Harrison's back and guided him to the door.

"That was quite exciting, don't you think?" Mother asked.

Smiling, Jessica didn't even try to feign confusion at her question. "I'm so happy I could fly."

"Don't do that," Mother chided playfully. "Flying is for birds and angels—not for people."

"I was afraid he might not ask."

"You two make a beautiful couple," Mother replied, leading the way back to the kitchen. "I can see your being attracted to him. He has a profession and plans for the future that would suit you well."

Jessica took up her apron but didn't put it on. Mother's words troubled her. "What do you mean?"

Mother was already donning her apron. "Well, it seems to me that Mr. Gable already does well for himself. He's been impeccably dressed each time I've seen him. He carries himself as a man of quality, and I believe he could provide the things in life that you love."

"Why does everyone think I'm interested only in *things*?" Jessica said, throwing down the apron. "I'm tired of people looking at me that way. I might have been spoiled and useless in the past, but I'm trying to change."

"No one said you were useless," Mother countered. "But you've always preferred nice things and expensive clothes. You've often said how much you enjoyed traveling with your grandparents and how much you love city life. It seems to me that Harrison Gable shares your interests."

Jessica knew her mother was right, but she still felt insulted. "Those aren't the only things that are important to me. I would never marry a man just because he had money. I would only marry if I loved him."

"I'm glad to hear it," Mother replied. "I know it was difficult for you to adjust after Robert married Alice. I have been more than a little worried that you would take up the first marriage proposal offered."

"I've been asked to marry several times," Jessica said, hands on hips. "You should give me more credit than that. I'm not a silly simpering girl. I know what's valuable in life, and I'm sick and tired of people suggesting otherwise!"

★

Harrison Gable enjoyed the ride north. There was still plenty of light, and Atherton had chosen to cut across his land rather than go all the way back to the road. It would shorten their trip by at least fifteen or twenty minutes, the older man had told him.

"I don't suppose you ride a lot back in Dallas," Atherton began. "Hope you won't be too saddle sore after all these visits."

"Surprisingly enough, I do ride quite often. I love it. I have, ever since I was a small boy."

"Me too," the older man admitted. "There's something peaceful about being out here in the fields—cattle grazin', clear skies, sun slowly settin'. If not for the fences, it might seem like old times."

Harrison glanced at the man. "You don't approve of fencing?"

Atherton shook his head and didn't look Harrison's way. "I can't say I'm very fond of it. I know it's helped cut down on damage done to some of the farms. I even understand it comes with the settlin' of a place. I just don't happen to like it.

"I suppose that might sound strange to you." He paused for a moment and seemed to be lost in thought as he studied the landscape. "When everything was open, it was like the entire state was yours to be had. You could ride from one area to another and never worry much about somebody takin' offense at you for crossin' their land. Seems like the fences have popped into place almost overnight. Feels kind of like a noose being tightened."

"But fencing helps in keeping your herds together," Harrison offered.

"Yup. I can agree with that. It's not nearly so difficult to round them up, and you don't have nearly the trouble with strays. In the past Will and I have run our cattle together with the Watsons' and Harpers'. And the Wythes', too, of course. Now with the town being platted, the Watsons and Harpers are putting in fence, and Will and I have set ours in place, as well. It's the end of an era, to be sure."

As they approached the northwest edge of Atherton's property, Harrison spied a gate leading out of the pasture and onto the road. Tyler managed the gate, never leaving the back of his mount. Harrison could see this was second nature to the man. Once they were on the road, he couldn't help but regard Tyler Atherton.

"You have the bearing of a man who's worked hard and accomplished much," he told Atherton. "Have you always lived here?"

"Pretty much. There were times when I had to be away. Before the railroad came to Cedar Springs, we had to drive the cattle north to Kansas each year. Then I was gone quite a time during the war."

"Were you in many battles?" Gable asked.

Atherton considered the question for a moment. "Enough to make me know I never wanna see another war."

Harrison nodded. "That's exactly what my father said. I was born during the conflict, and my mother was terrified we would be killed in the midst of it."

"A lot of innocent folk died. Those were sad times."

"Did you have to fight the Indians out here, or was the area already civilized?"

Atherton frowned at this. Obviously this wasn't a pleasant topic. He was silent so long, in fact, that Harrison feared he'd offended his host. Harrison didn't know what to say, so he said nothing at all.

Soon Atherton picked up the conversation again. "There were always Indians around when I was young. They would raid and threaten death. My people would rally and fight back. Eventually the Comanche managed to get the upper hand. They killed my father and several of his men. It wasn't easy to have much grace for them after that."

"I can imagine. If they'd killed my father, I'd feel the same way."

Atherton gave a heavy sigh. "It didn't serve me well to bear a grudge. I learned that revenge couldn't satisfy the void. I had to forgive and move on. I knew it was what God would have me do."

Harrison wasn't sure how to respond. It was clear the man didn't enjoy the subject. Who could blame him? Still, with his years of training to understand people by their actions and words, Harrison was certain there truly was a peace about Mr. Atherton.

"Looks like Austin Todd is headin' our way."

Gable looked down the road to see the same rain-drenched cowboy he'd seen sitting beside Jessica Atherton in church. Only this time he was dry.

"Afternoon, Austin," Mr. Atherton called out as they came together.

"Near to evening," Todd replied.

"Do you know Mr. Harrison Gable?" the older man asked.

"Only by reputation." He gave a nod and smiled at Harrison. "Mr. Barnett speaks highly of you."

"I'm glad to hear it. I have enjoyed doing business with both Mr. Barnett and Mr. Atherton."

Atherton chuckled. "He's only enjoyed doin' business with me because it got him a date to take Jessica to the harvest celebration next Saturday."

"That right? Well, I hope you have a good time."

Harrison wasn't sure, but Todd didn't sound any too sincere. Perhaps he'd better watch himself. This man might also be after the lady's affection.

"I intend to," Harrison said. "Thank you."

"I'm glad we ran into you, Austin. I have some things to discuss with you." Atherton looked to Harrison. "If you don't mind, I'll let you go on ahead by yourself. Just follow this trail north, and you'll come to the river, where there's a bridge that will bring you pert near to Harper's drive. Just cross the bridge, angle to the right, and you can't miss it."

"Thanks, Mr. Atherton. I'm obliged." He tipped his hat at the older man, then again toward Austin Todd. "It was a pleasure to meet you, Mr. Todd. I'll look forward to seeing you in the future."

But hopefully not sitting in church beside the woman I intend to marry.

Chapter 11

Jessica placed a china plate on the dining room table, then went to the silverware drawer. The day's work had left her feeling sluggish. She moved in slow, purposeful steps, as if each one needed to be thought out. Reaching the sideboard, she took up place settings for herself, Mother, and Father and put them around the table beside the plates.

"Jess, you'd better set another place. I see your father has brought Austin Todd back with him."

Her heart fluttered a little bit, and Jessica felt a burst of energy. She rushed to the mirror that graced the dining room wall above the sideboard and frowned. She looked so worn—tired, really. There were dark circles under her eyes, and her head was starting to hurt. She glanced down at her dress. It bore spots of pumpkin and flour.

Maybe I should go change my clothes. I don't want to appear shabby and unkempt when Austin sees me.

Immediately, Jessica stopped fussing and frowned. *Why am I so concerned about my appearance?* It was just one more reminder of her self-centered ways. It was painful to remember the many times when looking beautiful to impress someone had been her only thought. The guilt made her feel ill.

As penance, Jessica decided to remain as she was. She had spent most of her life primping and making certain that she wore the perfect outfit. It needed to stop. It was one thing to be concerned with look-ing presentable and dressing appropriately for the occasion, and quite another to do so for the sake of impressing others or, worse yet, making others feel inferior.

She lifted her chin and reached down to the sideboard to take up more silver and china. By the time her father entered the house with Austin, food graced the table and everything was ready.

Austin offered Jessica a smile when he and Father entered the dining room. "Your pa thought I needed a meal," he said and shrugged. "Who was I to turn down good food?"

"How do you know it's good?" Jessica teased.

Her father laughed and spoke before Austin could recover from his surprise. "Anything your mother makes turns out perfect. The fact that she still likes to have a hand in the kitchen, though she has hired help, always amazes me." He looked to Austin. "When I first met Mrs. Atherton, she was not as accomplished as she is now. She was rather spoiled and selective in what she would and wouldn't do. Her sister took her in hand, however, and taught her how to cook and clean."

"I can do more than that," Mother announced, bringing in the bread plate. She placed it on the table to reveal pumpkin bread.

"That she can." Father took hold of Mother and kissed her soundly. He held her for a few moments after the kiss ended. They were still very much in love. Jessica watched as her father helped Mother into her chair, then took his own place. He was a true gentleman.

To her surprise, Austin pulled Jessica's chair out for her and waited to seat her before taking his place. Jessica thanked him, barely able to say another word. Father offered a prayer and then began to help himself to the fried ham steaks. The other dishes were passed, and the men seemed in particular awe of the pumpkin bread.

"I don't think I've ever had anything like this before," Austin com-mented, taking another piece only after Jessica's father did. He slathered it with freshly churned butter and bit into it with a look of pleasure on his face.

Jessica found she wasn't all that hungry. She tried to keep up with the conversation, but she felt so tired and her head throbbed. They had worked hard that day, canning pumpkin and pressing clothes for Sunday. Then too, it had been very hot. Apparently it had taken more of a toll than Jessica realized. She poked at her food and hoped no one would see that she wasn't actually eating.

Father and Austin discussed the new town and their ideas for bringing in businesses. Even Mother added her thoughts regarding the church and school. She mentioned that Jake Wythe had a friend named Rob Vandermark who was a pastor looking for a church. His wife was an accomplished teacher. Mother thought they should write to him right away. If they could secure a schoolteacher and a preacher in one letter, they would be well ahead of the game. Father agreed and promised to speak with Jake.

"Are you planning to attend the party on Saturday?" Mother asked, perking Jessica's attention.

"I doubt it. When folks set to partying, that's usually the time rustlers get busy. I'll just keep an eye out, and you folks can have yourselves a nice time," Austin replied.

"I think Will wants you to be there. He's going to say a few words about the new town and the rail line, and he wants to introduce you as the new law for the town. I wouldn't be surprised, too, if folks will want to talk to you about the rustling."

"Well," Austin said thoughtfully, "I could probably come by for a little while and then head out to look for rustlers."

Mother offered him more coffee as he downed the first cup. He gave her a quick nod and waited while she poured it from a silver pot. Jessica felt as if her body were leaden. She was clearly coming down with something. A wave of dizziness caused her to drop her fork and take hold of the table. Mother immediately noticed her condition.

"Jess? Don't you feel well?" Mother reached out to touch her head. "You have a fever." She got to her feet and helped Jessica to hers. "If you'll excuse us, I'm going to put Jessica to bed. I think she's managed to catch something."

Austin was on his feet. "Is there anything I can do to help? I could carry her."

Jessica closed her eyes even as Mother assured him she could manage.

Feeling as she did, Jessica almost wished her mother would have let him assist. She wasn't at all sure she could make it to her bedroom upstairs.

"I'm so sorry, Mother. I haven't felt like myself all day. I thought I was just tired."

"Well, it's clear that you've taken sick. I'm not at all sure what the problem might be, but we'll get you to bed and then see what you feel like tomorrow."

Letting her mother take charge, Jessica was relieved when Mother finally managed to get her upstairs and settled on the bed.

"Let me undo the buttons on your dress," Mother said, reaching out to Jessica's collar. She unfastened the bodice and pushed it down to the waist. Careful to keep Jessica from collapsing, Mother managed to pull her to her feet so the gown and petticoat could slip to the floor.

Jessica's head throbbed all the more, and she longed for the comfort of her bed. She turned to climb in, but Mother stopped her again. "Let me unlace your corset and get that off, as well. You can sleep in your shift, if you'd like, but you'd probably feel better in a nightgown." She made quick work of the corset and eased Jessica onto the bed.

"Thank you," Jessica whispered. "I'm sorry to be so much trouble."

"You aren't trouble. You're my daughter and I want to see you through this. Now stay here," she said, pulling the covers over Jessica's body. "I'll be right back with some medicine."

Jessica wasn't about to go anywhere. She could scarcely settle the covers comfortably around her. Every muscle, every fiber of her being longed to be still. She thought of Austin downstairs. So close but so distant. He was a strange man—mysterious, quiet. She couldn't help but wonder at his past. Maybe Father could tell her more.

Mother returned and helped Jessica sit up a bit to take a spoonful of a nasty tasting liquid. "This will help you sleep."

"I don't think that will be a problem," Jessica replied.

"It will help with the fever, as well." Mother eased her back onto the mattress, and Jessica closed her eyes. "I'll check on you in a little while."

The sickness didn't lose its grip on Jessica until sometime in the night on Wednesday of the following week. Her fever finally broke after her mother had tried both to sweat and freeze it out of Jessica. The illness left Jessica almost more tired than she'd felt when this had all started. She got her first restful sleep in the wee hours of the morning and slept through until late Thursday afternoon. When she awoke she found Mother by her side.

"Are you feeling better?" Mother asked. She touched Jessica's head ever so gently. "Your fever is gone. You should start to feel much better."

"What was wrong with me?" Jessica asked, her voice weak and throat dry.

"The grippe or ague I suppose—I'm really not completely certain. You were delirious for a time and shivering, so I thought for sure it was ague. But then you started heaving, and I thought perhaps it was grippe. Either way, your fever was high and I feared it might cause harm to your brain."

Jessica sighed and closed her eyes. "May I have some water?"

"Of course. I have a glass right here. I've been trying to keep liquids down you since you fell ill."

Taking Jessica in her arms, Mother helped her to sit up long enough to take a drink. Jessica shook her head as Mother helped her to lie back. "I don't remember hardly anything after you helped me to bed."

"I'm not surprised." Mother got to her feet. "You rest and I'll fix some chicken broth for you."

The rest of the day Jessica focused on taking in fluids as her mother insisted. By night she felt a little better, and by Friday morning Jessica was able to sit up and not feel as though she might break in half.

She'd had a long time to ponder her life while recovering. Images of the past came to life to remind Jessica that she had often handled people harshly, without care for their feelings. She didn't like the girl she'd been, yet back then Jessica had seen nothing wrong in her actions. When her mother came in to check on her, Jessica posed a question.

"Mother, do you think I'm selfish?"

Her mother looked at her as if she'd posed a difficult mathematics problem. "What is this all about?" Mother asked.

Jessica pressed the question again. "Do you think I'm selfish?" Jessica looked at her hands and smoothed the covers. She was almost afraid to meet her mother's gaze. "Have I always been self-centered and more concerned about myself than others?"

"I wouldn't exactly say that. You've had your moments, but everyone does."

"But people think me to be shallow. You and Father even think me that way."

Mother actually laughed at this. She came and sat down beside Jessica and took hold of her fidgeting hands. "Hardly that. You are anything but shallow. In fact, you are by far and away my most complex child."

"How so? Was I that difficult?"

"You misunderstand me. You are rather like an onion with many, many layers. Each time one layer is pulled away, another appears. I've seen layers of your heart and mind stripped away over the years, but always there's another layer, and no one has ever yet reached the core of who you really are."

"And how does that happen?" Jessica felt perplexed by her mother's statement. "Is there something I can do?"

Mother shook her head. "Not in total. It's partly a matter of what other people think, but mostly it's how you stand in the eyes of God."

"I didn't used to care what people thought," Jessica said. "At least I told myself that. In truth, I really cared too much. I wanted to be the prettiest and the most fashionable girl. I wanted others to envy me—to wish they were me. I only cared about me," she confessed. "And now . . ."

"And now?" Mother asked in a gentle manner.

Jessica shook her head and looked across the room at the armoire that was filled with beautiful clothes. "I'm ashamed. I want to change, but I fear people will always believe me to be that same selfish girl. Even you and Papa tease me about caring for new gowns and other beautiful things. I overheard Papa once telling one of my beaus that the way to win my heart was with pretty doodads and plenty of attention, or something like that. First it made me angry, and then it broke my heart."

Mother tenderly stroked Jessica's hand. "Darling, you can change your ways, but people who've been impressed by them or fallen victim to them will need time to believe the change is real. You can start living your life in a way that will prove your heart has changed, and soon folks will come around. Take it to God and He will direct you."

Jessica bowed her head. "I'm afraid I've not concerned myself much with God. I doubt He'd even listen to me."

"Well, that seems to be the crux of your problem. Without God you are stuck making decisions on your own. And, Jessica, that's a very lonely place to be—troublesome, too. You've put God off for a long while. Why not try turning this concern over to Him. I think you'll be surprised by His answers."

"Maybe," Jessica admitted. After all, she hadn't yet tried that.

Mother smiled. "Where's your Bible?"

Jessica pointed to the chest of drawers. "In the top drawer."

Crossing the room, her mother found the Bible and brought it back to Jessica. "You might want to read this and pray. I find that reading God's Word and praying always brings me understanding." Mother turned. "I'm going to go prepare something for you to eat. Oh, I forgot to tell you. Your father ran into Mr. Gable and told him you were recovering from illness and wouldn't be able to attend the harvest party."

"But I might be strong enough by then," Jessica argued. She didn't want to miss getting to know Harrison Gable better.

"No. That's too soon. You are in no condition to get out of bed, much less take a long ride into town and participate in a large outdoor event. Now, try reading, and I'll bring you a little broth and a few crackers."

Disappointment settled upon her, and Jessica could only sigh for what might have been. *I hope this doesn't cause Harrison—Mr. Gable—to lose interest in me. After all, he might fear me to be a weak and sickly woman.* But even as she thought this, her gaze fell on the Bible. The book reminded her that once again she'd been thinking only of herself.

"I hope you have some answers here for me, God, because I sure don't have any for myself."

Chapter 12

Cedar Springs overflowed with visitors for the harvest party. Crystal blue skies and cooler temperatures made the affair too appealing to refuse. The streets flowed to capacity, and everywhere vendors were hawking their wares and enticing the people to buy. Jugglers and fire breathers came all the way from Dallas to entertain and impress. Children ran up and down the closed-off Main Street with squeals of delight. They seemed to think it novel to be allowed in the roadway when they'd so often been cautioned against it.

Austin had always avoided these kinds of things, but Will Barnett and Tyler Atherton had insisted he be there. They wanted to talk to him about Terryton and his agreement to be marshal. Sometimes Austin wondered if he'd made the right decision. With the Rangers he could move around all over the state. Being Terryton's marshal would keep him in one place for some time to come.

"I see you made it," Barnett said, coming up as Austin tied off his horse.

"I did, but I'm still not sure I should be here. Every rustler around these parts is gonna know we're celebrating up here today. It will be the perfect time to strike."

"Relax. You don't have to stay for long. I'm gonna make an announcement here in just a couple of minutes. We'll go over to the platform and speak from there." Austin noticed the makeshift structure and nodded. He looked around for Tyler but didn't see him anywhere. "What about Mr. Atherton?"

"Couldn't make it," Barnett replied. "Jessica was still pretty weak from her sickness, so they decided to stay home."

"But Miss Atherton is feeling better, isn't she?"

"That's what I hear." Barnett's expression changed. "The mayor is signaling for us to join him. Come. Just follow my lead. You know what's expected of a marshal, and the people who don't already know you, need to."

Barnett led the way to the dais. They shook hands with the mayor and awaited Will's introduction.

"I'm glad to have this opportunity to tell you about our progress in creating a new town about twenty-eight miles to the northwest. I donated land for the creation of Terryton to honor my old friends, Ted and Marietta Terry, who settled a good part of this county. Please understand this is in no way a decision made lightly. And we certainly do not anticipate harm to Cedar Springs."

Austin saw more and more people press in to hear what Mr. Barnett had to say. It made him nervous to be the focus of attention, but Barnett didn't seem concerned.

"As most of you already know, this area will no doubt be incorporated into Dallas as the city grows. Terryton will still be accessible if our plans go well. The railroad has agreed to our request for a spur line to Terryton, primarily for shipping cattle and goods. The only stipulation was that we have some form of legal authority in place prior to the ground breaking. For that purpose, we have hired Austin Todd." He motioned Austin to step forward.

Feeling all eyes on him, Austin did as instructed and tried not to concern himself with the crowd. He was glad when William continued.

"Austin, as most of you know, is currently a cattle inspector. He has extensive experience with law enforcement and, I believe, will be a real asset to our little town. Eventually, once the town is formed and running well, we will hold elections for this position. For any of you interested, I'd urge you to keep in touch. We will be looking for various businesses to join us, and I'd be happy to talk to anyone who would like to know more."

"What about the problems with rustling?" someone called from the crowd.

"Yeah," another man piped up. "I lost two dozen of my prime beeves."

William looked to Austin. The crowd did likewise. Austin felt the weight of their stares and fought back discomfort in order to answer the questions.

"The Rangers are well advised of the situation and have men staked in various areas. I myself plan to head out after this announcement. We believe we're close to capturing the men who've been particularly active recently. But that's all I can say regarding those responsible. I can talk to you individually if you have questions." He stepped back and swallowed the lump in his throat. Public speaking was something he did not enjoy at all.

Barnett had a few more comments to make, and then the two men descended the platform to find many people had additional questions. Austin found himself separated from Barnett as men and women pressed around the two for answers.

"Ranger Todd," one of the men began, "you boys gonna hang 'em when you catch 'em?"

Austin shook his head. "No. We'll see them brought to trial and let the courts deal with them. The days of lynching are a thing of the past. We're civilized now, and we'll abstain from taking the law into our own hands."

"Well, those rustlers sure don't care about the law," another man claimed.

"True enough," Austin said, feeling as if the pressing crowd would soon trample him into the dirt. "But we honest citizens do. Upholding the law is important—otherwise we're no better than the thieves stealing our cattle."

"If they show up on my land and I catch up to 'em, I'm puttin' a bullet in 'em," a stocky man declared. There were murmurs of approval, but Austin waited until the crowd quieted down before finally speaking.

"You can certainly handle things for yourself—protect what's yours—

and most likely you won't run afoul of the law. However, I know what it is to kill, and it's not a pleasant thing to live with. I doubt most of you have had to kill a man and watch the life go out of him." Austin looked around at the disgruntled men. "It's easy enough to talk about putting an end to a man's life and quite another thing to actually do it." This quieted any further comments about killing. It seemed his words had sobered even the angriest of men.

There was another round of rapid-fire questions, and Austin began to regret ever having agreed to come. Moments later, a rescuing angel came to his side.

"I'm sorry, but Austin is needed elsewhere," Marty Wythe declared. "You can speak with him later." She didn't wait for comment but pulled Austin by the sleeve, forcing him to follow.

Once they were well away from the crowd, Marty dropped her hold. "You looked like you were a drowning man going down for the third time."

"I felt like one," he admitted. "Folks definitely get themselves riled up over these things."

She shrugged. "Well, beef is their livelihood. Take that away, and we'll have another financial crisis on our hands."

"I'm sure that's true." He glanced around. "You here with your family?"

"Of course. Robert and Alice are showing off their baby over there." She pointed and Austin easily spotted the couple. "And Jake is over there, where they're roasting pecans and handing out samples. The older boys wanted to watch and, of course, eat." She smiled.

"And what about the two little ones?" he asked to be polite.

"With Jake. The baby was sleeping, and Johanna was her busy self. I did promise Jake I wouldn't be gone for long."

Austin started to say something, but the stunned look on Marty's face stopped him. He turned to follow her gaze and found the same tall bearded stranger he'd met in the jail. "Mr. Cuker." He gave the man a nod.

"His name isn't Cuker," Marty declared. "It's Paul Morgan. He once employed my husband." She shook her head. "I knew there was something familiar about you when I saw you from afar a while back. Why are you trying to conceal your identity with the heavy beard and change of name?"

Morgan smiled. "The years have been good to you, Mrs. Wythe. You are even more beautiful than you were when you first married our Jacob."

Her eyes narrowed. "*Our* Jacob?"

He chuckled and looked to Austin. "I don't believe I know you."

"Austin Todd, cattle inspector with the Texas Rangers," Austin replied, trying to reassess the man. Usually if a man hid from his name, he was up to no good.

"Glad to meet you. Always appreciate a good lawman." He turned to Marty. "I suppose you deserve to know why I'm here."

"I'd definitely like to know how you even found us."

"It wasn't the easiest thing in the world, but I had my ways," he said, grinning as if he'd really managed something good.

Austin could see that Marty didn't think it was good. Her brows were knit and her lips formed a frown. Usually nothing disturbed this strong woman overmuch. He couldn't help wondering what was wrong.

"You said you were good friends with the Wythes." Austin eyed the man, determined to get some answers. "How is it you really know them?"

"My dear sir, the Wythes are good friends," Morgan protested. "I gave Jacob his first banking job in Denver."

"You took it away from him, as well," Marty added.

Morgan looked at her with great sympathy. "Now, Mrs. Wythe . . . Marty . . . the financial troubles this country suffered robbed your husband of his job. However, I'm here to offer it back to him. It's taken a good two years, but I've managed to get back on my feet. That's why I'm here."

"To ask Jake to come back to Denver and work for you?" Marty gave a bitter laugh. "That will never happen. He hated banking then, and he hates it even more now. He's doing what he loves to do—ranching—and you can't say anything that will convince him to return to Denver."

"Still, I'd like to ask him about it myself."

Austin could see her apprehension. For the little time he'd known her, Austin had never seen her look so afraid. He couldn't help but wonder what her worry might be. Was this man a threat to her or to Jake? Austin gave the man another close look. He was well groomed and nicely dressed. He seemed friendly enough. Maybe Marty was just afraid her husband would agree to go back in this man's employ.

"I'll take you to Jake. He's with the children right now."

"I had heard you had a family. Adopted some boys, didn't you?" Morgan asked.

"Yes." Marty seemed unwilling to offer any more information. "Come along, Mr. Morgan. I don't wish you to have to wait for your answer."

Austin smiled to himself as Marty made her way through the crowd. She was a strong woman and could no doubt handle the matter on her own. Making his way back to his horse, Austin gave the scene one final look. Folks were enjoying themselves with the revelry. Celebrating the harvest was something everyone could get behind. Barnett had told him that next month they would begin slaughtering hogs and a few steers. Putting up food for the winter wasn't nearly so critical in the southern part of the country, but Barnett had maintained that his wife was a stickler for planning ahead. With that in mind, they had already ordered a large shipment of ice from Dallas in order to preserve the meat they didn't smoke.

Austin had to admit he admired these people. They were good, God-fearing folks who had a penchant for reaching out to those in need—like him. Heading for his horse, Austin almost wished he could stay and share their company a little longer. But deep in his mind a warning sounded that he was getting too close, caring too much. It was time to put some distance between him and the others.

As the band struck up a rousing rendition of "The Yellow Rose of Texas," Austin felt someone touch his shoulder.

"Hey there, Austin. Why don't you come join us?" Robert Barnett was all smiles. "Alice brought some mighty fine pies, and the town fathers roasted three of the biggest hogs I've ever seen."

His stomach rumbled at the thought of such a delicious meal. "I suppose I could force myself to stay a little longer," Austin said with a grin.

Robert laughed and slapped Austin's back. "That's the spirit. I knew you were a smart man."

★

Marty wasn't at all happy to see Paul Morgan. The man had all but left them to die back in Denver. He'd stripped away Jake's job and their home. How could he possibly think Jake would want to work for him now?

"I must say I'm surprised you would even attempt this," Marty told the older man. "After all, you deserted us in Denver."

"Not by choice, I assure you."

"Oh, well that makes it all better." Her sarcasm was not lost on him.

"Mrs. Wythe, you must believe me. We were all suffering. I had no choice but to close the bank. I lost a great deal, too."

Marty tried to rein in her anger. "I'm sure you did. I have to warn you, however, Jake is back to doing what he loves. He's not going to return to banking. I'd stake my life on that." She spotted Jake just where she'd left him and the children. "He's over there." She made her way to Jake. "Darling, look who's come to see you."

Jake was holding an exhausted Johanna. The two-year-old was sleeping peacefully in his arms and looked rather angelic, Marty thought. Jake glanced up and frowned in disapproval at the sight of the man standing beside Marty.

"Mr. Morgan? I hardly recognized you." He gently placed Johanna on their ground blanket, where the baby was sleeping, and got to his feet. "I have to say this is a bit of a surprise."

"Yes, isn't it," Marty declared. "I asked him how he found us, but he wasn't forthcoming with an answer. Perhaps you'll manage to get more out of him."

Morgan appeared to ignore her comment. Instead, he extended his arm to Jacob. "I'd like for you to join me for a little while. I have some things to discuss with you."

Jake shrugged. "I guess that's all right." He turned back to Marty. "The boys are gettin' some pecans. They're supposed to come right back."

"You could have your discussion here," Marty said, looking to Morgan.

"Nonsense. I wouldn't dream of imposing on your day of fun," the man replied.

But you already have. You have imposed and made me most uncomfortable.

The two men left her standing there, wondering what they would discuss and why Morgan had invaded their peaceful lives. She didn't trust him, especially now that he'd lied about his name and had worked to hide his face from recognition. He'd not done anything to help them when the economy went bad, yet here he was thinking Jake would just give up his dream and return to banking. Or was that not really what he had in mind?

"Wasn't that Mr. Morgan, the man Jake used to work for in Denver?" Alice Barnett questioned, coming alongside Marty.

"Yes. I'm afraid so. He thinks he's going to talk Jake into coming to work for him again."

Alice touched her arm. "How did he even find us?" There was real fear in her eyes.

Marty didn't wish to worry Alice, but she felt as fearful as the younger woman looked. "I don't know. He said it wasn't easy, but that's all he told me. He clearly had no desire to waste his time with me."

Alice glanced over her shoulder in a nervous manner. "But if he could find us, others could, too. We haven't exactly been hiding out, but I was hoping we were safe . . . from the past."

"Don't let your imagination get the best of you," Marty cautioned, hoping she sounded reassuring. She certainly didn't feel it. "The economy isn't doing so well that folks can afford to throw their money around. No doubt the men who hired Smith will be just as strapped for cash as many others. They wouldn't have been so frantic for the gold certificates if not."

"Yes, but that's what worries me—they were frantic. I'd feel better if I knew what Mr. Morgan had done to locate us."

"Even if we knew, Alice, we couldn't prevent others from using the same avenue." Marty frowned and shook her head. "No, we'll just need to be on our guard and keep an eye out for strangers. If Mr. Smith shows up, we're bound to see him before he sees us." At least she hoped it would be so.

★

Jessica smiled, feeling rather shy at the appearance of Harrison Gable in her bedroom. Mother had escorted him in only moments before. She had taken a seat in the corner in order that propriety might be observed and pretended to read. At least Jessica presumed it was pretense.

"I brought you these," Gable said, pulling a bouquet of roses from behind his back.

Jessica gasped at the sight of a dozen pink roses. "They're beautiful. Oh, Mother, look."

Her mother glanced up from the book. "They are lovely. If you give them to me," she said, getting to her feet, "I'll have Lupe put them in water."

Mother took the roses and headed for the hallway. Leaving the door open, she turned from the hallway. "I'll only be a moment."

Jessica knew it was her mother's way of letting them know there would be no time for anything untoward. This seemed to amuse Mr. Gable, who gave a low chuckle.

"She must think me the worst of rogues."

Jessica shook her head. "It's not that. She just doesn't want my reputation ruined. I've never had a man—who wasn't a relative—in my bedroom."

"Well, I'm honored to be the first." He pulled up the chair Mother had used during Jessica's worst hours of sickness and sat beside the bed. "I must say, you are looking quite lovely."

Jessica laughed. "You are a sweet-talker. I know how ghastly I look, so you needn't try to persuade me to think otherwise. This sickness took its toll."

"I'm glad to see that you've recovered, but you're wrong. You are far from ghastly in appearance. There are roses in your cheeks and a warm glow of joy in your eyes. Dare I believe it's because of my arrival?"

Her cheeks flushed hot. "I am happy for the company," she admitted. "It's been rather dull. Did you manage to attend the harvest party? I'm sure they're still having a wonderful time, so you might not want to remain here for long."

"I did indeed walk through the crowd of festive folk, but without you to accompany me, it wasn't nearly so pleasant. That's when I got the idea to leave and ride out here to see you. I had to assure myself that you were past the worst of the illness."

Jessica believed him to be one of the most striking men she'd ever known. His perfectly sized nose and thin, well-formed lips gave his face a dashing appearance. And those eyes—those dark, dark eyes—suggested power and capability and also passion.

Mother slipped back into the room and retook her chair. Jessica ignored her, but she knew that Harrison had noted her return.

"I appreciate your concern. I am feeling much better now."

"Perhaps we'll have a chance to try again," he replied, lowering his voice.

Jessica nodded. "I'd like that."

"I'll be tied up most of next week, but I'll do my best to call again on the Sunday after next, if that would be acceptable?"

Feeling overwhelmed with happiness, Jessica could only nod and smile. She didn't trust herself to speak. Gazing into Harrison's eyes, she found herself feeling rather consumed. He seemed to look right through her, almost as though he could read her thoughts and feelings.

"I see you've been reading the Good Book," he said, noting the Bible beside her.

"Yes," Jessica said and picked up the book. "It's afforded me a great deal of comfort."

"I can well imagine. I'm particularly fond of the Psalms. How about you?"

"I do love the Psalms, but of late I've been reading the Gospels— particularly John."

"I can't say that I've read that one lately. I'll have to give it a go when I can find the time." He glanced at his pocket watch. "Speaking of which, I must go. I have to catch a train this evening, and I still haven't packed."

"Are you going far?" she asked, trying not to sound overly interested.

He smiled, as if knowing her concern. "Not at all. I'm going to be in Dallas filing paper work and holding meetings with the railroad and with bank officials most of this next week."

He took hold of her hand and rubbed his thumb over the back of her knuckles. Jessica shivered from the sensation. The feel of his warm fingers upon her skin left her almost breathless. Looking into his eyes, she could see his desire. It both frightened and excited her. Jessica wasn't at all sure which emotion was stronger.

"I . . . uh . . . I'll look forward to your return," she finally managed to say.

Harrison lowered his lips to the back of her hand, and again Jessica shivered from the rush of emotions. He kissed her hand and stood. Looking not to Jessica but to her mother, he said, "I believe Miss Atherton is chilled. She seems to be shivering." He looked back at Jessica and winked.

She could see the amusement in his expression as her mother came forward with a shawl. "Here, this will help," she said, wrapping it around Jessica's shoulders. But Jessica knew from the look on Harrison's face that they both understood that it wouldn't help at all.

He took his leave, and Mother escorted him downstairs while Jessica threw off the shawl and leaned back against her pillows feeling rather breathless. How was it that this man should affect her so strongly? He was certainly handsome, but then, so was Austin Todd, and she hadn't gone all weak-kneed and silly over him.

At the thought of his name, though, Jessica found herself forgetting Harrison Gable. What was it about Austin that fascinated her? He clearly wasn't interested in her. Maybe that was the attraction.

Maybe I see him as a challenge.

She pondered that idea for a moment. Perhaps it was only because the man came across as aloof and disinterested that Jessica found herself wanting to know more about him.

"He's certainly a fine young man," Mother said, breaking Jessica's thought. "It was particularly thoughtful that he would come all this way to check on your health."

Jessica put aside her contemplations of Austin Todd and returned to the subject of Harrison Gable. "He was very thoughtful. I have to say I was surprised to see him."

"I don't think it was such a surprise to me. He seems quite smitten," Mother said, smiling. "I think the two of you make a handsome couple."

"Mother, please," Jessica protested but not too sincerely.

Mother laughed. "I'm not so old that I can't remember how it was to have young men interested in me. I can see that Mr. Gable has a strong interest in you."

"He doesn't plan to stay around here for long," Jessica reminded her. "Don't go marrying me off just yet."

"Your father told me of Mr. Gable's plans to one day work in Washington, D.C., but that doesn't worry me. There are trains between here and the capital." She looked at Jessica and shrugged. "I rather enjoy train travel, and I've heard that Washington is a wonderful city, with all the amenities you love."

"There you go again," Jessica chided. "I've not even had a proper outing with Mr. Gable, and already you have us married and living in Washington. Really, Mother, you are quite the hopeless romantic."

Her mother laughed and headed for the door. "I suppose a lifetime with your father has done that to me. Now, if you'll excuse me, I'll have Lupe bring up your flowers and also something to eat. I'm sure you're going to need your strength for the days to come. After all, you don't want to still be weak when Sunday after next rolls around."

Chapter 13

"We should tell Robert what's happened," Alice said, still looking quite worried.

"We should," Marty agreed. "It's important that the menfolk know about the possibility of others finding us. I know William will want to know. He doesn't take chances when it comes to the safety of his family."

Alice wrung her hands together. "I can't help but worry that Mr. Morgan might have been watched. Someone could have easily followed him here, and he'd be no wiser for it." Alice's face paled, and her tone revealed her fear.

Marty patted her arm. "Don't fret, at least not until we're sure there's something to fret about. I don't know exactly how he found us. He wouldn't say."

"I'm so afraid," Alice said in a hushed tone. "We aren't safe anymore."

"Nonsense. No one is going to try to hurt us here. We've family and friends aplenty, and Texans don't take kindly to anyone who threatens the well-being of their womenfolk." Marty shook her head and stared off into the crowd where she'd last seen her husband. "I know Jake will refuse the offer, and then Morgan will have no choice but to return to Colorado alone."

"I hope you're right, but I still can't help being afraid." Alice moved her hand upward to touch the fading scar on her right cheek. "After

603

all this time, it seems strange that Mr. Morgan would show up now. I want my family to be safe. I had so hoped it was over."

"You're borrowing trouble. As I said," Marty said, softening her tone, "Mr. Morgan didn't come here to harm you or your family. He wants Jake to return to Colorado. He no doubt is getting back on his feet and wants Jake's help in recreating his empire. But Jake won't go."

"I understand that," Alice admitted, "but you know there are plenty who would harm us. All they'd have to do is get wind of Mr. Morgan's plans to find us and follow him. I'm going to tell Robert. He should know there's a chance of trouble."

"I agree that he should know, but, Alice, please try not to worry. We'll be fine."

"Alice!" a feminine voice called out.

Turning in the direction of the cry, Marty found Alice's mother, step-father, and brother making their way to join Alice. Mother and daughter embraced, and the earlier fears seemed to give way to the joyous reunion.

"Mother, I'm so glad to see you." The relief in Alice's voice was apparent.

"Well, we knew this would be quite the affair, and it seemed reason-able to ride the train over. Roy gets some free passes from time to time for his work with the railroad and freight." She threw her husband an admiring smile.

Marty thought the man seemed quite happy, and the previously wid-owed Ravinia Chesterfield James looked positively aglow. Even Simon seemed to fit right in. The couple hadn't been married all that long, but already it was clear that they were a family.

"And look at you," Alice said to her young brother. "I think you've grown ten inches since I last saw you."

"I am getting taller," Simon replied. "Pa says he'll have to put a brick on my head to slow me down."

They laughed at this, and Marty was happy to hear that Simon was calling Mr. James *Pa*. The boy needed a father in his life, for his own had never been there for him.

"Pa, can we go watch the bronc riders?" Simon asked, quickly for-getting about his sister.

"Sure, son. We'll go in a minute. Just be patient." Simon clearly looked disappointed but said nothing.

Alice's mother looked to Marty. "I understand from Alice that you, too, have a new baby."

"Yes. John Jacob is just a little older than your grandson."

"John Jacob sounds like a fine name," Roy James interjected. "A strong name. That's always good for a boy."

Marty nodded. "We named him after my father and Jake . . . well, really after Jake's grandfather. The baby's sleeping just there on the blanket with his older sister."

Ravinia stepped aside to gaze upon the baby. "He's beautiful and so is she. What a joy they must be."

Marty laughed. "Johanna looks angelic when she sleeps, but when she's awake she is like a Texas twister, wreaking havoc wherever it sets down."

They all chuckled at this, causing Johanna to stir slightly. Marty couldn't imagine why their laughter would awaken the child when all the noise of the crowd hadn't. Perhaps she worried subconsciously that someone was having fun without her.

"And your older boys? The ones you adopted?" Ravinia asked.

"They are doing well. They're just over at the pecan vendor's stand. Jake sent them there with a little spending money. I'm sure they'll return stuffed to the brim with nuts."

"They could be interested in far worse things," Alice's mother said with a smile.

Johanna seemed to settle back to sleep, so Marty motioned them away from the blanket.

"It's so good to see you. Will you be staying in town?"

"No. We plan to take the early evening train back to Dallas. Roy is teaching Sunday school tomorrow."

Marty nodded. "Well, I know you're anxious to meet that new grandbaby of yours, so don't let me keep you. He's quite a handsome boy."

"Yes!" Ravinia said enthusiastically. "I can hardly wait to hold my grandson."

"That's all she's talked about since the babe was born," Roy declared. "I figured we had to get up here if I was gonna have any rest at all."

"It seemed that everything conspired against me to get here. If it wasn't one problem, it was another. I'm still bound and determined to come stay for a few weeks. Maybe next summer."

"You will be welcome to stay with us as long as you'd like," Alice told her.

Marty added, "And if the Barnetts run out of room, you can come stay with us. Our household is a sight noisier, but you'd be welcome just the same."

"See there, Ravinia." Roy gave her a gentle elbow to the ribs. "I told you they would be happy to have you and Simon."

"Well, I do want to make certain I spend plenty of time getting to know my grandson," she said in a serious tone. "A few years back I never thought this day would come, and now that it has, I want to enjoy it to the fullest. Now, where's my grandson?"

Alice laughed. "Robert is watching over him just now, but I'm sure he will be happy to see you three. We were just talking of making a trip to Dallas so you could meet little Wills."

After they'd gone, Marty gazed around the crowd. Here and there she recognized old friends, but there was no sign of Jake or of Mr. Morgan. She was beginning to worry about what might have taken place during their meeting. It surely wouldn't take that long to hear Morgan's proposal and refuse it. She saw her boys returning just then and momentarily forgot about anything being amiss.

"Look, Mama, we got roasted pecans," ten-year-old Wyatt announced. His brothers—Sam, nine, and Ben, seven—followed close behind.

"These have sugar and cinnamon baked on 'em," Ben announced, holding up a small spiraled cone of newspaper. Inside were a handful of the sweet nuts. "Try 'em, Mama."

Marty smiled at the threesome and sampled their treats. "They are delicious."

"I think we should plant some pecan trees," Wyatt said. "Then we could have our own all the time."

"Nut trees can be a lot of hard work. When they bear, you have to pick up the nuts from the ground, then dry them, and sometimes even husk them before you can get to the shell. Remember the black walnut tree at Auntie Laura's house?"

The boys nodded. "But that was fun," Sam said. "I like stompin' on the green balls and seeing the black balls with the nuts come out."

"And it made our hands black," Ben added, as though that were a particularly good point.

"Yes, so while I agree that nuts are delicious, we might be better off to focus on raising cattle."

"Papa's gonna teach me to rope a steer," Ben told her. "He said we could do it when we get home."

"Well, roping takes a lot of practice, but I'm sure you'll master it quickly." Marty smiled at the boy. Johanna began to stir and then sat up, rubbing sleep from her eyes. The baby slept on even as Marty lifted him and put him in the perambulator. "Boys, fold up our blanket here and bring it along. We need to find your father."

Johanna was all smiles as Marty hoisted the girl onto her hip. "Just look at you, sleepyhead. Your hair is all mussed."

The little girl laughed and patted Marty's cheeks. "Mama go now."

"Yes, we're gonna go find Papa."

Marty turned to Wyatt and Sam, who had completed folding the blanket. "Just tuck it into that pack Papa affixed to the back of the baby buggy. Wyatt, will you please push the carriage for me? Sam can carry your pecans."

"So long as he doesn't eat 'em all," Wyatt said, handing his cone over.

"I won't eat 'em all," Sam assured him. "Just a few."

"You got your own," Wyatt said, taking hold of the buggy's handle.

"Boys," Marty interjected, "no fighting."

"Yes, ma'am," Sam and Wyatt said in unison.

Marty didn't go far before running into Alice and her family once again. "I wonder if the children could stay here with you and your mother for a moment. I need to go see what's happened to Jake."

"Of course they can," Alice said. She looked to her mother. "You don't mind, do you?"

"Of course not," Ravinia James replied.

Alice frowned. "But maybe you shouldn't be the one to go. We can send Robert. Why don't you wait until he and Roy get back? They've just gone to fetch us some drinks."

"I don't want Robert to have to leave his family for this." Marty looked back in the direction Mr. Morgan and Jake had gone. Just then the baby began to fuss. No doubt he was hungry.

"Well, there's Austin. Why don't you ask him to go? Then you can tend to John Jacob, and I'll keep an eye on Johanna. The boys will be just fine." Alice smiled. "They are good boys, and look, they're already playing with Simon. It's been a long time since they've seen each other, so they'll keep occupied telling one another their adventures."

The boys were caught up in a game of marbles over to one side, where the dirt was level. They were carrying on a lively conversation as they knelt in the dust to eye their next move. *Oh, to be that innocent of trouble*, Marty thought.

She gave a sigh and made up her mind. It would be better for a man to go in search of Jake. Then, if there was to be any trouble, Jake wouldn't be distracted with worries about his wife. "I suppose I could ask Austin. He would obviously be the better one to intercede if something has gone wrong."

Alice waved Austin over. Marty could see that he was preparing to leave and hated to ask him for this favor if he planned to head out right away.

"Afternoon, ladies. I was just heading out to check some of the area ranches. I don't want the rustlers taking advantage of this gathering."

"That's a good idea," Marty said. "But before you leave, could you help me with something?"

He looked at her with a question-raising brow. "And what would that be?"

Marty hurriedly explained, then said, "They went in the direction of the train yard, but I can't be sure where they are now. I'm just worried that Mr. Morgan will try to bully Jake into something."

"I can't imagine your husband letting anyone bully him into anything, but if it makes you feel better, Mrs. Wythe, I'd be happy to help."

"Thank you. It would mean a lot to me."

"Then it means a lot to me, too. I'll go find him and tell him you're in need of his company."

Marty watched Austin disappear into the crowd. The band struck up a Sousa march just then. It almost seemed as if they were heralding Austin's search. Marty shivered for no reason. She knew she was being silly. There was no reason to worry about Morgan and the meeting. Jake was indeed as strong a man as Austin had implied. He would never let Morgan have the upper hand.

"Look, Marty," Alice said, holding up a large packet of letters tied together with a string. "Mother brought these. They were the final business correspondences of my father. They were in the box that was shipped to her from Colorado."

Looking at the letters, Marty couldn't help but wonder if they might provide any better understanding of what had gone on in the past. She knew Alice was still trying to fit the pieces together. Maybe the letters were the final element needed.

"Have you read them?" she asked, looking first to Ravinia and then to Alice. Both women shook their heads.

"I never saw a need, since they were marked as business correspondence," Ravinia answered. "I thought to throw them away and then decided I'd let Alice be the one to either keep them or discard them."

"Oh, I want to read them," Alice declared, adding, "as soon as we get home." She tucked the large stack of letters into her picnic basket. "Oh good, here come Robert and Roy."

Marty said nothing more, but she couldn't help wondering what the letters contained. She hoped Alice would be quick to let her know the contents. Maybe the letters would explain everything that had happened in Colorado.

---------------------------- ★ ----------------------------

Austin Todd waited until the older bearded man he'd known as Cuker departed. He could see Jake sitting on the edge of a stone bench. The look on his face suggested something bad had taken place during his encounter with Morgan.

"Mind if I join you?" Austin asked.

Jake shook his head. "I don't at all. In fact, I'm glad it's you."

"Why's that?"

"I want your advice on something, but first I need to explain my past to you."

Austin leaned back against some fencing. "Sure. What do you need me to know?"

"Well, you know Marty and I lived in Denver for a time. I worked at the bank for Paul Morgan. He was good to us—always giving me gifts. He arranged a house for me since I was marrying and gave me a really great deal on the mortgage and interest. He filled it with fine things and told me the contents of the house were his wedding gifts to me and Marty."

Jake fell silent for a moment, but Austin could see he had more to say. "Morgan advanced me in the bank very fast. I was branch manager in no time at all. I replaced Alice's father after he was killed couriering bank papers. That's when Alice was cut up."

"I remember you telling me about it, but why are you bringing that up now?"

Jake looked most uncomfortable. "A man named Smith was constantly following her after she healed from the attack and was released from the hospital. He pestered her at every chance and demanded she find those papers. She and Marty went to search for them but found nothing. They even went back to the house were Alice and her father had lived. A new tenant living there told Alice that the only things left in the house were her father's personal effects and correspondence. She had mailed everything to Alice's mother. Now keep in mind that Alice thought her mother was dead, because her father had told her so. It was quite a shock for her."

"I can imagine." Austin shook his head. "So this is far more complicated than you told me before."

"It is, and I'm sorry to have to fill you in on everything at once, but this entire matter has just taken a new turn."

"And that's why you wanted to speak to me?"

"Yes. Morgan is determined that he needs to find those certificates before his adversary does. He wants me to come back to Colorado and help him, since I worked with many of the banking customers and employees. He's quite adamant that I assist him."

"And if you don't?"

"There will be problems."

"And that's why you wanted to tell me all of this. Are you thinking I might have answers?"

"I'm hoping you'll have advice for me," Jake said with a heavy sigh.

"Advice on what exactly?"

Jake looked up with a forlorn expression. "On how to stay out of jail."

Chapter 14

Feeling nearly recovered from her bout of sickness, Jessica sat reading by the fireplace. The day was warm enough that a fire wasn't needed, but this chair was Jessica's favorite. Upholstered in a soft mauve color, the fan-backed chair was far and away the most comfortable. With an added ottoman, Jessica felt like a queen on her throne. Of course, she never told anyone that and would now have been quite embarrassed if she had. She'd given a lot of thought to how she might go about changing the way people saw her. Jessica wanted desperately to have people love her and respect her just as they did Mrs. Barnett or even Mother, and taking on queenly airs wasn't the way to accomplish that.

She was looking at the words of Matthew chapter five and pondering the meaning of the Sermon on the Mount when her mother ushered visitors into the front room.

"Look who I ran into, Jessica, as I was coming back from the spring-house."

It was Marty Wythe and her sister Hannah.

"Miss Hannah . . . Marty," Jessica greeted with a nod.

"How are you feeling, Jessica?" Hannah Barnett asked.

Jessica smiled. "Much better, thank you." She could see that the ladies clearly had something on their minds. "If you need, I can retire to my bedroom."

Hannah shook her head. "No. You can be of help in this matter. We are putting together a group of women to pray."

Jessica grimaced. For all that she had been doing to try to know God better, she wasn't at all sure her prayers would avail much. But already Hannah Barnett was looking to Mother.

"We have a problem, a family problem, and we need the Lord's counsel and protection."

"Why don't you sit down and tell me what's happened," Mother more insisted than questioned.

The two women took a seat on the sofa and began to share the story, first one explaining and then the other.

"We can't help but think that Mr. Morgan means to see Jake put in jail unless he goes to Colorado and helps him," Hannah told them.

"But how can he possibly do such a thing?" Mother asked. "Surely no one would believe that Jake embezzled anything."

Marty spoke up. "Mr. Morgan gave us everything and made us feel that it was a perfectly normal procedure for him to follow with his employees. We had no way of knowing that the money, gifts, and even the lower interest rate on our home were part of his scheme to control Jake. Of course, Mr. Morgan had no idea the financial crash would come and close down many of the banks."

"But Jake no doubt worked hard for the man," Mother countered.

"He did. He did all that he was instructed to do. But that doesn't seem to matter," Marty replied. "Jake said there's no way to prove that those things were gifts or that the extra money was given and not taken from the bank. Mr. Morgan told Jake that he has plenty of friends who will help him doctor the books and make it apparent that Jake stole from Mr. Morgan. So if Jake doesn't help him, he'll end up in jail for something he didn't do."

Jessica listened in fascinated silence. Such intrigue was not the everyday topic around these parts. The thought that someone innocent might be jailed was abhorrent to her. Just as it obviously was to the others.

"We will pray, and we'll get others to pray, as well," Mother offered. "I won't say who the family is or offer details. I'll simply say that a family I know needs prayer for a private request."

Mrs. Barnett nodded. "I'd appreciate that, Carissa. If we get folks praying, I'll feel better. The Lord has something in mind for all of this, but I surely don't know what it is. Alice spends most of the day in tears. She's been so upset since finding out about Mr. Morgan's threat that she's hardly had any milk to feed the baby. Marty has had to help a time or two."

"And Jake feels to blame," Marty explained, "even though he had nothing to do with the gold certificates."

Mother considered this a moment. "I'm sure he feels responsible, but we can clearly see he's not. He's not the type of man to do such a horrible thing."

"No, he's not," Marty agreed. "Jake was always meticulous in his dealings with Mr. Morgan and the bank. To have Morgan tell him now that he'll see him jailed for embezzlement unless Jake helps him . . . well . . . it's deeply wounded Jake."

"So you can see our need for immediacy where prayer is concerned," Mrs. Barnett added.

"I do," Mother replied. She looked to Jessica. "We both do."

Jessica nodded in agreement but had serious doubts as to how her prayers might help. She hadn't exactly been close to the Lord. Would He still listen to such a backslider?

Hannah and Marty got to their feet, and Mother escorted them out the front door while Jessica continued to ponder the situation. When her mother returned, Jessica was ready with her question.

"Mother, will God listen to me if I pray? I mean, I haven't been a good person. I didn't read my Bible for a long time, and frankly, I'm not sure I even knew what I was doing when I prayed for Jesus to forgive me and come into my heart."

Instead of Mother looking shocked, as Jessica had feared, she only smiled. "Jess, God listens to the earnest prayers of sinners seeking forgiveness. You've had a reckoning of the heart, so perhaps now would be a good time to offer up an earnest prayer."

Her mother's words stayed with Jessica throughout the day. By the time afternoon rolled around, Jessica was aggravated in even thinking about it, and the confines of the room only made matters worse. She was relieved when Mother shooed her from the house and suggested she sit on the porch or take a walk to get some air.

The day was warm but not unbearable. Jessica had only just settled herself on the porch when a horse and rider came loping up the long drive. It was Austin Todd. Jessica felt her stomach flip-flop. It wasn't the same as how Harrison Gable made her feel, but it was just as intense. There was something special about this man. It didn't hit her over the head like Harrison Gable's presence did, but rather it was like an all-consuming fire. The feelings had started small, but they were building with each encounter and now had become a threatening blaze.

"Miss Jessica," Austin called out as he dismounted. He left his horse to graze on the front lawn and joined Jessica on the porch. "I came by to see how you were feeling. It's been almost two weeks since you came down sick."

She smiled at his concern. "I'm doing much better. You were kind to concern yourself."

Austin looked almost embarrassed. "Well, since I was here the night you took ill, I've had it on my mind quite a bit."

"You have?" Jessica couldn't imagine that Austin Todd gave her a second thought, but she was delighted that he had.

"It seemed pretty bad. I wasn't sure if it was something contagious or serious, but it surely was a fearful thing to watch."

Jessica frowned. Had he only been worried about whether or not he might contract the same illness? Surely Austin wasn't that shallow. She glanced up to meet his concerned expression. He seemed sincerely worried for her sake.

"Mother said it was probably either a bout of the ague or the grippe. Could be contagious, I suppose, but I couldn't say. You might need to check in with Mother to be sure."

"Oh, that doesn't worry me," he replied. "I was just fearful for your sake. I figured you'd be pretty miserable in quarantine, and if it was life-threatening . . . I would truly regret that."

Jessica felt pleased at his response. "You needn't worry anymore. I'm recovered . . . well, very nearly in full. Mother wants me to continue to take it easy for at least another day."

"I'm sure that's wise." He seemed at a loss for words, and the conversation lagged. Tugging at his collar, Austin looked rather miserable. Jessica took pity on him.

"Father said there have been problems with cattle rustling."

"Yes, but the Rangers have caught up to most of them. The losses are way down."

"That's good news. I know there've been years when the rustlers were a worry to my father. Seems about six years ago we lost quite a few head."

Again strained silence surrounded them. Jessica was determined to keep Austin with her, so she hurried onto another line of questioning. "You once told me that you were from Virginia. Did you like it there?"

Austin looked at her for a moment, as if trying to figure out how to answer.

Jessica chuckled. "I apologize if I was too forward. You know that I speak my mind. It's just normal curiosity. Why don't you sit and we'll have a proper talk?"

He glanced at one of the nearby chairs and finally gave a nod. "All right. I liked Virginia for a great many reasons, but I also didn't like the area for other reasons. What else do you want to know?"

"I don't know." Jessica hadn't expected this at all. "I guess I would have to ask what some of those reasons were. For instance, what did you like best about Virginia?"

He looked away from her and gazed across the yard. She thought he looked almost sad. "The people. The people were good and kind. Not that they aren't here in Texas. Fact is, the people here remind me a good deal of the folks in Virginia."

"And what didn't you like?"

"The crowds. Too many people. For all the good ones, there were equal numbers of bad." He paused and looked back at her. "I told you that my mother was originally from Texas. She used to tell me stories about growing up here, and Texas sounded . . . well . . . peaceful and unpopulated."

"We're growing by leaps and bounds, my father says. Still, I can't imagine just up and moving because there were too many people."

He smiled and Jessica felt her stomach flip again. Goodness, but he was a handsome man. Not only that, she loved his rich baritone voice. Deep, but not too deep. And his eyes were just as enticing as Harrison Gable's, even if they were a lighter brown.

". . . because that kind of life wasn't what I wanted anymore."

She hadn't been listening and regretted it immediately. Jessica needed to know more about this man. "I'm sorry, would you say that again?"

"I said Virginia has some peaceful, less populated parts, but I lived near Washington, D.C., where there was constant noise. I decided to come west because that kind of life wasn't what I wanted anymore."

Jessica tried to keep her mind on their discussion. "What kind of work did you do?"

"Much the same as I do now. Oh, I don't mean inspect cattle, but working for the law."

"And do you have family back there?"

She couldn't be sure, but Jessica thought he frowned. He lowered his head rather quickly and blocked his face from view. For a moment she thought he might not respond, but finally he looked up.

"I had family, but they died."

"How tragic. That must have been hard for you."

"It was. Sometimes it still is."

★

Austin wasn't at all sure why he was telling Jessica all of this. His life had been a very private one, even before the death of his family. Now, however, he felt compelled to tell this woman everything. He supposed it had to do with his attraction to her. There was just something that drew him back to her no matter how hard he'd tried to ignore it.

"So you came west hoping for a new start and to escape memories?" she asked in a soft, gentle tone.

"I did." The admission wasn't as difficult as Austin had feared.

"And has it worked?"

He looked at the young woman with the beautiful dark brown eyes and smiled. "As well as anything has."

She pushed back reddish-brown bangs from her forehead and smiled

617

back at him. "Hopefully time will help. Mother always says that time heals our wounds. Time and God."

"God?"

Jessica nodded. "Mother believes that God cares deeply for our every need."

"But you don't?"

She shrugged. "I'm not sure what I believe."

This was something Austin completely understood. It gave him a sense of relief to find someone who felt just as he did. "I know what you mean."

Cocking her head to one side, Jessica seemed surprised. "You understand?"

"I do. I feel about the same as you do. I'm not sure what I believe anymore. I was raised in a God-fearing home. I even attended church with my . . ." He fell silent. He'd very nearly told her about Grace.

"With my family," he added. "I read the Bible and prayed, but when I lost my family, I lost my connection to God. It felt as if He'd removed His presence along with my loved ones."

"How awful," Jessica said, looking thoughtful. "My distance grew out of pure disinterest and self-centered sin."

Austin didn't say so, but he admired her once again for her straightforward conversation.

She continued. "I suppose I found other things far too fascinating. There were parties to attend and new gowns to be purchased. I'm ashamed to say I lived a spoiled and pampered life."

"Why ashamed? If your parents chose to lavish you with attention and possessions, I don't see anything wrong with that."

"It wasn't wrong in and of itself," she said. "It was the way it stole my focus—my heart." She looked at him with an expression of regret. "I don't like the person I became. That's why I'm working to change."

He was completely captivated by this confession. He'd never in his life heard a woman speak in such a manner, especially one so young and beautiful. Ignoring the sound of an approaching carriage, Austin said, "I understand what you mean. I've been working to change myself, too. It's not easy."

"No," Jessica said, shaking her head. "It's probably the hardest thing I've ever done."

For a moment they just sat there looking deep into each other's eyes. It was a silent sort of bonding that drew them together in an inexplicable manner.

"Well, I must say I thought to hear at least a hello."

Austin bristled at the sound of Harrison Gable's voice. He turned to look at the man and gave a terse nod. "Mr. Gable."

"Mr. Todd. What a pleasant surprise."

"How so?" Austin asked. He thought the man looked insincere and figured to put him on the spot. Gable was too experienced to fall into that trap, however.

"I had hoped to discuss your duties as marshal to Terryton. You need to know what the railroad expects of you. I have just returned from meetings in Dallas and have much to share. Hence my surprise to find you here."

Austin refused to let him off the hook. "So what does the railroad expect?"

Gable smiled. "Let's not bore Miss Atherton with such talk. I can speak to you another time. I'm sure you have somewhere you need to be."

Austin leaned back in the chair and shook his head. "Nowhere in particular." He saw a quick flash of irritation in Gable's expression. But just as quickly as it came, it was gone, and he returned to his smooth-talking ways.

"I must say, Miss Jessica, you are looking quite well. I am glad to see you feeling better. Perhaps you'll be up to an outing soon?"

"Of course. Mother says I only need rest another day or so. Perhaps we could go riding. My horse, Peg, needs to stretch her legs. She hasn't had a good run in some time. We could get Osage to come along with us."

Austin hated to hear her respond so positively. He wanted to say something but knew anything he said would make him sound like a jealous beau.

"I'm afraid I'm rather saddle weary. I've been riding a great deal back and forth from Cedar Springs to the railroad site. Perhaps we might borrow your buggy and take a ride?" He motioned toward the small conveyance.

The momentary relief Austin felt at the news that Gable didn't wish to ride quickly dissolved with his comment about the carriage.

No doubt you'd like to take her for a ride. That buggy is tight enough to keep you two snuggly fitted. You would just spend the time wooing her and trying to convince her of how dear she has become.

"I doubt that would meet with my father's approval," Jessica said with a smile. "He's very protective of my reputation—and of me."

Austin breathed a little easier at this. She was a woman of integrity. He realized in that moment how much he'd come to care for Jessica.

Don't let it happen, his heart warned. *Don't feel too much, or you'll just get hurt.*

In a most intimate fashion Gable reached out to Jessica and took hold of a loose curl. He let it wrap around his finger and then leaned down to whisper inappropriately in her ear. Austin noticed the way she shivered. It hit him hard.

She cares for him. She's enjoying his attention.

"I have the utmost regard for you and your reputation, Miss Atherton," Gable assured her.

Austin got to his feet. "I guess I need to be going. I'm due for supper with the Barnetts."

"What a pity," Gable said, straightening. "Perhaps we can talk another time."

Austin met the man's gleaming eyes. "I think that would be wise." He hoped the tone inferred the seriousness he felt. He intended to find out what Gable's intentions toward Jessica might be.

Again his thoughts were of warnings to back off—to distance himself from feeling too much. The memory of losing his wife pierced him, and he forced a pleasant expression. "After all, if we don't discuss it, I won't know what the railroad needs me to do. Good talking with you, Miss Atherton. Gable."

Gable nodded in a knowing fashion, then turned back to Jessica, as if dismissing Austin altogether. "So as I was saying, my dear, we need to put a little color back in your cheeks, and I have just the plan."

620

Austin ignored the anger that was building. Instead of saying anything more, he mounted his horse and headed for the Barnetts'. He couldn't understand why Gable's interaction bothered him so much. He wasn't about to give in to feelings that could only result in pain. Not even for one as beautiful as Jessica Atherton.

Chapter 15

Two weeks after his visit with Jessica, Austin sat at the Barnett dining table and shared his news with William, Robert, and Jake. Having been tied up with arresting a rustling gang, this was the first chance Austin had to explain what he'd learned about their situation.

"I wrote to my former boss, Ellery Turner, regarding Morgan and the counterfeit gold certificates. He wired me that the department had some knowledge of gold certificate counterfeiting, but they'd hit a stone wall in their investigation. He was excited to learn this new information and arranged with the Texas Rangers for me to begin a further search for them."

"That's wonderful news," Will said, looking to Jake. "Hopefully Morgan will find himself too occupied by that to cause you any further trouble."

Jake shrugged and looked less than convinced. "Morgan still says that I embezzled from the bank. It's his hold over me to get what he wants."

"I figure to let it get around that I'm investigating bank fraud," Austin replied. "I might even pay Mr. Morgan a visit on such pretenses and ask him about his banking practices."

"To what end?" Jake asked.

"I'm hoping it will make him nervous—maybe even make him leave the area." With that matter resolved, Austin pushed back the empty coffee mug and took some papers from inside his coat. "I have a list of questions that I'll need to ask you, Jake. This will help me get a better feel for the situation."

"I'll do whatever I can."

"Okay. When does Morgan plan to get back in touch with you?"

Jake's face took on an expression of confusion. "I don't know. He just said he'd be in touch." With a look of concern Jake continued. "I don't even know where he's staying. He could be in Cedar Springs or he could be elsewhere. I just don't know."

"I'll figure it out. Did he mention being here with anyone else, perhaps a cohort?"

"No. I think Mr. Morgan is alone." Jake looked toward the ceiling and seemed to grow thoughtful. "I'm sure that if his money is back in place, he'll have no trouble getting help when he needs it. He's never been shy about paying for what he wants."

Austin considered the matter for a moment. He had been rather excited when Mr. Turner let him know that the agency needed him for this investigation. There was always that old nagging doubt about his capability for such work. Doubt that seemed to grow daily since watching his brother die.

"Austin?"

He looked up and realized the other men were watching him. "Sorry," he said sheepishly. "I was pondering our next move."

"And what did you decide?"

"That I need more information. Robert, you said that Alice had been followed and even approached by a Mr. Smith. But he wasn't with the men who attacked her and killed her father?"

"Right. Mr. Smith appeared after the attack. Alice said she was still in the hospital when one of the nurses told her that a man had come to see her. The doctor turned him away, explaining that Alice was enduring a bad infection and couldn't be disturbed. The man left but tried again to approach her at the house of friends where she was staying after her release from the hospital. Finally, he took to followin' her, and any time he found her alone he would pester her about some missing papers that her father should have had on the night he was killed. Papers that we now realize were really gold certificates."

"And all of this took place in Denver?"

Jake piped up here. "Yes. We didn't know about it when Alice first came to work for us."

"I didn't realize she had worked for you," Austin said, writing this down for future reference.

"She came to us lookin' for a job. Her friends had left the area, and she was homeless, without hope for her future. Marty took to her right away and hired her as her lady's maid."

"Did the man who'd been following Alice approach her at your home?"

"He did," Jake said. "The man eventually started watching our house and following Alice to the shops whenever Marty sent her out for something. Eventually Mr. Smith got bold and showed up at the doorstep. Marty made his acquaintance with a shotgun in hand." He smiled. "She's quite a woman, my wife."

Will laughed. "You don't know the half of it, Jake. That girl used to keep us up nights just trying to stay ahead of her shenanigans."

"I learned some of my best orneriness from Aunt Marty," Robert admitted.

Austin immediately thought of Jessica Atherton. He imagined she had always been a feisty but ladylike worry to her parents.

"Do you suppose," Jake said, looking rather skeptical, "that Mr. Smith might know Mr. Morgan?"

Austin gave a slight nod. "Anything is possible. It would seem to fit, since Morgan has come here seeking help in getting those certificates back. On the other hand, it could be that he realizes others are looking for them and desperately hopes to find them first. There is a possibility that the man is completely on the up and up and has nothing to do with the counterfeiting."

"I suppose it's also possible that there is more to this than we realize," Jake muttered. "I, for one, am sorry I ever went to work for Morgan. I didn't wanna be a banker anyway, and I should have stuck with my resolve and told my father no."

"Actually, I can see the hand of God in all of this, Jake," Mr. Barnett declared. "If not for you going to work for Morgan, we might not be able to get to the bottom of this mess."

"He's right." Austin gave Jake a smile. "You have insight to the man, and now a connection that might very well allow us to get to the truth."

Jake seemed to think about this for a moment. He scratched his head. "I'll do whatever it takes. I want Alice and my family to be free of these threats."

"Can you take some time to join me in Dallas?" Austin asked. "I'd like to sit down and discuss this with a couple of my superiors. I think they can give us some advice for how to go about things."

"I can get away," Jake said, looking to his brother-in-law for approval. Austin knew the man still assisted the Barnetts with their ranch work from time to time.

Will nodded. "I think that'd be a good idea."

"But I can't leave Marty and the children alone," Jake said, looking back to Austin. "It wouldn't be safe. Mr. Morgan knows where we live, and he's bound to know I've talked with Marty. He might decide to threaten her in order to push me to a decision."

"They can all stay here," Will said. "We've got enough room, and Hannah will love having Marty here."

"Marty will enjoy being with her sister and Alice, as well," Jake replied. "I think that's a good idea. I know they'll be safe here."

"Any intruders will have to get through us and a good number of our men before they can cause harm to any of the womenfolk," Robert added. He grinned. "And then, God help them, they'll have to deal with our gals."

Will laughed. "He's right. You know, Hannah can be pretty fierce when she feels her family is threatened."

Jake nodded. "Marty, too."

Austin felt a deep emptiness as the men talked about their wives. It wasn't really a pain these days, but more of a dark void that seemed to go on forever. He wondered if he'd ever know the peace of mind he sought. He was so weary—so burdened.

Come unto me, all ye that labour and are heavy laden, and I will give you rest.

The words came as a nearly audible voice. Austin looked at the men who sat opposite him, but no one seemed to notice him. They were all busy talking among themselves. None of them had spoken that Bible verse from Matthew.

For a moment Austin remembered a time when he had shared that verse with Grace during morning prayer time. She had told him that the verse had always been a comfort to her, especially when her workload was heavy.

"So when do you want to go?"

Austin barely heard Jake ask the question. He put aside his memories and answered. "The sooner the better. We need to put an end to this." He put his thoughts completely back on the case. "I'm figuring it might be possible that whoever is involved in this may be after more than the forged certificates. I think it's quite possible they might be looking for the actual plates themselves. After all, a few forged gold certificates won't get them far."

"I'm guessin' you're right," Robert replied. His expression grew a bit darker. "But no matter what, they have hurt my wife for the last time, and I intend to see this through to the end."

"Agreed," Austin said, knowing he had the full cooperation of the men before him. Again he thought of Jessica and how willing he would be to protect her from harm.

Then protect her from yourself, Austin's mind seemed to mock. *You're the only real danger to her.*

"You look beautiful," Mother told Jessica as she descended the stairs.

Jessica hoped so. She'd taken great care to dress for her outing with Harrison. Robert and Alice would ride with her into Cedar Springs, and then Harrison would join them in attending a musical affair. Jessica was determined to look her best, as this was the first proper event she would attend with the handsome lawyer.

Mother motioned. "Turn for me."

Jessica did so indulgently. She knew her mother was anxious for everything to be perfect. The gown had a beautiful skirt of Muscovite velvet that had come all the way from Russia. The black velvet brocade set upon dark green corded silk gave the gown an opulent look. The high-necked silk bodice was a buttery cream color, trimmed with black and dark green bands, which served to enhance the beauty of the piece.

Mother plucked a piece of lint from one of the voluminous sleeves. "Harrison Gable will be completely captivated."

"So long as he's not too captivated," Jessica's father said with just a hint of disapproval. "I don't know that this is a good idea, but I won't take back my agreement to let you go."

Jessica stepped to where her father stood. Stretching up on tiptoes, she kissed his cheek. "You worry too much, Papa. Besides, I'll be with Robert and Alice."

"I know, but that's a long ride into town, and it will be an equally long ride home."

"But our house isn't nearly as far from town as the Barnett house, and besides, they've already arranged to have their baby cared for by Marty and Jake," Jessica argued. "Everyone thought this would be a good diversion for Alice."

"Tyler, you've already given your word," Mother declared.

He looked to the ceiling and shook his head. "I know. I know. I must have been crazy."

"Oh, Papa, don't fret." Jessica always called him Papa when she wanted to soothe him. "You needn't worry. We'll have supper and then attend the concert. I'll be staying in an adjoining room near Robert and Alice at the hotel. There will be locks on the doors. Mr. Gable won't even be at the hotel. He'll be in his own home. Tomorrow morning after breakfast and some shopping, Robert will bring me back safe and sound. You have no reason to doubt me."

Jessica knew her father thought highly of Robert. After all, he had hoped Jessica might marry the son of his best friend. And, while the current hotel arrangements had given Jessica a twinge of discomfort, she had been far more excited by the news that Harrison Gable would escort her that evening. It was worth it, even if she was being chaperoned by her friends.

"I wish you would have waited to dress at the hotel," Mother said, fussing with the velvet bands that encircled Jessica's waist. "You're going to be all dusty by the time you get there."

"Since Robert couldn't get away any earlier than this afternoon," Jessica reminded her mother, "we wouldn't have time for changing our clothes at the hotel. Besides, Robert has promised he'll bring Uncle Brandon's enclosed carriage. Alice and I will be quite comfortable."

The sound of an approaching carriage caused Jessica to rush to the window in a most unladylike fashion. "They're here. Where's my overnight bag?" She searched around the room and spied it by the front door. Excitement coursed through her like a steady electric current.

"Don't forget your wrap," Mother said and brought a long black cape to her. "It could be quite chilly by nightfall."

Jessica took the cloak and kissed her mother. "I'll be just fine."

She took up her bag, but her father reached out and claimed it. "I'll take this."

She followed him from the house. Robert had just brought the carriage to a stop near the house, and Jessica saw Alice give a wave through the window. It seemed strange that they should come together for this event. Alice had been her enemy at one time, but now Jessica only longed for a friend.

"I see you're ready to go," Robert said, jumping down from the driver's seat to retrieve the bag her father held.

"Robert, you take good care of my gal," Father told him and handed him the bag. He turned to Jessica. "And you, behave yourself. You know what I expect out of you." His voice was stern, but Jessica could hear the love in his voice.

"I promise, Papa. I will be a perfect lady, just as I've always been."

Her father gave her a skeptical look, then helped her up into the carriage. Jessica smiled at Alice as her father closed the door. Settling into the seat opposite Alice, she blew out her breath. "I wasn't at all sure he'd allow me to escape."

Alice grinned. "Well, I'm glad he did. I'm looking forward to spending time with you. Robert decided not to bring a driver. He said that way you and I could sit inside and talk up a storm and get to know each other. He thinks it will take my mind off of . . . everything."

Jessica noticed Alice's beautiful gown of turquoise. Lace edged the neckline, and the bodice was decorated with tiny silver beads. It wasn't anywhere near as fancy as her own, but in some ways, Jessica thought it lovelier. "Your gown is exquisite," she told Alice. "It complements your hair perfectly and gives you the tiniest waistline."

"Thank you. I was about to comment on *your* dress." Alice shook her head. "I haven't seen anything like it since Marty's clothes in Denver. They were all so beautiful and so delicate. I enjoyed helping her to dress just to feel the rich materials. I suppose you have a dozen such gowns?" The carriage lurched forward as they began to move out.

"I have my share, to be sure," Jessica said, feeling rather self-conscious. She gave her parents a wave and then turned back to Alice. "I used to worry about such things. I thought gowns and jewelry to be so important. Now I don't feel the same way."

Alice's expression grew thoughtful. "I suppose everyone comes to a place in life where they learn what truly matters most."

Jessica thought of how much she wanted to change. Life lessons had been slow in catching up with her, but now that they had, her reformation was all consuming.

"I like to think that I have changed for the better. Of course, I still have to prove myself," Jessica replied. "That's the hard work ahead of me."

Chapter 16

Being inside a bank on a Saturday afternoon seemed a little strange to Austin. However, the second-floor office of the National Exchange Bank of Dallas was exactly where they'd come to meet with a federal court judge and two Secret Service agents. The walls were papered with green and gold stripes, and of course there was a great deal of mahogany. The table and chairs were mahogany, as were the room's trim, doors, and floor. And, despite the fact that someone had opened one of the two windows, musty warmth made the room most uncomfortable.

The bank manager sat at the head of the table and began the introductions. "Gentlemen, I'm happy to be able to meet with you here today. As many of you know, my name is Claude Reiman. I am employed by the bank and will act as their representative. Mr. Todd, I believe you already are acquainted with Judge Weimer?"

"Yes," Austin said, nodding toward the older man. He'd known Judge Weimer through business with the Texas Rangers when certain situations had led them to federal involvement.

"Judge Weimer, this is Jacob Wythe," Austin continued. "Mr. Wythe is the reason we are here today." He turned to the two agents. "These are agents Carson and Deeters." The men gave a slight nod in unison.

"I'm pleased to meet y'all. Happy to have the opportunity to assist you in any way I can," the judge answered. His thick southern accent suggested he wasn't raised in Texas, but perhaps Georgia or the Carolinas.

He was an older man and, befitting his age and situation, made a stately figure in his dark suit and snowy white hair. Austin felt poorly dressed next to the others. He and Jake had worn their Sunday best, but their clothes lacked the refinement and newness of that of the other men's clothing. Normally that wouldn't have bothered Austin in the least, but at the moment he wanted to make it clear to these men that he and Jake were equal to the task at hand and not simply some bumbling backwoods ninnies.

Weimer gave Austin a stern gaze. "Why don't you tell us about this matter, Mr. Todd."

Austin looked to Jake and then stood. "Gentlemen, I will endeavor to explain our circumstance and to address our needs in as concise a manner as possible."

For the next hour, Austin and Jake shared the information they could. The judge took notes and from time to time asked questions to clarify the details further. To Austin's relief, a man showed up about forty minutes into his explanation and provided a tray with glasses and a pitcher of sweet tea. The refreshment did its job and Austin found it easier to continue.

"Most likely," Austin said in conclusion, "the certificates and possible plates are still in Colorado. Even so, we don't know if Mr. Morgan is involved with the counterfeiting or if he's simply trying to regain the forgeries for the sake of protecting the originals. After all, the trouble came from his bank and makes a mark against his reputation. Unfortunately, he believes in threats and has caused Mr. Wythe grave concern for the safety of his family and for his own well-being."

"To what purpose?" the judge asked.

"To the purpose of obtaining Jake's assistance in finding those certificates," Austin replied, glancing at Jake. "Or to see Jake sent to jail on trumped-up charges."

After answering a few more questions, Austin took a seat. He felt exhausted from the detailed explanation and request for assistance.

He knew the men at the table realized the importance of the situation, but nevertheless they talked amongst themselves as if trying to decide nothing more important than whether they'd buy the evening paper.

Last of all, the two Secret Service agents produced copies of several counterfeit bills. They pointed out some of the inconsistencies and mistakes.

"These are examples of some of the best," one of the men said and passed the bill around. Even Mr. Reiman agreed he wouldn't have known it wasn't a true piece of currency. The judge turned the twenty-dollar bill over in his hands. His expression grew thoughtful.

"Gentlemen, I believe you make a good case. Mr. Wythe, I am of the opinion that your appearance here today lends support to your innocence. I consider myself a man of discernment, and I will afford you protection from prosecution in any way that I can. Not many men have inspired me to pledge as much, but I feel certain this is God's will. I have friends in the Denver area and will take this up with them, as well, should the need arise. They will be most eager to see this worked out, as am I."

"Thank you, your honor," Jake replied. "I appreciate that. And my family does, too."

The counterfeit bills were collected as final comments and suggestions were offered. Austin felt that their time together had been beneficial. The meeting closed and some of the parties went their separate ways, each man with his assigned responsibilities. All were determined to put an end to the problem of counterfeiting.

Austin arranged for a private audience with Carson and Deeters over supper. He'd already informed Jake of the plan but now worried that maybe his friend would rather do otherwise. "I hope you don't mind if we do business with our meal," he told Jake. "I figured this would be our only chance unless we stay longer in the morning."

"I don't mind one bit. I'm anxious to get home, but this is vital to my well-being, and even more so to Marty's. And to the Barnetts'. Might as well make the best of our time, and if that means we work while we eat, then so be it."

"I suppose we could head out after our meeting. We could take the train from here to Cedar Springs. I understand there's a 7:45 this evening. It'd be difficult but not impossible."

Jake gave an appreciative grin. "You don't have to worry about me, Austin. I appreciate that you've been willin' to help us with this." He sobered considerably. "I figure we have to resolve this, or we'll always be lookin' over our shoulders. I can't live like that."

★

It was only a week before Thanksgiving, and Jessica felt the excitement of the season as well as the fact that tomorrow was her birthday. Her parents had always treated birthdays as a special event, but often Jessica's birthday got delayed and celebrated with Thanksgiving. She had no idea what her mother had planned this year.

"You're certainly quiet today," Mother said, motioning Jessica to raise her hands. She looped the yarn around Jessica's fingers and started to wind the yarn into a ball. "Is something wrong?"

"I've been thinking about Thanksgiving and then, of course, Christmas." Jessica glanced down at the dyed yarn. The rosy color would look nice made into a sweater for Johanna. At least that was what Mother had planned.

"And what of your birthday? It's tomorrow, or have you forgotten?" Mother asked, glancing up. "I can't believe my baby is going to be twenty-two."

"Me either," Jessica admitted. "All of my friends are married, and most have children, and I have nothing to show for my time on earth except myself."

"That is a matter of opinion. You've touched the lives of others and influenced them."

"Yes, but mostly in negative ways," Jessica replied. "I want things to be different from now on. I want this to be a new start."

Mother refocused on the yarn. "I think that's an admirable idea. But for now, wouldn't you like to know what I've planned for you?"

Jessica smiled. "Whatever it is, I will be content and happy."

"I'm glad to hear that," Mother said. "Since it's a Friday this year, I've invited a few people over to share dinner with us. The Barnetts and

Wythes will be here helping to butcher hogs, so it seemed only right to have them stay for supper and cake. Lupe has already been hard at work to create one of her delicious coconut cakes."

"Who else have you invited?" Jessica asked, quite curious. "Will the boys be home?" Her brothers had been absent for so long that Jessica feared they would make southern Texas their permanent residence.

"No, the boys won't be here. They've agreed to help build a church just across the border in Mexico. The minister of that congregation heard about the houses their teams had been building, and he begged them to help erect the church. It seemed they had some of the supplies needed but definitely could use more financial and physical help. We arranged some of the former, while the boys filled in the latter. Most of the other men had to return to their homes, but Howard and Isaac decided to stay—and with our blessing. What they're doing is important. So often people think of sharing God's love by preaching or reading the Bible to someone. More often, we can show people Jesus by demonstrating kindness and love in practical ways."

Jessica wasn't happy to know her brothers would remain in the South. It wasn't that she didn't believe they were doing good works, but she missed them and knew that Father needed their help with the ranch. "I knew they'd find some reason to stay. Sometimes I worry they'll never come back to ranching."

"Nonsense. It's in their blood. They'll be back. They're just enjoying their youth."

"They're older than I," Jessica countered. "Everyone is always telling me that I should already be settled with children. Why is it my brothers may continue enjoying their youth without correction?"

"That's how it is for a man. If he doesn't marry before he's thirty, people call him wise and laud him for his choice." Mother shook her head and reached over to undo a tangle in the yarn. "As for women, it's the opposite. A woman is supposed to marry young and have children. This is the way it's always been, and I doubt it will ever change. But, Jessica, I thought you wanted to be married. I remember your saying that with a wealthy enough husband you could see the world and all its splendors."

Jessica frowned. "That was the old me. The new me wants whatever is meant for me. I'm trying to understand what God wants. If it's marriage and children, then I believe I will be happy with that. If it's something else, then I will be content with that."

Releasing the yarn, Mother gave Jessica's knee a pat. "I'm glad to hear it. Wealth can buy only so much happiness. Real joy and peace come through knowing God's will and ways. Watch and listen for His direction."

Jessica knew her mother was right, but she couldn't really say she knew what was next expected of her by her heavenly Father. How did one learn to hear the voice of God?

"So do you want to know who else I've invited to share your birthday?" Mother asked.

Jessica had nearly forgotten that she'd asked. "Of course."

"Well, I gave it a lot of thought and even brought your father in on the decision. After we discussed it at length, I invited Aunt Laura and Uncle Brandon to come. And your father thought it would be nice to invite some of your . . . friends. Like Mr. Todd and Mr. Gable."

Jessica felt her face grow hot. Obviously her father and mother thought of Austin and Harrison as appropriate suitors for their daughter; otherwise they would never have considered such a thing.

"And did you invite them?" she asked, trying hard to sound as if she didn't care.

"I did. I am happy to say that both agreed to come."

Jessica glanced at the yarn in an effort to hide her delight. "I'm glad they can make it." She heard Mother chuckle and looked up to see her watching in amusement. "Why are you laughing?"

"You. You're trying so hard to convince me that it doesn't matter, but I know it does. I'm not so old that I don't remember the thrill of being pursued."

"You're not old at all, Mother. I heard Father say just the other day that you look as young and beautiful as when he first married you."

"His eyesight is failing." Mother smiled and continued with her task. "Still, I'm glad to hear he thinks I look the same. The evidence of the years is upon us both, and time is not always kind." She grew thoughtful. "But I really can't complain. The years have been good, and the holidays are always such a special time. I remember your first Christmas. Goodness, but you were just a newborn—barely a month old. I was so happy to have another girl. I feared Gloria would be the only one, and she did so much want a sister."

"It must have been difficult, what with so many little ones," Jessica said, thinking back on stories she'd heard of her mother and father's early years.

"It was," Mother admitted, "but good things usually come at a price." Her expression was reflective. "You must remember that I had my sister close by, and Gloria was eight years old and a lot of help. We were also starting to do quite well for ourselves. Your father hired a girl to come cook and clean for us. She was Lupe's older sister." She shrugged. "I don't regret any of it. Your father always made me feel safe and well cared for. I was seldom afraid with him at my side." She paused in her work. "I want that for you, Jess. I want that more than I can say. I pray all the time for you to find the right man to marry. I know that God has a man for you."

Jessica heard the sincerity in her mother's voice. It touched her heart that Mother should care so deeply about her happiness. She supposed no one could ever love her as much as her mother and father, but Mother believed there was one man out there for her who would try. Jessica wanted to believe with all her heart that it was true.

"But what if He doesn't?" she murmured, doubt creeping in.

"What?" Her mother looked perplexed.

"What if God doesn't have a man for me? What if I'm to remain unmarried?" Jessica wondered if God would punish her in such a manner for her selfish years. "Some women do, you know. Look at Eleanor Barnett. She prefers women's rights and politics to marriage and children."

"I know He has a husband for you, Jess. Don't ask me how; I just know it. One day you will marry and be happy. But don't take me wrong. Marriage will be work—the hardest work you'll ever do." Mother paused and smiled, adding, "And the most rewarding."

★

The next evening, Jessica found herself the center of attention. Well, at least most everyone's attention. Austin seemed rather distant, although he had made polite conversation and wished her well. On the other hand, Harrison was making somewhat of an annoyance of himself. He constantly sought to be at her side and whispered comments in her ear, as if they were already intimate. She couldn't help but thrill to his touch when he put his hand on her arm, but even so, it was Austin whose attention she was trying to get.

By the time supper was over and the birthday cake was served, Jessica found herself deep in thought. Harrison Gable was a stunningly handsome man with dark brown eyes and a gentle smile. He was obviously intelligent, having studied and practiced law with great success. He also had his eye on a future that included travel and living well. Austin, on the other hand, was equally handsome, but his features were completely different. Where Harrison's hair was brown-black, Austin's was a sun-kissed brown. Where Harrison had a bit of curl to his hair, Austin's was as straight as string. And to be sure, Austin was smart. He might not have Harrison's book learning, but he was nobody's fool.

"Do you like the cake?" Mother asked.

Jessica looked up and nodded. "It's delicious."

"And do you like the company?"

A smile crept across Jessica's lips. "Some of the best I've ever had."

Mother leaned in to whisper. "So who's in the lead?"

Jessica pulled back and looked at her. "What do you mean?" she whispered back.

"Austin and Harrison—who's winning the race to capture your heart?"

Jessica's confusion became feigned surprise. "Mother, really," she responded, her lips to her mother's ear. "You sound as if you're trying to matchmake. I thought we were just celebrating my birthday."

Her mother laughed and the melodious sound delighted Jessica's heart. She couldn't help but grin and give a little shrug.

★

Sunday morning dawned cloudy and cool. Jessica feared they might have to endure a cold rain on the way to church and was glad when her father brought around the enclosed carriage.

The weather, however, cleared a bit by the time they reached the church in Cedar Springs. Jessica was still reflecting on her birthday and how pleasurable her time had been with both Harrison and Austin present. She didn't even mind anymore that Harrison had acted so intimate with her in front of the others. She felt quite special and nothing was going to ruin her memories.

The Atherton family took their place in the family pew and awaited the beginning of the service. Jessica wondered if Austin and Harrison were in attendance but didn't want to look around for them. No doubt someone would see her and guess her mission.

The pastor offered a prayer and then invited the congregation to sing a hymn of praise. By the time they'd reached the fourth stanza, Harrison Gable had slipped into the pew beside Jessica. They exchanged a smile, but Jessica refocused her attention on the song. Then to her surprise as they started to sing the second hymn, Austin Todd appeared. He frowned at Gable but softened his harsh expression when Jessica met his eyes. To her surprise, Austin moved past both of them to take his place between Jessica and her mother. His nearness pleased Jessica, and his smooth baritone singing was most pleasurable to hear.

Jessica tried to keep her thoughts under control. This seating arrangement meant nothing. No doubt the other pews were full and the men had no other choice but to sit in her family's pew. Since her brothers were still away, it seemed the logical choice. Not only that, but Austin knew her parents better than he knew Mr. Gable. He most likely had made his choice based on the comfort of being with folks he knew. At least, that was her rationale.

As the music concluded and the congregation reclaimed their seats, Jessica had almost convinced herself.

The pastor offered another prayer and then encouraged the congregation to take out their Bibles. "In the second book of Corinthians, chapter five," he began, "the apostle Paul pleads the case for man to be reconciled with God. Let me share his thoughts." He leafed through several pages and began to read.

"'Therefore if any man be in Christ, he is a new creature: old things are passed away; behold, all things are become new. And all things are of God, who hath reconciled us to himself by Jesus Christ, and hath given to us the ministry of reconciliation.'" He looked up from the Bible. "Make certain you understand. We are only reconciled to God through Jesus. There is no other way, and the Bible makes this clear."

Jessica felt as if he were speaking directly to her. She swallowed hard, suddenly feeling very uncomfortable. What was it about these particular Scriptures that made her uneasy? The pastor continued reading.

"'To wit, that God was in Christ, reconciling the world unto himself, not imputing their trespasses unto them; and hath committed unto us the word of reconciliation.'" He looked up. "And here is the key: 'For he hath made *him* to be sin for *us*, who knew no sin; that we might be made the righteousness of God in him.'" Closing his Bible, the pastor stepped away from the small pulpit.

"Jesus made himself sin for us—that we might be reconciled to the Father in heaven. Jesus, who had never sinned, became the essence of sin that we might be saved. If that doesn't humble you, then something is wrong in the way you think."

Jessica's heart took on the full impact of the man's words. Reconciliation with God was something she'd not truly considered. In fact, she hadn't even been aware that it was missing. She'd never really felt the need to be reconciled with God. From the time she was small, church and its Christian teachings had been a part of her life that she took for granted.

"Paul urged people to be reconciled with God—to know the truth that comes to us through the Scriptures. Jesus is that truth. It is Christ and Christ alone who makes it possible for us—mere sinners—to be brought into right accord with the Father. It is nothing of ourselves and everything of Him who died to save us."

Jessica looked down at the floor. She was scarcely able to draw breath for the impact of the preacher's words. This was what was missing in her life. This was the oneness that she had longed for. It wasn't a husband or children. It wasn't wealth or new gowns. It was the need to truly belong—to be reconciled to her Father in heaven. It was Jesus whom she longed for. She couldn't make the past right. She couldn't change a single word or action, but she could become new through Christ.

The preacher continued to speak on the same passages, and by the time he concluded and asked if anyone in the congregation felt God's call upon their heart, Jessica could hardly sit still. She felt drawn as if someone were pulling her forward. Without any thought to what others might think, Jessica got to her feet, stumbled past Harrison, and made her way to the altar. She was becoming new—throwing off the old and the ugly, the sin nature that had done her no favors.

She wanted to cry and laugh at the same time. She was being reconciled, and it felt like a new birth.

Chapter 17

Sunday the sixth of December found Austin at the Barnett Ranch sharing the noon meal with the Barnett and Wythe families. Austin had found real love and acceptance from these people, and he didn't take that for granted. He had long since ceased to be just a man who inspected their cattle and agreed to patrol their new little town. He felt as if he'd been made a member of the family.

His mind warned him of the danger, but his heart craved the love they extended. Mrs. Barnett mothered him as his own might have done prior to his brother's death. Austin tried to force the memories from his mind and was grateful when Alice Barnett spoke up.

"Mr. Todd, I have something I'd like to show you. Robert said it might be useful to you in your investigation."

This surprised Austin, but he didn't show it. Alice was so like a little bird. She was lovely to look at despite the scar on the right side of her face, but she was easily spooked and unnerved by the things that were happening.

"I'd be honored to take a look," Austin replied, pushing back from the table. Already Hannah and Marty were beginning to clear the table.

"Well, I, for one, intend to take me a bit of a rest in the front room." Mr. Barnett looked at Jake. "Care to join me?"

"I would," Jake said, following Mr. Barnett from the room.

Austin started to get to his feet, but Alice bade him otherwise. "We can just stay right here. Hannah said it wouldn't be a problem. I'll go check on Wills and then bring the letters." She disappeared from the room, leaving Austin to turn to Robert.

"Letters?"

The other man gave a curt nod. "Correspondence between her father and mother, as well as business dealings. We were hopeful they might lend a clue to where Chesterfield might have put those plates and certificates."

Austin considered it a moment. "They very well might. I know the other two agents helping me in this are finding very little."

Alice reappeared just then, and in her hands she held two stacks of letters. Placing them on the table, she took a seat and pushed one stack toward Austin.

"These are the writings of my mother to my father and a few of his letters to her that Mother saved. They were not pleasant to read, by any means. My parents were unhappy with each other, and my father blamed my mother for things that were clearly untrue."

"I'm honored that you would trust me to read them. I promise to be discreet about their contents," Austin assured her.

Alice took a deep breath and reached for the second stack. "These are business dealings, invoices, and such. Mother said she very nearly burned them, not seeing any real purpose for them, but she thought perhaps I would want them. Now I'm of a mind they may be of use to you."

"They just might," Austin said. "There haven't been very many clues, and Mr. Morgan hasn't appeared again to Jake. Reading through these might give us some idea of where to look next."

Alice looked to Robert. He squeezed her hand. "Mr. Todd will see this brought to an end."

She looked back at Austin, and the pain and fear in her eyes were almost his undoing. He wanted more than ever to help her—to help them all be rid of the demons that tormented their family.

"There's one more thing," Alice said, reaching into a small bag she had attached to her waistband. From it she pulled a small bronze key. "This was in one of the envelopes. There were no markings on the envelope, but this key was wrapped in a piece of paper and left inside." She pushed the key across the linen tablecloth and left it to Austin's scrutiny.

He picked the piece up and pondered its purpose. It wasn't a normal door key, nor did it look like one used for winding a clock. The key resembled a tiny violin or perhaps a banjo. One end had a solid round piece of brass by which to hold the key. The end resembled the tuning pegs on the neck of a stringed instrument.

"I've never seen anything quite like it," Austin admitted.

"Neither have we," Robert said. The envelope had no markings and there was no indication as to where the key might belong.

"I'll check into it," Austin promised. "It might very well be important."

"I hope so. I hope all of this proves to be of use," Alice said, her eyes seeming to implore him to assure her it would.

"Thank you, Mrs. Barnett. I'm convinced this will lend me a clue or two." Austin put the key into his pocket. "I presume I may take the letters home with me?"

"Of course. Keep them as long as you like," Alice replied.

Rather than linger, Austin took up the letters and made his way to the front door. He gave a wave to Jake and William. "Thanks again for dinner. If you don't mind, I'm gonna take my leave. I have a bit of reading that needs my attention."

"Good to see you again, Austin," William said. "I'm excited at the turn of events regarding the rail line, and as soon as the officials come to see me, I'll be in touch. We're just about to get the tracks started. The railroad is gonna be doin' more detailed surveying most of December."

Austin nodded and headed from the house. His horse awaited him in the barn, where Robert had given it fresh hay to enjoy while Austin ate with the family. He quickly added the letters to his saddlebag, then readied his mount. He made his way from the Barnett Ranch with every intention of heading home. However, when he came to the turnoff for the Atherton place, Austin couldn't help himself. He had seen Jessica in church that morning, and she was all he could think about. He'd given up trying to guard his heart and knew the painful truth. He was falling in love with her.

His inner warning still attempted to make him turn back. He thought again of Grace and how awful it had been to lose her. If only he wouldn't have insisted on their living in the country, away from the dangers of the city.

"She's in a better place—the baby, too," he told himself aloud. "She loved me and would want me to go on living." He knew it was true, but there was a part of him that feared being loved like other men feared death.

At the Athertons', Austin was eagerly greeted by Mr. Atherton. "Welcome, Austin. Come on in. What brings you our way?"

"I shared lunch with the Barnetts, and . . . well . . . I thought it might be nice to check in with you."

Tyler Atherton assessed him momentarily. "I think I know why you're really here. Jess is down at the springhouse. You might wanna make your way there. It'll give you a nice walk back—together."

Austin met the man's smile and nodded. "Thank you, Mr. Atherton."

"My pleasure. Just go around the house to the back and make your way down the path to the right. It'll lead you to the springhouse . . . and to Jess."

Austin nodded again, nervous. He left Atherton and did as he'd been instructed, making his way down the path. His hands felt clammy and he wiped them on his Levi's, all the while chiding himself for letting the stress of the moment get to him.

He spotted the springhouse and the stream of water that ran under and through it. What a prize to have a cold spring on their property. Smiling, Austin thought this a rather secluded and perfect meeting place for young lovers. Not wishing to startle Jessica, he called out.

"Miss Atherton, are you here?"

It was only a moment before Jessica peeked out the door. "Mr. Todd, I wasn't expecting to see you again today."

"I hope you don't mind. I didn't have a chance to speak to you at church."

"I was just putting away some things for my mother. I'm finished now, so we can talk all you'd like."

He watched her secure the springhouse door. She was dressed very simply in a dark brown skirt and calico blouse, which could barely be seen under the oversized coat she wore. Perhaps she had borrowed one of her brother's work coats to keep warm in the springhouse. She wore her hair casually pulled back with a ribbon. He recalled that in church it had been pinned up in an attractive manner with a little hat. Austin preferred it this way, however. In fact, if he could have been so bold, he would have released it all together. There was something very intimate about seeing a woman with her hair down.

Jessica joined him. He could see she was fully aware that he'd been assessing her. She smiled. "Would you like to walk while we talk?"

He grinned. "I kind of liked it back here. Seems pretty out of the way."

She laughed. "There is a very nice path to the orchard. I think you'll enjoy it. Come on."

Austin let her lead him. The couple remained silent until they reached the orchard. "The fruit has all been harvested," Jessica began, "but it's still a lovely place. In a few months this will all be in bloom, and the scent will be wondrous. I love springtime with everything coming to life."

Austin struggled to put his mind on the conversation. "Uh . . . it can be a troublesome thing, too. What with twisters and such. We never had many of those back in Virginia."

Her expression grew thoughtful as she looked into his eyes. "I wonder if I might impose upon you?"

Austin could only smile. "In what way?"

"I want to know more about you."

He felt his breath catch deep in his throat. He cared about this woman, and he knew there could be no future for them unless he told her of the past.

"All right," he said softly. "What would you like to know?"

"Tell me about your family. Do you have brothers or sisters?"

"I did," Austin said, trying not to betray his discomfort. "I had a brother . . . Houston. My mother's way of staying connected with Texas was to name us boys after beloved cities. I think I told you that she was raised in Texas but moved to Virginia."

"Yes. You said you *had* a brother. Does that mean he's passed on?"

Austin took off his hat and pushed back his hair. Replacing the hat, he squared his shoulders. "Yes. It was a tragedy that involved us both. It started a terrible cycle of death in my life."

She looked at him oddly. "Will you tell me about it?"

He had thought it would be difficult to share his memories with Jessica, but it wasn't. As he began to tell her the sad story, Austin actually found comfort in the telling. It was almost like a confession of guilt and sin. By confessing the past, perhaps he could be made clean.

"Houston and I both worked for the Secret Service. I had helped him to get the job, in fact. I had recently married." He paused to see if she was shocked by this declaration. She didn't appear to be at all.

"We worked well as a team, but one night things went wrong just as we were on the verge of breaking a big case and arresting the perpetrators. Somehow the men became aware that the law was closing in, and they took up positions to fight." The images were still clear in his memory.

"I found myself in trouble—boxed into a corner, which, of course, was exactly what my adversary wanted. That left me no choice but to shoot my way out. Houston found me and helped subdue the attackers by adding his fire power. We had them pretty well beat, and when the last man took off running, we knew we'd won. We figured the other agents would easily take them in hand."

"And did they?"

"All but one. One hid out in the darkness, in the brush. He jumped us as we made our way to join the others. I raised my gun to shoot him as he aimed his rifle at me. For whatever reason, Houston felt certain the man would kill me. He jumped in front of me and took the bullet."

"That was very heroic. He must have loved you a great deal. Did you get the other man, the man who shot him?"

Shaking his head, Austin felt sick at the truth of the matter. Could he really tell her? He drew a deep breath. "The other man managed to slip away because I attended to Houston. He died in my arms. Killed by my bullet."

"Your bullet?"

He gave a heavy sigh. "Yes, my bullet. I fired just as Houston jumped in front of me. The other man was out of ammunition. I learned that

646

after one of the agents checked his discarded rifle. I'd killed my own brother for nothing."

Jessica shook her head vehemently. "Nonsense. It was a terrible accident and an act of supreme heroics by your brother."

"That's what Grace—my wife—said. But my parents didn't see it that way. My mother railed at me—blamed me and cursed me. She said it had been my responsibility to keep Houston safe, but instead I ended his life. She told me to leave and never return. My father felt the same way. It was just too painful for them.

"Houston was engaged to be married, and I had to break the news to his fiancée. She blamed me, too. She pummeled me with her fists and hit me until she was weeping so hard she collapsed. Her father had the servants put her to bed, then told me it would be best if I didn't come back."

"I'm sorry. They were wrong to treat you like that. You didn't mean for him to die. They had to know that."

He shrugged. "I'd like to think they did. I decided to give them some time. This was the end of January, and Grace was due to have a baby the following month. I'd moved us out to the country the previous year. I felt she'd be safer there when I had to be away, which was often. I was wrong. I was in Washington, D.C., when she went into labor. There was no one with her, no one to help. The girl I'd hired to keep house and help Grace with the laundry and meals was sick and couldn't come. If she'd been there, things might have gone differently, but I can't blame her. That'd be no different from my parents blaming me for Houston's death."

"What happened to Grace?" Jessica asked. She reached out as if she might take hold of his arm, but hesitated and then decided against it.

"Something went terribly wrong, and she delivered a stillborn son by herself and then followed him in death. I found them there on the bed, the babe held close in her arms. I was beyond grief. I wanted to die and gave strong thought to ending my life. That was February."

"How awful," Jessica said. "To lose two people—three really—in such a short time."

"By June both of my parents had passed away, as well." Jessica gave a gasp, then covered her mouth with her hands as if embarrassed. Austin felt bad for having just blurted it out like that. "My father hadn't been well for several years. We were never sure what the problem was, but the doctor was of a mind that he had a weakness in his heart. My father died in May of a heart attack. My mother died a month later from some type of consumption that wasted her away. The doctor said it was mostly likely that she had lost the will to live. That was something I could well understand."

"Had you reconciled before their deaths?"

"No. They went to their graves hating me, blaming me." Austin looked past Jessica to the line of trees. "That was probably the hardest truth I've ever had to face. My parents had taught me about forgiveness and love, but when I needed it most, it was denied me." He hadn't meant to add the latter and gave a nonchalant shrug. "After that I came west. I couldn't bear to remain in Virginia. I needed a fresh start."

"I can imagine it was just too painful to stay." Her words were offered in sincere understanding.

Jessica reached out again, and this time she took hold of his arm. She gave a light squeeze and continued to hold on to him. "I'm so sorry that you had to go through such terrible loss. It's no wonder you always have a certain sorrow in your eyes."

That she had noticed touched him deeply. Austin took hold of her hands. She shivered, much as he'd seen her do when Harrison Gable touched her. The tiny reaction made him happy.

"The pain is less now."

She gazed into his eyes for a moment longer, then turned toward the trail, forcing Austin to release her hands. "We should probably head back," she said, smiling. "I wouldn't want Father to come looking for us."

"I agree," Austin said and easily caught up to her. "I hope I didn't offend you with my story."

"Of course not. I'm so glad you told me. As I said, I could tell you were a man of sorrows." She glanced up at him and smiled. "Perhaps that sadness can be laid to rest now. Perhaps in sharing the burden with another, you will find peace."

"The peace has come gradually," he admitted. "I longed for many years to be able to go back and undo what had happened. I thought God didn't care about me or my family, so I chose to ignore Him. Now I find He refuses to ignore me."

Jessica nodded knowingly. "He has done the same with me. You were there when I went forward."

"Yes, it was a very special moment."

"I hope you can have a moment of your own. God's peace is so much better than anything anyone else could offer you."

Austin felt the urgency to tell her how he felt, but the words stuck in his throat. Instead, he stopped her from walking and turned her to face him once again. Reaching out, he gently ran his fingers along her jaw. This time he felt the trembling go through her. Her eyes were fixed on his face, and Austin could see she had feelings akin to his own. The intensity frightened him, although he would never have admitted it.

Jessica was the first to look away. She pulled back and began to walk again. "Come," she said, her voice hesitant and shaky. "Mother . . . uh . . . we have some cake." She twisted her hands together but kept walking. "Yes . . . we have some cake. I think . . . you . . . you should have some."

He chuckled, feeling mighty pleased with himself over her reaction. "Cake?"

She kept her gaze straight ahead, but Austin could see that her cheeks were bright red. "Yes. Cake."

Chapter 18

Christmas was an occasion Austin hadn't celebrated in over five years, but this Christmas Eve the Barnetts had insisted he join them. In fact, Mrs. Barnett had commanded him to plan on staying the night so he could share Christmas breakfast with them before going to church. After that the Athertons had arrived, and Austin found himself most uncomfortable. Jessica hardly looked his way, and he wondered if he'd caused more problems than good by having told her about the past.

After supper he'd joined the family in the front sitting room. But like a coward, when the suggestion was given to play charades, he slipped down the hall to his temporary bedroom. Now he heard the family laughing and having boisterous conversations, and he'd never felt more alone.

A light rap on the door immediately caused him to stand at attention. Tyler Atherton came in and smiled. "I thought I saw you head down this way. You're missin' out on the fun." He dusted his shirt and laughed. "Guess I got some powdered sugar on me when I tried to sneak a cookie and Hannah caught me."

Austin stretched his arms over his head. "I'm pretty worn out. Figured I'd get to bed early."

The older man gave a lopsided smiled and raised a brow. "You wanna try again?"

Austin looked at him in confusion. "What do you mean, sir?"

"I mean you didn't come back here because you were tired."

"Was it that evident?"

Mr. Atherton chuckled and pulled up a chair. "Why don't you sit and tell me what's botherin' you."

Austin reclaimed his chair and began to talk about the same things he'd told Jessica regarding his brother, parents, wife, and son. By the time he'd finished, Mr. Atherton was looking at him with an unreadable expression. Austin feared perhaps Atherton felt the same toward him that his parents had.

"Son, that has to be about the saddest story I've ever heard. What a heavy load to carry, and all alone."

"Well, sir, that's the problem. I'm not bearing it alone now. I told your daughter about it. I'm afraid I might have offended her."

Atherton shook his head. "Here I figured you were tryin' to work up the nerve to propose to my girl, when all the while you were sufferin'."

"I'm not really suffering," Austin admitted. "I've dealt with their deaths, but my folks died without ever forgiving me for my own brother's death. It's their anger and hatred that I can't seem to forget."

"Ah, Austin, good folks like you described couldn't have really hated you. They were grief stricken, and folks in grief often say things they don't mean. I remember during the war when I had to tell a young man that two of his brothers had been killed. I was his superior, but he looked me in the eyes and told me that if I'd done a better job of leading, his brothers would still be alive. Then he threw a punch at me, but I dodged it. Finally, he told me he was quittin' the war. He figured to head back here to Texas and break the news to his folks."

"What did you do?"

"I let him go."

"Just like that? I mean there would've been repercussions for desertion."

"Yes, if he had really deserted. He came back about an hour later, apologized, and said he was ready to take his punishment for what he'd said and done."

"But you didn't punish him, did you?"

Atherton smiled. "No. He was a good man, and I knew it was his

651

pain talkin', not him. After that we were good friends. He even worked several years at my ranch after his folks passed and their place had to be sold to pay off debts."

"I wish my folks could have forgiven me. I never saw them again after that night. They refused my attempts to reconcile and told their house servants to turn me away. I wanted to make things right, to be back in their good graces." He shook his head. "They were God-fearing people who raised me to believe in forgiveness, but they had none to offer."

"Don't be so sure, son. I would imagine your folks had a load of regret that overwhelmed the forgiving act." Atherton scratched his jaw. "Regret is a powerful thing. A lot of times folks give in to it, and it eats them up. Unless, of course, they learn to give it over to the Lord."

"For them, I guess that was easier said than done."

Atherton got to his feet and fixed Austin with a sympathetic expression. "I wasn't talkin' about them, son." He walked to the door and paused. "Come on back to the party. The gals will be breakin' out the Christmas cookies and candy, and I do not intend to miss out. 'Sides that, I'm bettin' my girl is wonderin' why you haven't been seekin' her out for conversation."

Austin was surprised, but he felt a sense of relief. He got to his feet and followed the older man back to the party. He'd no sooner rejoined the party when he spied Jessica stepping outside. Since it was already dark, Austin thought to see where she was headed.

He crossed the room, and those who were still playing charades roared with laughter as Jake did his best to act out something that looked rather painful to Austin. The feeling of happiness and family encircled him once again. If only it could last.

Stepping outside, Austin found Jessica standing on the porch just a few feet away. "I saw you come outside and thought maybe something was wrong."

"I just needed a little air," she said, smiling. "It was getting pretty stuffy in there."

"I thought maybe you were avoiding me." Austin couldn't help but remember the earlier dinner conversation. Jessica had referenced their being late because Harrison Gable had stopped by with a gift. "I guess you and Gable are getting pretty close." He tried to sound disinterested, even though he was dying to hear her response.

"Well, I must say he's certainly been attentive. He brought me a Christmas gift and told me how wonderful he thinks I am."

"And what did you tell him?" Austin knew it was a bold question, but he didn't apologize.

Jessica laughed. "I told him he wouldn't say those things if he really knew me. He only sees the me that has been fighting to change. He has no knowledge of the selfish, spoiled girl I used to be. I'm sure my former friends would be happy to inform him."

"That won't matter to a man if he cares for a gal." Austin didn't know why he had said anything in support of Gable, but he didn't intend to do it again. "And if it does, he's not worth your trouble."

She sobered. "I suppose that's true enough."

Her serious mood caused Austin some discomfort. He hadn't meant to cause her unhappiness. "I . . . uh . . . have really enjoyed sharing Christmas Eve with everybody. It's fun to see the little ones get so excited over lighting the Christmas tree candles."

"Wait until the ladies bring out the Christmas candy and cookies. They work for weeks on making them. Then they have to be very creative about hiding it all so the guys don't get into it before the holidays."

"And did you help in the making of these treats?"

She smiled. "I tried to help, but I'm not very good at such things. I always figured to have servants and didn't really care to learn. Mother mostly had me mixing ingredients together while she went to measure out a different recipe."

"So you decided to go back to the idea of servants doing it all?"

She shook her head and crossed her arms. "No. Now I figure I should learn all those things I put off—especially cooking. I don't know that I'll ever marry. After all, I am twenty-two, but if I do marry, my husband will probably want to eat." She gave a laugh, and to Austin it sounded like music.

"Most men do like to eat," he confirmed. "And twenty-two isn't all that old."

Jessica still smiled but said nothing for several seconds. When she did speak, she changed the subject. Now the focus was on him.

"I want you to know that I appreciate the things you shared with me about your family and the losses. As I told you that first time we met, I prefer that people speak their minds. I find that these days honesty is more important to me than just about anything else, and I know it wasn't easy for you to tell me."

"It wasn't as hard as I'd figured, Miss Atherton," he admitted. He could see in the glow of light from the windows that she was still smiling. "In fact, I find it kind of easy to talk to you."

Her smile widened. "Truly? Because I find it very easy to talk to you."

"Do you find it just as easy to talk to Harrison Gable?" He hadn't meant to speak the words aloud, but now that they were out, he couldn't take them back.

But Jessica wasn't offended. She seemed to really consider the question before answering. "Harrison is different from you. He likes to talk about intellectual and political things. He has all sorts of plans for his life that culminate in his becoming president."

"Really?" Austin tried to imagine even having the slightest interest in such an ambitious position.

"Yes. He told me he'd studied all of the presidents in detail as well as our constitution and history. After doing this, he just knew that he could do the job better than most have done."

"Seems a little confident of himself."

"Well, I suppose, but at least he was honest about his feelings. Like I said, I prefer that."

Austin thought perhaps he should open himself up to her—tell her how he felt. But there was always the chance that she would spurn his affection. Especially if Gable had given her any indication of proposing. Surely a man—even a man like Gable—didn't do that without having a sense of the woman being willing.

Cheers rose up from inside the house. Jessica grabbed hold of his arm. "Come along, Mr. Todd. You have to see this to believe it."

He allowed her to lead him back into the house, where everyone had crowded into the formal dining room. Jessica made a place for them as best she could, and Austin stared down at the fifteen-foot table in complete wonder. Every square inch was covered with sweet treats of every kind. There were platters of cookies and tiny cakes, tarts and candy—candy of every flavor imaginable.

"You must try Mother's fudge and peanut brittle. They are the best."

He could hardly hear her for the children's enthusiasm. They were all vying for the position of who would go first.

"Oh, be sure to get some of the divinity. Mrs. Barnett makes that, and it's very good."

"Anything else?" he asked with a grin. "Anything that you made?"

She met his gaze and shook her head. "I mixed those spicy oatmeal cookies, but they're pretty plain." She turned back to the table and motioned to him. "See those little sandwich cookies? My aunt made those. She calls them Melt Aways. She makes a little cookie with butter and cream and I don't know what else. Then she bakes those and makes a delicious frosting for the middle. You pop the whole thing in your mouth, and it just melts away. That's the cookie you really need to try."

He didn't get a chance to reply because William Barnett was tapping a glass with his knife to get everyone's attention. "If everybody will settle down, I'll announce the person who gets to start us this year. Austin, since you're our guest, I figure that job will go to you."

Austin was surprised by this, but the others seemed delighted and pushed him around the table to where the dessert plates awaited.

"I hope he hurries up. I'm starvin' to death for candy," Wyatt told his mother. Marty rolled her eyes, but Jake only encouraged it.

"Then maybe you'll need to go second," he teased.

Mrs. Barnett put a cookie in Austin's hand. "Take anything you like and as much as you like. There is plenty for everyone." She leaned in closer and said loud enough for everyone to hear, "But if I were you— I'd hurry." Everybody laughed at this.

Austin reached tentatively for a Melt Away. He looked up and saw Jessica smiling in approval. He moved on to a platter of white candy and raised his brows in question as he pointed to the divinity. She nodded. Then Mrs. Barnett handed Wyatt a plate, and the party began in earnest.

Jessica awoke on Christmas morning with a sense of peace and contentment that she'd never known. The evening before had been so much fun, and she'd very much enjoyed her private talk with Austin Todd. She knew she had come to care for him. She prayed for him constantly, knowing that his sorrow was great. Mother had reminded Jessica recently that Jesus had known great sorrow, and Jessica had been touched in a way she hadn't expected. Jesus could understand their hurts, their pain. What a comfort that was, and today was the remembrance day of His birth.

For Jessica, it was unlike any other Christmas. Before, she would have been concerned with what she might receive. She would lie in bed and imagine all the wonderful things her parents might have purchased for her. She had concerned herself very little with the true meaning of the day.

Mr. Barnett, however, had read the Christmas story the night before, and for Jessica it was like hearing it for the first time. He told of what Mary and Joseph each had to deal with. Mary was certain to face condemnation for having a baby before she and Joseph married formally. Joseph would no doubt have to deal with humiliation, as he would most likely be tormented and rejected by his friends, family, and the temple authorities. They both had to deal with the imposed taxes and the long trip to Bethlehem—an arduous trip that required them to travel a distance of nearly a hundred miles, mostly on foot, only to arrive and find that all the beds were taken and there was no room for them. There was nothing easy about the birth of Jesus.

Jessica found herself pondering the story for a few minutes more. Finally, she got up and dressed. The house was still quiet when she made her way downstairs. Feeling her way around, Jessica lit one of the lamps. She saw from the clock on the fireplace mantel that it was only four-thirty—not even light outside. But in another half hour her folks would be getting up. It might be Christmas, but the animals still needed to be fed. Several of her father's prized cows were due to calve most any time.

Putting fuel in the stove, she built up the fire and placed a pot of coffee atop. Next, she donned her brother's work coat, lit the lantern, and made her way to the hen house. The morning was chilly and she was glad for the warmth of the jacket. And for some reason it made her think of Austin. Perhaps because she'd been wearing it when he'd come to the springhouse. She smiled at the memory. It was funny, but she found herself thinking of him a lot.

It's just because he's had such a bad time in life.

The darkness outside seemed to wrap around her as she crossed the barnyard. Sunrise wouldn't come for another three hours, and the world seemed as silent as the grave. She shivered at the thought and picked up her steps. She wished Austin would show up, as he had done that day at the springhouse.

That was such a pleasant day, and I loved getting to know him better.

Harrison had promised to visit on Christmas Day, but Jessica wasn't sure she wanted him to come. The more she spent time with Austin, the less interest she had in Harrison. Besides, Harrison had already seen her the day before. He'd shown up without warning, bestowed a beautiful necklace upon her, and even brought a box of candy for her mother.

And all the while, I couldn't wait for him to leave so that I could see Austin at the Barnetts'.

Could this be love?

She shook her head at her own internal thoughts. She wouldn't know true love if it bit her. With all of her other beaus, she had only wanted to enjoy their company and the good time that could be had. But with her change of heart and desire to become a better person, she wanted more. And with Austin, she'd found that.

It must be love. I've never felt like this before.

She took up a basket that hung outside the door. Humming a Christmas tune, she stepped inside to the flutter of the winged animals. Several rushed past her in a flash, no doubt hopeful to be first in line for the feed she would soon drop. Father had placed a hook in the center of the coop just low enough that Jessica and her mother could hang the lantern while they searched the nests. Jessica turned up the wick and then placed the long handle over the hook and settled the lantern. The room lit up and Jessica continued her tasks. First she took up the feed and stepped outside to the collection of chickens. Her mother had over thirty hens, and most were good providers. Those who weren't were noted and lined up to become fried chicken at Sunday dinner.

Outside, the hens were scratching the ground, and the rooster let out a crowing that nearly caused Jessica to drop the basket.

"Silly rooster," she chided. "It's not yet sunrise and it's Christmas morning. Be quiet and let my parents sleep."

He immediately stopped, as if he'd understood her command. Jessica tossed a handful of feed as a reward. She then gave the hens a liberal portion and made her way back into the coop to gather eggs. It didn't take long to fill her basket and head to the house. Mother and Lupe would be surprised that she'd taken on this duty.

I am resolved to make myself useful rather than ornamental.

Lupe was already hard at work. Jessica hadn't noticed when the older woman had come to the kitchen, but she had several lamps lit and was working down the dough she'd left to rise the night before.

"Merry Christmas, Lupe," Jessica said, holding up the basket. "I gathered the eggs and thought I might make breakfast."

"*¿Es verdad?*" Lupe questioned.

Laughing, Jessica put the basket on the counter. "Yes, it's true. I may need some help, but I think I can manage bacon and eggs. And I can slice some bread for toast."

Lupe smiled. "You do not need to do my work."

"I want to, though. I want to do something nice for Mother and Father . . . and for you. It's Christmas, and I think I owe it to all of you." Jessica paused and grinned at the older woman's surprise. "It's my Christmas present."

Chapter 19

With the new year came new information, and it couldn't have pleased Austin more. After going through the business correspondence of Alice's father, Austin had determined that one bank in particular might lend them an answer. The bank was in Colorado Springs rather than Denver, and furthermore, it was clear from Chesterfield's correspondence that he had been making some sort of quarterly payment to the institution.

A letter that arrived for Austin Todd explained why Chesterfield was storing a locked box in their vault. The man said that a previous manager had made the arrangements with Chesterfield and the new manager had long wanted the box removed. He made it clear that if Austin would come with a letter of permission from Alice, he would be happy to relinquish the property to Austin's care.

Fingering the key Alice had given him, Austin felt confident that this would open the box. It wasn't like any key he'd ever seen, but even so he knew it must be the one. Why else would Chesterfield have kept it in his personal effects?

He looked at the bronze key a moment longer and then set it aside. Austin expected Robert at any moment. He'd stopped by the Barnetts' to tell them about the letter, but Robert and Alice and their baby had gone to visit Marty's family. Hannah had promised she'd send Robert over as soon as they returned. That was over three hours ago.

Tucking the key back into his pocket, Austin decided to put some coffee on to boil. He wouldn't say he made the best coffee, but it was pretty good. And on a chilly day the drinker might not be too picky.

With the coffee on the stove, Austin went in search of an extra mug and spied the cookies Tyler Atherton had brought him the day before. Jessica had baked them and wanted Austin to sample her very first batch. The memory made him smile. She was being true to her word on learning how to cook, and the outcome had been delicious. He couldn't remember ever having such delicious sugar cookies, and he wasn't of a mind to share them. Smiling to himself, he hid the remaining cookies in the cupboard. Robert got plenty of goodies at home, but he had a sweet tooth, and if he saw the treat he might be tempted to eat until they were gone.

After some time, Austin heard the distinctive sound of a horse approaching. He checked the coffee. It was ready. He took the pot from the stove and placed it on the table with the mugs. A loud knock sounded on the door.

"It's open. Come on in," Austin called, pouring coffee into each mug. He held up the pot. "Thought you might need a cup to ward off the chill."

"I do," Robert agreed. "Pa said it got down to thirty-five degrees last night." He rubbed his hands together. "And to make matters worse, I've lost my gloves . . . again."

Austin chuckled. "Maybe that was why you received so many pairs for Christmas." He couldn't help but think back to that morning and the family's exchange of gifts. There had been three for Austin. From the Barnett family he'd received a hand-knit scarf and a new shirt— both made by Hannah Barnett. The third present was a leather-bound copy of *The Time Machine* by H. G. Wells from Jake and Marty. He cherished all three.

"Seems I set the gloves down and they walk off. Or maybe it's me who walks off," Robert said, discarding his coat. He hung it on an empty peg by the door and made his way to the table. "Jake tells me I don't know anything about the cold since I live in Texas, but I'm pert near frozen to death."

Remembering a time in Virginia when snow had blanketed their town, Austin gave a chuckle. "It is a whole different situation, and I find I prefer Texas."

Robert ambled over to the stove to warm his hands. "Ma said it was important so I came over straightaway. What seems to be the problem? Have you learned something new?"

"I have. Take a seat and I'll show you. You want cream or sugar for your coffee?"

"No. Just black is fine."

Austin produced the letter and placed it in front of Robert. He gave the man time to read while he took his seat at the table and sampled the coffee. He smiled in satisfaction at the taste.

"Do you think this might be where the counterfeit bills are hidden?" Robert asked, looking hopeful.

"That's my thought. You'll note that the box is heavy, so I'm hoping that means the plates are in there, as well. I've contacted my superiors to see how they want to handle this. Most likely they'll have me travel to Colorado Springs to retrieve it."

"Then maybe all of this will be over with," Robert said, shaking his head. "Jake can tell Mr. Morgan and be done with it."

"Has he showed up again?"

"Yeah. We don't know where he was for most of the fall, but Morgan reappeared in mid-December and has been showing up from time to time, never planned or invited, but always persistent."

"Is he still threatenin' Jake with the authorities?" Robert asked.

"Not directly. When Jake suggested that perhaps Morgan himself was behind the counterfeiting and maybe he should take his suspicions to the authorities, Morgan changed his tune. He told Jake that he was just overstressed about someone forging certificates using numbers associated with his bank. Said he was worried about the effect it might have on the economy.

"Jake said Mr. Morgan was somewhat apologetic, like he expected Jake to understand it was his fear talking and not his reasoning. However, in the next breath, he muttered something to the effect that no one would believe he'd just handed Jake all that wealth and privilege. And, of course, there's really no one who can substantiate that Morgan did, in fact, give those things to Jake."

Robert considered this for a moment and took a long drink of the coffee. "It would seem Jake's comment threatened Morgan enough that he decided to move slower. Even so, I can't help but wonder if Morgan has a part in all of this. I have a hard time believin' he's just worried about the finances of the country."

"It's hard to say," Austin admitted, "but I tend to agree with you. I've gone over all the details given me by Alice, Jake, and Marty. I'm beginning to see a definite pattern. The one thing they all have in common is Mr. Paul Morgan. With that in mind, I've sent word to my associates in Washington to have him further investigated. I'm certain by now they've arranged for someone to look closer at his dealings. The man certainly lives above his means and did so even during the hardest times in '93 and '94."

"Well, he is related to J. P. Morgan. It is possible he's been subsidized by this distant cousin."

"I don't know. I guess that's just one more thing to figure out." Austin picked up the coffeepot and offered Robert a refill. He gladly took it.

For several minutes the two men drank in silence. The wind picked up outside and made a moaning sound in the cabin. To Austin it sounded sorrowful.

"What's your plan, Austin?" Robert finally asked. "Is there anything I can do to help get this resolved?"

"Well, as I mentioned, I've sent a wire to my former boss. I figure he'll give me the go ahead to retrieve the box and open it. If it holds the certificates and plates, then that's good news. If not, we're back where we started."

Robert nodded. "I can help you with rail fare."

"Thanks, but when I agreed to take this on, the agency set up an account from which I can draw. I won't need financial help."

"So what kind of help do you need?"

Austin thought for a moment and without really meaning to he replied, "Spiritual."

Robert looked surprised, even confused. "In what way?"

Leaning back in his chair Austin shared something of the past. It seemed to get a little easier each time he told it. Robert listened patiently, making no comment while Austin related his story.

"I faced a lot of loss." Austin paused, uncertain he should continue. Robert was a good friend and appeared to be in no hurry to leave. Austin drew a deep breath and added, "It left me feeling that God no longer cared for me, that I wasn't of importance to Him."

Robert gave a hint of a nod. "Because you'd lost your family." It was more statement than question.

"Yes, mostly. In the aftermath I felt so alone—even spiritually. The church folk I knew didn't bother to check up on me. I had moved back to the city after Grace died. I couldn't bear remaining in that house." He blew out a heavy breath and fell back against his chair. "Even though I rented an apartment in the town's central area near my old church, no one came to call. It was as if I no longer existed."

"Perhaps they didn't realize you'd returned."

"Oh, they knew. I still owed the pastor for Grace's services, and when I went to pay him, I mentioned having moved and gave him the address. He didn't call on me or check to see why I wasn't attending services. Of course, it is a rather large church."

"Still, you would have thought someone would have come to see you."

"I think my parents scared them off. They probably told everyone that I was to blame for Houston's death, as well as Grace's and my baby's." He shook his head. "If only they knew how I still carry that burden of responsibility. I loved my brother. I loved my wife and son. For my parents to suggest or think otherwise broke me in a way I wasn't sure I could recover from."

"I can see now what you meant by spiritual help." Robert rubbed his chin. "I'm no preacher, but I do know that God doesn't strip away His love when we make mistakes. You never meant to cause your brother or wife harm, so there was no sin on your part. The responsibility and blame you heap on yourself really aren't yours. You've taken on a burden that never belonged to you."

Austin stiffened. "It was my bullet."

"What was the intention of your heart?"

"I was going to wound the counterfeiter."

Robert raised a brow. "You mean to tell me you weren't plannin' to kill him?"

"No," Austin said, shaking his head. "We needed the counterfeiters alive so we might learn if there were others involved on a higher level. It turned out there were."

"So the intention of your heart was to capture this criminal and not to kill him."

Austin shrugged. "To tell you the truth, when I saw him aim his rifle, I feared for Houston and myself. I drew up my pistol, and like I said, the man moved to fire and I beat him to it. Unfortunately, Houston thought I'd be killed and jumped in front of me."

"Seems to me it was your brother's fault he got himself killed."

"That's a hard thing to hear. I don't look at it that way." Austin felt a sense of anger. "Houston was a good agent. He knew his job and did it well. We had always been a good team up until then."

"You were still a good team. In fact, I'd say his action proved that. He must have loved you dearly to sacrifice his own life for yours."

"He did." Austin's words were barely audible.

"And what about Grace? Was it your intention to kill her—to kill your son?"

Austin was indignant. "Of course not! But I took her from the city, fearing someone might try to hurt her because of my work. I thought I was doing a good thing, but the isolation proved to take her life."

"And you know for certain that had you been in the city, she would have lived?"

He thought for a moment. "No, but at least there would have been help available for her. Don't you understand? She was alone. I'd planned for someone to be there, but the woman wasn't able to come. So when Grace went into labor, no one was there to help her."

"Austin, women die in childbirth all the time. I feared I'd lose Alice, but she told me the sacrifice was worth anything to have a child."

For a moment Austin remembered Grace saying something similar. He didn't have a chance to think on it for long, because Robert continued.

"And with your folks . . . well, I think their deaths had little to do with you. No doubt they were grieved over the loss of your brother, but their own bitterness and the need to blame someone ate at them. We can't live under the pressure of hate and anger for long before it consumes us. It picks away little pieces of the heart day by day until there's nothing left—and a man can't live without a heart."

"My father died from a heart attack, and I believe Mother died in her grief—not anger at me."

"Which is my point," Robert said, getting to his feet. "This really isn't about you or what part you played. My guess is that your folks regretted what they'd said to you, but they didn't know how to make it right, so they just left it undone. They probably thought they had plenty of time to mend fences. But we never know how much time we have on earth, so it's best to treat each day as though it's our last."

Austin wanted to believe him. "And where was God in all of this?"

Robert never lost his smile. "God was there with your brother and you when a man threatened to kill you, and He took your brother's life instead of yours. He was there with Grace and your son when neither were strong enough to go on living. He was there with you when you found them dead. He was even there with your parents while they grieved and blamed you, and there, too, as they died in their sorrows and bitterness. He never left you, Austin. We are the ones who do the walkin' away."

Taking his coat from the peg, Robert donned it and opened the door. "Just think about it, Austin. Go look in the Bible and see if I'm not speakin' truth. That's the only place to go for confirmation. God will show you."

Austin followed him to the door and reached into his own coat pocket. "Here, take these. I have another pair." He handed Robert his leather gloves. "Thank you."

Robert grinned. "I'm probably going to lose these, you know."

"That's all right."

Austin stared at the door long after Robert had exited. He reasoned through all that Robert had said and did his best to find cause to deny its truth. He couldn't. He shifted his gaze to the ceiling.

"Are you really here with me?"

———————— ★ ————————

Jessica kneaded her dough just as Mrs. Barnett had instructed. Mother had sent her over to Hannah Barnett for lessons on making bread and cinnamon rolls. She assured Jessica that Hannah made the best in the county—possibly the state.

"That's looking good," Mrs. Barnett told her. "Now we're going to roll out the dough. Once we have it stretched out, we'll slather butter on it and sprinkle it with cinnamon and sugar. Will likes me to be generous with the sugar." She smiled at Jessica. "After that, we roll it up, stretch it out a little to make it longer, and then we cut it in inch-wide slices all the way down the roll. We put them out on a pan and give 'em room, because they're gonna double their size when we leave them to rise."

Jessica fervently hoped she'd remember everything, because Hannah had mentioned she'd be heading to Marty's and be gone for maybe an hour. Alice would be there to help if she got stuck, but Hannah assured her that she'd be back in time to help Jessica get them into the oven.

Alice popped into the kitchen, as if the thought of her name had drawn her there. "The babies are asleep, so now I can get some of that ironing done."

Hannah Barnett looked at her daughter-in-law with such an expression of love, it stirred something deep in Jessica's heart. "I told Jess that she could come to you if she gets perplexed in finishing up here."

Alice gave her mother-in-law a nod. "I'd be happy to help. I'll be in the back room. Holler if you need me."

Jessica couldn't help but sigh in relief. She was glad they had become good friends. Alice was the only woman her own age who spent any time with Jessica, and clearly she wouldn't have had to. No one could have blamed her after the way Jessica had treated her in the past, but Alice was full of forgiveness.

I want to be like that.

The two women left Jessica to her work, and by the time she had placed the last roll on the pan to rise, she heard a loud knock on the front door.

"I'll tend to it," Alice called out.

Jessica took up some large flour sack towels, covered each of the trays, and put them aside to give the rolls time to rise. Grabbing more wood, she stoked the fire in the stove so the heated air would help the dough rise faster.

Since she'd heard nothing more from Alice, Jessica presumed that the caller was for her and went about cleaning up the kitchen. However, when she heard Alice cry out as if in pain, Jessica hurried down the hall as quietly as possible.

"I don't know where those certificates are. Let go of me."

The sound of her friend's fear caused Jessica to freeze in place.

"I know that you're a busy . . . mother," a man declared, letting the word fade. The unspoken threat was there all the same.

"I can't help you," Alice insisted.

Jessica wondered what she should do. There was a shotgun by the back door. Perhaps she should retrieve it. She didn't recognize the voice of the man, but he wasn't a friend.

"I know Mrs. Barnett has gone. We saw her leave in the buggy."

"We?" Alice asked, her voice little more than a squeeze.

This put Jessica into action. There was more than one man and that could mean trouble. More trouble than two young women could handle alone. The shotgun would make a good companion.

Jessica quickly retrieved the weapon, checked to make sure it was loaded, then made her way back as the stranger announced, "I think you know my friend." Alice gasped and Jessica stepped around the corner, shotgun leveled.

"I think you remember Mr. Smith."

Alice promptly fainted.

Chapter 20

Austin got home late at night after traveling that day to Dallas and back. He'd made the long ride to Dallas early that morning to meet with a representative of his old boss, Ellery Turner. The man took detailed notes of everything Austin had done and learned. Then he gave Austin a letter from Mr. Turner. Austin perused it quickly, happy to see that it contained official approval for him to go to Colorado Springs. Once there, he would meet with two other agents Turner would send. They were men he would know, so there would be no question as to their identity. The trio was then to retrieve the lockbox from the bank and return to the hotel. There were further instructions, but Austin decided to give them a more thorough reading at home.

Happy to have his orders, Austin had grabbed a very late lunch before seeing Judge Weimer in order to brief the man on what was happening. However, that had been hours ago, and now he didn't know whether he was more hungry or tired or cold.

The little cabin sat by itself under the starry sky. Nevertheless, the sight welcomed Austin and made him feel better. The wind had picked up in the last hours, chilling him to the bone. All he could think of was being warm, but eating and sleeping continued to run a close second and third. First he'd have to care for the horse's needs, so getting thawed out would have to wait.

Glancing overhead at the stars, Austin thought of Jessica and how much he'd enjoy looking up at the night sky with her by his side. The horse whinnied, as if agreeing with his thoughts.

"You like her, too? Well, that just shows you have good taste," Austin said in the stillness. He smiled and continued thinking about the beautiful woman. He also thought for a moment of Grace and knew she'd want him to be happy. She wouldn't have liked the man he'd become since her death—lonely and haunted by the past. She would want him to marry Jessica.

"I've done my best, Grace, but I intend to do more."

He rode around to the small pen Mr. Barnett had made for the horse. There was a loafing shed with a suitable attachment where Austin could store his tack, and across the pen a trough of water sat by the main pump. It proved to be a good setup.

Once he'd finished with the horse, Austin made his way back around to the front of the house. It was only when he got to the door that he realized a note had been tacked to it. He pulled the paper off and took it inside with him.

Lighting a lamp, Austin turned up the wick a bit and read the missive. *Need to see you as soon as possible. R. Barnett.* Austin pulled out his pocket watch. It was nearly ten o'clock. Definitely too late to visit the Barnetts. No doubt Robert wanted to know about his trip to Dallas. He tossed the letter down on the table and yawned. Maybe he'd just wait until morning to eat.

★

Jessica could scarcely breathe. "Will I . . . what?"

"Will you marry me?"

She looked at the man kneeling before her. "This is rather sudden. We don't really know each other very well."

Harrison Gable got to his feet and pulled Jessica into his arms. "Believe me when I say that I want very much to know you and know you well." He pressed a kiss against her left cheek and then her right. Jessica pulled away as his lips headed toward her mouth.

"This isn't right. My father would not approve of the way you're acting." She moved to stand behind her chair, hoping that it might keep Harrison at bay.

He threw her a leering glance and laughed. "Your father won't long have much to say on the matter. Marry me and we can slip away tonight. We'll go to Dallas, where no one knows you. I have friends there—a judge who can marry us right away." He paused and took a step toward her. Jessica backed up. This only caused him to smile once again. "Marry me, Jessica. You know that I can make you happy. I know that you have feelings for me. I've seen you tremble at my touch. Don't think me unschooled. I know exactly what I'm doing."

"I'm sure you do, but what you don't realize," she said, moving once again to expand the distance between them, "is that my father and mother are just in the other room. It wouldn't be difficult to draw their attention."

He stopped pursuing her and folded his arms across his chest. "So draw their attention."

He'd called her bluff, and Jessica knew she would have to act quickly. "I don't need them to fight my battles for me. I have no desire to marry you, Mr. Gable. I have considered the possibility and weighed it in the scales. However, you have been found wanting."

Her bold words seemed to surprise him. For several seconds he said nothing, but his eyes narrowed and his expression appeared angry. "It's Todd, isn't it? You fancy yourself in love with that sad-eyed lawman."

"It's really none of your concern to whom I give my love. Now, if you don't mind, it's getting quite late, and you promised my parents that we would only spend a few minutes alone. I believe we should now rejoin them, and you should bid them good-night." She headed toward the door with false bravado. Without looking back to make certain he followed, Jessica opened the door and stepped into the hallway.

She heard Gable follow and was pleased with herself. Maybe being strong and assertive wasn't always a bad thing.

"Mother. Father," she said, entering the larger sitting room. "Mr. Gable has to leave."

"It was way too late to come over last night," Austin said apologetically. "I didn't want you to think I was ignoring you." He threw Robert a smile, but the man didn't return it.

"We've got a big problem."

Austin could see that Robert was more than a little agitated. "What's wrong?"

"Morgan was here. Worse still, he brought the same man who'd harassed Alice in Denver."

Austin twisted his hat. "Who was that?"

"He calls himself Mr. Smith. He always mentioned having worked for someone. We just didn't know it was Morgan. Alice is sick over the whole thing. She passed out cold. Lucky for her Jessica was here."

"Jessica Atherton?"

"The same." For the first time Robert smiled, but it wasn't joy filled. "She greeted the men with Hannah's double-barreled shotgun. She ordered them to leave, and I guess she must have looked menacing enough that they figured she'd shoot."

Austin couldn't help but laugh. "I would've liked to have seen that."

Robert lost a bit of his worried look. "Me too."

Austin could see that Robert was anxious to finish and sobered. "What happened next?"

"After they'd gone, Jessica bolted the door and put Alice to bed."

"Where was your ma and servants?"

Robert shrugged and began to pace. "Ma had gone to visit Marty. I guess everybody else was busy elsewhere. Jess said it happened in just a matter of minutes."

"So Morgan isn't just bothering Jake. Now he's after Alice. Well, I've got news that may change everything." A brilliant idea flashed through Austin's mind. "In fact, if you'll help me, I know it will."

"I'll do whatever I can to rid my wife of those men. I thought to track them," Robert admitted, "but my pa discouraged it. He said since you were now working on this, we had to lay low and give you a chance."

"I appreciate that," Austin said. "It'll help us with what I have in mind. I got the approval to go to Colorado Springs and retrieve the lockbox on behalf of the Treasury Department. All I need is a signed letter from

Alice stating that I have been given the key and have her permission to remove the box from the bank and take it into my possession."

"I'm sure she will be happy to oblige."

"There's more. I will meet up with a couple of agents the department will send via express train. Barring any complications, I should be able to be home in a week, maybe ten days."

"What will you do once you have the box?"

Austin pulled the key from his pocket. "I'll open it. I'm supposed to learn of the contents at the bank. If it's the forged certificates or the plates, we'll confiscate them and the agents will take them back to Washington. Otherwise, I'll bring whatever is in the box back to Alice."

Robert looked perplexed. "So what is it you need from me?"

"Well, the way I figure it, if Morgan and his Mr. Smith know what I'm up to, they'll follow me. They won't have any reason to stick around here once they know I'm headed out on the train and why. What I need is for word to get out about my plans. We need them to overhear what I'm doing and when."

"I'm bettin' you're right," Robert said, sounding hopeful for the first time. "I reckon they will follow after you."

"And that will take them away from your family and from Jake's." Austin considered the plan for a moment. "Since we don't know where they're staying or who they may have hired to keep watch on us, I'll have to make sure we have plenty of time to bandy the news about."

"How long do you think it will take?" Alice stepped into the room. It was clear she'd been listening from the hallway.

Austin didn't mind. "A day or two. I figure if we get enough folks talkin', Morgan is bound to hear about it."

"And you need me to write a letter?" Alice questioned.

Austin nodded. He could see the fear in her eyes. "I do."

"Then I'll get that for you now." She left the room without another word.

Robert stopped pacing and crossed his arms with a frown. "This had better work."

★

Jessica knew she would have to give her mother an account of her time spent with Harrison, but she wasn't looking forward to it at all. Thankfully, Father was off with William Barnett ironing out some final arrangements about the plans for the railroad.

At one time, what had happened the night before was something Jessica thought would make her the happiest woman in the world. But it hadn't. In fact, it had only caused her more problems.

"You have moped around here all day," Mother declared. "Now sit down and tell me what happened. Did Harrison get fresh with you? Did he try to take liberties?"

Jessica shook her head. "No. Well, yes, but not really." She sank into her favorite chair by the fire. "He proposed." Mother looked confused for a moment and then burst out laughing. Jessica frowned. "It's not funny, Mother."

"It is when you consider I feared something evil had happened. I'm relieved to learn it was just a proposal. So did you accept?"

Jessica met her mother's eyes. "No."

"Can you talk about it? You left so quickly for bed last night I was quite concerned."

With a sigh, the young woman began to share the details. "He wasted little time. With you and father otherwise occupied, I suppose he figured it to be the perfect time. So while we were in the sitting room, we made small talk about the evening and then without warning he asked me to marry him. I thought at first it was a joke."

"But he was serious?"

Jessica looked at her mother and nodded. "He asked me to marry him and to do so right away. He wanted me to run away last night to Dallas, where he has a friend who could marry us."

"Run away to marry? Didn't he know you would want a big wedding?"

"I don't think he truly knows anything about me, Mother."

"Goodness. I remember a few years back when you and I were dreaming about your wedding. We were looking at an article in one of the ladies' magazines about some royalty somewhere married in a lavish ceremony. It spoke of the princess wearing a gown embroidered with real silver thread. And her trousseau—do you remember what it said about that?"

Jessica shook her head. She longed to get back to her ordeal, but Mother seemed almost dreamy in her remembrance. "The magazine said her trousseau consisted partly of 'forty outdoor suits, fifteen ball dresses, five tea gowns, and a vast number of bonnets, shoes, and gloves.' I can still remember the exact number and wording, because it was so much more than anything I could imagine."

Jess gave a heavy sigh.

Mother seemed to understand her frustration and eased back against the sofa with a smile. "Sorry. I just think it unfeeling of him to expect you to give up a proper wedding."

For a moment neither woman said anything more. But Jessica couldn't leave the matter at that tentative point. "I don't love him," she confessed. "I don't have any feelings whatsoever for him. I thought at one time I might. He was thrilling and attentive, and I thought him very handsome."

"But someone else has caught your eye, or should I say your heart?"

"Yes."

Mother considered this a moment, looking thoughtful. "And you feel bad now? Perhaps you feel sorry for Harrison?"

"No. I'm afraid it's much more selfish than that." Jessica shifted uncomfortably. "I've tried so hard not to make myself the center of attention. I've tried to improve myself and be more focused on God, but . . . honestly, I'm worried."

"Worried about what?" This definitely had her mother's attention.

Jessica gazed upward, feeling unable to face her mother's reaction. "What if this is my only chance to marry?"

Mother lowered her gaze. Jessica thought perhaps her mother was disgusted with her shallow thinking, but Jess had to be honest. That was part of changing for the better. And, she'd always been one to say exactly what she thought.

"You can't marry a man you do not love," Mother finally said, raising her gaze to Jessica. "You told me that you don't love Harrison. Therefore, you did the right thing. Whether or not anyone else proposes marriage is immaterial. If you married Harrison Gable, you would come to regret it, and then hate might very well build instead of love."

Jessica found her mother's expression sympathetic and not at all ashamed or disappointed. She felt her fears release. Mother understood.

"I want very much to marry. It's just that I want to marry someone else. Someone I love."

"But Mr. Todd hasn't asked?"

She wasn't surprised that mother knew. She'd done very little to conceal her thoughts of Austin Todd and had spoken quite favorably of him on more than one occasion. She sighed and didn't bother to deny it.

"He hasn't, but I wish he would."

"Maybe you should tell him that," Mother told her. "You said he liked the fact that you speak your mind. Perhaps he would find it acceptable if you did the proposing."

"Mother!" Jessica snapped, sitting up. "That's hardly proper."

Her mother's laughter was unexpected, causing Jessica to get to her feet. "If you think this is a joke, then I'm going to go to my room."

Mother stood and took hold of her. "I don't think it's a joke, my dear girl. I only want the very best for you. I don't want you to lose someone because of traditions and proprieties. If you love Austin, you must tell him."

"But what if he doesn't feel the same?" The thought of Austin's rejection made Jessica feel almost sick.

Mother was unconcerned. "What if he does? What if he's just been waiting for some sign from you?"

Jessica thought carefully. What was the worst that could happen? If she told Austin about her feelings for him and he told her he wasn't inclined to feel the same way, she couldn't possibly feel any worse.

★

Austin made his way home from the Barnetts', taking the road rather than cutting across their vast pastureland. He'd come this way on purpose—that purpose being he wanted to see Jessica.

Directing his horse to leave the road and head up the path to the Atherton house, Austin knew he needed to square things with Jess before heading to Colorado Springs. He wanted her to know that he had feelings for her, that he cared very much for her, and he wanted to marry her.

But what if she doesn't feel the same way about me? What if Gable holds her heart and I'm too late? The thought of losing Jessica to Gable made Austin sick to his stomach.

I know she feels something. She trembled at my touch—surely that's a good sign. But even as he thought about it, a troubling idea came to mind. Maybe she trembled because she was put off by his touch. Maybe it was abhorrent to her.

He nearly turned the horse for home at that thought, but he'd already reached the house, and Tyler Atherton was waving to him from just outside the barn.

Austin drew a deep breath and dismounted. Pulling his mount along with him, he walked to where the older man was washing up.

"Good to see you again," Mr. Atherton said. "I was just heading into the house for some coffee. Would you like to join me? Jessica has been baking again. I think she's caught on to it pretty quick. She made some of the most mouth-watering cinnamon rolls you could sink your teeth into."

"Sounds too good to pass up." Austin nodded toward the horse. "I shouldn't stay too long, however. There's a lot going on, and I have to make some preparations."

Atherton dried his hands and face on a towel that hung nearby. "Well, let's get right to it, then."

Austin went along with the older man and soon found himself sitting at the long dining room table with Atherton. The ladies were strangely absent, and Austin found himself desperate to learn of their whereabouts. Especially of Jessica.

"Mmm, this is the best cinnamon roll I've ever had," Austin admitted. "And a perfect match to the coffee."

"I thought you'd enjoy it," Atherton said, then sampled his own roll. He ate for a moment and smiled. "Just as good as the first six."

Both men chuckled at the comment. "I know Jess will be pleased to know you've approved of them."

It was the opening he'd been waiting for. "Speaking of Miss Atherton, is she here?"

Tyler nodded. "She's helpin' her ma with one of the new calves. The mama won't nurse it, so my gals are seein' that it bonds with another cow. Carissa and Jess have always been good at that. But don't worry, she won't be much longer. I had just finished checking on them when you arrived." Then he quickly changed the subject.

"Say, that place we're building for you in Terryton is nearly done. I sure hope you won't mind havin' a jail on the front side of your house. We're building it with two cells and a small office. If we find we need more room, we can add some additional cells to the east and west walls. But your residence will be on the back side. We argued over whether to put an access to your living quarters from the jail or just have it on the outside free and clear. Will seemed to think you'd appreciate the internal access, and we fixed the door so you can bolt it from your side when you retire."

Austin didn't care where the jail or door was at this point. He thought perhaps he should just put his thoughts out there for Atherton to consider. It wouldn't be all that appropriate to ask Jessica to marry him without first stating his intention to her father. On the other hand, if he asked Atherton for his blessing, but Jessica had no feelings for him, then it would be for naught.

She has feelings for you. Stop being so bull-headed, his heart seemed to declare.

"Mr. Atherton, before the ladies join us . . . well . . . I wanted to talk to you."

"Oh? What about?" Atherton took up his coffee.

The laughter of women came from the kitchen. They were back already, and Jessica and her mother were definitely amused about something. The only problem was that Austin couldn't continue his conversation with Mr. Atherton.

"Ladies, look who's come to sample the cinnamon rolls," Jessica's father said as they entered the room.

"Oh, goodness, Austin," Mrs. Atherton said in surprise. "We'd have come sooner if we'd known you were here. We have a calf whose mama won't let him nurse. After we fed him we were watching his antics. Jess, you should take Austin out to the barn and show him."

Mr. Atherton looked at Austin and smiled. "I think you should go, son. The calf is quite the showman."

Popping the last of the cinnamon roll into his mouth, Austin got to his feet and followed Jessica through the house and out the back door. He loved watching the way her skirt swayed as she walked. Her hair hung down her back, tied with a single ribbon. A ribbon that wouldn't be at all difficult to pull loose. Austin felt perspiration form on his forehead at the thought of running his hands through her caramel and cocoa hair. He liked the way the sunshine lit glints of red amidst the browns.

"You're sure quiet," Jessica said, looking back at him.

They'd just reached the barn, and she swung the door wide. "Is something wrong?"

"Uh, no. Nothing's wrong."

"Well, you just seem . . . hmm . . . different." She grinned. "Not that different is bad." She smiled and motioned him to follow. "We have the calf over here." She led the way and stopped in front of a small pen.

The calf gave a pitiful cry. Jessica knelt down and reached through the rails, and he came to see if she had something to offer him. Austin thought the calf seemed surprised when all he found was her hand.

"He is a cute little fella," Austin said, giving the animal a quick glance. He'd much rather watch Jessica than the calf.

Austin wanted to say something more, but the words seemed to catch in his throat. How could he leave for Colorado Springs without telling her how he felt? If he didn't stake a claim, Harrison Gable might sweep her off her feet and carry her away.

"We will be pairing him with one of the other cows. Mother's been using a hide to put on the back of another calf. The scent will rub off, and then we'll put the hide on this little fella so that the mama cow will accept him. Mother feels certain she'll take him. He was just weak, but now he's doing better. Tomorrow we'll try to put them together."

Jessica continued talking about the animal, but Austin could only think of her and what he wanted to say. How could he just come out and declare his love for her? If he did that, would she think him too bold—too much the rogue?

Before he could answer that, however, Jessica got to her feet. Still facing the calf, she laughed. Having no will to stop himself, Austin reached out and plucked the ribbon from Jessica's head. The thick lustrous hair splayed out across her back.

In surprise, Jessica whirled around to face him, and without giving it another thought, Austin pulled her into his arms and kissed her soundly. He felt her melt against him with a sigh.

Maybe words weren't necessary, he thought, and deepened the kiss.

Chapter 21

Gasping for air, Jessica pushed away from Austin. "You kissed me!"

"Was that what it was?" he asked with a grin. "Well, I just might do it again." He stepped forward as if to follow up his words, but Jessica put her hands to his chest and pushed.

"Why did you kiss me?" she asked, searching his face.

"Why? You have to ask why?" Austin shook his head. "I've never heard of a woman having to ask why she was kissed."

"Well . . . I . . . I . . . don't understand. You've . . . never, I mean . . ." She stammered to find the right words, and finally she waved her hands in the air. "I don't know what I mean."

He chuckled and moved a step closer. This time Jessica didn't stop him. Her mind whirled with thoughts. Was this a declaration of love? Did Austin truly feel for her as she did for him?

"Look, Miss Atherton . . . Jessica," he said, reaching out to push her hair back, "I've been disturbed by you ever since I met you."

She regained her senses at this. "Disturbed by me? What kind of thing is that to say about somebody?"

He reached out again to touch her hair. This time, however, he toyed with the wavy strand as he'd once seen Gable do. "All right, you've been on my mind, and it's been almost torturous. I can't eat or sleep without thinking of you."

Inside, Jessica was cheering, but outside, she remained stoic. "Well, it sounds like you may be sick."

Austin looked incredulous. "I am sick. I'm love-sick. You've got me acting like a boy with his first crush."

She grinned. "What's so bad about that?"

He began to pace in front of her . . . only inches away . . . close enough that she could reach out and touch him if she chose to. With her heart racing and her breathing rather ragged, Jessica watched Austin's expression change several times before he stopped in front of her. His expression looked very much like an animal that needed to be put out of its misery.

"Well?" she asked, hands on hips. "What's so bad about being love-sick?"

"You know that I planned to never feel anything for anyone again. I told you about all the folks I lost . . . including my wife and son. I didn't want to go through that then, and I sure don't want to go through it now."

"And you figured that if you kept your heart as hard as stone you wouldn't have to. Is that it?"

"Something like that."

She shook her head. "It doesn't work. Believe me."

He put his hand to his face and rubbed his temples. "I just don't know what to do about it. One minute I'm sure I know what to say, and the next I feel tongue-tied. You've turned my world upside down and sidewise." He lowered his hand and studied her for a moment. "You are without a doubt the source of my disruption."

Jessica shook her head and started to speak, but Austin put his finger to her lips. "Hush. I know my words don't make sense. I know they sound harsh, but they're not intended to. Maybe I don't have flowery words like Harrison Gable, but I do have the truth."

She took hold of his finger and drew his hand away. Jessica didn't release him, however. She continued to hold fast to his hand. "I don't want flowery words."

"I don't have his kind of money, either. Never will, most likely."

Jessica shook her head. "I don't need money, either."

Austin looked deep into her eyes. Jessica could see a longing in his expression that matched her own. "What do you need?" he asked softly.

"You," she whispered. "Just you."

Stepping back as if burned, Austin seemed to struggle for words. "I love you, you know."

"I didn't, but I guess I do now." She wanted to jump up and down and shout it out to the world. Why did young women have to act so composed when moments like this were begging to be celebrated?

His mouth clenched for a moment and then Austin asked, "How . . . how do you feel . . . about me?"

Jessica surprised them both by throwing herself back into his arms. She reached up to pull his face to hers. It was the first kiss she'd ever initiated, and she liked it very much. Pulling back, she smiled.

"I guess you feel the same as I do," Austin said, shaking his head. "Poor woman."

"So what are we going to do about it?"

He chuckled. "Well, I thought I'd talk to your father about marrying you. That is, if you want to marry me." She raised a brow, but said nothing. It wasn't the proposal she'd looked forward to.

He seemed to understand almost at once and dropped to one knee. Reaching up, he took hold of her hands. "Jessica, will you do me the honor of marrying me?"

Laughing like a young girl, Jessica thrilled to the question. She felt none of the dread she had when Harrison had proposed. "Here I thought I might never marry, yet I've had two proposals in the last twenty-four hours."

He frowned. "Gable?"

She sobered. "Yes, but I told him no."

"May I ask why?"

"Because I don't love him, silly. I love you."

Austin met her gaze. "So will you marry me?"

Jessica pulled her right hand from his hold and reached out to touch his face. A tenderness and love she'd never known filled her with wonder. "Of course I will."

★

A half hour later, Austin was asking Mr. Atherton for permission to marry his youngest child. Austin knew the man to be fair-minded but worried that he wouldn't want his little girl marrying a lawman. The life of such a man could bring danger upon his family, and Austin didn't want to cause the Athertons any grief.

"Do you love her?" Mr. Atherton asked. He watched Austin carefully as he awaited the answer.

Austin didn't hesitate. "I do. I love her very much." He looked to the floor, unable to take the intensity of the older man's gaze. "I never thought I could love again."

"I remember you sayin' you lost your wife and baby."

Drawing a deep breath, Austin raised his head. "Yes. It was in child-birth. Folks told me it was for the best . . . that if I had to lose the mother, it'd be better to lose both, since the baby would have had a hard time surviving without the mother. I never quite saw it that way, though."

Tyler nodded. "Sometimes folks don't know what they're sayin', and by the time they do, it's too late."

"Some even said that I wasn't to blame, but whether I was or not, I vowed not to let it happen again. Then I met Jessica and none of that seemed to much matter. I guess that's my heart trying to comfort me."

"Maybe it's God trying to comfort your heart. He does that, you know. The Holy Spirit is called the Comforter in the Bible. I reckon God wants us to find comfort and peace of mind, or He wouldn't have given us a Comforter."

"Even if we walk away from Him?" Austin asked.

"And did you?"

Austin blew out a heavy breath. "I didn't stop believing in Him, if that's what you mean. I just stopped believing He cared."

"And now?"

He wasn't sure what to say. His thoughts were filled with doubt. "Now, I guess I'm a little confused. I want to trust Him, but it's hard."

"For sure nobody ever said it would be easy," Atherton countered. "We've all had our demons to wrestle, Austin. I had mine in learnin' to forgive. See, I suffered loss when the Comanche killed my pa. I hated them for that and wanted to take revenge on them."

"What happened?"

"God had other ideas. He had Carissa and her little girl needin' me and me needin' them. Of course, I wasn't good to any of us with all that hate inside. I had the opportunity to face my demon in person, and God made a way for me to lose my hatred and anger. I learned in that moment that I could let hatred have control of me for the rest of my life, or I could give up my rights to it and hand it over to God. I chose the latter, and I have to tell you, son, I haven't been sorry."

The older man's confession deeply touched Austin. "Guess I need to take it to God, as well."

Atherton pushed back his chair from the table. "Why not do it right now? I'd be honored to join you in prayer."

Austin hadn't expected this, but it felt right. It was time to set things straight. It was time to come home to His Father in heaven.

★

"Did you set a date?" Mother asked.

Jessica shook her head and fell back against her bed pillows. "No. I have to say both of us were so surprised by the proposal that we hardly spoke after I agreed to marry him."

"Well, no matter. I imagine you'll want to get to know each other better. Maybe a summer wedding would be nice."

"Summer? I don't think I'd want to wait that long," Jessica said, folding her hands together under her head.

"Well, you don't want to rush into anything. Getting married based on emotions alone is never wise. Make sure this is the man you want to spend the rest of your life with. Once you're married, there's no going back."

"Oh, I know that." Jessica didn't find value in her mother's warning. She felt as if she'd known Austin all of her life.

"So what kind of plans do you want to make for your wedding?"

"I'd like a big church wedding. I want a beautiful white wedding dress like we saw in *Peterson's Magazine*. You know, the one with the sweeping train and all the lace?"

"With the huge sleeves?" Mother asked.

"Goodness, no. It was the princess-style gown with the wide lace that came over the shoulders and made a V at the waist. It had no sleeves except for the lace hanging off the shoulder and over the top of the arms."

"Oh yes. I remember it. I suppose we shall need to find the pattern and have it made for you in Dallas."

Jessica nodded. "We could make a grand time of it. Just you and me." She was excited by the prospect. "And we could shop for shoes and maybe some new clothes." All at once Jessica sobered. She sounded just like her old self. Once again, she was focused on her appearance and the attention she knew she'd receive from having her mother to herself.

"What's wrong, Jess?" Mother asked, cocking her head to one side as she always did when assessing one of her children's health. Her eyes narrowed slightly in scrutinizing her daughter. "Are you ill?"

"In a way. I'm sick of myself. I hate that the first thing I think of is a grand wedding and new clothes. I've been working hard to put the old me away and let the new me take charge."

"It's really better if you let God take charge. I find that when I try to be in control, I lose control."

"But I'm trying so hard," Jessica replied in exasperation. "Why can't God just make me be unselfish."

"It would be nice if we could snap our fingers and become better people instantly." Mother sounded sympathetic. "Unfortunately, change is a journey we must take one step at a time. Give it over to God and rest in Him."

"I am—at least I'm trying to give it over. Then something like this happens, and I feel as though I go back ten steps." She paused and shook her head. "I'm sorry, Mother. I didn't mean to get carried away. The idea of planning my wedding just makes me giddy," she said, smiling.

"Jess, I don't think you're selfish to be happy about your wedding. Every girl dreams and fusses over it. I did. When I married Gloria's father I had a beautiful wedding with all the trimmings. That turned out miserably, and I was widowed with a baby. When I married your father, it was different. I wore a simple gown of white Indian muslin over yellow cotton, and we married at the Barnett Ranch so that Hannah could be

685

there. She'd just given birth to Sarah, and William wasn't letting her go anywhere." Mother smiled at the fond memory.

"When I think of all the money my father spent on my first wedding and how badly it ended up, well, I know what it is to be selfish and demanding." She met Jessica's gaze. "You are neither one. Now go to sleep and have pleasant dreams." She turned the lamp down until it went out, leaving just the light from the hallway.

Jessica snuggled down under the covers, feeling much like a little girl again. She gave a contented sigh and closed her eyes to dream of wedding gowns and flower bouquets.

Chapter 22

Two days later Jessica was still contemplating the kind of wedding she hoped to have when she glanced outside and saw Harrison Gable show up unannounced. She had no desire to see him and quickly ducked out to the kitchen to see if she could help Lupe with anything. Peeking around the arched entry to the kitchen, Jessica heard her mother's soft voice.

"Good morning, Mr. Gable. What brings you here today?"

"I am hoping to speak with your daughter."

Jessica contemplated running for the back door. She had nothing to say to Harrison Gable. She'd refused his proposal and clearly wanted nothing more of his desire to court. She glanced back at Lupe, and the older woman shrugged as if to say, *"It's your problem."*

Mother was telling Harrison that she'd go in search of Jessica if he would just have a seat in the front sitting room. Jessica drew a deep breath to steady her nerves and brushed her sleeves for any hint of lint. Mother came down the hallway smiling.

"You have a visitor."

"Yes, I heard," she replied in a whisper. "I wish I didn't have to speak with him. I don't want to hear his comments about how I should be marrying him instead of Austin."

Mother put her hand on Jessica's hand. "Don't make more out of it than it has to be. Just be kind and polite and let the matter resolve itself. Maybe he's come to congratulate you. After all, someone is bound to have mentioned your engagement by now. Your father was mighty excited about it—maybe even more than I was."

"I suppose he's been telling everyone in Cedar Springs," Jessica said, frowning.

"Just stop worrying. There's nothing Harrison can do about it. You love another."

She knew Mother was right, but it was so hard to ignore her feelings of anxiety. She wanted to celebrate and enjoy this wonderful feeling of happiness. Instead, Jessica knew that trying to explain the situation to Harrison wouldn't be easy.

"I'll go," she finally said.

"I will pray for you, Jess."

The words comforted Jessica. The thought of her mother taking time to pray about something as trivial as her encounter with Harrison touched her. She patted her mother's arm. "Thank you."

Smoothing down the front of her blouse, Jessica slowly made her way to the front sitting room. She felt rather like someone going to her execution. *I won't bring up the engagement unless he does.*

"Ah, here you are," Harrison said, getting to his feet. He gave her a broad smile, which revealed his almost perfect teeth. "And how lovely you look today."

Jessica bristled at his compliment. "Thank you. I wasn't expecting you, and I am rather busy."

He nodded knowingly. "I do apologize for coming so early in the day, but I felt I had to. Please sit down and I'll explain."

He motioned to the sofa, but Jessica took her place like a queen in her favorite chair by the fire. "All right, please continue."

Harrison pulled up another chair to sit directly in front of her. "I wanted to apologize for my actions the other night. I know I surprised you with my proposal of marriage. I realize we haven't done much in the way of courting, but I thought to do more of that after you accepted my proposal."

Jessica started to say something, but he held up his hand. "Please let me get this out. You see, I care very much for you, and because of that I felt it important to speak to you privately about this. It has to do with Austin Todd."

"Why would you come to me about Mr. Todd?"

Gable actually looked uncomfortable. "I've heard it said around town that you have accepted his proposal of marriage."

Jessica stiffened. "I have."

"I also heard about his plans. I thought you might be upset. I mean, there's no way of knowing whether he'll return."

Her eyes narrowed. "What are you talking about?"

"Oh dear, you don't know. I was afraid that might be the case." He gave the look of one who truly felt bad. However, Jessica knew it was a lie. "I've heard folks talking all over town about Mr. Todd leaving on the morning train tomorrow. He's going to Colorado, they're saying. I really don't know why he is heading there in particular, but I feared for you, since he didn't seem to have plans to return. He didn't buy a round-trip ticket. I knew you two had just become engaged, and I feared this would leave you in great shame."

"Colorado?" she murmured. Why hadn't Austin told her about this?

"I thought perhaps with his leaving, and it being uncertain that he would return, you might need the comfort of a good friend." He reached out to touch her hand. "I know you have no desire to marry me, but my offer does remain on the table. Truly I am only here as a friend."

Jessica felt momentarily sickened at the thought that Austin had skipped out on her. Surely this was a mistake. Even if it weren't, however, she didn't want to give Harrison the upper hand. She had to have faith in Austin—in their love.

"Austin will be back. He loves me and I love him. That's something I couldn't share with you. Austin no doubt has to go to Colorado on business."

But rather than appear surprised or even angry at her declaration, Gable seemed even sadder. Shaking his head, he gave her a look of pity. "Poor woman. No doubt he lied to you, especially since he hasn't bothered to let you know of his plans. What a savage thing to do to one so innocent."

Jessica squirmed in her chair and hoped Harrison Gable wouldn't notice how uncomfortable he'd made her. "Really, Mr. Gable, I hardly see why any of this is your business."

He threw her an apologetic look. "Of course you are right. You are the one he's made a fool of, but this isn't my business. I shouldn't be causing you more pain with the telling of that cad's actions. After all, you are my friend, and I don't wish to hurt you."

"He's not a cad!" Jessica jumped up from the chair. "He's a good man, and I intend to marry him. Now, if you'll excuse me . . ." She started to leave the room, but Gable crossed the room in a flash and took hold of her.

He dropped the façade. "I can give you a better life than he can. I would care greatly for your comfort and happiness." He pulled her closer, and though Jessica tried to push him away, he held her in an ironclad grip. "I know ways," he whispered against her ear, "to make a woman happy—and keep her that way."

She put the heel of her boot down on his foot. Yelping, Gable dropped his hold, and Jessica flew from the room, passing Mother on the way. She knew her mother would question her about what had happened, but at this point Jessica only longed to put some distance between herself and the vulgar Mr. Gable.

Seeking the sanctuary of her bedroom, she slammed the door shut behind her and locked it. The memory of Harrison's declaration gave her a tight feeling in her chest. Why hadn't Austin mentioned that he was leaving for Colorado? She didn't want to give doubt room to grow, but what was he doing? Was he truly not planning to return?

Jessica paced the room and tried to make sense of it all. She calmed a little as she remembered something she'd said to Harrison about Austin's trip. It might very well be that the Rangers needed him to travel to Colorado. Perhaps they'd asked him to bring back cattle rustlers for trial. Or maybe he was helping another Ranger. She frowned, running out of reasons for Austin to abruptly leave town without telling her. Suddenly, nothing made sense.

★

Having spread the word that he was headed to Colorado Springs on important business for the Secret Service, Austin felt certain word would get around to Mr. Morgan and his cohort. Robert, too, had helped spread the news, and it seemed to be all that folks were talking about.

Austin smiled to himself as he made his way to the Atherton ranch. "Let 'em talk," he said to the twilight. He would leave on the morning train, and he wanted to make sure that Jessica knew about his plans.

It was nearly suppertime when Austin arrived. He knew Mrs. Atherton would invite him to join them for the meal—at least he was counting on that. He gave a firm knock on the door, then dusted the tops of his boots off on the back of his Levi's.

Mr. Atherton answered the door with a smile. "Austin. Good to see you, son. Come on in. We were just sittin' down to supper. Can you stay?"

"I'd like that, sir. I was hoping to speak to Jessica after the meal."

"Of course. I think that's more than acceptable. Maybe I'll find an excuse to help her ma with the dishes. 'Course, I don't want her thinkin' it might become a regular thing." He chuckled and put his arm around Austin's shoulders. "Come on, son. I think the ladies will be pleased to see you."

When Austin entered the dining room, he found Mrs. Atherton and Jessica sitting before their empty china settings at a table laden with delicious-smelling food. He remembered just then that he still had his hat on and quickly remedied the situation.

"Look who I found at the door. I told him he needed to join us for supper."

"Of course," Mrs. Atherton said, getting to her feet. "Let me get another place setting. Austin, why don't you sit there beside Jess."

"Here, I'll take your hat," Mr. Atherton said. "It'll be on the coat-tree by the front door."

Austin moved to where Jessica sat and pulled the chair out. She didn't look at him, and it bothered Austin greatly. Why this sudden cold shoulder?

Mrs. Atherton placed the dishes and silver in front of him and asked if he wanted coffee or tea. "I've made both, so you have your choice. Either one will warm you up."

"Coffee's good for me," Austin replied, still concerned about Jessica's silence.

With the coffee poured, Mrs. Atherton retook her seat, and Mr. Atherton offered a short prayer. As the meal progressed, Austin's curiosity mounted. Jessica hadn't turned once to look at him, and it was starting to be quite annoying.

"So what brings you out this way?" Atherton asked. "Were you just hopin' to spend some time with Jess, or did you have other pressin' business?"

"Actually, I came to let you all know that I'm going to be gone for a while." This brought Jessica to attention.

"And where are you headed?" the older man asked.

"Colorado Springs. I'm helping the Barnetts and the Wythes with a matter." Jessica's tight shoulders seemed to relax just a bit. "It shouldn't take long," Austin added. "Probably no longer than a week or two. Either the item I seek will be there and be what we expect, or it won't."

"Does this have somethin' to do with the man who's been pesterin' Jake and Alice?"

"Yes," Austin replied, relieved that Atherton had been apprised of the situation.

The rancher nodded and cut into his meat. "I hope it will put the past to rest and give them the peace of mind they seek. William told me it was quite the conspiracy."

"It would appear that way," Austin said.

"And why are *you* going in particular?" Mrs. Atherton asked, a forkful of food midway to her lips. "Why not Robert?"

Austin had figured on this question. "I used to work with the Secret Service. As a part of the Treasury Department they deal with counterfeiting and fraud. I presume you know that this is part of the problem at hand."

"We know all about it," Atherton replied. "A big mess, if you ask me."

"It is indeed, but I'm hoping to put an end to it. My old boss asked me to come in on the investigation because I've had experience with this type of crime, and I am friends with the folks involved."

"I'm sure that put William's mind at rest," Jessica's father declared. "I know it would mine. We'll certainly be praying for you."

"Is it dangerous?" This came from Jess's mother, and Austin couldn't help but sense Jessica's tensing once again.

"No more so than anything else," he said with a smile. "I don't expect problems. And if there are any, I'll have the support of two other agents, who are even now taking a fast train to Denver and then to Colorado Springs. They're good men—men I know and have worked with before."

The conversation continued, but Jessica only spoke when her parents asked her something directly. Austin remained puzzled at her attitude. She almost seemed angry with him. Once supper concluded, Mrs. Atherton shooed the couple from the dining room, and Mr. Atherton made good on his suggestion to help wash dishes when Jessica protested.

"I'll help your mother. You two go on and enjoy the fire I started just before we sat down. That front parlor ought to be nice and warm for you now."

Jessica didn't so much as look at Austin but nodded and headed from the room. Austin followed after her like a puppy after his master. He figured it would be an uncomfortable evening of silence, since something had clearly disturbed Jessica. He was wrong. The moment they were in the parlor, Jessica turned on him to demand answers.

"Why is it that I'm the last to know of your plans? Harrison Gable said you were leaving me high and dry."

"And you believed him?" Austin frowned. "Besides that, what were you doing with him?"

"Oh, don't try to avoid the question." Jessica put her hands on her hips. "He told me that it was all over town about you heading off. Harrison said you were most likely not coming back, and since he'd heard that we were engaged, he thought he'd come and comfort me."

"He heard about our engagement, eh?" This made Austin smile. "I'll bet that was a sucker punch to his pride."

Jessica shook her head. "He pitied me. He told me in a most sympathetic way that I'd been a fool."

Austin's voice softened. "Jess, why would you believe him over me?"

"Because you weren't here. You hadn't told me before telling the entire town that you planned to leave. I don't want you to go—especially now. I want Harrison Gable to eat his words."

Stepping forward, Austin reached out to take Jessica's hands, but she refused. With a shrug, he continued. "I can't go back on my word, Jess. Not for you or for anyone else. I gave the Barnetts and Wythes my promise to see this through."

"But it's dangerous, and don't tell me it's not. If it weren't, there wouldn't be a need for additional Secret Service men."

"All right, it's dangerous, but I've been trained to handle situations like this."

"You're making me the laughingstock of town."

"Hardly that, Jess. Be reasonable." Austin decided it might calm her if they sat. "Come sit with me, and I'll explain."

She sat but folded her arms across her chest and fixed Austin with such a stare that he knew this wouldn't be easily resolved.

"No doubt Harrison will spread the news of my situation all over town, and everyone will laugh about how I've been duped."

Austin shook his head. "You haven't been duped."

Jessica's eyes widened. "But that's what everyone will think. If you leave me now, people will think that you are running away from our engagement. Especially if Harrison Gable has his say."

"Since when have you cared about what other people thought? Since we first met you've been unconcerned about others and what their opinion of you might be."

"That isn't true. I didn't use to care, but now I do. I don't want to shame my parents, and I don't want . . ." She let the words trail and fell silent.

"Jessica, I'm not leaving you. I'm simply doing a job. You have to understand that my job requires me to travel. Eventually, I'll be marshal of Terryton and stick close to home, but right now I have an important mission, and I'd like to go to it knowing I have your blessing."

"Well, you don't," she declared, getting back to her feet. "I don't want you to go. I won't come in second to your job. If I can't come first as your wife and friend, then maybe you should leave and not come back."

Austin realized that in her anger, they weren't going to accomplish anything. He rose and headed for the door. "I'll be back as soon as I can."

"Don't bother!" Jessica turned away from him and fixed her gaze on the fire.

Austin knew she didn't mean it. Grief, but that girl could work up a rage. He smiled to himself as he collected his hat and left the house. *I like a gal with spit and spirit. Grace was always so sweet and quiet. Like sitting in a beautiful garden.* Austin chuckled to himself. *Life with Jess is gonna be like riding in a runaway wagon.*

He rode back to the cabin and settled in for the night. He had already determined he would pen Jessica a letter. He wanted to make sure she knew his intentions were to return and bring a wedding ring when he did. That ought to give her something to think about.

★

Jessica couldn't sleep and tossed and turned most of the night. She regretted her anger and the words she'd hurled at Austin. She knew she'd acted inappropriately, but she had been so enraged that Harrison was right about Austin leaving that she hadn't been able to control her temper.

It was just the thought of being pitied by people who thought she'd been deserted. Jessica couldn't stand to be in that position. It was even better when folks didn't like her, but to pity her was more than she could bear.

You're being foolish. Even if they pity you, they'll see when Austin returns that they were wrong. It was little comfort, but she knew in her heart that Austin had spoken the truth. He would return.

But now he'll go away, and his last memories of me will be of anger and worry. She chewed on her lower lip. *I have to apologize. I have to see him before he goes. I have to tell him that I believe him and that what other people think doesn't matter.*

But how was she supposed to do that?

When light streaked the horizon, Jessica gave up on sleeping and dressed for the day. She had only one thought. She would ride into town and meet up with Austin before he caught the train. She would apologize for her actions, and then she would let him go.

"I have to trust that God will take care of him," she murmured.

She waited until she saw a light in the bunkhouse and then slipped out the back door and went in search of Osage. The old man was already putting a pot of coffee on to boil when Jessica found him.

"Osage, I don't mean to be a problem to you, but I need to ride into town."

The old man got slowly to his feet. "That's no problem, little gal. How soon do you want to head out?"

"Right away, if we can. I'll let Lupe know, and she can tell Mother and Father. I know they'll understand. I wasn't very kind to Austin last night, and I can't send him away without apologizing."

"Startin' to care for the fella?"

"More than that," she replied. "I've agreed to be his wife."

Osage chuckled. "Well, I'll be a three-legged cat." He motioned to one of the other cowboys. "You see to this coffee. Miss Atherton and I have to ride to town." He turned back to Jessica. "I'll have Peg saddled and ready to go in ten minutes."

"Thank you, Osage," Jessica said, surprising the old man with a kiss on the cheek. She could hear him whooping it up as she exited the bunkhouse. His enthusiasm made her smile.

The ride didn't take long. For an old man, Osage was still amazingly limber and able to sit a horse as well as he could when Jess had been a little girl. They didn't run the horses all the way but covered the distance in walks, trots, and gallops. By the time Jessica and Osage entered the city limits, the sun was up and the cool air was warming. Jessica went immediately to the train, only to learn she was too late.

"What do you mean he's already gone?" Jessica asked. "The passenger train doesn't even arrive for another forty minutes."

"Now, Miss Jessica, don't go gettin' all put out," the stationmaster admonished. "The schedule changed for the winter. But don't worry; he left you a letter. I was supposed to get it out to you today."

He rummaged around the papers on his desk and handed a folded piece of paper to Jessica. "I didn't snoop in it. I figured it was private." He grinned. "But I wanted to look. I heard you two were gettin' married."

Jessica nodded and took the letter. She thanked the stationmaster and hurried back to where Osage stood holding the two horses. "He's already gone," she said, opening the letter.

Jess,

 I'm sorry for the way things went last night. You had a right to be upset. I didn't handle this well. For that I apologize, and I hope you'll forgive me. I never meant to make you the last person to know about my plans. The only reason the word was sent around to the entire town was because we're hoping it will aid the case. I can't really explain in this letter, but will tell you everything when I come back. And I will *come back.*

 I love you, Jessica, and I know that you love me. I don't plan to be gone any longer than I have to, and when I come home, I plan to bring you a wedding ring.

Love,
Austin

She looked up at Osage and gave a heavy sigh. The old man cocked his head to one side. "That letter resolve everything?"

She smiled and tucked the letter into her jacket and let her worries fade away. "Yes. I suppose it does."

Chapter 23

Austin remained on guard throughout the trip to Colorado. He had established on the first day out of Cedar Springs that both Morgan and a man he presumed to be Mr. Smith were aboard the train. Neither man had made himself visible during the day until around five o'clock, when the elusive Mr. Smith joined Austin's car. Of course, he hadn't known for sure that it was Smith, but the man acted suspicious and seemed to be watching Austin closely.

Later that night Morgan and Smith had apparently thought him to be asleep when they met toward the back of his car. Austin happened to be facing the same direction, and though his hat was pulled low, he could still see from just under the rim. Morgan had appeared, now with his beard shaved off, only for a brief moment to notify his partner to follow him. Austin supposed they might be headed for the smoking car. Austin didn't know if Morgan's change of appearance was for the purpose of throwing Austin off Morgan's movements, but if so, it didn't work.

He was glad that the two men had learned of his plan and followed him. He'd worried they might not have received the news or had chosen not to follow him. It was good to know they wouldn't be pestering the Wythes or the Barnetts. When the train stopped in the next town to re-fuel, it allowed the passengers time to disembark for a short while. Austin took advantage of his time off the train to send a wire to Robert to let him know that the men were following him. He knew the information would help Robert to relax his watch and get back to the tasks at hand.

January in northern New Mexico made Austin realize his suit coat was hardly heavy enough to ward off the cold. By the time they reached Raton, he felt numb from the winter winds. There had been a blizzard just hours before, and the trains were delayed in getting through until the snowdrifts could be plowed from the tracks. This took a special rotary snowplow, the likes of which Austin had never seen. The huge machine was put on the front of the locomotive engine and pushed forward to remove the snow with its whirring blades.

Austin sat shivering in the poorly heated passenger car while one plow was used on the tracks about twenty yards to the east of them. He saw the blades cuts through the snow, which was blown out a chute over the top of the engine. It was quite interesting to watch, but it only served to make Austin feel all the more chilled.

Once they were finally on their way, it was slow going and caused Austin no end of anxiety. He wanted to see this investigation through, and do so quickly. He was anxious to return to Jessica and make plans for their marriage. If she'd still have him.

By the time they rolled into Colorado Springs, it was the following evening. Austin made his way to the nearest hotel and settled in for his first good night's sleep in a week. The delay on the train had given him a sore neck and backside. He could sit in a saddle for days on end, but the hard seat of the train car made him miserable.

He saw Morgan and Smith momentarily in the depot but had no idea where they might have decided to stay. Austin wasn't concerned that they might lose track of him, so rather than expend his energies keeping an eye out for them, he would let Morgan and Smith worry about keeping Austin under surveillance. After all, this was just as important to them as it was to him. For now, all he wanted was to sleep in a bed.

The following morning Austin awoke to even more snow. He felt chilled to the bone and longed for Texas . . . and for Jessica. He reminded himself over and over that there was a job to be done and it shouldn't take him long to retrieve the box and see if it held what they were looking for. If it did, then they could finally put this case to rest.

Dressing, Austin gave serious thought to buying a heavy coat. He quickly decided against it, however. The extra money he'd brought was going toward a wedding ring for Jess. He could bear a little cold. Besides, he'd have no need of a heavy coat in Texas.

But Texas seemed like a million miles away. Austin went to the window. The shop roofs were covered in snow, as was the rest of the town. At least it seemed that it had stopped snowing, and for this Austin was grateful. Hopefully he could accomplish everything in just a few hours and be back on the next train headed south. Then again, he might have come for naught and would find nothing in Mr. Chesterfield's box. He quickly shook off that thought.

"I can't let myself borrow trouble," he said aloud, noticing his breath fogged the window.

Dropping the draperies back in place, Austin checked his pocket watch. It was too early for the bank to be open, and he was hungry. A good meal seemed most important at that moment. Just then there was a knock on the door.

He frowned. No one knew where he was—not exactly. Unless, of course, they had managed to get the clerk downstairs to reveal his room number.

With great stealth he moved closer to the door. He was about to question the person on the other side when a youthful male voice called out. "Morning paper?"

Austin opened the door and nodded. "I'll take one." He flipped the kid a coin and told him to keep the change.

The boy's eyes lit up. "Thank you!" He hurried to the next room and began the routine again.

Austin tucked the paper under his arm and made his way to the hotel dining room, where the temperature was much warmer. He supposed it was because of the busy kitchen and the room full of guests. Despite the fact that he was still chilled to the bone, Austin chose a table by the window in order to keep an eye on both the entrance to the hotel and the street.

"Would you like to order?" A young serving girl smiled at him most generously.

"Yes. I need to thaw out, and a hot meal might just do the trick," Austin replied. "I wasn't at all prepared for winter weather."

"You weren't? Where are you from, mister?" She eyed him carefully. "Don't you have a warm coat?"

"I'm afraid not." Austin gave her a grin. "I'm from Texas, and we're not used to this white stuff." The girl giggled. Austin figured her to be about seventeen.

"Would you like some hot coffee?"

Austin nodded. "Lots of it. Maybe a bathtub full." He settled back against the wooden chair. "That might finally thaw me out."

She giggled again, but then appeared to get an idea. "I can seat you closer to the kitchen. Sitting here by the window is bound to be colder."

Austin appreciated her thoughtfulness but shook his head. "Nah, I'm all right. The coffee will do the trick. Oh, and I'll need a nice big breakfast."

"We have two breakfast specials," she declared. "Biscuits and gravy on one order, and eggs, bacon, and toast on the other."

"I'll take both."

The girl's eyes widened in surprise. "They're really generous with the portions here. Are you sure you want both?"

"Yup, I'm sure. I'm half starved." He'd not eaten much on the train. The prices were high, and he'd heard from other customers that the food was not that good. Short of buying some jerked meat and apples during one of their stops, Austin had eaten nothing.

The waitress disappeared into the kitchen. Austin busied himself with the newspaper he'd bought earlier. The *Daily Gazette* had very little of interest to Austin. Nevertheless, he forced himself to read the paper and sip the hot coffee his waitress brought. He didn't want to appear anxious to anyone who might be watching—especially to Mr. Morgan. As far as he was concerned, Morgan needed to believe Austin completely clueless to his presence.

When the girl brought two plates of breakfast with most wonderful aromas, Austin wondered if perhaps his eyes had been bigger than his stomach. Nevertheless, he thanked the young woman and put the paper aside. He offered a short prayer of thanks, then straightened and plunged his fork into the biscuits and gravy. A first taste revealed heaven on earth, and Austin quickly inhaled another two forkfuls. It wasn't quite as good as he'd had on the Barnett Ranch, but very nearly.

He continued to eat, pretending to be completely absorbed in the food while keeping an eye out around him. He wasn't worried about Morgan or Smith actually presenting themselves, but he figured they'd hire someone for the job. Morgan had to know that Austin would recognize him, and Austin doubted that he'd allow his henchman to get too far away from him. They'd no doubt pay some dim-witted ninny to watch him and report his movements.

By the time he'd finished the biscuits and gravy and started in on the eggs and bacon, Austin was fairly certain his hunch was right. At the far end of the restaurant, an older man, looking rather weathered, worn, and out of place, sat eating a huge meal as if he hadn't had food in a month. The man was dressed in layers that he began to shed as time passed. Whenever Austin looked his way, the man quickly returned his gaze to his plate.

Smiling to himself, Austin ordered more coffee and relaxed at the table. The bank wouldn't be open for another half hour, and he still needed to make contact with the Secret Service agents who were to have arrived in town prior to Austin. They had agreed to send him word as to where they should meet before Austin made his way to the bank.

He picked up the paper again and nodded to the girl when she offered more coffee. Just as he started on his fifth cup, Austin noticed two well-dressed men enter the dining room. They were impeccable in their appearance and furtively studied the room from hooded eyes. Austin knew them immediately. Five years hadn't changed them much. Marcus Kayler and Sam Fegel were two of the department's best men. They would get a message to Austin without anyone being the wiser. It was exactly what he'd been waiting for.

Austin decided it would be best to remain at his table, and when the waitress appeared to ask him if he wanted anything more, he decided on something else to eat. "Do you have any cinnamon rolls?" he asked, remembering how good Hannah Barnett's had been.

The girl grinned. "I can't believe you're still hungry, but yes, we have cinnamon rolls. My mother made them, in fact, and they're as big as plates."

"Sounds good." Austin delayed her just a moment longer. "So is this your family's restaurant?" He continued to glance toward his two friends.

The girl nodded. "My uncle owns the hotel. He's my pa's brother. They set this up when the Cripple Creek Mining District was formed a few years back, and the family's been here ever since."

Seeing the men move his way, Austin decided he'd give them the perfect opportunity. "Well, it's a mighty fine place. I can't remember ever eating this well on the road. I do believe I'd like to have a cinnamon roll and some more coffee. And if you could hurry, that would be great."

The girl seemed amused by his order. She whirled on her heel to head toward the kitchen and ran headlong into Marcus Kayler, just as Austin had planned. In the flash of a moment, Kayler steadied the girl while Fegel slipped a note to Austin. It happened so quickly that Austin was sure no one was the wiser.

The girl flushed in embarrassment, giggled nervously, then hurried for the kitchen. Austin thought of Jessica and imagined her in the same position. His Jessica would have probably berated the men for not watching where they were going. Austin couldn't imagine Jessica being nearly as giggly as this young woman. He frowned. The last time they'd been together, Jessica had been anything but giggly.

The thought of her still holding a grudge was most disconcerting, but Austin had prayed she would receive the letter and understand his heart, even if she couldn't accept his actions. He missed her so much, and had it not been for his promise to the Barnetts, Austin might have given up the job, turned the key over to the Secret Service agents, and headed back to Texas. He let go a heavy breath.

I gave my word.

Austin didn't have a lot in this world, but he still had that. He had his fledgling faith, as well. He knew God was with him, but the old memories fought against him like some kind of plague. How was it that he could lay Grace to rest and learn to love again, but he couldn't free himself of the guilt he felt over his brother's death?

"Here you go," the girl announced, putting a plate in front of him. On it sat the biggest cinnamon roll Austin had ever seen.

He stared at the roll for a moment and then looked to the server. "This is just one roll?"

She giggled. "I warned you. Ma believes in filling folks up. She said for me to tell you that this one's on the house."

"How come?" he asked. It seemed most unusual for a restaurant to give food away.

"Ma said that if you were hungry enough to eat both of her specials in one sitting and still want more, then you deserve to have it on the house." She picked up some of his empty dishes. "I'll be back with the coffee. Should I leave your check?"

"Yes, thank you."

The girl shifted the dishes with one hand and reached into her pocket with the other. She glanced at the check and then handed it to Austin.

"If you'll wait," he called loud enough for everyone to hear him, "I'll pay for this now."

The girl took his offered payment as well as the paper on which she'd written his total. "Now, you keep the change," Austin told her. The girl's eyes widened at the generous tip. He could see that she was more than pleased.

"Thank you, mister." She hurried away, as if needing to show someone her good fortune.

With the girl gone, Austin raised the newspaper and retrieved the note he'd slipped under there earlier. He kept the paper folded and pretended to read an article, all the while working to open the note Fegel had slipped him. After several attempts he managed the task and read the content of the message.

Will meet you in alleyway behind jewelry store across the street from bank. There's a place we can meet without being seen. We've arranged with the store to allow you access to the back from inside the store. Just go into the place and ask for Mr. Mitchell. Tell him you've always wanted to see his famous gold nugget but you haven't the nickel for a ticket. He'll show you to the back.

It was signed *Kayler* and *Fegel*.

Austin managed to tuck the note into his vest pocket before the girl returned with more coffee. She asked if he needed anything else, but Austin assured her he was fine. He looked across the room to where the man who'd been watching him sat. Again the man quickly looked away. This gave Austin a moment to look at the two agents and nod. The game was now afoot.

Getting to his feet in a slow, methodical manner, Austin gave a bit of a stretch and headed back to the hotel lobby. He wasn't surprised when the weathered old man followed him after a couple of minutes. Austin made it easy for him by heading up the lobby stairs slowly. He would return to his room, wait a few minutes, and then head down the back stairs, which he'd scouted out before coming to breakfast. Hopefully the old man would think Austin still in his room and continue to wait in the lobby.

This, Austin hoped, would throw off anyone's ability to keep him under surveillance. He didn't mind that Morgan knew he was in the area, but he wanted him to only know as much as Austin deemed necessary.

At the appointed time, Austin made his way to the jewelry store. He couldn't see that anyone had followed him and breathed a little easier. No doubt Morgan had already snooped around to learn the whereabouts of the bank Austin had come to find. Still, Austin hoped he might have time to go to the bank and retrieve the box before he had to encounter Morgan and his man.

The jewelry store owner looked up when Austin entered. There was no one else in the place, but still Austin felt it necessary to speak softly and maintain his cover. He browsed around the store for a minute before the owner approached.

"Welcome to my store. May I help you, sir?"

Austin rubbed his chin. "You're the owner?"

The man gave a tight smile. "I am."

"Well, I was hoping to see your famous gold nugget, but I'm afraid I don't have a nickel to spare—for the ticket." His voice was low, but nevertheless the man's eyes widened, and he gave a quick glance around the room as if fearful that someone had overheard.

"Come right this way," the owner said upon ensuring they were alone. He led Austin through a door and into a small stockroom. He pointed out the back door somewhat hidden behind a stack of boxes. Austin made his way to the door while the owner returned to the front of the store.

The two agents were awaiting his arrival in the alley. Austin gave each man a nod. "Did anyone follow you?" he asked.

"No," one of the men replied. "You?"

Austin shook his head. "I took the back stairs and a nondirect way here. If anyone followed me they did it in a very skillful manner."

"Well, it would seem to me these folks are full of skills," Marcus Kayler put in. He extended his hand. "Good to see you, Austin." Austin ignored the hand and the two men shared a hardy embrace. After giving Austin a slap on the back, Marcus laughed. "Wasn't sure we'd ever get a chance to work together again."

Sam Fegel likewise gave Austin a slap on the back. "I thought old Mr. Turner had gone daft when he told us we'd be working with you again." He shook Austin's hand and gave him a brief embrace. "I thought you were done with us."

"Yeah, well miracles do happen." Austin pulled out his pocket watch. It was nearly time for the bank to open. He shivered from the cold wind and snapped the lid shut.

"What's the plan?" Kayler asked.

"I'll go to the bank and retrieve the lockbox. If it is what I think it is, then I'll hand it over to you at the hotel. You'll be able to catch the afternoon train and head back to Washington."

"Sounds like a plan," the man replied. "We can keep watch from the store. If you have the box when you come out, then we'll know you have retrieved the contents. We'll head straightaway for the hotel."

"If the box is too large or heavy for one man but is what we've come for," Austin told them, "I'll step outside the bank and walk away without putting my hat on."

"Got it. If you're quick enough, a trolley will be there at half past the hour. It will take you on a route that passes the hotel. No one should try anything while you're so clearly in the company of others. If you miss it, another will be by at the top of the hour."

Austin nodded. "I guess that takes care of it. I'll see you at the hotel either way." He gave the men his room number, then headed back into the jewelry store. The owner looked at him with a worried expression. No doubt he feared the stranger's presence might bring problems for his store. Despite this, Austin paused for a moment at a case that held wedding rings.

"Are you looking for something in particular?" the owner asked.

Austin looked up with a grin. "A wedding ring. I promised to bring one back with me."

The man opened the case and pulled out the tray of rings. "We have many to choose from, as you can see."

Austin picked up a beautiful ring of gold with two tiny blue sapphires. "This one caught my eye." He held the piece up to catch the light from the window. "How much?"

The man quoted him a price. Austin arched a brow. "How much?"

"Well, I might be able to take off five percent."

"Still seems mighty high," Austin told him. "How about twenty percent?" He knew full well the man would never agree to such a large discount, but this way they could dicker to the percentage Austin expected to get.

"I should say not," the man replied, sounding most offended. He seemed to forget all about the covert reason Austin had come in the first place. "I could go maybe as high as seven percent."

"How about fifteen? I mean, that's me coming down five percent." Austin grinned. "And it's for a good cause. I have the prettiest gal waiting for me in Texas."

The man stiffened. "Ten and that's my final offer."

Austin pretended to be uncertain, even though ten percent was exactly the discount he was seeking. "I suppose if that's your final offer then I haven't got much of a choice. I'll take it."

The jeweler seemed surprised when Austin pulled out the cash and handed it to him. "I'll take it with me."

"But sir, what about the size? Will this fit your young lady?"

Austin looked at the ring and thought of Jessica's slender fingers. "I think it'll be fine. If not, we can take care of the matter in Texas." He tucked the ring into his vest pocket and bid the man good-day.

Pulling up the collar of his coat, Austin stepped outside and squinted against the morning sun. The light glinting off the snow all but blinded him. He drew a deep breath and felt the cold air sting his lungs. How in the world did people live in this frozen land? Without another thought he dodged a couple of men on horseback and crossed to the bank.

The bank was an older redbrick building that held a sort of warm grace in contrast against the snow. Austin had already been informed it was one of the local banks that hadn't needed to close for long during the recent financial crisis. Hence, they'd been able to keep Chesterfield's box locked in the vault until they could once again reopen. Austin walked into the building and pulled off his hat. Looking around the room, he saw tellers already busy receiving customers. Unfortunately, it wasn't much warmer inside than it had been outside.

A man at a desk to the left of him glanced up and smiled. "May I help you, sir?"

"I'm here to see the bank manager, John C. Espry."

The man stiffened. "Do you have an appointment?"

"Of sorts. I think when you let him know I'm here, he'll be more than happy to meet with me."

The man gave him a look of disbelief but nevertheless got to his feet. "Who shall I say is calling?"

"Austin Todd."

The man gave a curt nod and hurried to a closed door near the back of the bank. It was only a moment before he returned. "Mr. Espry will see you immediately." The man looked to be surprised by this turn of events but said nothing more. He showed Austin to the office and closed the door behind him.

"Mr. Todd," the older man said, getting to his feet. "Thank you for coming today. I received your note last night and am quite anxious to see this matter attended to. The president and owner of this bank wants it cleared up right away. He is making plans for changes in the future and feels this needs to be settled."

"I'm happy to oblige," Austin replied. "Here's the letter I've brought from Mr. Chesterfield's daughter, Alice Chesterfield Barnett, giving me permission to receive the lockbox and its contents."

Espry took the letter and, without even bothering to read the contents, instructed Austin to follow him. "The box is being kept in a private room. I'll take you there," he told Austin, glancing again at the letter. He tossed it to his desk. "Frankly, even without the letter, I was instructed to hand it over to you."

The older man pulled a set of keys from his pocket. "Come with me."

He led the way out a back entrance to the office and down a long narrow hallway. When they reached a back staircase, Austin thought they might be headed up. But Espry took a sharp turn to the right and led Austin to a large wooden door. Espry inserted a key and the lock opened. "It's just in here," he said. Espry turned on the lights and escorted Austin inside. Austin couldn't help but sneeze several times in a row. The room smelled musty. The cloying scent of cigars seemed to permeate the draperies and carpets. Espry seemed embarrassed and apologized. "This room was used just yesterday to hold a board meeting. I am sorry that we didn't think to air it out."

Despite sneezing, Austin assured the man it was of no concern. "I'm here for the box. I've endured worse smells than this." His glance went to the table where a black box sat. "Is that it?"

Espry looked to the table. "Yes, this is the box left with us by Mr. Chesterfield."

Austin stepped forward. The box was most unusual. It looked to be about twelve by twelve by twelve. Austin ran his hand over the ornate black lacquered piece and noted obvious Oriental touches to the box. He pulled the strange key from his pocket and inserted it in the lock. The moment of truth came as the key turned and the box opened.

Chapter 24

The contents of the box were better than Austin had hoped for. Not only were the counterfeiting plates within, but so too were the certificates, papers for additional certificates, and several bottles of ink. He snapped the lid closed quickly as Espry stepped forward to see the contents.

"Thank you," Austin said and relocked the box. Looking up, he could see that Espry was disappointed Austin hadn't shared the look inside. "I'll take this with me." He hoisted the locked box to his shoulder. "You've been a great help, and I know Mrs. Barnett appreciates your cooperation in this matter."

The bank manager seemed hesitant. "And the contents . . . were they what you'd expected?"

"Exactly so," Austin replied, heading out of the room and back down the narrow hall.

He didn't waste any time. Making a straight path through the bank, he exited the front door, knowing that his cohorts would see him and the box. The trolley was just approaching, and Austin quickly signaled with a wave and jumped aboard the crowded conveyance.

The box wasn't all that heavy, but its value was enormous. The contents could have easily caused massive problems with the monetary system. He would need to make a closer examination, but it was clear why this had cost Alice's father his life.

As the trolley reached the area of Austin's hotel, he paid the fee and jumped down from the steps. He shifted the box to his left shoulder and made his way into the hotel. The clerk looked at him in surprise and called out before Austin could make his way to the stairs.

"Sir, would you like a bellman to help with that?"

"No thanks," Austin said over his shoulder. "I've got it." He bounded up the stairs, as if to prove his ability, and quickly made his way down the hall to his room.

Once inside, he deposited the box on his bed and returned to the door to lock it. The room was warmer than it'd been downstairs, and sunlight shone brightly through the window. At last Austin was starting to warm up.

Taking the banjo-shaped key from his pocket once again, Austin inserted it in the lock.

Pushing back the lid, Austin reached into the box and began pulling out the contents. There were plates for the gold certificates, as well as plates for pressing twenty-dollar bills. Austin carefully examined each item, marveling at the work that had gone into putting together such a kit. The work was exquisite and no doubt done by one of the best in the business.

A knock on the hotel door brought Austin to attention. That would be his friends Kayler and Fegel.

"Just a minute," he called out and placed the items back into the lacquered box. He didn't bother to close the lid and lock it, but went to unlock his door.

"I'm glad you guys are here," he said and quickly realized it wasn't the agents at all, but rather Morgan and his man.

"We're glad to be here, as well," Morgan said, pushing Austin back.

Austin felt like ten kinds of fool for having let his guard down. He had been more than a little foolish to feel safe in his hotel room.

Morgan headed to the box and peered inside. "It's exactly as I had hoped. You've saved me a great deal of trouble, Mr. Todd."

His holster was hanging at the top of the bed. Austin moved slowly toward it. With a little luck, he hoped to pull his revolver without the men noticing. But even as he tried, Morgan's partner pushed Austin back and took the gun from the holster.

"You won't be needin' this." The man's icy blue eyes narrowed, and his expression seemed to dare Austin to fight.

Morgan looked up to see what had caused the exchange. "Glad to see you're on the job, Mr. Smith. That could have set us both back had Mr. Todd managed to get his weapon. I'm afraid I wasn't very observant, since I had my mind fixed on other things."

He went back to rummaging in the box while Austin tried to figure a way he might overpower the tall lanky Mr. Smith.

"I'm glad to see that Chesterfield was careful with this." Morgan looked at Austin and smiled. "When he told me he no longer planned to help me in my endeavors and that he planned to go to the police, well, I feared I might never again see these."

Snapping the lid in place, Morgan turned the key. "But now they are safely back in my care."

"You do realize that the Treasury Department is well aware of these plates and forged certificates. They've put more men than me on this case, so you can't hope to get away with this."

"I don't hope to get away with this, Mr. Todd," Morgan said, fixing him with a blank stare. "I've already gotten away with it. For some time before Mr. Chesterfield got cold feet, I had gotten away with it. Chesterfield caused me a most uncomfortable delay, especially in light of the financial difficulties of '93. However, now that my property has been returned to me, I shall endeavor to make up for lost time." He looked to Mr. Smith and shrugged. "I suppose the first thing we need to do is dispose of Mr. Todd."

The henchman stepped closer to Austin and put the revolver to his head. "That won't be no trouble."

A knock on the door startled the two thieves. With his eyes narrowed to slits, Smith lowered the gun to Austin's midsection.

"Austin, it's us. Open up."

Morgan moved to Todd. "Say nothing."

"Come on, Todd, we haven't got all day if we're going to catch the train to Denver."

Austin shifted uncomfortably from one foot to the other. He had to warn the men of what was happening, but how? Smith punched the barrel of the gun into Austin's stomach. Doubling over in a grunt, Austin managed to back into the nightstand. The lightweight piece of furniture toppled over, and all the contents on it spilled noisily to the hardwood floors.

"Fool!" Morgan exclaimed as the hotel door was kicked in.

Austin straightened just as the agents attacked. A gunshot rang out and Austin felt a burning sensation run through his body. Even so, he pushed forward to disarm Smith. The other agents were busy with Morgan, who had drawn a revolver of his own.

Austin kicked Smith in the shins, but the man held fast to the gun. The taller man had the advantage and held his ground. Forcing Smith's arm upward, Austin tried but failed to make him drop the weapon. Instead, as Smith's arm lowered, he somehow managed to get his finger on the trigger once again. The sound of the gun being fired was all that Austin heard as blackness overtook him.

★

It had been two weeks since Austin had headed to Colorado. Two weeks and no word. Jessica paced most unhappily through the house, wringing her hands and fretting about what might have gone wrong.

Perhaps Harrison had been right and Austin had changed his mind about returning. But even as the thought came to mind, Jessica did her best to take it captive, as the Bible directed. Her mother and father knew how worried she'd become.

"You're not helping yourself any by fretting," Father said when Jessica made her way back through the front sitting room.

"I know, but I can't put aside the feeling that something is wrong." She went to where her father sat and knelt. "Papa, can't you send a wire or contact someone who might know what's going on?"

Her father reached out and patted her hands. "Sometimes these things take time."

"But this has already taken far more time than Austin believed it would. Not only that, but he promised to wire as soon as his task was completed. He should have been able to send us a message, something telling us he was all right."

Gazing at her with a sympathetic look, Father reached up to gently take hold of her chin. "I hate to see you so worried. You're not eatin' or sleepin' properly, and your mother is beside herself. I guess I'd better do what I can, or she'll have my hide." He gave her his classic lazy smile, which eased Jessica's mind just a bit. "I'll check with Will and see if they've had any word."

Jessica threw herself against her father's seated frame. "Oh, thank you. Thank you. I'm so afraid of what might have happened. I can't rest until I know."

"I figured as much," her father declared. "If you'll get up off me, I'll go right now."

"Can I come with you?" she asked, her voice pleading. "Please, Papa, I promise to do whatever you say, and no matter what news we hear . . . I assure you I can bear it."

"Very well. Have one of the boys saddle our horses, and I'll let your mother know what we're up to."

The ride to the Barnetts' seemed to take forever. Jessica wanted to run Peg all the way, but Father wouldn't allow for such abuse. "We've plenty of time, Jess."

When they finally arrived, Jessica drew her leg up and over the horn of her sidesaddle as she kicked out of her stirrup. Without warning, she jumped to the ground.

"You trying to kill yourself?" Father asked. "Next time wait until I can help you down."

"I'm sorry. I'm just so anxious to know what's going on."

"I realize that," he said, tying off their horses, "but if you're dead, you won't get to know anything."

Jessica knew he was right, but she trusted her mount. Peg was used to her mistress taking chances. Father took hold of her arm, and together they made their way to the porch.

"Let me do the talkin'," Father said. "In your state of mind you won't make a lick of sense."

Jessica nodded but knew it would be hard to say nothing. Even so, she'd do her best. When Robert appeared at the door, she fought the urge to pounce on him and demand answers.

"Mr. Atherton . . . Jess," Robert said with a grin. "We weren't expectin' you to come visitin'."

"We came to see if there's been any word from Austin."

"Come on in." Robert moved away from the door. "I haven't heard anything since the wire tellin' me that Morgan and Smith were on the train."

"Jess is worried. I guess I am, too. He hasn't come back, and he hasn't gotten in touch with Jessica. I figure since the man plans to marry her, he'd at least let her know when he'd be back."

It was the first time Jessica realized that her father was just as concerned as she was. She looked to Robert. "Do you suppose your father has had word or maybe Jake and Marty?"

Robert shrugged. "It's possible, but Pa would have told me if he knew anything. As for Marty and Jake, I couldn't say. I haven't seen them in a couple days. The kids have been down sick, and they weren't at church yesterday, as you know. If they've had a letter or telegram in the last few days, I wouldn't know about it."

"I have to think that if they'd had any word," Father countered, "they would have let you know."

"We have to do something!" Jessica exclaimed. "We can't just keep waiting."

"Waiting for what?" Will Barnett asked, coming from the hallway.

"Howdy, Will. Jess and I were just trying to learn if there had been any word from Austin."

"None that I know of." He frowned. "And you've heard nothing?"

"Not a word."

Jessica stepped forward to the man who'd been a sort of uncle to her. "Please help us. We have to find out what's happened. I'm afraid something is wrong and Austin is in trouble."

"We could send a telegram to his old boss in Washington," Robert suggested. "What was his name?"

"Ellery Turner," Jessica replied without a breath. "Can you go immediately?"

Robert smiled and put his hand on Jessica's shoulder. "For you, I'd do most anything. Let me tell Alice, and I'll head out."

"You'll stop by the house as soon as you know something?" Jessica asked.

"Sure will. Just remember, it might take days to get word back."

Jessica nodded, knowing full well those days would feel like years.

———————————— ★ ————————————

Austin opened his eyes to a sight he'd never thought to see again. His brother Houston was perched on his bed, grinning at him like he'd just beat him at checkers.

"You're dead," Austin said, shaking his head.

"Well, from the standards of life as you know it—yes."

"Does that mean I'm dead, too?"

Houston chuckled. "Nope. It means you're dreamin'."

Austin looked around the room. It all seemed so real, so clear. How could it be a dream, a trick of the mind? "Where am I?"

"Does it matter?" his brother asked.

"I suppose not." Austin looked at his brother for a moment. "I've wanted to talk to you for a long time."

"I know," Houston replied, his smile fading. "You're wondering if I blame you for what happened, 'cause you blame yourself, and it's become a difficult burden to carry."

Austin nodded. "Yes." He tried to sit up, but pain caused him to fall back.

"You always were too focused on yourself," Houston said, shaking his head. "My dying wasn't your fault. It was an accident. I put myself in harm's way. You didn't make me do anything."

"But you were protecting me, and it was my bullet that . . ."

"That killed me?" Houston shrugged. "Didn't much matter if it was yours or his. I knew what my odds were, and I took them. I didn't want to see you die. Grace and the baby needed you."

"They didn't need me long. They died."

Houston nodded slowly. "I know. The folks, too. You've been alone for far too long."

Austin felt a rush of sadness. "But there wasn't even time to tell you goodbye. You died so fast. I watched the life go out of you, and there was—"

716

"Nothing you could do." Houston finished the sentence with a sigh. "I know. There still isn't. Moping around and feeling like you do won't bring me back. You need to stop letting this control you. You need to fight for yourself now. Fight to live."

Austin felt so very tired. He closed his eyes. "I don't know if I can."

"But you have a gal waiting for you back in Texas."

"Jessica." Austin opened his eyes.

Houston nodded and bent toward Austin. His brown hair fell over his left eye, causing him to reach up and push it back in his habitual manner. "She's a good woman. I think you two will be happy." He paused for a moment and smiled. "And that's what I want for you, Austin. I want you to be happy. Let the past rest." Houston got to his feet. "It can only hurt you if you allow it to. Let it go like the Good Book says. Let *me* go."

Chapter 25

Austin awoke to abdominal pain and a blinding headache. He felt as if every muscle in his body had gone to mush, and when he tried to move his arms, he found it nearly impossible. Rather than fight, Austin relaxed as best he could and closed his eyes again. He couldn't help but think of the dream he'd had. It had seemed so real. Houston seemed so happy and free of accusation. Had God used the dream to send him a message? Or had Houston's spirit appeared to him? Did God do that kind of thing? A memory came to mind of reading about Jesus and the appearance of Moses and Elijah, who had died long before.

"With God all things are possible," he murmured. But even as he contemplated whether or not the dream was real, peace like he'd never known settled over him. His brother was in God's care—as were Grace and his son and his parents. Somehow, he just knew they had come to realize his part in Houston's death had simply been an accident. A terrible, tragic accident.

Opening his eyes again, he stared up at the gray ceiling. The lighting seemed different. Had he fallen asleep again? Why was he here, and exactly where was *here*? It was obviously a hospital, but he didn't remember coming to it or why.

"Good afternoon, Mr. Todd. I'm glad to see that you're still among us."

Austin looked at the older man and gave a weak smile. "I'd shake your hand and make your acquaintance if I had any strength."

"I'm Dr. Kirkland. You were brought to my care nearly a month ago. You were in pretty bad shape, and we didn't expect you to live."

"A month? I've been asleep for a month?" Austin found it impossible to believe. Why, just yesterday he'd . . . he'd . . . His mind was blank. He strained his memory to search for what he last remembered.

"I remember I took the train . . . somewhere." He thought hard. "Colorado."

"Yes, that's right." The doctor picked up Austin's chart and studied it while Austin continued to search his mind.

"I live in Texas. I know that much."

"And are you married?"

"No. But I'm going to be." An image of Jessica came to mind. "She's the prettiest girl in all of Texas."

The doctor looked to Austin and chuckled. "I'd say then that you're remembering the most important things in your life."

"How did I end up here?" Austin shook his head. "Why does my head hurt so much? And my gut. I feel like I've been ripped apart."

"You suffered two bullet wounds, Mr. Todd. The first one was more serious. It entered about here." The doctor put his finger on his own body. "It pierced your small intestine and narrowly missed your kidney on its exit. It caused considerable damage. We operated on you twice. The other bullet grazed your head but didn't cause serious damage. However, you lost a great deal of blood and suffered an infection, as well. Now you're showing signs of recovery, and we are all most happy to see that."

"And you say this happened almost a month ago?"

"Yes. You've been a very sick man. It wasn't until a couple of days ago that we had real hope of your survival."

"I feel like a wrung-out dish towel," he said, trying to rise up. Intense pain ripped through his body, and now his back hurt as much as his gut. Austin felt as though his neck could barely support his head and fell back against the pillow. "Am I going to be like this forever?"

"No. You'll need time to recover your strength. You've been flat in bed for a month, and we performed the second surgery just four days ago. You aren't just going to jump up and do everything you used to do, but in time you will regain your abilities. Of that, I feel certain. Now, I plan to have the nurse give you something to help with the pain, but first I'd like to know if you feel up to some visitors. They've been here for a couple of days."

Austin nodded. "Who are they?"

"Let's see if you remember them," the doctor said, going to the door. "I'll be right back."

Austin frowned, trying to force his memories to return. He kept thinking about a box. A black lacquered box. What did it mean? He tried again to sit up but found it impossible.

Frustrated by his own weakness, Austin relaxed against the bed, determined that he would beat this. He'd do whatever the doctor said to do, and he'd recover.

"Austin!" A woman rushed into the room and to his bedside.

"Jess," he whispered. He remembered her.

She sobbed and took hold of him. "I was so afraid. When you didn't send us a telegram, I knew something must be very wrong."

Jessica hugged him tightly, and Austin's pain increased, but he said nothing. His joy at seeing her again and remembering who she was overcame any concerns about the pain.

"I don't remember what happened."

"Your Secret Service pals filled us in on that," a man declared.

Austin looked past Jessica to see Tyler Atherton. At the mention of the Secret Service, Austin had a flicker of memory. "I was working for them, wasn't I?"

Mr. Atherton came closer, and Jessica released her hold. "You were," she said. "You were trying to catch counterfeiters who were blackmailing Jake and scaring Alice. Remember?"

He considered this news for a moment and let the pieces fall into place. There had been someone bothering his friends. Austin could remember talking to Jake and Alice's husband, Robert. "I remember some. I took the train here, right?"

"You did," Atherton replied.

"That's all I remember. I don't remember getting here or what happened afterward."

"This kind of assault on the body often blocks the ability to remember," the doctor told them. He looked to Austin. "Your memory may return in time."

Austin hadn't realized the doctor had rejoined them. "I hope you're right, Doc. I sure don't like this feeling of not knowing what happened."

"Your friends said that you met them and were in agreement that you would go to the bank and retrieve the box belongin' to Alice's deceased father." Atherton paused a moment. "Do you remember that much?"

"The box. I was after the box." It made sense now why he kept pondering that black lacquered box.

"Yes, you were followin' a lead that brought you to Colorado. It was thought that perhaps the box contained the missing gold certificates and even some plates for makin' 'em. And it did. You took the box from the bank back to your hotel, where you were waylaid by Paul Morgan and his man, Lothar Hale. He went by the name Mr. Smith when he was stirrin' up trouble with Marty and Alice in Denver."

The story was coming together, and though parts of it remained veiled in a fog, Austin could finally recall his mission and the agents. They were Marcus Kayler and Sam Fegel. He'd worked with them in Washington.

"Were Kayler and Fegel hurt?"

"No. They heard the ruckus as they stood outside the door to your room. They rushed in and took Morgan and Hale into custody. Then they realized you'd been shot. The police arrived to assist them, and they got you to the hospital."

"Were they able to retain possession of the box?"

"Yes, and all the contents. There were certificates and plates and papers for making additional certificates, as well as ink and stamps and a few other things."

"They were all the working tools of Mr. Chesterfield, given to him by Mr. Morgan," Jessica added. "Apparently Mr. Morgan has been making counterfeits for a long time."

"It's all still rather foggy to me," Austin admitted.

721

"In time it may well clear for you," the doctor assured him. "You may retain some memory loss, but otherwise I'm hopeful you'll have a full recovery."

Austin gave Jessica a weak smile. "Then we can be married."

She began to cry again. "I'm so sorry for the things I said before you left. I didn't mean them. I love you." Jessica reached down to touch his cheek. "I love you dearly. Please forgive me. I'll never doubt you again."

"I don't think I remember much of anything bad being said," he replied, "so I hardly see the need for forgiveness. I love you, too, Jessica, and even if we had words, I know your love is true. It's a matter of heart." He smiled as she once again bent low to hug him. He remembered the argument in full, but he wasn't about to hold it against her.

She pulled back and wiped her tears with the back of her hand. "Yes, and my heart is full of love for you."

The doctor stepped forward. "These things were in your pockets when they brought you to the hospital. He handed a knotted handkerchief to Jessica.

"Open it," Austin said. "Maybe it will help me remember."

Jessica did as he said, and when she spread back the pieces of cloth, she gasped. Austin could see her expression was one of surprise but also of happiness.

"What is it?" he asked.

She held up a gold band with sparkles of blue. "You promised me a wedding ring."

"Do you like it?" He struggled to remember exactly how it had come into his possession, but he trusted God would return the memory in time.

"I love it. It's perfect." Her eyes welled again with tears. "I will cherish it."

"I know it's a bit extravagant, but I figure you're worth it. I wanted you to have the best." He knew that much was true. He also remembered where the money had come from. "I took my savings and brought it with me. I knew I was going to buy you a ring." He said the words more as an account of his agenda, hoping it would recall to mind the details.

"Austin, I don't need an extravagant ring," Jessica said, meeting his gaze. "I just need you. And you need to get well and come home. You need to forget the past and move forward. Your brother and Grace and I believe even your parents wouldn't want you to linger in guilt and sorrow. After all, your folks loved Jesus. They're with Him now, and they know the truth of what happened. They don't blame you anymore."

"Maybe you're right," Austin replied, feeling more tired than he could remember ever being.

"I believe my patient needs to rest," the doctor declared. "We're going to give him something to help him do so."

Jessica stood. "There's a pocket watch, some money, and your Ranger badge in this cloth. Shall I keep these things for you?"

Austin nodded and closed his eyes. "I'd feel better if you did. I don't know how long I'll have to be here, but as soon as I'm able to return to Texas, I will. I'll have the Secret Service wire me money for the trip home. They owe me that much."

"They're also paying for your hospital stay," the doctor added. "And all fees associated with your injuries. Your friends said that this was the wish of a Mr. Turner."

Austin smiled. "Sounds like him."

★

Jessica hated leaving Colorado Springs when Austin was still in such a weakened state, but she knew her father had to return to the ranch. Howard and Isaac were returning after a long time away, and Father wanted to be there when they arrived home.

"It won't take him any time at all to recover," Father told her as the train pulled out of the station. "And you will be so busy plannin' the weddin' that you won't have time to miss him."

"I doubt that is true, but I will endeavor to focus on my duties," Jessica replied. She grew thoughtful, almost fearful. "Father, you don't think things could go wrong now, do you?"

"With the weddin'?"

She shook her head and peered past her father to the window. "No, I meant with Austin's recovery. He couldn't get . . . well . . . sicker, could he?"

"The doc said he was strong and in good shape. He thought it would take a few weeks but that in time Austin would recover fully. I don't think he figures on Austin failin'. And if I know that boy, he'll recover in half the expected time."

"Why do you think that, Papa?"

Her father laughed. "Because I was young once, too. If I had a pretty gal like you waitin' for me to take her down the aisle . . . well, I wouldn't be abed for long. Injuries or no injuries, nothin' would keep me from my beloved."

Jessica smiled and put her head on her father's shoulder. "Thank you, Papa. Thank you for bringing me here and for encouraging me."

He slipped his arm around her and pulled her close. Jessica relished the warmth of her father's embrace. She tried hard to think of a hot Texas summer rather than the cold that nipped at her face and fingers.

★

"It's so good to be back in Texas." Jessica sighed. "I don't care if I never leave here again. It was so cold in Colorado." She glanced in the shop windows of Dallas's finest shopping district. She and her mother were making purchases for Jessica's wedding and having a wonderful time together.

"Before long the temperatures will be unbearable, and we'll be saying how much we hate it. Then you'll find yourself wishing for the cold," her mother said with a smile. "Oh look, here's the glove shop the dressmaker mentioned. I hope they have what we need."

Jessica followed her mother into the shop. She looked at the various sets of gloves Mother chose and tried on a couple of them. Mother wanted her to have full-length white gloves to wear with her wedding gown, since the dress was without sleeves.

"I think these with the tiny pearl buttons are perfect," her mother declared, once Jessica had donned the exquisite pair with silver embroidery vining along between the pearls.

"I do, too, Mother. I think they're the most beautiful gloves I've ever seen. But, you know, I don't really need them. I would probably never wear them again."

"Nonsense. You might attend the opera or the symphony and need them then. Many brides wear their wedding finery again on their first anniversary. Now, let's see what else you might need."

They spent a productive day shopping, and before they retired to their hotel room, Jessica and her mother shared supper in a restaurant a block away.

"When did you say Austin is due back?" Mother asked.

Jessica sampled the lemonade the server placed on the table. It was sweet, but not overly so, just as she preferred it. "He said he should be back by the middle of March."

"Are you sure you want to go ahead with the thirty-first for the wedding? That will give him only a couple weeks to get his affairs in order for the ceremony. Wouldn't you rather wait until next month? April is such a lovely time for a wedding in Texas."

Jessica shook her head. "I would have married him in his hospital bed if I'd thought I could get away with it. No. He wants us to go forward with the thirty-first. He's even arranged to buy a wedding suit in Colorado. The tailor has already come to measure and fit him there in the convalescent home. He'll be ready, Mother. Never fear."

Her mother laughed. "I suppose I should have guessed that much. Your father would have been the same way."

The waitress brought them veal cutlets and fried polenta with cheese. There were cooked greens on the side, as well as fresh dinner rolls. It was a veritable feast, and Jessica savored the aroma as she slathered butter on her roll.

Mother offered a prayer, and Jessica found herself thanking God for all that He had done in her life. She wasn't yet completely transformed, and some of the old selfishness still rose up in her occasionally. *I'm not perfect*, she mused, knowing that she would never be so . . . on earth. She would continue to work hard, however, to change her bad habits and selfish ways. She was determined on that point.

After a good night's sleep, Jessica dressed with Mother's help and accompanied her to breakfast and then to a final bridal gown fitting. As Jessica nervously stepped into the satin and lace gown, she couldn't help but gasp. The reflection in the mirror made it all seem the more real. She was truly getting married.

The dressmaker's assistant worked at pinning the gown until it met the approval of her employer. The dressmaker herself walked around and around, critically reviewing the work and looking for flaws. Jessica felt rather like a pin cushion as they reworked a piece on the bodice. Oh, but it was a lovely dress with its beautiful train—the stuff of little-girl dreams and big-girl hopes.

"I think you've done a beautiful job," Mother told the dressmaker. "And you say it will be ready in a week?"

"Yes, there isn't that much left to do. We will reduce the waist and adjust the buttons in the back, then sew the final pieces of lace to the bodice and smooth some of those seams. Do you still wish for me to ship the gown to you?"

Mother nodded. "Yes. Have it delivered to the depot at Cedar Springs in care of the stationmaster. He has already been instructed about it, but I will remind him that the dress is coming."

"Very good. I shall endeavor to have it on the train within the week."

Jessica looked once again at her reflection in the mirror. *It's really happening. I'm going to marry Austin Todd. I'm going to be his wife— the mother of his children.* She cast a quick gaze heavenward, scarcely able to believe it.

Thank you, Lord. Thank you so much for all that you've done to make this happen. I haven't always understood why my life took the turns it did, but I can see your hand in everything that has taken place.

★

Austin performed the exercises suggested by the doctor and felt his muscles growing stronger each day. He was anxious to return to Texas but wanted to do so as much a whole man as he could be. The doctor had told him he might struggle with pain for the next few months, but that it shouldn't be serious or last for long. Already the pain associated with the bullet wounds was so much better that Austin felt certain he could deal with anything that came his way.

March in Colorado wasn't as warm as he'd hoped. And because it was still just as likely to snow as it had been in February, the doctor had loaned Austin a coat for those times when he sat outdoors in the fresh air. For now, most of the snow had pretty much melted, thanks to several warm days. One of the nurses had informed him that the Farmers' Almanac suggested an early spring, with warmer temperatures than normal. If this was warmer, Austin didn't think much of it.

"Mr. Todd, you have a visitor," a young student nurse announced.

Austin felt a momentary hope that it might be Jessica. However, when Ellery Turner walked through the door, Austin was just as happy to see him.

"Mr. Turner, I never expected you to come to Colorado."

"It was necessary for some of the work related to the case against Mr. Morgan. I thought, why send someone else when it would benefit me to see you." The two men shook hands.

"Well, by all means have a seat." Austin motioned to the only chair in the room. "I'll sit here on the bed. So tell me everything. How goes the case?"

Turner sat and crossed his legs. "It goes very well. The evidence is vast, and as we've been able to uncover more details, the case has strengthened."

"Good," Austin said, knowing this would be good news to the Barnetts and Wythes. Not to mention everyone else. "I'm glad it's working out that way. I hope this won't be too big of an embarrassment to his family. J. P. Morgan has been most helpful in getting the country back on its feet."

"No need to worry. This Morgan isn't related in the leastwise to J. P. Morgan. He only told people that in order to win their trust. He was quite good at convincing people of his powerful connections."

"I'm glad you've been able to resolve this. I hope the courts send Morgan and his cohorts to prison for a very long time."

"We never would have had that chance if you hadn't gotten involved. That's another reason I've come. I'm hoping to convince you to rejoin the department. We need men like you, Austin. I know that business with your brother was devastating, but hopefully you can put that behind you and move forward."

"I am doing exactly that, but I'm afraid it won't be with the Secret Service." Austin noted the disappointment in the older man's expression. "I plan to be a town marshal in Terryton, Texas, with a wife and a passel of young ones. You see, God has sent a very special young woman into my life, and while I was certain I could never love another, He's given me that gift, as well."

Turner smiled. "I'm so glad to hear it, Austin. I can't say that I'm not disappointed, but I'm also very happy for you. However, if you should change your mind in the future, there will always be a place for you in my department."

"Thank you, sir. That means a lot to me."

Chapter 26

"You look so beautiful," Alice told Jessica as she put the final touches on the bride's hair.

"Thank you for saying so and for doing this. I know I could never have made such an intricate arrangement on my own."

Alice smiled. "I used to dress Marty's hair when I worked for her. It was my favorite part of the job. I love being creative and adding beauty to the world." She tucked one last piece of baby's breath into Jessica's hair.

Jessica watched from her seat in front of the dressing table. She had waited so anxiously for this day, and now that it was here, she could scarcely breathe. It was like holding her breath, waiting to see if all would go well.

"There. I think we're done. Is it what you'd hoped for?"

Jessica looked at the curls pinned high atop her head. "I think it's perfect. The veil will sit just right."

"We can see about that in a moment. But now we need to get you into your gown," Marty Wythe announced.

With a slight tremble, Jessica got to her feet. She couldn't help but wonder about the man who was awaiting her arrival at the altar. What would their life be like now that the railroad was finally building the spur line and Austin was acting marshal of the up-and-coming town of Terryton?

Marty smiled and helped Jessica step into her dress. "You are going to make a beautiful bride, Jessica. I've never seen anyone quite so radiant as you."

"It seemed like this day would never come, and now that it's here, well, it seems to be going by much too quickly." Jessica stood stock-still while Marty and Alice helped secure the skirt of the gown. Once this was done, Marty held up the boned bodice and helped Jessica to slip her arms through the lacey material. Alice immediately went to work pulling the bodice in place. She and Marty worked quickly to do up the thirty-some covered buttons. When this task was complete, the women set about straightening any wrinkles and repositioning the lace to lie properly.

"I think our work is done," Marty said, stepping back.

"Except for the veil," Alice declared, bringing it forward from the wardrobe where it had been hanging.

The hand-crafted lace and tulle veil crowned Jessica's head in a most elegant manner. The lace edging matched that on her dress and flowed so neatly against it that it appeared to blend into the gown itself as it extended down and past the train. Jessica thought she had never seen anything quite so lovely as her headpiece, which was adorned with a silvery band trimmed with white camellias.

Alice secured the flowery tiara while Marty helped Jessica into her gloves. "Be sure the slit on the ring finger offers easy access," Jessica reminded her.

"I have it perfectly placed," Marty assured her.

"I'll need your help to pull the blusher veil over her head to cover her face," Alice told Marty.

The two women worked perfectly together and adjusted the tulle to cover Jessica's face. "I'll get your flowers, and then we will finally be ready." Alice hurried to the table and retrieved the bouquet. She handed the exquisite arrangement of white jasmine, camellias, and very pale lavender lilacs to the bride.

Jessica felt butterflies in her stomach, and she bit her lip to keep her teeth from chattering. She knew she was being silly, but her anxiety was getting the best of her. What if she wasn't a good wife? What if

Austin saw her and changed his mind? What if he hadn't even arrived at the church?

Stop it. Austin loves you, and he's waiting for you.

She looked to the young woman whose scar she had once thought ugly. It had faded over the years, and now seemed far less noticeable. "I'm ready."

Alice smiled. Dressed beautifully in a new but simple lavender gown, Alice stood ready to act as matron of honor—the only attendant Jessica wanted. Alice's husband, Robert, would stand as best man to Austin. Jessica was grateful to both for having put aside her former transgressions. She planned for them all to be great friends for years to come.

"Shall we go?" Marty asked. Both Jessica and Alice nodded. "Very well, then. I'll go take my seat and signal the organ to start the wedding march."

Alice followed her out the door with Jessica slowly coming behind. As she exited the room, she found her father waiting to take her arm.

"My, but you take my breath away," Father declared. "I've never seen you prettier, Jess."

"Thank you," she whispered. "I'm afraid I'm feeling a little nervous."

He patted her gloved arm. "That's normal. I thought I might faint dead away when I married your ma."

Jessica didn't believe him. Her father had always been a pillar of strength. It was impossible to imagine him feeling weak in the knees over anything.

"You know, Jess, when I first held you in my arms all those years ago, I couldn't imagine this day. I never wanted to give you away to anyone because you were so special. You were the completion of our family, and a blessing to all of us."

"Papa, you'd best stop or I'll be in tears." She looked up to her father with a smile. "I love you."

Father smiled at her in return. "I love you, too, darlin'. But there's a young man waitin' for you who thinks he loves you even more. I guess we'd best go meet him at the altar."

Jessica nodded and held fast to her father's arm. "I'm ready."

Organ music filled the entire church as Jessica's father led her down the aisle. Although Austin stood waiting at the front of the church, Jessica couldn't lift her head to glimpse his face. She feared if she did, she might become overwhelmed, so she watched the church floor instead.

When her father stopped, she knew they'd reached the altar, but still she struggled with her nerves and refused to look up.

"Dearly beloved," she heard the pastor begin, and after that the words were something of a blur. She rallied when her father gave her over to Austin. His strong grasp on her arm felt reassuring.

When the time came to repeat her vows, Jessica did so in a hushed whisper. Her mouth seemed as dry as cotton, but somehow she managed to get the words out. When Austin prepared to put the ring on her finger, all Jessica could think about was the first time she'd seen it in the hospital.

Austin had been so pale, so wracked with pain as he lay on the hospital bed. But even in that condition, Jessica had seen in his eyes the love he held for her. It gave her strength, and Jessica raised her face to gaze into Austin's warm brown eyes as he found her finger and slipped the ring on.

He smiled and Jess couldn't help but smile back. What they were doing felt so right—so perfectly ordered—and Jessica's fears drained away. It truly was a matter of heart, and her heart told her that they would share a lifetime of love, and that made the future seem perfect.

When the pastor announced they were man and wife and that they could share a kiss, Jessica waited in anticipation as Austin carefully lifted her veil.

"Hello, wife," he whispered, his lips close to hers.

"Hello, husband," she replied, then fell silent as his mouth claimed hers.

Tracie Peterson is the award-winning author of over one hundred novels, both historical and contemporary. Her avid research resonates in her stories, as seen in her bestselling HEIRS OF MONTANA and ALASKAN QUEST series. Tracie and her family make their home in Montana. Visit Tracie's website at www.traciepeterson.com and her blog at www.writespassage.blogspot.com.

More From Tracie Peterson

Visit traciepeterson.com for a full list of her books.

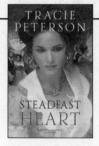

Brought together by the Madison Bridal School in 1888, three young women form a close bond. In time, they learn more about each other—and themselves—as they help one another grow in faith and, eventually, find love.

BRIDES OF SEATTLE: *Steadfast Heart, Refining Fire, Love Everlasting*

In the years surrounding the Civil War, loyalties in the Lone Star State remain divided. Amid the bitter prejudices on the harsh Texan plains, is there any hope that the first blush of love can survive?

LAND OF THE LONE STAR: *Chasing the Sun, Touching the Sky, Taming the Wind*

◊BETHANYHOUSE

Stay up-to-date on your favorite books and authors with our free e-newsletters. Sign up today at bethanyhouse.com.

Find us on Facebook. facebook.com/bethanyhousepublishers

Free exclusive resources for your book group! bethanyhouse.com/anopenbook

You May Also Enjoy...

A teacher on the run. A bounty hunter in pursuit. Can Charlotte Atherton and Stone Hammond learn to trust each other before they both lose what they hold most dear?

A Worthy Pursuit by Karen Witemeyer
karenwitemeyer.com

When Brook Eden's friend Justin, a future duke, discovers she may be an English heiress, she travels to meet her alleged father. Once there, she finds herself confused by her emotions and haunted by her mother's mysterious death. Will she learn the truth—before it's too late?

The Lost Heiress by Roseanna M. White
LADIES OF THE MANOR
roseannamwhite.com

Lady Miranda Hawthorne secretly longs to be bold. But she is mortified when her brother's handsome new valet accidentally mails her private thoughts to a duke she's never met—until he responds. As she tries to sort out her growing feelings for two men, it becomes clear that Miranda's heart is not the only thing at risk for the Hawthorne family.

A Noble Masquerade by Kristi Ann Hunter
HAWTHORNE HOUSE
kristiannhunter.com

◆ BETHANYHOUSE